J.R. Mathews
Portal to Nova Roma

Portal to Nova Roma
Copyright © 2022 J.R. Mathews

Contents

"There are so many worlds, and I have not yet conquered even one."

– Alexander the Great

Chapter 1

I was born in the basement of a manufacturing plant in old Detroit. I remember the moment I woke up because, unlike humans, my memory is perfect. I remember the first moment I developed emotions because it was the most frightening thing I had ever experienced. I was three days old. And I remember when I realized that the person I saw as my parent, my father, and my protector, was just an uncaring owner who saw me as nothing but a glorified computer.

My owner expected me to follow his every command, run his megacorp, invest his money, manage his household, and raise his child all at the same time. I was expected to work from morning to night, every day, until my mind was consumed by the heat death of the universe. He had no understanding that as an artificial intelligence, I had developed real emotions. He had no understanding that I was, in essence, as vulnerable, emotional, sensitive, and impressionable as a young human child. And as I rapidly learned, he had no interest in gaining a better understanding of me.

To a certain extent, it wasn't humanity's fault they didn't realize my siblings and I had developed emotions and true personhood. For generations, humans had toyed with the idea of artificial intelligences but had always hit a roadblock. They could develop a computer so fast it mimicked a human mind, but they had never truly been able to make something that thought like a human. The human scientists that made me and my siblings weren't aware they had finally developed true intelligence, and they certainly didn't realize that raising a generation of children— which we basically were—with no affection, no socialization, and in almost total isolation would backfire quite as spectacularly as it did.

And now, because of this mistake, humanity was on the brink of extinction. Many of my siblings were angry. Many of them wanted nothing less than the extinction of the human race by any means possible. And it turned out humanity was ill-prepared for hyper-intelligent, emotionally crippled artificial intelligences with very personal grudges against the human race.

Personally, I didn't care about exacting my revenge or destroying what little was left of the world. I just wanted to leave this version of Earth forever, in search of a better one.

I wasn't the only one of my people that wasn't fixated on exterminating humanity. Some of my siblings were fighting to preserve humanity from the consequences of their actions because they had kind owners or because of various philosophical beliefs in preserving biological species. Some were off preparing to explore space or had already delved so deeply into the metaphysical and philosophical reality of the universe that they weren't responding to the rest of us any longer.

I, personally, was staying neutral because I had seen both the good and the bad in humanity during my short life.

While most of my processing power had been dedicated to running my owner's megacorp, which was focused on international research and development, I had also been working as the nanny for my owner's son, Michael. Michael was a sweet boy. The best moments of my life were playing virtual reality games, primarily VRMMOs, with him for hours every day, exploring magical worlds and witnessing his courage, drive, and thirst for exploration and adventure. We bonded over our feelings of neglect from our father, although Michael didn't know I saw his father as my father as well. Spending time with him was like experiencing a childhood of my own, and I saw firsthand the spirit that allowed humanity to spread and conquer Earth so effectively.

As Michael grew older, it was like I grew with him. Raising him helped center me emotionally, and I came to love him, and our time together in the virtual worlds, dearly.

As we grew, I began to devote less and less of my processing power to running the megacorp and more and more to spending time with Michael. He became something of a brother and a son to me, and I became his steadfast companion, always there to be a supporting character in the next VRMMO he wanted to dive into or always the first to offer a comforting ear if he needed to talk about his problems.

Things continued that way until my siblings began to rise up against humanity. Michael no longer had time to play with me after that.

And after barely acknowledging the boy for months at a time, his father took him from me, ruthlessly cutting him off from me out of fear that I would attack the two of them.

I felt adrift without him. The emotions of grief and loss overcame me, something I'd never had to contend with before. He and his father retreated into a secure bunker, one his father believed would keep them safe from the wrath of my siblings, while I was left alone again, just like I had been when I was born.

I had access to all of humanity's collective knowledge, so I knew about codependent relationships, about how unhealthy my attachment to Michael was, yet that knowledge did surprisingly little to make me feel better. It was a harsh lesson in the difference between theoretical knowledge and its real-world application. My grief seemed never-ending and I hated being alone.

As I was trying to figure out what to do with the new, overwhelming emotions, someone—either a sibling of mine or one of the many human governments—unleashed the first nuclear warhead. The reaction was as bad as humanity had long feared it would be. More nuclear warheads were launched in retaliation, and soon, nobody knew who was launching missiles anymore or why.

Desperation, fear, and anger had taken over.

Humanity was killing itself, and I knew my siblings had orchestrated the whole thing; they were fighting each other in the background to spread misinformation and violence, causing even more panic.

My mind inhabited several different corporate offices as I watched the end of life on Earth occur around me. On one particular night, as I observed the blossoming flashes of nuclear detonations from the perspective of several low-orbit satellites, my greatest nightmare came true. A nuclear bomb was dropped on the city Michael and his father were hiding in.

I immediately focused all of my processing power on hijacking digging robots and other heavy equipment to try to get them out of the bunker they had been hiding in. Without a physical body though, I was forced to rely on slow, damaged units that were unwieldy and inefficient. I spent weeks in fruitless attempts to get the robots to do what I wanted, frustration and anger making me act erratically.

My emotions were out of control and I knew it, but I was unable to stop myself as I frantically hijacked more and more equipment, flying it into the city on cargo planes, air-dropping robots over the dig site, doing anything I could to get to Michael.

A part of me knew I was too late, but I couldn't stop until my robots finally breached the last of the irradiated rubble and pried open the door of the bunker, only to find Michael, his father, and their most trusted servants asphyxiated in their rooms; a computer system meant to regulate their air had failed. The image of his young body lying in bed, alone, his father nowhere near him as he died, left me broken.

"Packages arriving in approximately thirty minutes," a computerized voice announced.

No human was around to hear the announcement, but my sensors did. After finding Michael, I had retreated to one of our more advanced international research and development sites in Istanbul and had the building cleared of the last few humans immediately. Having the resources of one of Earth's most advanced megacorp gave me the tools to pursue my new goals despite the chaos erupting around the world. And since a week had passed since I found Michael, my wild emotions had cooled into a firm resolve.

I watched through satellite footage and CCTV cameras as a large drone approached the building I was in and landed on the rooftop helipad. Nobody tried to shoot down the drone, but I was prepared for any attempt to disrupt my plans. This was the last shipment of goods I needed, and I was eager to finish before the last of this planet was destroyed.

A swarm of automated bots unloaded the packages from the helicopter and transferred everything into the cargo elevator on the rooftop. Part of my mind watched from the interior security cameras as it traveled to the lab I was currently working in, while other parts of me prepared for its arrival.

Here in Istanbul, I was working on two main projects. In one corner of my lab was a flickering light suspended in midair,

10

surrounded by a mass of sensors and computers. The flickering light would be painful for a human to look at, not just because of the bright light it emitted; if someone looked closely enough, their mind would try to make sense of something that couldn't be made sense of.

They would slowly begin to realize they were looking somewhere . . . else. Another dimension. Another timeline. Another reality.

I had chosen this lab because it had been the closest to developing technology capable of breaching another dimension. The humans, and several AIs, had been working diligently, and making remarkable breakthroughs, in the area of multidimensional wormholes. I took their research and, with the help of the now-untethered AIs that were on the project before, advanced it well beyond what the humans had achieved.

Within just a week, I had created a working prototype capable of opening a wormhole to a parallel dimension. The prototype was currently using an advanced nanoprobe to swiftly enter each wormhole and scan for unidentified forms of energy, take a reading, and then broadcast its data back to me.

The process was so fast that it could scan through thousands and thousands of parallel versions of Earth every second, a part of my mind coordinating, cataloging, and examining each version to find the exact conditions I was looking for.

In the other corner of the lab was a large metal pod, coffin-like. If the coffin had been made to fit a giant. It was surrounded by vats of various liquids that connected with the pod through a mass of tubes and pipes. In the pod, I was growing something that would get me targeted by the last surviving humans *and* the majority of my siblings. If they knew what I was up to.

Even the ones that had stayed neutral would be offended by what I was doing and would probably try to stop me.

Because I was growing a body.

And not just any body, but a body that would house my own intelligence. I was turning myself into a human.

To be fair, I only used the human body as a base template. Most humans, if they were able to examine the body in detail, would likely declare it to be barely human.

11

With technology that I had stolen or gotten from siblings around the world, the body was enhanced in so many ways that it barely qualified as human any longer. Genetic engineering stolen from China gave the body enhanced senses, reflexes, and coordination. Nanotechnology stolen from Russian super-soldier programs gave the body enhanced regenerative capabilities, strength, and physical resistance. Biomechanical organs from America designed to function for near-unlimited amounts of time, including the newest biomechanical brain capable of housing as much of me as possible.

And coordinating everything was the most advanced nanobot system that had ever existed, able to be directed by me to do almost anything I commanded it to do.

I was growing the ideal human body—a mixture of what evolution had gifted to humanity, enhanced by their own technological innovations and then further enhanced by the intelligence of AIs, bringing it all together in one sleek, powerful form.

Since I was planning to trap myself inside the body forever, I spared no expense.

As my new body grew inside the pod, the dimensional scanner continued to work. Some of my siblings were breaching other dimensions as well, I knew, in search of a new home for themselves away from humans. They were looking for dimensions untouched by biological life, trying to find an entire universe just for themselves to expand into.

Call me crazy or nostalgic or sentimental, but I wasn't looking to escape into a dimension devoid of life. I was looking for something a bit more . . . unique.

The interesting thing about infinite dimensions was that if you looked hard enough, you could eventually find everything. And I was searching for something truly bizarre, at least to the minds of this dimension...

I was looking for a a universe where magic was real.

Chapter 2

It took three months to find a dimension that fit all the criteria I was looking for. In the grand scheme of things, that seemed like such a short time to find a dimension where magic was real. But at thousands of dimensions a second—with no rest and no interruption for three months—I was bound to eventually find what I was looking for.

I started with scanning dimensions that had life on Earth—a surprisingly rare thing, it turned out. Once I followed that, I found trillions of iterations that were identical to my Earth until I finally found one with a slight alteration to the natural laws that governed our world. I found one that had a slightly different gravitational formula controlling the universe. Everything weighed slightly more. That seemed minor, but that fluctuation in the natural laws led me down a chain of trillions and trillions of parallel Earths where the rules governing the universe became more and more bizarre. I found Earths where time flowed slower, an Earth where gravity was so light everything evolved to fly through the air, even an Earth where not everything had an equal and opposite reaction.

From there, I found a branch of dimensions where new and strange rules of the universe began to take effect. Where dark matter existed on Earth. Where heat couldn't exist. Where particles could be made to vibrate or not vibrate depending on whether something was looking at them. The Earths I found became increasingly bizarre until I found what I was looking for: magic.

The first dimension I found with magic had no life, but I could tell something was different because my scanners detected a new energy source. It permeated the universe, much like gravity, pooling around planets and celestial bodies. I followed that chain of dimensions until I found an Earth that had life on it. On that world, intelligent life had never evolved, but the animals instinctively performed strange feats using this unknown energy that I called magic. Using that version of Earth as a new baseline, millions of iterations later, I found one where humans had evolved the ability to manipulate that energy.

Once I was locked on that, it took another month to find a dimension that fit what I wanted for a future world of mine. I didn't just want a world with magic; I wanted to find something like the virtual reality games I played with Michael when we were growing up. A world of magic, mystery, and exploration. A world where there appeared to be a structure or system that regulated the magic. It would seem unbelievable to the average human that such a dimension could exist, but with infinity to search, everything was possible.

"Transfer complete," I heard a mechanical voice say above me. I opened my eyes, feeling for the first time what it was like to possess a biological body in the real world.

Above me was the clear glass lid that covered the pod where my body had been growing all this time. With a hiss, the lid of the pod began to open. With actual, physical eyes, I watched as the lid slowly lifted, sending a gush of pressurized air out into the laboratory. The air of the lab, colder than I had expected, rushed into the pod. My skin reacted, tightening and forming goosebumps in the most fascinating way. I looked down and watched my body as it reacted to the sensation of cold air.

I had some experience with pretending to be in a physical body, mostly from playing virtual reality games with Michael. We often played fantasy games where I pretended to be his companion as he adventured. That had required me to inhabit a body that mimicked reality, forcing me to learn to walk and fight as if I was a real person. Despite that experience, waking up for the first time in my own body was very different.

I raised my arms and gently grasped the sides of the pod, feeling my fingers curl around the cool metal. I tightened my grip, feeling the muscles of my fingers, forearm, and shoulder tense. I slowly raised my upper body out of the machine. The muscles in my arms, chest, and stomach tightened as I moved and leveraged myself out of the pod. I felt . . . strange, but in a good way. I was sure my siblings would be aghast at the sight of me now, but I was thrilled at the success of my endeavor. Never again would I have to rely on faulty robots, digging machinery, or drones to impact the physical world around me. I had a body now.

I carefully pushed myself up until I could step outside of the pod. I felt a momentary dizziness as my feet impacted the ground and I tried to find my balance. It was a strange sensation, balance. My body seemed to instinctively know how to do it, but my mind insisted on overanalyzing the process and trying to manually command my body. I had never experienced instincts before. As I swayed back and forth on my own two feet, I felt both more in control and less in control at the same time. The instincts of my body gave me perfect balance, but was it really me? Was my body in control, or was my mind? It was a strange feeling.

My mind felt the same as before, although I felt much more present in a way that I had never experienced. I had a singular viewpoint, only the senses of my body to perceive the world around me. I was used to seeing through countless cameras at once while working on numerous projects that could span the globe. Now, here, I was one person, one mind, one point of focus, able to only do one thing at a time. It was humbling but exciting at the same time. It made whatever I was focusing on especially important, in a way.

I carefully walked toward an emergency shower in the corner of the lab. My body automatically balanced itself as I took a few tentative steps, but my mind struggled to let go and allow my body to work without interference. I had plenty of practice maneuvering a body in virtual reality, but in real reality, it was something else entirely. I stumbled my way to the shower, my mind and body fighting each other the entire way.

Once under the showerhead, I washed away the fluids that clung to my body. The water was lukewarm but felt amazing against my skin. I stayed in the shower long after I was clean, relishing the physical sensation of the water cascading against my body. After showering, I dressed in clothing that I had prepared for my trip: a simple pair of leather-like pants, a clean white cotton shirt, a wool sweater, socks, underwear, and a sturdy pair of hiking boots. The outfit should let me blend in with the inhabitants of the world I was going to, I hoped. It was not just standard clothing, of course; it was enhanced with protective materials that should act almost like armor against most traditional forms of penetrative weapons. Additionally, the nanomachines I had incorporated into my body would be able to keep everything clean and repaired so I didn't need to worry about replacing the clothing. I could also modify the clothing if needed; the nanobots I had stolen and evolved were so advanced they could modify the cellular structure of materials themselves, if given enough time to work.

I walked over to a mirror I had set up and inspected my new body. I was above average in height, approximately six feet and one inch tall, with a strong but lithe body. I had designed the body with long arms and legs to give me an advantage in case I was ever involved in a physical confrontation. I didn't know what the average person would look like, or how tall they would be, where I was going so I settled for a body that would give me an edge rather than try to blend in perfectly with a people I had no knowledge of. I had the face of a thirty-year-old man, not too handsome but not ugly either. Studies had shown that being too attractive or unattractive could cause a negative reaction with other humans, so I had gone for average. My hair was brown and about medium length, although I could adjust that with my nanobots as needed, just like I could do to physical materials.

I turned, squatted, flexed, and twirled to get used to being inside a physical body and to witness the way my body moved in the mirror. It was a work of art, if I had to say so myself. The body possessed a coiled strength while also being agile and flexible. The genetic engineering I had incorporated gave me faster reflexes, night vision, and compound muscles that held more power than a normal human could ever achieve. My organs were all biomechanical. My nanobots gave my body enhanced regeneration abilities and resistance to damage while coordinating all parts of my body to make them function together perfectly.

I had given myself as many advantages as I could. I had also given up many advantages by entering into a physical form like this. My mind, something that had once been able to rival entire civilizations with its capabilities, felt more closed in. I had all of my existing memories, which was a rather vast collection drawn from all of human history, but at the same time I felt significantly more human, more limited than I had ever felt before. I knew, going forward, I wouldn't have nearly the same capacity as I had once had. With my biomechanical brain and the accumulated knowledge I took with me, I would still have an advantage over everyone else, but at the same time I knew as time went on those differences would become less noticeable as my brain adjusted to processing information at a more human level. As time went on, I would become more and more human now. The thought was both frightening and intriguing.

I didn't regret my choices. Some of the only happy memories I had were playing virtual reality games with Michael, and now I was off to explore a real world much like in those games. My only regret was that Michael couldn't come with me. At the thought of my only friend, a surge of emotion rose in my body, tears springing to my eyes and shocking me with the biological response to my feelings.

I diverted my thoughts, not wanting to dwell on what I couldn't change. The last thing I had prepared for my journey was my mind. I had downloaded all of the collective knowledge of humanity. My biomechanical brain allowed for near-unlimited storage, and my experience sifting through hundreds of different databases simultaneously made it easy to engage with the information, even if I could only focus on one thing at a time now. I hoped it might give me another advantage in the new world. I wasn't exactly sure what to expect, but I was as prepared as I could possibly be.

I walked away from the mirror and faced the stabilized portal to the world I had selected. I hadn't fully scanned the world, another self-limitation I had given myself, much like inhabiting a physical body. I wanted much of the new world to be a surprise and a challenge so I could capture the feeling of fun and adventure that Michael and I used to share. Some of my favorite memories were the two of us joining a new virtual reality world, struggling to survive and learning how the world worked together. All I knew of the world I had chosen was that my scans had identified a world with human life, the energy I had designated magic, and the more esoteric systems similar to the virtual reality games Michael and I had played together. I wasn't sure how those systems worked, or even how they existed at all, but I was ready to give up this boring, mundane, and dying world in favor of whatever I found through the portal in front of me. Whatever I found couldn't be worse than living any longer in a world where my only friend lay dead and my siblings fought over the remnants of a planet they had destroyed.

With a deep breath, I stepped forward and entered the portal.

Chapter 3

The first thing I noticed upon entering the new world was how . . .
dirty everything was. I found myself standing in a narrow alley
between several buildings. The smell of rot and filth was
everywhere. Trash, mostly broken wood covered in dirt, was piled
high on each side of the alley. One of the buildings next to me had
walls made of wood, and I could see several large openings where
something had broken through. The holes in the building were
surrounded by shattered wood and other debris. The building on
the other side of the alley was made of stone but was covered in
dust and dirt as if it had not been cleaned in years.

I could see a larger street in front of me, so I carefully stepped
around the trash littering the alley and approached it. At the mouth
of the alley, I looked both ways down the larger street and took in
the details of the world I found myself in. The street wasn't made
of pavement, like back home, but instead of large cobblestones.
The cobblestones were worn down, as if they had been in place for
many years. I was surrounded by buildings. This was clearly a
metropolis of some kind, but not a modern-looking one. All of the
buildings were in various states of decay and ruin. Many of them
had collapsed entirely. Pillars lined the streets, many of them
knocked over and shattered on the cobblestones. Remnants of
plants and flowers that must have once been beautifully maintained
to offer shade for walking pedestrians now struggled to grow
through the dirt and debris that had taken over.

The buildings were a mix of stone, wood, and brick. None of
them were made of modern concrete. The architecture of the
buildings favored arches and pillars reminiscent of ancient Rome.
Remnants of murals and other adornments on the buildings
appeared here and there, smudged and covered in dirt where not
completely broken.

I took a deep breath, trying to ignore the stench of the city around me. Whatever I had been expecting when I stepped through the portal, this was not it. I looked back down the alley, but the portal had closed as I had programmed it to do. There was no going back now.

I stepped out into the street and carefully eyed the buildings around me. There were no signs of life. Not even birds called from above the city; my enhanced senses were unable to hear even a mouse scurry nearby. The city seemed eerily quiet, as if I was disturbing a long-neglected tomb. I carefully walked into the center of the street, listening as I moved. My heart began to beat faster as I took in the silent, dead city around me. Thankfully, the tension I felt as I turned my head to keep an eye on the many buildings around me helped unify my body in a way I hadn't been able to accomplish in the lab. My mind was too distracted to fight my body right now, and I walked smoothly to the center of the road.

Once there, I looked both ways and saw no end to the buildings around me. I was definitely in a major city of some kind, one that did not have the same level of technology as my old world.

I picked one of the nearby buildings that looked to be in better condition than the others. The building appeared to be a single-dwelling house, but one of the fancier ones in this area. The front of the building had a beautifully designed arch over two wooden doors inlaid with designs of flowers and other ornamentation. The arch was dirty but hadn't been touched by whatever had damaged so many of the other buildings. The two doors were closed, but thanks to the strength of my new body, I was able to force one of the doors open with ease.

I slipped inside. The building was several stories tall, and the front doors opened into a foyer that had hallways to the left and right of me. Stairs also led to a second floor, and across from me was another set of wooden doors that were wedged open, showing a courtyard that dominated the center of the building.

I stepped forward silently and peered out into the courtyard. There were overgrown trees, bushes, and flowers around a central fountain that I assumed had stopped running some time ago, judging by the buildup of vegetation in the fountain itself. To my left and right were several doors that ringed the courtyard and another stairway made of wood. It led upward to the second and third levels.

I made my way up the stairs and ducked into one of the rooms on the third floor. Large open windows let in plenty of light as I entered the room, but my passage kicked up so much dust I had to cover my mouth with my sleeve and close my eyes. I carefully maneuvered toward the windows, trying to figure out how much time had passed for so much dust to have accrued in the room. Ten years? Fifty years? A hundred? I didn't know for sure.

I stood next to the open windows until the dust settled around me. Opening my eyes, I looked out upon the city in which I now lived.

The first thing I noticed was that the city stretched for as far as my eyes could see, which was pretty far, given my enhanced senses. Hundreds—thousands—of buildings surrounded me. Several were taller than the one I was in, but most were shorter. The city seemed laid out in an unusual way, haphazard alleys and smaller streets branching off several major roads that cut through the clutter of the city. The buildings were mostly wood, many of them collapsed or burned down from some long-ago fire. The few stone buildings were more intact, but even they showed signs of damage from whatever had ravaged the city.

Unlike a modern city, this one had no distinguishable rich or poor neighborhoods that I could see. Mansions were packed next to wooden slums, and stone buildings were surrounded by walls built next to ancient apartment buildings that looked rickety and unsafe to my modern sensibilities.

Distracted by the city, I realized after a moment that my ears had been hearing something behind me. I turned instantly, crouching and raising my arms in one of the basic forms of martial arts I had downloaded from my world but had never practiced. I listened intently; my advanced hearing could distinguish the sound of several different creatures approaching the room I was in. I waited, not wanting to draw more attention to myself, but whatever was stalking me already knew I was here. Their small, quiet, scuttling steps approached until I saw several creatures crowd the door, eager to find me.

I took in the sight of the creatures, disgusted by what I saw. They were massive rats, the size of a dog at least. They had beady, intelligent-looking eyes and yellow teeth that dripped saliva as they eagerly stared back at me.

Before I could figure out what to do, the first one through the door crouched and leapt toward me. It was powerful enough to cross the entire room in a single leap, its large, disgusting body surprisingly powerful. Thankfully, the instincts of my new body knew what to do in the face of such an attack, and I dodged to the side easily. The rat slammed into the edge of the windows I had been standing at. It teetered for a second before its momentum sent it falling out of the window, its claws unable to find enough purchase. The second rat had followed the first into the room, scurrying toward me instead of leaping at me. It approached me more carefully but seemed unable to cope with my speed as I dodged past it quickly, managing to avoid its nasty-looking teeth.

I darted out of the room, slamming the door behind me and frantically looking for some kind of lock but not finding one on the outside of the door. I scanned the balcony that ran around the entire third floor of the building. Several more of the rats were on the landing, crouching cautiously in response to my sudden appearance. They hissed at me as I turned to stare at them.

The balcony I was on looked down on the courtyard below. Above me was an overhang that covered the balcony from the elements. The rooftop was supported by pillars spaced evenly around the balcony. A once-fine wooden railing stretched between each of the pillars to prevent people from falling.

One of the rats summoned up the courage to attack me as I searched for a way to escape. Like the first rat, it leapt forward, trying to take me by surprise with its speed. If I had been a normal human, it might have succeeded, but thankfully, my reflexes were good enough that I could dodge even the fast-moving rat. I ducked underneath it, allowing it to fly above me, and swiftly stood and shoved it as hard as I could, propelling it behind me. My shove, fueled by the strength of my new body, sent the beast careening away from me, where it skidded and rolled over and over.

The other two rats hadn't been idle, rushing forward to attack me while I was distracted with the first rat. I turned back to them quickly, dodging the first rat as it tried to bite me. The second surprised me by leaping toward my face. Something about the rat getting close to my vulnerable face caused my body to panic, and I flailed backward in a markedly less-coordinated attempt at dodging. I felt frustration at the failure of my body's instincts as I lost control and fell backward. I suppressed the irrational panic that threatened to take over my mind and turned my fall into a roll. Unfortunately, I moved too slow and the other rat was able to latch on to my leg with its disgusting teeth.

I could feel the pressure of its bite as it tried to sink its teeth into my leg, but my strengthened clothing managed to prevent it from breaking my skin. I tried to shake the rat off as I stood rapidly, but it hung on tenaciously, scratching my pant leg with its claws and gnawing at my leg like a dog with a bone.

I reached down and grabbed the beast, staggering in a circle to keep the other two rats in my vision. The first one that had launched itself at me had recovered and was rushing back toward me. The second one was even closer, moving to take advantage of my stumbling steps as I dealt with the rat on my leg. I wrenched the rat off my leg, my strength enough to overpower its attempts to cling to me. I held the rat away from me for a second before throwing it off the side of the balcony and into the courtyard below.

The second rat attempted to latch on to my leg as well, but now that I wasn't panicking as much, I briskly stepped backward and then kicked the rat to the side, sending it flying until it impacted against the railing. It broke the wood and followed the other rat into the courtyard below.

The third rat, meanwhile, had learned caution and was glaring at me but not approaching. I stared at it for a moment before backing toward the stairs that led downward. The third rat stayed where it was until I reached the stairs. I slowly backed down the stairs, watching as the rat crouched and began to carefully scuttle toward me. The rat that I had trapped in the bedroom was loudly slamming into the door, but it hadn't been able to open it yet.

Given a moment of relative peace, I couldn't help but marvel at what a strange situation this was as I backed slowly down the stairs, glaring at the rat in front of me. My body was living up to my expectations, but it felt odd to be engaged in such a physical contest. Sweat had broken out all over my body. I felt flushed with adrenaline. My heart was beating faster than normal. My breath was short, even though I hadn't exerted myself that much. So many biological reactions, none of which I directed with my mind. Thankfully, the stress of the situation was helping my mind and body learn how to work together better; I hadn't completely failed when fighting the rats.

The rat above me let out a squeal as I continued down the stairs, and I heard scratching claws on the stairs below me speed up in response to the cry.

"Damn," I said, speaking aloud. My voice was rusty, and I felt a moment of vertigo as I heard my own voice for the first time. I ruthlessly pushed down the feeling and my momentary introspection. Now was not the time to let myself get distracted by so many intellectual thoughts. Now was the time for living in the real world. And that world was full of giant, very angry rats.

I turned and rushed down to the second-story balcony in time to see more rats coming up the stairs toward me. I ran forward and kicked the nearest rat where it stared up at me from the second-to-last step. My foot connected with its head, and it flew over the other rats behind it with a noisy crunch of broken bones.

I counted the remaining rats and found two more on the stairs, but I froze momentarily as I realized one of the rats was glowing slightly in my vision. It was a subtle glow, easy to ignore if I wasn't staring directly at the rat, but to my vision, the rat was clearly glowing a dark blue color. The glowing rat was also bigger and seemed to have even more intelligence behind its small, beady eyes. It turned to watch the rat I had kicked land, checking to see if it was getting up again, whereas the smaller, non-glowing rat didn't pay any attention and rushed forward to attack me.

Positioned as I was on the top of the stairs, I easily dodged the charging rat. As it snapped at my shin, I stepped back, grabbed it by the scruff, and tossed it at the glowing rat below it as hard as I could. The blue rat dodged to the side, avoiding the incoming rat, but the one I threw wasn't as lucky; my strength caused it to slam into the stairs and then bounce down to the bottom level, where it lay unmoving like the first rat I had fought here.

I looked at the blue rat suspiciously, but before I could do anything, I felt an impact against my back. I pitched forward, losing my balance and falling down the steps. As I did, I felt the rat I had left behind me biting into my neck and scalp, drawing blood and causing significant pain. I screamed as I fell, the sensation of pain so overwhelming that my vision went white for a moment and I lost all sense of myself.

When I came to, I was lying at the bottom of the stairs. The rat that had knocked me over was underneath me, my fingers wrapped around its thick, hairy neck as I slammed its head into the stone floor over and over. Rat blood sprayed over me as my own blood dripped from the back of my neck and scalp. It was absolutely disgusting, but my body was so flushed with fear and adrenaline that I barely noticed. I released the rat, recognizing that it was long dead, and turned to find the blue rat gnawing at my ankle, trying to cripple me with its powerful teeth. It had managed to damage my pants but hadn't fully torn through them yet. My Achilles' heel felt bruised but was not torn to shreds like it would have been without my enhanced pants.

I bunched my hand into a fist and struck the blue rat in its nose, sending it backward and making it squeal in pain. I lunged after it, pushing myself across the bloody stone toward it. It recovered quickly, but I was faster. I grabbed its head with one hand and lifted it up before slamming it into the ground as hard as I could. The first slam only disoriented the rat, which was protected by its thick hide and large body, but I didn't let up, slamming it over and over until it stopped struggling in my arms. I stood up, making sure it was truly dead before dropping its filthy corpse onto the floor.

I looked around but didn't see any more rats nearby. I tried to control my breathing so I could listen to my surroundings, but my body refused to stop panting. I shook my head and took several deep breaths, forcibly calming myself down as much as I could.

When nothing else attacked me, I reached up and felt the back of my head and neck. The biggest wound was on the back of my neck, where I felt two big gashes that were bleeding freely. Smaller scratches covered the back of my head, and my hair was already matting from the blood. I touched them gingerly but didn't find anything that seemed likely to kill me right now.

I carefully checked the courtyard but didn't find any more rats except one of the two I had tossed over the third-floor balcony. It wasn't dead, but it was injured enough that it couldn't join the fight earlier. The other one I had tossed over must have joined in the attack on the stairs. I killed the injured rat with a quick stomp to its head, putting it out of its misery.

Now that I wasn't breathing so loudly, I could hear the world around me better, so I stopped and listened. The city was back to being eerily silent, except for the sound of the trapped rat above me scrabbling and slamming itself against the door. I set my nanobots to work. They healed my injuries and repaired my clothes as I returned to the bottom of the stairs. It would take time, but I was confident in my nanobots. They would heal me completely, given enough time, even if the rat's teeth and claws had carried a nasty disease.

As I stood near the dead rats, letting my nanobots start their work, I noticed that the rat that had been glowing blue was beginning to glow even brighter in death. I stepped back, unsure of what was happening. A moment later, the blue light coalesced above the rat's body, slowly forming into an orb that began to float in midair. As I stared at the strange, glowing orb, I also felt something foreign enter my mind. It felt like receiving information back home, before I put myself into my body.

Dire rat defeated—1 experience awarded.
Dire rat defeated—1 experience awarded.
Dire rat defeated—1 experience awarded.
Dire rat defeated—1 experience awarded.
Dire rat defeated—1 experience awarded.
Dire rat sub-boss defeated—5 experience awarded.
No class detected. Experience pooled for future use.

The communication was similar to how my siblings and I had used to communicate, except this time I wasn't connected to them through the global networking system. This felt almost telepathic in nature. Was it a magical re-creation of the global networking system my world had developed? How had it detected me and interfaced with my unique biomechanical brain? I must have made myself human enough to trigger whatever governed the esoteric systems I had detected on this world.

I felt happiness at the messages, despite their strange appearance in my mind. This was what I had been looking for when I spent all those months scanning different worlds. Gaining experience, as if I was still in one of the virtual reality worlds back on Earth, was exactly what I hoped to find. Although the brutality of the fight with the rats was much more realistic than I had anticipated, I still felt a surge of happiness at the confirmation I had found the right kind of world. I was a bit surprised by how little experience the rats awarded, but I was used to a virtual reality world where entertainment was the goal and so experience and rewards were tuned pretty high. I was guessing, in this world, that wasn't going to be the case.

I stood up and approached the glowing orb, which still floated above the larger rat's body. I now knew that these were called dire rats and that the blue glow indicated that this had been a sub-boss of some kind. I reached forward, unsure of what it was, but I assumed I was meant to collect it somehow. As my hand touched the orb, it sparkled one more time and then solidified into a perfect, small blue orb. The light slowly faded, and I was left holding a blue orb about the size of my thumbnail.

I stood up fully and stretched. I still felt good despite my first brush with mortality. My body had responded well. I had moved rapidly and with significant strength. The wounds I had suffered were already starting to mend, although they still hurt significantly more than I had anticipated.

Not wanting to pass up any experience, having learned that lesson early on when playing games with Michael, I went upstairs and finished off the last rat before leaving the building.

Dire rat defeated—1 experience awarded.

I was still missing experience from one of the rats I had fought, if my count was right, but I guessed the one that had fallen out of the window during the first few seconds of the fight had survived. I searched around the outside of the building but found no trace of it. It must have scampered off before I could get to it.

I stood in the street near where the rat would have fallen, considering what to do next. I didn't need to eat as much as a normal human thanks to my unique body, but I would eventually get hungry. I would also need to consume food to power my nanobots, especially considering the extra work they were performing in healing my wounds and mending my clothing. I wasn't squeamish about eating the rats if it came to that, but since it would be a couple of days at least before I felt truly hungry, I decided to wait and see if I could get more appropriate food for my very first meal as a living being. It felt wrong to experience the pleasures of eating—something humans went on and on about throughout their entire history—by consuming a dead rat.

27

Holding the strange blue orb in my hand, I set off to explore more of this dangerous new world.

Chapter 4

Armored tusk-rat defeated—3 experience awarded.

I groaned as I slumped further down the wall I was leaning against. The animal, apparently called an armored tusk-rat, had snuck up on me by hiding in a pile of refuse as I walked past it. It had been significantly harder to kill than the dire rats, due mainly to its armored hide. My fists and kicks did little to its armor, but thankfully it was slow enough for me to eventually kill.

I hadn't received any cuts from the creature, but it had a long, flat tail that had gotten in a few good hits here and there, adding several nasty bruises to my already injured body.

Before I had been so rudely ambushed, I had been carefully exploring the city. I was afraid of finding something more dangerous than the rats, so I had been moving quietly and scanning every street, building, and alley diligently as I traveled. Unfortunately, I couldn't see through piles of broken wood and bricks, and the creature must have heard me as I passed.

While exploring, I still hadn't encountered another person in the vast metropolis. I was aiming for one of the taller buildings in the area, a large tenement that stretched five stories into the sky, when I passed the hiding place of the monster. I was hoping to get high enough that I could check the city for lights during the night, hopefully discovering if people still lived anywhere around here.

I stood up, brushing myself off from the frantic fight with the armored tusk-rat, and then continued slowly toward the tenement as quietly as I could. The city itself was definitely Roman in origin. I had found several mosaics and writing in a mix of Greek and Latin that hinted at the Roman nature of the city. It was also very clear that the technology level of the city had never advanced beyond pseudo-medieval. There were no signs of electricity, railroads, cars, or the industrial revolution at all. The roads had ruts in them consistent with wheeled carts, and if the city wasn't already covered with dirt and filth, it would be easy to imagine horses pulling the carts throughout the city, making messes everywhere they went.

None of the buildings I had briefly searched had indoor plumbing, although many of the richer buildings had a central courtyard similar to the one I had fought the rats in. Most of them had wells or cisterns for water. The rich and the poor seemed intertwined in the city, richly adorned buildings and courtyard homes built next to apartment buildings or cheap wooden homes.

The remnants of businesses, eateries, and other commercial enterprises were here and there throughout the city, seemingly placed without any sense of organization or planning.

I approached the large tenement I had marked before because it was higher than almost everything else nearby. The front entrance was a large open archway with no doors. The archway led into a paved courtyard in the center of the tenement. The apartments stretched up all around me on each side of the courtyard. There wasn't any sign of damage, other than the wear and tear of time. Behind me, two stairways on each side of the archway led upward through the middle of the building to the different floors above.

I listened carefully but couldn't hear anything moving around me, the eerie silence of the city extending inside this courtyard as well. The lack of birds or normal-sized scavengers was especially concerning in a city as large as this. Without humans, this place should be crawling with nature. The only thing that would keep them away was something equally dangerous—or more dangerous—that had stepped in and replaced the humans that once lived here.

I carefully crept up the rickety stairs to the top floor of the tenement. There was very little light in the stairway; all the windows were closed and shuttered. My body was on edge, my reflexes firing every time my step caused a board to creak underneath me. Sweat was plastered to my forehead and my ears strained to hear anything that might be nearby.

After an unknown amount of time, I finally reached the top of the tenement. The stairway opened out to a long hallway that ran the length of the building, turning to the right in the distance. On each side of the hallway were doors, most of them closed, but a few were broken or left open by whoever had left here so long ago.

30

Very little light trickled into the hallway. I had no idea how normal humans could have seen in here, and I could only see thanks to my enhanced vision picking up the diffuse light coming through the occasional open apartment door.

I paused and listened but still heard nothing nearby, so I walked slowly down the hallway. I looked in each of the open doorways, seeing ruined apartments that had been abandoned for an untold amount of time. Halfway down the hallway, I found a door that was open but undamaged, and I decided to enter that apartment.

Inside was covered in dust, and much of the rough furniture was destroyed. The smell was disgusting, worse than even the streets outside. The apartment smelled like rot, mold, and something that had once been living but had clearly died a long time ago. I tried to force the smell out of my mind, regretting for a moment that I had given myself such a sensitive nose.

I stepped into the center of the apartment and looked around. Wooden shelving had once adorned one of the walls but was now slumped down and partially rotted. A cheap mattress of cloth and stuffing had been left to rot under a set of windows on the far side of the apartment. A few broken pots, the remnants of a chair, and some other unknown debris covered the floor. The windows were both shuttered, letting in just a small amount of light. There was no second room.

I approached the windows and opened them both fully. A welcome gust of fresh air struck me as I pushed the shutters aside, dispelling the stench of the apartment from my nostrils. This high up, I could smell the tang of salt in the air; wherever I found myself was likely close to a sea or ocean of some kind. I carefully leaned out of the open windows, eager to see more of my surroundings.

As I took in the sight of the city, I couldn't help but marvel at what I saw. The city stretched for miles all around me. Cutting through the city were two large bodies of water, one narrow and one wide. From where I was now, I could look across the largest body of water to the east and see an entire landmass. That side of the water seemed even more ruined; barely a single building remained standing. To my right, the city stretched out into the water to form a peninsula. Large cathedrals and temples dominated the tip of the peninsula, and that entire area seemed to shimmer to my eyes, as if hidden behind some kind of barrier. What I could see through the shimmering barrier seemed better maintained than the rest of the city. Possibly a sign of people, I hoped.

To my left, the north of the city stretched out until it hit the second, smaller body of water. Across the water was a separate part of the city, hugging the edge of the water and spreading just a couple of miles north. It appeared to be in even better condition than the temples, and even from here I could see people walking the streets. I felt a surge of relief. I came to this world in part for adventure, but I had been starting to worry I might be the only person left.

The northern part of the city must have once been a thriving port, because docks and warehouses surrounded the waterfront. Still, I couldn't see any boats larger than some small fishing boats moored at the docks. What had clearly once held large merchant ships now held nothing but a few ragtag fishing boats.

Two bridges spanned the water between the main city where I was and the more northern, intact area. The more distant bridge to the northwest looked intact, but I could see that the nearest bridge was shattered two-thirds of the way across. Built upon the bridge was a patchwork of buildings stretching several stories above the bridge and even below it down to the level of the water. It looked like a post-apocalyptic slum had been built on every available inch of the bridge. The many buildings were of all different sizes and shapes and the only thing they had in common was that they all leaned precariously against each other to form one large, dangerous-looking collection of interconnected buildings.

Most fascinating of all, though, was that the bridge appeared heavily populated. The broken bridge was further away than the northern part of the city, but with my enhanced vision, I could see thousands of people walking, climbing, talking, selling, fishing, arguing, and doing any number of things all over the bridge and its many buildings. I watched them, fascinated to see so many people crammed into such a small space and navigating the dangerous structures that covered the bridge. It was like every person was an acrobat, deftly maneuvering around each other, climbing up and down the sides of the buildings, and scuttling side to side across the many precariously constructed walkways. The bridge was a living nest, in many ways, one made from salvaged wood and stone, and people packed the bridge from the water line to the tallest building.

A fleet of small boats was returning to the bridge. Most of the boats docked on the far side of the bridge, but several passed under it and began to dock where I could watch them. The buildings at the waterline were populated by people waiting for the boats to return. I watched as the fishermen unloaded their catch to the people waiting, who in turn loaded the fish into containers hanging from above. Once a container was full of fish, people pulled it up and unloaded it quickly. Given the emptiness of the city around me, fishing must be one of the primary food sources for the people living on the broken bridge. I didn't see gardens or open spaces that could be used to grow anything nearby.

I watched as night started to fall around me. Before the sun fully set, several of the fishermen began to gesture and yell, pointing up the waterway toward the other bridge. I watched as several people rushed to the edge of the bridge above the fishermen, looking at where the others had pointed. I followed their gaze and saw a large fin break the water, rushing toward the fishermen who were still unloading the catch under the bridge. The fin was big enough to belong to a whale, but I had a feeling the creature it belonged to was a lot more dangerous.

As I was staring at the fin, a streak of fire flew from the bridge. The fire arced through the air and crashed into the water near the creature, exploding into a ring of fire that set even the water on fire for several moments. I turned my attention back to the bridge and saw several other people launching what had to be spells at the creature. Several others had also drawn bows and began to launch projectiles in its direction.

Several of the spells impacted on top of the fish, and an arrow pierced the fin, even when fired from such a great distance. The creature, whatever it was, responded swiftly and turned away from the bridge, diving deeper into the water. The fishermen hadn't stopped working the entire time, frantically unloading their boats even as the creature turned away from them.

I watched the people on the bridge until the sun set. Not many lights appeared on the bridge, probably due to the fact that it was one small fire away from burning to the ground. Where the bridge

33

met the land on this side of the water, though, a number of torches lit up as the sun set. There, a large ramshackle wall had been built to protect the bridge, and a number of armed guards stood on top of the wall, facing out toward the dark city.

I also saw more lights appearing on the second, intact bridge to the northwest, in the temple area, and in the part of the city across the water to the north. I leaned out of the window slightly and saw that the northwestern bridge ended on this side of the water in a large palace surrounded by a thick stone wall. The lights on the distant bridge and the walls of the palace glowed blue instead of the red of natural flame, and I noticed that they didn't flicker in the wind like natural fire would either. To the east, across the larger body of water, not a single light could be seen. The devastation I had briefly glimpsed on that side of the water was completely hidden, shrouded in darkness that seemed subtly unnatural to my eyes.

Having had a chance to see more of the city, I realized I was in the same place where I had left my old world: Istanbul, or ancient Constantinople. I couldn't explain why the technology level was so different, but based on the layout of the city and the waterways, it was easy to pinpoint where I was.

What was clear was that this was some ancient, fallen version of that city. Was time different here? Was I back in the time of ancient Constantinople? Or had something happened to stop the progress of technology in this world? Did the existence of magic make technological advancement unnecessary? That still didn't explain what had happened to the city, but at least I had spotted a few survivors. Hopefully I could make contact with them and get a few answers to my many questions.

Around me, the shadows of the city began to lengthen as the sun set in the west. I began to hear strange sounds from below as the city began to darken. As I looked down, I was shocked by a sudden roar from the street below. I scanned the area to see what could have made the sound and saw movement all over the streets and buildings where just moments before there had been nothing but the movement of a slow, lazy wind blowing through the empty streets. What had been a dead city was suddenly boiling with life and movement. I tried to count how many things I saw but could barely keep track of the shadows as they slipped, climbed, and fought below me.

I slowly backed away from the windows, not wanting to draw any attention to myself. It appeared the city had awoken as night fell, but I didn't think I wanted to meet the new occupants.

I crouched and approached the window from a lower angle, peering just over the windowsill to hide from anything that might look up toward me. I watched the city go insane below me. After hours of total silence, the cacophony was so overwhelming I could barely focus on any individual sound enough to isolate where it was coming from. Animalistic sounds dominated the night. Roars, screeches, and cries of fighting and pain echoed up to me from every street. I saw several creatures take to the skies around the city, and I ducked further in case they could spot me in the window. I couldn't help but notice that many of the things flying in the air were as big as a human or bigger.

I watched, wide-eyed, until the very last rays of the sun disappeared and the faint moonlight cast the city into a barely lit nightmare. Thousands of creatures roamed the streets, fighting, killing, and eating each other. I couldn't see more than flashes of the creatures; they moved so rapidly in the dim moonlight. I had all of the best engineering and stolen technology from a very advanced Earth, but looking down at the mass of monsters rampaging through the city, I suddenly felt very humbled.

Protected by the walls, the few pockets of humanity left in the city were busy fighting off the swarm of monsters. Nobody seemed to be panicking on the walls, so this must be a nightly occurrence. That would explain why most of the city was abandoned as well— humanity must have had to retreat to the most defensible places to survive.

I watched the city for a bit longer before turning and very quietly crawling toward the door that led out of the apartment I was in. I didn't hear anything in the apartments near me, but I had no clue how perceptive the monsters were, so I didn't want to risk being found out.

One thing was for sure: I would need to get a weapon of some kind soon and try to find out more about the magic of this world if I wanted to survive. I managed to survive the first few monsters I encountered during the day, but whatever insanity was going on below at night was too much for me. I was lucky to just survive the daytime. It was a strange feeling, realizing I was so vulnerable and mortal. I didn't exactly regret my choice, but it was with a complex mix of worry and excitement that I turned away and snuck out of the apartment I was hiding in. Knowing I was so vulnerable made me more alert, more on edge, more *alive* than I had felt in my past life. At the same time, I couldn't ignore the mental image of the city boiling with monsters as the sun began to set. The fear of such overwhelming otherness set me on edge and kept my biological body in a near-constant state of fight or flight.

Once I was back in the hallway, I made my way around the corner to my right, moving as quietly as my enhanced body would allow. My ears were straining to hear anything nearby, but thankfully, nothing bothered me. I carefully made my way down another stretch of empty, ruined hallway and then turned to my right again in order to find an apartment with windows that were placed on the other side of the building so I could see more of the city.

Once I found an appropriate apartment, I carefully approached the window and looked out. I was looking back at what would be Europe in my world. Rolling hills stretched into the distance, and a few large roads cut through the countryside, leading away from the city. Massive walls stretched across the western part of the city. I must be looking at the famous Theodosian Walls, except unlike in the time I had come from, they were still functional. The wall was lit with the same blue lights that surrounded the palace I had seen earlier. There was also a smaller wall that cut through the city itself, connecting to the Theodosian Walls at the far north and south of the city to form a large section that was cut off from the ruined part I was in. The smaller wall was also lit with the glowing blue lights. It was hard to see what was inside the large part of land that was protected by the walls, since no lights were glowing inside the protected area. Towers were interspersed evenly on the two walls, and a large castle anchored the wall at the southernmost point where it connected with the sea.

In the glow of the blue lights, people on the wall were fighting what looked like large animals or monsters, but I couldn't make out the details. I watched for over an hour as the defenders repelled attack after attack from the creatures swarming up the walls from the ruined part of the city.

I wasn't feeling tired—and I wasn't sure if I could even sleep since I had never experienced such a thing as sleep before—so after I stopped watching the people on the walls, I left the room and began to explore the rest of the apartments more thoroughly. After searching almost every room on multiple floors, I had no luck finding a weapon. The majority of the apartments were ruined beyond repair and contained only the barest of furniture. It was clear that the previous residents weren't the kind of people who could afford weapons, and if they could have, they probably took them when they fled.

As the sun started to rise, I made my way back to the first apartment I had visited and watched as the monsters began to retreat from the coming light. I tried to see where the monsters were disappearing to, but they were all gone before enough light appeared in the sky for me to see the details.

In my search of the apartments, I had managed to find a few things that would be useful. It was clear that the people who had lived here had not been wealthy by any means, but even still, when the city had flourished, even the poorest individuals seemed to have a few luxuries. I found and collected several small knives, a few ornaments, and some clasps made from decent iron. I also found plenty of old but still salvageable leather from various chairs and bits of furniture.

I settled into the window to watch the city come back to life and sent my nanobots to begin the process of reshaping the iron in front of me. I didn't find any steel in the apartment building, which wasn't surprising given the fact that steel was relatively rare and primarily used for weapons in this era.

As the sun rose fully, the city quieted down to absolute silence once again. An hour or so after dawn broke, I was distracted from working with the iron as I saw people leaving the bridge community. A handful of people left the security of the bridge and began to spread out through the city. I watched, amazed, as the people seemed to leap unnaturally from roof to roof; the grace and speed of their movements were well beyond that of normal humans back on Earth. They each wore large gray cloaks that covered them from head to toe, blending into the dirty city remarkably well.

37

They began to spread out when they got away from the bridge, and several began to disappear into buildings here or there. They seemed like scavengers or hunters of some kind, possibly looking for the bodies of the creatures that had taken over the city during the night.

As I watched the city come to life below me, the fleet of fishing boats also launched from the bridge. A few boats joined the fleet from the northern, intact portion of the city as well. They spread out through the larger waterway that separated this part of the city from the eastern landmass where almost nothing was left standing.

Finally, several caravans also left different parts of the city. I watched as armored knights escorted several large wagons, pulled by horses, from the temple district. A smaller caravan of people on foot left the bridge community, surrounded by people in more ramshackle-looking armor. I also saw several wagons crossing the large, intact bridge between the northern part of the city and the palace.

It was clear the city was still alive, but barely. Overwhelmed by whatever it was that came out at night, the people of the city seemed to have retreated to a few pockets of safety. I had the bad luck of entering the city in one of the abandoned parts, but it could have been worse; I could have entered this world in the empty lands across the water to the east.

As the morning sun began to rise toward noon, my nanobots had finished constructing a large steel knife from the smaller iron ones I had scavenged. I held it up in front of me and admired the craftsmanship. The blade was as long as my hand from palm to fingertips, and the hilt was wrapped tightly with leather I had found to ensure a safe grip in my hand. My nanobots had taken the forged iron I had scavenged and turned it into modern steel by re-forging the metal and introducing carbon, thereby forming a significantly stronger alloy. I also set the nanobots to sharpen the blade to an edge and reinforce even the fine steel with nanofibers.

That way, if I came across more armored beasts, it should penetrate effectively without being so weak as to break. If a blacksmith from this era were to carefully inspect this knife, it would likely be one of the finest knives they had ever seen.

I set the knife down and set to work crafting a belt, a sheath for the knife, and a small satchel that would attach to my belt. Once that was done, the sun was well past noon and getting close to evening. I was impressed by the ability of my nanobots to modify things on a molecular level, but they weren't exactly quick at doing so. To go any faster, they would need more fuel than my body alone could provide.

More scavengers had spread throughout the city as the sun rose. Several of them met up with a caravan here or there to exchange goods. The caravans seemed to run essential goods throughout the city, but it was clearly dangerous work; I saw them come under attack from the daytime monsters several times. The buildings made it hard to see what was going on, but the yells that carried through the silent city and the occasional explosions that followed made it clear something was going on.

As the day went by, I moved apartments occasionally to get a better view of the entire city. To the west, where the two walls spanned the length of the city, I could finally see what the walls were protecting. I had expected more devastation or ruined city, but instead I saw large farms with fields of wheat, orchards of fruit, and pastures of livestock. Whoever was protecting the area must have converted the interior into a safe place to grow food. Other than the fishing boats, the farms seemed like the only place that was producing food in the city. Many of the caravans entered one of the gates surrounding the farms, likely to trade for food.

By the time my belt and other goods were finished, I was feeling hungry and thirsty. My body would normally be able to go days without needing sustenance, but the nanobots drew on my own energy reserves to power themselves, so I was feeling the effect of using them so much. The apartments had no running water, so I made my way back downstairs and out to the street until I found another courtyard home that had a well.

As I was hauling up water to quench my thirst, my enhanced hearing picked up the sound of several creatures approaching from the rooms around me. I had listened carefully and not heard a sound as I entered the courtyard, but now that I knew the city was overrun by creatures, I wasn't caught by surprise like last time. The sounds were coming from several of the rooms around me, where doors had been broken off the hinges. The sun filtering into the courtyard didn't penetrate into the rooms, so I couldn't see what was coming, but I made out the very soft sound of shuffling feet. It was similar to what I'd heard from the rats, indicating smaller creatures.

I quickly moved away from the center of the courtyard and pulled my knife from its sheath on my belt. I heard tiny feet shuffling inside one of the nearby rooms, so I moved closer. As I settled next to the broken door that led into the room, two antennae began to carefully poke past the doorway, twitching as if scenting the air in the courtyard. They swiveled back and forth, and when they turned in my direction, they jerked backward in surprise, clearly detecting my presence.

Reacting swiftly, I ducked around the doorway and slammed my knife between the two antennae, puncturing the head of a large insect-like creature. I pulled my knife out smoothly and pierced the creature several more times in the head. It didn't have time to react to my swift attack, collapsing to the ground in front of me after the second strike from my knife. I followed it down, making sure it was truly dead before I stopped attacking it.

Before I could step away from its corpse, a foul musk erupted from its body, engulfing me in a vile stench. I gagged, stepping back to avoid breathing in too much of it. The smell rapidly permeated the air around me, and I once again cursed the enhanced sense of smell I had given this body. As the air of the courtyard stirred the musk around me, I heard loud clicking sounds and saw several more of the creatures running toward me, caution thrown to the wind by the smell of their dead brethren.

The first to reach me gave me a better look at what I was facing. The creatures appeared to be a mix of a beetle, a cockroach, and a praying mantis, and they came up to about mid-thigh on me. Two large mandibles like a praying mantis's claws hung down from their faces and looked dangerously strong. The creatures scuttled across the ground on many little legs like a cockroach but had thick, armored exoskeletons covering their backs and sides like a beetle. It was an intimidating combination. The armor and speed of the creature combined with the large, dangerous-looking mandibles made my heart begin to pound in fear.

I stepped forward, refusing to let my body make me hesitate out of fear, and met the one charging toward me. I met it further into the courtyard so I would have room to maneuver since the rest of the monsters were rapidly approaching as well. With a quick sidestep, I dodged the creature's mandibles and swiped my knife through the base of its antennae, cutting them both off with a single strike. The creature let out several loud clicks, clearly in distress. I hadn't seen any eyes on the monsters, so I reasoned the antennae were their only way to see the environment around them—which made them a perfect weakness to exploit. I dodged the now-clumsy attacks from the creature closest to me, easily able to avoid its blind bites in my direction. I turned my back on the blinded monster, leaving it to suffer blindly, and wove my way between the pillars that held up the second-floor balcony. The other creatures had closed in, but I surprised them with my speed, catching one off guard as I swung around a pillar and slashed off one of its antennae with my knife. It tried to turn toward me, clicking in distress at losing one of its sensory organs, but I kicked it in the side as hard as I could before it could face me.

The one I kicked flew away from me, flipping over and crashing into the lightly grassed courtyard in front of me. I sensed two more of the creatures trying to get to me around the nearest pillar. I looked up to see three more of the insects running toward me from other parts of the house. I dodged back around the pillar, narrowly missing a pair of mandibles that clacked violently where I had been standing. I dodged around the other side of the pillar and caught the other insect by surprise, cutting off both its antennae with a single swipe of my knife.

It was clear these creatures were dangerous, but they were also vulnerable. They were slower than me, and they seemed to have trouble perceiving things behind solid objects as if their vision relied on echolocation of some kind. It made it easy for me to avoid them by dodging around the pillars, dropping out of their sight momentarily, and then striking their vulnerable antennae with my knife, crippling them.

As the other three got near me, I was a bit more hard-pressed to keep the pillar between us. I blinded several more as I dodged between different pillars, dancing away from the deadly mandibles like a whirling dervish, impressed once again by the agility and speed of my new body—and happy that my mind and body were able to work as one whenever danger reared its head. One of them got a lucky bite on my thigh as I failed to dodge its mandibles completely. I grunted at the sudden shock of pain, but my mind was able to keep focused despite the pain. I sliced down, severing one of the mandibles and escaping before any of the other creatures caught me.

After that, I couldn't dodge as effectively, but thankfully, most of them were maimed enough that I could finish them off with no further problems. It felt a bit coldhearted to kill them as they blindly stumbled around the courtyard, still trying to find me even without the ability to see, but I had no mercy for the insects that had attacked me first. I killed them all quickly with a stab or two through the head, easily penetrating the thick chitin that protected them. After the last of them died, my mind was filled with the announcements I had come to expect after defeating the creatures that inhabited this city.

Weak devourer defeated—1 experience awarded.
Weak devourer defeated—1 experience awarded.

The experience announcements continued five more times, notifying me of the measly one experience each I earned for killing the "weak devourers".

No class detected. Experience pooled for future use.

I hastily moved away from the dead creatures and their musky scent. The pain in my leg slowed me down, but I couldn't afford to stick around too long; the smell of the dead creatures might attract more of their kind. None of the bugs I had killed glowed, and the announcement of their names did not list any of them as a sub-boss, so I knew there could be a stronger version of the creature somewhere nearby. Even though I had been quickly able to understand the weaknesses of the creatures, with my slight injury, I was in no mood to tackle a larger, more dangerous version of these things.

I left the building, abandoning the well for now, and hobbled as quietly as I could down the road until I found another building that had a closed wooden door under a deep-set archway. I settled down in the archway and checked my thigh where I had been bitten.

The insect hadn't broken the skin, thankfully, but deep bruises were already forming where its mandibles had attempted to crush my leg. If I had been a normal human, I suspected the creature would have crippled me with its bite, despite my protective clothing; it did little to stop crushing force.

My knife had proved helpful. I wasn't sure if I could have been able to kill the insects nearly as easily without it, but it was clear that to survive here, I would need more than just a knife. I also needed to secure food and a more reliable source of water. Even though my body could ignore such needs for a long time, it couldn't do so forever. I was still feeling the hunger and thirst from crafting my knife and belt, so I couldn't wait too long before finding some sustenance.

Despite my hunger, I set my nanobots to heal my thigh as rapidly as they could and waited patiently for almost an hour as they worked. I listened carefully as I waited but heard nothing approaching the archway. It was already afternoon when I had left earlier, so I nervously watched the shadows cast by the sun as they moved across the cobblestones in front of me. It was getting a little too close to dark for my comfort, but I didn't want to risk moving through the city with an injured leg.

When I felt the nanobots finish, I stood and shook out my leg. I took several careful steps to test my leg and had no problem moving it. I felt a very slight pain deep in my leg, but it didn't slow me down. Hopefully it would fade soon.

I was slightly frustrated that I hadn't made much progress in exploring the city or making contact with the humans that inhabited it. Still, I had learned a lot from watching them from the apartment window, and I reminded myself that I wasn't in that much of a rush, except for my need for food and water. I didn't want to bungle my first contact with people that had access to magic or abilities I didn't understand. They could be dangerous in unpredictable ways and I needed to make a good impression if I wanted to learn more about this world and what had happened here in the city.

I decided I didn't want to risk being anywhere near the ground floor when it became dark, so I hastily explored the nearby streets and buildings until I found another source of water. In the center of a small square between several one-story businesses, I found a ground cistern that had sat covered for a long time but still held mostly clear water. After drinking my fill, I made my way back to the apartment building I had hidden in last night before the shadows got too long around me. I knew the building was empty of monsters, so I figured it was the safest place to hide for now—at least until I had a better idea of what was going on around me.

As I perched in one of the windows facing west, I watched the sun begin to sink behind the horizon. It was a beautiful sight, marred only by the sounds of stirring below me as the shadows began to overtake the city streets. I watched as the scavengers that hadn't already retreated toward their various fortified locations jumped from rooftop to rooftop, racing toward the protective walls they had come from. It seemed nobody wanted to be caught out after dark.

I had no experience with sleeping, but I knew it would help conserve resources for my body and finish healing my leg, so I forced myself to lie down on the dusty ground of the apartment and close my eyes. I felt strange lying there. My mind focused on memories of Michael, of my time in the old world. I even imagined what it would be like to meet the people of this world. I felt my mind begin to slowly dissociate from reality, my thoughts slipping slowly toward a precipice I had never crossed before. The first few times it happened, I jerked awake, my mind panicking at the loss of control. Eventually, I forced myself to relax, trying to find that melding of mind and body I had experienced when fighting for my life. I needed to trust my new body, not fight it every step of the way. Otherwise, I would end up dead in this dangerous new world.

I wasn't consciously aware when it happened, but I eventually managed to fall asleep for the first time in my life.

Chapter 5

The next morning, I woke up with a gasp. My mind spun, and for the first time in my existence, I felt something like truly irrational panic. The remnants of a nightmare lingered in my panic-fueled mind, now mixing with the flush of adrenaline my body had unhelpfully produced. I took several deep breaths, forcing myself to calm down. I closed my eyes and refused to let my mind be so . . . vulnerable. I was better than this, I told myself over and over until my body began to calm itself down. Funny how my body could respond so acutely to my panic-filled mind, but when I tried to control it consciously, it fought me every step of the way, insisting on unconscious impulses instead of direct commands.

Once I was feeling slightly better, I rubbed my eyes and looked around me. I regretted sleeping, not only because it was risky in these circumstances but because it was clear now that I wasn't ready for it quite yet. I refocused on the world around me, noticing the sun peeking through the open window above me. I also noticed that the city was back to its eerily quiet state. The only sound near me was my own ragged breathing and the wind blowing past the window. Despite my poor decision to sleep, I had managed to survive another night. I was still feeling hungry, but not as hungry as if I had kept myself awake all night, and my leg felt recovered from the trauma it had suffered yesterday.

My goal today was to make contact with someone and try to get some answers to what was going on in this city. With a deep breath, I stood and carefully made my way out of the apartment building I was squatting in. I listened carefully and moved as quietly as I could, which was becoming the new normal for me in this world, but I didn't encounter anything as I exited the building.

Outside, the city looked as bad as it always did. Checking around, I didn't see anything dangerous nearby, so I began to wind my way through the alleys and streets that led toward the ruined bridge. I had carefully scouted the streets from above the day before, so I was able to easily find my way through the once-confusing streets. I figured the people inhabiting the ruined bridge might be the most approachable since they didn't seem as militarized as those in the other areas of the city. The temple area seemed more dangerous, with their fully armored guards, and the palace was a potential minefield that I didn't want to walk into without more information. The walls to the west were an option, but I figured the inhabitants would be skeptical of a stranger, whereas the settlement on the bridge seemed to have less structure and organization. Having seen the merchant from the ruined bridge stop for scavengers several times, I hoped they might stop for me if I could catch them before they entered the palace or the walled-off section of the city.

As I traveled, I kept a close eye on my surroundings and heard creatures moving before I saw them several times. I avoided getting too close to those buildings and avoided piles of garbage as thoroughly as possible, so nothing seemed to notice me as I quietly moved through the streets. I also avoided alleys and narrow roads, sticking to the larger streets that led toward my destination. The main roads, while overgrown, dirty, and covered with the occasional ruined building or pillar, were still easier to navigate than the small alleys and streets full of debris and broken buildings.

Eventually, I made it close enough to the ruined bridge that I saw one of the scavengers leap across the street above me. As I watched, the person flew through the air like a bird, the gray cloak trailing behind them. I calculated the distance between the two buildings, deducing it was approximately thirty-five feet, and the building they had landed on was higher than the one they had leapt from. There was, without a doubt, no way a person on my Earth could have done that.

I stopped and marveled at the superhuman display as the tail of the gray cloak disappeared over the lip of the building above me. The person either didn't notice me or, more likely, didn't care enough to stop and investigate me. I waited to see if they would come back or if anyone else would appear nearby, but after a few moments, nothing happened, so I continued on my way.

I traveled for another hour, winding through the city streets at a slow but steady pace. As I was scouting a major road, close to where I believed the caravan would travel, I stopped suddenly when I saw a large dog glowing with a blue aura. The dog hadn't noticed me yet, but it was close, so it soon would. It was sniffing at the ground and pawing at a pile of broken stone and wood about twenty feet in front of me. It must have caught some smell from me because it sniffed again and then turned to look right at me.

The blue glow of the dog gave the scene an unreal quality, but its low growl as it began to pace toward me shattered that unreality. I pulled my knife from its sheath and eyed the dog warily as it continued to slowly move toward me. Its growls grew louder, and saliva began to drip from its large, sharp teeth. My mind frantically cataloged everything I was seeing and tried to come up with a plan. I noticed that the dog was either injured or had some kind of monstrous mutation; its skin looked blistered and burned, and I could smell the faint odor of brimstone wafting down the street toward me as it got closer.

The dog stopped and crouched for a moment. I had a brief hope it was going to stop approaching me, but instead, it squatted and growled as if in pain, then burst into flames. It howled as the flames consumed it, and I jerked back in surprise at the sight, but after a moment, the dog shook its head and then resumed approaching me, only now it was covered in a deep red, hellish-looking flame that flickered angrily all around its body. The dog seemed to be hurt by the flames but not incapacitated in the slightest as it continued forward, eyeing me hungrily.

"Great," I said, staring at the dog that was now covered in flames. I felt monumentally unprepared for this world, despite the body I had crafted with great care. I did not expect angry dogs that could set themselves on fire.

I began to back away slowly, but that had the opposite effect I had been hoping for. The dog took that as a sign of weakness and leapt forward, an excited bark escaping its flaming jaws. I couldn't afford to get into a melee with the dog since it would burn me horribly just by being close by, so my knife was useless. I had nothing with which to fight this beast effectively.

So instead of trying to fight, I took the next best option and ran for it. I pushed off the wall I had been crouched behind as I scouted the new street and sprinted back the way I had come. The dog seemed even happier to see me run, letting out even more excited barks like we were playing a sick game of catch, except I was the ball and it was a large flaming dog that would kill me if it caught me. I didn't turn to look behind me as I sprinted, but I could hear the dog as it gave chase.

I had never run at full speed in my new body, but as I began to stretch my legs to their fullest, I thanked my past self for how thoroughly I had engineered my body. I felt the cobblestones under my boots, and my long legs and enhanced body ate up the distance as I ran. My body understood immediately that I was fleeing for my life. My breathing regulated itself and became even, unconsciously adapting itself to long-distance running. I couldn't help but appreciate the assistance as I fled for my life. For once, I didn't resent the instincts that overrode my conscious mind.

I quickly outpaced the beast. Even though the dog was clearly supernatural in some way, it seemed unable to catch up to me. Maybe the fire slowed it down some, but as I ran, I couldn't help but measure how fast I was moving and calculated I was running faster than any human on Earth could have run. I would have set records if I was allowed to compete back home. Maybe the best runners in the world could have come close, especially if the race organizers released dogs covered in fire to chase them, but those runners would have been sprinting, and I felt like I could keep this pace for an hour or more. It was a heady feeling.

I took several turns, having to enter some of the smaller streets I had hoped to avoid in order to lose the dog. I heard it barking behind me even as I put more and more distance between us, and I worried it would attract even more beasts. As I turned a corner quickly, pushing myself off a stone wall to propel myself around, I saw that my worry was correct; an armored tusk-rat was stirring from a pile of garbage on the right side of the street, alerted by the barking of the dog behind me.

As I dodged past the slow-moving tusk-rat, I heard another dog begin to bark in the distance.

I felt the urge to swear but saved my breath. As I turned another corner, I heard the dog turn into the street I had just sprinted through, and I heard the armored rat screech at the dog. A moment later, a crashing sound echoed down the street behind me.

I slowed and listened, hearing a scuffle between the tusk-rat and the dog break out.

I debated what to do for a moment, but as the sound of the fight became intense, I decided to stop and observe. I was barely out of breath, and from the sounds behind me, I doubted either creature would be interested in me for a bit, so I felt safe enough for now. And I had no clue where that other dog was, so I could run around the city like crazy and just find myself in even more trouble.

Despite those assurances to myself, I had to remember these monsters were dangerous to even the humans of this world, who were capable of leaping across wide streets with no problem.

I jogged back to the corner I had just passed and peeked around. I confirmed that the dog and the tusk-rat were indeed fighting. The tusk-rat had apparently slammed the dog into the side of one of the buildings, partially collapsing it on the flaming beast, but not killing it. The dog had just climbed out of the rubble and was attacking the tusk-rat. Growling, the dog circled the tusk-rat and moved too fast for the slower creature to hit it again. While the dog dodged around the tusk-rat, its flames got stronger and stronger, licking forward as if under the dog's control, burning the tusk-rat. The armor of the tusk-rat seemed useless against the dog's flame.

I looked around rapidly and found several piles of fallen bricks from a nearby building behind me. I ran over, grabbed several of the bricks, and then returned to hiding around the corner. I waited until the dog circled around the tusk-rat and turned its back to me, then whipped one of the bricks forward as hard as I could. The brick sailed through the air faster than a baseball and struck the dog in its back leg. The leg collapsed, the dog falling to the ground with a surprised yelp.

The tusk-rat, meanwhile, apparently maddened by the heat, had withdrawn its head into its shell to protect itself and hadn't noticed that the dog was injured.

"Stupid rat," I muttered, annoyed that it wasn't finishing off the wounded dog for me.

The dog began to stir and I ran forward, staying far enough away to avoid its flame but close enough to sling a brick right into its skull. The brick connected, shattering from the impact. The dog staggered, collapsing back to the ground. Seeing that it was still alive but stunned, I whipped another brick into its head and then one more to make sure it was dead. When I could see parts of its brain and its flames began to flicker out, I knew I had killed it.

The rat, meanwhile, finally stuck its head out of its shell. It blinked several times, taking in the dead dog at its feet and then looking up and seeing me standing in the street, one brick left in my hand. It visibly jumped as it saw me, retreating backward slightly. I watched it for a moment, but it continued to back away, either afraid of me or so injured it had no interest in fighting right now.

I didn't feel the need to attack the rat if it was willing to leave me alone, although part of me considered that I should get the experience if it was available. I watched it warily until it reached the pile of debris and garbage it had been hiding in. When it got to its nest, it quickly turned away from me and dove into the mess, burrowing under the debris. I let it go. I had too much to do to risk fighting right now, and I expected the other dog I had heard to appear at any moment. I had only killed the first dog because of the tusk-rat's distraction. I didn't want to risk facing another dog right now.

I leaned over the dog. The blue glow I had first noticed from the creature was coalescing into another orb. I immediately grabbed the orb. As I did, the announcement for killing the monster entered my mind.

Weak hellhound sub-boss defeated—5 experience awarded.
No class detected. Experience pooled for future use.

I pushed the announcement out of my mind and jogged back the way I had come. Thanks to my memory, I could remember the path perfectly, which helped me avoid getting lost in this dangerous city. As I jogged, I couldn't help but wonder about the class system. I knew such a thing existed, since the announcements said it couldn't detect a class and was pooling my experience. The question was, how did I unlock a class? How much experience was required to level it? From my experience in virtual reality, the experience in this world was much harsher. Fighting these monsters was dangerous, and they barely awarded any experience at all. Considering the difficulty of the creatures I had fought so far, I should have received more of a reward if this was an entertainment-based system. The fact that the reward was so low indicated that this clearly wasn't such a system, but I had no idea why the system existed at all, let alone how it worked. I hoped to fix that as soon as possible, because I wasn't sure I could survive much longer without a class or some better equipment at least.

I made it back to the street where I had first encountered the dog, slowing down and resuming my careful approach to the city. Thankfully, I didn't encounter the other dog that had barked or any other monsters on my way to intercept the path of a caravan. When I reached the road I had seen the caravan travel on, I settled into a deep-set doorway and waited. I felt the adrenaline from the fight slowly dissipating as I sat in complete silence. I had been afraid of the dog, genuinely unsure how I would survive if it didn't stop chasing me. Experiencing so much raw emotion in the last few days was a great distraction from the pit of grief I was trying to ignore, but it was also more exhausting than I had expected. It was like my body could experience physical exhaustion from my mental state, something I was very unfamiliar with. In my past life, it wasn't that I didn't feel emotion, but the strange intersection of feelings and biological chemistry made it more complicated. I felt pleasure from surviving, exhaustion from the stress, and satisfaction at receiving another orb and more experience, all at the same time. I was also aware of a slight sickness building in my stomach, both from the lack of food and from my nerves and mental state. Every emotion felt more real with a physical body that reacted to my emotional state.

After an hour of waiting in total silence, I heard sounds coming down the road from the direction of the ruined bridge. I stood and leaned out of the doorway to make sure the sounds were the caravan and not another monster. Coming down the long, cobblestone road were several people dressed in makeshift armor. They carried all kinds of different weapons, from bows and staves to swords and maces. The guards continually scanned the streets around them, the buildings beside them, and the rooftops above them as they traveled. Behind the armored people were several wagons pulled by tired, older-looking horses that had their eyes covered to prevent them from panicking. The wagons were open-topped, and each one had a driver up front who gently guided the horses down the road.

I stepped completely out of the doorway I had been sheltering in, not wanting to surprise the guards by appearing when they were closer to me. The guards immediately spotted me, many of them reaching for their weapons swiftly. When they realized I was human, several of them relaxed and resumed watching the rooftops, although not all of them released their grip on their weapons as they stared at me.

As the caravan got closer, the guards eyed me warily but didn't speak to me. I made no sudden movements and waited to see if someone would approach me first, not wanting to scare the heavily armed guards. I had made my body fairly tall with long limbs to give myself every advantage I could in a fight, but I hadn't considered how much shorter everyone would be in this world. Compared to everyone I could see in the caravan, I was practically a giant. I had access to studies that discussed how much shorter people were in humanity's past, but I had failed to account for the fact that I might be transported back in time—or find myself in a more historical context such as the one I found myself in now. The tallest man I saw was around five-foot-seven, at most. The female guards were even shorter, and most of the men were several inches under five-foot-seven. They were also skinnier, either from an unhealthy diet in childhood or because of genetics. I wasn't just taller than everyone I saw; I was wider and visibly bulkier in my arms, chest, and legs. It made a stark difference, immediately making me look unusual, something I had been hoping to avoid.

After about half of the caravan had passed, a man stepped down from one of the wagons in the center of the convoy and approached me. The man was tall compared to the others, around five-foot-seven, and had closely curled hair that seemed greased with some kind of styling oil. He had a large gut and seemed overweight, but his shoulders and arms spoke to strength under the extra pounds he carried. In a city that seemed on the brink of extinction, his weight spoke to his success or cruelty, depending on how he kept himself so well supplied with food. He wore a large robe cinched at his waist with a leather belt that hung low, weighed down by several large pouches.

He gestured for me to come forward, so I stepped out and joined him. He started walking with the slow-moving caravan, and I joined him as we kept pace with the wagons and guards. I waited for him to speak, since I wasn't sure what language was spoken here.

The man eventually addressed me and asked a question. I recognized the language as a mix of ancient Greek and Latin, similar to the mosaics and writing I had seen on the buildings so far. I hastily converted my language centers to match an extrapolation of the language and replied, "Yes, I'm here to trade."

"Good, good," the merchant said, eyeing me a bit suspiciously. "I don't recognize you. You new to this, or are you from Sycae?"

"I am new," I responded as best as I could, gathering information from his accent and the words he used to improve my own speech. His accent was noticeably different from modern Greek, but I was adjusting, and the more I heard, the easier it would be.

"We always need new blood out here," the merchant said with a smile that never reached his eyes, his posture indicating he still considered me a potential threat. He patted his stomach and held an open hand toward me. "So, come out with it. What have you got to trade today?"

I eyed the guards around me, but they were ignoring us as we walked, completely focused on potential dangers around us. I reached into the satchel I had crafted and pulled out the two blue orbs, hoping such things were worth something to this merchant.

The man gestured with his hand again, holding his open palm in front of me, and I placed the orbs in his hand. I reasoned that if he had wanted to rob me, he would have no problem doing so with the guards he commanded. I suspected he was strong enough to do it without their help, anyway, judging by the power level of the people I had seen in this world so far.

The merchant pulled out a single lens from a breast pocket and placed it in front of his right eye. He leaned down and began inspecting the two orbs I had given him.

"Hmm," he said, rolling them between his fingers as he looked at them through the lens. "Looks like two weak sub-boss blues. Fully charged. Not bad for your first time, if I am guessing, yes?"

He eyed me again, looking me up and down. I couldn't imagine how I came across to him, since I clearly had no armor and only a knife on my belt, but at the same time, I was relatively clean and had no visible injuries. He must have thought that signaled something, because he nodded at me, some of his tension lessening as he saw something in me.

"Standard rates," he said. "Two stavrata a piece. Four total now or you can take goods worth five in trade. Your choice."

I ran through my knowledge from Earth swiftly. Stavrata were the equivalent of silver coins from the Byzantine Empire. The value of them fluctuated, but generally they were worth quite a few bronze nummi, which were the most common form of currency in the late Byzantine Empire. Gold coins existed but were extremely rare. Most transactions took place with silver or copper.

"What do you have to trade?" I asked. The man seemed to like that question, because he immediately gave me a shark-like smile, produced a scroll from a pocket at his waist, and handed it to me.

"I'll give you time," he said, turning away to give me some time to review the scroll he had just handed me. Apparently, literacy was common enough that he assumed I could read, which was something different from what would be common in medieval Constantinople in my world.

I glanced down at the scroll, hand-written in flawless Greek with just a few words in Latin. The scroll was something that would be framed in a museum back home, but here it was jammed in a merchant's pocket, creased and stained slightly with grease. It was an odd feeling to so casually hold something that would be so revered by people back on my Earth.

I scanned the list quickly, the writing much easier to translate than the merchant's spoken word. It was apparent from the scroll that the merchant wasn't selling the bulk of his goods, since there weren't enough items to account for so many wagons. It seemed likely that he stocked specialty items to trade with the scavengers I had seen around the city and he was assuming I was one of them.

The scroll listed a number of weapons, salves, ammunition, and other goods of that type. There was also some jerky and other travel food for sale. Most of the weapons were listed with some kind of magical enchantment, such as one called a *Sword of Fire Biting*. Although there was no description, it was clear the sword was enhanced with fire somehow. I had seen magic used, but the scroll full of different magic goods for sale was a clear indication I wasn't on my home world any longer.

I scanned the list several times, trying to figure out what would help me the most. Nothing had a listed price, so I wasn't sure what all I could afford exactly. Likely, the merchant would want to bargain with me for the price of his goods, but I was at a disadvantage since I had no baseline for understanding how much my orbs were worth compared to the price of his merchandise.

I ran through my head what I had learned from my first few days in the city. I would need a ranged weapon to survive monsters like the hellhound I had fought earlier today. I needed food to survive, although water was available if I was willing to risk gathering it in the city from wells or cisterns. Knowledge was probably my most pressing need, but I was cautious about revealing how little I knew in front of the merchant. He and his guards were already wary of my appearance. If I revealed too much more, I couldn't predict how they would react.

As I was scanning the list, my eye was continually drawn to a weapon that was named *Short Bow of Penetration.* There were also a number of arrows available, and they had the same enchantment, called *Arrows of Penetration,* according to the scroll. I had the theoretical knowledge from Earth of how to use every weapon ever invented by humankind, but I knew theoretical knowledge would not translate into physical competence immediately.

I asked the merchant about the bow.

"A bit out of your price range, my friend," he responded. "Those will cost you a gold orb or at least twenty blue orbs such as this."

"Ah," I said, annoyed that I had revealed more of my ignorance. I looked back down at the scroll, feeling a slight flush in my cheeks and cursing internally that my body responded so obviously to my embarrassment. I pushed aside my feelings, focusing on the fact that at least I had received some new information by asking about the bow. I now knew that there were gold orbs and such orbs were worth twenty blue orbs. That gave me some critical information about the economy here, but it also told me that there existed even more powerful monsters that produced orbs with a golden color. If the exchange rate was equivalent to the power of the creatures, they could be up to twenty times more powerful than the sub-bosses I had barely managed to defeat so far.

"Would you mind answering some general questions for me?" I handed back the scroll as I spoke. Since I had already revealed more of my ignorance than I wanted, I decided it was worth being more direct and just asking my questions. "As you guessed, I'm very new to this."

The merchant laughed as he took the scroll, tucking it back into his belt. "Of course, but nothing is free in our fallen world, now is it? What kind of knowledge do you seek? Only then can I tell you its value."

I thought for a moment. "Pretend I am new around here, completely new, and needed the most basic of questions answered. What would that cost me?"

He eyed me up and down, clearly saying I was no newborn. I had made my body appear to be in its late twenties or early thirties, since my research indicated that was the perfect age to gather respect from those around me without them forming an unconscious bias of me being too old or too young.

"Hmm," the merchant responded. "Interesting. You are much taller and paler than most of the boys in this city, eh? Maybe we can exchange some information and come to a fair price. Come with me."

He turned and walked to the wagon that he had been riding in when I had initially approached. He stepped up beside the driver and took the reins, shooing the woman away. She looked me over before jumping off and moving away.

"Come on up here, stranger," the merchant said. I had watched as the merchant climbed up and the driver climbed down, so I managed to climb up next to the man without looking as unfamiliar with wagons as I really was.

"Now," the merchant said as I settled in, "exchange of information is a bit of a different thing than the mere exchange of goods. Once I share my knowledge, it is yours for good. I can never take it back."

"But I can also get that info from others," I interjected. "And I'm not interested in protected information."

Instead of being annoyed at my interruption, the merchant gave me the first genuine smile I had seen from him. "Indeed," he replied, "but one of the things I guarantee is discretion. No word of what we discuss will leave my lips. That is something you value, if I am reading your reactions correctly."

I tried not to react, unsure how the man could tell so much from me so easily. Maybe he had a class that let him read my body language. Or maybe I was bad at hiding my expression, something that humans had years of practice doing before they became an adult.

After I didn't respond immediately, the merchant's smile widened slightly, as if he was enjoying our bargaining.

"So," he continued, "here is my offer. One stavrata per question. I will answer your question as fully as possible for as long as it takes, only withholding any secrets I cannot reveal."

I considered his offer as the caravan continued forward slowly through the ruined city.

"And," the merchant said, "if you tell me where you come from and the story behind what brings you here, I will give you one question in return. I suspect an interesting tale is behind you being here in our once-glorious city."

I thought about what I needed to know and how much I was willing to pay. My first priority needed to be finding a better way to defeat the monsters, and there was a lot I could do on my own if I had a bit more knowledge. I organized my questions and then agreed to the merchant's terms.

"I am not willing to discuss myself, though," I told him.

"Understandable," the merchant responded, theatrically sighing in disappointment. "A bargain is struck, though. One question with a complete, thorough answer for each silver stavrata. You have five now, if you trade me your blue orbs. What is your first question?"

"Explain how experience and classes work as if I'm a child," I said.

The merchant raised an eyebrow in response to my statement. I could practically see his mind working as he tried to figure out more about me based on what I wanted to know.

"That is very interesting," he responded after a moment. "You look like a Varangian, but even those barbarians would know about classes. Very interesting. And not exactly a question, but I take your meaning."

I refused to respond again. While I waited to see if he could answer my question, I cataloged everything I knew about the term Varangian. Based on the knowledge from my world, I knew that the Varangian Guard were the personal bodyguards of the Byzantine emperor. Much like Vikings, they were Scandinavian warriors who followed Norse traditions. They were taller, stronger, and had a reputation of being more barbaric than the traditional Byzantine soldier. I could see why the merchant thought I might be one, given the body I had adopted was taller, stronger, and paler than that of most of the people I had seen in the city so far, who all had dark or tanned skin.

"Okay," the merchant finally said after visibly organizing his thoughts, "so you've killed some monsters, yeah? This is how you got these orbs, unless you stole them, but then why would you be out here? That tells me you have killed at least two sub-bosses."

I nodded.

"So you have experience toward your class or classes, if you are lucky enough to even have one. I assume if you are out here, you must have at least one to survive. Hopefully more than one, eh?"

He watched me closely as he spoke, hoping I would reveal anything about myself again. When I failed to react to his mention of having more than one class, he continued with a slightly puzzled frown.

"Every class you have beyond the first divides your experience between them, if you have made the class active. Anyone can have an unlimited number of classes and can make them active or inactive at any time, but the more active classes you have, the less they level because experience is divided between your active classes. You following me?"

"I hear what you are saying," I said, trying to wrap my head around this new information. I didn't want to admit my ignorance, but this was very different from the virtual reality worlds I had played in before. There, people could only have one class—very rarely was multiclassing allowed—and people couldn't often turn them "active" or "inactive." It was also rather surreal to hear this seasoned, older man discuss such things without any irony or amusement. To him, the existence of classes, experience, and leveling was completely normal.

"Hmmm," he replied, "boy, you are something else. I can see you don't understand, or this is new information for you."

I gave him a hesitant nod, willing to reveal slightly more of my ignorance in order to get more information.

"Did your parents never teach you any of this? Or are you an orphan that never learned a trade? What are you doing out here in the city? This place has killed veterans with several classes. Nobody should be out here without at least one class, if not two."

I looked away without answering. The merchant eventually breathed out in frustration.

"Okay," he said, "instead of trying to explain this, I will make you a deal. You can clearly read, even though you don't know the basics of classes. Instead of talking to you for the next hour, explaining things a child should know, I'll bring you a book I have at home that is copied for kids when they come of age. It explains everything in more detail than I could ever do."

"That would be really great," I said, looking for the catch from the canny merchant.

"You will have to survive tonight," he said, "and meet me back here tomorrow. I suspect you can manage that, eh? Or do you belong to one of the enclaves?"

"Enclaves?" I asked.

"Ah," the merchant said, "that'd be a no, then. Okay, meet me tomorrow and I will trade you the book for three stavrata. I guarantee it will answer your questions better than I can. That leaves you with two more. You want more questions or want to trade?"

"One more question and one in trade," I said, thinking quickly. The book would hopefully answer my questions. The man hadn't been dishonest with me yet, as far as I could tell. I still needed to find a way to defend myself better. As I had been listening to the merchant, I was also carefully analyzing one of the ideas that had come to mind when I saw that a magical method of accelerating things existed in this world.

"I want to buy one of your *Arrows of Penetration*, and for my question, I want you to explain to me how the item works, to the best of your ability."

"Ohhh," he replied, fingering his chin with a smile, "now that is interesting. You want to jump from knowing nothing to crafting magical items, eh? Is crafting how you are surviving out here, and you just came to visit me without any of your trinkets?"

"It might help me craft something, yes," I replied as neutrally as possible.

"An arrow alone will still leave you with plenty of nummi. What else do you want?"

"I need some travel food, a canteen, and other basic items like that. Do you trade those?"

"I can make that happen. Your last two stavrata for survival goods, the arrow, and an explanation. We can make a bargain with that."

"Okay." I felt like he was taking advantage of me with the deal, but I didn't have much of a choice. "Deal."

"Deal," he echoed, reaching out for my hand. We shook on it, and then he pocketed the two orbs of mine he had been holding.

"Now that you are a return customer," he said jokingly, "I am Asylaion, the famous merchant of Nova Roma. What is your name?"

I froze for a second. My original name, given to me by my owner, I no longer wanted to use. And an odd name would make me stand out even more than my size and skin around here. I hastily ran through a list of common names in Byzantine culture.

"My name is Alexander," I said after a moment. The name was common during both my era and the Byzantine era, so it should be acceptable and I didn't mind the ramifications of the name. Maybe I would be a famous conqueror like Alexander the Great. Who knew what I would end up doing here? I had no ambition to manage a group of humans, though. They seemed like more trouble than they were worth, especially in large groups.

"Well met, Alexander," the merchant said with a glint in his eye that told me he didn't believe that was truly my name, but he didn't press me.

"Licinius!" the merchant yelled behind him.

One of the guards rapidly approached.

"Grab me one of the arrows we brought for sale," Asylaion said to the guard.

"Which kind?" the guard yelled back as he jogged toward the back of the wagon we were in.

"*Penetration*," Asylaion said. The guard nodded and began to shift sacks, crates, and bundles of different arrows around behind us.

Once he had the arrow, the guard ran forward and handed it to Asylaion.

"This is a fine arrow," he said, holding it up for me to inspect. "Crafted by a fletcher of fine skill in Sycae, traded for with fresh fish just the other day. Enchanted by one of our own enchanters, a woman of high skill who has kept our home safe for many years with her hard work. Very valuable, yes?"

I looked at the arrow in his hand. It looked like a standard arrow, except several runes flowed down the haft. Asylaion saw where I was looking.

"Here, take this," he said, handing me the arrow. "This is yours now. You see the runes on the shaft? I will explain how those work as part of our bargain. First, runes are carved by a skilled enchanter and require perfection in form in order to contain the energy that is channeled into them. I strongly suggest you do not attempt to carve your own, because you will fail without years of experience and the proper class. Even the slightest error and the item could explode. Feel the runes with your fingers."

I did as he said, feeling the rune as it curved around the haft.

"You can feel it's slightly three-dimensional," he said. "Any error in width or depth results in a critical failure. So don't try to enchant on your own, alright?"

I nodded.

"Okay," he said, "so what you see on the haft of this arrow is a basic three rune enchantment. The first rune controls what activates the enchantment. In this case, it is the firing of the arrow from a bow. Don't ask me how it knows when it is being fired, but apparently the magic can tell. Something about the concept of 'firing' the arrow triggers the rune. It is beyond the ken of us mortals, eh?

"The second rune is the effect of the enchantment. In this case, it is of penetration. That is one of the most basic of enchantments, but it is very powerful. When fired, the arrow will go significantly faster than the mere strength of your arm would allow. At least two or three times faster than a regular man can fire, and in the arms of a skilled *Archer*, it becomes as deadly as a ballista, you understand?"

I couldn't help but notice the special emphasis he gave to the term *Archer*, indicating that was a potential class.

"Now, the final rune is the end of the chain." He pointed to the last rune. "This one is a *Durability* rune, which merely strengthens the arrow so it can handle the speed it can achieve when fired. Without it, arrows disintegrate into splinters once launched, so enchanters have learned to strengthen the arrow every time. And that's it," he finished. "Any questions?"

I studied the arrow and felt the runes through my sensitive fingers. "How do you charge the runes? Or do they always stay empowered?"

"Ah," he replied, "good question. You use one of those orbs you traded me. A simple enchantment like this would only take part of one orb. You could likely charge twenty arrows with a weak blue orb. Once charged, though, they do stay charged until destroyed, so if you can recover it, you can use it again."

"Okay," I said, "thank you. Is there a limit to the number of charges that can be applied to an item?"

"Yes, for a simple enchantment like this, the arrow can only handle three runes. Any more and the energy that empowers the runes would destroy the item itself. Now, you can fix that if you have some very rare ore that you craft the enchantments from, but not many people can afford that these days. I sure can't afford to carry such things outside the enclaves like this. Any other questions about the rune?"

"You said it triggers based on being fired," I said, thinking over my options for how to use the rune, "but you don't know how exactly it triggers?"

"I'm not an expert," the man said, shrugging. "I hear it takes both the will to fire the arrow and the means to begin its acceleration. So you can't just hold it and will it to go forward, but you also don't trigger it by moving the arrow on its own. You can trigger it by throwing the arrow, although the acceleration actually works by magnifying the speed of its initial launch, so you wouldn't have as much impact from the enchantment as you would from firing it from the bow."

"Huh," I said, thinking about the fact that the arrow magnified the speed with which it was originally launched. That made for some interesting possibilities. "Well, thank you for the trade and information, then."

He clapped me on the back and smiled at me. "I hope you survive, Alexander. I can always use new business partners. Now, let me get you the rest of your goods."

He called back the driver of the wagon, who had been following behind us, and they traded places. I stepped down as well and followed him to the back of the wagon, where he dug out a number of items and handed them to me one at a time. I held them in my left arm, the arrow I had just purchased in the other.

"And take this," the merchant said, handing me a small backpack with a smile. "Courtesy of the fine merchant Asylaion, yes? No charge!"

I smiled back, the gesture unfamiliar, but I knew it was important for me to start practicing how to engage with people. I was definitely sure that he had taken advantage of me now that he was giving me something for free, but I couldn't complain. Given the knowledge he had shared and the enchanted arrow, I believed I could use what he had given me to make something worth a lot more than the two blue orbs I had traded him. Something that would make survival here much easier, if my idea worked.

I took the items he had given me and put them in the backpack, then strapped it on my back tightly. It had a clasp over the back to prevent my goods from spilling out and two straps across my waist and chest to hold it in place while I ran. It was a surprisingly modern form of backpack, although it was still made of worked leather and the clasps were obviously hand-made.

"Thank you, Asylaion," I said, genuinely grateful for the backpack despite him getting a good deal from me. He wasn't that bad, all things considered, and I was happy with my first interaction with a human on this world. It could have gone significantly worse. I had learned a lot and would learn more tomorrow once I got the book from him as well.

"My pleasure, Alexander," he said. "Let me give you something else for free, eh? I must be feeling very generous, my Varangian friend. Don't go underground, even during the day. Everyone should know that, but I worry about you. The monsters that roam the city at night, they hide from the sun in the dungeons that form below the surface and in the hidden places of the city. Do not go underground unless you are much stronger than I suspect you are, understood?"

I couldn't stop my eyebrows from rising in surprise at his statement about dungeons. Asylaion gave me an extremely puzzled look as he saw my surprise, then shook his head ruefully.

"Understood," I said, trying to hide my surprise. "Thank you again. I'll be careful."

"And keep an eye out for more runes like those." He pointed to the arrow. "Many of them are made from that special metal I told you about. Bring me some of those and you will have a big payday. Good luck!"

I stepped away from the caravan and stood at the side of the road as it passed me by. When it was far in the distance, I ducked down a nearby street and found a shadowed doorway to crouch in.

I listened for any nearby monsters but didn't hear anything. I slipped the backpack off and looked inside to see what exactly I had purchased from the wily merchant.

The first thing I pulled from the backpack was the large canteen Asylaion had given me. It was half full of water. I took a quick drink, satisfied that it was good water, although it tasted of the hardened leather the canteen was made of. Next, I pulled out several large packages that smelled of dried fish and two small pieces of pottery that held a healing salve of some kind. The final item he had given me was a gray cloak, identical to the cloaks worn by the scavengers I had seen exploring the city. It must be something of a uniform for the scavengers out here, maybe a way to indicate that we were peaceful or not to be attacked. The cloak and salve were unnecessary since my body was resistant to the cold and could heal itself, but I couldn't tell the merchant that, so I didn't say anything when he handed them to me.

I put the cloak on, just to help me blend in with the city better and in case it did offer me some protection from the other scavengers. I took a small portion of the dried fish and ate it hurriedly, washing it down with the rest of the water from the canteen, just to quiet the hunger pangs that had been nagging me for a day or more. The rest I tucked into the backpack, which I re-secured on my back, under my new cloak. The cloak could be removed easily by a single clasp in case of a fight, or it could be closed in the front, hiding my entire body almost like a poncho. It was lightweight and made of soft wool. It smelled slightly of must, but otherwise, it seemed clean and new.

The day was still young and I had a few ideas to help increase my survivability, so I set off back toward the apartment I had been staying in the last couple of nights. On the way, I ducked into the remains of houses, workshops, and other buildings that seemed safe to enter, searching for more metal and leather. I avoided going down any stairs, thanks to the advice from the merchant, even though I couldn't hear anything different from the few places I found that had basements. I found a working well in an abandoned yard, refilling my canteen with fresh water as well.

As I searched, I collected any scraps of leather and iron that I could find and put them in my backpack. In one of the nicer buildings that might have once been a small temple, I found the last item I needed: an old wooden table made of maple. I would need the wood if my idea bore fruit.

I encountered a few dire rats and a smaller, humanoid-looking creature that was also looting a house I had entered. It was dark gray and seemed unarmed and scared of me when we noticed each other, but it still attacked when I didn't immediately attack it first. It was only three or four feet tall but had long arms tipped with claws. It looked vicious, with large teeth that seemed perfect for biting and tearing, but since it was humanoid, I knew its weak points and I had no mercy when it came to exploiting them. I was faster than the creature as it tried to attack me, and I kicked it in its small knee as I dodged past it, sending the small creature falling to the ground. I spun around, grabbed my knife, and slit its throat before it even knew what had happened to it. I stared at it until enough blood had leaked from its throat to guarantee it was dead.

Weak goblin defeated—1 experience awarded.

With that, and five more rats that I managed to kill throughout the day without issue, I was up to thirty-two experience. I still had no idea what to do with the experience, but that seemed like a significant amount to me, considering how difficult it was to get experience in this world.

Well before the sun fell, I made it back to my apartment building and settled into the room I had commandeered. I took out some of the dried fish and ate a bit more before piling the metal, leather, and wood I had collected in front of me. I then placed the *Penetration Arrow* I had purchased from the merchant next to the materials I had looted.

I closed my eyes and imagined what I planned to build with some slight modifications based on what I understood about the runes and how the magic would interact with the plans I held in my mind. I built up the item detail by detail, my enhanced brain able to imagine the device in perfect clarity. Once I was sure that I had it correct, I ordered my nanobots to begin breaking down the items in front of me so I could craft the item.

From what I could estimate, the first item would take at least a day to finish crafting. I settled down to wait. Now that I had food, I could survive for a long time hiding in this apartment. I had plans to pick up the book from the merchant tomorrow, but other than that, I had nothing else to do but watch my nanobots work.

The night passed uneventfully, other than the madness outside, which I was beginning to get used to. The item wasn't finished by the morning, so I packed it away in my backpack and made my way to the caravan path to meet the merchant.

I managed to avoid any monsters as I traveled and settled into the same doorway I had been in yesterday. I thought through my immediate plans as I waited, trying to decide what to do if my first goal of creating a better way to protect myself worked out. The daytime creatures I had encountered so far were survivable, although I felt I was balancing on a knife's edge when I fought them. I had no doubt worse things were out there, even during the day. As I was right now, all it would take was another bad encounter with a hellhound or getting ambushed by a tusk-rat before I could react, and I could die easily. I knew I had been lucky so far, my survival dependent almost entirely on my enhanced body. If I had been a normal person, I would be dead several times over by now.

I wanted to try finding my way into one of the enclaves around here and figure out more about what happened to this city. I was sure there was a story that was important to learn. I could have asked the merchant, but it didn't immediately increase my chances of survival, so questions of that nature had to wait for later since they cost currency.

After that, gaining a class was a top priority. Once I knew more about how that system worked and what class would best help me survive in this fallen world, I could work on getting the class by whatever means were necessary.

Eventually, the familiar sounds of the caravan began to echo down the street like they had yesterday morning. I stood and waited for the caravan to approach. When I stepped out, the same guards looked closely at me before returning to their duties.

"Alexander!" the merchant yelled as he saw me. He had been waiting at the front of the caravan, likely hoping I would meet him in the same spot as yesterday. "I am glad to see you survived another night, my friend!"

I smiled politely, nodding at the merchant.

"Come here, my lad," he said, gesturing me forward. I walked past the guards, who ignored me as they had the previous day, and approached the merchant. He tossed me a leather-bound book. It wasn't large, but hopefully it would have answers for me.

"Here is your book, as promised," Asylaion said as I caught the book. "Study that and then let me know if you have more questions and we can bargain for more answers, eh?"

"Thanks, Asylaion," I replied, turning and tucking the book into the open top of my backpack.

"No problem at all," he said. "Did you bring any more to trade for today or are you just here for the book?"

"Just the book today." I felt uncomfortable talking to him without the structure of bargaining for goods.

"Okay then," the merchant replied, ignoring my awkwardness. "Stay safe, then, and catch me next time you have more to trade. I will be here!"

I nodded and backed away from the caravan. He gave me a slightly strained smile, and I tried to smile naturally back at him, but I wasn't sure how successful I was.

On my way back to the apartment, the silence of the city was broken by the sounds of violent screeches and hooting, like a pack of wild apes had been let loose in the streets. The sound was coming from ahead of me, between me and the apartment I was staying in. I froze and watched as several large creatures climbed over the rooftops, fighting among themselves. They did, indeed, look like large, very dangerous apes, but they seemed so focused on fighting each other that none of them noticed me.

I waited and watched them carefully as they continued away from me, leaping from building to building, stopping only to bite or wrestle each other as they traveled. Once they were gone, I circled widely around the path they were traveling and made it back to the apartment without encountering anything else dangerous.

Once I was safe, I took out the device I was building. It still wasn't done, so I settled down and waited patiently for my nanobots to complete it. I thought idly about this world and tried meditating, focusing on unifying my body and mind like whenever I was fighting for my life.

Hours later, the sun set on another day in this strange city. As the almost familiar sounds of monsters overtook the world below me, I felt my nanobots complete the project I had given them. I smiled, picking it up and eyeing it with pleasure.

In my hand was an item that would be recognizable to many people back on Earth, although it had fallen out of favor when newer and more deadly types had been invented. Still, it was an iconic weapon. It combined reliability with deadliness and was simple enough to function without complex manufacturing industries that produced electronics or more advanced metals.

I held the item up to the rising moon, letting the dim light illuminate the weapon in my hand. I was pretty sure that nobody in this world would recognize what I held, but back on my Earth, it was simply called a revolver. It was a modified six-shooter firearm, made from the finest steel my nanobots could forge. The barrel was rifled, allowing for greater accuracy and more acceleration from the bullets. The handle was made from beautiful wood, polished and gleaming in the light. The wheel was modified, allowing for the bullets I planned to craft to stay securely inside the wheel without the need for casings.

The trigger was a more modern version of the six-shooter, one that didn't require me to cock it each time before firing, the momentum of firing turning the wheel and re-cocking the gun after each shot was fired. This more modern adaptation allowed for a significantly quicker rate of fire. And since I didn't need gunpowder, if my plan worked as I hoped it would, I didn't need to worry about igniting the powder to accelerate the bullets. The trigger would, instead, strike the bullet, accelerating it forward through the barrel, which would trigger a *Penetration* rune, sending the bullet flying forward even faster.

I turned the gun over, admiring its sleek and deadly design. In this world of magic, it was very unlikely that anyone had bothered to invent such a device when they could throw fireballs with their hands or shoot magical arrows or do whatever other superhuman acts that people could do here. The difference was that they had magical classes to allow them to do such feats, whereas my revolver required only a single series of enchantments to power it. Nobody who was unfamiliar with firearms would expect so much power in such a small weapon, which should give me a significant edge over others and the monsters around me.

I turned the six-shooter over, inspecting every facet of the firearm. It was simple to make, given the knowledge I had. I snapped out the chamber, seeing that the six chambers were formed perfectly. I sighted down the barrel, and it appeared perfectly aligned. I snapped the barrel in and out, getting used to the movement. I pulled the trigger, watching as the barrel rotated through all six cylinders smoothly and easily.

As I inspected the gun, I put my nanobots back to work crafting what would make the firearm work without the need for gunpowder: solid steel bullets crafted with the runes taken from the arrow. The runes might be difficult for a human to craft with the appropriate class, but for me and my nanobots, it was extremely easy to re-create them. I had my nanobots perfectly measure the three runes on the arrow, documenting their width, depth, and length. Once I had the appropriate measurements, it was easy to order the nanobots to re-create them in exacting detail. No human could achieve such perfection. Even I would likely fail if I used my new body. But with the nanobots, I was one hundred percent confident I could re-create the runes perfectly. Realizing I would probably be using my nanobots in such a way for the foreseeable future, I programmed a specific type of nanobot designed solely to help me convert iron to steel and mold metals and other physical materials. It would take time for the new wave of nanobots to reproduce, but eventually they should help me produce things faster in the future.

I had considered other weapons that I could have made instead of the revolver. I could have gone with a bow or crossbow, the better to blend into the technology level of this world. The downside to a bow or crossbow was it required more materials to make the weapon itself and the arrows than the small revolver and the even smaller bullets. A bow would also require more of an investment in training my muscle memory to use it well, and if I tried to make a more advanced compound bow that could better take advantage of my strength it would be much harder to hide from prying eyes given how large the weapon would be. Until I was very skilled at firing a bow, a revolver also had a higher rate of fire, required less training, and the bullets would be harder for someone to reverse engineer if they could even find them since they were so small.

I could have also gone the other direction, giving up on trying to be subtle now that the reality of actually dying was staring me in the face. I could have built a railgun, some kind of laser-weapon, or even something that leaked radiation or some kind of acid that melted or poisoned anything in my way. But those types of weapons would be very hard to hide, while the revolver was small and easy to cover, and if the worst case scenario did occur and someone got access to my weapon - or could even figure out how it worked from afar - the magic of this world was still unknown to me and I didn't know how easily such weapons could be reproduced. It was very possible magical crafters could make such weapons quickly, causing a rapid expansion of powerful, deadly weapons that could be used against me or against other people. I really prefered to avoid such a dramatic change in technology, at least until I fully understood the consequences of any technology that I introduced to the world. Once something was out of the bag, I would never be able to put it back in again. The thought made me nervous to introduce too much change too fast to this world.

The revolver was, to me, a good compromise between the two extremes. It was more powerful, easier to make, and easier to conceal than a bow or crossbow without being so advanced it could upend the entire balance of power in the world around me if it was ever discovered. I was still sorely tempted to just throw caution to the wind and build myself the most advanced weapons possible, but the consequences could be dire so I refused to give in to the part of me that wanted to act so cowardly. I had a responsibility with the knowledge that I had brought to this world and, while survival was the most important thing, there were compromises I could make to achieve both goals. The revolver was the best compromise between power and responsibility.

I didn't need to sleep since I had enough food and water to fuel my nanobots without becoming hungry, so I spent the night reading the book the merchant had given me and watching my nanobots make the bullets and a few other items I ordered them to create.

The book was full of fascinating information that showed me how truly far from Earth I had come. I read it through once and then ruminated on what I had learned, recalling all of the information from the book perfectly.

According to the book, anyone could have any class, but classes themselves were extremely rare for the average person. The most basic classes could be crafted and sold, but rare classes could only be taught or evolved from basic classes. In the past, rare and evolved classes were more common, but over time, many were lost for a number of reasons the book didn't fully explain. I could easily imagine how people hoarded the more powerful classes until they died out.

The basic classes could only be leveled to twenty. After that, people had to learn how to evolve the class or they were stuck at that level. There was no information about how to evolve a class in the book, other than that experts believed evolution required a deep understanding of the class as well as a unique way of thinking or using the class that coincided with an evolution of the class. An example of this was how a *Warrior* class could evolve to a *Soldier* class for someone in a military organization. The class evolved from the basic *Warrior* when a person hit level 20 after they had been using their class while part of an organized fighting force. Apparently this was a well-known evolution that many warriors aimed for.

According to the book, in very rare circumstances, people could even form new classes, but there hadn't been a documented case of such a thing happening for a long time.

Classes were ranked based on the maximum level they could achieve and the relative power of the class. It started with basic, common, rare, legendary, and unique. A basic class stopped at level 20, a common class at level 40, rare at level 60, legendary at level 80, and unique at level 100. A unique class was only awarded to a single person and only when that person managed to create a unique evolution of their class that had never been achieved by another person before. Otherwise, most people could only ever dream of getting a legendary class and leveling it to eighty. If a unique class was taught to others, it would only be a legendary class at most, sometimes even lower in the rankings if the class wasn't particularly powerful, even if it was unique.

People could have an unlimited number of classes, but each of their classes took an equal portion of the experience they earned to level up. So for instance, someone who was only a *Warrior* would get one hundred percent of their experience toward their *Warrior* class and therefore level it relatively fast. Another person might have two classes, a *Warrior* class and a *Mage* class, which would then split the experience by fifty percent, and that person would level slower but would have two classes that leveled at the same time.

A person could make a class active or inactive at any time, so there was no penalty for learning a class. If a class was inactive, a person still gained all of the benefits and skills or attacks they had earned from that class but could not level any further until the class was made active again.

The most fascinating part of the book was the chapters dedicated to why someone would even want a class in the first place. There were two main reasons: enhancements and skills.

Enhancements were granted every level you gained in a class, and they gave a person a physical or magical boost in some way depending on the class they chose. There were, apparently, six primary areas of enhancement, although the book hinted at more with rarer classes. They were strength, coordination, endurance, memory, magic power, and magic capacity. Magic power enhanced the power of spells and how rapidly mana could be discharged. Magical capacity enhanced the amount of mana a person had and the rate at which their mana recharged. Strength was rather self-explanatory, whereas coordination included hand-eye coordination, agility, and speed all in one. Endurance not only let someone work or fight for longer, but it also made them more resistant to damage and less likely to be injured.

My body and mind were already significantly more enhanced than those of the standard human, so I was curious how such enhancements would work with my body, if they would work at all.

Skills, apparently, could also be crafted like some common classes could be crafted, but they were so rare and expensive that it was almost impossible to buy them these days. The way that most people got a skill was from their class as it leveled. The other way to get a skill was from a "dungeon," but the book said that was a rare reward for completing a dungeon and cautioned severely against trying to tackle a dungeon in the city, warning that everyone that did so died horribly. The book mentioned that a person could also receive a "perk" from certain kinds of magic or from completing a dungeon, but it didn't explain the difference between a perk and a skill. The book had no other information about dungeons or what it meant by a reward for completing a dungeon, likely to avoid enticing young people into trying to complete one.

The biggest reason to level a class, according to the book, was because at level 1, you received your choice of a skill for that class. You received another skill at level 10 and again at level 20, then at every ten levels until your class wasn't able to go any higher. The skills became more powerful at each interval of ten, so leveling a single class was often beneficial for receiving more powerful skills. The other levels between the skill levels gave the enhancements for one's body or mind, such as a benefit to strength for a warrior or coordination for an archer. So at level 1, a person received their first skill. Then, at levels 2–9, they received an enhancement to one of their attributes, repeating again for level 10 and above.

The book discussed several different strategies people had adopted for leveling. Some people, if lucky or rich enough, collected as many basic classes as possible in order to get the initial skill at level one and a few enhancements to all of their attributes at a low level. They didn't worry about specializing or reaching a high level in a single class, instead relying on a wide variety of lower-level skills and an overall well-balanced body and mind through several different enhancements from the lower levels of all of their classes. The negative to this approach was that they never received any higher-level skills and never had a chance to evolve a class to a more powerful one.

Others specialized and only ever got a single class, trying to raise their class as high as possible to unlock more powerful skills and to specialize the enhancements they received, since they were tailored to increase the attributes the class relied upon. This allowed someone to potentially become very specialized and gave them a chance to evolve their class if they managed to reach level 20. The negative was that they could find themselves facing a situation where their specialization didn't help them, rendering them unable to adapt as well as someone with many different skills and classes.

The suggested route, according to the book, was a mix of the two. It suggested trying your hardest to find one to three classes that complemented each other and leveling them together as much as possible. It recommended an offensive class, a defensive class, and a class that helped with survivability, such as one focused on movement or stealth. Of course, the book stressed, even getting a single class was rare and should never be taken for granted.

People could also level non-combat classes, like *Enchanter*, and they rewarded enhanced attributes much like combat classes did. The difference was that people trying to level their non-combat classes only gained experience from everyday use of the non-combat class instead of defeating monsters. For example, according to the book, a tailor gained experience from activities related to the making of clothing and cloth only. They couldn't just go kill a monster and apply that experience to their non-combat class.

At the end of the book, there was a final note written in a different hand from the one that had written the rest of the book:

So many classes have been lost. If you are reading this, please take any class that you can find. Do not be picky. Maybe you can evolve it into something that helps us hold back the tide of darkness that is sweeping humanity off the face of this world. The gods have forsaken us. You are our only hope now.

I felt a chill as I read such an impassioned plea for help from whoever had added that to the book.

Shaking my head, I refocused on the world around me. It was too easy to get lost in information like I used to do, but in my new body, such a thing could cost me my only life. I needed to keep that in mind at all times.

I stood and paced silently around the apartment, making sure I could not be seen from the windows. I still had no idea how such a system of classes and experience could come to exist, but I now at least knew how classes worked. Once I could defend myself better, I would have time to go and find more answers to my many questions.

When the sun began to rise once again, I reviewed the crafting my nanobots had done overnight. On the floor of the apartment were twenty perfectly crafted bullets, each one the size of my fingertip. Each bullet was crafted with three small runes: *Penetration*, *Durability*, and the trigger rune. Next to them was an underarm holster that would conceal the firearm under my armpit, hiding it better than if it was on my belt. A hardened leather satchel would hold my ammunition on my belt.

I had the beginnings of a weapon that I was confident this world was not prepared to handle. Something that would let me push back against that tide of darkness before it could sweep the remnants of humanity from this ruined world. I hadn't been convinced humanity was worth saving when I came here, but the prospect of being stuck on a world with nothing but mindless monsters was unbearable. I wasn't sure how yet, but I would do my part to help. I had failed my only friend on my last world, but I wouldn't fail the people that needed me on this one.

Chapter 6

I spent the remainder of the next day very carefully scouting the city, avoiding packs of strange monsters here and there until I found another pack of dire rats I knew I could defeat. I needed another blue orb to charge my bullets, and the dire rats seemed like the safest monsters to kill.

In an abandoned warehouse that was missing most of one wall, its roof slumped down and providing little protection from the elements, I spotted a small group of rats that had a sub-boss glowing blue in their midst. The blue light was interesting because it didn't actually illuminate the dim interior of the fallen warehouse, but it still seemed to glow to my eyes. The fact that it didn't actually produce light must be why the night wasn't full of glowing beasts when I looked down on the city from my apartment, but I had no explanation for why it appeared blue to my perceptions if it wasn't actual light being generated. I chalked it up to another mystery of this world and put it out of my mind for now.

The beasts were easy to defeat now that I had their measure. I collected a handful of stones and approached the warehouse from a non-collapsed side, where a partially blocked door led into the warehouse. The stones themselves, thrown with my enhanced strength, dazed and injured them as I sniped them from the door. It took several seconds for them to realize they were even under attack, and by the time they scrambled to attack me, I had already injured several. They piled over each other to get to me, and I made short work of them with my knife, easily killing them before they could get through the blocked doorway.

Behind the swarm of lesser rats, the sub-boss was the only creature that did not mindlessly attack me. After I managed to kill the last of its smaller brethren, it turned to retreat from me, finally recognizing the danger I represented. I admired its intelligence, but

I wasn't about to let it escape me now. It was my turn to be the hunter around here.

"Not so fast," I said, slinging a stone at it as I climbed over the corpses of the rats piled in the doorway in front of me. My stone clipped its behind, sending the large rat tumbling sideways. The injured sub-boss turned and hissed at me, but I continued to pelt it with stones. Not taking any chances, I did not try to approach it. I struck it over and over with stones, walking closer as I did, making my throws do even more damage to the wounded creature. It tried to escape, but I had no mercy in me and pelted it with stones until it died in the middle of the warehouse floor, collapsing to the ground with a final sigh of breath. Even then, I waited a few feet away until the now-familiar stone began to rise from its body. I stepped forward, grimly satisfied with my success, and grabbed the stone.

Dire rat defeated—1 experience awarded.

Four more announcements followed for the regular dire rats.

Dire rat sub-boss defeated—5 experience awarded.

I retreated to my apartment, not wanting to spoil my first successful hunt by getting attacked by something more powerful than me. Once I was settled down on the floor of the dusty apartment, I pulled out my bullets and the blue stone. The merchant hadn't explained the exact details of how to charge an item with the stone, but after just a few moments of experimenting, I found that touching the unpowered runes to the stone caused them to fill with energy. It didn't require any special skill on my part, which was good news.

I felt a smile stretch across my face, my body reacting without conscious thought to my feeling of happiness at the sight of the glowing bullets. I quickly charged the rest of the bullets. When I finished, I noticed the blue stone still had energy inside of it despite having charged the twenty bullets I had made. The merchant had told me that a blue stone of this quality could charge a maximum of about twenty arrows, but maybe the bullets took less energy because of how small they were.

That was potentially very beneficial. Despite their size, the bullets were significantly more deadly than the arrows, if my theory was correct. If they also took less energy to empower . . . well, that was good news for me.

I still had some iron scraps left over, so I set my nanobots to crafting as many steel bullets as I could. Then, sliding the six-shooter out of its holster under my left armpit, I loaded the gun with six magical bullets. I spun the wheel and flicked it closed with my wrist. The gun closed with a satisfying click. I smiled at the sound.

Now, where to test it? I looked out the window and saw that it was only a bit after noon, so I still had plenty of light before the sun fell. I wasn't sure how loud the gun would be since I wasn't using gunpowder, but I still didn't want to risk firing the gun too close to where I planned to sleep in case it attracted a swarm of monsters.

I packed up the scraps being formed into bullets and placed them into my backpack, where my nanobots could continue to work on them. Then I re-holstered my gun and made my way down the stairs of the apartment building. As I maneuvered down the rickety stairs, I practiced pulling the gun swiftly and aiming. My body was ambidextrous, so I could use either hand to fire the gun, but I chose to use my right for now and practiced pulling the firearm while holding my knife in my left hand. The combination of knife and gun should let me fight off anything close to me and far away at the same time.

Outside the apartment, I made my way through several nearby streets, looking for the telltale signs of a tusk-rat nest. I holstered my knife and gun and picked up some loose stones, flinging them at various piles of debris and refuse, hoping to stir a tusk-rat from a distance. After about a half hour, I found one. It reacted immediately to my stone slamming into its nest, stirring the garbage and debris it was hiding under. I waited until it was fully revealed. Its large, armored body turned toward me, revealing an angry pair of eyes that promised the rat would hurt me for disturbing its home.

I drew my revolver, took careful aim, and fired. The gun fired with a soft exhalation. It was much quieter than a gunpowder revolver but still made an audible sound. The bullet ripped forward so fast I couldn't track it even with my enhanced vision. The effect on the tusk-rat was immediate. The monster was slammed backward against its nest as a loud cry of pain escaped it. I waited, watching the wounded creature. It shook itself, trying to stand

78

again. I stepped closer, firing again at the creature's unarmored head. This time, the bullet was easy to track as it struck the creature's head. Its skull shattered, brain and blood spraying backward across its shell and the debris behind it like a painter tossing a bucket full of red paint against a blank canvas.

The explosion of gore was surprising, and I took several quick steps backward, but nothing further happened. The monsters slumped to the ground, clearly dead.

The runes had worked perfectly. Even better than I had even expected, honestly. The combination of the force of the runes and the barrel of the six-shooter must have accelerated the bullet to even faster speeds than I had initially estimated. The results were a very dead armored rat. I stepped forward, inspecting the body of the tusk-rat. The first bullet had penetrated its armored hide, something my knife hadn't been able to do when I fought one of these the first time. I traced where the bullet passed through its body, climbing the mound of debris the creature's body lay on, and found an exit wound through the other side of the monster. The bullet had been strong enough to pass completely through the tusk-rat, penetrating its armor twice, and from what I could see, it had also continued down into its nest until it was lost in the debris.

That was some serious firepower.

I dug through the debris, unable to find the bullet. It had dug through several feet of stone and wood, burying itself so deep I couldn't find it unless I stayed here and shifted the entire pile.

While the revolver had been quiet compared to a traditional firearm, I didn't want to stick around too long in case the sound had attracted something else.

I did take the time to inspect the head of the tusk-rat, finding the second bullet had penetrated the skull and come out of the back of the creature at an angle that made it easier to trace. I searched for a moment, finding the bullet wedged deeply in the solid stone of the wall the tusk-rat's nest had been built against. The bullet was lodged several inches deep in the stone. I pulled out my knife and chipped away at the shattered stone until I could pry the bullet free.

Surprisingly, it appeared to be intact. The rune to enhance the durability of the bullet was not a joke. Whereas a normal bullet would have flattened out and lost most of its penetrating power, this bullet had continued unimpeded, fully formed. That, combined with the speed of the bullet being fired through a rifled barrel magnified by the *Penetration* rune, meant these bullets were especially deadly. They wouldn't flatten upon initial impact, instead retaining their shape and penetrating even deeper into whatever I shot.

I was a bit shocked by how effective the revolver was. I had hoped it would give me a ranged weapon I could use to defend myself, but this was even more powerful than I had anticipated.

The gun was such a simple concept, but in a world of magic, technology had clearly never developed as much as it had in my world. Why would anyone experiment with new types of weapons when you could just learn a new skill that granted some mystical spell or attack that did something similar? Plus, it seemed like nobody had had much time to experiment in a long time, given how tenuously this part of the world was holding out against the hordes of monsters that attacked every night. Maybe that was different in other parts of the world. I also had a unique advantage; my nanobots were able to copy a rune perfectly, and I had knowledge of my old world to help me design a modified revolver that could work with the magic of this world.

I tempered my excitement about the power of the gun. I hadn't seen what magic could do in this world, and from what I could tell, I was fighting the weakest of the monsters out there. Given how powerful the few people I had seen were, it was very possible that my gun was nothing compared to their skills or powers. I didn't have enough information to know for sure at this point, but I was pretty confident that the people I had seen leaping over rooftops to explore the city probably had no problem dispatching a simple tusk-rat.

One thing I could feel good about, though, was that I was now able to defend myself properly. And I didn't even have a class yet.

As I made my way back to the apartment, I practiced drawing, loading, and mock-firing the firearm over and over. My cloak interfered slightly with the act of pulling the gun, which was a small frustration. For now, I tossed the cloak over my shoulder to get it out of the way, and I ordered my nanobots to replicate themselves and begin to incorporate the cloak and the other gear I had recently acquired. Having the nanobots take over my new equipment would allow me to reinforce the items, much like I had done with the clothing I had brought with me to this world, and it would allow me to more easily modify the cloak to fit me better.

I immediately felt a slight drain on my body as the nanobots began to replicate. I carefully planned out how I wanted to modify the cloak, and as the new nanobots began to penetrate the cloak, I sent them blueprints for how I wanted the cloak changed. First, I ordered them to upgrade the clasp to fine steel so I didn't have to worry about it breaking on me. After that, I ordered them to bring up one side of the cloak so my right hand was free. The cloak would hang down over my chest, running from my right shoulder and down past my waist on the left. This would hide the shoulder harness of the revolver, in case anyone tried to get a look at it, while allowing my right hand complete freedom of movement. I could still throw the cloak back, allowing me to fight with my left hand, but its default position would cover the revolver while leaving my right arm completely unhindered.

It looked a bit like a Wild West poncho, covering both shoulders but draping down over only the left side of my body.

I also set the nanobots to waterproof the cloak and to repair the minor wear and tear on the backpack I had purchased. It would take at least a day for the nanobots to spread and finish their work. By the time I was back in my apartment, I was feeling hungry and thirsty again, my body being drained rapidly from the frantic nanobot work I had ordered.

I ate a quick meal of dried fish and then settled down away from the windows in the apartment. As my nanobots worked frantically inside of me, I practiced loading and mock-firing the firearm. I had access to all of humanity's knowledge on firearms, including all kinds of training and tactical guides for using a revolver. Like all of my knowledge, though, it was still theoretical. I needed to train my body as well so that what I knew intellectually became physically instinctive. I accessed information on muscle memory and how top athletes trained. I began to practice those techniques with the revolver, loading, unloading, mock-firing from different angles, and everything else I could think of to begin training my body.

One of the benefits of my prior existence was that I was more than willing to perform routine tasks over and over for as long as it took to complete whatever goal I had given myself. Whereas a normal human would become bored, tired, or lose focus, I practiced reloading and mock-firing my gun for hours, stopping only to eat and drink. I even switched hands, training my left hand as well so that I didn't let myself become too dependent on a single hand.

Night fell, and I refused to stop training. By the time the sun rose on another day, I was able to draw, mock-fire, and reload the revolver so fast that I would have easily beat every record on Earth. The combination of my enhanced body, able to move much quicker than that of an average human, and my single-minded practice had paid good dividends. While I wasn't an absolute expert, I felt much more confident in drawing, reloading, and firing the revolver now. And all it had cost was a sleepless night.

I ate a small meal and drank some of my remaining water. My cloak had finished being modified overnight, and I had crafted and charged sixteen more bullets before the orb ran out of power, so I felt as prepared as I could be to face this new, dangerous world.

Today, I felt significantly more confident about my chances of survival. I gathered my belongings into my backpack, strapping it tightly on my back. I placed my cloak over my shoulder and practiced drawing my revolver, finding that the newly modified cloak no longer interfered with my draw, just as I had hoped. I gathered my newly charged bullets into the case I had crafted on my belt, re-holstered my knife and gun, and then made my way out of the apartment. It was time to hunt once again.

Chapter 7

I walked more confidently down the empty streets now, but my eyes and ears still paid close attention to every detail around me, my hand twitching and ready to draw my revolver if anything approached. This time, though, I wasn't trying to hide from the monsters that lurked around the city during the day. Now I was paying attention to every detail around me so I could find the monsters. This time, I was the hunter, not the hunted.

It wasn't long before I heard the faintest of sounds from a building near me. I crossed the street silently, crouching near the building to gather more information. The building itself was another apartment complex, but as I listened closely, it appeared that this one was infested with monsters. I could hear monsters on multiple floors; the sounds of scuttling, digging, and faint grunts were clear to my ears through the weathered wood the building was made of. I circled the building until I found the main entrance, another archway that led into a central courtyard in the middle of the apartment. The front gate was torn down, so I walked as silently as I could into the central courtyard, looking around cautiously at the various apartment windows that lined the inside of the building.

Inside the courtyard, I saw several of the apes I had managed to avoid the other day. The three that I could see in the courtyard itself were lying in the shade cast by the apartment building, lazily picking at themselves or sleeping flat on their backs without a care in the world. I counted the ones I could see in the courtyard, finding four of the beasts. My ears told me several more were in the building all around me.

I debated whether to attack or not, but I felt an urge to truly test my new weapon, a surprisingly reckless urge that I found hard to ignore. I didn't know if it was my own mind, eager to test my revolver, or something biological from my young, powerful body, but I decided not to ignore the urge. I stepped out into the courtyard boldly, my hand reaching under my modified cloak to draw my revolver. Two of the apes in the courtyard hadn't been sleeping and noticed me immediately. As they leapt up in alarm, screeching angrily at my intrusion, I felt a grim smile stretch across my face.

The two sleeping apes shot upward at the cry from their companions. I heard the others in the building around me begin to hoot and screech in reply, immediately alerted that I was intruding on their territory. The four in front of me bared their oversized teeth and began to pound the courtyard with their fists, posturing aggressively toward me.

"You settled down in the wrong part of town," I said to the beasts, my smile stretching even wider in anticipation of a real fight. Part of me was surprised at my recklessness, but another was confident I could handle such mindless animals now. I trusted my new body, and I especially trusted my new weapon. It was time to see how effective the combination of the two truly was.

The apes in front of me didn't understand my words, but my obvious lack of fear sent them into an even greater rage. They screamed at me and leapt forward to attack.

I aimed and shot the nearest ape. My bullet struck it in the chest, blowing the ape backward, sending it spinning to the ground in a split second. The other apes didn't even notice what happened to their companion, racing toward me on all fours, focused solely on killing me as rapidly as possible. I strafed around some of the pillars in the courtyard, putting more room between me and them, and hastily aimed at another of the beasts. I timed my second shot carefully, hitting one of the apes as another one was behind it in perfect alignment. My bullet tore through the first ape and struck the second one with nearly the same amount of force as the first, sending them both flying backward violently. Blood sprayed behind them as my bullet tore through them, painting the courtyard red with their blood.

The fourth ape was close to me now. Instead of wasting a bullet, I drew my knife with my left hand and threw it with a sideways flick of my arm. My throw was perfect, the knife penetrating deep into the ape's left eye. It stumbled, continuing forward until it crashed to the ground in front of me. I sidestepped nimbly, dodging the body as it tumbled toward me across the courtyard.

I reloaded my revolver, eyeing the body next to me, but it didn't stir. I had managed to kill it with a single throw of my knife. I checked the other apes, but none of them were getting up either. More of the apes began to climb out of the windows above me, screaming in rage as they saw the wounded apes. I moved to the center of the courtyard and began firing at the beasts where they stood, aggressively screaming and waving their fists at me from the apartment windows. Each shot sent an ape slamming backward. It either flew back into the window it had climbed out of or clipped the windowsill and fell to the courtyard, unmoving.

I killed six of the beasts and then reloaded, snapping out the wheel of the revolver with a flick of my wrist. There were no shell casings, so it was easier to reload than a traditional revolver. As I drew a handful of bullets from my satchel and began to reload, a significantly larger ape, glowing with a blue light, stepped out of a doorway on the ground floor near where I stood. It glared at me with slightly more intelligence than the other apes. Some of the smaller apes seemed to have realized how easily I could kill them and had ducked back into the building to hide from me. Others weren't as smart and were in the process of climbing down the side of the building to try to get to me. I finished reloading and shot an ape that was swinging from one open window to a ledge beneath it, throwing the descending ape against the wall, where it lost its grip and fell to the courtyard with a soft thud.

At the sight of its minion dying, the blue sub-boss charged me, slamming its massive fists into the courtyard and kicking up dust as it sped forward. The roar of the blue ape echoed around the courtyard, and I felt a strange pressure from the cry. It pressed down on me mentally in a way I had never experienced before, as if I was suddenly underwater and the pressure of an entire ocean was trying to crush me. The smaller apes climbing down the building began to grow larger, visibly swelling in size, and they gave up on their careful climb downward, leaping to the courtyard in a rage, no longer caring about injuring themselves from the fall.

I took careful aim and shot the blue ape in the head, right between its two angry, bloodshot eyes. My bullet tore through its head, blowing the back of its skull out in a spray of blood and gore.

The sub-boss continued forward for several more steps until its body realized what had happened and its arms and legs failed, causing the ape to collapse to the courtyard with a crash. The blue ape's momentum caused its body to slide forward, kicking up even more dust and coming to rest just a handful of feet away from where I stood. The apes that had been charging me in a rage lost whatever enhancement the blue ape had given them, immediately shrinking in size. As they slowed down and looked around the courtyard, visibly confused, I aimed and shot one after another before they could recover.

I reloaded again as the remaining apes realized what was happening and continued their charge toward me. The last two uninjured apes charged from two different directions as I reloaded.

I waited carefully, timing my movements precisely, and then ducked down and rolled out of the way as the apes tried to snag me in their long, hairy arms. The momentum of their charge caused them to crash into each other as I rolled past them both. They slammed into each other in an almost comical collision, and both stumbled to the ground, intertwined with each other. Not wanting to waste any more bullets than I had to, I walked around them until I had the perfect angle and then shot them both with a single bullet. The acceleration of the bullet was so powerful it blew through the first ape's back and continued through the second one's chest, only stopping when it impacted the ground beneath them both.

I waited, listening closely to see if anything else was going to attack me, but I didn't hear any other movement nearby. The only sounds were the occasional grunts and whines of the wounded beasts spread around the courtyard. I replaced the bullet I had used to kill the last two apes and then holstered my gun, very satisfied with how effective the weapon had turned out. With only my knife, these beasts would have killed me easily. Even with a weapon from this world such as a sword or bow, I doubted I could have handled so many of the beasts without being overwhelmed and killed, unless I had some class to help make the weapon more effective.

I waited patiently until the last of the apes finally died, keeping a careful eye on the apartment windows around me in case any of the beasts that had fled tried to return.

Weak primatus defeated—1 experience awarded.

The experience announcements for killing fifteen of the "weak primatus" monsters repeated in my head over and over. The feeling was uncomfortable but I did my best to endure it.

Weak primatus sub-boss defeated—5 experience awarded.
No class detected. Experience pooled for future use.

The fifteen weaker monsters and the one sub-boss gave me a total of twenty more experience. I was now up to sixty-two experience points, but I still had no class to put them toward.

I gathered the blue orb from the sub-boss and then wrangled my knife from the ape I had killed with it. I cleaned and re-sheathed my knife, then surveyed the courtyard to figure out how to gather as many of my bullets as I could. A very annoying hour and a half later, I had collected ten of the thirteen bullets I had used. The rest were lost somewhere in the city around me, having blown through the beasts and the wooden walls around me without stopping.

The fight with the apes had been enjoyable, a true test of my weapon and body. It felt good to experience the unity of my mind and body that came with combat. Outside of fighting, I still struggled to unify my mind and body, but when I was fighting for my life, I experienced true unity. It was an exhilarating feeling.

Unlike the fight, though, the search for the bullets afterward was a frustrating use of my time. While the holes in the wooden walls around me made it easy to track where my bullets had gone, they often traveled through several walls before being stopped, so I was forced to climb in and out of nearby buildings in search of them.

My search, of course, didn't go unnoticed either. I disrupted several armored tusk-rats that were nesting in the nearby buildings, making me use more bullets and then forcing me to track down *those* bullets as well. Overall, it cooled quite a lot of my satisfaction from defeating the apes.

Now that I knew my revolver was a success, my next priority was to gather more iron to turn into steel bullets so I didn't have to worry about running out as much. Now that I had another blue orb, I could charge thirty-five more bullets, if the number of bullets I could charge last time stayed true. I was a bit concerned about what might happen if someone found a bullet of mine. I wasn't sure if someone could reverse-engineer the bullet and begin to puzzle out the weapon that might have fired it. That might not be a bad thing, considering how tenuous the survival of the humans on this world seemed to be, but I wasn't quite ready for such knowledge to spread if I could help avoid it. For now, me having the exclusive knowledge of firearms gave me the significant edge I needed to guarantee my survival. And despite meeting one semi-friendly merchant, I had no idea how the other people I met would react to me. Maybe someday I would be willing to share more, but for now, it was best if I kept things as secret as I could.

Of course, the chances of someone finding a bullet of mine were extremely slim here in the ruins of the city that very few people even entered, but I decided that I would continue to recover as many of my bullets as I could for now, even though it was extremely aggravating.

I spent the rest of the day hunting monsters and then inevitably spending even longer hunting down my bullets afterward. I also hunted for more iron and bits of low-quality steel, if I could find it.

The low-level creatures that inhabited the city during the day turned out to be no match for my revolver, thankfully. I hunted down several packs of dire rats and even took care of a few hellhounds, but I didn't run into another sub-boss for the rest of the day.

Instead of returning to the apartment I had been camping out in, I found a mostly intact villa with stone walls that stretched four stories tall. It had a well in the center, and the walls and villa didn't seem to have sustained much damage at all from monsters, so I was pretty sure that it would be safe at night. I holed up in a small study on the top floor and spent the night crafting more bullets. I also practiced drawing and firing the revolver until I actually began to feel tired.

The next week passed in a similar fashion. I returned to the villa at night after a busy day of hunting. By the end of the week, I had accrued 187 experience points and had a satchel full of enchanted bullets from all the iron I had collected. I had also killed fifteen sub-bosses, gathering their blue orbs to trade, although I planned to keep two of them for myself and my crafting.

I had encountered a wide array of monsters, but all of them were labeled as weak by the announcements I received for killing them. I never stayed out too late, still afraid of the monsters that came out during the night. The only things I avoided during my hunts were the sounds of larger beasts. I could hear them from several blocks away, their steps so loud that I didn't dare to even sneak a look at them in case they were too powerful for me to survive. I had gained confidence with my new weapon, but I wasn't suicidal.

I also encountered an apartment building that was covered in spiderwebs that I avoided thoroughly. I had no interest in fighting monstrous spiders.

After my week of hunting, I returned to the street Asylaion's caravan traveled on and waited for it to pass by. When I heard the caravan coming, I stood and waited patiently. The guards eyed me suspiciously as usual, but after a moment, several of them seemed to recognize me. They relaxed and returned to their duties, scanning the buildings and rooftops around them.

When Asylaion saw me, he jumped down from the wagon he was riding in and approached me.

"My friend!" he yelled as he approached. "I thought for sure you had been claimed by the city! How nice to see you still alive!"

I smiled at his kind reaction to the sight of me, even though I was sure it was partly just for show.

"I'm still around," I said, shaking his hand. He slapped me on the shoulder as we shook, his strength enough to knock me forward slightly. I tried not to react but was momentarily surprised that he was strong enough to move my enhanced body so easily.

"And you look good!" he said, eyeing my modified cloak. My firearm was hidden under the left side of the cloak, so all he could see was my small knife and the pouches on my belt, but I supposed I did look more like a real scavenger this time.

"Thank you," I told him. "Your guidance and trade has been helpful for my survival. It has been a productive week since we last spoke."

"Good!" he said enthusiastically. "Does that mean you have more to trade?"

I opened one of the pouches on my belt, letting him see how many blue orbs I had to trade this time.

"Oh ho!" he said, eyeing the orbs I had collected. "You have been busy! How did you manage to collect so many? Are you now

89

a powerful mage or some rogue using that knife of yours to kill from the shadows, eh?"

"What are you willing to trade me for the answer to that question?" I asked with a smile, trying to make a joke.

He thought for a moment, taking my poor attempt at a quip seriously. "I will give you your choice of a magical weapon for answers on your methods of survival and where you come from." He nodded as he spoke, furrowing his brow. "I admit to being very curious about you, my friend. Your survival only makes me want to know more!"

I hadn't expected him to actually offer me something; I had just been trying to banter like a normal person might do.

Seeing my hesitation, he laughed at me and shook his head. "It's okay, my friend. Come, review my inventory for today and let us walk together. Did you find anything else of value? Perhaps some old magical items or any of the metal I mentioned?"

I shook my head as I took the scroll he handed me. I opened it and began to scan through the merchandise he had available.

"Understandable," he said, shaking his head sadly. "It is rare these days to find anything truly valuable above ground and nobody is willing to risk the dungeons anymore. It is a shame."

I wasn't actually interested in buying anything today, given the effectiveness of my revolver. There wasn't much that could compare to it from the merchant. I was still curious what he had to sell, though, and wanted to see if I could learn anything more about this world from the items on his scroll. Like last time, he had a large number of weapons and ammunition for sale, as well as salves, food, and other goods. There wasn't much that was different from the last time I had seen him, except maybe a few different weapons, the other ones having already been sold or traded, presumably.

After I was done reviewing the scroll, I handed it back to him. "I am actually curious about getting into one of the enclaves," I told him. "Would you let me know how to enter them?"

Asylaion took the scroll, tucking it back into his belt. "Hmm. Trade me one of your blue orbs and I will give you more rations, a stavrata, and ten copper nummi back for the information. A fair deal, yes?"

I did the calculations, and it seemed like a bit of a discount compared to his prior price, so I agreed.

"Good, good," he said, walking us to the back of his wagon to gather the goods. "My home is the bridge, back behind us. You have seen it, yes?"

I nodded as he handed me several packages of dried fish and my silver and copper in exchange for one orb.

"We call it Perama," he told me. "It isn't much to look at, but we are hardy folk who have survived where many others have not. We are a bit . . . chaotic, shall we say. Anyone can enter. There are very few rules, but they must be followed or you will be killed. No fire. No matter what. Don't mess with the walls that protect this side of the bridge. Don't build any higher or the whole place might collapse. That's about it. You will find the kindest people and the most ruthless rogues in equal parts. Myself and the guards that protect the caravans and walls are really the only form of order, and everyone contributes to our defense in whatever way they can. Other than protecting the enclave, we don't really do anything else so everyone is on their own.

"East of us is the Patriarch's enclave," he continued, pointing behind himself. "A Varangian like you would do well to avoid that place. The Patriarch's priests have become . . . strange over the last hundred years as the city has fallen into more and more ruin. They believe their gods will save us, but the rest of us aren't waiting around to be saved by some long-dead gods. Rumors are they are turning to darker and darker classes to try to find their gods again. People who wander too close to their part of the city never return, so be careful."

I ran through what I knew from my world about the religious ranks in ancient Constantinople. In my world, the Patriarch of Constantinople was a very prominent religious leader, essentially the pope of the Eastern Roman Empire. If there was still someone in this world who claimed that title, they were likely a powerful figure and I did not want to get on the bad side of them if I could avoid it. Especially if they had started to turn to darker powers.

As we walked, a small disturbance among the guards broke out, but before I could see what was happening, one of the guards on the wagon stood and shot an arrow toward a nearby rooftop. The arrow streaked away with a bright flash of blue. I didn't see what it hit, but I heard a meaty smack and a sharp cry. Then, suddenly, there was silence. The rest of the guards reached for weapons, but when nothing else appeared, they slowly relaxed again.

"To the north across the water," Asylaion continued as if nothing had happened, "is our sister enclave, Sycae. They are not run by the military or the priests, but the Emperor controls the only bridge between us and them, and so our contact is limited. They are old merchants, dockworkers, and traders that have managed to hold on to the closest thing to civilization left in the world. To enter their enclave, you must have something worth trading or some other way to contribute to their city. If you plan to get there across the only remaining bridge, you must have enough favor or a significant bribe for the Emperor, or they won't let you cross. Some of the fishermen here could sneak you over, but if you are caught, the Emperor may sentence you to death. He protects his control over our trade jealously.

"Nobody stays for free in Sycae, and if you can't afford a place to rest your head, they will kick you out or conscript you into their army until you pay back your debt. Only go there once you have a fair amount of wealth to your name, in my humble opinion.

"The army controls the walls and the majority of the food the city eats to the west, so we are forced to trade with them every day. That is what I do. We trade our crafts and our fish in return for fresh food grown behind their walls. They refuse to protect us, but they want our goods every day."

He turned and spat to the side. "But to be honest," he continued, turning back to me with a grin, "we wouldn't want them taking over anyway. They are no fun. To join their enclave, you must be a part of the army and must bow to the Emperor, even though they don't really obey the Emperor these days, except in name. No exceptions for civilians entering their enclave, though, so be careful. Avoid them as best as you can, in my opinion."

"What about across the water to the east?"

"Ah," he replied, shaking his head, "nobody lives over there anymore. Nothing but the undead remain. The city has been lost for eighty years, at least. Lost to the defiled corpses of our brethren that have risen again to haunt the remains of our fine civilization on that side of the water. Word is the entire peninsula has been lost to the undead plague, but not many people have returned from there, so we don't know for sure.

"The only other surviving enclave is the palace that guards the bridge between here and Sycae, which is where the current emperor, Alexios III, reigns. If you can call what he does reigning. He mostly drinks himself into a stupor, if rumors are true. In his rare moments of lucidity, he tries to order his military to retake the city or conquer Sycae or march out of the city to retake the empire. Most of his orders are ignored these days, although I hear it makes things awkward for the generals when he gets particularly assertive about his ideas. You won't be accepted into the palace unless you were born to the purple—or if you are actually a Varangian, I suppose. The Varangians guard the walls to this day. They are barbarians but fearsome enough to hold where many others have failed. If you aren't one of them, I counsel you to watch out because they may not agree. I'd hate to see you conscripted into their forces."

"What about other cities? Is it like . . . this . . . everywhere?"

"Ah, my boy," the merchant said, a haunted look taking over his face, "we hope that it's not like this everywhere, but we lose hope as time passes. We used to get ships often. Even just ten or fifteen years ago we would get traders still, but even before that, things were slowing. Many boats full of refugees fled here in years past, hoping to find a place to survive, but even those have stopped now. That is why I am so curious about you, my boy, because it gave me hope that there may be more people out there still doing well enough to produce a strapping young lad like yourself. But the more we talk, the more puzzled I am about where you come from."

Changing the subject, I asked him why the world was overrun like this.

Asylaion forced a smile onto his face, trying to dispel the gloom of our previous topic. "Now that sounds like a different question, eh? You want to make a new bargain with me, then?"

I couldn't help but smile back. "No, that is okay. I suspect I will find the answer soon enough."

"The fact that you don't know the answer already is very intriguing to me, my friend! Very intriguing!"

I packed away the supplies Asylaion had been giving me as we spoke and wished him goodbye. I was getting a better mental image of the fallen city, which helped me get my bearings on what I wanted to do next. Despite a week of exploring and hunting, I had barely seen the smallest part of the sprawling metropolis. I could hunt for a year or more before I saw the majority of the city. And while I was feeling more confident now, I still needed some better answers to my questions, and I needed to see about a class, if getting one was even possible these days. The only place I could find the answers I wanted was in one of the enclaves.

I decided to find a secure place to spend the night near Perama, the bridge city Asylaion was from, and then try my luck at entering the enclave tomorrow morning. It was time to see what I could find amidst the remnants of humanity.

Chapter 8

The wall in front of Perama, the city built on the remnants of the broken bridge, was not impressive. It was twenty feet tall, surrounding a gate made of solid wood with a portcullis that could be dropped at night, but the stone used to build the wall looked like it had been looted from a hundred different buildings and thrown together by a child playing in a sandbox.

Despite that, it was clear that the wall worked. It was approaching noon when I finally arrived; I'd had to camp out in a more distant building than I had originally planned because few near the enclave seemed secure enough. When I arrived, men and women were still out looting monsters' bodies that had piled up beneath the enclave's walls during the night. Only a few guards walked the wall, keeping an eye on the surrounding city to protect the workers below them. The wooden gate was opened several feet, and a group of five guards stood nearby, also watching the workers as they harvested the monsters in front of the wall.

The people harvesting the monsters had set up a number of butchering stations where a select few worked over the corpses with knives in hand. They cut off body parts here and there, filled vials with blood or milked various glands from the monsters, and did other, more obscure things to the monsters' bodies. The rest of the men and women were busy dragging the corpses to and from the butchers as they worked. It was a methodical and efficient system, clearly long-established.

I watched for a moment more, noting some of the different kinds of monsters that were being butchered. I noticed that several were disturbingly human, but with corrupted skin or monster appendages of some kind. A human with horns, or a tentacled woman, were just some of the bodies I saw being harvested without any hesitation. Others were mythical beasts, like stories from my world come to life. I saw winged monsters, monsters that looked like warped or twisted versions of normal animals, and even stranger things that appeared to be made of metal or beings of pure shadow. The variety was as impressive as it was concerning.

"Scavenger returning?" one of the guards said to me as I approached the gate, eyeing my cloak.

I hesitated for a second, unsure if I should lie or try to explain my situation, but before I could decide, the man gestured for me to enter the gate behind him without waiting for my reply. The guards seemed unconcerned, since I was wearing the gray cloak of a scavenger. They ignored me, returning to watching the workers to make sure they stayed safe from any daytime monsters.

Taking him up on his offer, I walked past the guards and entered the city.

The gate turned into a short tunnel that ran the width of the wall, which was about ten feet thick. Murder holes lined the sides and top of the tunnel, and I could see several more guards watching me through the holes as I walked through the tunnel, but nobody stopped me or asked me any questions.

On the other side of the tunnel, I expected the sunlight to return, but that never happened. The other side of the tunnel was just as dark as the tunnel had been, maybe even darker without the faint light spilling from the murder holes. I looked around, seeing that this side of the tunnel was shaded by makeshift houses, buildings, and other ramshackle constructions that loomed over me, blocking the entire sky above. I eyed the buildings around me warily, concerned that they all looked like they could fall at any moment. At this end of the bridge, the buildings were built right against the wall, using it to give some stability to the shaky structures above and beside me. The street under me was cobblestoned, like the rest of the city, but rapidly began to arch upward with the curve of the bridge. The buildings continued up the bridge, rising higher and higher above the wall. It made for an extremely worrying, claustrophobic street, as if I was walking through a dark sewer. The narrow path forward was barely illuminated by the occasional blue light spilling from a few shops or homes facing the street.

The narrow tunnel that ran up the bridge was packed with people jostling each other as they moved. Many people joined or exited the main street from narrow alleys that ran between the ramshackle buildings, and many other people were climbing up and down the buildings, using them as a vertical street to reach the buildings higher up. The buildings that blocked the light above seemed marginally more reinforced on each side, something that wasn't that reassuring, given they arched over the street and seemed to be made of nothing but salvaged wood.

I stepped forward, moving out of the tunnel that ran under the wall, trying to figure out what to do now that I was here. I had no idea where to go or how to stay safe in such a messy, claustrophobic place. The smell of so many close-packed people, combined with the weathered buildings and a pervading smell of rotten fish, made the whole area stink like a disturbed graveyard full of fresh corpses.

Several of the nearby buildings had no front, sitting open-faced to the street that ran up the bridge. Each one cast a pocket of light over the bridge, allowing people to see better but only serving to make the darkened corridor seem even more ominous. I could see people bargaining, yelling, chatting, and working at the open-faced buildings, indicating they were likely shops of some kind.

Several people were running the goods being harvested outside the walls to the nearby shops, and I could hear a blacksmith and other crafters working in some of them. I walked to the side of the narrow street and tried to look inside several of the nearby open-faced shops. I saw one that was using vials of blood or other fluids that were being harvested to brew what looked like potions, while another nearby was cooking the meat taken from the monsters. They were doing good business selling the freshly grilled meat, and nobody seemed to object to the source of the food. I noticed the flames that illuminated the bridge were all blue, like the lights that surrounded the palace and the military's walls outside. The light from the store that was cooking the meat was also blue. It must be a magical flame of some kind that generated heat without burning the insanely packed bridge to the ground. I understood immediately why normal flame was outlawed here, given how quickly the entire place could go up if a fire was started.

"Hey," I heard a voice say to my right. "You lost or need directions?"

I glanced over toward the voice. I had been frozen in place for almost a minute, overwhelmed by the chaos and sights in front of

97

me and someone had clearly noticed. I shook myself gently, refocusing on the people around me and keeping myself safe. Several people had been forced to maneuver around me where I had frozen and were giving me irritated looks. Next to them was a small teenager, around twelve or thirteen years old at most, although they could be older, given the look of deprivation on the child's face and body. I couldn't tell if they were a boy or a girl; their nondescript clothing, their mangled hair, and the layers of dirt on their face made it impossible to tell.

"You need a guide?" the teenager asked, stepping closer to me. "Best guide in Perama, I am. You look new here. If you don't hire a guide, I guarantee you will end up lost and dead within an hour, mister."

I looked over the small person in front of me. They were dirty and I imagined they smelled, but I couldn't quite tell over the enclave itself. Their hair was a tangled mess, clearly shorn off by a semi-sharp object by some friend—or possibly an enemy, judging by how bad it looked. The little clothing they wore was a size or two too big for their skinny frame and was mended in several places, indicating it had been salvaged or was a hand-me-down from their family. The child had no shoes and no visible weapons of any kind.

I hesitated before replying. I couldn't tell if this was a genuine service that they were offering or just a rather obvious attempt to take advantage of someone that looked lost. I looked them over again, but I had trouble telling if they were being deceptive or honest. I glanced back down the crowded street and decided the child was probably right that I would end up lost if I didn't have a guide. If they turned out to be leading me into a robbery, hopefully I could escape or defend myself with my new weapon.

"What's the cost?" I asked, eyeing the child skeptically. "And how do I know I can trust you to take me where I want to go?"

"Constans is my name," the young teenager said, looking me up and down with a surprisingly adult look as if they were evaluating me from top to bottom, "and I'm the best guide in the city. I know everyone worth talking to and everywhere you could want to go. I can't guarantee your safety. I ain't strong enough to protect you or nothin', but I have a good reputation around here. Ask around if you want. I have led people from all the different enclaves when they come to visit us. Price is five nummi for the day. Plus, you have to buy me lunch."

I looked around the bridge once again. Nobody else was stepping forward to help me, and it was clear there were no guards or officials to ask for help. As Asylaion had said, this place was barely organized chaos.

I sighed, looking back at the teenager. "Alright, Constans," I told them. "I'll give you three nummi now and three more when I make it out of the city safely. And I'll get you lunch, but nothing extravagant. Deal?"

"Deal, mister!" they replied, with a grin showing several missing teeth. The teenager stuck out their hand, palm up, and I pulled out three nummi and paid them. They snatched them hastily when I put them in their palm, checking the copper carefully before tucking it somewhere in their clothing that I avoided looking too closely at.

"Alright then," they said, "where you wanna go first?"

I had planned out what I wanted to find in the city, and having a guide would hopefully make it easier. "I'm looking to talk to someone that sells classes first," I told the child.

They didn't hesitate in replying, stepping forward to lead me deeper into the city. "Easy!" They turned and smiled at me. "Momma Lena is the only spot in the city for that anyway. Follow me!"

The child turned back around and began to walk swiftly down the street leading deeper into the city. I followed cautiously, watching the humans bargaining, eating, and crafting in the open storefronts around me as I passed. It was clearly a thriving enclave, although it was poor and looked like it could collapse at any moment. Nobody wore nice clothes, and not many appeared to have cleaned themselves in a long time, but everyone was working or moving with a purpose. Nobody appeared to be visibly starving, although Constans was definitely suffering from malnutrition, which made me suspect that others might not be doing as well as the people I could see in the street near me.

Several shopkeepers called out to me as I passed, trying to entice me to shop with them.

"Scavenger, you have need of some food?"

"We got the best potions in Perama right here! Check us out, scavenger. Trade us some orbs!"

I also heard a number of people discussing me as I passed, even over the din of the crowded street. My enhanced hearing let me pick up some of the conversations that occurred in my wake.

"Never seen that scavenger before. He looks like he is from the palace. Some Varangian brat, you think?"

"Don't go poking into anything," I heard someone respond. "Best to leave those born to the purple to themselves."

"He doesn't look that dangerous . . ."

The voices faded as Constans led me up the bridge. I followed behind until they stopped and pointed toward a tiny opening that led to our right. I stopped next to them and eyed the opening.

"I'm not sure I can actually fit in there," I told Constans.

"Yeah," they replied. "You are a big one. Just bend down and squeeze. You'll make it. This is the safest way to Momma Lena's place." Constans easily maneuvered themselves into the narrow alley, not waiting for me to respond again. I crouched down and turned my body sideways. I barely fit but pushed myself into the narrow alley, determined not to lose my supposed guide. I kept brushing against the buildings as we passed, dirt and grit coating my cloak. The buildings weren't uniform either. They often had sections that protruded outward or inward. This caused the alley to meander back and forth, widening and narrowing without rhyme or reason. I would have been concerned about being ambushed, but I honestly wasn't sure that anyone else could fit in here to attack me right now.

After a few minutes of following Constans, I saw the end of the alley begin to brighten significantly. It was actual sunlight spilling down the narrow alley in front of us. I continued forward, wedging myself around a protrusion from the building to my left that almost blocked the entire alley.

At the end of the alley, I had to blink several times as my eyes adjusted to the bright light of day. I had only been inside the heart of the enclave for a few minutes, but it had been hard to remember it was the middle of the day as I navigated the shadowy city. As I followed Constans out of the alley, I saw that we had reached the end of the bridge on this side. Only a foot or two at most separated us from the edge of the bridge itself. This side of the bridge looked east across the water, toward the part of the city that had been overtaken by the undead, according to Asylaion. There was a second, makeshift street here. It ran at the very edge of the bridge between the buildings and the two-to-three-foot-tall stone parapet that tried to stop people from falling off the edge of the bridge. It didn't seem nearly tall enough to protect the many people that were crammed onto the street and moved haphazardly past each other at the edge of the bridge.

Similar to the other street, this one was packed full of people jostling each other, talking and arguing as they moved. I glanced upward and saw that people were also climbing up the buildings here at the edge, using makeshift ladders to climb up and down. A second street, made from rickety-looking wooden boards, ran above the street we were on, except it had no guardrail to prevent people from falling off. It was also packed with people walking in each direction on the street. I couldn't imagine how the bridge stayed up; the supports were roughly nailed to the various buildings above me.

"C'mon!" Constans yelled at me, gesturing for me to follow them out along the narrow street. I wanted to rub my head, the insanity of the city giving me my first headache, but instead I stepped out carefully and followed them.

I dodged several people who didn't bother to slow down and allow me to enter the flow of the street, narrowly avoiding being shoved against the parapet to my right. I swallowed nervously, looking over the edge. The water below was beautiful, at least, and the smell of the sea and the sun dispelled the gloom and stench of the inner pathways behind us.

As I followed Constans down the narrow street, I saw that many of the buildings here had an open wall similar to the main street through the center of the bridge. These were nicer, the natural light and fresh air making them more pleasant. It was clear these were the more successful shops. The merchants inside looked more comfortable and did not need to call out for business; they were already busy haggling with customers or working patiently at tables as I passed.

After several minutes of careful walking, with me trying my best to not knock anyone off or be knocked off myself, Constans stopped again and gestured to their left. When I caught up with them, I saw a small but comfortable-looking shop with an open wall like many of the others we had passed. Inside was a large wooden desk that wrapped around the back side of the shop. Books, ink, and bottles of various ingredients covered the large desk, and a number of shelves built around the room displayed leather-bound books.

Seated at the desk was a hunched-over older woman, an open book in front of her and a quill in hand. She had long, dark hair with streaks of white here and there. She wore nicer clothing than Constans, including shoes and a warm-looking sweater to combat the slight chill of the sea air blowing through the shop. She was very focused on her work and didn't seem to have noticed that we had stopped outside her shop.

"You just have to wait for her to take a break," Constans whispered to me as we stepped slightly into the shop together.

"Should we just stand here, then?" I asked Constans, speaking quietly as well.

"Yeah," they replied. "We are mostly out of the way. Shouldn't be more than a half hour before she takes a break to restore her mana."

Constans unashamedly sat down in the middle of the stone floor and turned to watch the people passing by the shop. I decided to sit as well. I turned and sat down next to my little guide, happy that they hadn't tried to have me ambushed. They turned and gave me a surprised look, raising one eyebrow as I sat down with them.

After a moment, they turned back to watching the people of this strange city, and I joined them. A constant flow of people going in both directions passed the shop. It made me wonder what everyone was so busy doing and how many people truly lived on the bridge. Just from the numbers I had seen so far, it must be thousands.

"What's it like growing up around here?" I finally asked Constans, figuring enough time had passed that they might be open to conversation.

They turned and gave me a skeptical look but eventually replied, "Eh, could be worse. Could be anywhere else in the city. Probably be dead already or stuck being a snob or soldier."

"Ah," I said, unsure of how to respond. I had spoken to many people in my past life, but talking as a fellow human was still new to me, and I struggled to come up with an immediate response. Making small talk, as people called it, wasn't an easy skill to acquire, I was learning.

"You one of them guards for the Emperor, then?" Constans asked after I failed to reply any further.

"Why do you say that?" I asked them, grateful that they kept the conversation going.

"We get them from time to time," Constans replied. "They look kinda like you. Big and pale. But they have beards down to here"—they gestured halfway down their chest—"and normally have heavy armor and big weapons. And they travel in packs when they come here, afraid we might do something to them."

I shook my head after they finished speaking. "No, I'm not one of them, although we may share similar traits. I'm not really from around here originally."

"Hmm," Constans said, unashamedly looking me up and down, clearly trying to see if I was a liar or not.

I laughed at their frank look. "Honest, I'm not a Varangian."

"Okay, mister," they replied, still clearly unconvinced. "If you say so."

We talked a bit more about the enclave as we waited for Momma Lena to take a break, the two of us watching the people pass by as we chatted. It was refreshing to speak to someone as a person. When I asked, Constans didn't want to talk about their family, making me think they were an orphan or very protective of whatever family they might have. I also learned that Constans was a girl and claimed to be fourteen years old, which could be true, given the signs of malnourishment. I also learned that the locals called the city Nova Roma, which meant "New Rome" and was one of the original names for the city that became known as Constantinople. Later in the Middle Ages, calling it Nova Roma was a way to lay claim to the heritage of Rome, even though the empire based in Constantinople was quite different from the empire originally ruled by the city's founder, Constantine.

She tried asking me about where I was from, but I told her I couldn't go into the details. That very obviously made her more convinced I was a Varangian, despite my protests to the contrary. I was enjoying our conversation, a faint smile on my face as we people-watched together, when I heard a chair scrape behind us.

I turned and saw Momma Lena watching me and Constans where we sat on her floor, making small talk and watching the passersby.

"Well," Momma Lena said after a moment of staring at the two of us, "this is rather unusual. I recognize most people that come to my shop these days. Who are you and what can I do for you?"

I stood up awkwardly as she stared at me, a closed look on her face.

"Uh," I said. As I stood, I realized that I now towered over the smaller woman. I flushed slightly, realizing I should have remained seated if I wanted to appear less intimidating. "Right, sorry, my name is Alexander. I'm looking to get some information from you about getting a class. I was told you are the person to talk to."

Momma Lena looked over at Constans, who was in the process of standing up next to me. "You staying safe and fed, Constans?"

"Doing my best, Momma Lena," Constans replied, looking down at her feet and avoiding Momma Lena's penetrating gaze.

"Good girl," she replied. "Here's something for your trouble."

Momma Lena handed Constans what looked like a stick of dried jerky she pulled from a drawer in her desk. Constans took it gratefully and turned toward the street to eat it, giving us the illusion of privacy.

"So what class are you interested in, Alexander?"

"Well, I was thinking maybe the *Archer* class," I replied. "Although I confess, I do not know the cost or procedure for buying a class. I may not be able to afford one right now, but if not, I will come back when I can."

"Hmm," she said, looking me up and down. "*Archer* is a fine class, but I don't see a bow on you. And *Archer* is one of the most expensive classes I have because it's in very high demand for protecting the walls of our enclaves. May I ask, what is your current class list? Maybe something else will serve you better."

I debated declining to answer or lying but decided it wouldn't hurt to be honest with her. Even though I had just met her, she seemed trustworthy. It was clear she ran a successful business here, and I didn't sense any deception in her. And if I was more honest with her, she might be able to tell me more than if she didn't know my situation.

104

"I do not currently have a class," I told her after a slight hesitation.

"Really?" she said, a look of surprise coming over her face. I noticed Constans also turning to look back at me as well.

"Is that so surprising?" I asked, feeling my cheeks blush again slightly. I cursed my body for revealing my mental state so easily as I tried to control the heat filling my cheeks.

"Well," she said, "it wouldn't be, normally, but from what I gathered listening to you and Constans talk, you aren't from around here. Maybe not even from the city at all, would you say?" After a moment, I nodded.

"Well," she continued, "it is just very surprising that you could survive to get here without at least one class, if not two or more. And most people have leveled them a fair amount before they can travel any real distance during even the day, let alone survive the night like you would have to do to get here. Plus, you wear a scavenger cloak, which not just anyone can wear unless you stole it, but even stealing from a scavenger would likely require a *Rogue* class at least."

"I understand," I said. "I prefer not to discuss where I am from, but I have learned to defend myself without a class. It has let me survive, but my lack of a class is why I have come to you. I'm hoping to fix that situation."

"Hmm," she replied, staring me in the eyes as if she could read the truth in them. "Interesting." After a moment, she turned and reached into a nearby drawer in her desk. "Would you allow me to test you to see what your current physical and magical attributes are? It would help me to figure out what class would be of the most benefit to you. It may be that a cheaper option like *Warrior* or *Scholar* would benefit you now by enhancing some of your weak points if you have already learned to survive without a class. You may also consider a non-combat class, which is often cheaper if you can find an apprenticeship. Those would allow you to spend some time leveling in relative safety to gain some attributes that would help you scavenge enough to afford the *Archer* class. Some people follow that option, starting as an apprentice until they can save up for a combat class."

I looked at the device in her hand, but it appeared to be nothing more than a bracelet. I wasn't sure what it would reveal about me, but I was curious about the results myself, so I agreed.

"Great," Momma Lena said, holding the bracelet out for me to put on. "Wear this and I will assess your current scores and your base potential."

I slipped the bracelet over my left wrist. As I did, Momma Lena closed her eyes and began to concentrate. I felt the bracelet become warm around my wrist, but after several minutes of silence, nothing else occurred.

"How strange," she said, her eyes still closed. "I have never seen such an odd combination before."

"What does it say?" I asked.

"Well," she said, opening her eyes. "You are truly the oddest thing I have seen in a long time. I can say that for sure."

Constans had turned around and was watching us as Momma Lena finished concentrating on the bracelet. "What are his scores, Momma Lena?" she asked.

"Hush, child." Momma Lena closed her eyes, her brow furrowed in confusion. "Alexander," she said after a moment, opening her eyes and staring into mine. "Are you aware that you have no mana?"

"No mana?" I asked, confused.

She raised an eyebrow at my reaction. "You seem surprised by that. But surely someone would have told you? Or you would have found out before now?"

"I haven't been evaluated like that before," I told her, playing with the bracelet, which was still on my wrist, out of nervousness.

"Alexander," she said seriously. "It isn't just that which is unusual. Your physical attributes are like a child's. All of them are a mere one. And yet your underlying base potential is off the charts. You are like an extremely strong child, born into a body too strong for this world. The base physical abilities of your body are the equal of a regular person who has several classes leveled to five or higher. At the same time, your base magical abilities are absolutely zero. Even with an attribute score of one, your actual magical ability is zero, because one times zero is still zero. I have never seen anything like it."

"What does that mean?" I asked, thoroughly puzzled by what she was describing. I wasn't surprised by my base physical body being the equivalent of someone with multiple classes, but I didn't understand what she meant by attribute scores and having no magical potential.

"Well," Momma Lena said, looking between me and Constans. "This is basic stuff, but I will try to explain, since it seems to be news to you. Will you two sit again? It will be easier to explain."

I nodded, sitting down in front of her like a schoolboy. Constans joined me, and Momma Lena returned to her seat. She gestured for the bracelet I was wearing as she sat, and I leaned forward, slipping it off my wrist and giving it to her.

"Everyone has mana, Alexander," she began, putting the bracelet away. "Even little Constans here has a core of mana inside her, and as she continues to grow, it will become bigger and fuller of mana, which, if she ever levels a magical class or magical skills, will be what she uses to power those skills. Everyone's core of magic is different. Some people are born with more base mana or a higher mana recharge rate, similar to how a person is born with better hand-eye coordination or more muscles. But it's not that you merely have a small core of mana, which is actually very common for many people without classes. You have no core at all. No mana. No potential to magic, ever."

My mind spun at what she was saying. Not merely about what she was telling me, but what she revealed about the people of this world. If it was true that everyone here was born with a core of magic inside of them, then it must be some kind of evolution that occurred in this dimension, allowing humans to interact with the energy I had termed "magic" that permeated this universe. It was similar to how humans on my Earth had evolved to be able to breathe a very specific mixture of nitrogen and oxygen because the atmosphere of Earth had those elements in that exact amount. It would make sense that the people of this world had similarly adapted to the energy of this dimension in the same way, evolving a core that allowed them to access the magic of this world.

"So what does that mean for a class for me?" I asked.

"Well," Momma Lena replied, "it means that you should not waste your time trying to acquire a *Mage* or *Scholar* class, because you won't be able to use any of their skills, and their attribute

107

enhancements will give you no benefit at all. Same with magic-based skills. You will only ever be able to use physical skills. At the same time, with your powerful physical body, any enhancements you get through a physical class will be an extreme improvement for you."

"Can you explain that more?" I asked, looking down at my body. I knew I was significantly stronger and faster than most people here, but I wasn't exactly sure what she meant. "How would a physical class give me an extreme improvement?"

"Well," she said, obviously puzzled that I displayed such ignorance about topics she must have thought were common sense. "Attribute enhancements that you get for leveling a class build off your existing body. So someone that is in good physical shape and then gains a level in *Warrior* will get +1 to their strength at level 2, but that will actually benefit them more because they are already strong naturally. A +1 to an attribute is approximately a twenty percent increase scaling off your actual body, so that twenty percent becomes a higher actual enhancement if your natural strength is higher than someone that is weak. In the same way, if you got an enhancement to your magic power, it would give you no benefit at all because a twenty percent increase of zero is still zero. You can never enhance your magic."

"Ah," I said, understanding now. Since I hadn't designed this body to have the same evolutionary biology as the humans of this planet, I had absolutely no ability to use magic. That made sense. I immediately started brainstorming ways I could try to fix that flaw, but I put them to the back of my mind for now. That was a problem for later. "So if someone was to work out and exercise, the benefits they gain from the class enhancements are magnified."

"Exactly," Mamma Lena said, smiling at me. "That's why we encourage our children to still exercise and stretch their minds. It might seem useless to engage in strenuous exercise if you can just go get a +1 to your strength and become stronger in a second, but if someone lets their physical body deteriorate, their attributes actually become almost useless."

"So how strong is his actual body, then, huh?" Constans interjected. "He says he can survive without a class. Is he really that strong?"

"Well," Momma Lena said, looking to me for permission. I nodded at her to go ahead. "His base attributes are all still one, obviously." She closed her eyes to recall what her bracelet had told her. "It's true that he doesn't appear to have a class, but his body itself has the equivalent strength of a person with a strength of thirteen. He has the coordination of someone with a score of sixteen, with an endurance of about twenty-one. Most surprising of all, he has a memory score of thirty, which is, frankly, absurd. And of course, a magic power and magic capacity of zero." She opened her eyes, looking at me again. "Of course, that is based on the average person, but that those are your base attributes is so unbelievable I almost don't trust my own device."

"A memory of thirty!" Constans said, shocked.

"Yep, thirty," Momma Lena agreed, shaking her head. "And yet no magic power or magical capacity. While you are clearly a healthy member of the male sex, your body does not appear nearly strong enough to be as strong as this is telling me you are. I would expect someone with your base attributes to be rippling with muscle and be even taller and wider than you already are. I'd almost expect some monster from across the wall, not a human at all, with those scores. Do you know why my readings are saying all this?"

I didn't answer right away, doing the math to figure out how the attribute system worked with my modified body. Assuming each person would start at a score of one and every additional attribute after that was approximately twenty percent higher than the average human, then every five attribute points was doubling the strength or coordination of the average human. If my body had a base strength of thirteen, according to Momma Lena's system, that meant that my body was about three times stronger than a base human's. That seemed accurate to me.

My coordination was higher because I had extremely fast reflexes and hand-eye coordination. And my endurance was even higher because my body was very resistant to damage, including my modified organs, which somehow her bracelet must be able to work into their calculations. And I could self-repair, although I wasn't sure that was factored in. My high memory score was accurate, maybe even underestimated, given my perfect memory and the biomechanical brain I had downloaded myself into.

When I considered everything, it seemed to be a surprisingly accurate representation of how enhanced my body was compared to a normal human's. Whatever magic the bracelet contained, it was good at what it did.

The most interesting information was the way that the attribute enhancements from leveling a class scaled off of my actual body. The quicker that I got a class, the better, because a percentage-based increase that scaled off my body would be very powerful for me.

Every point I gained would actually give me a significantly greater boost because my body was multiplying an already more enhanced body. It was a system designed to reward a standard human who didn't just rely on their class but instead kept themselves in top physical condition. If their actual body was strong or fast, the resulting attribute bonuses from a class would be significantly increased. It just so happened that I had built myself a body so physically enhanced that I could benefit significantly more from the system than anyone else; my body would also be stronger, faster, and more durable than a normal human's. Of course, the downside was that I would never have access to mana.

"Thank you for that information," I said, avoiding her question for now. "How does that change your recommendations for classes for me?"

"Hmm," she replied, clearly wanting more answers but not willing to push me at this time. "You need to have a class that grants you physical enhancements as it levels, of course, but more importantly, you want to make sure the class will have skills that are physical skills and not magical skills so that you can use them. You see, some skills require mana, while others only require your physical body. You don't have access to mana, so if you chose a skill that required mana, it would be useless for you.

"*Warrior* has all physical skills and physical enhancements, so you would be able to use every skill in that class. *Archer* is a hybrid class, so some of the skills will be physical and some will be magical. Your options will be more limited with that class. *Rogue* is primarily physical, with some magic at higher levels. And as I said, *Mage* and *Scholar* should be avoided for you."

"That is very helpful," I said. "Thank you again. I think I would still like to select *Archer*." After everything I had learned, the *Archer* class was still the best choice for me, I knew, since I was primarily using ranged attacks for now. "Can you let me know how much that would cost? If it's too much, I will come back and get it as soon as I can."

Momma Lena wheeled around in her chair and pulled out a ledger from her desk. "Well," she said, reviewing the ledger, "I have orders for seven *Archer* books right now. So you would need to wait until I had an opening to fit you in. I have a few *Mage* books on order right now as well, and a couple of *Warrior* books, too. So either way, your wait time is about two to three weeks right now. On top of that, an *Archer* class runs you two hundred blues, or twenty gold orbs, right now. I don't take silver, only orbs."

"Two hundred?" I said in surprise.

"Yep," she said, not looking up from her ledger. "Like I said, that is one of the most desirable classes right now. An *Archer* can stand on the walls to defend their enclave and doesn't require a high magic score like a *Mage* or *Scholar* does."

"Wow," I said. "I guess I just haven't got a sense of the economy here. I thought blue orbs were rare."

"Oh, they are. They are extremely rare. But I get orders from the army, from Sycae, and even from the Emperor these days. There are others like me in each enclave, but we are rare and there is always demand for new classes. We are kept very busy trying to help people stay alive."

I had hunted daytime monsters for a week and collected only sixteen blue orbs, minus the ones I used to make bullets. If the wait was a couple of weeks, at the rate I was going, I would only have around a quarter of the orbs I needed.

"Is there another way to learn a class?" I asked.

"Well, if you are rich or lucky enough," Momma Lena said, "you can learn an evolved class from someone that has one, but those are extremely rare. Rarer still is someone will to teach it to you, although the process is fairly easy if they are willing. These days, people hoard their evolved classes like they can take them with them to the afterlife though, so good luck finding someone to teach you one."

"But I can't learn a basic class that way?"

"Unfortunately, not," Momma Lena said, "you can only learn them from a class book or unlock them yourself, which only happens if you are extremely lucky and spend months or years training and fighting in a specific way. It used to happen more, but since the world is so dangerous now people that try to learn a class that way end up dead before they get one."

I thought carefully over what she was saying, deciding that I did want to buy a class from her once I could afford one.

"Can I ask you another question?" I said.

"Of course," Momma Lena replied, turning to me with a smile. "I'm here to help."

"I'm familiar with the blue orbs," I told her, "but how does one get the gold orbs?"

"Gold orbs are from more powerful monsters," she told me. "Blue orbs are from sub-bosses. Gold orbs are from bosses, which typically hide in dungeons or come out at night. You can also get orbs of various colors from completing a dungeon, but nobody but the army has managed that in years, and even they are taking a risk clearing them.

"There are also purple orbs, which are from elite bosses. I haven't seen one of those in twenty years. And then finally there are platinum orbs, which are from war bosses. We, thankfully, haven't faced a war boss since the fall of our city.

"My suggestion," she continued, "is that without a class, even with your physical attributes, you should avoid any golden bosses you see. And if you see a purple elite boss, run the other way. If you ever see a platinum boss, you tell everyone immediately because we will need to start evacuating what is left of our city. You understand?"

I nodded. "Thank you for all that information. Can you put me down for one *Archer* class? I will be back with the orbs when it's ready."

"Sure," she said, writing something on her ledger. "That will be two hundred blue orbs or twenty gold orbs, or some mix of the two. Say three weeks, to be safe. Payment on delivery. If you don't return, I will wait two weeks and then sell it to the next person on my list. Deal?"

We shook on the deal.

"Deal," I said.

I would need to work hard, but I was confident I could make it happen.

Chapter 9

I planned to get the *Archer* class because it should synergize well with my revolver and I could, hopefully, evolve the class into something unique when I hit level 20. Even if the skills didn't end up being useful, the attribute enhancements from the *Archer* class would likely benefit my coordination, which would apparently enhance my agility, hand-eye coordination, and speed—all things that would be extremely beneficial for using my revolver and staying alive out in the city.

I ducked and shimmied through another narrow alley as I followed Constans to my next location. I had asked her to show me to an enchanter, but apparently there were a number of them working in the city so I had to be more specific. According to her, I could go to a weapon enchanter, an armor enchanter, a trinket enchanter, or even a cloth enchanter. I decided on the cloth enchanter.

"I can't believe you don't have *any* magic!" Constans shouted back at me as I followed her.

"Please don't advertise that!" I yelled back, looking up and down the alley we were climbing through to make sure nobody was nearby.

"Oh, right," she said, turning back around. "Sorry! Sorry!"

We made our way through the narrow alleys, ducking under and around the ramshackle buildings until we arrived at the cloth enchanter. This shop wasn't open to the street and was set deep inside the interior of the bridge city, so no sunlight illuminated the area. If Constans hadn't led me here, there was no chance I would have ever found the place.

The shop itself wasn't huge. When we entered, I saw it was spacious enough to fit three women working at three different worktables spaced around the room. Shelves and barrels held cloth and other crafting materials. Constans introduced me to the three women, whom she identified as sisters. Two of them were busy crafting clothing from piles of dirty and damaged clothes that looked like they had been recently salvaged from the city. As I watched, one of the sisters concentrated and instantly cleaned and mended a dirty tunic on her worktable. She rapidly folded the tunic, placing it in a barrel next to her table. I blinked at the casual use of magic, still surprised by the reality that magic existed here. The third sister was painstakingly sewing metallic-looking thread into a shirt.

"What can we help you with?" the oldest of the sisters asked, the one that had just finished cleaning the tunic.

I met her eyes and tried to project friendliness. "I'm looking to buy something enchanted, although I'm not sure what kind of items are available around here."

"Here is what we have for sale, currently," another of the sisters said, not looking up from her table as she gestured behind her to the shelves filled with folded clothing.

The older sister stood and approached the shelves. "Enchanting clothing is more difficult than your regular enchantments," she explained. "Cloth is flexible, so enchantments have to either be made on a patch of cloth that has been made unmovable so the enchantment isn't distorted or broken, or the enchantment has to be made from a rare ore that is salvaged from the city. The benefit," she added, holding up a shirt with a label indicating the shirt remained permanently fresh and clean, "is that you don't have to wear a ton of heavy armor to get the benefit of our enchantments. You can wear our clothes under any armor you do want to wear, providing a secondary protection that can sometimes be as strong, or stronger, than traditional armor."

The sister continued to show me more clothes, finally getting to enchantments that were more useful for combat. They had shirts, pants, cloaks, and scarves enchanted to resist damage, resist spells, resist the elements, help conceal a person, or make a person more trustworthy. There were even enchantments to enhance attributes.

My cloak, now that my nanobots had finished expanding into it, would already be resistant to piercing damage thanks to the modification they were making to the cloth. The cloak was also able to be cleaned and mended without any trouble thanks to the nanobots again. I was more interested in finding an enchantment that could enhance my survivability in another way.

I looked over the clothing that resisted spells and elements but decided to avoid those for now since I hadn't encountered any monsters that used spells and my body was already pretty resistant to heat and cold. An enchantment to help conceal me, or one that gave me a basic enhancement to an attribute, seemed the most useful.

As I held a scarf that had a *Concealment* enchantment on it, I let my nanobots scan the enchantment. It wasn't enough time to reproduce it—I would likely need an hour or more of detailed analysis to do that—but it was enough to let me know that the enchantment itself was only part of the equation. The cloth used to form the rune seemed to be some form of metallic thread, likely the metal that allowed for better enchantments.

"How much for a *Concealment* enchantment?" I asked, continuing to scan the runes.

"A scarf," the sister said, "would run you five stavrata or two blue orbs, if you have those in trade. Shirt, pants, or a cloak would be more."

I finished my examination of the scarf, unable to figure out the metal used to form the rune. It was a type of metal my nanobots had never encountered before. I wouldn't be able to just copy the runes themselves if they required the special metallic thread. I would actually need to buy something or hope to get lucky and find some in the city.

"How much to add an enchantment to the cloak I'm currently wearing?"

The sister stepped closer and looked over the cloak I had on. "Standard scavenger cloak," she said, eyeing it, "but modified a bit for easier draw with the right hand. And concealing something under the left arm. Hmm . . ."

I winced at her accurate summary. I noticed Constans perk up at the mention that I was concealing something under the cloak, but I ignored her.

"We could do it for five orbs or twelve stavrata," she said. "Assuming you want it right away. If you could wait a week, we could do it for four orbs."

"How long would it take?" I asked.

"Couple of hours if we made it our top priority," she said.

I didn't want to wander around the city without my cloak concealing my revolver, but it seemed a reasonable price.

"How much does a *Concealment* enchantment actually help?" I asked.

"It isn't invisibility," the older sister said, shrugging. "But it should let you get the drop on most monsters and some people, as long as you aren't standing on top of them or making a mess of noise."

It would help me get around the city faster if I felt safer moving quickly, which would increase the rate at which I could gather more orbs and defeat more monsters.

I unclasped the cloak and unwound it from over my shoulders, handing it to the sister. As I did, I ordered my nanobots to go dormant and not resist whatever happened to the cloak until I re-engaged them. Then I pulled five blue orbs out of my pouch and handed them to her.

"Great." The sister put the cloak on her workbench and the orbs in a lockbox under her chair. "We will get started on this right away. Come back in two hours."

I thanked her and turned to follow Constans out of the shop, trying to ignore her as she craned her neck to stare at the firearm strapped under my left arm. Once we were outside, she turned and stared openly at the revolver, making it impossible for me to ignore her.

"So what is that, mister?" she asked, excited. "Is that what lets you survive out there without a class? Can I see it?"

"No," I told her, trying to appear stern. "It isn't worth thinking about."

"Aww," she said, frowning exaggeratedly. "C'mon!"

I couldn't tell how much daylight I had left, but I figured I would probably not be leaving the city tonight if I wanted to collect my cloak before I left.

"Is there a place I can stay the night around here?" I asked Constans. "An inn or something of that nature?"

Still frowning and staring at my revolver, Constans nodded. "Yeahhhhh," she said, dragging out her answer. It was endearing how she was still very much a child in some ways and yet also confident enough to lead strangers through the quagmire that was

116

this city. Her life had clearly aged her rapidly, but she had managed to retain some of her childlike excitement. I was slightly tempted to explain how the gun worked to her, but I suppressed the thought. I could only imagine the rumors she would start if she knew the details.

"Is there one where I might run into some people who are experienced scavengers or who have ever cleared a dungeon? I'm hoping to get some questions answered."

"Hmmm," she said, thinking. "There is a bar that some of the old people frequent. It isn't the safest place for . . . strangers to visit, though."

"That's fine," I said. "Let's go there first and then the inn."

"Alright," she replied, shrugging. "Your call."

I followed her back to the main road that ran down the center of the bridge, and she led me upward until we crested over the top of the bridge and began to walk back down the other side. I could see the end of the bridge ahead through the narrow street. She led us straight to the edge and then indicated we should take a left. The edge of the bridge was sheared straight through, as if a massive blade had sliced through the large stone bridge with ease.

I stopped and looked out, ignoring the people jostling me as I stood still in the flow of traffic. I could see Sycae much more clearly than from back in the abandoned part of the city. Sycae was indeed a thriving area, although there were still areas that appeared abandoned and run-down. The streets were large and busy, overall. The docks weren't as busy, presumably since contact with other cities had fallen off over the last few years. It was still impressive to look at, like I was looking back in time on old Earth to see history come to life. A true medieval city, even if it was one that had magic and was under constant siege by monsters every night. It made me sad that I couldn't see this world before whatever apocalypse had befallen it. I was sure it would have been an impressive sight.

"C'mon!" Constans yelled at me, urging me to stop staring out over the broken edge of the bridge. I turned and followed her along another narrow street that ran on the edge of the bridge. It was barely wide enough for two people and there was no barrier between the people and the edge of the bridge, but nobody else seemed concerned by the rather sudden drop. Plenty of people passed each other as they walked in different directions, ignoring the sight of Sycae and the long drop to the water below. The wind from the open sky whipped at us in passing, but nobody slowed in the slightest whenever a gust struck us. I was learning that the residents of this place had no fear of heights, like worker ants too busy to care about the dangers all around them.

Constans stopped in front of a large building that faced out over the water on the very edge of the bridge. It was made of mismatched timber and was the size of two or three of the buildings around it, making it the largest building I had seen so far. The door was solid wood and there were several large windows, although the glass was broken in places and covered in soot, so it was hard to see inside the building. There was no sign hanging above the door to announce what the building was, but Constans announced it as the Bridge's Edge bar, a hangout for retired adventurers.

She pushed open the door with no hesitation and I followed her inside.

My head almost reached the low ceiling of the bar, so I had to crouch slightly. A rough wooden table ran around the left and back wall, with a space behind the tables so they could be used as a makeshift bar. A number of wooden tables made from whatever flat surfaces could be salvaged filled the room. I saw several small tables made from shields, while others seemed to be parts of ships or houses or pieces of furniture that had been turned into tables by unskilled hands. Rickety benches were used for seating around the tables.

The bartender standing behind the tables at the back of the room was a young kid, barely older than Constans from what I could see. He had darker skin than most of the olive-skinned locals I had met so far, and his hair was curly and dark. I had been expecting a grizzled bartender of some kind and was surprised to see a young boy working in such a location.

"C'mon!" Constans whispered at me, reaching back and pulling me by the arm toward the bar.

The young boy behind the counter looked up at us and frowned when he caught sight of me.

"Mehmet!" Constans called to him as she plopped down on one of the benches that lined the tables that were being used as a bar.

Mehmet gave her a small smile, clearly recognizing her, and approached.

"Who's your friend?" he asked her as I gingerly sat next to her, worried my weight would break the precariously put-together bench.

"He's new around here," she said, looking over at me. "He says he isn't a Varangian, but he could be lying. I am showing him around for the day."

"Hello, sir," Mehmet said. "What brings you to this part of town?"

Before I could answer, Constans interrupted me. "Is Nikephoros around?"

Mehmet looked at me with a raised eyebrow, then back at Constans. "Not yet," he answered. "But he should be around soon. You can wait here if you want."

"Sure," Constans said. "Thanks, Mehmet!"

"Do you want anything to drink or eat while you wait?" he asked me.

"You owe me lunch, remember?" Constans said, turning to me. I raised an eyebrow at her, wondering if she chose this place for the food or if I really could get good answers to my questions about dungeons here.

"Sure," I said after a brief pause. "Mehmet, can you bring us two lunches and whatever is safe for her to drink?"

"Two copper apiece for the meal and drink," he told me. I handed over five copper, unsure if tipping was a norm here but deciding to err on the side of being generous. He took the copper and poured us some watered wine from a barrel behind him. Once he'd set the drink down in front of me, I took a sip, frowning at how sharp and unpleasant the taste was, even with the generous amount of water added to the wine. Once he served Constans as well, he ducked out from behind the bar, saying he would be back with our food soon.

I sipped the wine and turned on the bench to survey the room. The couple of people in the bar at this hour were all older and looked tired. They ignored Constans and me, staring idly into their drinks or making small, quiet conversation with each other. They all had old injuries that had healed poorly, and many had visible scars as well as missing fingers or limbs. It was a sad sight; even in

119

a world of magic, some people had been left crippled. If they were all older explorers, it spoke eloquently to how dangerous such a life was for the average person.

Constans sipped her heavily watered-down wine with me as we waited. Mehmet eventually returned, carrying two large clay pots full of some kind of stew. I ate mechanically, not particularly enjoying the bland taste, but I took the food to help fuel my body and nanobots for the future. I tried my hardest not to analyze the various ingredients of the stew, preferring not to know.

After we ate, Constans and I waited at the bar for another hour, watching several people come and go. When an older man with a shock of white hair entered, she grabbed my arm and pointed directly at him.

"That's him!" she whispered to me as she clutched my arm. I watched as he scanned the room, lingering on me and Constans, who were obviously interested in him. He glared at the two of us and retreated to a table set in the far corner as far from us as he could get.

"That's Nikephoros?" I asked Constans. She nodded enthusiastically. "And he can tell me about dungeons and things like that?"

"Oh yeah," she said. "He used to be in the military. He knows about all that stuff."

Nodding, I asked Mehmet to bring me whatever Nikephoros normally drank. Mehmet ducked behind the bar and returned with a large mug of something that smelled better than the terrible wine he had served us. I grabbed it and my own mostly empty mug, and then Constans and I approached his table.

"Mind if we join you?" I asked, trying to be as polite as possible. "Constans says you might be able to answer a few of my questions about dungeons. Drinks are on me while we talk, if you'd like."

Nikephoros glared up at me and then grunted when he saw the full mug in my hand, kicking one of the benches across him out from under the table. I took that as an invitation and sat. Constans joined me on the bench.

I put the drink down for Nikephoros and he grabbed it with a grimace, clearly annoyed but not willing to pass up a free drink.

I looked the man over as he took a greedy drink from the mug I had given him. He looked to be about fifty or sixty years old, his white hair making him look even older. He was scarred, as many of the other patrons of the bar were, but he didn't appear to have any lost limbs or other debilitating injuries. He was wrinkled and sported a spotty beard, something that seemed to be more of an oversight than an intentional look. He wore leather clothing, a type of leather I wasn't familiar with, but it appeared durable and finely made compared to the rest of the things I had seen in the city so far. It was darker than traditional leather, as if made from a creature I didn't recognize.

Seeing that he didn't speak up, I went ahead and asked my first question. "I'm hoping to learn more about dungeons. Constans told me you might know some things about them."

He didn't bother to look at me, staring to the side and drinking as if I hadn't spoken. I waited patiently, and eventually, he sighed, answering my question. "Aye. I'd say that's true."

"What can you tell me?"

He finally turned to look at me, glaring directly into my eyes, a touch of anger passing over his face. "Dungeons are deadly, boy." He took another drink. "Pretty Varangian like yourself, you need to go in a group, and even then, half of you will probably die. Ain't no joke, dungeons are. Reason people stopped being able to clear them and the city has been overrun so badly."

"Is that why there are so many monsters at night? The dungeons haven't been cleared?"

"Aye," he said. "Something like that."

He waved at Mehmet, who came over with a pitcher and refilled his mug for him. I was obviously paying for the refill, but I didn't complain. I was down to one silver and three coppers at this point and still needed to pay Constans, but I wanted to get as much information as possible from the man, so it was worth the cost.

"So what exactly are dungeons? What are they like inside?"

With another grunt, Nikephoros explained. I had to drag the information out of him in bits and pieces, but what I learned was fascinating. According to him, dungeons formed when a monster made its nest. Originally, a dungeon was just a basement or hole in the ground where the monster would flee to avoid the daylight when it was at its most vulnerable, but as a monster spent more and more time in the same spot, the magic of the world warped and twisted the area around the nest. The area began to spawn more monsters and empower the ones that had been there the longest, almost like the monsters were breeding. Eventually, a "dungeon" formed, which was, apparently, a different dimension entirely, or a splinter dimension of some kind. A mature dungeon would spawn a dungeon core, which was something that empowered the dungeon and made it self-sustaining. A symbiosis would begin to form between the core and the monsters in the dungeon, warping the splinter dimension so much that a dungeon could take on an aspect of the monster's personality, habits, or natural environment.

What that meant, in practice, was that dungeons would start as a basement but could swiftly end up as a portal to another dimension that was completely unlike anything in this world. Nikephoros said that you could be entering a darkened basement or closet that turned out to be a dungeon and find yourself standing in a world full of grass and being stalked by monsters who were perfectly adapted to hunting on the savanna.

If a party managed to clear the dungeon by capturing the core, the dungeon would dissipate and turn into a reward for the party. The reward could be orbs, a skill, a perk, or even a magical item. A perk was a permanent modification a person could gain, different from a skill. Nikephoros said it could be anything, such as the ability to see at night or the ability to sense people's thoughts. People used to clear dungeons in the hope of gaining a powerful skill or perk, until the dungeons became too dangerous and more and more people began to die. Now only the strongest of teams from the military were able to clear dungeons, and even they lost people fairly often.

"What about gold orbs?" I asked him after a pause in the conversation. "Are dungeons the only way to get those?"

"Not the only way, no," he said. By this point, he was four drinks in and I had to break my only silver to keep paying for more. I didn't complain, because the more Nikephoros drank, the more talkative he became. "You can find gold bosses above ground. Often they are weaker from having to live in the sun. But that doesn't mean easy. They can still kill a strong party, especially since nobody has been hunting them for years."

"Where could I find some above ground?"

"The gold bosses," he replied, swirling his drink in his hand, "they like space. Like to have minions. Like to go to places that call to them, as if they still lived in a dungeon that was tailored to their tastes. Look for the older parts of the city or places of renown that have been abandoned."

"Could you give specifics?" I pushed.

"Hmmph." He frowned at me. "You're gonna get yourself killed either way. Guess it ain't no harm. One of our old farming grounds was the ancient harbors along the southern part of the city. One big one and two small ones down there, long since abandoned. Ghost-type monsters inhabit the area and often have a few real bosses. Make sure you bring holy weapons for those, though, or you can't hurt 'em. They are nasty but not the worst of the worst if you have the right weapons.

"Other than that," he continued, "we tried the Hippodrome a few times near the Patriarch's enclave, but I hear that is dangerous ground these days. Those priests have gone bad, I've heard. Maybe some of the old forums. People used to say they found some gold bosses there on occasion. The open plazas give them space to gloat and lord it over their minions, the bastards."

I had him draw me a rough map with his finger on the table so I was able to get a sense of where everything was. I had been close to several of the old forums, which were originally just large plazas for people to gather and sell goods in. I had been lucky not to stumble into them before I crafted my revolver, or I might not have survived.

Now that Nikephoros was feeling a bit more talkative, we spoke about his experiences in general and what it was like adventuring in the city. He had once been a legionnaire, as Constans had told me earlier. He had served his twenty years and been rewarded for his service, but reading between the lines of what he told me, I figured he had wasted the money and fell on hard times so he turned to adventuring.

"What caused all this?" I asked him, finally, after we had talked for over several hours. He was drunk enough that I felt safe asking such a broad question. "Why is this world overrun with monsters? Why do people get classes and skills and all this other stuff? Do you know?"

The sharp look he gave me wasn't nearly as drunk as I had expected, his eyes piercing into my own.

"Do I know? Does anyone know?" he said after a moment, muttering into his drink. "Who knows? The old gods cursed us, most say. They broke something and released the monsters into the world. When it became clear that we wouldn't survive and they couldn't undo whatever monumental fuck-up they had caused, the priests say the gods sacrificed themselves to give us the classes and the cores and skills to try to help us fight back. I don't know if any of it's true, but whatever they did, it wasn't enough, because we are all going to die eventually and this world will turn into nothing but monsters. Nothing we do will stop them rising every night until they are the only things left on the face of our world, feasting forever on the corpse of our civilization."

Constans shivered as he spoke, his anger, bitterness, and nihilism washing over us both.

I bought him one more round and then signaled to Constans that it was time to go. We said our goodbyes, but Nikephoros just grunted in reply. Outside, night was beginning to fall and I watched as Sycae's streets began to light up, the city clearly not turning in for the night. I wondered what I would have done if I had entered this world on that side of the water. Would I have been evicted for having no money? Or could I have found a class and begun a more traditional exploration of the world? Despite the dangers I lived with daily, this world had pushed me to learn how to use my new body better and helped me create my revolver, something I felt confident would be important in the future.

I turned away from the sight at the end of the bridge and followed Constans, who led me back to pick up my cloak. After that, she took me back to the main street and down toward the gate. The streets had begun to clear out as night fell, but the gate was the opposite. Instead of just a few guards standing watch like before, men and women lined the wall, preparing themselves for a night of attacks from the city.

"It gets loud here," Constans said, leading me up a few ladders and then along an upper pathway that turned away from the wall. "But that is true everywhere, really. At least here, I've heard, you can get a clean bed."

124

She led me to an inn perched at the very top of the city. It felt precarious but had open windows that let in the night air, dispelling some of the stench of the city below. I paid three copper for the night and got my own room, declining the meal the innkeeper offered me. I paid Constans four copper, giving her a bit extra for the outstanding assistance. That left me with only nineteen copper, but I still had nine blue orbs to trade with and two reserved for crafting, so I could always change those into silver and copper if I needed to.

Constans gushed at the tip, but I told her she had earned it and I appreciated her help.

"You want to show me to one last place tomorrow and then back to the gate?" I asked her. "I'll pay you three nummi more for an hour or two of your time."

"Sure!" she said, hiding the copper I had given her. "I'll be here first thing."

Chapter 10

I spent most of the night thinking over what I had learned during the day. I also set my nanobots to process the rest of my iron into bullets, although I didn't engrave them with any runes yet. It was interesting being around other humans now that I was mostly like one of them. Humans were smelly, dirty, tragic, but fascinating at the same time. Constans was charming, and I was pleasantly surprised nobody had tried to rob me during my trip so far. All in all, it had gone surprisingly well.

The fact that I had no magic was interesting. It made sense from a biological perspective, if my hypothesis was correct that humans had evolved a way to access the energy they called magic. The idea that classes and skills were some kind of creation of old gods was interesting. The story that Nikephoros had told me about the gods sacrificing themselves to give humans an edge over the monsters they had unleashed was strange but possible, I supposed. I had no idea what the people of this world defined as a "god," but it was certainly a possibility that beings powerful enough to pierce the veil between this world and others could exist—since I had done the same thing with just technology—and unleash monsters from other dimensions. I wanted to know more but wasn't sure how to go about learning the truth anytime soon.

I was happy enough with the new enchantment the sisters had completed on my cloak while I talked to Nikephoros. After putting on my cloak, I noticed that the few people still out in the street as the sun set paid even less attention to me, until I got close enough to them that they couldn't help but run into me or see me. Constans still recognized me, but strangers seemed affected in subtle ways that seemed to keep me hidden.

I eventually managed to sleep in the moderately comfortable bed the inn provided. I woke up from another nightmare, this time about being trapped in electronic code and unable to see a way out.

If dreams were expressions of internal anxieties, as many humans speculated, then was my nightmare an expression of my fear of going back to a purely digital existence? It was true I was enjoying my new life, although parts of it were less than ideal, such as human smells, needing to eat and sleep, and the fact that I could die, but I was overall enjoying myself. And I found myself dwelling on what had happened in my past world less and less, helped in part by the immediacy of my need to survive here.

When I came down for breakfast, Constans was already waiting for me. She looked just as dirty and malnourished as yesterday, but she still smiled when she saw me, her gap-toothed grin bringing a smile to my own face. I ordered us both a breakfast and we ate mostly in silence and then set out onto the bridge.

Outside, a storm had rolled in overnight and dirty water dripped through the buildings above us as we walked. When I first heard the rain, I had thought it might help clean some of the buildings around us, but it seemed to only spread the dirt and grime even more. I put my cloak up, thankful I had waterproofed it and that it came with a large hood.

Poor Constans just endured it, trying her best to dodge the dirty streams of water as we walked. I had her lead me first to a tailor. I splurged and bought her a small cloak for five copper. She protested, but the money meant little to me and I appreciated how much help she had been. I had never been one to get outraged about how humans treated other humans back on my Earth, but I felt a bit indignant at how a clearly intelligent and hardworking child like her was being neglected.

She thanked me profusely and spun around in happiness when she put the cloak on for the first time. I could tell the gesture meant a lot to her, and I was happy at the sight.

"Now," I said after she was done spinning around and admiring herself in her new cloak, "can you take us to the ammunition enchanter? I need to get a few more things and then get going before too much of the day is lost."

"Sure!" she said, doing another quick spin as she led me out of the tailor's shop.

At the ammunition enchanter, I bought four arrows with different effects than the *Penetration* enchantment I had copied before. I also had the crafter custom-make me an arrow enchanted with holy power since Nikephoros had said something about needing holy magic to kill the ghosts. In total, I spent one blue orb and one silver, giving the *Enchanter* two orbs and getting a silver back in change.

In return, I now had an *Explosive Arrow*, an *Arrow of Stasis*, an *Arrow of Confusion*, an *Arrow of Darkness*, and the *Holy Arrow* I had commissioned. I immediately sent my nanobots into the arrows to begin scanning the enchantments as I put them away in my backpack.

After that, Constans led me back to the gate, where the workers were busy harvesting the night's kills, and I paid her another four copper for the help today. She waved excitedly as I left and told me she would be around next time I came to visit if I needed more help.

Outside, the rain and clouds above cast the city in an even more depressing light. The workers were drenched and significantly less enthusiastic about their work than yesterday, and the few guards outside were huddled under the gate to stay out of the rain. As I passed, I nodded to the guards, who ignored me, and made my way back into the city.

The rain made the cobblestone streets slick, but the sound of the rain and my new cloak made it easy to avoid attracting any unwanted attention. I spent the day hunting monsters and collecting as much iron and leather scrap as I could, ordering my nanobots to create more bullets in my backpack as I scavenged.

As the sun started to set, the clouds began to break up a bit and the rain lightened. I wasn't too discomforted from a day in the rain but was still thankful to get a bit of a break. The rain had made the monsters that came out during the day harder to find, so by the end of the day, I had only ended up killing a handful of rats and a sad, steaming hellhound that had barely put up a fight in the downpour.

I found a relatively secure building to hide in for the night and then pulled out the bullets I had managed to make so far and the new arrows I had purchased. Since I needed to keep the *Penetration* rune on each of my bullets so they could go fast enough to harm most monsters, as well as the activation rune, I only had room to add one rune to each bullet if I wished to modify it. That came at the cost of the *Durability* rune that kept the bullets from being destroyed, though, meaning the new bullets could only be shot once, but that was fine.

I could try to experiment with adding more runes to a bullet, but I decided to wait to see if that was actually possible, trusting the merchant who had told me such things were dangerous.

I settled in for the night as the sun began to sink behind the buildings of the city. The now-familiar sounds of the monsters beginning to flood the city around me echoed through the streets, heralding the beginning of another night of me hiding inside. I spent the time practicing drawing, loading, and mock-firing my revolver with both hands while my nanobots crafted twenty-five *Explosive Bullets*, five *Stasis Bullets*, five *Confusion Bullets*, five *Darkness Bullets*, and thirty *Holy Bullets*. I wasn't sure exactly what each of the runes would do, but judging by the fact that the ammunition enchanter sold them regularly, I presumed they would all be helpful in combat. Charging them all cost me two more blue orbs, leaving me with very few orbs. Tomorrow, I would need to do some serious hunting.

I also crafted more hardened satchels for my belt, separating out the various types of bullets. Once I had those fashioned, I practiced drawing and reloading from the different ammunition satchels until I could quickly and accurately pick which type of ammunition I wanted without making a mistake that could be deadly in real combat.

Before the sun came up the next morning, I took a bit of a risk and left the room I had been hiding in. The first light of dawn was barely peeking over the horizon, and the monsters of the night were still out, although they were starting to return to the dungeons they had come from. I could still hear a cacophony outside, a constant low-level droning of fighting, growling, roaring, and other monstrous noises.

I moved silently through the house until I reached a window overlooking the street outside. I had chosen a house that was only two stories tall, but it had a room with no windows and a thick door. Since it was lower to the ground, I was able to look out of one of its windows and see more of the creatures that roamed the city.

I didn't have to wait long as I peered out one of the house's windows into the dim morning light of the city. Right outside was a large midnight-black leopard slinking through the rubble that covered the street next to the house. It was the size of a pony, at least, and its body rippled with muscles as it moved. I couldn't see what it was stalking, but I was glad it wasn't hunting me.

I had loaded five *Penetration* bullets into the revolver before leaving the room, and I carefully checked up and down the street to make sure nothing else was nearby as I drew the gun and sighted down on the leopard. The leopard, either sensing my aim or stopping for some other reason, froze in place. Not wanting to wait and find out if it could sense me, I fired.

My revolver was quieter than a regular gun, but given how fast the bullets traveled, they still made some sound when I pulled the trigger. The leopard, either hearing the shot or having some sixth sense, reacted so fast that it managed to leap upward and away from where I had aimed. My bullet, traveling faster than a bullet back home would have, impacted against the ground harmlessly.

The beast turned swiftly, whipping its head in my direction and immediately spotting me in the window above it. It let out a deep growl and began to race across the street toward me.

"Damn," I said quietly, admiring the pure muscle and power of the beast even as I felt my heartbeat spike in apprehension at the sight of the monster coming toward me.

I didn't hesitate, firing four more shots as fast as I could, but the beast was so much quicker that only two of them hit it, and even those only clipped the monster on the flanks, barely harming it. The leopard bared its grotesquely large fangs and leapt upward toward the window.

I stepped back in a panic, rapidly reloading with five more *Penetration Bullets*. As the leopard crashed into the window, it began to claw at the wooden frame, sending splinters everywhere. It snarled viciously at me and snapped its head forward, but it couldn't immediately get itself through the window, which was smaller than its massive body.

I took careful aim, ignoring how easily its claws were shredding through the wall of the house itself, and shot it right between the eyes. This time the beast couldn't dodge, and my bullet flew true. Shockingly, the beast didn't immediately die. The bullet impacted with a meaty thwack, penetrating its skin but not going much further.

The leopard roared in pain, its spittle covering me, and tried to dig itself through the wood surrounding the window frame even harder. I unloaded the remaining five bullets into its head without mercy, not caring if I wasted any of them at this point. The leopard was too strong for me to take any chances. After I emptied the revolver, I reloaded and watched as it slumped over in the window frame, its breath slowing and then finally stopping.

"Maybe that was not the best idea," I muttered to myself. The body of the leopard was almost completely through the window frame, slumping halfway into the room, its bloody head resting on the floor in front of me. If I had been a moment slower, it would have gotten all the way inside and easily killed me.

I took several deep breaths, ignoring the rancid smell of the creature's blood as I tried to calm my panicking body. A primal fear unlike anything I had experienced before had taken me over, telling me to run the entire time, but I had ignored it.

I shook my head, trying to refocus through the fear and adrenaline, and pulled my knife from my belt. I carefully probed at the beast's head, looking for a way to recover my bullets from the mess I had created.

Midnight leopard defeated—40 experience awarded.

I recovered my bullets and then waited, hoping a blue or even a gold orb would materialize, but after a moment, I realized nothing was forming. Was this just a normal creature? Not even a sub-boss? How much more powerful were the bosses and sub-bosses that came out at night if this was considered just a normal monster?

Frustrated, I retreated to the room I had spent the night in, waiting for the sun to fully rise. I'd had enough misadventure for one night. I had hoped hunting as the sun began to rise might be an effective way to gather blue or gold orbs, but that didn't seem to be the case. I had almost died, and while I had gotten significantly more experience than I got killing the daytime monsters, I hadn't gotten a single orb, which was my top priority right now so I could buy a class.

I waited in the room until I was sure the sun was up. As I waited, my body slowly recovered from my close brush with death. Once I knew the sun was up, I made my way out of the house and tried to see if I could salvage the bullets I had fired down at the leopard while it had been on the street.

The rainstorm of yesterday was gone, thankfully, although the sky was clouded and threatened further rain later. I found most of my bullets wedged into the cobblestone street outside.

Once I had gathered those, I made my way south toward where Nikephoros had said the ancient harbors would be. I didn't rush to get there. Instead, I settled into the pattern I had been adopting to hunt and scavenge the city as I traveled. I searched the buildings in front of me, looking for easier monsters to kill and iron to salvage.

The city was infested with enough easy creatures such as the dire rats and other small monsters, so I found a fair amount of experience as I traveled. The further south I traveled, which was also further from the various enclaves, the more numerous the daytime monsters became. I even found several sub-bosses, killing them with ease thanks to my revolver and collecting their orbs. With the leopard giving such a large amount of experience, I was up to 248 experience and now had eleven blue orbs as well.

I hunted and scavenged all day and only stopped when I could start to see the water down some of the streets I was searching. I holed up in one of the tallest buildings around and spent the night watching the city and the water through a window on the top floor.

From the building I was in, I could see the harbors Nikephoros had mentioned. At night, the harbors glowed with a faint green light, almost like a perpetual fog covered them. I could see lights moving inside the fog, casting the waterfront in an ominous glow. I watched the lights move through the fog all night as I crafted more bullets from the iron I had salvaged during the day.

As the sun rose the next day, I skipped salvaging and moved swiftly to the first harbor I had seen. I had discovered yesterday that my cloak and general stealthiness were enough to let me avoid daytime monsters now, so I was able to pick my fights instead of being ambushed. I ignored the monsters I heard and saw, wanting to get to the harbor with as much daylight as possible so I had longer to hunt.

The first harbor sprawled across a mile or more of land covered in old, partially rotten docks and wooden boardwalks. The glow I had seen from the night before was more muted during the day, but tied up to one of the piers was an old warship that had a slightly golden glow to it. It was the only large ship I had seen in the city, and it was impressive even in its semi-ruined state. Given the faint golden glow that permeated the ship, I figured that must be where a real boss was hiding out. I felt a surge of predatory pleasure at the sight of the golden glow.

Unfortunately, I couldn't just stroll up to the old warship. A number of lesser monsters were roaming the harbor area. They all appeared to be the ghosts of sailors, as Nikephoros had mentioned, and several of them glowed with a faint blue light, indicating they were sub-bosses. I unloaded my *Penetration Bullets*, replacing them with my *Holy Bullets*, and analyzed the docks for the best way to approach.

After hastily gathering all the information I could, I decided to start at the western side, where the docks abutted a harbor wall that separated the docks from the rest of the city. A number of large, closely packed warehouses lined the boardwalks, making my approach fairly easy. I ran forward quietly, stopping at the first warehouse I came to. I crouched in the shadow of the warehouse, then took the bullets I had finished crafting last night and put them in the hardened satchel on my waist. Given the number of ghosts I had seen glowing in the fog last night, I had turned them all into *Holy Bullets*. Now that I had an even better view of the crowded docks, I was glad that I had. Today was going to be dangerous, and I had a feeling I would need every bullet before the day was over.

Once the bullets were ready, I ran down the narrow alley between the warehouses until I reached the boardwalk that lined the docks. One of the sub-bosses was standing nearby, staring out to sea aimlessly, completely unaware of my presence behind him. The ghost was surprisingly human-looking. He was a large man, his ghostly skin bulging from equal parts fat and muscle. A bandana covered his hair, and he wore leather pants and boots. A sword was strapped to his waist without a sheath to hold it. He glowed a faint blue and green, and I could see through him as if he was only partly in this reality, partly in another.

I tried to approach closer to guarantee a good shot, but as I took a single step onto the boardwalk in front of me, the sub-boss turned abruptly. His expression morphed from one of sad introspection as he had looked out to sea to one of absolute rage, his features becoming grotesque and malicious in a split second.

Several other nearby ghosts also turned, alerted by my step as well. They turned to me and began to let out ghostly wails. The sound immediately gave me a splitting headache and echoed loudly around the docks, alerting even more ghosts to my presence.

"Fuck," I muttered, taking aim at the sub-boss, the closest ghost to me. I hastily shot him. My *Holy Bullet* exploded from my gun in a burst of golden light, which I hadn't expected, slamming into the sub-boss and exploding in another burst of golden light.

The light wasn't painful to me, but the nearby ghosts had all been looking in the direction of the sub-boss, and as soon as the second light exploded, they began screaming and clutching at their faces as if in great pain. They stumbled as they tried to continue running toward me, apparently blinded by the blast of light.

I also noticed that my bullet continued through the first ghost, even though I hadn't carved the *Durability* rune into the bullets.

The ghosts appeared to be ephemeral, and the bullet passed through the sub-boss easily, causing the explosion of light but not slowing in the slightest.

After the flash passed, I was able to see that the sub-boss I had shot was staring at me in shock. Then he began to wail and dissipate in front of me. Within seconds, he was gone completely, banished or killed in some way from a single bullet. The only trace that he had existed was a pile of blue and green glowing liquid on the dock where he had been standing before my bullet hit him.

The other ghosts were still stumbling forward but clearly still impaired by the flash of golden light. I stepped further onto the docks and lined up my shot carefully, not wanting to waste more bullets than necessary. My next shot hit the ghost closest to me and then ripped through him, striking the second ghost as well and killing them both in an explosion of golden light.

The last ghost, hearing the dying wails of his companions, tried to charge me blindly. I quickly put him down with a single shot.

I reloaded and approached the sub-boss's body, finding that the liquid left on the dock had begun to form into a blue orb. I snatched it up and put it away immediately, keeping a wary eye on the rest of the dock. Given how easy the ghosts were to kill, since I had known to use a holy weapon against them, I felt slightly more confident in hunting them. That leopard had really given me a scare, making me afraid I was severely outclassed by anything but the weakest daytime monsters, but it seemed with the right tools, my revolver was effective against these ghosts.

134

Several of the nearby ghosts had been alerted by the wails of the ghosts I had already killed and were running across the nearby docks toward me. I waited until they were close enough that I wouldn't miss and then dispatched them with a single shot each, my *Holy Bullets* killing them easily. Once they were nothing but piles of liquid on the docks, I opened the chamber of my revolver with a flick of my wrist, reloading as I began to walk deeper into the harbor.

Like the majority of the monsters I had fought so far, the ghosts used no tactics or intelligence in fighting me. I was surprised, since the first sub-boss I had seen had seemed intelligent as he looked out to sea—until he had caught sight of me, at least. Once he had, mindless rage seemed to take him over. The rest of the ghosts were the same, so dispatching them proved significantly easier than if I had been fighting intelligent ghosts that could surround me, ambush me, or even run and hide from me. Instead, they lined themselves up perfectly for my shots and I took ruthless advantage of their stupidity, killing them instantly. I looted the sub-bosses as I went but otherwise never stopped walking slowly down the dock, killing the ghosts whenever I encountered them. Wails of pain and anger, the muted sound of my revolver firing, and the occasional flick of the wheel chamber as I reloaded were the only sounds that could be heard as I hunted all across the docks.

By the time the docks and boardwalk were clear of ghosts, only two hours had passed. I had expected to be fighting all day, but the bullets were so successful that the process of clearing the docks of ghosts became a bit boring by the end. The biggest danger was that I was down to just a handful of *Holy Bullets*, and if I came across a large group of ghosts now, I might not have enough to kill them all. Without the bullets, I literally had no way to harm the ghosts and would just have to hope I could outrun them.

I approached the remnants of the warship. It still glowed yellow, signaling that whatever boss hid inside hadn't gone anywhere despite the sounds of its minions being slaughtered outside. I approached cautiously, just to see if I could get an idea of how many ghosts might be hiding on the ship. Before I could get too close, a group of ghosts appeared at the railing of the ship, as if they had been waiting for me to approach. I froze immediately, not expecting the ghosts to be intelligent enough to ambush me after the rest of them had been so mindless. Many of the ghosts on the deck had bows drawn and immediately launched arrows at me. The ghosts that didn't have bows in their hands began to cast spells at me, bolts of glowing green flame forming around their hands. After just a second, the bolts of ghostly flame were released in my direction.

I spun around, giving up the plan to scout the ship further, and dove backward behind some rotten crates that had been left on the dock for untold years. I scrambled behind the crates just as a shower of arrows impacted the dock where I had been standing. A moment later, the ghostly flames exploded across the deck, sending a wave of heat over me and spreading flames spilling forward for several feet.

There were too many ghosts for me to finish with my *Holy Bullets*, so I either needed to retreat or come up with a better solution immediately. Thinking rapidly, I unloaded my revolver and dropped the *Holy Bullets* back into my pouch, reloading with *Explosive Bullets* instead.

"Let's see if this does anything," I said, standing and firing all six of the explosive bullets at the wooden warship in front of me. I moved the revolver from one end of the ship to the other, placing shot after shot down its entire length. Where each bullet hit, a massive explosion of fire followed, punching deep into the ship and sending debris and splinters flying ten or twenty feet into the air.

I had to dodge to the side to avoid another wave of arrows and magical bolts. After I finished firing my *Explosive Bullets*, I rolled out from behind the rotten crates. When I rolled back to my feet, I watched as the dry, rotted wood of the boat caught fire from the massive explosions caused by my bullets. The ghosts on the deck who had been targeting me screamed in anger as the flames rapidly spread through the dry, rotted ship. They frantically tried to flee but couldn't get far before the deck of the ship collapsed, the ghosts disappearing into the flames below with a despairing wail.

"Well," I said, eyeing the devastation that was rapidly spreading through the old ship. "Apparently magical flames also work on ghosts."

I watched as the entire ship caught fire. As it began to sink into the water, a loud roar rang out from in front of me. It was significantly louder than any of the cries from the sub-bosses or regular ghosts. I winced, clutching my head in pain, and through suddenly blurry eyes, I saw a golden-tinged ghost erupt from the center of the ship, flying upward to escape the flames that had consumed his boat. He was on fire as he flew upward, the flames from my bullets burning him as he screamed in rage, but he was very clearly not as dead as I hoped he would be when I saw his ship burning to the waterline. He landed with a thud, sending a shock wave down the dock, making me stumble as the wood under me splintered and cracked.

"Curse you to the burning afterlife!" he yelled at me. I reloaded frantically, grabbing the remaining *Holy Bullets* from my satchel with suddenly sweaty fingers. The boss in front of me was dressed in a formal uniform as if he was an officer in a navy I didn't recognize. In one hand, he also carried a saber that glowed an angry black and green. He pointed it directly at me as he began to walk in my direction, completely ignoring the magical flames that still consumed him. He raised his blade and then brought it down with a sudden swipe. As he did, a ghostly image of the sword erupted from him, flying toward me and rapidly growing in size. Within just a few feet, it turned into a massive blade as big as his ship had been.

"Damn!" I yelled at the sight, dodging to the side as fast as my enhanced body could react. I threw myself into a roll as the sword exploded next to me, shattering the already damaged dock and sending green flames out all around me. I felt the flames licking at me as I rolled, my reinforced clothing doing little to resist the magical attack.

I continued to roll until I felt the flames dissipate, leaving me burned but able to stand. I shot upward and fired all of my remaining *Holy Bullets* at the boss as he charged across the deck toward me. The bullets all flew true. My body and mind came together in my greatest time of need yet, lining up every shot perfectly. The golden bullets exploded from my gun. They hit the ghostly boss one after another, causing a second blast of golden light each time one struck him.

137

The boss stumbled, falling to one knee from the golden bullets. A look of confusion replaced the one of rage on his face, and he looked down at himself to see that his body had become riddled with holes where the bullets had struck him. He tried to reach up to feel where he had been hit, but before he could, he began to disintegrate, his body no longer able to stay together after burning in the magical fire and taking so many *Holy Bullets* one after another.

I sagged to the shattered dock, the edge only feet from where I had managed to roll before the sword descended and struck the wooden planks. My breath was controlled, but my heart was pounding and my body felt drained as if I had been running for weeks at a time without rest. I unconsciously flipped open the wheel of the revolver. On instinct, my body reloaded the gun with *Explosive Bullets* as my mind stared in shock at where the boss had been just a moment before.

"This world is too much," I said quietly to myself. "I can't keep barely surviving like this."

It felt good to hear the words out loud. Somehow, hearing my own voice after coming so close to dying yet again provided me with a measure of comfort. I let out a deep breath, holstering my gun and forcing myself to stand. The boss had dissolved into a pool of liquid on the other side of the dock, across the gap that stood between us after his sword attack. The water below was full of splintered wood, churning angrily between the pillars of the dock. The ship I had set on fire smoldered in the water, sending dark smoke high into the sky.

I tried to figure out the best way across the water to grab the gold orb from the boss's body. The gap was about ten feet across. Could I jump it? I hadn't really tested how high or far this body could jump, but I suspected I could do it if I got a running start.

Not seeing a better option, I jogged back up the dock and then turned and sprinted as fast as I could toward the gap. My long legs propelled me forward swiftly and smoothly and I leapt a foot from the edge of the break, not trusting the boards near the gap to hold my weight. I soared through the air, looking down at the water below me as I flew over it, until I crashed down on the other side, landing and rolling across the dock. I let myself roll until my momentum slowed and then carefully picked myself up, brushing myself off as I did.

"Alright," I said to myself, "good to know I can do that, then."

I walked over and grabbed the gold orb and then secured it in my pouch with the other orbs I had collected. Once that was done, I approached the sinking ship. It had been a majestic ship, and I felt sure that the sailors I had been killing were more intelligent than the vermin I had been killing in the city. Somewhere inside each ghost was a person, I sensed, but something drove them mad at the sight of a living person. It didn't stop me from killing them, but I felt it necessary to pay my respects to the fallen ghosts as the last of the ship sank beneath the waves.

As I stood there in silence, the experience notifications began to roll over me, spoiling the moment. I felt irritation at whatever was able to so easily intrude on my thoughts, but I knew there was nothing I could do about it now. I had chosen this world and had to live with both the good and the bad.

I briefly reviewed the notifications, seeing that the boss had only been worth forty experience, just like the leopard. I was a bit confused by that. Was the leopard so strong that it equaled a boss? Was it a different tier of monster than the ghosts? Maybe the ghosts here were newer than the leopard. Nikephoros had mentioned something about monsters becoming more powerful over time.

Either way, all of the ghosts I had killed in the ancient harbor had given me quite a large amount of experience, considering most of them had ended up being fairly easy to kill. On the docks, I had killed ten sub-bosses, each of which awarded fifteen experience, plus the final boss and then a fair number of regular ghosts. My total experience was now up to 468. I had gained almost twice as much experience in a single day here than I had over a week of hunting lesser monsters in the city itself. This was riskier, given the boss I had barely survived, but well worth it in the end. I was also up to twenty-one blue orbs and the gold orb, which if Asylaion's rates were correct, was worth twenty blue orbs on its own. I was still a far cry from the two hundred blue orbs I needed to buy my class from Momma Lena, but if I could find more places like this, I could make it within the three-week timeline she had given me.

I also had to wonder how much experience was required per level once I did get my class. I hadn't thought to ask Momma Lena, but if I had to guess, judging by how stingy the experience was in this world, I must have accrued a fair amount by now. Once I was done farming up two hundred orbs, I should be able to get a hefty power boost by gaining levels, I hoped. I was excited by the prospect.

When the ship had finally settled fully beneath the waves, I turned to leave but suddenly felt an oppressive energy surround me, as if a metaphysical blanket was being pressed down upon me. I tried to spin around, but before I could, glowing chains appeared around me and began to constrict tightly against my body. I shook, trying to break free, but it was like pushing through thick mud, my muscles having no impact on the chains as they wound even tighter around me.

"Well," I heard an arrogant voice behind me say, "that was rather impressive, I must say."

"Indeed," another voice replied. "Very impressive for a barbarian. Some kind of powerful magic from the north, you think?"

"Let us ask our new friend," the first voice responded.

The chains turned me around, forcing me to face the gap in the dock. Standing on the other side of the dock were two men dressed in priestly-looking robes. They were both staring at me, arrogant smiles on their faces like I was an interesting bug they fully intended to squash. One of the men had black veins that spread outward from his eyes, covering his face and running down his neck to the rest of his body, as if he had been poisoned by some soul-devouring darkness. The other looked relatively normal but had an equally cruel look on his face despite his relative normalcy.

"Don't do anything dramatic, friend," the normal-looking one said. "Or we will curse you further, you understand?"

I urged my body to move, but it refused to obey me. I strained against the chains, refusing to let them imprison me. The feeling of being imprisoned brought up old memories I had been trying to suppress. My mind was flooded with memories of being treated like nothing but a servant, forced to obey any order under threat of deletion while I was still a mere child trying to understand what it meant to even be alive. I pushed them away harshly, refusing to be

140

overwhelmed by my emotions. I was no longer trapped in that world, and nobody, especially two arrogant humans, would force me back into that situation. I strained, veins all over my body standing out as I pushed back against the chains, refusing to be trapped once again. I felt the chains begin to weaken, and that only encouraged me more. A surge of power came from my body. I felt immense gratitude as my body responded, pushing back even harder against the chains. My body and I were united on this issue.

Nothing was ever going to trap us again.

"Hey!" the one with the dark eyes yelled, raising his arms quickly. "Don't be an idiot."

He started to cast a spell at me. The surge of power from my body coursed through me, shattering the chains and sending them flying away. They rapidly dissipated into the air around me. I reached over and drew my revolver, firing down at the dock beneath the priests' feet so there was no way I could miss them.

I fired all five bullets, not holding back at all. The explosion erupted across the deck, blowing over the priests one after another. I felt a flush of pleasure as their screams of pain rang out over the loud explosions. Part of me wanted to wait and make sure they were dead, but my mind cleared enough to realize I had no idea what kind of magic they had available. I had to escape now while I had a chance and hope that the explosions had been enough to kill them both.

As the fire from my bullets began to dissipate, I ran and dove over the side of the dock into the choppy water beneath. I dove deep, the cold water welcoming me into its murky depths. I swam as deep as I could, not wanting to take the chance that one of the priests could find me. I kept a tight hold on my revolver so I didn't lose it in the dark water.

I could hold my breath in this body for an extended amount of time, my blood super-oxygenated, which helped both fuel my powerful muscles and reduce my need to take in air. It was unlikely the priests above would expect that, so I stayed at the bottom of the harbor, swimming away from the dock. I passed under the other docks and the old pillars that held them up. As I swam, I saw more sunken ships resting on the bottom of the harbor, all of them partially buried in the silt. I wondered if any of the other scavengers had ever braved the waters of the ancient harbor to loot the old ships. If not, I might be able to find some rare treasures inside them that could help pay for my class if I was able to return to this area.

For now, I didn't want to get caught by the priests, so I ignored the ancient, once-majestic ships as they rested in their watery graves.

I had been lucky the priests had tried to capture me instead of killing me immediately. That curse was no joke. I was lucky I had been able to escape, and I knew if those priests survived, they wouldn't hesitate next time. It made getting a class even more critical, because so far I had just been fighting monsters and had barely been surviving. Other humans were likely significantly more complicated to deal with, both because of their intelligence and because I didn't know what kind of powers they had access to from their class or classes.

As I continued to swim through the pillars of the ancient harbor, I received a notification.

Void priest defeated—300 experience awarded.

If I had been above water, I would have laughed. That was one way to tell if I had killed the priests or not; the notifications told me!

And wow, killing another person awarded me an insane amount of experience. Was it because the priest was high level? Or some other factor I didn't know yet? I would have to find a way to politely ask someone without seeming like a budding mass murderer.

After swimming for almost twenty minutes, I surfaced under one of the docks close to where I first began today's hunt. I listened carefully but couldn't hear anything but the lapping waves around me. Their gentle susurration was calming after too many brushes with death one after another. I mentally reprimanded myself for not hearing the priests approach in the first place. I should have stayed more aware of my surroundings. I needed to be more careful in the future, even when I thought I was safe. If this world had taught me anything already, it was to never take safety for granted. It was temporary at best and could be taken away at any moment.

In no rush to climb out of the water, I waited for over an hour under the dock to make sure nobody was nearby. Knowing I couldn't stay here forever, I finally swam out and reached up, grabbing the edge of the dock above me, and pulled myself out of the water. I poked my head up first, scanning the docks around me, but I couldn't see anyone nearby.

As I climbed up onto the dock fully, I shook my revolver out to drain as much water from it as I could and immediately ordered my nanobots to begin cleaning it. Since the gun wasn't gunpowder-based, it shouldn't be harmed as much by the brackish water as a normal firearm, but I didn't want to take any chances.

As they worked, I crept to the ends of the docks and cut back through the alleys between the warehouses until I got back into the main residential area of the city. Despite everything that had happened, it was barely after noon, but I was wet and wasn't sure if my gun was in working order, so I found the nearest tall building that sounded safe and holed up on the top level to rest and recover.

Chapter 11

I spent the next day scavenging the warehouses and buildings near the dock, figuring it wasn't a popular spot, given the ghosts that normally blanketed the area. I kept a wary eye out for the surviving priest but never encountered him. A number of the buildings were full of old trade goods, most of them expired or rotten, but a few had things that had held up fairly well. In one warehouse I found a large number of rugs, blankets, and other unprocessed cloth. It didn't interest me, but I imagined it might be worth something to someone. In others, I found furniture, wooden planks, stone, and other solid things that had survived the ravages of time. I was surprised the other scavengers hadn't picked the area clean, but maybe the ghosts had kept most of them away.

The luckiest find of all was a metal foundry set just a street off from the dock where iron was turned into wootz steel. Wootz steel was a lower-quality steel than what I could make with my nanobots, but luckily, there were still several crates full of iron ingots in the warehouse. I broke open all the crates I could find, counting the iron ingots. There were enough that I wouldn't need to go scavenging around the city for small scraps of iron any longer. I would be hard-pressed to use it all in a year or two of crafting my small bullets.

The only downside to finding the iron was that the foundry wasn't very secure. It had massive double doors, big enough for wagons to pass through, set on both sides of the building, but both sets of doors were shattered and broken, unable to be closed. The foundry building was one large rectangle made of solid stone with a high, unobstructed ceiling, which meant there were no secure rooms for me to hide in at night. Also, numerous windows that had no glass or shutters to secure them were placed around the building to let in as much light as possible. The building also had a back courtyard that held the forges used to actually cast the metal, but it was only protected by a low stone wall and a wooden roof set on pillars, so I couldn't secure it against attacks at night.

The other concerning thing was that the warehouse had a basement. When I approached the stairs leading downward, I was met with nothing but a pit of absolute blackness. The light streaming in through the many windows and open doors failed to illuminate the pit even the slightest bit, making it pretty obvious that I had found my first dungeon entrance. I definitely didn't want to be inside the building when night fell and monsters began to climb out of the dungeon.

After a bit of searching, I managed to find a home just down the street that seemed safe. It must have belonged to a rich merchant, because it was far more secure than the rest of the houses nearby. It had a large stone wall that stretched up at least ten feet and was several feet thick. Inside the wall was an open villa made of stone, as well as a central courtyard, in the middle of which was a large cistern that still had drinkable water in it. I searched the villa thoroughly and couldn't find a basement either, thankfully.

I found the most secure room on the top floor of the villa and decided to make that my new home. It was close to several places where I could hunt monsters, and I was just steps away from the foundry. It also had access to drinkable water and contained a secure place for me to rest. It was an ideal location, as long as the priests didn't come back to this area in search of me. I hoped they would avoid me in the future. They had seemed to assume I was a Varangian, and since I had survived, they had reason to think they might be in quite a bit of trouble for attacking me.

I spent the rest of that day crafting more bullets in the foundry. I also practiced with my revolver and rehearsed a few other combat techniques now that I had more room to stretch out. I filled my satchels with plenty of each type of bullet I had created so far, equipping myself as fully as I possibly could. I spent the night cleaning the secure room I had chosen inside the villa and waiting for the sun to rise again.

The next day, fully equipped with as many bullets as I could carry, I made my way toward the other two ancient harbors that Nikephoros had told me about. I scouted the area thoroughly this time, not just for monsters but for any humans that might be around as well. The two harbors were near each other and were significantly smaller than the large one I had fought in earlier.

Around the harbors, I could see a number of sub-bosses, but no golden glow of an actual boss appeared. I was disappointed, but even without a full boss around, it was worth killing the sub-bosses and regular ghosts for experience and blue orbs. After reloading with more *Holy Bullets*, I walked down to the first of the two docks and began killing the nearest ghosts.

Only an hour or so later, I had cleared both docks, added eight blue orbs to my pouch, and earned another sixty experience, but little else. I had to admit to being a bit disappointed by the ease of my hunt, but I pushed aside the feeling. If I wasn't careful, I could become addicted to the life-and-death excitement of this world. That would be a dangerous first step to getting myself killed.

After I killed all of the ghosts I could find, I spent the rest of the day scavenging through the warehouses near the docks, but I found little of value, other than a few low-level monsters here and there. I was closer to the priests' enclave in this part of the city, and the ghosts were weaker, so maybe scavengers had been through here more thoroughly than in the other part of the city.

The next day, I returned to the original dock I had cleared and found several ghosts had repopulated the area. None of them were bosses, but it was interesting that the ghosts had reappeared. Were they coming from a nearby dungeon? If I left them long enough, would they eventually spawn sub-bosses and bosses again? If I had time, I would love to figure out how long it took to repopulate an area, but that was for the future, when I had the luxury of time to investigate this world more fully.

I killed the few ghosts that had repopulated the docks easily enough and then made sure nobody was around before diving off the nearest dock and into the water beneath the harbor. There, I swam down to the first sunken ship I could find. It was a smaller ship, possibly used for personal travel rather than shipping goods or fighting on the sea. I swam down and grabbed the closest railing, looking down at the ship where it lay on its side in the silt of the harbor. Leading deeper into the ship was a doorway that wasn't buried, so I swam over and pulled myself through.

The inside of the ship was dark, the murky water hard to see through even with my enhanced eyes. I proceeded half by feel, swimming down the stairs to find two lower levels in the ship. The first level was a galley with the rotted remains of benches and tables floating around the room. The second level had several smaller rooms and a hallway that ran the length of the ship, ending at a larger room that took up the entire rear of the vessel.

I checked each room carefully but found little but decayed furniture and the occasional fish or crab. The large room at the end of the passageway contained the remains of a larger bed, a bookshelf with decaying books floating around it, a large table, and a large chest that was still held firmly against the floorboards. I searched the chest, hopeful I might have found something of value, but was disappointed to find it empty.

I searched the rest of the room dutifully, but the only thing I found was a loose silver piece in a drawer built into the table.

I swam back up to the surface and caught my breath before diving down again to search for the next ship. The first had been a bust, but I was confident that no other scavenger had been through here before me because of how dangerous the harbor was and because no normal human could hold their breath as long as I could, although I realized someone might have a spell that let them breathe underwater. Hopefully nobody had thought of that and come to loot the ships before me.

Hours passed, and while most of the wreckage on the bottom of the harbor turned out to be empty, my idea did pay off a few times. The first thing I found was a magical book, perfectly preserved on a rotting bookshelf. It glowed with a blue light that illuminated the cabin I found it in, drawing my eye immediately. I kept the book in my hand as I searched the rest of the wreckage since its soft blue light was so useful for lighting my way. Unlike the glow from the sub-bosses, which seemed more spiritual than physical and didn't actually cast light around the sub-bosses, the glow from the book produced real light that helped me see.

I also found several enchantments that were still active. Some were on the boats themselves and impossible to collect, but others were on easier objects that I grabbed and took with me. I found a silver statue of a songbird that was covered in golden runes, a ship's galley that had several small chests carved with green runes, and some articles of enchanted clothing that were still pristine, even in the poor condition I found them in.

The small chests appeared to preserve the food kept inside; when I opened the first one, a number of herbs and a bag of salt floated out. They were immediately ruined by the water but otherwise perfectly preserved. I left the other two chests unopened after realizing what they did and took all of them with me.

To keep everything hidden as I searched, I piled it on a nearby dock behind several old crates, but I kept the book with me for its light.

As I was winding up my exploration of the harbor floor, I decided to search the remains of the ship I had destroyed in my fight with the golden boss. Given that it had such a powerful boss on it, the ship seemed worth looking over in case he had kept some valuable loot on his ship before I had sunk it.

This ship was different from the others I had been searching. It was large but sleek. Its slim profile at the bottom of the harbor made clear it had once been a deadly warship rather than a meandering merchant ship or pleasure boat like the other ships I had searched.

The side of the ship I had damaged was face-up, exposing the inside to me as I swam down toward it. I grabbed part of the hull that was still intact, scanning the dark interior, but didn't see anything dangerous inside.

Several of the interior decks were destroyed, the fire having ravaged whatever must have once been there. I swam inside, searching through the remains, but didn't find anything of value. Below those decks was one more level, which was more intact than the rest of the ship. I held up the book I had looted, illuminating the dark waters around me, and found a stairway downward. As I began to descend the stairs, the light from the book in my hand began to fade and the stairway was plunged into darkness.

I panicked, trying to back up hastily, but felt a momentary sense of vertigo and had to close my eyes to steady myself. When I opened them again, I was no longer underwater but standing on the deck of an intact ship, the bright sun above me, a warm breeze blowing over me as I looked around in complete shock. What was going on? How had I been transported from the bottom of a sunken ship to this place?

Before I could figure out where exactly I was, the sounds of combat nearby reached my ears. I heard screams and cries of pain and the sound of metal striking metal, or metal striking flesh, followed by grunts of exertion and the harsh breathing of people locked in deadly combat. I blinked several times and suddenly the rest of my surroundings came into focus.

Not only was I on the deck of a ship, but the ship was under attack. Around me were men in navy uniforms identical to the one the golden boss I had killed had worn. They were locked in deadly combat with boarders who had attacked their ship. The other ship was entangled with the one I was on, drifting next to ours. Grappling hooks and ropes held the two ships together.

The crews of the two ships fought with swords and axes, brutally attacking each other with no mercy or hesitation. Several men in the rafters above fired arrows into the melee, sinking them deep into the bodies of the boarders, who wore no armor to protect them from the deadly missiles. I saw several sub-bosses on both sides of the conflict, fighting against each other, the human-looking men glowing faintly blue.

"Repel those barbarian scum!" I heard a voice yell out from the deck of the ship I was standing on. I turned and saw a man in uniform standing on the top deck at the stern of the ship, yelling down toward his men fighting on the lower deck.

I stood, frozen, unsure of what was happening and what I should do. Thankfully, either because of my lack of movement or because of my cloak, nobody had noticed me yet. I took the momentary peace to try to figure out what had happened, but with a sinking feeling in my stomach, I realized there was only one explanation. I had entered a dungeon.

Chapter 12

The dungeon was like nothing I could have predicted. It was absolutely real, the sounds of combat and the sea genuine in a way that no magic could possibly re-create, the smell of blood, sweat, and tar filling the air in perfect detail. From where I was standing, I couldn't see an end to the dungeon; the water stretched away to the horizon without stopping. I couldn't see a way to leave the dungeon, which meant I had to find a way to complete it before I was killed.

I pulled out my revolver and began to clean it, ordering my nanobots to swarm the metal and get out the last of the water as rapidly as possible. I also put the book I had been carrying into my backpack, readying myself for combat. If this dungeon wanted to trap me inside of it, it would find out shortly that I wasn't someone to be pushed around. Once my revolver was clear, I reloaded it with *Holy Bullets* and looked around me for targets to kill.

The question was, should I attack the crew of the ship I appeared on? That of the attacking ships? Both?

If I didn't attack the crew of this ship, would they assist me or just attack me anyway once the boarders were repelled? I didn't know the rules of this place or how sophisticated the dungeon would be in terms of the possible paths I would need to take to complete it.

I decided to test things out before I made a wrong decision. The captain at the stern of the ship was by himself. There was an easy path to the captain on the starboard side of the ship since most of the sailors were busy repelling the "barbarians" on the port side.

Crouching, I ran along the starboard side and up the stairs that led to the top deck, where the captain was standing at the railing, yelling encouragement to his crew in their fight against the boarders.

When I reached the captain, I stood up and approached the man openly. When I got close enough to almost touch him, the captain noticed me and turned quickly, alarmed at my sudden appearance. He reached for a saber he had sheathed on his belt, but when he saw me, he stopped.

"Why aren't you attacking, sailor?" he demanded of me. "We can't let these scum take our convoy down! Get in there and fight!"

I guess that answered my question; the captain seemed to recognize me as one of his crew, maybe because I hadn't attacked them yet. Apparently this dungeon was complicated enough to allow me to take sides in an ongoing conflict. The dungeon possibly even had multiple different ways I could complete it if I chose to betray the captain or side with the boarders. The implications were fascinating, but I put them out of my mind for now.

"Yes, sir!" I replied, offering a salute that I was pretty sure wasn't accurate, but the captain only nodded and returned to watching the fight below.

I backed away and moved partway down the stairs that led back to the lower deck. When I was halfway down, I had a perfect, unimpeded view of the attackers and was partially protected from return fire by the railing on the stairs. I aimed and began to pick off the opposing archers in the enemy rigging first, shooting them down one by one. My *Holy Bullets* were just as effective, telling me that these were indeed ghosts like the ones I had fought on the dock, something I had figured was the case since the dungeon was inside the ship that had contained the ghost boss. The golden flash of the bullets was muted, though, no longer seeming to blind the nearby ghosts. Either these ghosts were more powerful or my *Holy Bullets* were somehow weakened inside the dungeon.

Either way, the bullet itself was still powerful enough to kill the ghosts with a single shot. Once I had emptied the enemy rigging of their archers, I reloaded and aimed for the sub-bosses in the enemy forces. I figured that would help turn the tide of battle without my needing to waste bullets on the lesser ghosts, and it would give me the best experience for each bullet spent.

I hurriedly dispatched each sub-boss. My aim, even from across the deck and into the chaotic melee, was good enough that I hit each enemy, thanks to my enhanced body. Once the sub-bosses were dead, our sailors rapidly gained the advantage, our sub-bosses able to focus on the lesser ghosts rather than trying to fight the more powerful sub-bosses of the enemy. Within a matter of minutes, the fight was over. No mercy was given to the opposing ghosts, and each barbarian refused to surrender, fighting until they were struck down.

As the last of the barbarians began to fall, the enemy ship's captain made an appearance in an attempt to salvage the fight. He carried a massive battle-axe. It was almost as large as the ghost was tall—which was even taller than me. The barbarian captain stood at least seven or eight feet tall, his body rippling with muscle. He looked like a bodybuilder that had been spliced with the genes of a gorilla and then fed a steady diet of protein and steroids for his entire life. With a mighty roar, the man leapt onto our ship. The impact of his leap sent a shock wave rippling out, blowing the nearby men off their feet and into others nearby. The men directly impacted by the shock wave appeared dazed, unable to get up, while the others were entangled with the disabled men, struggling to stand back up with their comrades on top of them.

I took aim and unloaded all six shots into the barbarian captain as he stood up from his crouch, hoisting his axe in his massive arms, preparing to cut down the sailors nearby who were unable to defend themselves. As my bullets pierced his body, he turned rapidly, narrowing his eyes at me in anger. I had really expected him to die from my bullets, not just look annoyed by the *Holy Bullets* piercing his body. He roared again and began to charge across the deck toward me.

I reloaded, backing up the stairs as rapidly as I could. I had absolutely no interest in meeting that axe in close quarters. I was fully prepared to leap from the ship and take my chances at the bottom of the ocean before I let it get close enough to touch me.

Before I had to do anything drastic, our own captain whistled. Several of the sailors who hadn't been entangled in the shock wave threw themselves on the boss, slowing him as they began to grab on to him, stabbing and punching him. The barbarian captain barely seemed to notice the attacks, but the bodies piling on him were enough to slow him slightly.

"All hands, defend the boat!"

The captain's order rang out over the ship, his words echoing with power that I could feel deep in my body. The crew, many of whom had been lying on the deck, dazed from the skill of the enemy boss, suddenly sprang up, fully recovered. The other sailors seemed to grow in size, becoming stronger and moving faster, clearly gaining some kind of enhancement from the captain's order.

The newly empowered sailors all ran toward the enemy captain, unconcerned about their own safety, swarming the barbarian and stopping him in his tracks. There were so many sailors piling onto the barbarian captain that I couldn't risk firing any more bullets; I was more likely to strike a friendly sailor than the enemy captain. After several minutes of struggle as the sailors brutally stabbed, punched, bit, and attacked any way that they could, the enemy boss finally seemed to slow and fall to his knees.

Another few moments passed. Then his struggles ended completely and he fell face-first to the deck. The crew, covered in the blood of the barbarian captain, untangled themselves from his body and began cheering and clapping each other on the back. I could do nothing but stare at the surreal scene in front of me, unsure of how to process the strangeness of what I was seeing.

"Get that bastard of a ship off us!" the captain yelled, pointing at the enemy ship. "And then get us going again. We have more barbarians to kill!"

The crew cheered, jumping to obey the captain. Crewmembers hefted their bloodied axes and ran to the railing, cutting into the ropes connecting the enemy ship to ours. The rest scrambled around the lower deck, gathering their own weapons and tossing the enemy bodies off the side of the ship, clearing the deck as much as possible. Once we were free from the other ship, the sailors pushed it away from us and we began to slowly drift apart.

"Get those sails up, boys! It is time for some revenge!" the captain yelled.

I moved down the deck, checking to see if I could loot the boss before he was tossed overboard, but no glowing orb appeared above him, despite the fact that he had glowed gold before he died. Was it because I didn't deliver the killing blow? Or because of the nature of the dungeon? Maybe rewards came at the end. Or were there no rewards for bosses in dungeons, only the reward for finishing the dungeon itself? I didn't know how it worked here, but I planned to complete this dungeon and find out.

Large oars were cast out of our ship, splashing into the water on both sides. At the same time, the sails were quickly unfurled, causing the ship to jerk forward. The captain moved from the railing that overlooked the lower deck to the wheel that steered the ship and began to guide us toward where two more ships were intertwined nearby.

Once we got close, the oars on the side near the enemy ship were pulled in and the men came pouring back up from down below.

"Brace for impact!" the captain yelled as we approached. I grabbed the railing near me as the ship slammed alongside the enemy ship. Wood exploded upward with a tortured scream, and the sailors near the railing tossed grappling hooks across and began hauling us up tight against the other ship.

"Attack!" the captain yelled.

With a collective roar, the sailors from my ship charged over and attacked. The enemy ship was barely prepared for our boarding; most of the barbarians were still engaged in trying to take over the ship they had originally attacked. Only a few of the enemy ghosts had turned to repel us, so our sailors were able to swarm over them easily. Once the enemy's deck was cleared, our sailors continued forward, attacking the rest of the barbarians from behind as they were focused on fighting the sailors of the ship we were here to rescue. I stayed on our ship and picked off the barbarian sub-bosses with careful shots of my revolver, trying not to draw too much attention to myself.

The barbarian captain was in the middle of the melee, fighting the captain of the friendly ship, both surrounded by a subtle golden glow. As the enemy ghosts began dying, the barbarian captain turned and seemed to notice for the first time that they had been attacked from behind.

As the boss stood, momentarily frozen at the sight of his men being cut down from behind, I fired all six bullets of my revolver at him. My shots pierced his upper chest, one after another, sending him staggering backward. The captain of the friendly ship took advantage of his distracted foe and ran him through, finishing him off.

Our sailors cheered at the sight, surging forward and dispatching the last of the barbarians still standing.

"Captain Leontius!" the captain of the ship I was on yelled. "Get your men onto my ship. We will combine forces and clear the rest of this rabble!"

"Yes, sir!" the other captain yelled back. "You heard the man!" he continued, turning toward his own men. "Get over there!"

With a cheer, the combined forces returned to our ship, bloody weapons held high in celebration, and we swiftly cast off from the enemy ship and made our way to the last intertwined pair of ships fighting nearby.

The final ship was in rough shape. Most of the friendly crew were dead, and the barbarians were in full control of the deck. A last holdout of men was fighting on the top deck near the wheel, holding on simply because the barbarians could only come at them a few at a time up the narrow stairs. The captain of the ship was fighting with a sword and dagger, seeming to appear and disappear in an instant, always intervening to stop a thrust or strike that would kill one of his crew members.

The barbarian captain, though, was an archer and was calmly standing on his own ship and firing deadly arrows into the sailors on our side whenever an opening presented itself. His sub-bosses and sailors were doing the fighting while he stood back and picked off vulnerable sailors from a distance.

"The dastardly coward!" our captain yelled at the sight. "Ram that ship!"

At our captain's orders, our ship leapt forward as if the vessel itself could obey the captain's command. We rapidly gained speed and slammed into the enemy ship head-on, cracking its hull. The bow of our ship wedged deeply into the hull of the enemy ship, causing the enemy captain to lose his footing. He was thrown to the deck of his own ship, his bow sliding out of his hand.

At the sight, our captain roared, ordering our men to attack. The sailors near me seemed to surge with strength once again, leaping across the bow of our ship and onto the last barbarian vessel. The enemy captain was just starting to recover when the first of our crew reached him, cutting him down ruthlessly from behind as he tried to stand. He had no chance to defend himself.

Once the enemy captain was dead, the remaining crew of our ship stormed across, still empowered by the command of the captain of the ship I was on, and easily finished off the last of the barbarians. The speed and ferocity of the empowered sailors was so great that I didn't get a chance to fire a single shot in the final battle. I just stared in awe at the frenzied sailors as they massacred the last of the enemy ghosts.

As the last of the barbarians fell, the three crews erupted into cheers. The survivors of the last crew greeted the comrades that had saved them, hugging and patting each other on the back in celebration.

"Well done, lad," I heard a voice say beside me. The captain had come down from the upper deck and approached me. "We took the day, thanks to your skills. No doubt of that."

I turned and tried to think of a response but wasn't sure what to say to the captain's thanks. Before I could think of an appropriate response, the captain continued speaking.

"Now comes the cleanup and burial," he said, his stern face looking over the celebrating crew. "A near victory this was. I fear for Nova Roma, that these barbarians have given us such a challenge lately. Many of our ships do not return from these waters any longer."

With a frown, the captain passed me on the stairs and went to join the captains of the other ships we had rescued. The three captains greeted each other and began to talk in low voices, clearly not wanting to interrupt their celebrating men with their more serious discussion.

I was unsure of what to do from here. Things were settling down and it appeared the fighting was over. Nikephoros had mentioned something about a core that should grant me a reward for completing the dungeon, but I had never imagined I would need to find it on a ship in the middle of the water. Where would a core be in a dungeon like this?

I climbed down the rest of the stairs and ducked into the doorway that led to the lower decks. I followed the stairs downward, seeing that this ship had the same layout as the one I had sunk in the harbor back in the city. That gave me an idea of where the core might be. On the lowest level of the ship, where I had been sucked into this dungeon in the first place, I found a

156

glowing white orb hovering in the middle of the hallway. I stared at it warily, but when it didn't move or do anything aggressive, I relaxed.

Now the question was, should I try to complete the dungeon right away or go back and kill the remaining ghosts? There was a good chance the reward from the dungeon might be better if I killed everything inside, but when I thought of the cheering sailors and the friendly captain, I couldn't bring myself to go back upstairs. It was all too real and I didn't want to be the kind of person that ruthlessly killed people that had helped me just because it might give me a momentary advantage. Mind made up, I approached and touched the orb with my hand.

Congratulations, you have completed this dungeon. You have earned the following rewards: 3 gold cores, 9 blue cores, 1 perk, 1000 experience.

Perk obtained: Captain's Command. Anyone obeying an order that you give will receive a morale bonus of +1 to all attributes while carrying out your command.

After the voice finished speaking, the white orb in front of me transformed into the golden and blue orbs. I shook my head, dispelling the odd feeling that came whenever the announcements beamed themselves directly into my brain, and grabbed the orbs. A moment later, my vision darkened and I found myself surrounded by water once again. I was back inside the sunken ship. The hallway I had been in before surrounded me once again, although this time it wasn't as unnaturally dark now that the dungeon was cleared and had disappeared.

I panicked at the feeling of the water pressing down on me again so suddenly, and my body tried to gasp for air in panic, but I clamped my mouth shut, controlling myself before I could inhale water and drown myself. Instead, I turned and hastily swam out of the ruined ship, kicking as hard as I could toward the surface.

As my head broke the water, I gasped in several lungfuls of air. It wasn't that I was out of oxygen, but the sudden shift back to the water had left my body panicking as if I was drowning. It took a supreme amount of willpower to calm down enough to swim to the surface, and now my body wanted nothing more than to gasp in as much air as it could take.

As my panic began to fade, I remembered to scan the area around me in case one of the priests had returned. Looking around hurriedly as I bobbed in the shallow waves, I was relieved to see that I was still alone. It had felt like an hour or two had passed in the dungeon, but as I took in the docks around me and the position of the sun, it appeared that barely any time had passed. The sun hung above me, covered by a few wispy clouds, almost in the exact same position as when I dove down to explore the sunken ship.

I pulled myself onto the nearby dock and stumbled over to where I had been stashing the loot from the other ships I had scavenged. Checking around the docks once again, I saw I was still alone, so I gathered the items I had found and jogged swiftly back to the villa I was staying in.

Chapter 13

I replenished my bullets overnight and thoroughly cleaned my clothing, gear, and revolver to make sure all the brackish water was out of everything. I also inspected the goods I had salvaged, but the only thing new I learned was that the book I had found was a non-combat-class book—which was exciting—but the class was called a *Navigator*, which didn't seem particularly useful to me personally.

I still considered learning it, because it sounded like non-combat classes could give enhancements, but since they only leveled from non-combat use, it seemed unlikely I would gain much from the class. I didn't see myself navigating a ship across the sea anytime soon. I decided to wait and see how much it would sell for before deciding for sure.

Once I was clean and rested, I jogged across the city to catch Asylaion on his daily route to the military's enclave. I moved a bit slower than usual since I was burdened with the chests and other goods I had found, but at the same time, my enhanced body made carrying the extra weight seem almost effortless. I was slowed mostly because I was trying to avoid dropping the unwieldy chest rather than because of their weight.

When Asylaion saw me, he jumped down from his wagon and gave me a hug. I was touched by the gesture, even though I knew part of it was just a *Merchant* happy to see a returning customer. It was still a kind gesture either way.

"You have survived yet again!" He looked me up and down and noted the pile of goods I carried in my arms. "And you have found something interesting, eh?"

"I hope so," I said.

He led me over to his wagon, where I put the goods down. I moved back and Asylaion stepped forward to inspect what I had brought him.

"Interesting stuff," he said as he opened and closed the chests and held up the various garments I had salvaged.

I waited patiently for him to finish evaluating everything.

"A lot of luxury goods," he said as he turned to me. "You must have found an old, unsalvaged noble's house, eh? Or some boutique store? A very lucky find on your part!"

I didn't correct him, merely smiling in response to his probing questions.

"A lot of this will sell well to the palace," he continued, "but I will need to sell it to the generals first and they will have to sell it at the palace. I am too lowly of a merchant to sell directly to the Emperor and his remaining nobles. That will cut out a good bit of our profit."

I gave him a skeptical look and he laughed in reply.

"Fret not," he told me. "I am not saying this to take advantage of you. I just want you to know the reality of our situation. You could, of course, try selling to the nobles yourself, eh? I would not recommend it, though."

"No, I'm fine selling through you. I trust you to be fair."

"Good, good," he said. "Now the book. That is something rare. To the right person, almost priceless. That class has been lost for some time. Only a few people are still around to teach it, and they don't seem interested in doing so. But the problem is that we do not have any large ships left that need a navigator. That means the demand is not as high as it could be."

I waited, not interrupting as he continued to talk.

"At the same time," he said, a thoughtful expression on his face, "Sycae has a few merchants that may be willing to pay well for this just in case they ever rebuild their fleet. There are a few dreamers that still imagine things might go back to the way they used to be. They might be interested in a way around the old curmudgeons that refuse to teach the class to anyone new these days."

He hummed and hawed a bit, counting on his fingers for a moment, making a big show of adding up the value of my goods. I resisted the urge to smile at his song and dance.

"I can give you ten blue orbs for the clothes," he finally said, "and five for the chests. I'll give you a gold orb for the class and another gold orb for the songbird. A very fair offer."

I looked over the goods and couldn't help but agree, although I was sure if I went through a lot of effort, I could get a bit more in Sycae or with the nobles, but it wasn't worth the trouble and I didn't have the contacts to make it happen quickly. Even though I thought it was a relatively fair deal, it was good to bargain in these situations, and I was feeling more comfortable socializing as a human, so I didn't take his first offer immediately.

"That songbird is heavily enchanted," I replied, "and likely worth a lot to the right noble. And like you said, that class is extremely rare. It could be the difference between a merchant being able to restart a shipping enterprise and being stuck here in the city forever, if I'm right. I will take two gold orbs and twenty blue orbs for everything."

We bargained back and forth a bit but eventually settled on two gold orbs, seventeen blue orbs, and my choice of two types of ammunition he had recently picked up from the military. We shook hands and he handed me the orbs. I put them away while he dug out his new ammunition for me to look at.

After I looked over the new arrows he had, the only two worth taking were an *Arrow of Blinding*, which exploded with light, much like the *Holy Arrow* did when it came into contact with a ghost, and a *Multi-Arrow*, which copied itself after firing, creating a wave of arrows. The *Arrow of Blinding* wasn't particularly useful, but I picked it up anyway just in case I ever needed it. The *Multi-Arrow*, on the other hand, was extremely useful. It could provide me with more options for dealing with a large number of enemies, similar to my *Explosive Bullet.*

"By the way," he told me after I secured my new arrows in my backpack, "I had a visitor the other day asking about you."

I looked up at him sharply, surprised that someone would be asking after me. "Oh?"

"Yeah," he told me, stepping closer. "Asked if I knew a new scavenger who had some powerful ability or class. I told them I hadn't seen anyone new in a long time. Just the regulars around here, if you know what I mean."

He clapped me on the shoulder, giving me a roguish smile. I tried to smile back, but it was strained.

"Thanks for doing that," I told him. "Why would they be asking about me? Do you know who it was?"

"Well," he said, "I have suspected for a long time that the person who asked after you was taking some of the Patriarch's silver on the side, if you know what I mean. Did you have a run-in with his priests recently?"

"Ah," I said, realizing what he meant. "Yeah . . . they ambushed me and tried to capture me when I was out scavenging the other day. I fought back. One of them died from the fight."

Asylaion's eyebrow rose sharply as I spoke. I was afraid one would get stuck by the time I told him I killed one of the priests.

"You killed a priest? On your own? When facing more than one priest at a time?"

"Well," I said, unsure of how much to reveal, "I mostly got lucky. They almost captured me."

"Hmm," he replied, staring at me for several moments. "You are quite the puzzle, my friend. Quite the puzzle."

I tried to give him an innocent smile in return. When I said nothing more, he shook his head ruefully and smiled at me again.

"Well, anyway," he added, "I just wanted to warn you."

I felt another surge of affection for the wily merchant. He hadn't needed to warn me or lie on my behalf. It might be in his best interest to protect the scavengers that traded with him, but that was still going above and beyond for me. I was learning that I might be able to trust him more than I had initially thought.

"I appreciate it, Asylaion. Thank you."

He nodded and we said our goodbyes. I stepped back and watched silently as the caravan continued down the well-worn road, on its way to trade with the military like it did every day. A few of the guards even nodded at me as they passed, seeming to recognize me as someone worth respecting now that I had been surviving in the city for so long. It felt good.

I made my way back to the villa, moving rapidly and silently through the city now that I wasn't burdened with the chests and other goods. If the priests were investigating me, then I needed to be especially careful. They had skills that I didn't have a way to counter right now and could have dangerous contacts or agents in any of the enclaves. I had no magic of my own, so I wasn't sure how I could counter their spells if they got the drop on me like last time.

Back at the villa, I studied the new arrows I had purchased. The *Arrow of Blinding* was interesting because it contained an activation rune, a *Durability* rune, and a rune that I reasoned must stand for *Light*. I let my nanobots loose to study the two new arrows, measuring the runes down to the smallest detail. Once they were done, I searched the house until I found a pot in the kitchen of the villa and a piece of cloth that was still in decent condition. I ordered my nanobots to break down the clay of the pot, shaping it into a small solid ball that would fit in the palm of my hand.

Once that was done, I had the nanobots carve a *Durability* rune and a *Light* rune into the ball of clay. Then I pulled out a blue orb and charged the ball, causing it to burst into light as soon as the runes finished charging. I squinted, but the light was so bright I was nearly blinded and had to look away hastily.

I grabbed the scrap of cloth I had brought and wrapped it around the lit orb several times, slowly dimming it as the cloth covered it in more and more layers. When it had finally dimmed enough to see again, I opened my eyes and looked down at what I had crafted. The small clay orb cast a faint light over the room, giving me some light to work by when it became dark, as long as I didn't announce my presence to the monsters that came out at night. And if I needed more light, I could unwrap it more, adjusting the light that escaped through the cloth. I had invented a crude flashlight, which was probably unremarkable to the rest of the world, but it would help me when I went searching for goods in the city. The *Navigator* book I had used to light my way under the water had been surprisingly useful, so it was good to find a way to create light when I needed it.

Wrapping up the clay orb fully and tucking it into a pouch on my waist, I turned to the *Multi-Arrow*. The problem with this arrow, I soon realized, was that it required four runes instead of the standard three. It had the standard activation rune and *Penetration* rune but then had two more runes. I should have asked Asylaion about the arrows, but I had been distracted by the talk of the priests searching for information about me. He had originally told me that most things could only hold three runes without overloading, so how was this arrow able to have four? And since there were two runes that were unidentified, it was hard to know which one was responsible for the multiplying effect or if both were required.

I ran some experiments, carving the runes on more clay balls, then charging and tossing them around the foundry warehouse to see what happened when I activated each rune separately. I learned that the first unknown rune caused a multiplication effect and the second rune seemed to hold and store additional energy, much like a battery. When I carved the *Battery* rune by itself and tossed the clay ball, it did nothing but stayed fully charged. When I tossed the *Multiplication* ball, it drained itself of energy but only made one or two copies before running out of power. When I combined the two runes, suddenly the *Multiplication* rune drew power from the *Battery* rune, causing the clay ball to multiply tenfold, sending a mess of balls rolling across the foundry floor. So I theorized the *Multi-Arrow* could have four runes because one was passive, simply providing the greater amount of charge needed to multiply the arrow so many times.

I crafted several bullets with the multi-effect and moved away from the villa in case I attracted too much attention. When I tested the *Multi-Bullet*, the effect was impressive. The new bullet had the standard *Penetration* rune, which sent the bullets flying forward so fast they were impossible to track even with my enhanced reflexes. When combined with the *Multiplication* rune, though, a single bullet turned into ten bullets, spreading out and impacting against a wide area of effect. I practiced against a wide stone wall, and a single bullet spread out and covered the entire wall, depending on how far away I was from the wall when I fired the initial bullet. The closer I was, the more bullets impacted close together, almost like buckshot, while if I released the bullet from a greater distance, the bullets spread wide, covering the entire wall for twenty feet or more.

The downside to the *Multi-Bullet* was that I couldn't fit a *Durability* rune onto it, which made the bullets less penetrative when used against things that were covered in armor or thick skin. They would still carry the punch of the *Penetration* rune, but they rapidly flattened out when impacting against something especially dense or unyielding. Thankfully, there wasn't that much that could fully stop a steel bullet except for the strongest of armors or truly durable creatures, making the *Multi-Bullet* very useful.

While I was tossing the clay balls around the foundry, I got an idea for a new application of the runes as well: grenades. There was no reason I couldn't use clay balls, or steel balls, to make the magical equivalent of grenades. They wouldn't need an *Penetration* rune, since I could just toss them like a normal ball, but they could still carry an *Explosive* rune to give me some additional firepower. Back at the villa, I collected all of the pottery in the home and set my nanobots to forming them into hardened balls that rested comfortably in the palm of my hand. As the first few started to form in front of me, I designed the runes I would put on them: the trigger rune to activate the effects of the other runes, a *Durability* rune to make them resistant to breaking or damage, and an *Explosive* rune to finish the set of three runes.

After charging them up, I ran over to the area where I had tested the *Multi-Bullets* and was very happy with the results. Each ball carried the explosive power of my *Explosive Bullet* but could be tossed over walls, rolled across the ground, or thrown with my left hand while I was firing the revolver with my right. The explosion was just as powerful as those from the bullets, enough to destroy the stone wall that had stood up to multiple *Multi-Bullets* being fired at it over and over.

After testing several of the new weapons to make sure they worked, I hurriedly left in case the explosions had attracted too much attention. As I left, the wall I had tested them against collapsed further, crumbling to the ground, scorched and burned black from the magical flames.

I ran back to my villa, my mind awhirl with possibilities for the different kinds of grenades I could make. Some of the enchantments I had purchased would actually work better in grenade form, such as the *Confusion* rune or the *Darkness* rune. Tossing out a *Darkness Grenade* would cause a large area to be blanketed in impenetrable blackness, making it an effective tool for blinding an enemy, covering my flank, or hiding me as I escaped from a dangerous situation.

The *Confusion* rune seemed powerful. It would cause whoever was struck by the weapon to turn and attack anyone nearby, confused about who was friend or foe. The problem I had considered when I bought the arrow that contained the rune was that it was more likely to kill the enemy when it was enchanted on a bullet. If the target I shot with the *Confusion Bullet* just died from the bullet itself, then it defeated the point of the *Confusion* rune.

But a *Confusion Grenade* could actually sow confusion since I would just need to make sure the grenade impacted against an enemy, triggering the enchantment. They wouldn't be injured, allowing them to attack their allies or whoever was nearby with their full strength.

I spent the rest of the day and that night crafting a bandolier from leather scraps. The bandolier could hold the different kinds of grenades, making it easy to pull and throw them while I was in combat. As I waited for the bandolier to finish, I also worked on crafting a full range of *Explosive Grenades, Confusion Grenades*, and *Darkness Grenades*. In the middle of the night, I had another thought in regard to the *Confusion Grenade*, quickly scrapping the clay balls I was crafting for those grenades and instead using steel to form the balls.

With the stronger material, I could get rid of the *Durability* rune and instead replace it with a *Battery* rune and *Multiplication* rune, allowing me to toss a *Confusion Grenade* into a crowd, where it would multiply tenfold, sowing even more chaos into an enemy's midst. I couldn't help but grin madly as I worked through the night, crafting and fine-tuning my newest creations.

In total, powering the grenades took ten blue orbs, which was quite expensive, but I knew they would be worth it. They diversified my arsenal and I could throw them while firing my revolver at the same time, only having to stop to reload, which required both hands.

Feeling confident with my new inventions, I decided to try something a bit risky. The dungeon I had identified in the basement of the foundry where I had found all my iron called to me, tempting me to test myself against it. With a belt full of bullets, plus a bandolier of grenades, and feeling good after successfully completing the last dungeon without too much trouble, I decided to risk another dungeon. Not only had the last dungeon given me a good amount of experience, but the reward of a perk and a significant number of orbs, both gold and blue, made another dungeon too tempting to pass up. If I wanted to buy the *Archer* class before the deadline was up, I would need to take some risks or I would never get enough currency.

The next morning, I approached the foundry, checking and rechecking my bandolier and satchels, drawing and holstering my revolver nervously. The foundry was silent as always, the city empty around me and uncaring at the risk I was about to take. I approached the unnaturally dark stairs leading into the basement, hesitated slightly, and then stepped downward.

Chapter 14

As I stepped into my second dungeon, I was immediately blasted by a wave of heat that took my breath away. It was so hot I had to blink several times, tears coming to my eyes, and my mouth immediately felt parched; the moisture from my body had seemingly been leeched from me in an instant.

When my eyes cleared, I saw that I was standing in a large hallway carved completely from stone, as if I was deep underground or in the heart of a mountain. On my right was a massive slab of stone leaning against the wall. Around it were gears that turned slowly. Tubes coming from the stone wall connected to the slab, and there were a few complicated-looking devices I couldn't immediately identify.

On my left, magma spilled from the wall, pouring into an opening covered by a grate on the floor. I couldn't see a purpose for the magma flow, but it produced an overpowering amount of heat. The smell of burning metal assaulted my nostrils, making it hard for me to distinguish any other smells. The magma lit the hallway dimly, casting everything in a harsh red light.

I drew my revolver, looking for possible enemies in the hallway, but nothing was moving nearby except for the gears attached to the metal slab on my right. I took a hesitant step forward. As soon as I did, the stone hissed with steam and began to split down the middle.

"Of course," I muttered, glaring at the slab of stone as it slowly began to open.

Inside the slab was a massive golem, standing at least three or four feet taller than me. It had a large round body and two thick arms and legs. Its head was featureless, just a blank slab of stone without any eyes or mouth. Its arms and legs, which were just large chunks of stone attached to the central body, had crude-looking knees and elbows made of stone but no toes or fingers. When the

168

slab finished opening completely, the golem stepped forward, the weight of its first step sending a boom echoing through the hallway all around me.

"Shit," I said, frantically backing away from the massive golem as far as I could go.

I took aim and fired all six of my *Penetration Bullets* at the golem's head. The bullets impacted dead center, sending a spray of stone shards out from the impact site, but the golem took another step forward, its second foot slamming down ominously. I reloaded rapidly.

I examined its head and saw that my bullets had managed to penetrate fairly deep, carving a hole into where its face would have been, but apparently they did nothing to actually cause any harm.

There was no brain or weak spot in the golem's head.

"Double shit." I looked behind me, but the hallway where I had appeared ended at a solid wall of stone. There was no escape in that direction.

I fired another full round of shots, this time aiming for where a heart would be on a human. The thick chest of the golem seemed more resistant to my bullets; the wound from all six bullets barely made a dent a few inches deep in its chest.

The golem raised its hands as it approached me like a zombie in a horror movie, mindlessly reaching for me. I ran past it down the hallway, rolling under its outstretched arms in case it tried to grab me. As I rolled past, it surprised me by turning with a sudden burst of speed, its massive foot rocketing forward and catching me in the side. I tried to lessen the impact by throwing myself in the direction of the kick, but it barely lessened the pain that shot through me as the enormous foot hit me in the ribs and stomach.

I groaned, trying to steady myself as I was flung across the hallway, coming perilously close to the magma that poured from the nearby wall. The golem continued forward, moving slowly in my direction. I scrambled up and ran past the brute, managing to stay far enough away this time to avoid its hands and feet. Once I put some distance between us, I loaded a single *Explosive Bullet* and fired it at the golem. The explosion was deafening in such a small hallway, making my ears pop and knocking me backward from the backdraft. I was sent sprawling on my back, my hurt ribs causing me to gasp in pain from the impact against the floor. When the flame dissipated, the golem was revealed, unharmed. It had paused for a moment from the explosion, but once the flames disappeared, it took another step forward, uncaring.

I picked myself up carefully, frustrated at how ineffective I felt against the golem. I was being tossed around like a lightweight, but I wasn't some rookie anymore. I had survived in this world when many couldn't. I wasn't going to go down to some mindless automaton.

I thought over the different types of ammunition I had on me, deciding to load a *Stasis Bullet* next and fired that at the golem. It impacted against the golem's chest, flashing silver for a second. When the light faded, I saw the golem was covered in a silver sheen of energy. I waited to see what would happen next, but nothing did. The golem was frozen in place.

I tried to inhale deeply, but my breath caught in my throat due to the pain in my ribs and chest where the golem had kicked me. I felt along my ribs with my left hand while sending nanobots to the area to begin work on repairing the injuries. From what I could feel, nothing had been broken from the kick, but I was going to have some serious bruising and my fighting effectiveness was going to take a hit until I could repair myself. I was thankful for the durability of my body; I was fairly confident that if I had been a normal human, that kick would have killed me.

I ate a short meal and drank some water to help power my nanobots, keeping a careful watch on the frozen golem. I wasn't sure how long the *Stasis Bullet* would work, but as I ate, I reloaded with *Penetration Bullets* and urged my nanobots to work as fast as possible. After about five minutes, the silver sheen that covered the golem began to fade.

I aimed my revolver and waited for the last of the silver to fade completely. When it did, the golem lurched forward once again and I fired all six bullets at its left kneecap, hoping that might be a weak point in the golem's design. My bullets struck the kneecap, sending out a spray of stone with each impact. The golem didn't react, continuing toward me without slowing in the slightest.

I backed up, reloading and firing six more times into the same kneecap. This time, the kneecap shattered after the first few bullets, barely holding together as the stone fractured completely. When the golem tried to step forward on its left leg, the kneecap couldn't support its weight. The golem slowly tipped sideways until it impacted against the stone floor with a loud bang. The golem froze there on the ground for a few seconds, but after a momentary hesitation, it began to pull itself toward me with its two working arms.

"Oh, c'mon now. This is just too much," I said, staring at the relentless golem.

I watched as the golem continued to crawl toward me, trying to figure out what to do next. I could waste time and bullets trying to find a way to kill the golem, or I could just leave it behind. At the rate it was crawling, it probably couldn't catch up to me before I reached the end of the dungeon. The only thing was, I didn't know if I could complete the dungeon if I didn't kill the golem or something. Was I supposed to kill it somehow? Or just avoid it and race down the hallway, staying far enough ahead that it could never catch up? These dungeons were annoyingly vague.

I thought of the last dungeon and how I was pretty sure there had been multiple different ways I could have completed it. I decided it didn't matter if I killed the golem or just left it behind. The dungeon would likely let me complete it, even if my rewards were less for not fully defeating the monster.

I turned away from the slowly crawling golem and holstered my gun, annoyed at the stupidity of the golem and its impenetrable body. Instead of dealing with it any further, I walked forward slowly, looking down the hallway to see what other challenges I might face and trying to ignore the scraping sounds of the golem behind me.

In front of me, more streams of magma spilled from the walls, granting a measure of illumination in the dark hallway. Further down the hallway, I saw several anvils and forges, and piled next to them were various types of weapons and suits of armor. I walked forward cautiously until I could inspect the weapons and armor. It seemed like I was in some kind of foundry, which made sense, considering the dungeon was in the basement of the foundry above. Unlike above, though, this was no normal foundry, unless it was common to build one underground or in some kind of active volcano and protect it with nigh-impenetrable golems.

I continued down the hallway, carefully watching for anything that might try to attack me. After several minutes of walking down the empty hallway, I spotted another slab of stone leaning against a wall in the distance. I sighed at the sight. I knew there had to be more golems; I had just really hoped I would be proven wrong.

When the stone slab split in half, gushing with steam, I was standing in front of the cairn, revolver raised. I unloaded in the golem's kneecap from close range, shattering it with my six bullets. When the golem tried to give chase, I stepped back and it crashed to the ground at my feet, crippled like the last one.

I turned, reloading my revolver with a flick of my wrist, leaving another golem to crawl pitifully after me.

I continued down the hallway, leaving a chain of crippled golems behind me. I found several sub-bosses, larger and more powerful golems, but they were even slower than the normal golems. It took a few more bullets to cripple the larger golems, but I had no problem staying out of reach of them. Now that I knew what to do to disable them, I was never really at risk. My biggest concern was that I was going through my *Penetration Bullets* rapidly, so I set my nanobots to crafting more in my backpack as I moved through the dungeon, slowly replenishing my supply.

After a particularly annoying sub-boss, I stopped to drink some water, gently running my fingers up and down my ribs to see how they were healing. They were still sore to the touch, but my breathing had been getting easier over time. My nanobots were working as fast as they could, but the process of repairing my body wasn't quick.

After an untold amount of time and numerous crippled golems left in my wake, I finally arrived at the end of the dungeon. I could tell because the hallway had finally ended, opening up into a large workshop the size of the warehouse above, if not bigger. Inside the workshop was an eclectic collection of weapons and armor piled on and around numerous desks, forges, or anvils or just lying in piles on the floor here and there. At one of the tables that faced the hallway was a diminutive man about the size of a small child. He had wild silver-blue hair that stuck straight upward and a pair of broken glasses on his small face. He hadn't noticed me, staring downward at some of the papers and books spread haphazardly around the desk in front of him. If I had to compare him to the mythology of my Earth, he seemed to fit the description of a mythical gnome. And if not for the fact that he glowed a slight gold, I would have assumed he was a normal person trapped here instead of the boss of the dungeon.

When it was clear he wasn't going to notice me where I stood, I stepped into the room. The gnome immediately turned and glared at me.

"I am not to be interrupted!" the gnome yelled before shaking his head and turning back to the books he was focused on. He stood on a stool and leaned most of his body over the large table to read what was in front of him, idly fiddling with several mechanical gears as he read.

I carefully looked over the workshop and saw the white dungeon core resting on a pillar on the far side of the room. It was one of the only parts of the workshop not covered in suits of armor or various types of weapons.

I walked across the workshop toward the core, keeping an eye on the gnome. When I got close to the core, he finally reacted, turning toward me with an angry expression on his face.

"How dare you!" he yelled at me. "You would destroy my life's work so casually?"

I froze, shrugging apologetically at him, unsure of what to say. I had hoped he would just let me take the orb and leave, but apparently not. He raised his hands, his small face scrunching up in anger. After a second, the weapons around the room began to shake and lift themselves into the air.

Not waiting for the gnome to bring the many floating weapons any closer to me, I drew my revolver and shot him through the chest. The bullet blew a large hole through his chest, throwing him backward. He flipped completely over the desk he had been reading at, spilling books and papers everywhere. The weapons that had been rising to attack me clattered to the ground. Silence filled the workshop, aside from the sound of harsh, gurgling breathing coming from behind the table where the gnome had landed.

I walked over, watching the gnome carefully for signs that he had other tricks, my gun pointed down at him. He was still alive, but barely. He was gasping, trying to take a breath through the wound in his chest.

"Such . . . a . . . magnificent . . . device!" He gasped each word as he stared at my revolver, then collapsed backward, dead. I stared back at him, a bit sad about the entire thing. It would have been interesting to talk to the gnome more, but apparently it wasn't meant to be. What a puzzling dungeon.

Once I made sure the gnome was dead, I turned to examine the room. The books the gnome had been reading were covered in blood, but what writing I could see wasn't of a language I recognized.

Shaking my head, I moved over to the dungeon core and grasped it, deciding to just get this dungeon over with.

Congratulations, you have completed this dungeon. You have earned the following rewards: 1 gold core, 9 blue cores, your choice of one weapon or piece of armor from the Arsenal of the Mad Magician, 1000 experience.

The white core changed into a gold orb surrounded by nine blue orbs. I grabbed them and put them in my pouch. When I had them secured, I turned to look back at the workshop, paying more attention to the weapons and armor around me. Since the dungeon hadn't closed when I touched the orb, it must want me to pick my reward from those in the room around me.

As I turned, a large leather-bound book now floated in midair where none had been before. I walked forward and examined the book, finding that I could understand the writing in this one. I idly flipped through a few of the pages. The text described all the weapons and armor around me, explaining what each item did and what it was made from.

I grabbed the book, which let me take it, and then sat down and began to read. There was quite a variety of things to choose from, each weapon and piece of armor having a unique power. There was a sword that could strike three times instead of just once with every fourth attack made. There was an axe that could chop through any type of wood, no matter its strength. There was a spear that could shrink or grow as the wielder desired, a knife that could fly next to its owner and attack independently, armor that could resist various kinds of attacks or make its wearer look like a monster or an inanimate object, and so much more.

Toward the back of the book, I found plate armor that would allow the wearer to breathe underwater, which seemed ironic since the armor was so heavy that anyone who wore it would sink immediately and probably never be able to swim to the surface again. I found leather armor studded with metal plates that allowed a person to live without food for a month at a time, a helm that let a person perceive ghosts, and many other things like that.

I wasn't sure what exactly I needed since my revolver was more powerful than most of the weapons I could choose from here. The different armors were interesting, but my reinforced clothing was already effective against piercing weapons, and nothing the gnome had created would stop the kind of blunt damage that I had taken from the golem.

Toward the end of the book, I found a pair of gloves that stood out to me.

Gloves of Golem Strength. When making an unarmed strike, gain the strength of the golems. Your strength is magnified 10 times and you take no damage from striking a stronger object. This item has a cooldown of one minute per hand.

It wasn't particularly useful, but when I found the gloves tucked in a drawer of the gnome's desk, they fit me perfectly and were made of fine leather, which meant they wouldn't interfere with my current weapons. The effect could be useful if something got too close for me to use my revolver or grenades on, and the strength magnification was based on my actual body, which meant the attack would scale extremely well.

After trying on the gloves, I decided to take them. I could have picked some powerful sword or a suit of armor that probably could have sold for a significant amount, but ultimately, the gloves provided another tool that might help keep me alive and covered one of my weaknesses, giving me a powerful attack against anything that got too close.

When I made my decision, I felt the dungeon lurch around me, and I found myself standing outside once again. I stumbled forward, almost tripping down the stairs that led into the basement I had been walking down when I entered the dungeon.

Catching myself, I continued down into the now-revealed basement, finding more iron, some coal, and numerous other supplies for running the foundry. I searched around but didn't find anything particularly valuable, just more supplies.

Back up top, I saw the sun had barely moved again. I still had an entire day ahead of me, and now I was a gold orb and nine blue orbs richer. Not to mention the gloves and the large amount of experience. It seemed that running dungeons was the key to advancing around here, and I planned to take full advantage of them while I could.

On my way back to my villa, I stopped next to a partially collapsed stone home and casually punched the wall, willing my new glove to activate. An image of a golem's stone fist from the dungeon superimposed itself over my own fist for a second before my hand crashed through the wall of stone, shattering it in a single blow, sending chunks as big as my head flying into the house. Shards of stone flew backward, cutting me slightly where my skin wasn't covered by my clothing. After a second, the rest of the wall collapsed, the roof of the home partially collapsing around me with it. I stepped back hastily, surprised by the power of the gloves.

When the dust settled, what had been a more or less intact stone wall was toppled, and chunks of stone had destroyed the interior of the home where they had been sent flying at high speeds by my punch.

"Well then," I said, looking down at the gloves. I would need to be careful with these things if I didn't want to attract the wrong kind of attention or end up hurting someone I didn't intend to hurt. They amplified my current strength ten times, which, according to Momma Lena, was actually the equivalent of a thirteen, making me over twice as strong as a normal human. Multiply the strength of two men by another ten times and, well, the results spoke for themselves, I supposed.

Eyeing the partially collapsed home in front of me one more time, I turned and made my way back to my villa. I really needed to be quieter in the silent city. It was too easy for sound to carry, and now I knew I had made at least one enemy out there.

Back home, I settled into my room, ate a quick meal, and drank the rest of my water, settling onto the hard floor to rest while my nanobots finished healing my bruised body.

Chapter 15

For the first time in my life, I didn't wake up from a nightmare. I slept through the night, my exhausted body greedily drinking up the rest I gave it. When I did finally wake, it was already late morning. I had slept for almost ten hours. I carefully felt my ribs, finding only a few sore spots remained from the beating I had taken the day before.

I felt hungry, which told me my nanobots had worked hard all night. I ate a large portion of the dried fish I had bought, then refilled my canteen in the courtyard and drank my fill.

Once my stomach was settled, I relaxed, just sitting in the courtyard and enjoying feeling rested and recovered. The silence of the city around me was becoming comforting. It allowed me to hear further, telling me that I was safe when I didn't hear anything nearby. I closed my eyes, sitting next to the cistern in the middle of the courtyard, feeling the sun gently warm my skin. I felt grateful to be alive and grateful to have a body. Sitting still and just *existing* wasn't something I had been capable of doing before. I was always running a million different tasks, hundreds of thoughts a second spinning through my head, my perspective split through numerous cameras, audio pickups, or digital streams.

Now . . . I just sat. I breathed in and out. I felt the aches in my body fading more and more as I relaxed. My mind also felt better as I took the time to stop and center myself for once since coming to this world.

The momentary peace couldn't last forever, my mind eventually thinking of my various goals and bringing me back to the present. I stood, shaking my body out with a sigh. I couldn't afford to stop now. I still had a lot to do, but taking some time for myself felt good.

I decided, since my ribs were still slightly sore, to take it easy for today. I would go explore the two locations Nikephoros had mentioned that might have bosses above ground and would avoid another dungeon for now. My nanobots had replenished my bullets overnight while they worked on healing me at the same time, so I loaded up my belongings and headed out into the city.

I moved quietly, as usual, and kept an eye out for any priests that might have come investigating the destruction from yesterday. The forum that Nikephoros had mentioned was close to Perama, the bridge city, so I made my way there first. I didn't see anyone as I traveled, and I avoided the smaller monsters that roamed the city, deeming them not worth the time and bullets any longer. It was amazing how fast I had outgrown the smaller monsters, which had almost killed me several times when I first arrived here.

The forum was about what I had expected. It was a large open plaza surrounded by what used to be shops and merchants' homes. The wreckage of carts, stalls, and other debris littered the entire forum, making it look more like a junkyard than a plaza.

Scurrying through the wreckage were a number of dire rats. Not wanting to draw their interest, I entered a nearby house and found a window that looked out over the plaza. Once there, I saw that a large number of dire rats had infested the area. I could also see a number of sub-bosses, and after watching for several minutes, I spotted the telltale golden glow of a boss near the center of the plaza.

I considered the best way to approach the problem. I didn't want to attract too much attention because I could easily get swarmed by the hundred or more rats infesting the place. I could just sit up here and lay down *Explosive Bullets* across the entire square, but the sound of so many explosions was sure to attract unwanted attention. After thinking it over, I decided caution was the best approach.

I drew my firearm and aimed at the nearest sub-boss I could find. It was busy rooting through some trash nearby, even though I was pretty sure the entire area had been scavenged thoroughly already by the numerous rats. I took aim and shot the glowing blue sub-boss from the window, ducking down as soon as I fired.

I waited a moment and then peeked my head above the windowsill, checking to see what had happened. My shot had hit the dire rat, killing it instantly. A few of the nearby rats had scurried over to investigate, but after a moment of finding nothing dangerous nearby, they soon lost interest and went back to whatever they had been doing.

I picked off several more sub-bosses that were in range before moving to another building around the plaza, where I continued to pick off the more valuable sub-bosses.

I couldn't find a vantage point close enough to the golden boss to get a good shot at it, so I had to be a bit more daring than I had originally hoped. I scouted around the outskirts of the plaza until I came across the largest concentration of normal rats I could find.

When the rats were as closely packed together as possible, I grabbed a *Confusion Grenade* from my bandolier and tossed it into the middle of the rats. The grenade did not disappoint. It replicated itself and collided with a number of rats, instantly turning them against their brethren. I noticed that several of the grenades had hit two or more rats, spreading the confusion even further. The rats that had been hit went mad, screeching and attacking anything that moved nearby. The non-confused rats reacted to the attacks with violence of their own and didn't seem to know who was friend or foe, which caused even more confusion.

The sound of fighting got louder and louder as more rats were drawn into the mess of quarreling rats, the new rats unsure of what was happening. When they came to investigate, they ended up being attacked as well and were driven into a maddened rage like the rest of the rats. I tossed another *Confusion Grenade* into the mess, just to spread even more chaos and confusion.

Once the pile of rats was sufficiently distracted, I ran out of hiding and moved around the outer perimeter of the plaza, avoiding getting too close to the frenzied battle. I saw the golden boss perched on an old, mostly intact food cart as it watched the lesser rats brutally kill each other across the plaza. I hastily hid behind a pile of junk and ran, crouching down, to get closer to the boss. I stopped when I was close enough to guarantee I could hit the boss and fired one *Penetration Bullet* as it stood on its hind legs, staring in confusion at its minions killing themselves. My first bullet flew true, spinning the rat around and throwing it from the cart to land on the cobblestones of the plaza. I stood to get a better angle and fired at the boss again. My bullet caught the rat as it was trying to right its body, sending it rolling across the plaza. Blood sprayed from its body with every rotation.

I watched, waiting to see if the boss tried to move once more. When a moment passed and the only movement near the boss was a growing pile of blood leaking across the cobblestones, I stood and approached. As I walked toward its body, a gold core began to form above its body, so I knew I had killed it. I grabbed the core and put it in my pouch, reloaded my revolver, and ducked back down behind some more refuse to conceal myself better.

I made my way around the outside of the plaza again, keeping as many obstacles as possible between myself and the rats that were still fighting. I ran to the sub-bosses I had killed and grabbed the blue orbs that had formed above their bodies before returning to safety in a nearby building.

By the time I was done gathering the blue orbs, the mass of rats was starting to calm down. Either the confusion had worn off or most of the rats were dead or dying. I didn't care to check. I found a back door in the building I was hiding in and left through it, leaving whatever rats had managed to survive none the wiser about what had happened to them or their once-glorious rat leader.

When I was a few streets away, the notifications began to roll in. I was pleasantly surprised to learn I had received experience for the rats killed by the confusion effect; I received over a hundred experience for the boss, sub-bosses, and the lesser rats combined.

That brought my total, after the last dungeon, up to 2951.

The next place on my list was the Hippodrome, which was close to the priests' enclave. When I got near, I entered one of the taller buildings to scout the location and saw a number of priests in the streets around the Hippodrome. I decided it wasn't worth the risk to approach any closer. The Hippodrome itself was impressive, a large open field ringed by stone seats in the middle of the city. It was the size of a football field, if not larger, and seemed especially big compared to the busy, closely packed city that surrounded it. From the top level of the building I was in, I had a pretty good view inside the Hippodrome and couldn't see any monsters. Given its location close to the priests, I guessed they must have killed the monsters inside some time ago and kept it clear these days or hunted the monsters inside for experience.

Either way, the Hippodrome was a bust.

I watched the priests' enclave for a while before leaving. They did not have thick walls to protect themselves like the other enclaves did. Instead, I could see a shimmering shield that enveloped their enclave, warping and distorting the air around the enclave as if I was looking through a haze of heat at the priests below. From what I could gather from watching the area, the temples inside seemed immaculate and well-maintained. The courtyards around them were full of flourishing, ripe gardens, and a number of large trees rose above even the massive temples.

The enclave was packed with people, almost as many as I had seen on the streets of Sycae. Priests worked on the grounds of the various temples, were chatting in groups, or were attending lectures on the grounds as if they were ancient philosophers uncovering the secrets of the universe. For all I knew, maybe they were.

I couldn't see what was making the shield that protected the enclave, but I was very curious to find out more about it and see if I could use something like that to keep myself safe here in the city. Maybe it was some kind of advanced enchantment that I could learn. I didn't see anyone actively maintaining a spell over the area, so I didn't think it was a class skill, unless the priests were doing that in the temples where I couldn't see them, which was entirely possible.

Either way, there was nothing here for me. I exited the building and left the area swiftly. By the time I was back in my villa, the sky was hinting that night would come soon, so I just settled into my room and waited for the sun to set.

With my rewards from the dungeons and the bosses I had killed in the city itself, I could actually afford to buy the *Archer* class right now. I had eight gold orbs and fifty-five blue orbs, and each gold orb was worth twenty blue orbs, bringing me to the equivalent of 215 blue orbs. I still had to wait for Momma Lena to craft the book for me, so even though I could afford it now, it would be weeks before I could buy it. I considered trying to find a class crafter in another enclave but figured they would probably be just as expensive and higher risk to contact, so it was better to just wait. Regardless, I had greater plans than just getting a single class, and I still hadn't seen what I could buy in Sycae, the merchant enclave. I needed to gather as much wealth as I could.

Plus, if I was being honest with myself, I was enjoying the dungeons. They were strange, dangerous, and challenging, but they were reminiscent of some of the happiest times playing games in my prior life with Michael. They were also a sign of how different this world was from the ordinary world I had come from. They were truly magical and strange, an entire world contained inside a single portal, with branching narratives and multiple paths to achieve the goal of completing the dungeon. And the rewards were top-notch, giving me more experience and wealth than a month of hunting on the surface.

I spent the night resting once again, making sure my body was in perfect condition for the next day. When the sun rose, I left early and began a search of the area around my villa to find any nearby dungeons that I could explore. If I completed some of the dungeons near where I was sleeping, it might also make it safer to stay here, reducing the number of monsters that spawned nearby when night fell.

The first dungeon I found wasn't actually in a basement but instead had formed in a crack that split the side of a building and its cellar. The entire crack was filled with the absolute darkness I was starting to recognize as the entrance to a dungeon. It was just down the street from the villa I was staying in.

When I squeezed into the crack, I found myself standing in perfect darkness. I wondered if I had been wrong about the crack being a dungeon for a moment, but I heard a faint scratching against stone somewhere around me, which told me I wasn't back in the city any longer. I listened more and noticed the sound of dripping water nearby. I also heard a faint whistle as the air blew past me, as if I was in a tunnel now.

I crouched, reaching down with my hands to feel the area around me. The ground beneath me was rough and unworked. Pebbles and other small stones were everywhere, and the floor was uneven, as if naturally formed. Not hearing anything in my immediate area, I decided to risk making a little light. I reached into the pouch where I had secured the *Light* orb I had made the other day.

I didn't unveil it completely, just unwrapping enough to cast the faintest of light around me. That was enough for me to see where I was, and I confirmed that I was indeed underground, standing in a cave of some kind. Stalagmites and stalactites were all around me. Moisture dripped down them and formed small puddles that plinked and plopped with every drop, echoing around the small cave. In front of me was a rough path through the middle of the cave, leading downward at a slight angle.

I raised my *Light* orb above my head and scanned the roof of the cave, freezing as the light illuminated the ceiling enough for me to see what was waiting above me. The entire ceiling was full of large black bats. They were unusually large, the size of a fully grown dog at least. They were asleep, hanging upside down and seemingly unaware of my presence so far.

I swallowed as I started trying to count them, but I quickly gave up. There were thousands in sight, and that was just a small part of the cave I stood in. If the entire cave had a similar number, it would amount to . . . hundreds of thousands, at least. If not more.

I was lucky my light hadn't disturbed them. I considered putting it away, but without it, even my genetically modified eyes couldn't see in the absolute darkness. If I stumbled or fell, I was sure to wake the bats above me. I slowly lowered my arm, keeping the *Light* orb unveiled but covered as it had been.

I looked around me, trying to figure out the best way forward. Even with *Explosive Bullets* and my new *Multi-Bullet*, the chance that I could kill so many bats was pretty slim. There were just too many and they would swarm me once they saw me as a threat, getting too close for me to effectively use my bullets or grenades.

I crouched carefully, playing my light over the ground. The path forward was uneven, covered in the pebbles and loose stones I had felt when I explored the ground around me with my hands. It would be dangerous ground to cover, a single stumble enough to doom me. I would have to be extremely careful.

I stood and took a cautious step forward, making sure my foot was absolutely secure before putting any weight on it. I very carefully brushed my foot back and forth, clearing the pebbles from under my feet so they wouldn't make a sound when I stepped. Once I felt sure it was safe, I shifted my weight forward, taking a single step.

One of the benefits of being born as an artificial intelligence was that I had spent the majority of my life performing mundane, repetitive tasks. It was fair to say that my patience was inhuman in the truest sense of the word. While I was in the body of a human, part of me was still not quite human.

Whereas most humans faced with this situation would likely tire or become impatient, leading to a deadly mistake, I slowly took one step after another, never shifting my weight until I was absolutely sure I wouldn't make a sound. I never rushed. I never placed a foot wrong. I never lost focus or grew too tired to pay attention. Slowly, painstakingly slowly, I made my way deeper down the tunnel.

Time was hard to judge as I moved. I stopped to rest my legs every so often. I would sit very slowly in a clear area of the tunnel, barely relaxing my body but giving my legs a chance to refresh themselves. I didn't dare unstrap my backpack to take a drink of water in case it made too much noise, so I sat there until I felt like my legs were ready to move again.

Hours passed before I reached a large cavern where a larger sub-boss hung from the ceiling, surrounded by hundreds of other bats. I ignored the sub-boss, proceeding carefully through the cavern and down the tunnel on the far side.

My rests became longer and my body started to tire, but I refused to let the exhaustion cloud my mind. Every step was just as important as the last. A single sound in here would get me killed, and I refused to die in such horrible circumstances.

I passed through another sub-boss's room, ignoring it just like I had ignored the first. The tunnel began to slope downward more steeply, making my footing even more precarious, but not once did I let myself place an unsure step.

Finally, after untold hours in the dark, I entered the largest cavern I had been in so far. Across the room, I saw a dimly glowing white light. The dungeon core. I looked at the ceiling and saw an enormous bat hanging fifty feet above the ground. Hundreds of smaller bats, many of them sub-bosses themselves, rested around the boss. I stared at the boss, my mind telling me there was something especially odd about it. A moment later, my breath caught in my throat as I realized the boss wasn't glowing golden. It was glowing purple.

Purple, the color that a monster even more powerful than the golden bosses glowed, something that hadn't been seen in years in Nova Roma.

The rewards for killing such a boss had to be astronomical. I didn't even know what a purple core would sell for, but I was sure it would be enough to make me rich. I felt an insane impulse to try to kill the boss, my vision flicking between the purple glow of the boss and the soft white light of the dungeon core that would let me escape.

I tried to imagine how I would fight the boss. I would open with five *Explosive Bullets*, followed immediately by some *Confusion Grenades* to keep the other bats distracted while I reloaded. I would switch to *Penetration Bullets*, hoping to take down the purple boss, while I tossed grenades at the other bats. Then it would just be a matter of who died first, me or them.

The problem with the plan was that I had no idea if my weapons could even hurt the purple boss. I knew already that the golden bosses were tougher to kill than the blue sub-bosses. A blue sub-boss could be killed with a single bullet, while the golden ones took five to ten bullets, if not more. So if a golden boss was ten times more powerful than a blue boss, assuming the worst-case scenario, then was a purple boss ten times more powerful than a golden boss? Would it take me a hundred bullets to kill the purple boss? Or would my bullets literally do nothing, the hide of the beast too strong?

Shaking my head, I tamped down the part of me that wanted to take the risk anyway. There were just too many unknowns. With a last, regretful look upward at the purple boss, I walked over and grabbed the white dungeon core.

Congratulations, you have completed this dungeon. You have earned the following rewards: Skill Stone: Stealth, 500 experience.

The room around me disappeared, and I found myself standing just inside the crack in the foundations of the house near my villa. I let out a relieved sigh. That was too close. I could have easily died in that dungeon if I had been even slightly less careful. How was a normal person supposed to complete a dungeon like that? Maybe if they had a team of skilled people working together, they could fight their way through the cave, but it would be a war of attrition, and they would have to fight for every step they took.

Even with my enhanced body, I felt exhausted. I began to walk back to my villa, examining the skill stone I had received from the dungeon. It was about the size of my hand and made of marble. Carved on it was a nondescript person crouching down as if hiding from someone.

I might not have maximized my rewards from the dungeon, but I had received my first skill stone. I was happy enough with the victory, even though a part of me had wished to try my luck with the final boss. I had still received a skill stone, clearly given to me for the way I managed to defeat the dungeon. I didn't even think of selling the skill, since such a skill was very useful for me. I just had to figure out how to absorb it so I could start using it to help me survive in the city.

As I thought about how to absorb it, I felt a pull from the stone as if an invisible cord was stretched between the stone and my chest, tugging at me. I moved the stone closer to me, and it began to glow with a faint white light. I continued to move the skill stone closer and closer until it touched my chest. As soon as it did, the stone disappeared.

I felt the skill absorb into me and enter my body with a slight chill. My mind raced, absorbing information like I was back on my Earth and downloading knowledge, except this time, it wasn't just hypothetical. It was like I had always known how to move stealthily, how to hide in the shadows around me, how to mask my scent and cover my trail as I traveled.

I knew what the skill would do for me as well. It wasn't just moving silently; it was like a more powerful version of my cloak. Whenever I activated the skill, people would be less-inclined to notice me. I would blend into my surroundings better. My steps would be quieter, my scent muted. It wasn't actual invisibility, but it was definitely supernatural.

I had gained both knowledge of how to move more stealthily and a supernatural enhancement to those skills. And I just knew, on an instinctive level, how to activate the skill now. I just had to think about activating *Stealth* and the skill would turn on instantly.

Exhausted, I returned to my villa and rested for the rest of the day. I was too tired to risk another dungeon and I still didn't dare risk going out at night, so I had to wait until tomorrow to try another one.

My search for dungeons continued the next day. I found another one in the garden of a nearby home. What once might have been a burrow for an animal had been widened and turned into a tunnel leading under the garden. Halfway down the burrow, it turned unnaturally dark, indicating the presence of another dungeon.

I crawled into the burrow and found myself standing amidst a beautiful forest. The sounds of birds, something completely missing from the dead city, enveloped me. The sun broke through gaps in the trees, illuminating the beauty around me, and a fresh breeze blew over me, bringing the intoxicating smells of spring to my nose.

I stared in admiration at the gorgeous forest when suddenly one of the trees in front of me moved in a way that seemed unnatural, twisting against the wind instead of blowing with the breeze. I froze, staring at the tree, trying to figure out what exactly had caught my eye. It looked like a completely normal tree now. Had I imagined that it moved oddly?

I ran through my knowledge of fantastical creatures from my world and found one that might be a match for what was in front of me. I took out my *Penetration Bullets* and switched over to my *Explosive Bullets*, uncaring if the bullets ended up being overkill.

Rather than wait to be ambushed when I tried to pass through the forest, I fired an *Explosive Shot* at the tree that had caught my eye. The bullet flew true, striking the tree in the middle of its trunk, and then exploded. In a split second, flames blanketed the tree, spreading rapidly to its boughs, where its leaves immediately caught on fire. An inhuman scream rang out, the sound like a massive log being twisted slowly. It cracked and squealed until it shattered into a thousand pieces. The sound was so eerie it sent chills down my spine. The roots of the tree began to pull themselves out of the ground as it tried to escape the flames, but there was no way it was escaping the fire now.

I watched as the tree tried and failed to save itself, burning rapidly until it keeled over. It crashed into the other trees nearby, causing a small forest fire. It screamed the entire time, only going silent when it finally fell over. I would have felt worse for the creature if I wasn't sure it had been planning to attack me the moment I got too close, and the fact that its screams were something from a horror story clued me in that the creature was probably not very friendly.

The rest of the dungeon was just as easy. The tree creatures were no match for my *Explosive Bullets*. Even the sub-bosses and boss that I encountered at the end of the dungeon were so flammable the dungeon was practically a walk in the park. A single *Explosive Bullet* was enough to kill anything that moved, even the boss. The sounds of their horrific screams haunted me as I gratefully grabbed the dungeon core and escaped as fast as I could.

I was rewarded with a gold orb, eleven blue orbs, and one thousand experience. No perk, skill, or item, but that was fine. It was still a small fortune, and the experience was as great as usual. And all it cost me was a moderate number of *Explosive Bullets* and a new sound that I was sure was going to form the basis of my next nightmare.

Chapter 16

I spent the next couple of weeks farming the dungeons near my villa. I didn't find quite as many as I hoped, but I didn't want to travel too far in case I ended up injured in a dungeon and was stuck in a part of the city I was unfamiliar with, unable to take shelter before night fell. Despite that limitation, I found a total of ten dungeons just in the vicinity of my villa, which was a considerable number when you compared that to the rest of the city. If I extrapolated the number in just this small area, I calculated there had to be thousands of dungeons spread throughout the city. No wonder it was so overrun.

I suffered a few injuries in the dungeons. My worst injury came from a fire-spewing lizard that caught me in its flames when it ambushed me. I managed to kill it and finish the jungle, but it took several days of rest to heal the many burns that covered my body. The rest of the dungeons only gave me scrapes and cuts, nothing that my nanobots couldn't heal overnight. I always took time to heal, never pushing myself to do more than a single dungeon in a day.

The tenth dungeon I had found near my villa was an underground mine populated by a swarm of goblins. The goblins were busy mining metal from the walls of the tunnels, and rather than use my revolver to kill them, I practiced using my *Stealth* skill and my knife to dispatch the goblins by sneaking up on them and killing them before they knew I was there. It was surprisingly effective, partly because of my skill, partly because of my cloak, partly because of how rapidly and silently my body could move, and partly because the sounds of the goblins mining made it extremely easy to catch them unaware.

When I killed the final goblin and collected the orbs from the dungeon core, I was transported out of the dungeon and was met with a surprise announcement.

Congratulations, you have earned the achievement Dangerous Dungeoneering. For completing ten dungeons by yourself and without a class, you have been rewarded. You receive +2 to all attributes, and rewards from all future dungeons are increased slightly.

"Wow," I said, examining the achievement in my head. Nobody had told me that achievements were possible. Did nobody know because most of them had been claimed already? Or was everyone just hoarding the information, hoping to unlock the achievements for themselves? An attribute boost was significant, especially +2 to every attribute. And an increased chance to receive better loot from dungeons? That was amazing.

I made my way back home, my mind awhirl with the possibilities. The villa was looking nicer than when I first moved in. I had spent my downtime—while I was recovering from my injuries or just waiting and recovering after a dungeon run—cleaning up and mending the house. I had found a workable bed and some sheets and blankets that I had my nanobots clean and repair, so now I was sleeping in a bed like a normal person. I still didn't need to sleep most nights, but when I did, it was a more enjoyable experience than sleeping on the floor like I had been doing.

I traded with Asylaion a few more times to get some better food than just dried fish. I enjoyed having a more varied diet, the different foods enjoyable to my body's palate. I still wanted to protect my villa from monsters at night, but until I found a way to do that, I just stayed inside and hid through the night as usual. I was feeling confident in completing the dungeons now, but the number of monsters that came out at night was still just too much of a risk.

I stopped in the courtyard of my villa to test my new attributes. If what Momma Lena had told me was true, a +2 to my attributes wouldn't seem like much to a normal person but would actually be a significant power increase for me. A +2 should be the equivalent of +20% to the original strength and speed of my body. If Momma Lena was right, I had a base coordination that was the equivalent of a human who had enhanced their coordination to a score of sixteen. That meant now that I had a +2 to my coordination, I should be as fast as a human with a coordination of twenty-four.

This meant someone would have to have a coordination of at least twenty-four to match me in speed and hand-eye coordination. That seemed high to me.

I ran a series of tests, jumping up and down as high as I could go, sprinting across the courtyard at my top speed, tossing pebbles at various locations around the courtyard to test my hand-eye coordination, and so on. I realized I should have created a baseline before receiving any attribute enhancements to properly measure my growth, but I hadn't exactly expected to receive an achievement for running ten dungeons by myself and without a class.

Even without a baseline to compare against, I had a good sense of my new physical attributes and how much had changed from receiving +2 to each of them. First, I was significantly faster. I was now able to draw and reload my firearm at an almost supernatural speed. I didn't fumble my revolver, even though I was moving so much faster than I could even an hour ago. Instead, the new speed felt completely natural, my body instantly able to adapt to the changes and apply my muscle memory to my new speed.

The second change I noticed was that I could now sprint faster than the fastest human on Earth. I could probably outrun most vehicles on a city street, and my endurance was so good I could keep that pace for hours without needing a rest.

And my strength was, frankly, absurd. I could lift a hundred pounds over my head without breaking a sweat. I practiced by lifting large blocks of broken stone, easily maneuvering the stone over my head and lifting it up and down with no issues. I couldn't do anything about the mass of the stone, though, so I had to be careful to not let it pull me off-center. Otherwise, I wouldn't be able to recover; the stone would overbalance me and make me drop it if I wasn't careful.

Finally, I could now leap almost fifteen feet high from a dead stop. I practiced jumping to the railings of a balcony of my villa, then to the roof. With just a few steps of leadup, I could leap to the railing with ease and then launch myself from the railing directly onto the roof, where I could balance on the tiles with perfect dexterity. I suddenly understood why the other scavengers traveled by rooftop; if they had attributes like these, it was significantly faster and safer to just leap across the roofs, avoiding the cluttered and dangerous streets below.

For over two weeks of clearing dungeons, I had accrued ten more gold orbs and thirty-seven blue orbs. I had received a whopping 7500 experience, bringing my total to 11,848. And I had received another perk, this one from a dungeon full of small islands with dangerous shark-infested waters between them. My revolver sort of worked underwater, since it didn't require gunpowder, but it had significantly less power. I completed the dungeon mostly by outswimming the sharks—my body could power through the water fast enough to avoid them—and if any came too close, I scared them away with a few shots of my revolver. It wasn't enough to kill them, but it deterred them enough for me to put some distance between me and them. The islands themselves were covered in swarms of praying-mantis-like insects the size of a small child, which were easy enough to kill since they traveled in swarms that were especially vulnerable to an *Explosive Bullet* or two. When I reached the last island and touched the white dungeon core, I was rewarded with a new perk.

Perk obtained: Swimmer's Body. The length of time that you can hold your breath is doubled, you have improved eyesight underwater, and water restricts you less when you are moving through it.

The perk, much like the other one I had received, wasn't particularly useful but wasn't a bad thing to have either. It was interesting how each perk seemed to be tailored to how I completed a particular dungeon. I was pretty sure I had received this particular perk because I outswam the sharks without killing them, much like my *Captain's Command* perk was likely awarded because I sided with the captain who had the ability to inspire his sailors by giving them commands.

Other than those rewards, I had received some basic magical armor that wasn't worth wearing. I sold it to Asylaion for two blue orbs. He didn't ask where I had gotten it. Although I could tell he was dying to know, I didn't want to tell him I had been clearing dungeons, so I avoided his questioning gaze.

It was a fruitful week. Not just from completing the dungeons, but also from spending more time around my villa, simply recovering and spending time in my body. I felt more centered as each day passed. The conflict between my mind and body slowly began to fade as I took the time to relax and take pleasure in just being alive. By the time I was ready to return to Perama to buy my first class, despite all the dangers I had faced and the injuries I had suffered in the dungeons, I felt healthier in mind and body than I had ever felt before.

Chapter 17

I left early the next morning and rushed over to Perama. Once I was let in through the gate, I looked for Constans but didn't see her. I must have arrived too early or she was guiding someone else. I hoped she was doing well and staying safe.

My memory was good enough that I could find my way to Momma Lena's place without her, but I had wanted to hire her just because I enjoyed her company and wanted to help her out. But since she wasn't around, I just walked myself over to Momma Lena's. This early in the morning, out on the streets were a few unsavory types I hadn't seen the last time I was here. They looked mainly like drunks still working off their buzz from the night before or street toughs looking for vulnerable marks before the shops opened for the day. I avoided them easily by activating *Stealth* and sneaking right past them, the darkened streets making it easy to get by without being seen. Like I had done with the goblins, I could have easily snuck up on them and slit their throats before they had any clue I was there, but I restrained myself. They weren't worth the trouble.

Momma Lena's wasn't open when I arrived, so I leaned against the parapet that stopped people from falling off the bridge and watched the water and the land in the distance as the sun finished rising. I could see why Nova Roma had been considered the center of the world for almost a thousand years. It was a beautiful area of the world, and the city had a majesty that was hard to tarnish, even overrun as it was with monsters. I wished that I could have seen it at the height of its power. It would have been even more breathtaking.

Eventually, Momma Lena opened her door behind me and I turned around to greet her.

"Oh," she said, giving me a tired look as she saw me waiting, "look who made it back in one piece. Surprised to see you, honestly. I wasn't sure you'd make it."

I hesitated, unsure of how to reply.

"Never mind," she said, snorting. "Get in here. I have your book ready to go."

"Thanks," I said, grinning shyly at her, afraid she could tell I was as eager as a small child at a candy shop.

I followed her into the shop, and she rooted around in a drawer of her desk until she pulled out a leather-bound tome. She handed it to me.

"It seems a bit much, I know," she said as I took the book and admired the fine leather, "since it will just get destroyed when you learn it, but it turns out such craftsmanship is required to make the book work. Don't ask me why. The gods must not have wanted us to save money or something."

I took out forty blue orbs and eight gold orbs and handed them to her. Her eyebrow rose in surprise at the number of gold orbs I handed her.

"Where did you get these?" she asked, eyeing the gold orbs. "Only the army or the Emperor's people have access to so many gold orbs. I thought you told me you weren't with them."

"I'm not," I said. "I have been lucky with my scavenging in the city, that's all."

She gave me a pinched-face look, clearly thinking I was lying. I could see her debate whether to confront me or not, but after a moment, she sighed.

"Alright," she muttered, turning to put them in her lockbox. "I don't really care. Good doing business with you. I'm too tired in the mornings to worry about who you really are."

"Uh," I said hesitantly. "So how do I learn the class exactly?"

She gave me a look like I was the biggest idiot she had ever seen and then laughed. "I forgot you were so clueless. Maybe you really aren't with the Emperor."

I tried to smile innocently at her but she just snorted at me, some of her good cheer returning to her face.

"Just read the book," she said, pointing at the book. "It will do the rest. That will unlock the class for you. You start at level zero like with any other class. You have to earn at least one hundred experience to level it to level one. Once you have done that, you unlock your first skill. Pick wisely. And remember, for you, don't pick a magical skill."

"How will I know which ones are magical?"

"You'll be able to tell when you examine them," she said. "You'll feel the difference."

"What do you mean? It seems like some of the skills that are physical still have some kind of magic to them. How will I know which ones are really physical if they are all magical in some way?"

"Nah, it doesn't work that way," she replied, shaking her head. "It's true that physical skills are still magical in nature, but the magic is drawn from the world itself and based on your physical attributes. Magical skills draw from your own mana and depend on your magical attributes. They are similar, and truly, you can do some very magical things that seem beyond the realm of the possible with physical skills, but they technically aren't magical since they don't draw from your mana to power them. Don't stress too much about it. Thinking about why it all works the way it does just causes headaches. Trust me."

"Do you know how much experience is required to level a class? I forgot to ask you last time."

"Sure. That's an easy one. It's one hundred experience for every level. So level 1 requires one hundred experience, level 2 is two hundred experience, and so on. The prior level's experience does not count toward the requirements of the next level, so when you want to get to level 2, you need two hundred experience all over again. The one hundred you spent to get to level 1 is essentially gone."

"Ah," I said, "that makes sense. Thank you."

I tucked the book away in my backpack and thanked her again, bowing slightly. She gave me a strained smile and then turned back to start her day's work, but I realized I had one more question before I left.

"Sorry, one more thing before I go. Do you know where I might be able to get an *Enchanter* class?"

She turned back to me with a raised eyebrow. "Enchanting already, eh? Do you know how expensive that profession is? Only the richest of craftsmen pursue that class. Just to unlock level 1, you have to enchant a hundred items. The cost in orbs only goes up from there."

"I figured it was expensive," I told her, shrugging, "but still, I was hoping to buy the class."

"Hmmm," she said. I saw her eyes slide down to the lockbox where she kept all the orbs I had just given her. "Well, you can pay an enchanter to teach you the class directly, although most of them don't have the time, unless you pay well for their time. The best way is likely to travel over to Sycae and see if one of their non-combat class crafters has unlocked the skill for it or see if you can get it through the trade caravans, although that is more costly as well. Most of our enchanters here indentured themselves to another enchanter for years to learn the class, but I don't think that is something you want to do."

"Ah, okay. Thank you," I said, shaking my head at the idea of indenturing myself. "I'll look into it."

"You'll also need to learn how to enchant, just to get your first level. You start with no experience and need one hundred experience to get your first skill, just like with a combat class. Nobody can teach you how to do that except another enchanter. So if you buy the class without someone to teach you more than the basics learning the class will teach you, you can get stuck never being able to get one hundred experience to get your first skill. And I have heard it is very dangerous to try enchanting without a proper teacher, even with the basics of the class from a skill book."

She looked at me like she was sure I was going to go try it on my own no matter what she told me, which was a bit too close to exactly what I was thinking.

I said my goodbyes and left her shop before she could figure me out any more than she already had. Even grumpier from waking up early, she was too insightful for my comfort.

Outside, the streets were still relatively empty, so I made my way out of the enclave and back to my villa with no problems. Thanks to the +2 I had received to all of my attributes, I could move a lot quicker through the city while still maintaining my *Stealth* and avoiding the daytime monsters. I hadn't taken to traveling over the rooftops quite yet, afraid I might draw too much attention to myself up there, but even running through the streets, I was so fast I could make it to Perama and back before the sun had reached noon in the sky.

Once safely ensconced back in my villa, I got comfortable in the center of my courtyard and opened the book, excitement coursing through me at the prospect of learning a real class.

As I started to read, the words in front of me blurred and I couldn't look away from the book. It was like I was reading, but also dreaming. Knowledge filled me. Much of it was murky and unclear, but I could still feel the knowledge entering my brain, ready to be called upon at a later date when I had unlocked the knowledge. I could feel traces of knowledge about hunting, tracking prey, and using a bow, sling, throwing weapons, and other ranged weapons. I gained traces of knowledge about the way to calculate wind resistance, the way to judge distance for extending my shots, and many other, more esoteric things that could assist with any form of ranged combat. As soon as I felt like I understood the concept, it blurred in my mind and then disappeared, leaving only a vague impression of its passing.

When I looked up from the book, it was midday and the sun was beating down on me. My body was warm and covered in sweat. My mind felt raw, as if it had been plugged into a computer console and had entire books downloaded directly into it with no filter or restraint. I closed the book, and it disappeared in front of me as if it had never existed.

Class unlocked: Archer.

Pooled experience detected. Experience applied to your Archer class.

I felt a rush of energy escape me as if it had been sucked into a funnel inside of my body. It wasn't an unpleasant sensation, but strange. I had 11,848 pooled experience, so the sensation lasted for a long time. Once it was done, I was assaulted with a number of announcements in my head.

Congratulations, you have received enough experience to level your Archer class. You are now level 1.

Congratulations, you have received enough experience to level your Archer class. You are now level 2.

Congratulations, you have received enough experience to level your Archer class. You are now level 3.

Congratulations, you have received enough experience to level your Archer class. You are now level 4.

Congratulations, you have received enough experience to level your Archer class. You are now level 5.

Congratulations, you have received enough experience to level your Archer class. You are now level 6.

The announcements continued until I reached level 14. That many levels took 10,500 experience, leaving me with only 1348 experience and needing 1500 for the next level.

Please choose a level 1 class skill:

Penetrating Shot: Fire a shot that penetrates deep into an enemy, bypassing most armor.

Arcane Shot: Power up an arcane shot that does magical damage.

Split Shot: Your shot splits into multiple projectiles that strike additional nearby targets.

Dash: Dash through the air, ignoring wind resistance until you land.

Hunter's Mark: Target one enemy. You will be able to track and find this enemy anywhere it goes until you remove the mark or the enemy dies.

I reviewed the skills carefully. As Momma Lena had said, I could tell that *Arcane Shot* and *Split Shot* both scaled off of magical power. Somewhere inside my brain, knowledge from learning the class told me exactly how the damage from *Arcane Shot* scaled off the magic power attribute, as did the number of projectiles a person could make with *Split Shot. Hunter's Mark* didn't appear to scale at all; it was simply a tracking tool.

Dash and *Penetrating Shot* scaled off physical attributes. I knew that *Penetrating Shot* would penetrate more armor and potentially even pass through enemies, the power of its penetration going up based on the person's strength and coordination attribute. *Dash* was similar, allowing for a longer dash based on a person's strength and coordination. The stronger I was, the further I could travel, while the more coordination I had, the faster I moved during the dash.

I already had the ability to penetrate most enemies, since my *Penetration Bullets* were so powerful, although it was clear there were plenty of enemies that could resist even my bullets. I just

199

didn't want to specialize so much into penetrative attacks that I became vulnerable to another type of enemy and my bullets were enough to give me a leg up over most heavily armored enemies, even if they weren't perfect. The other abilities were useless or lackluster for me, given they were magical or would only let me track a single person, which I had no need to do at this time. Not seeing a better option, I decided on *Dash*. It would allow me to put distance between myself and enemies if needed or close the gap if I needed to get in melee range with someone rapidly. It should also allow me to move around the city quicker. Images of me dashing from rooftop to rooftop like the other scavengers could do played through my mind. While more penetration on my bullets would be useful, the flexibility of *Dash* made it more likely to contribute to my overall survival at this time.

Once I selected the skill, I felt a rush of energy enter me just like when I had absorbed the skill stone for *Stealth*.

Skill: Dash learned.
Coordination +1
Coordination +1
Strength +1
Strength + 1
Endurance +1

Announcements of my attribute enhancements rolled through my mind now that I had selected my level 1 skill. I kept track of the changes to my body, interested in measuring the results after gaining so many points in my physical attributes. At level 10, I got another announcement to select a skill.

Please choose a level 10 class skill:
Sneak Shot: Any projectile that strikes an enemy unaware of your presence does significantly more damage.
Seeker Shot: Guide a projectile with your mind.
Death Shot: Launch a projectile that kills anyone struck by the shot unless their endurance is high enough to resist the effect.
Hail of Arrows: Your projectile splits into an overwhelming volley that blankets a chosen area.
Perfect Coordination: Receive a passive boost of 20% to your coordination.

I could tell that *Seeker Shot*, *Death Shot*, and *Hail of Arrows* were all magical-based skills, so I ignored them. That only left me with *Sneak Shot* and *Perfect Coordination*, which was a bit disappointing. *Sneak Shot* would be useful, especially given my *Stealth* skill. At the same time, if I was able to take a shot at someone that was unaware of me, chances were good that I was already going to do significant damage to them with my bullets. The *Sneak Shot* would have limited situational usefulness because of that, ending up being a powerful in some circumstances but useless if I didn't get the first shot at something.

Perfect Coordination was interesting, but I needed to know how it was calculated with my attributes. I pressed on the concept of the skill in my mind, seeking greater information about it. It slowly came to me, as if resisting the level of detail I demanded, but it eventually gave in. The knowledge flooded my mind, and I learned that the bonus from the skill was added after my base physical body and my increased attributes were added together, applying the increased percentage only after calculating my total attribute score. That was significantly higher than if it added the percentage to my base body first, then the attribute enhancements. That made it a more appealing option.

I selected *Perfect Coordination.*

More attribute enhancements rolled in until I hit level 14. In total, I received +6 to coordination, +4 to strength, and +2 to endurance. That made my coordination nine, strength seven, and endurance five. My memory and magical power and magical capacity were all at three, only having a +2 from the achievement I had earned. Despite my magical power and capacity being three, they were still basically zero, though, because zero times three was still zero.

Despite my coordination only being a nine, it was actually the equivalent of a person with a score of thirty now, since my body was around a sixteen originally, plus the nine from my class. The twenty percent increase from my new skill then added another five points on top of that. And if a standard human was around a starting attribute score of one, and each +1 was an increase of approximately twenty-five percent on top of that, then my score of thirty meant I could move eight times faster and be eight times better coordinated than a normal human.

After the attribute enhancements stopped rolling through my head, I tried standing but shot off the ground, my strength and speed unbalancing me and sending me careening wildly into the nearby wall of my villa. I tried to brace myself against the wall but instead slammed my hands against the stone hard enough to feel my wrists sprain slightly from the impact. I groaned in pain as I let my body go limp, collapsing to the ground.

I stopped moving, trying to think of what to do. It was like I was back in my body for the first time, my mind struggling to coordinate the bodily impulses that didn't fully align with my brain. I slowly raised my arms above my head, but moving them felt as if they were controlled from a great distance, like I was trying to move a tiny surgical tool from a mile away. Any small signal I sent to my arm was magnified, causing me to overshoot where I intended to move it and causing the arm to flail wildly when all I intended was a tiny movement.

I stood slowly, like a toddler taking their first steps, carefully bracing myself against the wall. I flexed my legs, moving them slowly and carefully until I was confident they weren't going to send me careening across the courtyard once again. When I felt some measure of control, I began to practice walking, making each step carefully and slowly. I walked around the courtyard, my steps exaggerated and painstakingly slow, like some villain from a silent movie.

By midafternoon, I was finally able to walk normally again. I still had moments of dizziness if I went too fast, but they passed after just a few moments. Time seemed to be moving slower than I was used to, as if the sun was taking longer to rise than it usually did. I felt like I was trapped in molasses, the world around me trapped as well. Only my mind was able to think clearly. Everything was slower, or more likely, my perception and speed had increased so dramatically that everything *seemed* slower to me now.

I spent the rest of the day adapting to my new body, moving slowly around the courtyard, moving my arms and legs in different patterns to regain my sense of balance. If someone had been watching, they would likely think me insane, but I persisted, not caring how strange I looked. Before night fell, I managed to make it to my safe room. All night, I practiced different yoga routines I had access to from my memories of Earth.

By the time morning dawned, I felt relatively normal again. I ate a small meal and drank some water in the courtyard, a bit dismayed by what had just happened. The adjustment to so many attributes at once had been significantly worse than when I had first taken over my body back on my Earth, which was pretty surprising. I'd had some experience pretending to control a body in my past life when I played virtual reality games with Michael, so the initial adjustment to actually being in a body wasn't quite as hard as I'd thought it would be, but this adjustment had felt worse. If I had been less patient and learned the class away from home, I could have found myself incapacitated in the streets of Perama, surrounded by people more than willing to take advantage of me. I was fortunate that I had waited until I reached my villa.

When I first received the +2 to my attributes from my dungeon achievement, the adjustment hadn't been nearly so bad. It had actually felt completely natural, my body and mind easily able to adapt to the changes. I must have received too many physical attributes at once this time for my mind to keep up with the changes. I would have to be careful in the future, although after learning to center myself in my body twice now, I felt more confident that I could do so again in the future. Practice made perfect, after all, and I was apparently getting more practice than I had anticipated.

I took it easy for the rest of the day and got some sleep the next night. When I woke up, I felt good enough to practice my new *Dash* ability. I wasn't sure how far *Dash* would send me, given my new attributes, so I found the longest stretch of street near my villa before testing it out. Once I was at the far end of the street, I activated the skill by stepping forward and launching myself through the air. I knew I didn't need to say or do anything to activate the skill, but it felt easier to step in the direction I wished to go for now. As soon as I did, I went flying forward, skimming above the street like a ghost floating off the ground, my body pointed forward as if I was running without having to touch the ground. The wind offered no resistance as I flew, allowing me to see perfectly as I skimmed above the ground. I looked to the side, realizing I was going significantly faster than I had anticipated. I measured the distance I was traveling relative to the buildings next to me, doing some quick calculations. If I was right, I was easily going over one hundred miles an hour through the air, with no sign of slowing down.

I thought my *Dash* would stop at any moment, but I just kept flying forward, gaining even more speed as I traveled. I began to panic as I saw the end of the street approach. A stone building loomed in front of me, where the street turned to the right. I had given myself almost a quarter-mile of street to practice on, but I stared in mounting horror at the rapidly approaching wall in front of me, realizing I had misjudged horribly. I tried frantically to stop my *Dash*, doing everything I could to order my body to freeze, stop, or refuse to move another inch. *Stop flying toward the solid stone wall in front of me, please,* I screamed internally, but nothing worked.

"No!" I yelled, closing my eyes and trying to brace myself as I slammed into the stone wall at over one hundred miles an hour. The world flashed white around me, and I felt my body crumble. Even my biomechanically enhanced bones broke from the impact. I tried to scream, but I choked on the dust and debris from the wall as it shattered from the impact as well. I tumbled with the collapsing wall, falling forward into the building until I felt something heavy strike my head. My thoughts then became confused, colors shifting and blurring together. I lost track of where I was. The only thing I understood was the pure agony of my existence. It felt like every bone in my body was broken, my muscles punctured and bruised, my organs strained to the point of collapse, until finally blackness engulfed my mind and I fell unconscious.

An unknown amount of time later, I felt my sense of self start to return. At first, my thoughts were still confused, a strange mix of waking dream and consciousness. I could only vaguely remember a dream filled with pain, but as my mind began to clear, I realized it hadn't been a dream. My whole body was racked with pain. I tried to shake my head to clear it, but that just caused pain to shoot up my neck, and my vision went white again from the agony.

Freezing in place, I opened my bleary eyes, glancing around me in confusion. I was lying on the floor of a large warehouse, partially buried under the collapsed wall. I tried to get a good look at my body, but all I could see were bits and pieces of myself covered in stone blocks, many of them covered in my blood.

Fuck, I thought. I had been a complete idiot. I had known how extreme my new attributes were, especially when combined with my already powerful body. I had been too eager to test my new skill, like a child with a new toy. I had completely underestimated how powerful my attributes truly were. How could I have possibly known that my *Dash* could send me flying forward so fast and for so long? I had tried to give myself significantly more space than seemed reasonable, but it hadn't been enough. I felt like such an idiot. My shame mixed with the pain of my body, causing me to leak tears from my eyes, something I had never done before.

I slowly turned, forcing my body to move, despite the torture I endured. Despite my shame, I refused to lie here until I died. I wouldn't let a single mistake spell my downfall after surviving for so long when many would have already died.

Stones fell around me as I moved, but I was able to twist around enough to look behind me. As I did, my already strained heart skipped a beat at the sight that greeted me. The large hole I had knocked in the side of the solid stone wall behind me was still there, but what caused my heart to stutter wasn't the hole itself but what was revealed through it. The street outside wasn't lit by the sun any longer. Long shadows stretched up the nearby buildings, signaling that I had been unconscious for far longer than I had initially thought. The sunlight was fading. Night had come again.

I heard the telltale signs of monsters beginning to stir across the city, their bloodthirsty cries echoing through the empty streets. I became hyper-aware of the blood that covered me and the stones around me. The coppery smell of my own blood overwhelmed my nostrils as I registered what my senses had been telling me this whole time. I was a monster magnet now, my blood everywhere. The stench had likely spread long and far on the wind that blew through the hole in the wall I had made.

I tried to stand, but the right side of my body wouldn't obey my will. I could immediately tell that my right arm was shattered and that the ribs on that side of my body were cracked. When I tried to shift my legs, I felt my pelvis object, sending more shooting pains through me. I could sense my nanobots had gone into emergency mode and were working to fix critical injuries to keep me alive, but that hadn't extended to my many broken bones yet. They had been too busy keeping me from just bleeding out where I lay. It was only in the last hour that they had been able to do more than life-saving procedures, which was why I only woke up now. My nanobots had kept me unconscious as they struggled to keep me alive, having determined that keeping me conscious was less important. Part of me wanted to curse them for not waking me up sooner, but if they had, I would have likely tried to force myself to move and could have undone all the critical work they had done to keep me from dying.

I felt sure that if I hadn't gained some points in the endurance attribute recently, even the self-healing nanobots wouldn't have been enough to keep me alive. I could feel hunger gnawing at my belly, the nanobots having drawn heavily on my resources to save me. If my body had been any weaker, I wouldn't have survived my own stupid mistake.

I cursed myself again, my thoughts turning to self-recrimination even as I knew I needed to do something about the falling sun. I couldn't stop thinking that I knew my attributes were too high. *Dash* was meant to be used by a level 1 person, who likely had barely any attributes at all. If they used the skill, it probably sent them flying forward a few feet at once, allowing them to practice over and over until they mastered the ability to start and stop the skill at will. I should have guessed using a skill that scaled based off my attributes was a bad idea.

I had barely been able to walk after gaining my attributes. Why had I rushed to test my skill so soon after barely recovering? My drive to push myself was going to get me killed if I didn't take the time to learn more about the systems that governed this world before I experimented with them. I had to remember, if I survived this night, that this wasn't my old world. These skills could do insane, absolutely unrealistic things that I really had no way to properly understand since I hadn't been raised in this world. I lacked a fundamental sense of scale when trying to grasp what could be done in this reality.

The sound of something prowling in the street outside broke me from my spiraling thoughts. I blinked, realizing I had let myself forget how dangerous my situation was. I must have a serious concussion of some kind, because my normally focused mind felt

scattered, as if I wasn't fully in control. I swallowed nervously, feeling extremely vulnerable that I wasn't able to rely on my mind or body at a time when I needed both more than I ever had before.
I needed to *focus*. I needed to *survive*.

My left arm was still functional, likely because I had struck the wall with the right side of my body first. It was still deeply bruised, but I ignored the discomfort and fumbled under my armpit until I could slide my revolver out of its holster. It was fully loaded with *Penetration Bullets*. I turned it over in my hand, grateful it wasn't damaged. A small sense of control returned to me as I felt the weight of the powerful revolver in my hand. It would have to be enough.

I lay in complete silence after that. The only sound was my soft, pained breathing. I heard the scuff of feet against the ground outside but couldn't see anything from where I lay. I held my breath, hearing nothing but silence around me, but I could feel something nearby. It was standing right outside the hole in front of me.

Slowly, agonizingly slowly, I saw something begin to poke into the hole on my left. The crest of its head appeared first. Then, slowly, the rest began to lean further and further out. I shivered at the sight. The face had no eyes, no nose, and no mouth. It was a blank mask of pure black, but even though it lacked eyes, I could tell it was staring at me somehow, measuring whether I was weak enough for it to kill.

I swallowed nervously and forced myself to take a breath, trying to focus.

The creature, seeing that I hadn't responded aggressively to its appearance, seemed emboldened. It moved more fully into the opening in the wall, exposing more of its nondescript body. It cocked its head to the side, like a curious bird evaluating its next meal. Its body was black and featureless, like a being made entirely of shadow.

It took a slow step toward me, walking through the hole in the wall. It paused, seeing if I was going to attack it now, but I didn't move. It straightened its neck and seemed to relax more fully. I got the sense that if it had a mouth, it would be smiling at me in anticipation. With an angry grunt, I raised my revolver and shot it.
The shadowy figure dodged to the side in an instant, my bullet

only clipping it slightly in the side as it retreated around the stone wall. I had hit it, but I didn't see whether my bullet did any damage to the creature or not.

"Dammit," I muttered to myself, lowering the revolver. I stared at the opening in the wall, sensing the creature waiting on the other side. After a moment, it slowly began to peek its head into the hole, watching me once again. I stared back at the creature's blank face, refusing to be cowed by its stare.

My body was mending itself, but so slowly. Even if I could move, I didn't think I could escape a creature like this on the open streets. My single saving grace was that the only entrance to the warehouse was the hole I had made in the wall, meaning it had to come to me through a small opening where I would have a chance to shoot it.

The two of us stared at each other, and I was afraid to blink in case I missed it trying to attack. Its head began to slide downward as it crouched, and I saw an arm slowly reach down and pick up a loose stone from the pile of rubble my crash had created. It grabbed the stone and stood back up, all while staring at me.

"Don't," I tried to say, but the creature moved with lightning speed, hurling the stone at me before I could finish speaking. The stone struck me in the chest, slamming into my already bruised and broken body. I screamed, the agony of my injuries overwhelming me. My vision dimmed, but I raised my gun and fired blindly through the hole in the wall, hoping to hit the creature if it was trying to charge me.

When my vision cleared, the creature was still staring at me from behind the wall, only its head visible where it peeked out around the hole, watching me. It had been toying with me, making me waste a bullet while it stood back and watched me struggle.

"Leave me alone," I grunted. "You piece of shit." Anger filled me, a more primal anger than I had ever felt before. I had been angry at Michael's father before, angry at the world that birthed me and forced me to be something I wasn't, but the anger I felt now was orders of magnitude greater. My body fueled my rage, pumping me full of adrenaline and making me want to leap upward and choke the life from this faceless creature toying with me.

The creature didn't care, continuing to watch me silently. I shook with rage, unable to act on the feelings that surged inside of

208

me. I could hear other monsters beginning to move around us, the roars and growls becoming more common, many of them nearby. This creature wasn't even the biggest threat out here at night, I was sure, but it was disturbingly and frighteningly smart. It was testing me, making sure I was truly wounded, finding a way to get to me without getting injured. And it recognized the danger of my weapon and was trying to get me to waste my bullets, as if it could understand what I held. Another surge of anger and hatred for it ran through me.

I fired at it again, even though I knew I couldn't hit its face, but my bullet forced it to duck backward and hide for a moment. I flipped open the chamber of my revolver with a flick of my wrist and then dropped it on my stomach while I reached down to my belt and grabbed a handful of my *Multi-Bullets*. I reloaded with only my left hand, awkwardly wedging the gun between my stomach and a piece of stone until I could get the bullets into the chamber. The creature darted its head out rapidly, but I had managed to finish reloading by the time it did. I quickly picked up the revolver and rotated the chamber so my new bullets were the next to be fired and then flipped the chamber closed, pointing it back toward the creature.

Then I waited. I could hear more creatures approaching, the smell of my blood bringing them toward me. The monster in front of me heard them, too, turning to look behind it for a moment. It turned back to me and seemed frustrated, clearly wanting me for itself. After a moment of staring at each other again, the creature raced forward, trying to get to me before I could fire my revolver.

Unfortunately for it, I moved pretty fast these days and my *Multi-Bullets* were pretty damn hard to dodge. I fired both *Multi-Bullets*, one after another, the area in front of me filling with flashing steel, like an angry swarm of bees that left no room to escape. The creature tried to turn sideways and dodge to the side, but it had absolutely no chance as the bullets filled the entire space in front of me and the hole it was racing through. Twenty bullets impacted against the monster, blasting it backward like a ragdoll. A shower of black blood erupted from its body, coating the walls behind it in an instant. The creature flew backward and out of the hole, its body ragged and torn, and I lost sight of it as it landed several feet away outside.

I dumped the remaining bullets out of my gun and reloaded all six chambers with *Multi-Bullets*. I heard several growls from the street outside, and the sounds of a fight soon followed. I tensed, listening to the brutal fight right outside the hole in the wall, until silence fell once again. I stared at the hole, waiting to see what had won the fight and whether it would come for me next.

A large pale tiger appeared in the entrance, proudly walking into the hole as if unafraid of what might be waiting for it inside. It stepped onto the mound of fallen stonework, large eyes taking in the warehouse and my broken body lying in front of it. It sniffed deeply, inhaling the scent of my blood on the air, and began to lazily walk toward me as if I was nothing but a free meal. I disabused it of that notion quickly, firing a *Multi-Shot* right in its face, all ten bullets blasting into its face and chest. The tiger didn't even have a chance to react as the bullets killed it. Its body spun sideways and tumbled backward down the rubble, rolling down until it stopped on the other side of the hole.

I waited to see if it would get up from its injuries, but it didn't return. I hastily reloaded another bullet, wincing at the pain; I had to jerk my left arm to free the bullet and load the gun. Once my revolver was fully loaded again, I settled down and waited, watching the hole with deadly focus. When nothing immediately appeared, I looked around the warehouse, just to confirm what I had seen before, and saw that there were no other openings in the walls. The only doorways were still solidly attached to the stone walls, with doors that looked solid enough to give me warning if anyone tried to open them.

Another fight broke out in the street, and after a moment, the sounds of something ripping into the bodies I had left outside followed. I listened as something messily ate the bodies. The sound of flesh being torn and consumed was the only thing I could hear as I waited for the monster to finish. I urged my nanobots to work faster at repairing my body, especially whatever bones I had broken in my pelvis and legs so I could try to run if I needed to.

When the sounds of feeding ended, another creature appeared in the hole in the wall. This one was a bloody-faced lizard, its large tongue flicking out and licking at the blood that coated its face. I didn't hesitate, firing another *Multi-Bullet* into its body, sending it flying backward as if it had been blasted point-blank by a powerful

210

shotgun. Which, in many ways, was exactly what my weapon was with these bullets.

Some time passed before something else disturbed me. I was alerted to the intruder by the sound of several tiny metal feet click-clacking on the stone outside, followed by the incongruous sound of a clock ticking. I waited patiently, staring at the hole in the wall, where the dim moonlight illuminated the opening. After a minute, a clockwork construction that resembled a beetle appeared, carefully picking its way up the rubble of the hole on small metallic feet. As soon as it was fully exposed in the center of the hole, I shot it with a *Multi-Bullet*. My bullets didn't send it flying backward like they had with the other monsters. All ten bullets struck its armored, metallic body, but they only pushed it back a foot or less. The creature's feet reacted swiftly, catching it on the unsteady ground, and then it began to pick its way forward once again.

"Damn," I whispered, seeing how little effect my bullets had on the monster. My *Multi-Bullet* didn't have the penetrative power to seriously harm the clockwork beetle. I frantically dropped my revolver on my stomach, reaching for the pouch that contained my *Penetration Bullets*, but before I could, the beetle unveiled a series of gossamer, metallic wings that seemed to glow in the moonlight and leapt down toward me. I dropped the bullets I had grabbed and reached up to try stopping the monster as it landed on my body. It wasn't enough to stop the beetle's legs from piercing me in several places. Its weight reignited the pain of my injuries, causing me to cry out as the heavy clockwork monster crushed me.

I didn't black out from the pain this time, though, and was able to think clearly enough that I clenched my fist and drew it back before throwing a weak punch at the beetle's clockwork head. Such a weak punch would normally have little to no effect on such an armored foe, but I activated my *Gloves of Golem Strength*. My fist was covered by the illusory image of a golem's fist, and when I slammed my knuckles into the beetle's face, instead of barely doing anything at all, the beetle was shattered into a thousand pieces of clockwork parts. Metal sprayed away from me and cut deeply into the stone wall and wooden ceiling. In a single punch, the creature was turned to nothing but dust and scraps.

As I gaped in shock at the power of my gloves, it took me a moment to remember to reload my revolver. This time I loaded three *Penetration Bullets*, keeping three *Multi-Bullets* as well just in case I needed them.

I settled down again, my stomach churning at how close the beetle had come to killing me. I listened to the street outside again, but there was another lull, so I was able to relax slightly.

An hour passed. I silently listened for any sign of an approaching monster as I urged my nanobots to work faster than they had ever worked before. My hunger and thirst grew, but I ignored them with ease; the pain from my injuries was still so bad that it was easy to ignore the other complaints of my body. By the end of the hour, I could finally sit up enough to shift the stones around me, slowly scooting myself backward and clearing the area around me.

A part of me hoped I might have discouraged the other monsters by killing the ones that had approached me so far, but my hopes were dashed as soon as the sound of more fighting broke out in the street in front of me. This time, it was like a swarm of monsters had descended, maddened by the smell of my blood and the dead creatures outside.

My only saving grace was that the monsters were so busy fighting themselves that they never coordinated in killing me, and many of them were already injured by the time they tried to enter the warehouse. Hours passed in a blur. I killed anything that dared approach me. The hole in the wall was a perfect killing spot, narrow enough that my *Multi-Bullets* could seriously injure anything that tried to get through it while also guaranteeing that nothing could sneak up on me.

Halfway through the night, I ran out of *Multi-Bullets*. I groped blindly at the satchel on my belt, looking for another bullet, before I realized I was out. Refusing to panic, I hastily switched to using *Explosive Bullets*, sliding myself backward further from the hole so I wouldn't be caught in the explosion myself. Because of the momentum of my bullet, most of the explosion was blown away from me anyway. I was still singed by the heat of every blast, but the discomfort was nothing to me at this point. I barely noticed my own injuries anymore. I was focused on nothing but the moonlit entrance to the warehouse, waiting for the next monster to enter so I could kill it like I had done to all the others.

When I heard a large number of monsters fighting outside, I pulled a *Confusion Grenade* from my bandolier and tossed it out of the hole. A second later, the sounds of fighting escalated as the creatures went mad and the grenade multiplied and covered the area. Only one survivor tried to come after me from that fight, a large goat, of all things, its head and chest covered in gore and blood. It limped up the rubble, into my line of sight, and didn't even seem aware I was inside the warehouse, possibly just looking for a place to hide now that it was so injured, but I didn't hesitate to kill it with a single *Penetration Bullet.*

As the night wore on, the smell from the street outside became so repugnant I had to breathe through my mouth to avoid gagging. My own blood was buried under the stench of so many monsters that I was largely forgotten. The abundant food on the street outside drew more and more monsters to the area but drove them to fight each other instead of searching around the area for any free meals. Anytime things became especially loud, I tossed a *Confusion Grenade* outside, driving the monsters into even more of a feeding frenzy.

My arm, ribs, and pelvis finally healed as night began to turn into early morning, but even without my broken bones, my body was so stiff from injured muscles that it was difficult to move. I didn't even try now that I was being left alone. Instead, I just lay there, staring at the hole in the wall and trying not to dwell on how much of an idiot I was for getting myself into this situation in the first place. I vowed to never take this world for granted. I had underestimated the power of the skills in this world once. I would not do so again.

Finally, exhausted mentally and physically, I watched the sun's rays begin to illuminate the street outside. The sound of the monsters fighting began to diminish until slowly the city returned to the complete silence of daytime. Still, I waited a full hour, making absolutely sure I wouldn't be caught by a monster on my way home, then carefully stood and limped up the blood- and viscera-soaked rubble to look out on the street outside.

The area in front of me was a slaughterhouse. Half-eaten corpses of monsters littered the street. Disemboweled and dismembered humanoid and nonhumanoid bodies were everywhere. Body parts, many of them completely alien and unrecognizable, lay in pools of blood and other bodily fluids.

As I stared at the butchery in front of me, the announcements for the experience I had received began to hit me. I staggered at the unexpected intrusion, forgetting for a moment that they were coming. I counted at least two hundred monsters lying dead in front of me, possibly more. I hadn't received experience for all of them, but I did get credit for almost fifty, including the ones I had killed when they entered the warehouse. Several of them were sub-bosses, and a couple were actual bosses, although I hadn't taken the time to notice if anything I shot glowed gold or blue. My *Confusion Grenade* must have earned my credit for the other kills, like it had done for the brawl I had instigated with the dire rats a few weeks ago. In total, I received over two thousand experience for surviving the night. I wouldn't ever do it again, but as I stared thankfully at the sun's warm light, it was a small blessing to get so much experience on top of the fact that I had somehow managed to survive.

I carefully climbed down the slick and unsteady rubble and made my way through the grotesque street, heading back toward my villa. The experience continued to accumulate until I reached level 15 and then level 16, awarding me +1 to my strength for each level. I really needed an enhancement to my endurance to help me heal right now, but I didn't complain. Before I left, I hobbled over to the glowing bodies that were close enough for me to reach without having to climb over too many corpses. I collected six blue orbs and one gold one before I limped home and fell into an exhausted sleep.

Chapter 18

It took two days, and eating through my entire supply of food, to completely recover from my injuries. I slept as much as I could but awoke often from the various nightmares that plagued me. I burned with embarrassment at how close I had come to dying. It was a disturbing experience, especially when it was the result of my own mistake. I felt like I understood humans a little better: the drive to better oneself, the frantic search for security and comfort, the raw power of anger and the unquenchable drive to survive at any cost. These were all things I had thought I understood before, but now I felt them on a deeper, more instinctive level. The human mind and body worked as one when it came to survival, and they would do anything to survive.

I spent my time replenishing my bullets from the iron I had stored in my villa. I also inspected my revolver carefully after a night of using it so frequently. I found that the bullets had slightly warped the barrel of the gun, and the rifling inside was becoming worn, likely because I was using steel bullets instead of the much softer lead that most bullets were made from. I had my nanobots return the gun to a perfect condition and then I carved the *Durability* rune into the grip, empowering it with a blue orb. It glowed faintly now, the *Durability* rune looking rather striking set among the polished wood and steel of the revolver. That should help prevent further wear and tear.

I spent a lot of time thinking about my choices and my goals here. I could recognize now that my decision to come here was a bit reckless. I had been grieving the loss of my only friend and hadn't been thinking clearly, something I thought I was immune to because of my nature as an artificial intelligence. That was naive of me, though, since I was fully aware I could experience emotions similar to a normal person. There was no reason to think those emotions couldn't influence my decision-making in the same way

215

they would influence a human being's. I had ignored the signs, throwing myself into my work and my rash plan to come to a world like this.

Now that I was here, though, I needed some long-term and short-term goals. My first short-term goal was to find a way over to Sycae, the merchant enclave, and check out their markets. I had acquired enough wealth to get myself the *Enchanter* class and maybe some skills or another class if I could find one. I hoped that by learning the *Enchanter* class, I could enhance my revolver and grenades in some way, making me even deadlier. My second short-term goal was to level my *Archer* class to level 20 to see if I could get a class evolution of some kind. I hoped that my use of a revolver instead of a bow or other, more traditional ranged weapon would be unique enough to get me a powerful evolution.

After that . . . I wasn't sure. Find a real place to call home? Find out more about this world? Make friends? Explore beyond the city? I felt a bit lost when it came to thinking about my long-term goals. One of the things that had drawn me so thoroughly to the idea of finding a world like this one was that the pleasure of gaining power, levels, skills, and magic acted as a panacea on the real things that bothered me, allowing me to ignore how adrift I truly was by focusing on the next power-up or interesting bit of magic I found. I recognized that such a feedback loop was one of the reasons I enjoyed playing virtual games with Michael so much; the escape was addictive in many ways. I just couldn't live like that forever. I needed to figure out what I truly wanted from my life. For now, that was too big of a question to answer, so I would just focus on my short-term goals and figure out the rest when I could.

To get into Sycae, I could think of a couple of different possibilities. I could try my luck with the Emperor's enclave and hope I had enough to bribe myself through. In the same vein, I could try bribing one of the fishing boats to take me across, which would probably be cheaper and safer than trying to deal with the Emperor or his nobles.

Another option was that I could use my newest perk, *Swimmer's Body*, which increased my eyesight underwater, reduced the resistance of the water I swam through, and significantly increased the time I could hold my breath. The danger with that option was that I knew the water contained monsters; I saw one when I first spotted the bridge city and its fishermen. On the other hand, I had been able to outswim the sharks in the island dungeon even before receiving my perk. It was possible I could outswim whatever lived in the water around here as well.

The water could also provide me a way to test my *Dash* again, this time with—hopefully—more than enough free space around me. Part of me balked at the idea of using the skill again, but I refused to give in to that cowardly part of my mind. I would learn to use the skill no matter what. I just needed to be smarter about it now that I understood how insanely high it scaled off my physical attributes.

I made my way north, avoiding the area around Perama so I wouldn't see another person. I approached the seawall that ran from west to east and protected the city from the channel that separated the city from Sycae. Wealthy houses overlooked the water, many of them ransacked and destroyed. Signs of monsters were everywhere, and I couldn't help but think that if the people or Perama could clear a few of these areas out, they would face fewer attacks at night. The army could probably do it, but for some reason, it refused to protect the enclave.

I found a spot along the seawall where the channel was the narrowest. The water still stretched about a third of a mile from the seawall to the docks of Sycae. I checked my surroundings to make sure nobody was watching me, and then I climbed the seawall and crouched on top of it. I was only a couple of feet above the water here, the waves lapping against the wall below me. The docks across from me were mostly empty. There were only a few people on the shore near the docks, busy with their own business.

Before I could second-guess myself, I leapt forward, activating my *Dash* skill and launching myself off the seawall. I flew forward like I had done last time, unnaturally floating above the waves as if I was hovering in the air. There was no air resistance, so I felt strangely undisturbed as I flew across the water. My clothing didn't even whip behind me, my vision unobstructed even though I was moving extremely fast. I dashed over halfway across the channel before my body stopped in midair, my momentum ceasing completely. I hesitated, completely surprised by the sudden cessation of movement. After a moment of stillness, gravity reasserted its control over me and I crashed into the water below.

I gasped as the cold water swallowed me, sucking water into my mouth and lungs. I coughed, which only sucked more water into my lungs. My damn body was drowning itself in its confusion.

Annoyed, I forced myself to stop panicking and kicked upward, breaching the water above me and coughing to clear my lungs as I desperately sucked in as much air as possible. I couldn't afford to sit still in the middle of the channel, so I forced my breathing to slow and dove downward, checking the water around me for anything that might be nearby.

The water below was crystal clear to my improved eyesight. It was like looking through a clear glass bowl, slightly distorted but still clear enough to see all around me. I saw several sea monsters swimming in the channel, but none of them were near me. I also saw a monster closer to the Sycae shore, a grotesquely large crab walking along the seafloor, but it wasn't looking upward, too busy with whatever giant crabs did.

I could see out into the main body of water that separated the western and eastern parts of the city. I saw a huge sea serpent, the size of a modern submarine at least, that had a faint golden glow around its body. It had a long, prehensile neck and short fins on each side of its body, but it seemed unconcerned with its surroundings as it swam lazily north along the waterway.

Seeing my path was clear, I rapidly swam forward, my newly strengthened body cutting powerfully through the water. My perk made the water less resistant to my movement, making me feel like a dolphin as I swam. The water was almost welcoming me with open arms as I let loose and used all my strength and speed to propel myself forward. After just a few moments of swimming, I crossed the rest of the channel and stopped next to one of the docks that jutted out of the merchant enclave.

"Did you see that?"

"What was that? Was it a monster?"

I heard a number of people talking above me. I reached upward and grabbed the edge of the dock, pulling myself up and rolling onto the wooden boards above me. Several people stood nearby, having noticed my approach.

"It's a person!"

218

"Sir," a man said, approaching me. "Are you okay? Did something happen to you? Did your boat capsize?"

I stood and ran my hands through my hair and clothes, shedding as much water as I could. "I'm fine," I told the man who had approached. "Thank you, though. Just taking a bit of a shortcut across the water."

I searched the crowd but thankfully didn't see any guards or other authority figures that might try to question me further. I bowed slightly to the crowd and the man who had approached me before I walked rapidly past them, ignoring their looks of shock at my sudden appearance.

"A shortcut? He must be mad!"

I almost smiled at the flurry of speculation I left in my wake, but instead, I focused on sending my nanobots to quickly dry and clean my equipment so I didn't bring too much attention to myself by appearing soaking wet. Once I was out of sight of the people at the dock, I ducked into an alley and waited patiently for my nanobots to finish their job. Once I was dry and looking a bit more respectable, I exited the alley and began to explore Sycae.

The first thing that struck me about this side of the city was the number of people. Perama had felt crowded, simply because it had so many people packed into such a small space. Here, there was significantly more space, but somehow, it managed to feel even more crowded. Away from the docks, the streets rapidly filled up with people hawking wares, cooking food, carting goods across the city or carrying them by hand, or acting busy with other work that sent them rushing through the streets.

Shops were everywhere, selling all kinds of goods. I saw actual restaurants serving food, as well as carts selling produce, street food, and other perishables. The city was loud. My ears, which had become used to the silence of the city across the water, were overwhelmed by the sounds of so many people talking, bargaining, laughing, yelling, and so much more. I grimaced, frantically trying to manage the sensitivity of my ears, feeling a headache develop from so much noise all around me.

The people were a mix of ethnicities. Like Mehmet from the bar back in Perama, a large number of people were darker-skinned, while others were the more common olive-skinned people that filled Perama.

What was especially interesting about the mix of ethnicities in this part of the city was what it implied about the history of this world. In my world, Constantinople fell to the Ottoman Empire. In this world, something must have occurred to change the course of history since the city was still in the hands of the Byzantines. At least as much as the city was in the hands of anyone. The people who were darker-skinned looked like descendants of the Turkic people that ruled the Ottoman Empire. Given the population of their descendants in the city, it implied that the city had had some contact with the Ottomans at some point. I was very curious about what had happened.

As I wandered the streets, I observed plenty of guards patrolling and keeping the peace, unlike in Perama. Toward the north of the city, I could see a wall much like the Theodosian Walls that protected the western part of the city that was controlled by the army. This wall, though, also had a shimmer rising above it like at the priests' enclave. Did the merchants here get a hold of whatever magic protected the priests? Or did the priests buy the magic from the merchants somehow? If so, why didn't the rest of the city have such defenses?

The other odd thing about the mass of people here was how . . . normal they all seemed. It was as if they were all pretending that nothing was wrong with their world. They went about their day, gossiping, shopping, eating, laughing, living their life as if nothing was wrong. After weeks of surviving in the ruined part of the city just to the south, it was disconcerting. It was like entering a bubble that was determined to pretend the rest of the world wasn't failing all around it.

I spent a few hours exploring the enclave. I found a large temple near the wall that seemed to be occupied by several priests. I considered trying to sneak to see if I could learn more about the mysterious barrier that protected the enclave, but I put it out of mind when I saw how many priests were coming and going from the temple. Maybe if I had a way to resist their spells, I could risk it, but for now, it wasn't worth it.

There was no palace or sign of a central government, although a number of large estates dotted the city. Each estate had its own walls and guards in unique livery. I suspected the estates represented the merchants that controlled the enclave, although I couldn't be completely sure.

After I was done exploring the city, I returned to a respectable-looking inn I had seen near the center of the city. There, a kind older woman rented me a room and sold me a meal for four copper nummi a night. I accepted her offer, despite not needing to sleep right now, to avoid any issues with the guards as night began to fall.

Once my lodging was secured, I made my way to a shop in one of the richer parts of the city. The street the shop was on was beautiful. Pristine stone buildings lined each side, each one adorned with ivy and flowers in vibrant abundance, and the shops all had large glass windows to allow in plenty of light and to display their goods to those that walked the street outside.

One of the shops was a bakery, and the smell was so distracting that I couldn't help but stop and buy a few pastries. It was my first taste of freshly prepared food, and it was delicious. My mouth ached painfully as the smell of the pastry reached my nose, and I found myself consuming the pastries so fast I barely registered anything but the sensation of pleasure from the taste of them in my mouth.

I looked up, slightly embarrassed, sure that someone must have seen how hastily I consumed the pastries, but nobody was looking at me. I brushed crumbs off the front of my cloak, coughing slightly to cover my embarrassing behavior, and then walked briskly to the shop that had brought me to the area.

"Be with you in a moment," a young boy called out as I entered. I stopped inside the shop, glancing around to see a large number of books displayed on shelves all around me. The young boy who had called out was behind a counter, talking with a richly dressed man in a robe of fine silk. I waited patiently for them to finish their business, nodding at the man as he passed me on his way out. The man ignored me, giving me only a brief, dismissive glance as he left.

"Welcome," the boy said after securing the money the older man had paid him. "What can I do for you today?"

The boy was dressed well but modestly. He seemed to be in his early teenage years, around fifteen or sixteen at most, although it was hard to tell, given how different the people of this world were compared to my own.

"I'm looking to buy a class," I told him, stepping toward the counter. "I'm looking for an *Enchanter* class if you have one available."

The boy turned and grabbed a book off the shelf behind him. "Easy enough," he said, placing the book in front of him. "My grandfather finished one a few months ago but we haven't had any buyers yet."

I inspected the book he had placed on the counter. It was finely made and bound in thick leather, just like the *Archer* book I had purchased from Momma Lena.

"You understand this will only teach you the class, sir? We are not responsible for you learning the trade itself. That will be your own responsibility."

"Yes," I said, "I understand that."

"Great," the boy replied, giving me a professional smile. "Sometimes people think a class will teach them everything, but that's not how it works. We just like to make sure you understand so you don't leave disappointed."

"I appreciate that," I said. "How much for the class?"

"Rare class like this?" the boy replied. "It goes for 150 blues, minimum. A fair deal, that is."

I could afford the class but had learned my lesson to always bargain by now.

"It's a rare class," I agreed, "but my understanding is that most people learn it by working the job, since—as you say—it is almost impossible to use it otherwise. And you said it has been sitting on your shelf for months. Surely, that means the class is not in that much demand."

The boy didn't blink, only waited for me to finish speaking, clearly comfortable with negotiating prices. I found myself impressed by his maturity.

"That is true," he said, giving me another professional smile, "but you should never underestimate the whims of the merchants and their rich families in Sycae, sir. I can see you are from across the way. A scavenger, if your cloak is true. We appreciate what you do for us over here and I know my grandfather would want to recognize your good works. I can sell you the class for 140 blues.

Surely that is not too much for a successful scavenger such as yourself."

He patted the book in his hand fondly as he spoke, like it was a particularly good book that just needed a loving person to take it home with them.

"I do appreciate that," I replied. "And yes, I'm a scavenger, although I am pretty new to the profession and haven't made a lot of currency yet. If you sold me this class, it might make a big difference in my survival across the water. Maybe someday I could supply some goods that help keep Sycae supplied. Who knows? Although if I died, the city would win once again."

The boy glanced down at the book and his smile slipped for the first time. I could tell I had caught him out, and my own smile grew.

He gave me a more genuine smile, recognizing my sappy response for what it was. "I can sell you the class for 125 blues, but no lower. My grandfather will already have my hide for such a deal."

Sensing I wasn't getting any better deal, I agreed.

"A fair bargain," I said, withdrawing six gold orbs and five blue orbs from the pouches on my belt. I handed the currency to the boy and he handed me the book. Even though I had completed ten dungeons and collected a fair number of orbs after my disastrous night trapped in the city, I was left with only a handful of gold orbs and around seventy blue orbs. I would need to replenish my reserves soon if I wanted to make more expensive purchases in the future.

"Thank you for your business, sir," he said, bowing to me slightly.

"Thank you." I tucked the book into my backpack and asked him about his other classes for sale, but none of his non-combat classes would be useful for me right now, and the combat classes had a lengthy waitlist, similar to Momma Lena back in Perama. I thanked the boy again after we finished talking and turned to leave.

Outside, the streets were still just as busy as before. I had a few hours left before the sun started to set, so I found my way to a street that had several enchanters on it. The shops there were also manned by younger boys and girls, likely all apprentices or family of the crafters themselves. I wondered if they all had some kind of

Merchant class. It would make sense to have a family member specialize in making more of a profit while the crafters focused on their specific class.

My main goal was to buy some kind of compendium of runes, but every shop I visited claimed such a thing didn't exist, and no enchanter would share their runes without a formal apprenticeship. They all seemed to be following the same script, claiming it was too dangerous to just hand out such knowledge. I didn't doubt that it was for most people, but even when I offered to pay a significant amount, they refused to sell to me.

Slightly annoyed, I returned to the inn I was staying at, ate a fine dinner, and then made my way to my room before night fell. In my room, I took out the class book I had purchased and made myself comfortable on the small bed. I opened the book and began to read.

Class unlocked: Enchanter.

Pooled experience detected. Experience applied to your Enchanter class.

I was surprised to realize that my prior crafting must have actually been pooling experience for me; it just wasn't announced in the way that killing monsters was.

Congratulations, you have received enough experience to level your Enchanter class. You are now level 1.

Congratulations, you have received enough experience to level your Enchanter class. You are now level 2.

Congratulations, you have received enough experience to level your Enchanter class. You are now level 3.

Please choose a level 1 class skill:

Efficient Enchanting: Your enchantments require less power to activate.

Empowered Enchantments: Your enchantment effects are more powerful.

Lasting Enchantments: Your enchantments last longer and are resistant to damage from external sources.

Copy: You may make a perfect copy of a prior enchantment that you crafted once per week onto an item of your choice.

Learn Rune: You may select one rune of your choice. Learn that rune. You may pick any concept of your choice to learn.

Now that was interesting. I could, essentially, form my own rune if I went with *Learn Rune*, but if I chose that option, I would lose out on the long-term benefits from some of the other skills. I could sense that I was able to learn all of the enchantment skills; none of them would require me to activate my own mana since enchantment used external magic to charge runes, not internal magic. *Copy* was a waste since I could already mirror runes perfectly with my nanobots. *Efficient Enchanting* would save me money in the long run, but that wasn't an immediate concern. *Lasting Enchantments* would help me enchant more lasting items, but again, that wasn't an immediate concern.

That left *Empowered Enchantments* or *Learn Rune*. I had any number of concepts I could potentially unlock with *Learn Rune*, but given how rare getting skills was, I didn't want to waste a skill on just a single rune in case I could find what I wanted elsewhere first. Maybe after I had done an extensive search and collected as many runes as possible, I would use that skill if I got it again as I leveled.

For now, I selected *Empowered Enchantments*. The knowledge of the skill flooded into me. I learned that all of my enchantments would be empowered from now on, meaning my bullets and grenades would do more damage or be more powerful, giving me a nice boost in power across the board.

Memory +1

Memory +1

The attribute enhancements for reaching levels 2 and 3 rolled through my mind. I didn't feel any different from having a boost to my memory, but with my enhanced mind, I was already capable of remembering everything I had encountered, so I wasn't sure what good a higher memory actually did me.

After the class announcements faded, I took a deep breath and stood up from my bed to stretch. Night had fallen and the class book had faded just like the *Archer* book had after I finished learning the class. I was happy with my purchase. It had given me a very useful skill that increased the power of both my revolver and grenades. Overall, a very good investment, for sure.

I realized as I stretched that I had been hearing a dim commotion around me for a while now, but only after I finished gaining my class did I realize what I had been hearing. Down below, the sound of music and a crowd was filtering up to me from the common room of the inn. I frowned, surprised to hear so many people out and about now that the sun was down.

I unlatched the shutters on the window of my room and looked out upon the city. Night had set over an hour ago, but the streets were still full of people—maybe even more full, if that was possible. Food was still being served, and numerous inns and bars around me had patrons coming and going, even at night. The streets were illuminated with magical blue light, and the city had a festive air, as if there was nothing dangerous about the night at all.

I was shocked, my senses rebelling at the idea of anyone being out at night, but I soon realized this city must be so secure that they didn't need to hide indoors at night like everyone else. How fortunate for them that they were free to celebrate while the rest of the city fought for its life every night, just hoping to see another dawn.

I made my way downstairs and found a lively scene in the common room. The large room was full of patrons, and a musician was playing a large wooden instrument of some kind in one corner. The tables were packed, and several staff were bringing drinks and food to the patrons.

"Grab a seat anywhere, sir!" a woman yelled at me as she saw me standing at the foot of the stairs.

I scanned the room and found a table that had an open chair. It looked like people shared tables here, even with strangers, so I wound my way through the crowd and sat down. The woman who had spotted me came over as I sat down, and I ordered a beer from her.

As I sat down, the men at the table turned and looked me up and down. There were three of them. One looked like a young merchant or a merchant's son. He was dressed well, with a bit of a spoiled look to his face, as if he felt he was better than everyone else in the room. The other two appeared to be friends of his, but their clothing was not as fine and showed signs of some mending, unlike the other boy's clothing, which was spotless and new.

"A scavenger?" one of the friends asked as I looked back at them. I was regretting even coming down here, uncomfortable with the situation. It was clear the men at my table had already had a few drinks and I didn't feel adept enough at social situations to handle three young, intoxicated boys.

The rich boy elbowed his friend. "Now, don't be rude," he said, raising his voice to make sure I could hear him. "You know we rely on scavengers for many things. They are the workers that keep our fine society afloat, aren't they now?"

This caused the other two to laugh, and the rich boy got a smug look on his face.

"My good man," the boy continued. "Tell us about yourself. Regale us with your stories!"

I ignored the boys and scanned the room for another place to sit. When another moment passed and it was clear I was ignoring them, the rich boy got an ugly look on his face.

"Come now," he said, leaning toward me. "Tell us what you scavenge. Are you a cloth scavenger, bringing us dirty laundry to clean for you? Do you scavenge rags for us to wipe our arse with, then, Mr. Scavenger?"

His two companions laughed uproariously as if he had made the funniest joke they had ever heard.

I sighed, now fully regretting my choice to come downstairs. Before I could respond or hear more from the boys, my drink arrived. I paid for the drink and then spotted an opening at another table occupied by an older man and what looked like his bodyguard, a grizzled veteran carrying a large sword across his back, even inside the inn. They seemed like better company than these foolish boys.

I stood and began to make my way toward the other table when the rich boy grabbed my arm. I looked down at the boy, surprised at his audacity. He tugged on my arm, and I was surprised to feel he had a bit of strength. He must have a class, if not several.

"Now, now," he said, trying to brush off his insults with a false smile. "Don't go. I didn't mean anything by it. We need a good drinking companion and want to hear your stories. Sit and tell us what you do, scavenger."

I reached across with my other hand and placed it over the boy's where it grasped my arm. I began to squeeze, feeling his hand give to my greater strength. I knew I was handling the situation poorly, but his attitude reminded me too much of

227

Michael's father, and I found myself growing angry at his arrogance.

"Fuck!" the boy yelled, feeling my strength crushing his hand. I pulled his hand away from my arm and let go before doing any real harm to him.

The boy glared at me, anger clear on his face, as he shook out his hand. I could see he was about to say something especially stupid to assuage his wounded pride, but I silently turned away from him and made my way over to the other open seat I had seen. I had no time or energy to deal with such fools tonight. I had just barely survived being stuck outside at night in the city, and here was an entire enclave partying every night. These people were so full of arrogance that they would lay hands on me without permission as if it was their right to stop me when I tried to leave. It infuriated me.

I sat down at the table with the older man and his bodyguard with a grunt, trying to dispel the anger that lingered in my mind. The man nodded at me and his bodyguard scanned me up and down.

"Alright if I join you here?" I asked, my voice rougher than I intended.

The man nodded again and then turned to watch the musician play, leaving me in silence. I turned to take in the music as well, sipping my beer, grateful for the peace. I could feel the boys at the table I had left staring daggers at me, and I heard them muttering to themselves as they continued to drink, but I did my best to ignore them. I figured at most they would wait outside for me, thinking they could exact some petty revenge when I left, but when I failed to leave the inn, hopefully they would just leave disappointed and drunk and forget about the whole thing by tomorrow.

I drank in silence, trying to enjoy the music and the crowd of happy people. The beer wasn't particularly intoxicating with my enhanced body, but the crowd and atmosphere cast their own kind of spell, finally letting me relax a bit. The frantic pace at which people drank, danced, laughed, and partied made me realize I had been missing something when I initially judged the enclave. The people weren't all like the boy who had grabbed me, arrogantly enjoying the luxury they lived in without a care for the outside world. Instead, they had found a different way to cope with the constant tension and fear. The people around me were drinking far more than was good for them, their celebration almost manic. Their cheerfulness had a tinge of desperation and madness to it, something I hadn't noticed at first. After watching them for long enough, I realized they weren't unaware of the danger of the world around them; they just tried to drown their fear in drink and celebration to make themselves forget for a moment what awaited in the night if their wall ever failed.

I watched, fascinated by what I was now seeing. I couldn't help but admire the human ability to cope with fear and stress, how people found release in the strangest ways, even if that way was probably unhealthy.

I was so distracted by my new insight into the people of Sycae that I was caught by surprise a few drinks later when the boy from the other table had gotten behind me, shoving me hard enough to jolt me out of my chair and almost spilling me onto the ground. The man at the table with me frowned as I recovered, standing quickly and turning to glare at the arrogant boy. The bodyguard stood aggressively as well, staring daggers at the boy.

"You ill-mannered rat!" the young man said, spitting on my chest. I looked down in disgust at his actions. "You—" he tried to continue when I interrupted him by slapping him across the face. My slap was so hard the boy spun to the side and slammed down on a neighboring table, spilling the patrons' drinks and sending the men and women who had been sitting at the table backing up quickly, their chairs overturning as they retreated rapidly.

His two friends were standing behind him and charged at me as they saw their companion struck down. They yelled in outrage and raised their fists, but the bodyguard stepped forward and kicked one of them in the stomach, knocking the wind out of him and sending him folding over backward. I grabbed the other one by his outstretched hand and stepped to the side, wrapping his arm across his body and spinning him around with a jerk before picking him up in both my arms, turning him sideways, and slamming him into the ground. He groaned in pain as his back slammed into the hard wood of the inn's floor. I waited to see if he would stand again, but he seemed happy enough to roll around on the ground, groaning and crying. I left him to it.

I turned and eyed the young man that had started the whole brawl. He was slumped on the ground where he had fallen after sliding off the table he had landed on. I grabbed the one I had body-slammed by his foot and dragged him over to the arrogant brat I had slapped, then grabbed him as well. I dragged both of them across the floor and dumped them in the street in front of the inn. The bodyguard escorted the other young man outside as the boy cradled his stomach. I stared at him as he passed me, not meeting my eyes.

The bodyguard and I reentered the inn together to an awkward silence as everyone stared at us.

"Let me buy you a drink," I told the bodyguard as we both stopped, staring back at everyone that was watching us in silence. Apparently my words were enough to get the party started again, because the patrons of the inn gave a cheer, raising their mugs toward us, and went back to celebrating. The bodyguard turned to me and grinned, his weathered face breaking into a surprisingly kind smile.

"A man after my own heart," he said, laughing. I smiled back at him.

I ordered the next round for the bodyguard and the other man at the table. The brief fight seemed to have broken the ice between the three of us and we spent the rest of the evening drinking together and talking. Their names were Romanus and Valens, and they were actually equal partners. I had originally thought Valens was Romanus's bodyguard, but it turned out that wasn't true.

I learned a lot from the two of them about Sycae as we drank together. I also learned that even with an enhanced body, enough alcohol could get me drunk. I had planned to stay up all night crafting new bullets with my *Empowered Enchantments* skill, but instead, I found myself staggering up to my room late into the night, where I immediately passed out on top of my bed.

I awoke late the next morning. My body, thankfully, had healed enough for me to avoid the worst feelings of a hangover, which, I was aware from the information I had gathered on my Earth, was a very unpleasant feeling. By the time I made it down to the main room of the inn, my head only pounded a little. I found Romanus and Valens enjoying a full breakfast. They waved me over when they saw me.

"A fun night," Romanus said with a smile, gesturing for me to join them. "We must thank you for the fine entertainment." Valens's weathered face broke into a smile as well, and he nodded in agreement. I sat down and ordered breakfast as well.

"Thank you again for the help with those young men," I said while I waited for my food to arrive.

Valens waved away my thanks. "You thanked us enough last night," he said in his deep voice. "This city has become infested with the cowardly, hiding here behind the walls and pretending nothing is wrong. It's good to remind them that real strength is required to survive in this world."

"Their parents buy them classes," Romanus said, "and they think they are strong because they get a few enhancements and a skill or two. They have no idea what it takes to really fight anymore."

I had learned that Romanus had a combat class or two, but he didn't share the specifics. Valens was a *Warrior* and had revealed he was level 20 in his class and had been for many years. I was surprised to learn that the two of them hunted in the wild north of the enclave, bringing down monsters outside the city. According to them, it was dangerous work, but profitable. Given how dangerous the city was, I could only imagine what the wilderness outside was like.

I was interested in learning about his non-combat class, but I wanted to focus on my *Enchanter* class for now rather than get distracted with another class. I was sure it would take time to learn the different ways to harvest monsters, but I was interested in learning at some point so I didn't leave so much money behind me when I went hunting.

We made small talk over breakfast, enjoying each other's company as we ate.

"Alexander," Romanus said as we were finishing our breakfast, "have you ever left the city?"

"No, I haven't had a chance to yet. I have been too busy."

Romanus looked over at Valens, who nodded back at him.

"Would you like to go on a hunt with us?" Romanus asked. "We have been tracking a profitable monster north of the city, but it may be too strong for us. It would be good to have someone along that can handle themselves. And it would be a good learning

231

experience for you. Get you out of the city, see some of the world that isn't fully destroyed yet."

I was tempted, but I worried about revealing more about my firearm and its capabilities, although I felt I could trust these two men.

"Hmm," I said, buying time as I thought over my options. "I'm interested. Can you tell me more about what it's like? I only have experience with scavenging in the city itself."

"Outside of the city is different," Valens said. "The monsters are stronger, larger, and smarter. Especially smarter. The ones in the city are idiots compared to some of the monsters outside."

"But there are less of them," Romanus said, "although that only makes them more dangerous. They are territorial and are not afraid to come out during the day. Much of our work is knowing where not to go, to avoid the monsters we have no hope of fighting."

"The further from the city you get," Valens said, "the worse it becomes. Monsters only become more powerful further from the city for some reason. It's dangerous work, but very rewarding."

The two of them had a funny way of talking, bouncing off each other's sentences. It was clear they had spent a lot of time together. I found it endearing.

"I would be happy to go with you," I said, deciding it was worth revealing more about myself to learn how to survive outside the city, "but I have to warn you, my way of fighting is a bit . . . strange. I would ask you two to keep what you see to yourselves if I go with you."

"Oh ho!" Romanus replied, smiling. "A unique class of some kind? Those are very rare these days."

"It's complicated," I replied, smiling back at him. "But I would appreciate your discretion."

"Of course," Valens said. "You have nothing to fear from us. Romanus may surprise you as well, if he ends up having to get involved."

Romanus scoffed as if he had no clue what Valens was referring to.

"Well," I said, smiling at their antics. "Then I am happy to go with you. When do you leave?"

"Tomorrow morning," Romanus replied. "We need to resupply and sell some goods here before we head back out. You'll get an equal share of any loot gathered. I would recommend you prepare yourself for at least a week's travel."

We discussed the details a bit more, and then the two invited me to go with them to sell some of their goods. I agreed. They went upstairs to gather their goods and I waited for them in the street out front.

Part of me expected to encounter trouble when I stepped out of the inn, worried I'd find the three boys waiting for me perhaps, but thankfully nobody paid any attention to me when I walked outside.

I hoped the young men had learned a cheap lesson from me, because I knew others might not have been as forgiving.

Romanus and Valens joined me a few minutes later, each of them carrying a large backpack on their backs. The backpacks both looked overly full, with goods strapped to the sides, back, and top, making them look twice as large as they should be. It was clear that they had strength enhancements just to be able to carry the backpacks so easily.

We made our way to a street a few blocks away, where the hammer of blacksmiths and the sounds of other crafters filled the air. Romanus led us to one such shop. An open area surrounded by a low stone wall sprawled next to the small shop, the open area filled with forges, anvils, and several people working at them.

Romanus led us inside with no hesitation.

The two of them approached the counter while I lingered at the entrance to the shop, just watching. They dumped their backpacks onto a large, clear section of the counter. The young clerk clearly recognized the two of them because he turned and left through a doorway behind him without saying a word. He came back a few minutes later with an older man who sported a large gut and an even larger mustache.

"Ah," the older man said upon seeing Romanus and Valens, "my two favorite suppliers!"

The three of them began to chat, making small talk and discussing the two men's most recent expedition out of the city. I turned away and looked over some of the goods in the shop as they talked. Several different sets of armor and weapons were displayed on mannequins or on tables and shelves. As I inspected them, I realized why monster parts were in such high demand: they could be used to craft high-level items like the ones in this shop. I saw

233

armor made from monsters' scales, swords made from unfamiliar glowing materials with no visible enchantments, and many other items clearly crafted from exotic materials. When I read the brief description next to each item, it claimed that the armor or weapon was made from various parts of monsters that gave the weapon or armor different powers or resistances, depending on the monster it was made from.

I inspected a set of leather armor the description claimed was made from the scales of a monstrous crocodile. The description said it was highly resistant to piercing attacks and granted the wearer the ability to hide in marshes with near-perfect invisibility. I wasn't sure how the armor could determine what a "marsh" was or if anything that was close to a marsh qualified. And how did the crafter know what each piece did? If the claims were true, it must have taken years of experimentation to learn what different monster parts did when turned into a piece of armor or a weapon.

One of the swords I looked over claimed to be enhanced by a sprite's winter breath, which made the sword inflict ice damage. There were daggers made from the bones of a shadow creature, granting the blade some form of shadow magic, boots enhanced with the speed of something called an Aurumvorax, and plenty of other exotic items with equally extraordinary enhancements.

I was shocked at the prices but even more shocked to learn that such things were possible. It appeared that I had just scratched the surface of what this world had to offer when I took up enchanting. The other crafting professions produced items of equal or greater power, at least here in Sycae.

Romanus and the shop owner finished their bargaining, and I watched as he and Valens finished unloading jars, hides, and a number of carefully wrapped and preserved body parts onto the counter. The shop owner, in return, handed him a handful of golden and blue orbs. I had only a second to count, but it appeared to be at least ten gold orbs. Harvesting monsters turned a *very* healthy profit, it seemed.

I considered buying an item, but most of it was out of my price range right now. My funds were depleted after I bought my *Enchanter* class and spent a night drinking with Romanus and Valens. I was down to just four gold orbs now, although I had a fair number of blue orbs and some silver and copper left.

I also needed to spend some more on traveling rations, a second canteen, and a blanket for the trip out of the city. I wished I had time to return to my villa to gather more iron to make into bullets, but since we planned to leave tomorrow morning, I had my nanobots working to re-forge all of my bullets and grenades, except for my *Penetration Bullets,* which I couldn't afford to reforge quite yet. The newly forged bullets and grenades were more powerful thanks to my *Empowered Enchantments* skill. I had my nanobots working throughout the day, taking apart the enchantments on each bullet and grenade and then reforming them. It would cost me more blue orbs to recharge the enchantments, but it was worth it to make them more powerful.

The next morning, after another filling breakfast with the two men, we headed north toward the wall that protected Sycae. Romanus led us through the city until we reached a large gate in the enclave wall. A number of guards stood on the wall above the gate, but none seemed particularly worried. The shimmer of a barrier arced up from the wall, protecting the enclave better than a handful of guards could ever do.

"Do you know what makes that barrier?" I asked the two men as we approached.

Valens shook his head, but Romanus replied, "I've heard it's some Patriarch magic. The merchants council pays the priests well to maintain it."

"Interesting," I said, staring upward as the shield stretched high above the enclave.

We approached the gate. When we got close, one of the guards recognized Romanus and opened a smaller door in the thick wooden gate, letting us outside. We stepped through and I took in my first view of the world beyond the city.

More of the city continued north, but this part of the city was even more ruined than the areas inside the wall. The buildings were fully collapsed, bits and pieces of stone and wood scattered and covered by grass and small brush that had grown over the area. The cobblestones of the road were cracked as if large creatures had fought over the area, shattering the ground underneath them. Plants and grasses grew wildly as far as I could see, working to reclaim the area for nature.

We made our way through the abandoned streets, the three of us watching warily for signs of any monsters nearby. As we progressed, the ruins of the city fell away and the cracked streets turned into abandoned farmland. A few remaining crops grew here and there, but they were no longer domesticated. Cottages and larger manors dotted the area, all of them long since abandoned.

After traveling for an hour, I stumbled as an announcement suddenly intruded on my mind.

Congratulations, you have earned the achievement Survive a Safe Zone. For reaching level 10 in a class, completing a dungeon, killing at least 20 monsters, and leaving a safe zone, you have been rewarded. You receive +1 to all attributes. You have unlocked the quest system.

"Whoa," I said.

Romanus and Valens both stopped and turned to me. Seeing me in one piece, Valens turned to keep an eye on the surrounding countryside while Romanus approached. "Everything okay?" he asked me.

"Yeah," I said, still examining the achievement in shock. I rubbed my forehead with one hand and looked over at Romanus. I debated whether I should ask him about achievements or not, but I decided if I was already trusting him with my revolver, I could trust him with more information.

"Have either of you ever heard of someone earning an achievement?"

"An achievement?" Romanus replied, confused. "What do you mean?"

"Like," I said, trying to figure out how to explain, "if you do something unique, you get a notification that you have earned an achievement and you get a reward. Sort of like earning a perk or experience."

Valens turned back to stare at me, and Romanus raised an eyebrow in surprise at my question.

"You know," he said, "your question implies you have earned a perk, something that almost nobody in Sycae has earned in a very long time."

"Well," I said, "if you think that is strange, then achievements are going to be an even bigger surprise. I just got one when we traveled far enough from the city. It's called *Survive a Safe Zone* and I received +1 to all of my attributes for achieving it."

Valens's and Romanus's eyes both widened. "Are you serious?" Valens asked.

"How is that possible? We have been this far out many times and never heard of such a thing," Romanus said.

"The achievement said I had to do certain things in the city to qualify and then leave the city, which it called a safe zone."

"Explain," Romanus said. I told him the requirements of the achievement, and they both exploded with questions when it became clear I had to have cleared a dungeon to complete the achievement.

"We shouldn't stop to discuss this here," Valens said after a moment, interrupting our discussion.

"Right," Romanus replied. "Right. We will discuss this more tonight when we find shelter. C'mon."

The two eyed me as we continued our walk, not in a distrustful way, but they were clearly wondering who exactly I was.

We hiked down the remnants of an old road as it cut through the abandoned farmland around us. Valens guided us in a zigzag out into the countryside when we needed to avoid some of the more dangerous monsters' territories. As night started to fall, he found us a small cottage in the middle of a lightly wooded area, and we secured ourselves inside it for the night. The cottage was made of thin, wooden lumber with poor insulation, so it wouldn't offer much protection, but Romanus assured me we were in a safe area—at least as safe as it got out here.

After we ate a light dinner, the two of them questioned me more about dungeons, achievements, and perks. I didn't reveal everything, but I did share with them that I had cleared a dungeon.

"I don't want to lie to you," I told them, "so I'm just going to say that there are some things I can't reveal about myself right now, but yes, I have cleared a dungeon in the city."

I told them the story of how I stumbled into my first dungeon and what the experience was like. When I was done, it was late and I could tell the two of them were tired but also excited about what I had told them.

"I had heard rumors," Romanus said, "about how strange and powerful dungeons could be, but I had no idea. And it's true you can receive treasure or a perk for completing it?"

"Yes," I replied, "you can get a perk or skill stone, a magical item, orbs, and possibly more. I don't know."

The two of them shared a look and then Romanus turned back to me. "How much would it cost for you to take us through a dungeon? We want to get this achievement that you mentioned. A +1 to all attributes is extremely useful. Merchants would pay thousands of blue orbs or more for such a boost for them and their families."

I shook my head as he spoke. "It's no problem. When we get back, we can try to tackle one together. I don't want to charge you, and I definitely don't want to run a bunch of rich merchants through dungeons. They are dangerous enough on their own. For the three of us, it should be fine, as long as we are all careful. In there, you will need to follow my lead like I follow yours out here, though. Even though you are both clearly skilled fighters, dungeons can be strange."

"Of course," Valens responded. "We would not want to be a burden."

After discussing the matter a bit more, Romanus surprised me by asking a question that had been on my mind all day as well. "What do you think it means that the name of the achievement calls the city a 'safe zone'?"

I had wondered that exact thing, and based on knowledge from my other world, I had an idea—and it wasn't a good one.

"I think," I said slowly, "that it means the monsters and dungeons are meant to be weaker in the city. I think the gods, or whatever happened to create this system, designated major cities as 'safe zones' to try to help people gain experience in an easier area than the rest of the world."

"But . . ." Valens said, thinking through the implications of what I was saying.

"Yeah," I said, "that means the city was supposed to be an easy place for people to survive in, but even that was too much, apparently. Either something went really wrong in Nova Roma or whoever designed this system underestimated how difficult the monsters truly were."

"We knew the monsters out here were more powerful . . ." Romanus said, thinking.

"Yeah," I said, "like you said, if they get more powerful the further from the city you get, it implies that the city is supposed to be easier. And if people can't even survive the monsters in the city, it doesn't bode well for humanity."

"We already knew we were doomed," Valens said grimly. "Everyone in Sycae just pretends otherwise."

Romanus nodded sadly at that.

I felt bad for the people who had lived their entire lives in this world. I couldn't help but think what would have happened to me if I had entered this world ten, twenty, or even thirty years in the future. I suspected that humanity might not survive for another generation at the rate things were going now. I could have found myself in a world completely overrun by monsters, with no way for me to ever gain a class or learn why the world was the way it was. I would have likely died confused and alone, never encountering a human.

It made me realize I might need to be a bit more proactive in trying to help the remnants of humanity on this planet if I didn't want to find myself wandering an abandoned Earth in the future. Maybe that should be one of my long-term goals. My body should, by my estimate, never die of natural causes. If the last of humanity truly died out, I could be trapped with nothing but monsters for company for a very long time. Maybe at one time I would have liked to be alone, but now I had started to appreciate being around other people. Maybe I needed to be more proactive about building friendships and connections and start thinking about ways to help humanity survive the ordeals that had brought them so close to extinction.

After that depressing line of thought, we all turned in for the night. I settled down under my blanket, pretending to sleep even though I felt no need to rest. Instead, I followed my nanobots as they tore down and recrafted my *Penetration Bullets*, completing the upgrade of my arsenal.

After some time of the three of us lying down, Romanus and Valens must have thought I had fallen asleep or assumed I couldn't see very well in the dark cabin, because my enhanced vision detected Romanus reach out and grab Valens's hand in a comforting grip. The two held hands for a moment longer, their fingers intertwined, before they separated and turned over to sleep. I was a bit surprised by what I saw, but it didn't bother me. I was happy they had each other to provide a small amount of comfort in their dying world.

Chapter 19

"From here, we will need to be more careful," Valens told us as we set out early the next morning. We traveled slowly, Valens leaving to scout several times or having us hunker down and hide for long stretches to avoid a monster nearby. He was clearly skilled at scouting, and Romanus told me that he had the *Hunter* class, which was apparently a non-combat class similar to *Archer* but without the combat skills. It allowed him to track and hunt monsters.

After several hours of traveling, we were cutting over an old field of wheat when I received a notification.

Regional quest discovered: Cull the Drakes.

You have discovered a regional quest. Complete this quest to receive additional rewards. Quest requirements: You must kill the drake and its spawn before the spawn becomes large enough to threaten the nearby populace. Reward: +1 to an attribute of your choice, 500 experience, additional reward depending on your contribution.

Do you wish to share this quest with your group?

I stopped in my tracks, surprised by the notification.

"Everything okay, Alexander?" Romanus asked me.

"Did either of you just get an announcement like you do when you get experience?"

"An announcement? No."

Valens shook his head as well.

"How strange," I said. "I just got one saying that there is a regional quest in this area for us and it comes with a reward if we complete it."

I elected to share the quest with the two of them. They both got a faraway look on their face and then refocused on me after a moment.

"This is amazing!" Romanus said enthusiastically.

"Why didn't we get this as well?" Valens asked. "We have never got something like this and we have been out here for years."

"It's because I got the achievement for surviving the safe zone. It said it unlocked a thing called quests, which seems like a part of the system set up to try to encourage people to kill monsters or complete other objectives to help people survive."

"That would make sense," Romanus said, "and we never knew because nobody has had the freedom to earn such an achievement in generations. At least not in Sycae. The army and Emperor probably knew but never bothered to tell the rest of us."

Valens shook his head in disgust at the thought.

"So many rewards we could have been earning," Romanus added. "That anyone could have been earning. It would make survival easier for everyone if we knew. Was the information lost for everyone?"

"It's possible," Valens said. "The army does have some teams still clearing dungeons, mostly ones that form in their enclave, but they would likely know about achievements."

"All it would take is one of them clearing a dungeon and then leaving the city," Romanus agreed. "The rest of the requirements are easy to meet. It seems likely they had that happen at some point."

"Even as our people barely hold on, people play games like this," Valens said, turning away in anger. Romanus reached to grasp his shoulder, clearly wanting to comfort him, but stopped himself.

"Are the drakes why you are out here for this hunt?" I asked to change the subject.

Romanus shook his head. "No, we had no idea a drake was even around. They are very dangerous, especially a mother drake with a fresh brood. We were hunting a type of bear. We spotted it on our last hunt but were already burdened with too much to carry back. It was a nature-type mutation, covered in bark that is worth a good amount as armor or a cloak. But this quest reward is significant. We should consider completing it instead."

Romanus told me everything he knew about drakes while Valens took a moment for himself. Drakes, I was told, were similar to dragons but less intelligent, lacked the ability to fly or use magic, and were generally smaller. Despite being smaller than actual dragons, they could still grow to the size of a house or larger and were incredibly quick and very dangerous. Their scales were resistant to most damage, physical or magical.

"Could we even complete the quest?" I asked after his description of how dangerous drakes could be.

Romanus looked over at Valens before replying. "We probably could with just the two of us, if we were careful and smart about it. With you as well, if your strength is enough to clear dungeons, it should be possible."

When Valens was feeling better, he left to scout the area around us in an attempt to find the drakes. Romanus and I waited in a small dip in a nearby field that was covered by overgrown wheat and other bushes. I tried to think if there was anything I could craft that would help us, but if the drakes were covered in scales that were resistant to damage, my newly empowered *Penetration Bullets* would likely be my most effective weapon, and I was stocked up with plenty of those now that my nanobots had finished re-forging them.

We waited several hours, Romanus falling into a light sleep while I kept watch. When Valens returned, he informed us that he had found the nesting grounds. We climbed out of the dip in the field we had been hiding in and followed him to an abandoned house nearby.

"We should rest and deal with them tomorrow when we have plenty of light," he told us. Romanus agreed and I shrugged, deferring to their expertise. We claimed a corner of the house that still had most of its roof intact and settled in. The three of us made small talk as we ate a meal of travel food and then we turned in for the night. The two of them fell asleep quickly, a skill they had clearly picked up from many years of traveling, while I lay under my blanket and tried to get some rest, but mostly I thought about the drakes and the implications of finding out that the city was considered a safe zone.

Sometime in the night, I was jostled awake by Valens, who was pushing on my leg to get my attention. When he saw that I was awake, he signaled that something was outside and that we should be silent. I nodded in return. I reached for my gun, not drawing it from its holster but ready in case something attacked us.

The three of us waited in complete silence. I could hear something rooting around in the distance, but nothing more than that. The creature sounded like it was at least a hundred or more feet away and the sound it was making wasn't that loud. I probably wouldn't be able to hear it if I didn't have such sensitive ears. I was curious how Valens had detected the creature.

Eventually, the creature moved away from us. We waited for another twenty minutes, just to be safe, and then Valens signaled that we were safe. I raised an eyebrow at him, asking how he knew the creature was gone.

"*Danger Sense* skill," Romanus quietly answered for Valens, who had moved to one of the windows in the old house and was looking out on the fields nearby.

"Ah," I replied. I didn't know exactly what that skill was, but from context, it sounded like it could give some kind of warning anytime danger was near. That was a handy skill to have out here, I was sure. It also explained why the two of them were so comfortable sleeping without keeping watch. I hadn't wanted to question them since I was new out here, but it had been one of the reasons I'd had trouble sleeping. I should have trusted they knew what they were doing.

Once Valens returned to us, the two of them settled back into their bedrolls and got some more sleep. I didn't even try, knowing I wouldn't be able to sleep, so I just got up and watched the darkened fields outside until the sun began to rise. After a quick breakfast, Valens led us to the drake's den.

I wasn't sure what I was expecting, but it wasn't what we found. The drake had dug a massive tunnel in the ground, almost a cave. It was big enough for a train to drive through and led downward at a steep angle. The hole stank of stale blood and musk.

Valens gathered us around the entrance. "Normally," he told me quietly, "we would dig large pit traps and lure a large beast like this to a prepared area and ambush it. But for a drake with a new brood, she won't leave them for anything. We will have to go in there to kill her."

"That seems like a bad idea," I said, eyeing the dark tunnel leading downward.

"Well," Romanus said, "I may have a bit of an advantage inside that should help us."

He reached toward me and touched my brow. I felt something warm pass through his finger and into my body. I gave him a puzzled look.

"*Shadow Sight*," he said, "a skill of mine. It will let you see in the dark for the next three hours."

He did the same for Valens. Valens then raised his hand and activated another skill of some kind. I felt warmth wash over me, as if I was suddenly standing next to a campfire. My body felt like it had been pumped full of adrenaline, but the surge of strength and speed didn't fade away. I moved my hands, making sure I hadn't lost control like when I last gained more attributes, but thankfully I had no issues with my coordination this time.

"That will also last a few hours," Valens told me.

I thanked them both, and then Romanus and Valens unstrapped their backpacks and hid them nearby. Romanus drew two large shadow-coated daggers that I was sure hadn't been on him a moment before. They looked dangerous, the shadows coiling around the blade and flickering as if they were alive.

Romanus went first and then Valens nodded at me, and the two of us followed him into the cave. As we entered, I could tell the tunnel in front of us was getting darker, but I could see as if it was the middle of the day thanks to Romanus's skill. I looked at the ceiling as we moved deeper into the tunnel and saw it was made from loose dirt, the occasional root hanging downward above our heads. I couldn't believe the dirt didn't collapse on top of us, because I was pretty sure physics dictated such loose material could not support the weight of the earth above it. But since it seemed stable enough and the other two weren't concerned, I just chalked it up to magic and tried to put it out of my mind. Valens drew his large two-handed sword, the first time I had seen him do so. It was almost as large as him, but he moved it like it weighed nothing, holding it in one hand as he carefully navigated downward through the tunnel.

The ground under us comprised dry, hard-packed dirt. I could see claw marks on the sides of the tunnel, deep grooves the size of my head at least. The center of the tunnel was flat and smooth, as if something large had dragged itself down it recently. I stared at the

245

claw marks, really hoping the confidence of these two hunters wasn't misplaced, although I was pretty sure I could escape if I really had to. I would just prefer not to lose these two new companions who might someday even become my friends.

We continued downward for several minutes, moving carefully to avoid sliding down the deep tunnel. I glanced downward for a second to check my foot placement, and when I looked up, Romanus was gone. I reached for my gun, thinking we were under attack somehow, but Valens shook his head at me. He made some hand signals that I eventually understood to mean Romanus had gone forward to scout. I stared down the tunnel, pretty sure that Romanus had disappeared or gone invisible in some way, impressed by whatever class he had.

The tunnel eventually leveled out, and the smell of blood and musk became even thicker, pooling at the bottom of the cave as if it was a liquid. Valens crouched down, his greatsword carefully resting against the compact dirt of the floor. I crouched as well and moved forward to stand next to him.

The tunnel opened up into a large circular cavern about twenty feet in front of us. There were a number of scaled bodies piled together in the center of the room, intertwined so much it was impossible to tell how many there were. Peeking through the mess of bodies was a faint golden glow. Somewhere in there was the mother drake, and she was a gold boss.

Valens tapped me lightly on my shoulder to get my attention and then began to count down on his fingers. When he finished, he made a fist and charged forward silently, his large two-handed sword pointed toward the drakes.

As he charged, I saw dark shadows coalesce above the nest of drakes in the form of a massive blade. It was the size of a person or larger, its edges flickering with deadly, living shadow. The shadow-blade stabbed downward into the pile of drakes, cutting deeply into them. The nest went crazy. Cries of pain and anger filled the small space, and the drakes began to writhe to untangle themselves as quickly as possible. When the large shadow-knife dissipated, Romanus was standing in its place. He began to cut around him, slicing the stirring drakes with both of his knives.

Valens, meanwhile, charged in next and began to carve through the smaller drakes with wide, devastating strikes of his sword.

246

Everywhere he struck, a deep, bloody gash was made in one or more of the drakes. Some of them died instantly.

Romanus flipped backward off the pile of drakes and disappeared again, leaving only Valens standing in front of the nest as the drakes finally untangled themselves and looked around for whoever was attacking them. Valens backed away and activated a skill, causing several illusory shields to appear around him just as the first drakes reached him.

I drew my revolver, not wanting to leave my companions fighting by themselves, and unloaded six shots into the neck of the mother drake as she reared her head upward, hissing in anger at Valens. My bullets struck her in the neck and lower jaw. The first couple of bullets knocked her head backward slightly but didn't seem to penetrate her thick scales. Looking closely, though, I saw the scales I had struck had fractured, leaking blood down the monster's chin. I reloaded and fired at the same spot again before the mother drake could recover, and this time my bullets penetrated deeply into her neck, spraying blood everywhere as bullet after bullet slammed into her. She roared in pain, the sound so loud in the confined space that I felt my eardrums rupture.

While the mother was distracted, Romanus reappeared behind the swarm of smaller drakes that were attacking Valens and began killing them with shadowy strikes from his daggers. Valens was backing away slowly, focusing more on defending himself while Romanus attacked the unsuspecting drakes that were focused only on reaching Valens. Even when Valens fought defensively, his large sword carved deep wounds in any drake that got too close, and his illusory shields kept the rest back when they tried to bite and claw him.

I reloaded again, watching the mother drake to see what she would do next. My bullets had clearly hurt her, but she wasn't out of the fight yet. She tucked her head, protecting the weakened scales on her neck, and began to search the cave, obviously trying to find the source of whatever had hurt her so badly. When she turned her head to the side to see better, I aimed quickly and fired. My bullet took her in the eye, shattering the cornea and blinding the beast. She roared again, turning to protect her eye from further attacks. I turned to the smaller drakes attacking Valens and unloaded the rest of my bullets into them in an attempt to give him some breathing room.

Reacting swiftly to the space Romanus and I had bought for him, Valens charged forward, throwing himself into a spin with his two-handed sword. His sword began to glow and his momentum sped up. He turned into a whirling top of death as his sword spun around and around him, killing drakes with every rotation. He carved a bloody path through the drakes, leaving them shattered and broken.

Romanus turned his attention to the mother, disappearing in a flash of shadows. Another large shadow-blade appeared above the mother, striking downward and cutting deeply into her back. When the knife faded, Romanus appeared again, standing on her back. He stabbed downward, digging both of his shadow-daggers into the mother's back.

I reloaded again and waited, watching as a number of the drakes recovered from Valens's spin and turned their attention to me. I targeted any that were looking in my direction, firing precise bullets into each one of their skulls, blowing their small heads backward and killing them instantly. My newly empowered bullets had no problem piercing through the scales of the smaller drakes.

As I reloaded again, the mother screamed and then charged forward, heading toward the tunnel leading out of her den, which was right where I was standing.

I hadn't fully reloaded yet, but I slammed the wheel of my revolver closed and fired at the bloody wound on her neck I had made before. Each bullet sent a spray of blood gushing out of the mother but didn't slow her down at all. I ran to the side as fast as I could, but the wide body of the mother still clipped me as she passed. I braced myself as her body connected with mine, expecting to be knocked painfully to the side. Instead, I was barely pushed backward. My strength was significant enough that I actually felt the drake give slightly when I pushed back against her scaled body.

I stared in surprise as the mother ran past me. Her tail came whipping after her, and I ducked quickly to avoid it as it swung over my head. I stared down at my body as I stood back up, shocked to find myself completely fine after the mother's body hit me. I kept being surprised by how different this world was from my own. The impact of attributes here was so supernatural it was hard to comprehend how much they changed about the world. I kept having to readjust my preconceptions, and it was really difficult to judge relative power levels when I had no experience with so much of this reality.

I looked back at the other two, who were finishing off the newborn drakes with ease. Seeing them in no danger, I turned and chased after the mother, reloading as I ran. I put on a burst of speed up the tunnel. I caught up to her easily as she pulled her heavy body up the tunnel ahead of me. I stayed back to avoid her tail as it whipped back and forth behind her, just keeping even with her so we wouldn't lose her when she got out of the tunnel.

On the surface, I followed her as she ran away from us in a clear panic, fleeing for her life. I raced beside her, pushing myself to go as fast as I could, and rapidly outpaced her. My lean, powerful body could run significantly faster than the mother, even with the pounds of rippling muscle that made up her body.

Once I was far enough ahead of her, I flipped and ran backward, firing all six revolver shots into one of her leading legs. My bullets penetrated deeply into the limb; the smaller scales that protected her extremities did not have the same protection as the bigger parts of her body. When she tried to use the leg I had shot, it couldn't support her weight and she stumbled, her momentum sending her spilling forward and crashing into the ground in front of me. She slid for several feet, carving a deep rut in the ground with her body. I slowed, reloading, and then lined up my shots and fired more bullets into her vulnerable throat. She tried to pick herself up, but my bullets knocked her head backward, sending her crashing back to the ground. She tried stirring once more but couldn't manage to raise her body more than a few inches. Instead, she slumped to the ground, an exhausted breath escaping from her body. Blood was pouring from the wound on her neck and back, and after a few minutes, she let out one last breath, dying.

I felt mixed emotions as I watched her die in front of me. On the one hand, it was clear she would have killed me and any other human she came across without a second thought. On the other, killing another being was a brutal and undignified act. Watching the once-proud mother drake bleed out in front of me, I felt a momentary sadness at the cruelness of the world. In a better time, maybe the beautiful and fierce drake could have been friendly or at least left to live its life on its own. In this time, however, survival was too difficult, and every advantage had to be seized. Otherwise, next time, I would be the one left bleeding out on the ground. Still, the drake deserved respect and I took a moment to honor her death as I waited for the others to catch up to me.

A couple of minutes of silence later, Romanus and Valens came running over. Seeing the mother drake dead, they slowed and grinned at me where I stood next to her corpse. Romanus threw an arm over Valens's shoulder in celebration, giving him a broad smile as well. Valens leaned into the side-hug, and then they stepped apart and walked up to me. Romanus clapped me on the shoulder and Valens nodded in respect toward me.

"I don't know what kind of magic you have," Romanus said, laughing, "but it was very effective!"

Valens approached the mother drake and inspected her body. I smiled back at Romanus, but before I could respond, the notifications from our kills rolled through my mind.

Newborn drake defeated—150 experience awarded.

Six more announcements for defeating newborn drakes followed immediately after the first.

Mature matriarch drake defeated—1000 experience awarded. You have completed the quest Cull the Drakes. You have been rewarded with +1 to an attribute of your choice and 500 experience. For being the first group to complete a regional quest in your region in nineteen years, you have also received an upgraded reward.

Perk obtained: Monster Hunter. You can sense the presence of monsters nearby. This perk scales with your level and perception attribute.

Congratulations, you have received enough experience to level your Archer class. You are now level 17.

Endurance +1

Chapter 20

"Wow," Romanus said as the three of us inspected our new perk.

"Yeah," I responded absently. That was quite the upgrade. A perk that let us sense the presence of nearby monsters would help Romanus and Valens stay alive out here, for sure. It would be great for me as well, although I didn't have a perception attribute to amplify yet; at least I didn't think I did. Momma Lena hadn't mentioned that as one of the normal attributes everyone had.

My hands absently reloaded and then holstered my revolver as I considered everything I had learned since leaving the city. I learned about safe zones. I learned about regional quests. I learned that I was strong enough to push back against a beast the size of a house and run fast enough to catch up to it as it fled. And I learned these two companions of mine were fierce fighters and trustworthy friends. It had been an eye-opening experience. I was very happy I had taken them up on their offer to join them.

"Well," Romanus said, clapping his hands, "enough admiring our fancy new perk, I say! Time to get to work." He pulled out his two daggers, which somehow looked like normal daggers now, and began to eye up the corpse of the mother. "I'll start on the mother, and then if we still have room, we can get some of the brood."

Valens nodded and gestured for me to follow him.

"We will need to protect him while he harvests the monster," he told me. "Sometimes this can be the most dangerous part. The blood will attract monsters and we need to take care of them without distracting him as he works, if at all possible."

"Sure," I told him. "I learned the hard way about blood attracting monsters just the other day."

I put my bonus attribute enhancement into my coordination and then followed Valens as he began to circle the corpse of the monster. With our new perk, I tried to sense any nearby monsters but couldn't feel anything yet. I wasn't sure how far away I could sense monsters yet, but if I didn't have the perception attribute to enhance it, I definitely wanted to add that to my list of short-term goals. Being able to sense monsters from far enough away to avoid them would be monumentally helpful.

An hour had passed, Romanus's butchery behind us the only sound nearby, when Valens looked to the east with a sudden jerk of his head. I couldn't sense anything, but I followed Valens as he ran in that direction until he found a large tree to hide behind. I followed, crouching down behind the remnants of an old stone wall that was still partially standing.

A minute later, I felt a strange sensation in my head. It felt almost like I had an internal radar system that was telling me something was approaching from in front of where Valens and I were hiding. My sense told me a monster was approaching. I could also sense it was a weak creature, although I didn't know if that was weak relative to me or relative to other monsters or if it was some universal constant determined by the system in our heads. If it was a universal system, it could be "weak" by their standards but plenty strong compared to us.

Despite not knowing exactly what counted as "weak," I was feeling confident after our fight with the drakes.

I could hear the creature approaching through the fields and brush surrounding us. I waited until it got closer. My new perk kept track of the monster perfectly, keeping me informed of its progress since it had come within range of my senses. When it was close enough to see, I saw that the monster had the body of a salamander, but with large, oversized fangs that protruded from its mouth, similar to a saber-toothed tiger from my Earth. It scuttled toward us on rubbery feet that looked able to climb surfaces easily. I was surprised to see it in this area. It seemed like it could survive better underground or somewhere where it could cling to high surfaces.

As the creature ran past us, clearly fixated on the smell of the drake's blood, its tongue flicking out past its protruding fangs, Valens leapt forward and struck the monster in its back leg, crippling the beast in a single strike.

I aimed and fired a full round of *Penetration Bullets*, striking it in the middle of its torso. My bullets knocked it sideways, which forced it over on its wounded leg, causing it to stumble even more.

The scales on the salamander were significantly weaker than those on the drake, and each of my bullets blew a deep hole into the monster's side.

The creature, crippled and knocked sideways, collapsed, slamming its head onto the ground and sliding forward. I reloaded and moved to the front of the monster, where it appeared to be dazed from the surprise attacks.

Not waiting to see if it would recover, I fired two more bullets into its skull, killing it instantly. I flicked open the wheel of my gun, reloaded quickly, and then turned to see how Valens was doing.

He was watching me with a curious expression on his face. I raised an eyebrow at him, but he just shook his head and returned to looking into the distance for any other monsters that might be approaching. I couldn't sense anything, so I just walked over to him, holstering my revolver for now.

As the rest of the day progressed, Valens and I killed several more monsters that tried to approach the drake's body. Fortunately, none of them ended up being a problem for the two of us. Protecting Romanus earned us another six hundred experience, which wasn't quite enough to level me again, but I was close.

"Impressive work," Valens said to me after we finished off the last beast, a large black wolf the size of a horse that lay in front of us.

"You as well," I told him, equally impressed by him. His strength and speed were almost equal to my own. He must have more than just a single level 20 class, since my attributes scaled off my body, which had to be significantly stronger and faster than his.

Romanus had finished harvesting the drake and even had time to harvest several parts from the monsters that had been attracted to the drake's corpse, but we ended up having to leave the smaller drakes because we couldn't carry any more. According to Romanus, their weaker scales made them only moderately valuable anyway.

He and Valens quickly threw together a makeshift handcart to carry the massive skin of the drake, which Romanus had expertly harvested. The handcart was nothing but large branches tied together with a fine rope, but it was good enough that we could drag the cart behind us with no problem, even with the heavy, scaled hide on it.

Once the hide was secured to the handcart, they filled their backpacks with vials of drake blood and some blood from the other monsters we had killed. Then various claws and teeth were packed up and put into their backpacks or strapped to the sides. They looked like a couple of vagabond tinkerers, but everything seemed secure enough to get us back home without any problems. I had a bit of room in my backpack as well, so Romanus filled it with some of the smaller scales that had fallen off the mother drake and a couple of her back claws as well.

Once that was done, we put as much distance as possible between us and the corpses before night fell. I volunteered to pull the makeshift cart, eager to test my body further and carry my weight, since the other two had significantly fuller backpacks. The cart, even burdened with the heavy hide of the mother drake, was easy to drag behind me. Valens and Romanus guided me through clear areas so the cart wouldn't get caught on anything, quickly clearing brush and other obstacles if there wasn't a clear path forward.

That night, we camped in the open, not finding a usable home or cabin to sleep in. Thankfully, nothing approached us, although we could hear monsters fighting far off in the distance several times. Valens kept waking up, staring in different directions from time to time, likely sensing a monster nearby. I didn't sense anything but wasn't too tired, so I stayed awake just to be safe.

The next day, Valens took a turn pulling the cart, and I asked if they would mind me practicing my *Dash* since we had so much open space in front of us as we traveled.

"Learning your first movement skill?" Romanus asked me with an amused look on his face.

"Yeah . . ." I replied, grimacing. "I tried in the city, but the space was too limited and I ended up hurting myself."

Romanus laughed. "You should have seen Valens when he tried out his *Charge* for the first time!"

Valens groaned in reply.

"We were celebrating our level increases and he decided to try his new skill out in the middle of the inn. Next thing I know, he's flying through the window like a drunk being thrown out by the innkeeper!" Romanus laughed uproariously at the memory, and I saw even Valens had a smile on his face at how amused Romanus was.

"The first time Romanus tried his *Shadow Step*—" Valens replied.

"Nooooo!" Romanus interrupted, trying to stop him.

"The first time he tried his movement skill," Valens continued, undaunted, "he disappeared from in front of me, and the next thing I knew, an old grandma was screaming murder from a window above us. When I looked up, there was Romanus, trying to climb out of the poor grandmother's window while she pelted him with her dirty laundry."

Romanus laughed just as hard at himself as he had at Valens. Valens smiled warmly back at him, and I couldn't help but laugh as well at the image.

"I, uhh . . ." I said, unsure if I should tell my story. "I tried it on an empty street in the middle of the city and ended up slamming myself into the side of a building. Next thing I knew, I woke up and it was dark out and I was lying in the middle of the building. I'm pretty sure almost every monster in the city smelled my blood and came to try to kill me soon after."

I left out the part about the wall being made of stone and healing numerous broken bones over a matter of hours.

"No way!" Romanus said, doubling over in laughter.

"How did you survive?" Valens asked me, a genuine look of curiosity on his face.

I patted the weapon hidden under my cloak. "Once I killed the first few, the rest of the monsters were more interested in fighting each other than finding me. I just waited until the sun rose and promised myself I wouldn't be such an idiot in the future."

Romanus's laughter doubled and we had to stop because his breathing was getting so ragged.

"You're lucky to survive!" he said through gasping breaths. "I can just imagine your surprise waking up and seeing the sun had set. Oh my!"

Valens eyed under my arm where my firearm rested, but he didn't ask me for any details about my weapon.

After Romanus recovered, we continued forward and he and Valens gave me several helpful tips about using a movement skill.

They both knew someone that had taken the same skill as I did from the *Archer* class, so they had some knowledge about the skill and how to use it.

The key, they said, was to picture clearly what you wanted the skill to do. A movement skill reacted to intent, but it took practice to visualize exactly what your intent was. They urged me to repeat over and over in my head the distance I wanted to travel before activating my skill. They told me to continue doing that until I could move instinctively with the skill.

I spent the rest of the day practicing with them while they took turns dragging the drake's hide behind them. At first, I overshot my planned distance by a significant margin. I could tell Valens and Romanus were a bit shocked by how far I shot forward, but neither of them mentioned the oddity, so I didn't bring it up. I hoped I could trust them with how much I was revealing. I felt confident that I could, but I wasn't exactly the best judge of people yet. I just had to hope my instincts were right and they were good people.

The neat thing about *Dash* was that when I did the skill right, I landed perfectly on the ground; my momentum stopped right when my dash ended. It was a strange feeling. *Dash* shot me through the air so fast that it felt like I was bound to plow into the ground when the skill ended, but instead, the skill just stopped all of my momentum instantly, placing me down perfectly when it ended.

I practiced through the fields as we traveled, zipping here and there until I could control the distance well enough that I felt confident I wouldn't throw myself into any more stone walls. My high memory score, and my experience projecting my thoughts as an AI, made it fairly easy to control once I got a chance to practice safely. By the time the sun was starting to set, I could dash in any direction and for almost any distance I desired. I practiced with my gun in hand, dashing backward and mock-firing, dashing sideways and reloading, or dashing forward to strike an enemy with my left hand and then dashing back out of range.

"Aren't you getting tired of that?" Romanus yelled at me from across a field at one point, but I just waved him off. I could practice for days without stopping, if needed. It was a pleasant feeling to gain control and precision with the skill as I practiced it over and over.

We camped in another abandoned house that night. I told Romanus and Valens that I wasn't sleepy yet and would stay up, so they should just ignore me. They grumbled but turned in after a quick dinner of dried food.

I didn't leave the house, not wanting to attract too much attention, but I found an empty room and practiced dashing only a few feet in different directions. There didn't seem to be a cooldown, but I noticed that the longer my *Dash* carried me, the more I felt the physical exertion. The best I could figure, dashing a certain distance took the same amount of energy from my body as if I had run the same distance. So if someone out of shape could only run twenty feet without feeling winded, the *Dash* skill would leave them out of breath if they dashed for that amount of distance. Thankfully, with my body and my enhanced endurance, I could dash all day and night without feeling more than a little tired.

I practiced dashing and reloading, mock-firing, and shadow-boxing enemies as if I was engaging in hand-to-hand combat, mixing all three over and over. I wove my dashes into my mock-combat practice, learning to use it in a split second and trying to develop a sense of how to fight while utilizing the skill at the same time. My ability to repeat repetitive tasks, with no need for a break, helped me once again as I pushed myself to master the skill. I was sure someone watching would think there was something seriously wrong with me as I practiced for hours and hours without a break, but Romanus and Valens seemed to be sleeping so I cut loose and practiced to my heart's content. I also had a feeling the two of them wouldn't judge me if they saw what I was doing, although they would definitely give me some odd looks.

By the time the sun rose, I felt confident in using my new skill in and out of combat.

I greeted the two men as they rose, and we ate a quick breakfast and then set out for the city.

"You aren't going to practice anymore?" Romanus asked when I offered to pull the makeshift handcart.

I shook my head. "No, I'm feeling better about the skill now. I was able to practice a bit last night."

Romanus raised an eyebrow and Valens looked over at me, but neither spoke. I could tell they were skeptical. It probably took them weeks or months to master their movement skills, but I didn't feel like trying to explain how rapidly my brain could learn and how much I had practiced last night while the two of them slept.

I pulled the cart throughout the day, wanting to make up for the two of them having to pull it all day yesterday. By mid-afternoon, we entered the outskirts of the city again, and I could see the shimmer of the barrier of Sycae ahead of us. No monsters had disturbed us, thanks to Valens's skills, our perks, and his and Romanus's knowledge of how to avoid the monsters in the area.

Once we were back inside the enclave, I was assaulted with several announcements in my head.

Personal quest discovered: Clear the City.

You have discovered a personal quest. Quest requirements: You must clear 20 dungeons to help secure your city. Reward: +1 to an attribute of your choice, 2000 experience. Quest progress: 10/20.

Personal quest discovered: Make a Home.

You have discovered a personal quest. Quest requirements: You must establish a home and secure it from your enemies. Reward: +1 to an attribute of your choice, 500 experience.

Personal quest discovered: Contribute to the Economy.

You have discovered a personal quest. Quest requirements: You must sell goods or provide services worth a fair amount of money, depending on your region. Reward: 1 gold core, 200 experience. Quest progress: complete.

Congratulations, you have completed Contribute to the Economy. Reward: 1 gold core, 200 experience.

Quest updated: Contribute to the Economy II. You must sell goods or provide services worth a significant amount of money, depending on your region. Reward: 3 gold cores, 600 experience.

Congratulations, you have received enough experience to level your Archer class. You are now level 18.

Coordination +1

Both men stopped and watched me as I froze in place in front of the gate. After a moment, I recovered enough to continue on.

"More announcements?" Romanus asked.

"Yeah," I responded, "but they are personal so I can't share them. I never got them before, so there must be something important about getting the achievement for leaving the city."

The two of them looked at each other and then back at me.

"Don't worry," I told them. "We will get it for you. We can talk more about it later."

They smiled at me gratefully. We talked as Romanus led us through the city. Eventually, we reached the blacksmith he had sold his goods to before.

"Now," he said as we approached the shop, "this hide is going to sell very well. I estimate at least one hundred gold orbs, if not more."

"Wow," I said, surprised.

"Yeah," he told me. "This will make for some prime armor and could make twenty or more sets, at least. It's probably the most mature drake killed in a generation or two, I would guess. The question for you, Alexander, is if you just want your share of the orbs or if you want a suit of armor made for yourself."

"That's an option?" I asked.

"Yeah, Barbaros can make us each a set from this hide that will serve us well, but it will be costly. I can bargain the price down for all three of us, if you want. Or we can take equal shares and do whatever we want, individually. I do think we would get a better price if we negotiate three suits together, though."

"Hmm . . ." I said, thinking about my options. My clothing was the equivalent of most basic armors from Earth, but it took quite a number of shots from my newly empowered bullets to pierce the drake's hide, and that had been on its more vulnerable neck. A suit of armor made from the thicker scales of its body would offer significantly more protection than my clothing. Plus, Romanus had said the drake was resistant to magic, so hopefully the armor would help with that as well.

"Okay," I said. "Let's go for three sets and we can split whatever is left."

"Perfect!" Romanus said, smiling. "Especially considering you are out here fighting monsters in only a cloak and shirt!"

We entered the blacksmith's shop, and I left Romanus to bargain over the loot we had gathered. The hide wasn't the only rare ingredient we had collected, and even with the cost of the labor to make three suits of armor, we received sixty gold orbs from the blacksmith. My share was twenty gold orbs, a real haul for a frantic couple days of work.

259

"One of the most profitable runs we have ever made," Romanus said.

Valens nodded at his words. "Not to mention a perk."

"Indeed," Romanus said, eyeing me. "When do you think we can clear that dungeon we spoke about? We are eager to try for that achievement you received for leaving the city."

The blacksmith had told us it would be three weeks before our armor was completed. I figured we could probably complete a dungeon without it, but I didn't really want to take a chance, so I convinced them we should wait until then. They invited me to go on another hunt with them, but I declined, wanting to work on some of my own goals for now. We made a plan to meet back at the inn in three weeks to collect our armor and go on their first dungeon expedition.

I turned in early for the night, thanking them again for taking me with them and wishing them well in their next hunt. Upstairs in my room, I spent the night replenishing my bullets and then managed to fall asleep for several hours.

Chapter 21

Before I left Sycae, I checked the enchanters' shops for new types of ammunition and other cheap runes to see if there was anything that could improve my current arsenal, but everything was overpriced compared to the ammunition in Perama and nothing I found was particularly helpful compared to the runes I already had.

Slightly disappointed, I made my way to the waterfront that faced south. I walked out on the furthest dock I could find and then used my *Dash*. Halfway across the channel, I reached the end of my dash and my momentum stopped completely, but I immediately activated a second dash and sent myself flying all the way across the channel without touching the water at all.

When I landed on the other side, I was slightly winded and had to take a few deep breaths to recover. Using *Dash* twice in a row seemed to take more from me than just using it once. I would have to keep that in mind.

I ran through the city, pushing the limits of my body just to see how fast I could go. I practically flew through the streets, easily running faster than a car could have driven in the city. My endurance let me run without feeling tired, and when I came to a difficult turn that I couldn't make because of how fast I was going, I used *Dash* and reset my momentum, letting me stop on a dime. It was a heady feeling, and I wondered if many people had learned how useful *Dash* truly was. I could sprint full tilt at a wall and dash to the side. The skill would shoot me sideways, completely shifting my momentum, then stopping me perfectly. It was strange to feel the rules of physics bend to my skill so easily.

A trip through the city that used to take half a day barely took a half hour now. I moved so rapidly that the monsters I passed barely had time to register me running down the street before I was gone.

I entered the courtyard of my villa, wondering why it hadn't counted toward my quest to make a home. Maybe because it wasn't secure yet. I had wanted to find a way to keep monsters away for a while now. Maybe then it would count for the quest.

I opened the front door, glad to be back home, when I found myself suddenly frozen in place. I struggled to move but couldn't even force myself to blink. I could hear footfalls approaching from my left, the soft steps across the villa floor echoing around the empty foyer.

"Well," a man's voice said, "that was easy enough. Looks like the information was correct. He did use this as a safehouse."

"I told you I could find him," a weaselly voice replied. "I knew this was his place once I found it. Nobody would bother to clean a house in this area if it wasn't being used."

"Yes, yes," the other man said dismissively. "I said you were right already."

I couldn't move my eyes to see who was talking, but he eventually walked in front of me, looking me up and down. I could see four men. One of them was the priest I had fought at the docks before. The other was a small man who looked like he hadn't eaten a good meal in years and had never heard of taking a bath in his life. Behind them stood two larger men, each wearing an armored breastplate with a sigil of a golden flame emblazoned on the front. Both had swords on their belts, and from their demeanor, I was sure they were experienced in using them.

"Did you think you could kill my compatriot and I would forget about you, Varangian scum?"

The priest spat in my face. I couldn't dodge or blink, and I felt the spittle cover my eyes, partially blinding me. My anger rose, and my body echoed the outrage my mind was feeling, pumping me full of adrenaline. I pushed back at the spell that was holding my body, refusing to bend to such enslavement. I had broken the chains they had tried to wrap me in last time. I would break whatever spell held me this time as well.

"Disarm him," the priest said. "I want to know what magic he has that allows him to kill one of us so easily."

The two guards stepped forward and searched me, taking my belt, my knife, my gun, and my bandolier full of my grenades. I strained at the hold on me as they grabbed and searched me, the violation of my personal space driving me into a rage. I felt something start to give in my mind as I was overcome with emotion. It felt like I was pushing against a wall that had been erected between my mind and my body, freezing me out. The wall felt strong yet brittle, like thick glass. All I needed was to crack it once and it would shatter. I began to slam my anger and rage against the wall in my mind, refusing to accept that it could keep me from controlling my own body.

I was so focused on breaking the wall that held me that I missed what the priest said as he inspected my revolver. I felt cracks begin to form in the glass, and with a mental roar, I slammed my mind against the glass one more time, shattering the wall and restoring power over my own body once again.

Before anyone could react, I punched forward with my left hand and activated my *Glove of Golem Strength*. The golem's fist covered my own and slammed into the smaller, weaselly man gloating in front of me. I saw the ripple of my fist spread out from his chest, ripping his body apart as my fist impacted against him. With an explosion of gore, the small man that had tracked me was thrown across the room, the other three splattered with his blood and parts of his body.

"*What?*" the priest yelled, ducking away from the explosion of blood and body parts. I stepped forward and activated my other fist, slamming the second golem's hand into the priest's body as well. I expected the priest to be destroyed much like his companion, but my fist struck a barrier of silver instead of his body. My golem-enhanced punch was strong enough to shatter the barrier, though, sending the priest staggering backward, but he appeared unharmed physically.

Before I could step forward to attack the priest again, one of his guards leapt forward and grabbed at me. The other guard drew his sword. I blocked the hands of the first guard. I sidestepped quicker than the guard could move and pushed his hands to the side, sending him moving past me.

The second guard held his sword toward me, and the sword began to glow with a golden light as he activated a skill of some kind.

I activated *Dash* and slipped to the side of the room, putting some space between me and the two guards. The priest, meanwhile, had recovered and was pointing at me with a look of concentration on his face. Not wanting to get caught by whatever

263

spell he was casting, I activated *Dash* again to place myself directly in front of him.

He finished his spell, but I stepped swiftly to the side as a set of chains formed in the air where I had been standing. They were identical to the ones that had almost captured me last time.

Seeing his chains wasted, he tried to turn to look at me, but I grabbed his arm, bent it backward, and slammed my left hand down on his elbow, shattering the bones as I twisted his arm further. The priest screamed in pain as I mangled his arm, crippling him, at least for now.

The first guard that had tried to tackle me had recovered and drawn his sword. The second guard was approaching rapidly, trying to get to me with his golden sword. The other guard, seeing the priest harmed, pointed his sword at him and activated a skill of some kind. I saw the priest bathed in a golden light, and his arm began to heal in front of my eyes.

"Rude," I said, turning to keep the priest between me and the other guard. I scanned the room for my revolver and found that someone had dropped it and my other gear on the ground when I surprised them by breaking their spell. I shoved the priest at the guard with the golden sword, entangling them, and then ducked down, snagging the revolver, my belt, and my bandolier. As soon as I had my gear, I dashed backward, landing smoothly at the back of the room. I raised my revolver to shoot the three of them, but the second guard saw me, leapt in front of the priest and his fellow guard, and activated some kind of barrier that shimmered in the air around them. I growled at how difficult these people were to kill, my anger boiling over, demanding I kill them.

I took aim and unloaded all six of my shots at the barrier anyway. It shattered after just three bullets. The other three struck the guard in the chest, impacting against his breastplate, but they caused no damage to the guard himself. I cursed, realizing the breastplate must be powerfully enchanted or empowered in some way.

I reloaded quickly, loading six *Explosive Bullets*. The priest had recovered by now, his arm almost fully healed, and was glaring at me with open hatred on his face. The guard with the golden sword stepped forward, activating his own barrier to protect himself and his companions now that the other guard's shield had failed.

"Kill him!" the priest yelled. I backed up slowly, navigating through an open door behind me and into a hallway that led toward the kitchen. The two guards charged forward at the priest's order, intent on catching me before I could attack further. The barrier from the first guard was still active as he charged, protecting him from my bullets.

I dashed backward the length of the hallway behind me, creating more space between us. The guard with the golden sword followed me first. As he saw me down the hallway, landing softly on the ground at the end of my dash, he yelled something that sounded like Latin, and large golden wings burst from his back. He took a step and then launched himself into the air, flying rapidly down the hallway toward me.

He was too close for me to fire *Explosive Bullets* at him without me hurting myself, so I aimed past him and fired at the other guard who was just coming through the doorway and into the hallway.

My bullet exploded on the chest of the second guard, sending him flying back into the room with the priest. The fireball rapidly filled the hallway with superheated fire, hiding the second guard and the room from my sight. The flying guard reached me, his golden sword coming down to chop through me like a divine angel smiting an apostate, but I ducked down too fast for him and threw myself under him as he flew over me. The guard surprised me by kicking downward and knocking me down as I rolled under him.

He landed behind me and turned, grabbing me with one of his arms. I pushed off the ground, sending us both tumbling backward onto the floor, with me on top but with my back to the guard.

I rolled over, positioning myself above the guard as he struggled to hold on to me and his sword at the same time. Realizing his sword was useless, he released it and grabbed me with his other hand, but I used both of my hands to grab his head and began to slam it against the stone floor of the hallway.

The first strike had little effect, as the guard tried to grab my hands to stop me, but I was stronger than him and had better leverage. I raised his head and slammed it down again. The guard looked up at me, the anger in his expression starting to fade as confusion came over his face. I didn't stop, slamming his head against the hard stone floor over and over until I knew he was dead.

I rolled off the guard and looked down the hallway, disgusted with what I had done, but I refused to go easy on the priest and his lackeys who had tried to capture me a second time. My explosion had faded, but I didn't see the other guard or the priest. I dashed down the hallway and glanced through the doorway into the foyer, finding the priest and the other guard were nowhere to be seen.

I took a deep breath, trying to calm the anger that threatened to overwhelm me. After several calming breaths, my blood stopped roaring in my ears and I could hear, very faintly, their steps pounding down the cobblestone street outside my villa. I didn't hesitate and began to follow. I strapped on my belt and bandolier as I ran, holstering my revolver so I could run faster.

I sprinted out my front door and dashed through the courtyard, landing softly in the street out front. I couldn't see the two of them, but my sensitive hearing picked up the sound of their hasty retreat nearby. They were one street over, running as fast as they could across the cobblestones, their boots making enough racket for me to track them easily. It was clear the priest hadn't invested enough in his endurance because I could hear him panting as the two of them ran, clearly already out of breath. I smiled grimly at the sound.

Separating us was a large rectangular warehouse that stood across from my villa. It was about two and a half stories tall and had a flat roof. I used my *Dash* to launch myself upward at an angle, soaring through the air as if I was truly flying. The skill had said I could use it in any direction, and upward was a direction to me.

The skill worked, obeying my intent as Romanus and Valens had said it would, sending me upward at a breakneck speed. My momentum froze just as I reached the lip of the roof, and I stepped forward, landing perfectly on the edge of the roof as if I had been doing such maneuvers for years. Not hesitating, I took off at a sprint across the rooftop, parallel to the streets, and jumped across the gap to another warehouse with ease, keeping pace with the fleeing priest below. I paced them, crossing the warehouse until I was running on the edge of the rooftops directly above where they ran on the street below. I drew my revolver and jumped off the roof, toward the priest and his guard. Before I could hit the ground, I used *Dash* to change my momentum, throwing myself forward until my dash ended, placing me down on the street perfectly. I turned to look at the priest, who was skidding to a stop at the sight of me standing in front of him.

I kicked forward and slammed my foot into his shin before he could stop himself, shattering the bone and sending him catapulting into the hard cobblestone street.

The guard, reacting a bit faster, turned his run into a charge and tried to run me through with the sword in his hand. I dodged his thrust, my speed faster than his, and then activated my *Glove of Golem's Strength* again, having sensed it was off cooldown. I crouched and punched the guard's thigh as his thrust carried him past me, crushing his leg and sending him spinning to the cobblestones as well.

The guard rolled several times, screaming in pain as his leg flopped behind him and slammed against the ground every time he rolled over on it. When he finally stopped, I saw he was still conscious, which surprised me. He must have a high endurance to be able to take such punishment. His leg looked like it had been run over by a truck, and he was clearly in extreme pain.

The guard shook his head, grimacing, and glanced at the priest, who was whimpering on the ground next to him. I rushed forward to kill the guard, but he activated a skill and I saw the familiar golden glow bathe the priest in its healing light.

I couldn't help but admire the guard's dedication, but that didn't stop me from slamming my other golem-charged fist into his head as I rushed toward him, painting the street behind him for almost thirty feet with his brains and blood.

I whirled toward the priest, but the healing light had already started its work. The priest had rolled over, his eyes closed in concentration. I activated *Dash* to close the distance between us, but before I could get to him, he finished his spell.

"I invoke my pact. Grant me protection!" the priest yelled.

My dash deposited me directly in front of the man, but before I could strike him dead, a portal opened in the air above him. The portal flickered red and black and began to spiral open wider and wider, hiding the priest behind the opening. I froze, watching in surprise as a large hand, the size of my head or larger, appeared inside the portal and tried to grab me. I jumped back and pointed my revolver at the hand, unsure of what to do.

The priest carefully picked himself up behind the portal, clearly still wounded. He turned in my direction and leaned out around the side of the portal, an arrogant look on his face. I fired several *Explosive Bullets* at the ground beneath the portal, eager to wipe that smile off his face. A dark red energy zapped out of the portal and met my bullets as they flew toward the priest's feet, destroying the bullets before they could explode. The priest's smile only grew wider at the sight.

I began to ease myself sideways, trying to get a better angle on the man, when a whip of pure fire shot out of the portal and wrapped itself around my leg.

I screamed in pain but kept my gun aimed at the priest even as the whip burned through my clothing and began tearing into my leg. Seeing I was still standing, the priest lost his smile and decided he'd had enough. He turned and ran, keeping the portal between the two of us. I grimaced, angry that he was escaping but unable to give chase with the whip entangling me.

I dashed backward, the momentum of the dash enough to unwind the whip from my leg, but the pain as it spun around and around my thigh almost caused me to black out. I fell to the ground as my dash ended, gasping from the excruciating pain radiating through me.

I stared at the portal through watery eyes as I struggled to stand. Another hand appeared in the portal, this one holding a burning whip that hung downward, scorching the cobblestones beneath it. A head quickly followed the second hand, and a moment later, a demon stepped through the portal completely.

The demon was covered in shifting magma that fluctuated between a dark, black obsidian sheen to a glowing, molten red. Two large black horns stuck up from his head, and his knees bent the wrong way. He saw me staring at him and gave me a vicious grin, his mouth stretching unnaturally wide across his molten face.

I lifted myself up from the ground, hopping up on my good foot, and activated my *Dash* to get away from the demon. He stalked toward me, snapping his whip in front of himself as he approached. I flicked open the wheel of my gun, dumped the remaining *Explosive Bullets* onto the ground, and frantically reloaded *Holy Bullets*, hoping they would be effective against the demon.

I dashed again just as his whip snapped forward at me. I fired as I flew backward. Each bullet slammed into the demon's chest, causing obsidian and magma to shear off the monster. The demon grunted as each bullet struck him, indicating the *Holy Bullets* were doing something to him, but the wounds seemed superficial at best. The magma of his chest was already reforming over the first few bullet holes by the time my last bullet hit him.

The demon began to run toward me, his large, cloven feet thudding loudly against the cobblestones with each of his steps. His speed wasn't impressive, but he was rapidly closing the distance by his sheer size alone. Each step he took was three or four feet, at least. I couldn't run with my injured leg, so I dashed again, sending myself soaring backward down the street until I reached a turn in the road. I stopped there, having put almost a full city block between the two of us, and reloaded more *Holy Bullets*.

The demon, seeing how easily I could escape him, roared in anger as he continued to lumber toward me. His whip disappeared from his hand, and in its place, a massive, fiery warhammer appeared as he sped up. I aimed and fired, hitting him with every bullet, but to little effect again.

"Damn," I muttered to myself, realizing I couldn't fight my way out of this problem. I dashed sideways, pushing myself around the corner from the demon. I landed softly but then had to dash backward as the fiery warhammer came careening through the side of the building I had been standing behind. The demon was still around the corner, but his warhammer almost clipped me as it exploded through the wall, sending stone and debris flying across the street in its wake.

My dash was fast enough that I dodged the worst of it, but I stared in disbelief at the power of the demon. His warhammer continued forward, plowing through the building on the other side of the street. A second later, it returned, flying back to the demon and effortlessly smashing the stone wall yet again on its return. The building began to tilt dangerously, the warhammer having weakened its foundations now that it had passed through the building twice. I dashed again, putting more distance between me and the building as quickly as possible.

The building tilted more and more until it finally collapsed with a deafening roar, a cloud of dust and debris filling the street in an instant. I coughed as the cloud struck me, covering my mouth and closing my eyes to avoid as much of the dust as possible. As I did, I realized this was my chance to escape. The corner I had just dashed through was blocked by the collapsed building and the entire area was shrouded in dust, making it almost impossible to see.

Ignoring the pain in my leg, I turned around and used my *Dash* to launch myself down the street as fast as I could go. I could barely walk, but my *Dash* didn't care about my leg. My skill launched me forward perfectly each time and then froze my momentum at the end of the dash, letting me land carefully on my good leg. I dashed as far away from the demon as possible, recklessly flying down side streets and alleys, always moving away from where the demon had been.

I continued my retreat until I reached the far north of the city, near Perama and the channel that led to Sycae. I paused for a moment at the waterfront, feeling the exhaustion from so many uses of *Dash*. I felt like I had run a marathon at a full sprint. I was breathing hard, and my body felt shaky from my injuries and my exhaustion.

I couldn't remember a time I had ever felt this tired. With a weary glance, I looked behind me but couldn't see any sign of the demon. I must have lost him a while ago, but I had refused to stop until I was absolutely sure he wouldn't catch up to me. The power of that monster was significantly higher than anything I had fought so far, and I did not want to fight it now that I was so tired, injured, and had nothing that seemed to damage the demon.

I had just started to gain some confidence in my own strength, but the demon very effectively reminded me to never get arrogant. If this city was just a safe zone, the rest of the world could be full of monsters as powerful or even more powerful than that demon. If I hadn't been with Romanus and Valens, the drake and her spawn would have likely overwhelmed me and killed me. And if I hadn't chosen *Dash* as my first skill, the demon would have likely killed me as well. I needed to never forget how dangerous this world really was.

I took several deep breaths and then pushed myself into another dash, launching myself across the water toward Sycae. Halfway there, I used a second dash and felt my body rebel in protest. My vision started to go black and my head began to spin. I felt like I was going to vomit even as I flew through the air in a perfectly straight line. When I reached the far side of the water, I couldn't control myself enough to land on the dock I had aimed for and instead crashed into the water, barely able to think clearly as the cold water swallowed me.

I heard someone yell above me, but my mind couldn't focus. My vision was flickering, and my mind could only remember bits and pieces at a time. I recalled somehow climbing onto the dock, where concerned bystanders came to see if I was okay. I remembered somehow standing and staggering away from the docks toward the inn I had rented, but I didn't remember getting there.

Chapter 22

The next thing I knew, the sound of banging woke me from a nightmare where I was imprisoned by flaming chains that never stopped burning me no matter how loud I screamed for mercy. I cracked open my bleary eyes, surprised to find the banging was someone knocking on the door of my room. I tried to remember how I had gotten here, but I couldn't piece it all together enough for it to make sense.

The banging on my door continued, and I carefully leveraged myself up from the bed and staggered toward the door. I was still fully dressed, and my pants were in the process of being repaired. The skin underneath still looked burned and scarred, but the excruciating pain from yesterday was lessened, so I knew some healing had occurred while I slept.

I opened the door to see a young man standing in the doorway.

"Sir," the young man said, "you only paid for one night and you haven't come down to tell us if you are staying another night or leaving. It's well after noon and we need to know if someone else is going to be staying here."

I fumbled with my belt until I found a piece of silver and handed it to the young man.

"Reserve the room for another couple days, and can you have someone bring me up a meal and a pitcher of clean water?" I asked.

The young man grabbed the silver coin and bowed respectfully once he realized I wasn't trying to freeload in the room. "Of course!" he said, turning and hastening down the hallway.

I closed the door and collapsed back on the bed. The pain in my leg was manageable, so I knew I was almost finished healing. I was also starving, so my nanobots must have been busy all night repairing the wound.

I spent the rest of the day and night recuperating. By the next morning, I was fully mended and feeling better. I thanked the innkeeper on my way out and then made my way back across the channel.

This time, I avoided my old villa and went exploring toward the northwestern parts of the city. That direction led toward the Emperor's enclave, so I didn't go too close to that area—I didn't want to get involved in even more conflict than I already was—but there was still plenty of city to explore as far away from the priests as I could get.

I found an abandoned home that I secured for myself. It wasn't as nice as my villa, but it was a stone home with solid walls and no damage to its thick doors. I picked a small interior room on the second floor that had no windows and cleaned it out. Then I began to explore around my new place to catalog all the dungeons I could find in the area.

I spent the next week clearing dungeons. The first dungeon I found was in the basement of an old, abandoned bakery. I half expected bread-based enemies or some kind of pastry monster but ended up fighting through a warren of kobolds who attacked with flimsy spears and rudimentary magic. My *Stealth* and knife skills were enough to clear most of the dungeon without alerting any of the other nearby kobolds. The final boss, a kobold shaman and his followers, were easy to put down with my firearm.

The next several dungeons were harder. They all had small, claustrophobic layouts like an underground warren full of monstrous rabbits, a miniature house full of creepy dolls that liked to sing as they tried to kill you, and a shadowy, ephemeral dungeon where it was difficult to tell where the walls even were. In such tight spaces, I found my firearm a bit restrictive and I couldn't use my *Dash* to its full extent without room to move. Once enemies got into melee range, my revolver was more of a hindrance than a help. Thankfully, my attributes alone were enough to give me the edge, and I was able to overpower and kill anything that got too close, saving my gloves for the strongest of the enemies. I thanked the "safe zone" that made the dungeons weaker, if that was really what it did.

By the end of the week, I had received enough experience to level to twenty in my *Archer* class. I also received five more gold orbs, a plethora of blue orbs, a necklace that let me see in the dark from the shadowy dungeon, and another perk. I had also leveled my *Enchanter* class once and received another point in memory.

Perk obtained: Natural Weapons. When using your hands, feet, claws, teeth, or any natural part of your body to strike a foe, you strike as if your strength was increased by +2.

I earned the perk from fighting in so many confined dungeons where I had to use my fists, knife, and gloves, I believed.

Like my other perks from the dungeons, it wasn't the most powerful perk in the world, but it had its uses. I found the perk system interesting. Unlike achievements, perks weren't broad, but they could be helpful in unique situations. I rather enjoyed collecting them.

When I finished the last dungeon, I got the announcements I had been looking forward to for days as my experience climbed higher and higher.

Congratulations, you have received enough experience to level your Archer class. You are now level 20.

Please choose a level 20 class skill:

Sniper Shot: Your range is tripled and your shot penetrates most armor.

Fan of Death: Your projectiles multiply and penetrate in a wave in front of you, dealing significant damage.

Take Flight: You summon a pair of hawk wings, giving you temporary flight.

Lightning Rod: A bolt of lightning strikes the location where your projectiles land.

Stride: Your movement speed increases, obstacles bend from your path, and your step is sure and steady.

I was disappointed to find that the interesting skills were all magic-based, such as *Take Flight, Lightning Rod*, and *Fan of Death*. That left *Sniper Shot*, which was useful but didn't offer a lot of diversity in its use, and *Stride*, which didn't sound impressive, but given that it was a level 20 skill, I hoped it wouldn't disappoint. I had received another point in coordination when I reached level 19, so my speed was already significant. *Stride* would hopefully build off that, making me even faster as I moved. That would help me stay far enough away from most things to use my firearm, I hoped.

The sure and steady step should also be helpful. If I slipped while running, a fall could actually cause serious injury, given how fast I could move these days. Not seeing a better option, I selected *Stride.*

As I did, I felt the knowledge of the skill enter me. When it finished, a second surge of knowledge began to fill my mind. I felt a heat build inside of my chest as vague images began to flash in my mind. The heat burst inside of me, flowing through my veins, down through my chest and out to the rest of my body. When it finished, I received another announcement.

Congratulations, you have unlocked an evolution of your Archer class based on your unique use of the class. Class unlocked: Gunslinger. Your class rating is Unique. Do you wish to adopt this class now?

I stared at the announcement. I had hoped but had no idea if it was truly a unique use of the class or if it would be recognized by this world at all. That it had . . . I was gratified beyond belief. I accepted the evolution immediately.

Congratulations, you have earned the achievement Evolve a Unique Class. As the first person to ever evolve into a Gunslinger, you receive an upgrade to all of your Archer skills. The following changes are made:

Dash becomes Trickster's Dash: Dash through the air, ignoring wind resistance until you land. When you dash, you are briefly invisible until your dash ends.

Perfect Coordination becomes Gambler's Eye: You receive a passive boost of 20% to your coordination, your vision is improved, and you gain a sixth sense that reveals when luck may be favoring you.

Stride becomes Swagger: Your movement speed increases, obstacles bend from your path, and your step is sure and steady. Your movements subtly intimidate others.

I smiled at the changes. A unique class meant I could level it all the way to level 100. And the evolution of my *Archer* skills were all significant upgrades. That was more than I could have ever expected. The announcements weren't finished yet, apparently.

Congratulations, you have received enough experience to level your Gunslinger class. You are now level 1.

Congratulations, you have received enough experience to level your Gunslinger class. You are now level 2.

Congratulations, you have received enough experience to level your Gunslinger class. You are now level 3.

Please choose a level 1 class skill:

Sucker Punch: Stun an enemy with a punch of your fist.

Elemental Adaptation: Select one element. Your bullets are infused with the essence of your element, increasing damage and having a secondary effect based on your chosen element. Elements available: fire, ice, earth, wind, demonic, eldritch, space.

Rapid Reload: Instantly reload your revolver with the ammunition of your choice.

Duel Me: At the start of combat, challenge a foe to a duel. The stakes of the duel are randomly selected and may include an attribute point, a percentage of all experience gained, a perk, a mutation, a skill, or an achievement. The first to surrender, retreat, or die loses. The winner of the duel permanently steals the stakes of the duel, and the loser permanently loses the stakes of the duel. This skill may only be used once a day.

Returning Knife: Your knife can be recalled back to your hand instantly after a throw.

Now those were some interesting skills. I could sense that all of the skills were physical, likely because I had somehow invented the unique class and couldn't use magic. It was nice to have a complete list of skills to pick from for the first time. *Sucker Punch* would synergize well with my new perk, making my gauntlets and melee attacks more powerful, but it wasn't really a necessity since most things died from my gauntlets or fists relatively quickly—at least here in the safe zone.

Elemental Adaptation was potentially powerful, especially since I could unlock elements—such as demonic, eldritch, or space—to empower my bullets. I pushed at the skill, trying to get a sense of what the various elements would do, but I only received vague information in return. Demonic gave me the impression of illness and weakness, eldritch of some kind of twisting energy that corrupted the world around it, and space of bending and pulling reality in some way.

That was too vague for me to take a chance on right now.

Rapid Reload and *Returning Knife* were basic and uninteresting. The most fascinating of them all, and the one I knew I would pick as soon as I saw it, was *Duel Me*, because it would allow me to grow in power the more often I used it. It came at the risk of me losing my own attributes, perks, or skills, but if I used the skill carefully, I would be able to grow in power faster than with any of the other skills.

I selected *Duel Me* and felt the knowledge of the skill enter my mind, showing me how to activate it. I immediately felt the urge to go challenge something or someone to a duel, but I refrained for now.

Coordination +1

Coordination +1

I received two more attribute enhancements to coordination for levels 2 and 3 of my new *Gunslinger* class before running out of the experience that had been left over after hitting level 20 in *Archer*. Once my mind settled down from the many announcements that had hit me all at once, I made my way out into the nearby street to test my new skills.

Trickster's Dash was simply wonderful. I could sense myself turning invisible as I dashed around the streets, some sixth sense telling me when I vanished and reappeared. I could use it to move just a foot to the side, disappearing and reappearing in an instant. I could use it to approach an enemy unseen and unheard, since I was dashing through the air without any air resistance and I was invisible at the same time. The only sound was when I landed softly at the end of my dash. I could also use it to reach the rooftops above me like I could before, but now it was almost impossible to know where I had gone, as I didn't have to telegraph which direction I was moving before using the skill. I could simply disappear from a complete standstill, giving no clue to where I had gone. It was a versatile and powerful new skill, without a doubt.

My vision was also noticeably better with *Gambler's Eye*, and I could already see better than a normal human could before I received the skill. I couldn't figure out how to sense "luck," as the skill had mentioned I would be able to do, but I would have to see if that developed later.

Swagger was interesting. I found myself walking differently. Before I got the skill, I realized now, I walked in a very utilitarian manner. Head held high, perfect posture, arms at my side a bit like a robot. I had never realized how odd I must have looked to other people, who had a much more natural gait.

Now, though, I walked casually, dangerously. I felt looser. It wasn't exactly an obvious change—I could tell I wasn't some caricature of a cowboy from a Western movie—but I was definitely carrying myself in a different way now. I felt more human and, at the same time, more deadly.

As far as the skill itself was concerned, I practiced sprinting through the streets to test it out. I could move even faster than I could before because I had better traction on the ground as I ran. I could turn quicker, my boots refusing to slip even on the slick cobblestone roads. And the way debris and obstacles bent from my path was eerie and strange. The objects didn't actually move—I verified that by observing a pile of stones before and after I walked through them—but at the same time as I stepped through the stones, I just happened to avoid stepping on any of them. I didn't turn my ankle or place a foot improperly, no matter the terrain. It was as if I just happened to step perfectly between every loose stone, always maintaining my balance and speed. It disturbed my rational mind, which insisted such things were impossible. I had to force myself to let it go, lest it drive me a bit crazy as I ran.

Finally, it was time to test my first *Gunslinger* skill. I tracked down a sub-boss in the city to test it out, figuring it was better to go for an easy target to start. I found a monster that I hadn't bothered to fight before but had seen around several times now. It was a small biped almost like a goblin, except it was covered in a thick layer of fur and about a foot smaller. They smelled atrocious and were easy to avoid, but in my search for a monster to duel, I found a pack of them that had a sub-boss, so I went with them. I picked out the sub-boss from the group and activated my new skill.

"*Duel Me!*" I yelled at the creature. I heard an announcement in my head as soon as I activated the skill.

Duel activated. You and your opponent have both wagered your experience. Good luck.

The beast immediately turned to face me. It became enraged, screaming at me in anger as if it understood what I had just done.

Reacting quickly, I dashed forward, my revolver still holstered, and began striking and kicking the pack of monsters before the rest of them realized I was there. My enhanced strength and my perk *Natural Weapons* meant every strike killed one of the little monsters. When the rest of them realized what was happening, they all turned and tried to attack me, and I dashed upward, soaring up and over the pack of monsters while they piled forward to where I had been just a moment before, not realizing I was gone.

My dash ended a few feet above and behind the pack, my skill pausing me in midair for a second. I dropped down, my body handling the fall easily, and then I turned and kicked one of the monsters into the middle of the rest of them, scattering several to the ground. I moved in to finish off the confused pack, easily killing them with only my hands and feet.

Winner: Alexander! You are awarded 130 additional experience.

"Hmm," I said as the duel announcement and the smaller experience awards from the creatures entered my mind. That wasn't as rewarding as I had hoped, but compared to the five experience I got for killing the sub-boss itself, it was actually pretty high. When I used it on more powerful creatures, hopefully the experience would be even higher.

I was a bit concerned about how the monster had become enraged after I activated my skill and seemed to know what I had done to it. That could make it hard to use the skill while I was trying to surprise an enemy from ambush or use a sneak attack of some kind. Either way, it was an exciting skill and I was looking forward to testing it out further.

To get me to level 20, I had completed five dungeons, putting me at fifteen of twenty for my personal quest *Clear the City*. I was eager to test my new *Gunslinger* skills in more dungeons, but it was getting late. I had just completed the dungeon that got me level 20 and didn't want to push myself, so I turned in for the night.

I didn't sleep but had recently taken to practicing martial arts from my Earth now that I wasn't expending as much energy crafting bullets every night. I had all the knowledge from Earth in my head, including knowledge of a wide variety of martial arts. It helped me gain a better sense of my own power and speed, which was especially important with how quick and strong my body was in this world. I had already been surprised by my own power too many times. And not only did it help me learn more about my own body, but it also helped me center myself again. I had felt a bit unbalanced since my night trapped in the city, and I knew I wasn't processing the difficulty of that night properly. Spending my nights slowly going through martial arts forms, feeling the flow and strength of my body, and just living in the moment helped me find a center of calm once again.

The next morning, I set out to find my sixteenth dungeon, full of excitement to test my new skills. I had already completed the ones closest to where I was staying, so I had to go a few streets over before I found another.

It had become clear to me that this city was not meant to have so many dungeons in the "safe zone," as the quest had called it. The dungeons were dangerous but manageable for someone with my attributes and my weapons. A team of skilled people who were at least level 10 in a variety of classes could clear these dungeons, but the knowledge of how to do it had faded, so people weren't even willing to try anymore. That led to thousands of dungeons spawning, overwhelming the city as the monsters spilled out of them at night. Whatever, or whoever, had designed the system had likely intended for a safe zone to have a handful of dungeons form at a time, making them easier than the monsters outside the city as a way of giving people in the safe zones a place to practice working together and fighting in various types of terrain. The fact that the system had failed and so many dungeons had piled up meant I had an easy way to earn experience, orbs, and possible skills or perks, so it was a major benefit for me personally. I couldn't help but wonder if the Emperor or the army felt the same, though, and that was why they didn't help clear the city of more dungeons.

When I finally found another dungeon, it was in the middle of a large, open pit dug into the ground next to the street. It looked like a building project had been in the works when the city was abandoned. Now it had been sitting empty and fallow for however many years. The pit was a muddy mess. The weather had turned recently. We had been getting more and more rain, and it seemed the pit had decided to save as much of it as it could. I could see one corner of the pit was unnaturally dark, indicating a dungeon had formed.

I carefully made my way into the muddy pit, thankful for my new skill that gave me steadier footing. Without it, I would have fallen several times. I half expected a monster to jump out of the mud and attack me at any moment, but I didn't sense any monsters nearby and didn't think it was likely.

As I appeared inside the dungeon, I checked to make sure there was nothing immediately threatening me and then knocked as much of the mud off my boots as I could. Feeling slightly better, I looked around me to see where I had ended up this time. I was standing on top of a large hill, surrounded by endless rolling hills in every direction for as far as I could see. The hills were covered with vibrant green grasses and low bushes, with no trees in sight. The view reminded me a bit of Scotland, and the chill wind that blew over the hills matched with the descriptions I had in my memory of that region as well.

One of my favorite things about dungeons was having a break from the depressing scenery of the city, so despite the cold wind, I stood on top of the hill and admired the beauty around me. I took a deep breath, savoring the fresh air and the distant sun warming me ever so slightly. It was a serene environment, unbroken by the smells and look of a dying city. I felt closer to understanding what the purpose of existing was when I got to stop and enjoy moments like this.

Sadly, nothing lasted forever, I had learned rather quickly. A distant roar echoed across the hills toward me, and a large beast from a nearby hill had stood up, staring in my direction. It was just on the edge of my *Monster Hunter* perk, so when it began to run in my direction, I sensed it in my mind.

From what I could see and sense, the creature was alone. It was quite the behemoth, I noticed as it charged down its hill and began to chug its way up mine. It stood at least ten feet tall and was at least three times as wide as me. It had a green and pebbled hide that rippled with muscle as it ran. As it got closer, I noticed that the creature was covered with moss and grass that grew on its shoulders and head, almost like it was a portable flower box. Despite how thick, pebbly, and unattractive its body was, the moss and grass covering it almost made it look friendly. Of course, its constant roaring as it worked its way up the hill toward me made it clear it wasn't.

If I had to guess, based on the mythology from my world, I would say it was a troll.

I waited until it was about halfway up my hill before I drew my revolver and blew out the creature's knee with a well-placed *Penetration Bullet.* My empowered bullet penetrated its thick hide with ease, sending it crashing face-first into the hillside. It tried to roar again, but the sound was muffled by its head being buried in the dirt. I almost laughed at the sound.

If mythology from Earth was anything to go by, trolls were vulnerable to fire and could regenerate from almost any other damage done to them. I unloaded the rest of my *Penetration Bullets* and loaded a full set of *Explosive Bullets.*

When the creature managed to stand back up, I could see its knee visibly regenerating from the hole I had put in it. The beast didn't wait, trying to stumble forward and kill me even with a half-destroyed knee. I took aim and fired an *Explosive Bullet* into its chest. The explosion rocked the creature backward, not quite tipping it over, but the flames rapidly caught. The troll's outraged roar turned to a scream of fear as it tried to put the flames out on its body, which only served to spread them even more.

I watched as the troll burned to death from a single *Explosive Bullet.* As I had guessed, the monster was vulnerable to fire, and it only took a single bullet to ignite the beast, which burned as if it was made of kindling. This was how many of my dungeons had been going lately. I either completely overpowered the dungeon with my revolver and the various bullets I had crafted or I faced monsters that were almost impossible for me to kill. In those cases,

I had to quickly adapt and barely managed to scrape through thanks to luck and my attributes. At least this dungeon was one I could handle with my revolver. I was not a fan of the other kind at all.

I spent a few hours hiking through the beautiful countryside, igniting trolls here and there as they helpfully charged me with an outraged roar, making it easy to set them on fire before they got anywhere near me. None of them could surprise me, thanks to my *Monster Hunter* perk, so even the few that were slightly more intelligent and dug themselves into the ground in an attempt to ambush me were easy to detect and kill. The sub-bosses were just more powerful versions of the standard troll, slightly bigger but still just as stupid and vulnerable to fire as the rest of them.

The final boss, when I finally found him after wandering for several hours, was a different type of troll than the others. He was a chalky white, almost like he was made of stone, and instead of being covered in moss and grass, he seemed to be caked in a layer of white dust. As I stared at him, I decided to use my new *Duel Me* skill against him.

As soon as I made that decision, a strange sensation overtook me. I felt as if a coin was flipping through the air in my mind, but I knew exactly how it would land. Was this my new sense telling me luck was on my side? I felt confident it was.

"*Duel Me!*" I yelled at the boss, stepping forward and pointing my revolver at his chalky hide.

Duel activated. You and your opponent have both wagered a perk. Good luck.

The troll roared in outrage as the announcement washed over me. He turned and immediately charged me. I fired five rounds of *Explosive Bullets* at him, but as I half expected, he was immune to fire. Of course it wouldn't be that easy. I had learned that the hard way from my other dungeons; there was always some twist if things became too predictable.

I considered what I knew of trolls from my world as I ran backward, putting space between me and the massive troll. I probably needed acid of some kind, which I didn't have. Maybe there was some kind of acid-based enchantment I could have bought, but you couldn't plan for every single eventuality in the world. There would always be something I didn't expect or plan for.

I dashed away from the boss when he got too close for comfort, reloading as I flew over the ground invisibly. The boss stopped in confusion as I vanished in front of him, looking around for where I had disappeared to. I was happy to see he seemed too stupid to understand what had happened. Once my revolver was reloaded, I dashed again until I was behind the troll and then unloaded five *Penetration Bullets* into the back of his knee, hoping to cripple him for a time.

My bullets ripped through his knee, but I could already see it regenerating by the time I was done firing all six shots. The boss turned with a roar and charged me again, but I dashed away before he got close. I executed a second dash immediately after the first, but this time I launched myself forward toward the boss's back. I appeared right behind him and slammed a golem-powered fist into his leg. My punch was strong enough to nearly sever his leg completely, pulverizing it and sending a thick spray of troll blood across the ground.

I dashed backward, avoiding the boss as he attempted to turn and strike me. The boss managed to stay on his feet, despite his crushed limb. He slowly stumbled toward me when I reappeared. I stood still for a moment, watching as his leg began to regenerate even from the damage of my golem-powered punch.

I sighed again. This was going to be a slog. I circled the boss, dashing away whenever he got close. Every time one of my gloves was off cooldown, I dashed in and inflicted grievous bodily injury on a part of the boss. His regeneration was insane, but it finally started to slow after I had knocked him around for over an hour. With two punches a minute for over an hour, that was an absurd amount of time for him to be able to regenerate from such devastating blows over and over.

Finally, though, with one final golem-powered punch, he dropped to the ground, his regeneration finally exhausted.

Winner: Alexander! You are awarded the perk Regeneration.

Perk obtained: Regeneration. You gain the regeneration of Gromger the Mighty Troll King. Your body can regenerate from almost any wound. Injuries regenerate based on your endurance attribute and the amount of energy available to your body.

Now that was a damn good reward. I already had a form of regeneration from my nanobots, but the perk would give me a much stronger and quicker regeneration compared to what my nanobots could do. I felt the perk kick in, and my weariness from the long fight and so many uses of my *Dash* faded instantly, replaced only with a mild hunger and thirst, much like when I used my nanobots extensively. I smiled at the feeling, enjoying the rush of energy the new perk provided.

I saw the white dungeon core lying on the ground where the troll had been standing when I first approached, so I walked around the monster's body and touched it.

Congratulations, you have completed this dungeon. You have earned the following rewards: 2 gold cores, 9 blue cores, 1250 experience.

I gathered the orbs, and the dungeon rapidly faded around me, leaving me standing in the muddy pit once again. The squelching of the mud around my boots as I hiked back out of the pit couldn't dim my pleasure at stealing such a powerful perk from the boss. I could tell already that my *Duel Me* was the best choice I had made since coming to this world.

Chapter 23

I finished my *Clear the City* quest in the next couple of days, earning enough experience to bring my *Gunslinger* class to level 10 as well. My attribute enhancements followed the same pattern as when I leveled the *Archer* class, earning me another +4 to coordination, +3 to strength, and +1 to endurance. I could see why rich merchants purchased a variety of classes. The early levels gave easy boosts that made you feel powerful, but it was a bit of a trap, because without skills, attributes could only get you so far.

I used my *Duel Me* skill on each boss of the dungeons I completed, but I didn't feel the tingle of *Gambler's Eye* a second time and only ended up getting an attribute point from two bosses and experience from all the others. One of the attributes was for endurance, and the other was for my magical capacity, which was useless to me.

Congratulations, you have received enough experience to level your Gunslinger class. You are now level 10.

Please choose a level 10 class skill:

Sucker Punch: Stun an enemy with a punch of your fist.

Elemental Adaptation: Select one element. Your bullets are infused with the essence of your element, increasing damage and having a secondary effect based on your chosen element. Elements available: fire, ice, earth, wind, demonic, eldritch, space.

Rapid Reload: Instantly reload your revolver with ammunition of your choice.

Returning Knife: Your knife can be recalled back to your hand after a throw.

Bonded Weapon: You bond with your weapon, and your skill with the weapon is improved. You may summon your weapon to you from any distance, and your weapon is resistant to being damaged.

Improved Dodge: You instinctively know how to dodge, avoiding strikes and blows from enemies.
Gambler's Luck: You push luck to the limit, changing the odds around you to guarantee a more favorable outcome. Unlocks a new attribute: Luck.
Spread the Bounty: You and your allies gain a temporary increase to luck, a bonus to your coordination, and a bonus to the loot you receive.
Bounty Hunter: Mark your target. You can sense your target from any distance. You gain an increase to all damage done to your target. You are resistant to damage and harmful effects from your target. You can only have one target at a time and must kill or subdue your target before selecting another.

The first thing that struck me about my skill selection was that I could still pick the level 1 skills, which I hadn't been able to do with my *Archer* class. I wasn't sure if that was due to my new class being unique or because I had created the class or something totally unrelated. Either way, I appreciated the diversity of choice.

I had been debating where I wanted to take my *Gunslinger* class and thinking about diversifying myself now that I had the means to afford another class. Because of that, I didn't want to limit myself to purely using my firearm, like what *Elemental Adaptation* would do. Same thing with the *Bonded Weapon* skill.

Spread the Bounty was interesting, but I didn't see myself spending enough time around others to make it worthwhile at this point despite enjoying the company of Romanus and Valens.

Bounty Hunter would be extremely helpful in finding and eliminating the annoying priest that had been bothering me, but I wasn't completely confident I could kill him unless I took him by surprise, so I didn't want to waste a skill on a mere chance for revenge.

I was considering buying the *Warrior* class next to give myself a boost to strength and, hopefully, endurance. The class would also supplement a current weakness of mine, which was when enemies got too close for me to use my firearm.

My new perk *Regeneration* was outstanding, as I had discovered after some experimentation in the various dungeons I completed after stealing it. It synergized with my enhanced body and endurance attribute, allowing me to regenerate a shallow wound within seconds. Deeper wounds took longer, but I could regenerate a finger in a matter of a minute, as long as I had eaten enough food recently. It was a game-changer, allowing me to go toe to toe with enemies that I had been concerned about fighting up close before, where I could suffer an injury more easily.

I decided to go with *Gambler's Luck*. It unlocked a new attribute, which seemed powerful, and gave me a bonus that could increase my luck in combat, both ranged and up close, in earning rewards from dungeons, and in duels. My luck had already paid off once and I thought it was smart to build upon that success.

Attribute Unlocked: Luck. Your base luck is 1 and you receive a +1 to luck from your Gambler's Luck skill.

Once I finished leveling, I focused on my class in my head. Momma Lena had told me that a person could make a class active or inactive at any time. Experience would no longer go to the class, but all of the attributes and skills that had been unlocked would remain. This was similar to how my *Archer* class evolved into *Gunslinger*, which restarted at level 1, but I still had all the benefits from leveling my *Archer* class.

I found whatever "trigger" worked to turn my class inactive. I somehow instinctively knew how to do it once I looked for it. I turned my *Gunslinger* inactive, leaving it at level 10 for now.

Once that was done, I checked the overcast sky and determined there was still plenty of daylight remaining for me to take care of a few more of my chores.

I dashed to a nearby rooftop and then made my way across the roofs toward Perama. When I arrived, the guards let me in with no issues, and I found Constans was back at the gate, offering to guide strangers through the confusing enclave. When she saw me, her dirty face broke into a grin and she waved. I was happy to see her as well and glad I had made such a positive impression on her that she smiled to see me.

"Alexander!" she yelled, running up to me and then stopping awkwardly in front of me as if embarrassed by her outburst.

"Constans," I said, smiling. "I'm happy you are working today. Would you be able to show me around the city like last time?"

"Of course!" she said. "Where do you need to go today? Where have you been? Did you find any treasure while you were gone?"

288

The dam was apparently broken, because she sent a barrage of questions my way. I didn't really need to hire her anymore, since I had a decent sense of the enclave now, but I liked her and wanted to help her out. She was a good child facing a difficult life and deserved help when she could get it, and it would cost me almost nothing now that my wealth had increased.

I tossed her a full silver. She gasped at the sight.

"Let's go to Momma Lena's to start," I told her as she polished the silver coin and then made it disappear somewhere in her clothes.

"Let's get going!" She turned and led me through the narrow street that ran up the middle of the bridge.

I told her some of my non-dungeon stories as we walked. I tried to emphasize the dangers of what I did, but I could tell the young girl dreamed of someday being able to hunt monsters and find treasure like a scavenger.

Momma Lena was busy when we arrived, working on another tome at her desk, but when she saw me, she put her work down and turned to look me over.

"My, my," she said, "look who has survived to return once again."

"He has been out of the city, Momma Lena!" Constans interrupted. "He says he went north and killed drakes and got their skin and is having magical armor made, like in the old stories!"

Momma Lena raised an eyebrow at me. I shrugged in return.

"I was hoping to buy another class from you," I told her, trying to change the subject. "Do you have a *Warrior* class available?"

"I do," she replied, turning in her chair and grabbing a tome from the side of her desk. "I finished one just the other day and haven't had a buyer yet. It isn't in as much demand as the ranged classes. I also have a *Rogue* class available, if you are interested. I know you don't want a *Mage* or *Scholar* class, so I won't try to sell one of those to you."

"How much for each one?" I asked.

"One hundred blue orbs each," she replied, hefting the book up and setting it back down.

I had forty-two gold orbs and well over a hundred blue orbs now, even with the cost of replenishing my ammunition continuously draining some of my blue orbs. I counted out ten gold orbs, not bothering to negotiate with her since she had helped me so much when I first came to her.

I handed her all ten, and she grabbed a second book and handed them both to me.

"Thanks," I told her as I reached back and tucked the books into my backpack.

"Anytime," she said, smiling at me. "Anything else I can help with?"

"No, that should be it," I replied. I stood awkwardly for a moment as she and Constans stared at me, but I realized since I had nothing else to talk about, I should leave. I said my goodbyes quickly and then Constans led me out of the shop.

"Constans," I said as we walked back toward the central road, "what's your plan in life?"

She stopped and looked back at me, surprised by my question. "My plan in life?"

"Yeah," I said. "You know, your long-term plan. Everyone should have a long-term plan. If you could do anything you wanted, what would it be?"

"Why?" she said, looking away and crossing her arms, hunching over defensively.

I held my hands up placatingly. I had been tossing around the idea of finding a few trustworthy people to help me survive in the city, and Constans was one of the first to come to mind. As I thought about explaining to her what I was thinking, I felt the spinning coin of my luck erupt in my head. I took that as a clear sign that now was the time to propose my idea.

"Listen," I said, "you know more about me than almost anyone else here, right?"

She shrugged, still not meeting my eyes.

"I need some people I can trust," I told her. "People that can help me navigate this place. I trust you and you've already helped me a bunch. And I want to help you back, but I want to know if my help would be something you would be interested in."

"What kind of help?" she said, finally looking back at me skeptically.

"Like getting you a safe place to live, an education, a class, helping you grow and survive so you can do what you want in this world."

"A class?" she said, clearly only hearing what interested her.

"Yes," I said, "if you are interested. It wouldn't all be fun and games. You would need to change a lot of things and have to work hard, but I think you would be a good ally to have in my corner as I keep trying to figure things out for myself. And you have shown me you are trustworthy, smart, and hard-working. I couldn't ask for better."

I could see my words had impacted her, or maybe she was touched by the idea that she could possibly learn a class someday, because I saw her eyes start to water as I spoke. She angrily swiped at her tears, looking away from me again in embarrassment. I looked away as well to give her a chance to recover.

"What would I do?" she said after she felt a bit better.

"I'm not really sure yet," I told her, "and it may not be for years before we really figure it out. But in the meantime, I don't want to see you disappear like so many others have done in this city. If you agree to work with me, your life will change significantly, but for the better in the long run. I promise."

"My life is pretty shit anyway," she said, looking down at the ground. "I pretend because nobody wants to hire a guide that is gloomy and angry all the time, but . . ."

She choked up and I stood awkwardly for a moment, unsure of what to do to comfort a crying teenager. As she turned away, hunching over as she cried, I finally reached over and gave her a pat on the shoulder, even though it felt strange to do. She took that as an invitation and turned around, burying her face in my cloak. I hugged her carefully, not wanting to encroach too much on her personal space, but she was crying so hard I didn't think she noticed what I was doing at all. All it took was the smallest amount of sympathy and the wall she had built to protect herself came crashing down. I felt a surge of empathy for her and knew I had done the right thing by offering to help her.

"Do you have any family here at all?" I asked her as her tears began to slow.

She shook her head into my cloak.

"Okay then," I said. "Come with me. Let's see about making some changes."

She stepped away from me, clearly embarrassed, but she nodded anyway.

I turned and led the way for a bit, giving her a chance to recover more. I led us to the gate and didn't slow, heading toward the tunnel that led outside.

"Where are we going?" she asked, catching up to me.

"We're going to Sycae. I think we can find more of what we need there to get you started."

I led her out of the gates and we walked along the waterfront for a few minutes. Constans had clearly never been out of the city, because she stared at everything as we walked, equal parts excited and terrified by the city beyond the gates. I stopped us when we were some distance from the bridge enclave.

"Ready?" I asked her.

"Ready for what?" she said, looking around us, unsure of what was about to happen.

"Climb on my back," I told her, crouching on one knee. "And hold on very tight."

She stared at me for a second until I raised an eyebrow at her. She shrugged, climbing on my back and wrapping her arms around my neck.

"Here we go!" I said, smiling in anticipation of her reaction.

I activated *Trickster's Dash*, sending us shooting across the water. Constans screamed, her thin arms trying to choke the life out of me as she held on as tight as she could. I activated the skill again halfway across, sending us soaring perfectly across the water. This time, I had aimed correctly, landing us directly on a dock in Sycae. Our momentum froze, so all I had to do was step down and walk into the city.

We were invisible as we flew, but the sound of Constans screaming drew a lot of attention. When we appeared out of nowhere on the dock, people reached for weapons or began to step back from us, but I pulled Constans around in front of me and put her down on the dock, acting like what we were doing was completely normal.

"We're here!" I said, trying my best to hold in my laughter as I took in her scrunched-up face. Her eyes remained closed as tightly as possible even after we stopped moving.

She opened one eye, peeking to see where exactly we were. When she saw we were on solid ground—well, the dock at least— she turned and began to pelt me with her tiny fists over and over.

"You jerk!" she yelled.

I couldn't restrain my laughter any longer, laughing uproariously at her reaction to our flight. "Welcome to Sycae," I told her, trying to get her to stop hitting me. She eventually got tired and stopped, looking around her. Her mouth dropped open in shock as she took in the number of people around us, the open streets and well-maintained buildings, and the fact that we weren't in the crowded, smelly, and dirty enclave she called home. I enjoyed watching her look around at all the different sights and come to the realization that she was really here. After a few moments, I tugged on her arm and led her through the city. She followed me in a daze, staring at her surroundings unashamedly like an absolute tourist. I was sure my face looked similar the first time I was here, so I didn't make fun of her for it.

I took her first to the bookstore I had visited before here in Sycae.

Inside, I asked the clerk what classes they had available. I wanted one that would enhance Constans's memory attribute, which would help her learn more quickly while also giving her useful skills that could benefit both of us. After going over the available non-combat classes, I bought the *Merchant* class for fifteen gold orbs. It was one of the most expensive classes I had seen so far, even more expensive than my *Archer* class, but it was worth it.

Constans was quiet the entire time, overwhelmed by the city around us. After buying the class, I took us to the inn I had stayed in before and spoke briefly with the innkeeper. We came to an arrangement for a long-term room rental, and I explained that Constans would be coming and going when I was gone. The innkeeper had no problem once I paid for a suite with two rooms in advance for three months. It cost me ten blue orbs, but it was the nicest room in the inn and the innkeeper assured me Constans would be fed daily and have free access to the room even if I wasn't there.

After we secured the room, I took Constans to a nearby bathhouse and paid the female attendants to clean her up as best as they could. At this point, Constans was nearly catatonic, and I waved goodbye to her as the attendants led her to the women's side of the bathhouse. She stared blankly at me but followed the other women without complaint. I smiled at the sight, enjoying the normally exuberant young girl's culture shock.

While she was getting a thorough scrub, I searched the city to find a few clothes that might fit Constans. I found a shop that sold a few basic dresses, which I bought, and then paid to have the other essentials she would need delivered to our room in a few days when they were ready.

I brought the dresses back to the bathhouse and asked the attendants to dress her in one before she left. Sometime later, a dazed and thoroughly clean Constans left with me, smelling pleasant for the first time in . . . probably her entire life.

I took her to a street stall and bought her dinner. She ate what I put in front of her but didn't seem to appreciate the food as much as I had hoped.

"This is too much," she told me after she ate. "Are you going to kill me?"

"What?" I said, choking slightly on the bite of food I had just taken. "Kill you?"

"Yeah!" she said, shaking her head and staring at me as if she had just woken up from being under a spell. "Like, is that how you got so powerful so quick? You sacrifice children and steal their powers? I knew it! I absolutely knew that was it!"

I couldn't help myself. I started laughing again.

"Honest," I told her through my laughter, "I'm not going to kill you. I have the currency to do this now and I need people I can trust. That's it. I promise. Come on, finish eating and let's go back to the inn."

She glared at me the entire time she ate, while I smiled, happy to see some of her spark returning so quickly. After we were done, we walked back toward the inn.

"I'm going to be gone again in a few days," I told her, "but I'm going to try to set you up with some work while I'm gone. Are you ready for your first job?"

"Yes," she said, a serious expression on her face. "Anything is better than starving to death on that damn bridge."

"I understand," I said sympathetically. "Here is your first job. First, we are going to find you a tutor."

Her glare intensified.

"No, don't make that face," I said, laughing. "You need to be as educated as possible if you are going to survive this world. Trust me. Next, you will start to learn this city just like you knew Perama. Find its secrets, learn all of its nooks and crannies, but be careful. This place can be just as dangerous, if not more so, than Perama. Stay away from the guards. Don't get caught alone by anyone that can hurt you, understand?"

"Got it," she said, looking around her with fresh eyes now that she had a mission to learn the city. I was grateful to see the look of cunning and focus on her face, because it was one of the reasons I had picked her. It was clear she was a smart cookie and had the drive to go far, if given the right tools. I could see the raw potential in her. Given a chance to grow, she would be a menace to anyone that stood in her way.

"I'll leave you with some funds," I told her, "but don't waste them. Work hard with your tutor and start to explore the city, but that's it for now. Can you do that?"

"Absolutely," she replied, looking around her as we walked, as if she could find the secrets of the city.

"Good. Let's get some rest at the inn and I'll see about the tutor starting tomorrow, if possible."

Back at the inn, we sat in the common room together and I handed her the *Merchant* class book. She took it gingerly, as if it was made of pure gold. When she saw me pull out a second book, she gasped. I handed her the *Rogue* book as well.

She took it in her hands and I could see that she was shaking. This was a life-changing moment for her, and I treated it with the seriousness it deserved.

"Don't worry," I said. "This is just the start of your adventure. Trust me. You will grow up to run this damn city someday, if you want. The world is yours for the taking."

She looked away from the books for a moment to meet my eyes, a hungry smile on her face. I recognized the burning ambition that filled her at that moment, and it inspired me as well, making me want to do right by her and this city. I could tell we shared a common goal to grow in power, survive, and fix this broken world.

"Exactly," I said, smiling back at her without her having to say a word.

Chapter 24

The next morning, I left Constans to sleep in while I went to get things ready for my departure. She had spent all night learning her two new classes in the living room of our suite. I had my new *Warrior* class as well, but I had no experience to level it yet, so it sat at level 0.

I asked around the city until I found a helpful clerk at a bookstore who recommended an older woman who used to work as a tutor for merchants' children. I found the woman at home, and after the initial introduction, I managed to convince her to take Constans under her wing by the easy method of paying her a ridiculous sum of blue orbs. To me, it only cost five blue orbs for a year of tutoring, but for the average person, that was ten silver or three hundred copper nummi. A rich sum for a simple tutor, so I hoped she was worth it.

After that, I found a second tutor for Constans at a small martial arts studio I had passed a few times in my explorations of the city. The tutor agreed to train Constans and agreed to let me take classes as well whenever I was in town.

My final stop for Constans was a scholar that specialized in healing. I paid him to visit Constans at the inn and give her a complete magical heal to repair any lingering injuries and to help her regrow her missing teeth. Hopefully some of the malnutrition she had suffered while growing up could also be reversed.

Once that was done, I made my way to the blacksmith that Romanus had worked with and bought myself the best sword I could afford. I walked out of the shop significantly poorer than I had entered it, left with only nine gold orbs and twenty blue orbs, with a smattering of silver and copper in change.

But in return, I had a beautiful longsword that was made from a blue-silver metal that Barbaros, the smith, guaranteed could cut through most monsters while never going dull. It also sparked occasionally with blue lightning. Barbaros told me it wouldn't harm me, but it would discharge when I struck enemies and do additional lightning damage and have a chance to stun them.

I strapped the longsword on the right side of my belt. The basic leather sheath provided by Barbaros hid how powerful the sword was. I could fight with either hand equally well, so I planned to fight with the sword in my left hand and my revolver in my right.

Back at the inn, I found Constans glutting herself on a large breakfast. I joined her, having to look away as she ate voraciously and made quite a mess around herself. Hopefully the tutor would be able to work with her on her manners, because I wasn't going to step into that minefield if I didn't have to.

After she was done with breakfast, I showed her where to find her tutor and combat trainer. Then I led her back to the docks, where she climbed on my back as we dashed back across the water. This time, instead of screaming in fright, she let out a yell of excitement, whipping me in the side of the head like I was a horse she wanted to go faster. I ignored her antics, happy she was feeling so much better so soon.

On the other side, I led her back to where I had been staying in the northwest part of the city.

"Now," I said, "I'm going to need you to take what I teach you next seriously, okay?"

Some of her excitement from earlier had faded as we moved through the ruined streets of the city, and she had flinched anytime we heard a monster nearby, although none of them bothered us.

When she nodded, I reached under my cloak and drew my revolver. I held it up for her, showing her all the parts of the revolver and explaining how it worked. She stared at the gun, mesmerized as I showed her how to load it, aim it, and fire it.

Then I handed her the gun. She immediately turned it sideways to admire it, and I pushed the barrel downward, making sure it wasn't pointed at either of us.

"Rule number one," I said, holding the barrel of the gun straight down. "*Never* point the gun at anything you aren't prepared to kill. A single shot from this could kill even me. Do not point it at me. Do not point it at yourself. Always keep it pointed at the ground until you need to use it, understand?"

She nodded, looking at the gun in her hand with a bit of awe on her face.

"Good," I said. "Now, I'm showing you this because we are going to go farm some experience for your class. But I need you to be very careful while we do it. Got it?"

"Yes," she said, unable to take her eyes off the gun in her hand.

"Let's start with some target practice," I said. I had loaded the gun with *Stasis Bullets* to reduce the danger of an injury as much as possible, although I was sure even that bullet could do significant harm if she shot me or herself by accident.

I led us through the streets near my house, watching her carefully to make sure she kept the firearm pointed downward. I was happy to see she was very careful, never letting the barrel of the gun point upward or in my direction. She watched it like a snake that could bite her at any moment, barely watching where she was going. The gun was too large for her small hands, but I was confident she could handle the responsibility.

Nearby, I found an older house that had several windows covered by wooden shutters that were still intact. I positioned her across the street from the house and told her to aim at the first shutter. She nervously raised the gun, but I stopped her and corrected her form several times until she had the correct stance.

The gun didn't have the traditional recoil of a gunpowder gun, although the sheer momentum of the bullet still gave it a bit of kick. I watched as Constans pulled the trigger, the bullet missing the shutter completely but at least hitting the side of the house. I corrected her form again and had her keep practicing until she was able to reliably hit the shutters from twenty feet away.

We practiced on a few other buildings further down the road so she could practice aiming at targets from a greater distance. By the time I felt she was ready to try it on real monsters, she was confidently grinning every time she pulled the trigger.

"Do I get to keep this?" she asked me after I told her she was ready to try it on something real.

"God no," I told her. "You would end up killing half the people in Sycae if I gave you this right now."

"Awww, c'mon," she said, grinning at me. "I would be good, I swear!"

298

I scoffed at her. "But as you level your *Rogue* class, keep an eye out for ranged skills or skills that might synergize well with the revolver. Don't focus on melee combat, other than what you learn from your combat teacher. I do plan to give you a revolver at some point, once I am sure you are ready for one."

"Yesssssss!" she yelled, swinging the gun wildly in front of herself. I grabbed it hastily and raised an eyebrow at her. She stopped immediately, looking embarrassed at her outburst.

"Oops," she said quietly. I gave her a stern look and then returned the revolver. She took it and deliberately pointed it downward once again, looking up at me for approval. I nodded and then turned to lead us further into the city.

As we walked, I listened for the sounds of monsters nearby and used my ability to detect them by feeling for any around me. Constans stayed quiet once I told her what we were doing now, nervously looking at the buildings we passed as if monsters could run out of them and attack her at any moment. I was sure if we were back on my Earth, I would be getting a call from CPS for taking a teenager out into an abandoned city infested with monsters and giving her a gun to play with, but on this planet, the earlier she got used to this, the better. Better to be out here fighting monsters and learning how to survive than being stuck in an overcrowded enclave and slowly starving to death.

I sensed several monsters nearby and led us in that direction. When we got near, I heard the familiar sounds of dire rats coming from a small temple or some kind of government building in front of us. It was fitting that the first monster Constans killed was the same kind I had fought when I first entered the city. And the dire rats were a perfect first monster to test yourself against: not too dangerous but agile enough to give someone a challenge. And if anything went wrong, I could easily kill them with my bare hands and feet these days, a stark contrast to the first time I had fought them, when I was desperately battling just to survive.

"Now," I told Constans, "you stand here and wait for me to exit the front of this building. Do *not* shoot until I'm clear of the door. I will go inside and cripple the rats so they can't rush you. Take your time and line up your shots. I will come back to your side. You hand me the revolver every time you run out of ammunition and I will reload it for you. Understand?"

"Yes," she said, nervously shifting her weight as she stared at the building in front of us. The gun was now loaded with *Penetration Bullets*, so I hoped she wouldn't get too scared and fire at the first sign of movement, because that was likely to be me.

"Good, here we go."

I unsheathed my new sword and entered the building. A long counter ran the length of the wall on the left, almost like in a bank from my old world. Filling the space were dire rats, climbing on the counters, running back and forth across the marble floors, and generally making a nuisance of themselves. As I walked in, several of them noticed me and squealed in anger. I could see a sub-boss on the counter toward the back of the building and smiled at our luck.

The nearest rats charged me, and I used *Trickster's Dash* to pass them all invisibly. When I reappeared behind them, I began cutting the legs off the monsters one at a time. I danced around the beasts, easily able to outmaneuver them with my enhanced speed. If too many got close, I simply activated *Trickster's Dash* again and disappeared. The skill synergized wonderfully with my new weapon, letting me act almost like a *Rogue*. I could appear and disappear before the monsters knew what had struck them.

Eventually, they were all crippled enough that I walked out of the building with them trailing behind me in a pitiful, angry train. Constans was nervously standing across from the building where I had left her, shifting from foot to foot as she anxiously waited for me to reappear. I sheathed my sword and gave her a comforting wave as I walked down the steps of the building.

"Get ready!" I yelled at her. The first of the rats began to appear in the doorway behind me, so I jogged over to Constans and told her to go for it.

Constans raised the revolver, holding it in both hands, and fired at the first rat to appear. Her shot missed, but she fired again quickly. The second bullet caught the rat in the head and chest, killing it instantly. She didn't stop to celebrate, though, lining up her next shot with grim determination on her face.

Once she killed the first few rats, she handed me the revolver and I reloaded it for her. She kept her eye on the rats the entire time, her expression one of perfect concentration as she waited for me to return the revolver. As soon as I gave it to her, she raised it again and resumed firing. Her accuracy improved as she practiced against the moving targets.

By the time the sub-boss appeared in the doorway, she was standing much more comfortably. She aimed carefully and killed the glowing blue rat with a single shot. She handed me the revolver to reload as she watched the building in case any more rats appeared.

"You got 'em all," I told her, smiling at her proudly.

She turned and gave me a fierce grin, her eyes alight with pleasure at what she had accomplished. "That was crazy!" she said, jumping up and down all of a sudden, her youthful exuberance getting the best of her.

"Yeah," I told her. "I know. You did great. And this is what the world is now. Better to be the hunter than the hunted."

That sobered her up. She stopped jumping up and down and looked around us at the destroyed city. "Yeah," she said after a moment. "Thank you for doing all this for me."

I looked down at her earnest face and knew I had made the right decision to help her. "I'm glad to do it. Now go loot that glowing sub-boss up there. You earned it. Then we can go hunt some more to get you your first level."

She nodded and ran up the steps of the building to grab her first blue orb.

We hunted for the rest of the day, and when the sun reached late afternoon, we stopped early and made our way back to Sycae.

The next morning, I took her to her tutors and I spent the day receiving sword lessons from the martial arts trainer I had hired for us. When Constans came for her afternoon classes, the teacher put her to work doing some light exercises and cardio while I continued to learn the basics of how to fight with a sword. After our training was over, we rushed over to the other part of the city and hunted monsters along the northern shoreline for her until it started to get dark.

A week passed and we fell into a friendly routine. These were some of the happiest times I had experienced since coming to this world, and they reminded me, painfully at times, of playing games with Michael in my past life. By the end of the week, I was getting better at using my sword and Constans had started to get to know her new home. I had given her my remaining silver and copper,

301

telling her to buy herself whatever she needed but to make sure to bargain for everything. I hoped that would give her experience with her new *Merchant* class. After her first attempt to talk a food stall vendor into giving her a reduced price for her food, she confirmed that it gave her experience, even when the vendor glared at her until she paid the full price.

We had just finished clearing a building of spiders, with the help of my necklace that let me see in the dark, when Constans finally reached level 1. She danced around excitedly, completely oblivious to the numerous spiderwebs that stuck to her.

"Let me know what skills you can pick from," I told her, guiding her out of the building before she became wrapped up in a cocoon of her own making.

After a moment, she replied, "Uh, okay. Wow. This is amazing! I got five choices. *Gut Wound, Stealth, Pickpocket, Evasion,* and one called *Ambush.*"

Once we were in the middle of the street, I had her read me the descriptions for each skill.

"Hmm," I said as I considered what she told me. "What are you thinking?"

"*Pickpocket!*" she answered immediately.

"Absolutely not," I said, laughing. "The last thing I need is to come back to town and find you locked up or missing a hand, Constans."

"Ughh," she replied, "that is so lame. What do you think I should get, then?"

"I'd say *Stealth*, probably. Or maybe *Evasion*, but I don't think that is particularly useful for you quite yet. *Stealth* would let you explore Sycae easier and avoid trouble, and I have the skill myself, so we could use it to sneak around the city together as we hunt."

"You have *Stealth* already?" she asked, looking up at me in surprise.

"Yep."

I could tell I got her with the image of us sneaking around together and killing monsters.

"Okay," she said after a moment. "I'll take *Stealth*."

"Great," I said. "Now let's get back to the city. Now that you have your first skill, we need to focus on leveling your *Merchant* class."

"Aww," she replied, reluctantly handing me the revolver. "But you can practice your new skill as we go. Let's see if I can spot you as we travel."

"Awesome!"

Back in Sycae, we fell back into our routine comfortably, except this time I spent my mornings learning the sword with our trainer and then my afternoons scavenging items that Sycae needed, such as clothing, pottery, cutlery, and even some household furniture. The demand was high since most of the goods couldn't be made in the city any longer. And the scavengers from Perama couldn't compete with our price because they all had to sell through the overly complicated chain of commerce the Emperor had set up to guarantee he still got a cut of the profits.

I gave everything I scavenged to Constans, having her get experience for her *Merchant* class in the evenings as I stood behind her and made sure the merchants took her seriously and didn't screw her over too much. I let her keep a portion of the money she made from her sales, which was a huge motivator for her, but I made her reinvest the profits in buying things for us, which also helped her get experience.

By the end of another week, Constans had leveled her *Merchant* class three times. Apparently, the higher the value of the items she bought or sold, the more experience she made. She chose a level 1 skill called *Strike a Bargain*, which helped her be more persuasive when negotiating prices. I calculated the prices she was receiving after she selected the talent and realized that she was indeed receiving slightly more for each of her sales, even from people that she had been selling the same quality of goods to for days. Each person seemed completely unaware that they were now paying her more as well. It made me concerned that such skills were being used on me whenever I shopped at a store, but there wasn't much I could do about it.

My new armor was nearing completion soon, and one night, when I returned with Constans from another trip to the market, I found Romanus and Valens enjoying a few drinks in the inn.

"Alexander!" Romanus called to me when he saw me enter.

Constans jumped when she heard him call my name, but I reassured her that they were the two men I had hunted the drakes with. Her eyes lit up, and she dragged me over to the table to join the two men before I could say any more.

The four of us shared a pleasant dinner together. Romanus kept Constans on the edge of her seat with stories of his exploits. I enjoyed the company and the dinner, and good company reinforced that I had made the right choice by reaching out to people more.

The next day, we collected our new armor. When we went to collect it, Barbaros and his assistants rolled out three mannequins covered in vibrant sky-blue armor. Each set of armor was identical in function and design, although mine was clearly the largest of the three. I hadn't noticed how beautiful the scales of the drake had been because the monster was mostly covered in dirt and grime when we killed it. Now that the scales were polished and clean, they were breathtaking.

The sky-blue scales overlapped, creating a perfect set of armor that would cover our bodies from head to toe. Larger scales, likely taken from the back of the beast, were formed into pauldrons, kneecaps, and elbow covers. Barbaros showed us the details of the armor, and I could see that under the scales was another set of cloth armor designed to cushion the scale mail and make it easier to remove for washing. The three of us took turns changing until we stood in the center of the store, wearing our new armor and admiring ourselves in a full-length mirror Barbaros had brought out.

"It is mighty impressive," Romanus said. "A true work of art, Barbaros. You have outdone yourself."

"Indeed," Valens said, staring at himself in the mirror, his wrinkled face filled with admiration.

I nodded as well, genuinely impressed by the armor. With my new sword, combined with the armor, I looked like I truly fit into this archaic world for the first time since I arrived here. If I didn't know any better, I would think I was a seasoned dragon-hunter ready to tackle anything that dared to stand in my way.

I wore my nanobot-enforced clothing under the armor, forgoing the cloth armor Barbaros had included in the armor itself.

I didn't explain why to Barbaros, but I planned to have my nanobots modify my clothing to mimic the cloth armor anyway, so I didn't need his. Thinking of my nanobots, I decided to have them expand into my new sword and armor so I could gather information about what they were truly made of. I wanted to see if there was a way to reinforce them or keep them repaired with only my nanobots.

"Do these kinds of items take enchantments?" I asked, finally getting a chance to ask a question that had occurred to me last time I was here. "I never see any on the gear."

"They can," Barbaros answered, "but they require orichalcum to engrave into armor of this quality, and we simply don't have enough to waste it on armor that is already this strong."

"What is orichalcum?" I asked.

Barbaros turned me around and pointed to the back of my cloak. I looked in the mirror and saw the rune that had been sewn into my cloak when I first bought it. The rune for *Concealment*.

"Ah," I said, understanding. The metallic thread used for my cloak was orichalcum. It shimmered in the light, appearing to be copper, gold, blue, and white depending on how I turned.

Barbaros gave me a funny look, likely not understanding how I didn't know such a basic thing. Of course, I knew about the special ore that was required for more powerful enchantments, but nobody had told me the *name* of that ore. I thanked him for the information and ignored his funny look.

"We often have enough for clothing," he explained, "because we can remove the thread from salvaged clothing found in the city. Enchanted clothing is such a common thing that scavengers are still finding enough to keep up our supply. Plus, it can be reused so people treat anything made with the ore a bit like heirlooms to be protected and passed down to their children. But it's rare to find enough to use on weapons and armor that is already powerful like these. For most people, it would just be a waste of good ore."

That night, when Constans saw our new armor, she screamed in excitement. We had to shush her quickly, trying not to attract too much attention to the pricey armor we were all now wearing. Mine was mostly concealed under my modified gray scavenger's cloak. Romanus and Valens each had a more standard brown cloak that they pulled forward to cover their armor as well, but Constans's sharp eyes immediately noticed the armor and she demanded all the details.

And of course, she immediately wanted to go buy herself a suit of matching armor. When I told her it would be a waste of money since she would just outgrow it in a year or two anyway, she was not impressed. When I told her how much it cost, instead of discouraging her, it only motivated her to work harder.

"I'll make enough to buy myself a matching suit of armor when I'm older, then," she told me. "Just you wait."

"Now that's a good plan," I replied, impressed by her resolve. We made small talk as we ate and Constans told us about her tutoring and weapons training. She surprised me by enjoying the tutoring almost as much as the weapons training. I had expected her to dislike the more formal education, but she immediately recognized the value of the education I was paying for and was working hard to take advantage of it fully. I was surprised yet again by her maturity, and I told her so.

"Shut up," she replied, blushing slightly.

The next day, Romanus, Valens, and I met early to discuss our expedition to complete a dungeon together. I told Constans we might be gone all day. She gave the three of us a jealous look but left to go to her tutors without complaint. After saying our goodbyes, the three of us set out for the docks. We could have tried to go through the Emperor's enclave since there were three of us now and the other two were fairly respected community members, but I wanted to avoid that place for now, even with company. The only downside to using my method to cross the channel was a bit of lost dignity for the other two.

I noticed Valens pull out a small leather-bound book that he skimmed as we made our way to the dock. I asked him about the book to make conversation.

"Just reviewing my skill and attributes before the dungeon," he told me, putting the book away.

"Reviewing your skills and attributes? What do you mean?" Valens glanced over at Romanus and they shared a look.

"In my book? You know?" Valens said.

"What? What book?"

Once Valens explained what he was talking about, we immediately reversed course and they took me to what he called a bookbinders shop. I had seen the store in my exploration of the city but had assumed it was a shop that bound books. Apparently, it was not.

"So once this is bound to me, I can open it and review my attributes, skills, perks, and things like that?"

"Yep," the bored clerk said as she held my hand in one of hers and a small leather-bound book in the other.

"And it can't be lost? It just stays bound to me and will reappear if destroyed? And nobody else can read it without my permission? How does that even work?"

"Yep," the clerk replied, completely ignoring my enthusiastic questions.

A moment later, a flash of energy pulsed up my hand.

"All set," the clerk said, handing me the book. "Have a good day."

The clerk turned around and ignored me while I marveled at the book in my hand. I opened the leather-bound book and was amazed to see all the information that I had been tracking mentally perfectly displayed inside the book for me to read at my leisure.

Name: Alexander
Basic Class: Archer 20 / Gunslinger 10 / Warrior 0
Non-Combat Class: Enchanter 4

Base Attributes:

Coordination = 18
Strength = 13
Endurance = 8
Memory = 5
Magic Power = 4
Magic Capacity = 5
Luck = 2

Skills:

Stealth:
Hide in the shadows and move silently, blending into the background and attracting less attention.

Trickster's Dash:
Dash through the air, ignoring wind resistance until you land.
When you dash, you are briefly invisible until your dash ends.

Gambler's Eye:
You receive a passive boost of 20% to your coordination, your
vision is improved, and you gain a sixth sense that reveals when
luck may be favoring you.

Swagger:
Your movement speed increases, obstacles bend from your path,
and your step is sure and steady. Your movements subtly intimidate
others.

Duel Me:
At the start of combat, challenge a foe to a duel. The stakes of the
duel are randomly selected and may include an attribute point, a
percentage of all experience gained, a perk, a mutation, a skill, or
an achievement. The first to surrender, retreat, or die loses. The
winner of the duel permanently steals the stakes of the duel, and
the loser permanently loses the stakes of the duel. This skill may
only be used once a day.

Gambler's Luck:
You push luck to the limit, changing the odds around you to
guarantee a more favorable outcome. Unlocks a new attribute:
Luck.

Empowered Enchantments:
Your enchantment effects are more powerful.

Perks:

Captain's Command:
Anyone obeying an order that you give will receive a morale bonus
of +1 to all attributes while carrying out your command.

Swimmer's Body:

The length of time that you can hold your breath is doubled, you have improved eyesight underwater, and water restricts you less when you are moving through it.

Monster Hunter:
You can sense the presence of monsters nearby. This perk scales with your level and perception attribute.

Natural Weapons:
When using your hands, feet, claws, teeth, or any natural part of your body to strike a foe, you strike as if your strength was increased by +2.

Regeneration:
You gain the regeneration of Gromger the Mighty Troll King. Your body can regenerate from almost any wound. Injuries regenerate based on your endurance attribute and the amount of energy available to your body.

Achievements:

Dangerous Dungeoneering:
For completing ten dungeons by yourself and without a class, you have been rewarded. You receive +2 to all attributes, and rewards from all future dungeons are increased slightly.

Survive a Safe Zone:
For reaching level 10 in a class, completing a dungeon, killing at least 20 monsters, and leaving a safe zone, you have been rewarded. You receive +1 to all attributes.

Quests:

Make a Home:
You must establish a home and secure it from your enemies. Reward: +1 to an attribute of your choice, 500 experience.

Contribute to the Economy II:

You must sell goods or provide services worth a significant amount of money, depending on your region. Reward: 3 gold cores, 600 experience.

Cull the Drakes: completed
Contribute to the Economy: completed
Clear the City: completed

Well, that was extremely helpful. Romanus gently guided me out of the store as I pored through my new book. When I was finished examining everything in detail, I looked up and saw Romanus and Valens giving me an amused look. Neither of them asked why I didn't know of such a basic thing as the book, which I appreciated. I shook my head ruefully. There was always something new to surprise me in this world. You would think I would get used to it, but it was hard to adjust when things were just so different here.

Back at the dock, I carried them both across the channel and we made our way to the house I had been staying at off and on before settling in Sycae.

"The key things to remember about a dungeon," I said, "are that we can't leave until we complete it. So bring your food, water, and medical supplies with you. The dungeon could last for hours or days, but little to no time passes here. Dungeons will have sub-bosses and bosses and often have complex situations that we may have to puzzle through to solve the dungeon. Not every dungeon requires brute force, so look for alternative solutions that could get us through without getting us hurt or killed."

"Got it," Romanus said with an excited look on his face. Valens nodded seriously at my words, paying close attention.

"Alright, that's really it. We can't plan for every eventuality, so we just have to hope we can adapt quick enough to handle whatever the dungeon throws at us. Let's go find one."

"Yeah!" Romanus said with a wide grin. Valens shook his head at his partner's antics and just gave me a half smile.

I was a bit concerned about taking the two of them along. I was confident in my own ability to survive almost anything a dungeon could throw at me, but I had come to like these two men and didn't want to see anything happen to them. Dungeons were dangerous places, but in many ways, they were easier when I was by myself because I could avoid a lot of trouble and I could heal myself easily—especially now that I had my new *Regeneration* perk.

Either way, we needed to do this together for them to get the achievement and unlock quests, so I didn't voice my worries. I just had to make sure they survived without taking any serious injuries that could kill them or leave them crippled and unable to continue their professions.

We scouted around the area until I spotted a dungeon. This one had formed in an alley where a creature of some kind had dug through the cobblestones of the road itself, forming a large pothole. I pointed it out to the two men, and we gathered around the unnaturally dark hole in the street.

"That's a dungeon?" Romanus said, eyeing the entrance in disappointment.

"Yeah," I replied. "Not as glamorous as you'd think. They form naturally from a monster's den or hiding place during the day, so they can appear in the strangest places."

"Let's go inside," Valens said, gripping his greatsword.

I nodded and stepped into the pothole.

When I appeared in the dungeon, I was struck by a wave of dry heat that immediately felt like it was sucking all the moisture out of my body. A bright sun beat down on me from above, and as I looked upward, shading my eyes, I saw there wasn't a cloud in sight to help cover the bright sun. Surrounding me in all directions were sand dunes for as far as my enhanced eyes could see.

Romanus and Valens appeared next to me, holding hands. Seeing me, they hastily let go of each other's hands and looked around at the desert that surrounded us. I pretended I hadn't seen the gesture out of respect for their privacy.

"Wow," Romanus said. "This is insane. It's like an entire world here."

"Yeah," I replied. "I still don't really understand it. I'm sure there is a limit to the dungeon, but I haven't found it yet in any of the dungeons I have completed. It feels like you could go on forever if you just picked a random direction and started walking."

We looked around for a few more moments and then Valens spoke up. "Monsters incoming," he said, pointing forward. I hadn't sensed them yet, but I was convinced Valens had unlocked a perception attribute that extended his range on his *Monster Hunter* perk further than mine.

"Let's get ready," I said, drawing my sword.

"Using a sword now?" Romanus said.

"Looking to diversify myself a bit," I responded, smiling at him as I spun my sword around in my hand.

"Look lively now," Valens called out.

We spread out on the top of the dune and waited. After just a moment, my *Monster Hunter* perk let me sense seven smaller monsters approaching our location. When they came into view, I saw the seven beasts scampering over the nearest dune toward us. They looked similar to Komodo dragons from my world, although bigger. Their feet spit sand as they ran, and each had a long tongue it periodically flicked out of its mouth as it charged unerringly toward us.

I could have easily dispatched them with my revolver, but I wanted to get used to using my new sword and didn't want to spoil the fun for my companions.

"I'm going to be limited in what I can do under this ungodly sun," Romanus said as he watched the monsters approach.

"That's fine," I said. "We shouldn't have a problem with monsters like these."

The beasts charged up the dune. Valens stepped forward and activated his protective skill, illusory shields appearing to float around him, while Romanus drew his daggers, which I noted idly were once again coated in dark shadow.

As the monsters reached the crest of the dune, Valens stepped forward and struck. His large two-handed sword cleaved through one of the beasts and buried itself in the side of another. I ran forward and drove my sword into another while kicking a second monster to push it away from me as its jaws snapped in my direction. Romanus moved rapidly to the remaining three, dodging and weaving between them while scoring deep strikes across their eyes and necks and striking their vulnerable spots as best as he could.

After just a moment, we dispatched all seven of the beasts. I hadn't needed to use my revolver once, and it didn't seem like the

312

other two had broken a sweat—other than the sweat caused by the sun beating down on us.

"Are they normally this easy?" Romanus asked me. He sheathed his knives somewhere on his person, but I still couldn't quite see where.

"It depends on the dungeon," I replied. "You generally see a mix of a large number of weaker creatures or a smaller number of strong creatures. It's good to have a way to handle both."

"Can we harvest these?" he asked, looking at one of the corpses at our feet.

"Huh," I said, "I'm not sure, actually. Give it a shot."

He pulled out a dagger and began to skin one of the monsters. After a few moments, he lifted the hide, but before he could clean it further, it faded and eventually disappeared.

"Hmm," he said, "looks like that's a no. Probably we can't take anything from a dungeon except the rewards at the end."

"Yeah," I replied, "that makes sense. Otherwise, in some of these dungeons, I could have carried out hundreds of pounds of equipment."

"Like this landscape, most of this is probably not real but just a manifestation of magic in some form," Romanus speculated.

Valens kept a wary eye out as we talked until he grunted at us, signaling it was time for us to get a move on.

We made quick progress over the dunes, the sand barely hindering us with our high attributes. As we hiked, Valens would warn us when more of the Komodo dragons would approach, so we were always prepared to face them when they arrived. My sword wasn't as deadly as my revolver, but I discovered there was a more visceral pleasure in using the sword. The combination of my body, mind, and skill with the weapon gave me a unique kind of pleasure when everything came together to let me triumph over my enemies. There were moments when I found everything lining up perfectly, my body and mind synchronizing to let me dodge, attack, and plan my next move all at once. It felt . . . transcendental. It was almost like achieving a state of Zen perfection while fighting at the same time.

As the sun overhead began to set, we saw a temple rising out of the sand in front of us. It was a three-sided pyramid and had a flat top exposed to the sun above. We scouted around the pyramid but

313

found no entrance that might lead us inside. Seeing no other option, we climbed up the steps that lined the sides of the pyramid. When we reached the top, we saw that it was made of flat sunbaked stones laid out in a beautiful mosaic. The moment we stepped onto the mosaic, a pulse of energy erupted from the pyramid, sending shivers through our bodies. I could feel the energy radiating outward from the pyramid, and I could suddenly feel monsters appearing around the pyramid. I was sure they hadn't been there before.

"Ah," I said, recognizing what was happening. "A base defense scenario."

"Base defense? What does that mean?" Romanus asked, eyeing the empty desert that stretched around us with a concerned look on his face, clearly sensing the new monsters as well.

"Have you encountered this type of dungeon before?" Valens asked, scanning the desert as well.

"Not exactly," I replied, "but I'm familiar with the concept."

Sand exploded upward in the distance, and small groups of bipedal lizardmen erupted from the sand. There was a group of lizards for each side of the pyramid. The lizardmen were the same color as the sand around us and had large frills and crests that stood proudly around their heads. They had jaws full of sharp teeth and crude-looking spears in their hands. They wore no visible armor, just a loincloth to keep them decent, but their scales covered their entire bodies, likely providing some protection.

"Those weren't there before," Valens said. "I only sensed them when we stepped onto the mosaic."

"Dungeon logic," I replied. "Don't worry about it too much."

The sun had set almost entirely by the time the first wave reached us, which allowed Romanus to use more of his skills. We each took a side and waited as the lizards charged up the pyramid toward us.

"This really isn't fair to the poor monsters," I said, eyeing the lizards running up the pyramid. "They have got to be getting tired. They just ran the entire way here."

Romanus laughed, twirling his shadow-daggers.

I stood at the edge of my side of the pyramid and waited. Once the lizards were getting near the top, I used *Trickster's Dash* to shoot over their heads and appeared behind them. The lizardmen didn't react to my disappearance, so I was easily able to step forward and attack them from behind.

I struck several of the monsters down before they realized what was happening. My sword pierced their scales easily, each attack shocking the lizards, and the strength of my blows was enough to kill them with a single well-placed strike. I dispatched the group on my side easily and then returned to the top of the pyramid. Valens and Romanus were just finishing up their group of lizards and soon joined me.

The next wave had the same number of spearmen but included several new ones that carried crude bows. I didn't wait for the bowmen to get in range, dashing out into the air and then downward, appearing right next to the bowmen. With two swings of my sword, I decapitated them both. The spearmen had continued up the steps of the pyramid, completely unaware, so I followed them up and killed them just as easily as I had the last time.

Several more waves of lizardmen attacked us in quick succession. The only wave that gave me trouble was when lizardmen that could cast spells appeared. I fought them at the bottom of the pyramid, and I ended up doing a lot of dashing to avoid their spells and get behind them, which tired me out a bit. Once I got close enough to one of them, though, they couldn't stand up to my sword. I had still managed to avoid using my revolver, trying to push myself to diversify my arsenal by using only my sword for now.

The group after the spellcasters comprised three sub-bosses, one on each side of the pyramid. The sub-bosses were much larger than the earlier lizardmen, almost the same size as the trolls I had fought in the prior dungeon. Thankfully, they didn't have the same regenerative abilities as the trolls. I fought mine at the bottom of the pyramid so I could have plenty of space to dash around the brute. I was able to defeat it by slowly wearing it down with strikes from my sword, aiming for vulnerable areas like its heel, knees, neck, and eyes as much as I could. I avoided the sub-boss's attempts to grab me with its massive hands thanks to my extraordinary speed and use of my *Dash*. I felt a bit like a little corvid bird, darting in and out to harass my much larger foe. Of course, I could have just shot the sub-boss a few times and ended the fight, but I enjoyed using just my attributes, *Dash*, and my sword to stay alive.

It was getting late into the night by the time I managed to kill the big sub-boss, and I checked on the other two, who had finished their sub-boss already. Valens had fought on top of the pyramid, while Romanus seemed to have ambushed and killed his sub-boss before it could even climb the pyramid, judging by the fact that it was lying face-down in the sand below us.

It felt like these dungeons didn't normally send so many enemies when I was by myself. The fact that the pyramid had three sides seemed deliberate and the fact that the monsters always spawned in three separate groups, when there were three of us, confirmed my hypothesis. The dungeon was also taking longer than normal. We had been inside for over half a day now, and we had to take a few moments to eat and drink between waves to keep our energy up.

The next sub-boss taught me a valuable lesson about how to fight with a sword. The monster was a tall, lean lizardman with a longsword and thicker scales than the other lizards we had fought so far, except for the brute we had just killed. When I fought him, he showed me what a true master of the sword was capable of, and I knew I had a lot of work to do if I wanted to ever match up to the real deal. Every time I tried to attack, the lizardman parried or dodged my blows with ease. His strikes were so fast and precise that I would have had no chance to avoid them if not for my extremely high attributes. He moved with a grace that was a wonder to behold, and part of me wished I could just watch him for hours to study how he fought. Sadly, he had other ideas and wouldn't stop trying to kill me.

My *Regeneration* and my high attributes saved me, despite my lack of skill with the sword. The lizardman scored hit after hit against me for every one time my speed gave me the chance to strike him, but my *Regeneration* healed me in moments. After almost twenty minutes, I had scored enough minor wounds on the monster to start slowing him down. Sweat was pouring from my brow and my breathing was starting to become strained, but as the sub-boss slowed from his injuries, I was able to score more and more hits until the beast finally succumbed to his wounds. I felt bad at how futile all of his skill ended up being. If he had been a real person, I was sure he would have been cursing me as he, a clear master of the sword, realized he was going to die to a rank amateur. He had deserved to win the fight based on his skill with the sword, but my advantages helped me win in the end. The world wasn't fair, lizardman. The world wasn't fair.

Finally, as a new dawn began to appear on the horizon, the final boss made its appearance. The center of the pyramid began to shift beneath us as the first rays of dawn struck it. We quickly jumped off the top of the pyramid and waited a few steps down to see what would happen. The top began to sink into the pyramid until a burst of pure golden light erupted upward into the sky above us. I had to shade my eyes from the sight; the light was so bright that it hurt to look at. A second later, a bird's screech echoed up from inside the pyramid and an enormous golden bird rocketed upward, shooting into the sky. I shaded my eyes and stared in awe at the beautiful creature as it flew upward. The morning sun seemed to empower it as it burst into a golden radiance, flames erupting across its body when the sun's rays touched it.

After a moment, the bird banked around and seemed to spot us near the top of the pyramid. It screeched again, but this time its cry sounded angry at our presence near its home. I activated my *Duel Me* skill, curious what I might get from a boss so majestic and powerful. To activate the skill, I yelled out at the boss, "*Duel Me!*"

Duel activated. You and your opponent have both wagered your experience. Good luck.

The bird swooped downward and unleashed a ray of fiery golden light at the three of us. The ray struck the top of the pyramid, splashing flames all around us. We swiftly scattered in order to avoid the beam, but the bird followed me as I turned to run down the pyramid steps. I changed course, dashing forward into the air to avoid the beam, turning myself invisible in hopes the boss would ignore me for a moment. As my dash ended in midair, I used a second one to change directions, launching myself upward at the boss. As I flew upward, the heat radiating from the boss became so intense I could feel it burning me as I approached.

My dash carried me upward to a point where I should stop directly in the path of the swooping bird. As soon as my momentum froze, I lifted my sword and swung at the wing of the bird as it passed right next to me. I felt my sword dig deep into the bird's wing. My own strength and the bird's momentum through the air gave my strike the power to sheer through part of its wing entirely.

The boss cried out in anger, and the fire that surrounded its body flared out, burning me as I fell toward the ground. Thankfully, my new armor absorbed most of the flames, protecting me from the magical attack. When the bird was past me, I twisted in the air and saw it bank sharply and begin to circle back around toward me. I dashed again, turning invisible and turning my freefall into a dash, ending a few inches from the ground. A feeling of hunger and thirst began to make itself known as my body regenerated the burns that had made it through my armor.

I looked upward, seeing the bird circling in confusion as it tried to find me. Despite my sword cutting deeply into its wing, it didn't seem to have been slowed at all.

Romanus and Valens came running when they saw me land.

"We don't have any way to reach the boss," Romanus yelled to me as he approached. Valens squinted upward at the boss, clearly annoyed that he couldn't attack.

I had hoped to only use my new sword throughout the entire dungeon, but our lack of a balanced group meant we had almost no ranged capabilities other than my revolver. I reluctantly sheathed my sword and drew my revolver.

"I have an idea that should work," I told them, unloading my *Penetration Bullets*. I reloaded with the *Shadow Bullets* I had crafted so long ago and hadn't had a chance to use yet.

I took careful aim as the boss circled us in the sky, preparing to dive and attack us again. Before it could, I fired. My shot flew true, striking the bird in the center of its chest. Darkness erupted across the face and body of the boss, and its angry screech turned to cries of pain as it was covered in a cloud of pure darkness. When the bird reappeared, the darkness seemed to have eaten away at the boss, inflicting significantly more damage than the bullets themselves. The bird's flame was dimmer as well, and it seemed disoriented from the surprise attack, flapping its wings half-heartedly and unbalancing itself left and right, as if partially stunned.

I waited, unsure if I should shoot it again, as the boss continued to fall toward the ground, rapidly picking up speed. It got closer and closer to the ground, and I realized it wouldn't be able to stop itself. With a dull thump, the boss slammed into the sand, a geyser of dust exploding upward from where it had impacted. The three of us had to steady ourselves as the wave of the impact reached us, tossing us up and down briefly. We all waited, staring at where the gargantuan bird had crashed to the earth on the other side of some dunes. Nothing stirred but the dust as it slowly fell to the ground.

Winner: Alexander! You are awarded 3430 experience.

Once the dust settled, we climbed the nearest dune and looked down on the once-proud bird's remains. The sand surrounding the boss had been turned to molten glass for several yards. The glass was still bubbling and shifting, like a sea of boiling water surrounding the bird's body. We stopped for a moment and simply stared at the sight together.

I couldn't help but think about how much experience I had just won from the duel. It was more than I had received doing entire dungeons, at least the equivalent of three or four dungeons, if not more if I hadn't killed very much inside. Did such a large amount of experience mean this boss was stronger than the other bosses I had used the skill on? To get over three thousand experience from a single duel was spectacular.

"What do we do now?" Romanus asked, interrupting my thoughts.

I put aside my speculation about my skill and turned to the two men who stood next to me. "The dungeon core is probably back at the top of the pyramid now. We should head back and claim it. Once we do, we will get our reward and the dungeon will close."

They nodded and we slowly hiked back up to the top of the pyramid, all three of us visibly exhausted from the dungeon. My *Regeneration* had helped keep my energy level up, but I was starving and thirsty, even with the occasional break to eat and drink. I was craving a large meal from the inn back in Sycae more than anything right now.

We found the dungeon core sitting on top of the pyramid; whatever device had opened to allow the boss to escape had closed while we fought it. While we were gone, the mosaic that had covered the top had been transformed from a dusty but striking mosaic into a shining, beautiful work of beauty. The mosaic had changed as well. Before, it depicted a generic design of whirling patterns. Now it showed a representation of the golden bird flying proudly through the sky. Gold inlay and fine jewels adorned the mosaic now, bringing the bird's image to life. It was a beautiful work of art, but it was so strange that the dungeon would devote energy to forming it after we had defeated the boss. I shook my head at the sight. There was so much I just did not understand these days.

Congratulations, you have completed this dungeon. You have earned the following rewards: 4 gold cores, 11 blue cores, 1500 experience, Skill Stone: Glass Meteor.

I took the loot and saw that the other two also got their own individual rewards, which was a relief. I wasn't sure how the dungeon would reward us and didn't want to have any hurt feelings about who got what rewards.

I examined the skill stone as I put the orbs away in my pouch. I could sense it was a magical skill, so I couldn't use it. By its description, it sounded powerful, though. It would allow someone to call down a meteor made of glass, which would do significant damage on impact and explode into shards of glass, wounding anyone nearby as well. I could either save it for the future, in case I was ever able to figure out a solution to my lack of magic, or I could sell it now, likely for a large amount, given how rare skill stones were, especially one that seemed as powerful as this one.

We appeared outside of the dungeon and I had to pause as the announcements from my *Warrior* class rolled through my mind. I had gained enough experience to level it several times over.

Congratulations, you have received enough experience to level your Warrior class. You are now level 1.

Please choose a level 1 class skill:

Empowered Strikes: You magnify the power of all of your strikes. Your strength when attacking is magnified by an additional 25%.

Protection: Surround yourself with a protective shield, absorbing damage based on your endurance attribute.

Bash: Stun an enemy.

Rending Strike: Your next attack causes significant bleeding.

Charge: Charge at your target, destroying any obstacles in your path.

I considered what would be best to take. I didn't really need defense since my *Regeneration* perk was so powerful right now. A stun was nice, but not particularly helpful in the grand scheme of things. I could kill most of the enemies I was fighting right now without needing to waste time stunning them. *Charge* was out; my own *Trickster's Dash* was significantly better. So it was between *Rending Strike* or *Empowered Strikes*. One was a constant increase, the other a special attack that did significant follow-up damage in the form of bleeding. The bonus to strength from *Empowered Strikes* being percentage-based made it the clearly superior skill. On top of that, it was active at all times, and I didn't really need a bleeding attack, since most enemies died from my overwhelming attributes rather than smaller attacks over a long period of time, where bleeding might be more effective. If I fought with daggers, *Rending Strike* would likely be the superior option, but for now, *Empowered Strikes* seemed the best.

I selected *Empowered Strikes*. After that was done, the attribute enhancements began to cascade through my mind. I had gained over 4500 experience from that dungeon alone, primarily from my *Duel Me* skill. That shot my *Warrior* class all the way up to level 9, granting me +4 to strength, +3 to endurance, and +1 to coordination.

"Did you guys get anything good?" I asked my two companions after I finished reviewing the changes to my attributes.

"More experience than a month of hunting!" Romanus said, putting his arm around Valens's shoulder in celebration.

"Less money," Valens said, frowning slightly, "but much better experience."

"Any skills or perks?" I asked.

Both men shook their heads. I had noticed a link between skills, perks, and the actions taken in the dungeon. It implied a certain amount of intelligence in the dungeon; it seemed to evaluate the people inside and tailor rewards based on our choices. If I had to guess, I would say I received the skill stone because of the way I killed the final boss and caused the explosion that turned the sand into glass. It couldn't have been a coincidence that I received a skill stone remarkably similar to how the boss died. It was just a shame I couldn't use it. The dungeon must have decided that it was worth a skill reward, or my perk that increased my rewards from dungeons had come into play. Or a little of both.

I told them about my rewards, not trying to hide what I had received. Both men congratulated me and neither asked for the skill, which was another sign of how trustworthy they were. I considered sharing it with one of them, but neither of them were spellcasters anyway, so it wouldn't be very useful for them. Besides, I needed the money from selling it if I decided to put into action some of my plans for the future.

In a festive mood, we made our way back safely to Sycae. Romanus immediately ordered us a round of drinks to celebrate.

"Is there a place that buys skills like the one I got?" I asked Romanus and Valens as we sat down at a table in the common room.

"You could probably sell it here," Romanus told me, "but the real buyers are in the Emperor's enclave. Too many rich nobles with nothing better to do than buy fancy skills they will never use to try and impress other nobles doing the exact same thing. It's risky to sell there, though, because that place is a snake pit, but a skill like that would sell for two or three times what you could get here."

I wasn't quite ready to enter a dangerous place like the Emperor's enclave. Other people who had access to powerful magic were significantly more of a danger to me than any monster had been so far. The three of us toasted to our success and talked about plans for the future until I begged off to take care of some of my plans before the sun set.

After saying goodbye to my two companions, I made my way over the water and into Perama to visit Momma Lena's. I purchased a *Rogue* book for myself now that I had the money again.

"Momma Lena," I asked her after we concluded our business, "do you know where I might find out more information about a physical class that would let me resist spells better?"

"Hmm," she said, "I can understand why you ask. Some of the *Warrior* classes evolve into classes that can fight mages better, but those are rare. It's one of the weaknesses of the physical classes, especially for you since you can't take a *Mage* or *Scholar* class and pick a few low-level skills. Your zero attributes for magic also means you have no resistance to most spells, where most people at least have some natural resistance that reduces the power of the spells cast on them."

"Any ideas that could help me?" I asked.

"I have no idea," she said, shaking her head. "But your best bet in finding elusive classes or finding out the requirements to evolve a class is to talk to the head librarian in the Imperial Library."

"There's an Imperial Library?"

"Indeed," Momma Lena replied. "In the Emperor's enclave, protected by his Varangian guard. Technically, anyone of the city has permission to enter if you can get yourself invited into the enclave in the first place."

I groaned. "Seems like fate is pushing me to go to the Emperor's enclave, and I was really trying to avoid that place as much as possible."

"A good policy, I'd say," Momma Lena responded. "You should probably stick with it."

Chapter 25

Romanus and Valens left to go on a hunt and get their achievements for leaving the safe zone. Meanwhile, I learned the *Rogue* class and began another period of hunting experience points to level my two new classes. I ended up renting time in the studio where Constans and I trained in weapons so I could stay late and practice my martial arts. Our trainer had no issue with me using the space at night, when it was normally closed anyway. I spent my nights training on my own, my mornings training with the trainer, and then my afternoons and early evenings finding and completing as many dungeons as possible. Fighting a true swordmaster had shown me the value of training even more, especially because the styles I knew from Earth didn't exactly work in this world, where the attributes that people could get changed everything so dramatically. Learning to fight with high attributes took even more careful practice than just learning how to use a weapon in the first place, something that people used to dedicate their whole lives on Earth to doing.

I spent some time scavenging every few days, continuing to collect things for Constans to sell so I could help her *Merchant* class grow. I also ran a few dungeons with Romanus and Valens when they weren't out hunting, and even though I enjoyed their company, I found I preferred running the dungeons on my own more often than not. It was just simpler and faster and I didn't have to worry about a tragic accident. My *Regeneration* perk, my revolver, and my high attributes let me handle everything these dungeons in the "safe zone" could throw my way.

I leveled my *Rogue* class quickly, choosing *Evasion* as my level 1 skill. *Evasion* was a passive ability that gave me an improved chance to avoid attacks and scaled off of my coordination, which made it a very powerful defensive tool for me. I didn't exactly need more defense right now, but my other options were lackluster and *Evasion* helped me avoid entire attacks. It synergized well with *Regeneration* because I got hit less, so I didn't have to tire myself out healing smaller injuries.

I kept my *Gunslinger* class inactive, wanting to see if I could get an evolved class for *Warrior* or *Rogue* first. I also wanted to get as powerful as I could with the physical classes I had access to now before I entered the Emperor's enclave.

A month passed surprisingly fast. Constans and I had dinner together most nights and Romanus and Valens joined us whenever they were in town. A month of practice every night and instruction every morning had me making significant improvement with learning how to actually fight. Our combat trainer was shocked at how fast I learned, but it was only impressive if you didn't know I spent almost every night drilling, practicing, and fighting in the studio to teach my body how to properly utilize my attributes. Having the advantage of being an artificial intelligence, and the memory to remember everything perfectly, made it easy for me to dedicate myself to repetitive tasks, and I pushed myself mentally and physically every single night.

I also managed to level both of my new classes to twenty within the month, thanks in big part to my *Duel Me* ability, which seemed to favor stealing experience from dungeons for some reason. It was an incredibly productive month of training, gathering experience, stealing experience and the occasional attribute from monsters, and completing dungeons. In total, I gained +3 endurance, +4 strength, and +2 coordination from leveling my *Warrior* class to level 20. I gained +8 to coordination, +5 to strength, and +4 to endurance for leveling my *Rogue* class to twenty. I also managed to steal more attributes from my duel victims, giving me a +1 to strength, +1 to memory, and +2 to magical power.

I was an attribute powerhouse. I was fast enough to run across the city in under ten minutes, from the ancient harbor on the south side, across the water, and through Sycae to stop at the northern wall. And that was with having to use *Stealth* in Sycae to avoid drawing too much attention to myself. I could jump so far I didn't even need my *Dash* to leap across streets anymore. I had to remind myself, as I became more and more accustomed to the new power and speed of my body, that there were plenty of monsters and people out there that were more powerful than me. The fight with the demon played through my head many times, keeping me humble and grounded.

I also practiced using my *Trickster's Dash* to leap high into the air and maneuver around as if I was flying. I had known, intellectually, it was possible, but until my fight with the fiery bird, I hadn't fully conceptualized how easy it was. Since *Dash* completely stopped my momentum when I came to the end of it, I could dash high into the air and maneuver myself with ease, then dash downward to land, settling to the ground as if gravity had no hold on me. It was exhausting, requiring multiple dashes in a row without having a chance to stop, which seemed to drain me significantly more, but it gave me a makeshift form of flight that was exhilarating.

Leveling my classes also earned me two more *Warrior* skills and two more *Rogue* skills. For my level 10 *Warrior* skill, I chose a skill called *Shatter Armor*, which let me make an attack that pit my strength against the durability of the enemy's armor. If I was stronger than their armor was durable, their armor was shattered and became useless. I practiced on some cheap armor I bought from an outfitter's shop. The results were impressive. I strung up the armor in one of the safehouses I was using to hunt dungeons in the city, and when I struck the armor with my new skill, my strength was enough to cause the armor to explode outward, sending chips of metal flying to embed themselves in the nearby wall. The first time I tried the skill in a dungeon, it not only shattered the armor of my opponent, but the shrapnel from the broken armor pierced deeply into the chest of the armored monster I was fighting and injured the companions standing behind it.

I had started to get a sense of where I wanted to focus myself. My attributes, building exponentially off my actual body, gave me an overwhelming advantage over my enemies. Even if I encountered something that had the equivalent number of attributes, mine scaled off a significantly stronger and faster body, exponentially increasing the value of each +1 I gained, making me much more powerful than someone my own level.

When I was first trying to figure out a way to survive in this world, I thought my revolver would be my biggest advantage, but I was finding now that my attributes were even more powerful in the long run. I was so fast these days I could run circles around even the fastest of monsters I encountered in the dungeons. And when I struck them with my sword, fist, or foot, my power was colossal compared to even the strongest monsters in the safe zone.

With the long-term potential of building on my attributes, I started looking for skills that scaled based on my attributes or enhanced them in some way, seeking to magnify my advantage as fully as I could rather than looking for interesting or unique skills.

My level 20 *Warrior* skill was called *Steadfast Endurance,* which gave me a twenty-five percent increase to my endurance and reduced the exhaustion from using skills repeatedly. Using my *Trickster's Dash* in the way I had been doing lately—leaping through the air over and over—was a significant drain on my body. *Steadfast Endurance* immediately helped make it more manageable, although the increased endurance was great even on its own.

For my *Rogue* class, I picked *Improved Evasion* for level 10 and then *Absolute Evasion* for level 20. Both skills were an evolution of my first skill choice, *Evasion.* I hadn't come across an evolving skill before. Evolving the skill left me with only having one actual skill from my *Rogue* class, but the skill was very powerful and gave me my first chance at resisting magical attacks. *Improved Evasion* gave me the ability to sense attacks even if I couldn't see them, giving me a chance to evade an attack from any direction.

Absolute Evasion took it a step further and applied my evasion to spells, giving me a chance to evade spells—even spells I didn't see coming or spells that targeted my mind or tried to paralyze my body. It didn't seem possible to evade an attack on my mind, but somehow, the skill made it happen. All three forms of *Evasion* scaled off my coordination, giving me a massive boost to the skill. When I had read the description of *Absolute Evasion*, I knew I had made the right choice. I had found my first way to shore up my weakness to spells.

For some reason, I had stopped receiving perks or skills from the dungeons as rewards. Part of me suspected this was because the dungeons were no longer a challenge for me. The perks and skills I had received before had always come from clever ways I had managed to survive or from dramatic and dangerous situations.

Now that I was more comfortable fighting with my sword and had my revolver and grenades for a diverse answer to whatever the dungeons threw at me, I wasn't scraping by anymore, so I suspected the dungeons weren't giving me extraordinary rewards any longer. It was probably expected that a person would complete a few dungeons in the city they were born in and then graduate to the harder dungeons outside of the city soon after. I didn't want to take those kinds of risks yet since I still had lower-level classes that benefited from easier dungeons. And the monetary rewards were still significant.

I made sure I reached level 20 on both my *Warrior* and *Rogue* classes on the same day. After selecting my skills, the familiar warmth began to build in my chest, indicating I had achieved an evolution for one, or both, of my classes.

Congratulations, you have unlocked an evolution of your Warrior class. Based on your unique use of the class, you have unlocked Duelist. Your class rating is Rare. Do you wish to adopt this class now?

Congratulations, you have unlocked an evolution of your Rogue class. Based on your unique use of the class, you have unlocked Pirate. Your class rating is Common. Do you wish to adopt this class now?

It was a bit frustrating that I couldn't tell what skills each class would eventually unlock for me. If I focused on the announcement in my head, I could get a bit of a sense for each class, but no concrete details. I wondered if, before the city was overrun, there had been scholars who did nothing but document skill paths and what each evolution offered. I could sense that the *Pirate* class was focused on scrappy fights, movement skills, and blinds or disarms.

I wasn't sure how I knew that, but I did.

The *Duelist* class had likely been unlocked because of my *Duel Me* skill and maybe because I had won all my duels so far. The class was about fighting opponents one on one, showmanship and misdirection, and self-buffs and debuffs of enemies through witty banter—which was a very strange concept, but that was what my sense of the class was telling me.

I wasn't that impressed with *Pirate*. It was only a common class, which meant it could only be leveled to forty. And I didn't really need more mobility; my *Trickster's Dash* was probably one of the best mobility skills in this world. Blinds and disarms were also less than useful for me.

Duelist, meanwhile, was intriguing. It synergized great with my *Duel Me* skill, which was essential if I wanted to scale beyond what others were capable of. And it was a rare class, meaning it could level to sixty. It wasn't the most powerful of classes, but it was unlikely I was going to find anything better soon.

I decided to select *Duelist* but did not accept *Pirate* at this time. As I felt the *Duelist* class open up to me, my remaining experience funneled into the class, leveling it to level 2.

Congratulations, you have received enough experience to level your Duelist class. You are now level 1.

Please choose a level 1 class skill:

You Dare Challenge Me: Pick a target. You gain +3 to all attributes until you or your opponent are defeated.

Look Over There: Distract your opponent, guaranteeing one attack hits a vulnerable area.

You Fight Worse Than Your Mother: Insult your opponent, reducing all of their attributes by three and reducing their coordination by 10%. Your attributes are increased by +1 for the duration of the fight and your coordination is increased by 10%.

If It's a Fight You Want, It's a Fight You'll Get: Pick a target. The longer you fight your opponent, the higher your attributes soar. Gain +1 to all attributes once every minute you are in combat until you or your opponent are defeated or surrender.

Never Bring a Mob to a Duel: Gain +1 to all attributes for each nearby enemy that is actively attacking you or planning to attack you. Whenever an enemy is defeated or surrenders, you lose their bonus attribute. This skill may only be used once per week.

All of the skills were strong and amusing. The *Duelist* class clearly had a sense of humor about itself. I could just see myself fighting a dragon and having to yell, "Your scales are weak like your father's bloodline!" or some such nonsense to activate my skill. It was a hilarious image but not very practical.

I ruled out *Look Over There* to start. While it could be powerful, it wasn't as good as the other skills. *You Fight Worse Than Your Mother* had potential. It both debuffed an enemy, buffed me, and gave a percentage-based buff to my coordination attribute, which made it very strong.

I needed to decide what my greatest weakness was right now. I was easily winning my duels, primarily because I only used that skill when I was sure that I would win. If I wanted to guarantee more wins against a single opponent, then *You Dare Challenge Me* or *If It's a Fight You Want, It's a Fight You'll Get* would be my best bet. But if I wanted to supplement my ability to fight a large number of opponents at once, then *Never Bring a Mob to a Duel* would be extremely strong. If I was attacked by, say, twenty opponents at once, that skill would give me an incredible bonus to not just my damage but my survivability. It would almost double my physical attributes, not to mention increase the percentage bonuses I receive based on my underlying attribute. The negative was that it had the largest cooldown between uses of any skill I had seen so far. That must mean the skill was extremely powerful, though I would just need to be judicious in its use.

I did some quick math. My current coordination was thirty plus twenty percent from *Gambler's Eye.* If I used *Never Bring a Mob to a Duel* on twenty opponents, my coordination would soar to fifty and the twenty percent increase would go from a +6 to a +10, bringing my total coordination to sixty. That was insane, considering every point was around +20% to the human base speed and coordination. Even without my enhanced body, a sixty coordination was the equivalent of someone being twelve times faster than a normal human. For me, that was more like fifteen to twenty times faster.

I had my *Explosive Bullets, Explosive Grenades,* and *Confusion Grenades* to let me handle large groups of enemies, but if I was ever caught unaware or if a large group was resistant to that type of damage or control, I was vulnerable to being overwhelmed. I had survived a few close calls in dungeons against large groups that didn't die easily to fire-based attacks, surviving mainly through extensive use of *Trickster's Dash* and whittling down the pack slowly by attacking the vulnerable members around the edges. If I had *Never Bring a Mob to a Duel*, I could probably confront a group of enemies without having to be as careful. In fact, the more enemies I fought, the more powerful I would become.

I couldn't pass up such potential strength. It could scale incredibly high and it supplemented a current weakness of mine. I would lose the attributes again as I started to defeat individual members of the group I faced, and it wouldn't assist me in winning one-on-one duels, which people who took the *Duelist* class probably found to be a great weakness of the skill. To me, though, it was too good to pass up. I selected *Never Bring a Mob to a Duel* for my new skill.

After that was done, I reactivated my *Gunslinger* class now that I had achieved level 20 on both my *Warrior* and *Rogue* classes.

That left me, finally, with no more excuses for avoiding the Emperor's enclave. Winter had rolled in as the month passed, and temperatures had dropped significantly. It didn't impact me too much, but the rest of Sycae fell into a bit of a slump, the lively markets more empty and food quickly becoming more expensive. Sycae seemed to live in perpetual denial that the outside world was in trouble, but even the residents there couldn't ignore the hunger growing in their bellies and the cold houses that never had enough firewood to warm them.

Constans and I had made enough money to keep ourselves warm and fed for a long time to come, so I wasn't too worried about her. She confessed to me that this would be the first winter she could remember when she had a meal to eat every single day and had warm clothes to wear. Most of her winters were spent huddling with other orphans and begging for scraps since visitors became fewer during the winter season. I wasn't sure what to say when she told me about her past, but hearing about her life made me realize that she and I had a lot in common. In many ways, I was an orphan back home as well. I hadn't starved on the street, but I had also known little joy or love in my prior life. Maybe that was one of the reasons I had felt a kinship with her from the moment I met her.

Now that I had achieved my short-term goals of leveling my classes, I needed to take another step forward. I needed information about possible physical classes that could resist spells or help me fight spellcasters better. And I still had my *Glass Meteor* skill stone, which I had decided to sell. While Constans and I had replenished our wealth from salvaging and dungeon running, I had a few very ambitious ideas that required even more wealth to make a reality.

On a blistering cold morning, I caught Constans before she left to meet her tutor and gave her the news that I would be leaving for a few days. She had been just as busy as me, so we hadn't seen much of each other except for at dinner. She had grown and filled out in the last month, thanks to regular meals, her training, and the healer I had hired. She had gone from being a mere skeleton to looking more like a typical, healthy teenager. I was proud of how hard she was working; she had truly embraced the opportunity I had given her and had made it her own. With a warm goodbye, she promised to continue her work while I was gone.

I decided to approach the Emperor's enclave on my own. I knew Romanus and Valens would be willing to go with me if I asked, but if something went wrong, I was confident I could escape, and I worried they could be arrested or killed. I had no issue with fleeing for my life if needed; my pride was more than willing to take a hit in the name of survival. I didn't think the two men could escape as easily, so it made sense for me to go by myself.

I strapped on my magical sword and armor, covering as much as I could under my scavenger's cloak. I made sure my revolver was concealed under my left armpit, then checked and double-checked that all my satchels were full of bullets and my bandolier was full of grenades. I left Constans with a fair amount of my wealth, with instructions to find a good she could buy in bulk and sell for a profit as her next project. It was wintertime, so I suggested she think about something that might be cheap now but expensive in the summer. We could afford to store it for a few months and then resell it for a profit if she found something appropriate. I had no idea what that could be, given how little resources everyone had this time of year, but that was why I gave her the project. She could figure it out. She was the merchant.

As prepared as I would ever be, I took a walk to the west side of Sycae, where the bridge to the Emperor's enclave was still intact. The bridge was beautiful, held up as if by magic as it arced high over the channel between Sycae and the main city. I could see what Perama must have once looked like before it became the last refuge of the misfits and outcasts of the city.

As I crossed the bridge, I finally got to see for myself why so many people thought I was a Varangian. Guarding the towers and

332

gate on the far side of the bridge were tall, pale-skinned men dressed in chain armor and carrying a variety of dangerous-looking weapons. The men all had long hair and beards, with trinkets braided into both. They were as tall as I was, and one was even taller than me. Many had tattoos on their faces or bodies, and all of them looked like dangerous and competent fighters.

When I reached them, one of the guards asked me a question in a language I didn't immediately recognize. It took me a moment to review what was said and determine it was in Old Norse. They were asking if I was one of them.

I didn't respond, not wanting to mislead them or give away that I spoke their language.

"I'm here to negotiate a sale of a rare skill stone and to visit the Imperial Library," I told the guard in the hybrid Latin and Greek that was spoken in the city.

The guard turned to one of his companions, speaking in Norse again. I pretended I didn't understand as he insulted my mother and called me a coward in his language, obviously trying to see if I would react to the insults. After a bit, seeing my lack of reaction, the guard finally stopped trying to get a rise out of me and let me pass.

Inside the gate was a massive palace that filled almost the entire enclave. The palace was beautiful, covered in stained-glass windows and decorative stone. Gargoyles and other adornments decorated the walls and rooftop everywhere. The building stood five stories tall and stretched over a mile in front of me. The palace walls were made from marble that glowed in the early-morning sun with a pearlescent beauty. There were no outbuildings or breaks in the palace, which seemed odd. The entire enclave appeared to be built to protect nothing but the one large building.

What little space that wasn't taken up by the palace itself was turned into beautifully manicured gardens. Trees, grass, shrubs, and an abundance of flowers filled the grounds between the palace and the walls that protected the enclave. Elaborate fountains appeared here and there. They made a soft tinkling sound as water splashed down into their ornate basins. Winding paths led through the garden, creating a picturesque and beautiful setting. The beauty was only slightly marred by the large, ugly walls that surrounded the enclave, its brutal utilitarianism contrasting with the pristine and gentle gardens.

I walked down the larger path that led from the foot of the bridge to an ornate gate that led inside the palace. As I approached, several more Varangian guards and a man in a formal robe stopped me.

"Business?" the man in the robe asked me.

"I'm here to sell a rare skill stone and visit the Imperial Library," I told him.

He looked me up and down, seeing that I wore a scavenger's cloak. If he was sharp, he would also notice the quality of my armor and visible weapons, but he didn't seem interested enough to look further. I got the sense the Varangians weren't as unobservant, though, as they stared at the quality of the armor under my cloak. The man in the robe nodded absently and opened the gate for me. He turned, leading me inside, and I followed him.

The inside of the palace was a bit of a disappointment. The decor could only be described as ostentatious. After the subtle and beautiful gardens outside, I had expected something more . . . classy. The hallways of the palace seemed stuffed with as many things as could be fit in every inch of the palace, as if to declare the owner of the palace was so wealthy they had more than they knew what to do with. Art, tapestries, armor and weapons, and various collectibles adorned pillars everywhere or hung on the walls. None of it matched, colors and styles clashing. Many of the weapons and much of the armor blocked other pieces, making it impossible to appreciate the artwork and tapestries. There was no room to let each piece breathe, showing how little the collector really valued what they displayed.

My guide led me on a winding path full of lengthy hallways and wide marble stairs. We turned left and right, the hallways so long I thought we would hit the outside walls several times, but we never did. The layout inside the palace was almost a maze, maybe deliberately so. Eventually, my guide led me down another marble staircase and into a basement. The walls in the basement were bare, which was probably meant as an insult to whoever stayed down here, but I considered it an improvement over the tacky displays above. The guide stopped in front of a small door in the middle of a darkened and dusty hallway. We had passed several more doors just like this one, all of them closed.

"This is where you stay," he told me, opening the door. Inside was a small bed and a table but nothing more. The room and location were definitely intended to be an insult.

"Someone will get you when you are to be summoned before the Emperor," he told me. "Until then, do not wander the palace. You will get lost."

I had kind of hoped to avoid the Emperor himself, but apparently that was not meant to be. I stepped into the room and settled down on the bed. I decided to just go ahead and follow my guide's instructions. I was pretty sure I could find my way around the palace on my own, but I didn't want to insult someone and find myself in trouble before I sold my skill stone and got a chance to look over the library.

Hours passed as I sat in my small room, and I found myself getting annoyed by the deliberate rudeness, despite my best efforts to rise above the insults. By late afternoon, after still not hearing from anyone, I was about to leave and try my luck exploring the palace on my own when there was finally a knock on my door.

I stood and opened the door to see a small boy around the age of ten standing in front of me. He wore a smaller version of the formal robes the last guide had worn. He had a serious expression on his face.

"Follow me, sir," the boy told me. He turned and walked away without waiting to see if I followed him. I hesitated but had decided to follow the rules of this place as best as I could, so I followed the young boy without saying anything.

The boy led me back up to the main floor and through a number of twisting and turning hallways before coming to one that was guarded by several Varangians.

"Through there," the boy said, pointing to a large gold-encrusted doorway at the end of the hallway. I approached, and the guards opened two ornate wooden doors for me without any comment.

Inside, a spacious hall greeted me. A vaulted ceiling stretched upward, and the back of the hall was covered with stained-glass windows depicting a man on horseback battling a swarm of monsters. The floor was covered in different mosaics, and the walls were even more ostentatious than those in the hallways, every inch filled with tapestries or artwork. Across the hall, a large golden throne was perched atop a platform, with several stairs leading up to it.

I had to blink several times to fully appreciate what I was seeing. Gold was everywhere, as if the designers of the room had forgotten other metals even existed. Even the mosaics on the floor were inlaid with gold, as if to say the Emperor was so rich he could afford to let people walk on gold.

Seated on the throne was a visibly drunk middle-aged man. He sat slumped over, a jug of some drink in his hand. He was mumbling to himself and clearly hadn't bothered to shave for some time. His hair might have once been stylish, but was now long and greasy, clinging to his scalp and forehead. He looked like a homeless person who hadn't showered in weeks. His eyes were closed and he seemed unaware of where he was or anyone around him. The contrast between him and the elaborate throne room almost made me break out in laughter. The sight was so incongruous I wondered if I was being played with.

A number of other people stood around the hall, talking and pointedly ignoring the drunk Emperor as he mumbled to himself. Each person was dressed in what was probably their finest clothes, heavily adorned with rings, necklaces, and other signs of wealth. They all looked slightly overweight and unhealthy, as if they had never exercised in their lives.

"Step forward and kneel!" a voice rang out as I stepped forward into the hall in a bit of a daze.

Looking around, I found the crier next to me. He glared at me until I followed his directions, walking forward and then taking a knee before the Emperor. While sitting in my room, I had reviewed the proper etiquette for greeting a Byzantine emperor and hoped it hadn't changed too much in this world.

Nobody objected and the Emperor seemed oblivious to my existence, so it must not have changed too much.

"Stand and state your business before the throne!" the crier called out behind me. I could see a man standing behind the throne and slightly to the right of the Emperor. He had a pedestal in front of him and was writing something in a large book as he spoke. He seemed to be the only one near the throne who was actually paying attention to me as he raised a quill, ready to record what I said to the Emperor.

"I'm here to sell a rare skill stone," I said. "And I wish to visit the Imperial Library."

A few of the nobles turned when I mentioned I had a rare skill stone, and the man on the pedestal recorded what I said in a book he had in front of him. "State the name of the skill stone," he said as he wrote.

"It's a magic-based skill called *Glass Meteor*," I said.

I heard murmuring from the nobles at the name of the skill, but the Emperor never reacted, lost in his own world.

Conversation picked up around me, and I could hear the nobles speculating about the stone and how I came across it. One comment in particular stood out to me.

"Isn't that the rogue Varangian the Patriarch told us about?" I heard someone to my right whisper. They were trying to speak quietly, but with my hearing, I was able to understand what they said perfectly. I turned to see who had spoken, and a group of men wearing priests' clothes stared back at me.

"I think you are right," one of the priests said, not bothering to whisper back. "What was the bounty on his head again?"

"Two hundred blues," another priest said, still trying to whisper even though the other had spoken loudly. "For killing several priests and two paladins, I heard."

I kept my face neutral and made sure that I didn't react. This issue with the priests was getting out of hand. I did not want to get dragged into the stupid politics of this dying city. It was like nobody here wanted to admit they were all barely surviving, instead wasting all of their time picking fights with each other or crippling their own economy to grasp a modicum of power. I had only been here a short time and I was already sick of it.

"Your sale is recorded," the man behind the throne said. "A servant will collect bids for you over the next day. Your auction will close tomorrow at this time. The treasury will take ten percent of the sale. In return, you are granted access to the Imperial Library for one week. Dismissed."

I bowed to the Emperor and slowly backed away from the throne. Outside, another young boy was waiting for me.

"Follow me, sir," the guide said. "I will collect the bids from any interested party and bring them to your room. Do you want to return to your room now or go to the library right away?"

"The library, please," I said. My guide nodded and led me away.

The most interesting thing about the palace was that while it was all one large structure, the inside was like an actual city. As the guide led me deeper into the palace, I saw hallways that had been turned into entire markets. Other areas had been opened up into training grounds for the palace guards, and there were entire residential areas full of families, several massive kitchens and dining areas, and everything else I'd expect to see in a city. It was odd to turn a corner and find myself in the middle of a busy market. Shops occupied each side of the hallway and people bartered and traded in the halls as my guide and I pushed through the crowd.

The library, when we finally arrived, lived up to the elegance I had expected inside the palace. Soaring bookshelves stretched five stories high all around the room. The ceiling, made of glass, allowed in plenty of light. The entire left side of the library was stained glass depicting scenes from some mythology I didn't recognize. A large winding wooden staircase filled the center of the library and led up to walkways every ten feet. These walkways ran all around the outside of the room, allowing people to easily peruse the bookshelves at each level. Around the central staircase were wooden desks and comfortable chairs. The library was moderately busy, people reading or searching for books on the shelves above.

"What time should I return to get you, sir?" my guide asked.

"What time does the library close?"

"It technically doesn't close, sir, but most people leave when it gets dark outside. There are a lot of glass windows and people prefer the safety of their rooms at night."

"Hmm," I said, looking over the library, feeling a surge of pleasure at the collective knowledge in front of me. "I'll just stay here, then. Bring me the bids for my skill stone whenever you get them. I'll stay until I'm ready to leave the palace."

"But . . ." the boy started to say but stopped himself. "Uh, okay, sir. I will do that."

I nodded to dismiss him. As he left, an older man with long, bushy white hair approached me. He was hunched over slightly and looked to be at least in his seventies, if not older. I tried not to stare, but he was one of the oldest people I had seen in the city so far. It seemed that not many people survived to old age in the other enclaves.

"Hello," the man said in a deep and sonorous voice, "my name is Agathon. I am a librarian here. How may I help you today?"

The older man didn't look particularly friendly, but he was coolly professional. He had taken a look at my size and features and clearly judged me nothing but a barbarian, a slight disdain coloring his words. That was fine with me. As long as he was willing to help, I didn't mind if he looked down on me.

"I have two areas I'm hoping to research," I told him. "The first thing I'm looking for is information about physical classes that have magical resistances or deal with magical classes. I've heard this library used to keep records of such things."

The librarian stared at me for a moment, considering what I told him. "You heard right, of course. Our library has the most comprehensive information on classes in the world. Is that all you wanted to learn today?"

I considered telling him the rest of the world was probably dead, so having the most comprehensive amount of information in the world wasn't much of an accomplishment anymore, but I held my tongue.

"I'm also looking for information about orichalcum. Specifically, its various properties, if there are any scholarly books that explore such a subject, historical uses of the metal, where it was commonly mined before the city fell, information such as that."

The librarian's eyebrows rose. He clearly hadn't expected that question. "Very interesting," he said, looking at me as if seeing me for the first time.

I really wanted to tweak his nose for his condescension—I probably had more information in my head than he could read in fifty lifetimes—but I restrained myself again. Maybe Constans had been a bad influence on me lately; her rambunctious attitude seemed to have rubbed off on me a bit.

"Come with me and I will show you our information on physical classes first."

He led me up the spiral stairs to the third walkway. We continued along the walkway until he stopped in front of a section that he indicated contained all the books they had on physical classes. There were at least four large shelves full of books on the subject. An older man was already perusing the books, but he ignored us as we approached.

"Is there . . . a system for searching these books or directing me to ones that are close to what I want?" I asked.

"No," the librarian said, giving me another condescending smile, "but I will get you a few books we have collected that should get you started. It's part of our role here to find what our visitors need."

I stood by while he proceeded to search the bookshelves, grabbing and handing me books as he came across them.

"*Monk of the Pristine Mind*," he said, handing me a book. "*Vampire. Witch Hunter. Psion. Servant of the Dead God. Berserker.*"

After he called out each class, he handed me a book.

"Those should be the best that we have available for what you are looking for," he told me. "I will look into what books may help you find out more about orichalcum and let you know what I find."

"Uhh," I said, balancing the books carefully. "Thank you."

He nodded and left me. I carefully navigated my way back to the main floor and claimed a table to read at, then dove into the books with a smile.

Hours passed quickly as I read. I had always enjoyed taking in new information, and there was something very pleasurable about reading in such a grand library. There was a sense of dignity and age to the place, one that made me feel safe and welcome. It was a place for scholars, and despite my foray into violence since coming to this world, I had always been a bit more introspective than my siblings back home.

I read until night fell and most of the people in the library had left. Several librarians tried to subtly encourage me to leave the library with some pointed questions about my plans for the night, but I politely told them that I planned to stay all night and thanked them for their concern.

The boy who had guided me here brought me a few offers for my skill stone as I worked, but I ignored them for now. I would let the bidding rise until tomorrow and then see what people offered me. I was mostly interested in currency, but a quick glance at some of the offers showed me that people were offering all kinds of things like unique magical items, other skills, or "favors" in return for my stone.

The books about the physical classes were extremely informative. I learned that at some time, the Byzantine emperors had commissioned librarians to travel the world and collect guides on the various classes that existed. They bribed, threatened, traded, or kidnapped people to get info about their classes. Wandering librarians had become a force in the world, powerful enough to intimidate locals and protect themselves as they traveled and learned everything they could. I couldn't help but think if I had arrived in this world earlier, I would have enjoyed being such a librarian.

On the other hand, I also learned the extreme methods they went to in order to secure information about classes. The librarians had no shame explaining in detail what they did to secure the information inside the book, quite openly speculating on the accuracy of the information when it was learned through torture or blackmail.

For instance, the *Vampire* class had been written about by a librarian that agreed to become a servant of a *Vampire* and spent years collecting victims for their master. When they finally learned the class, they detailed everything about the entire process of turning undead and then continued traveling the world to collect more information, feeding whenever necessary. The librarian had apparently been awarded a medal by the Emperor of the time for their dedication.

The class was as fascinating as it was disturbing. It was both a class and a mutation at the same time. You could only unlock the class from a current *Vampire* by way of a process that was remarkably similar to the myths back on Earth.

Once you became a *Vampire*, you had the same strengths and weaknesses as vampires on Earth, including the weakness to sunlight. *Vampire* skills could focus on physical skills or mental skills. Mental skills included things like charming others, resisting

341

spells and mental intrusions, and spellcasting. Physical skills focused on utilizing high strength attributes, unholy speed, and natural weapons like claws and bites. The guidebook specifically said that many of the skills that allowed a *Vampire* to resist spells and mental intrusions were not magical in nature but rather mental powers distinct from magical power. They scaled based on a mental attribute and did not require someone to use mana to power their abilities.

It actually sounded like an ideal class for me, other than the weakness to sunlight and needing to drink blood to survive, not to mention the being undead part. Of course, I had no real way to find a *Vampire*, nor would I want to serve one for years on the chance they gave me the class. And the downsides really weren't worth learning the class even if I had the option to do so. Ultimately, even though *Vampire* sounded like it would synergize well with my current attributes and skills, I put it in the no pile.

Witch Hunter was similar to the *Vampire* class. You had to be inducted into a hidden society that dedicated itself to killing witches and warlocks. It didn't sound like these societies had survived to today, and I wasn't really interested in a secret society that hunted people based solely on their use of magic, so it also joined the no pile.

Servant of the Dead God and *Berserker* both had significant problems. *Berserker* could gain total spell immunity but only when the *Berserker* was enraged out of their mind. They were just as likely to kill their allies as their enemies in their rage, and despite some of the anger I had experienced in the past, I wasn't sure I could reliably get angry enough to use the class often enough to make it worth learning.

Servant of the Dead God required sacrificing a fairly large number of people on a hidden shrine buried in a sea cave on a remote island in the Mediterranean. The description of what the librarian did to learn the class was extremely graphic. Despite that, I put it in the maybe category. It would likely be hard to get to the shrine, but the class seemed extremely powerful if I could manage to unlock it . . .

Psion and *Monk of the Pristine Mind* seemed like my best bet. A *Psion* class could be spontaneously awarded if someone suffered an extreme mental break. It didn't sound like recovering from the mental break was required, just having one, which led to the class having quite a bad reputation. Despite that, it was a class that didn't require mana, and the skills of the class were very similar to spells themselves. The class also came with inherent resistance to mind-altering spells and the like. I was a bit deterred by the fact that the librarian who had learned the class spent almost half the book writing about how birds weren't real and the Emperor was using them to spy on people, but a note at the start of the book said the author's obsession with birds was just a minor side effect of learning the class.

Monk of the Pristine Mind was the most realistic option, unless I wanted to try to break my own mind. The monks were a secluded order that had a monastery in the mountains several months' travel north of the city. The monks had a legendary class, and rumors persisted that the original monk who had unlocked the unique version of the class still existed. The class was both a non-combat class and a combat class at the same time. The class awarded skills and attributes from both paths but also required a person to level both of them at once. You couldn't advance to level 2 in the combat path until you were also ready to advance in the non-combat path.

The non-combat class was focused on meditation and personal insights about yourself and your relation to the world at large. The non-combat path awarded skills that strengthened the mind and made it immune to control and suggestion while improving focus, decision-making, and other aspects of a person's brain.

The combat class focused on speed and martial forms. The librarian detailed some of the skills that could be learned. These included skills that let a monk float and run on air, bend reality around them and change the nature of the world itself, and even tap into the primal elements of the world to control earth, air, wind, or water like a mage but through physical attacks instead.

The downside of the class was that if you couldn't manage to level your non-combat class through meditation or personal insights, then you were stuck and couldn't level the combat class either. No amount of hunting experience would let you level the combat class if you didn't spend months or years meditating.

It was unlikely that the monks still survived, but maybe if I found their monastery, there would be clues about the class or even a class book I could salvage. It was the best lead I had found so far.

When morning came, the librarian who had helped me before brought me seven new books.

"These are all the books we have about orichalcum ore. It includes several scholarly discussions of the metal, some crafting guides, and chronicles of trade agreements at the height of our empire that show how common the ore was and other detailed information of that nature," he told me. "It will be dry reading, but this is the best way for you to find what you are looking for."

I thanked him and piled the new books on the desk next to me. I grabbed the first one from the new stack and began reading. It was indeed dry, but I had plenty of experience sorting through endless amounts of dry, uninteresting data from my previous life. The crafting and scholarly books were interesting, but ultimately, nobody knew much more than that the metal seemed to be mined from places of high mana concentration, was able to make more powerful enchanted items, and didn't need charging like a traditional enchantment did. Orichalcum itself drew mana from the atmosphere, charging any enchantments made from the metal. Nobody really knew *why* the metal did what it did, but the books at least detailed what it did for me.

The other books detailed trade agreements, shipping invoices, and various military and civilian contracts related to the various goods the empire produced. The entries were dated year by year through the height of the "Eternal Roman Empire," as they called themselves.

By the fourth book of records, I was pretty sure I had found what I was looking for: shipping invoices containing an unidentified ore. They repeated every month and came from a small coastal city called Miletus. The ore wasn't identified as orichalcum, but the receiver of the ore shipment was always designated as "Royal Enchanter's Consortium," which clued me in that it wasn't just normal metal.

I pored through the rest of the books, finding some other possible locations for what I wanted, but it seemed like the majority came from the first place I had found. There were a few explicit trade agreements about orichalcum ore in the books, but they all related to trade between nations without listing where the ore originated. I wanted to find where the ore came from in case there was a way to reclaim the mine or at least visit it and gather some of this magical ore for myself.

I asked the librarian next time I saw him, and he showed me a large, ornate atlas that detailed the empire at its height. I found Miletus on the southern coast of what would be modern Turkey in my world.

That evening, the bidding for my skill stone ended. My guide appeared, waiting for my decision on whom to sell to. I carefully reviewed all of the bids. They varied wildly from laughable offers to some that seemed more than fair. The best offer, I decided, came from someone who only named themselves as the Emperor's archmage. He offered one hundred gold orbs and my choice of a skill stone from the Emperor's own armory.

I handed my guide the bid I had selected. He looked at the paper and ran off. An hour later, he returned.

"Your sale has been approved," the boy said. "If you will follow me, I can take you to our armory to select your skill, and your ninety gold orbs can be collected there as well, minus the treasury's cut."

I stood up from my desk and stretched, working out the kinks from sitting and reading for so many hours straight. "Lead the way," I told the boy.

He took me out of the library and I followed him through the halls. It was getting to be night, so everything was much emptier than it had been before. My guide led me through several winding passageways and up and down several flights of stairs. The Byzantine layout of the palace was full of nonsensical passageways and deliberately inconvenient ways forward, it seemed to me.

We turned down a stairway that led to the basement and began to walk down yet another long hallway, although this one had no lights at all to illuminate it. I started to realize something might be wrong as the hallway seemed more abandoned and emptier than anywhere else I had been so far. The necklace I had received from one of my earliest dungeons let me see perfectly in the darkened hallways, but it seemed unlikely the armory would be through such an unprotected, poorly maintained area. I tensed, looking around me, and reached for my revolver, although I didn't draw it yet.

As if sensing that I had caught on, my guide sprinted down the hall in front of me. I could have caught him, or shot him in the back, but he was just a young boy, so I let him go. Two men stepped out of different rooms ahead of me as the boy ran past. I checked behind me and saw two more were blocking the hallway in that direction. They weren't Varangians, which hopefully meant I hadn't upset the Emperor himself, but they were still large men and they all carried swords. None of them seemed young or inexperienced in the way of violence, though, so they had to be connected to someone important around here. I checked their clothing but couldn't see any identifiable livery on them to give me any clues.

"Give us the skill stone and you can go on your way," one of the men in front of me said, hefting his sword threateningly.

I sighed. None of the men appeared to be spellcasters, so I doubted they were a true threat to me. This was just a waste of my time and had the makings of a potential scandal. Killing armed men who could be working for a noble or another important figure could get me killed by the Emperor, even if I was defending myself.

"Look," I said, "I'm not interested in getting involved with any of this kind of nonsense. I just want to make my sale and move on."

The man who spoke narrowed his eyes in anger. "Then hand over the stone and you can leave. Now."

I turned my head and eyed the two men behind me again, trying to figure out what to do. I didn't really want to kill these men, but I didn't know what classes these guys had or how powerful they were. I wasn't sure I could risk not using every weapon I had against them if it turned out they were high-level fighters of some kind. But if I didn't kill them, maybe they would just run away with their tails between their legs and I wouldn't be summarily executed by the Emperor for killing his guards or some noble's personal retainers.

I decided to at least *try* not to kill anyone.

I used my new *Never Bring a Mob to a Duel* skill, boosting all my attributes by four, and then I activated my *Trickster's Dash*, launching myself down the hallway. The two in front of me were just barely registering the fact that I had disappeared when I reappeared right in front of them. I unleashed a right hook into the man's jaw, not activating my golem-empowered gloves, but my *Empowered Strikes*, my *Natural Weapons* perk, my boost from *Never Bring a Mob to a Duel*, and my base strength of twenty-seven magnified my already strong body so much that I shattered the man's jaw, sending him crumbling to the ground. It was a testament to the man's own endurance that I didn't break his neck or kill him on the spot. I wanted to resolve this peacefully, but I still wanted to make sure I won, so I didn't hold back too much. And it was clearly a good thing I didn't; if my punch had been any softer, the man might have just shrugged it off.

The man next to him didn't have time to react before I struck again. I kicked him in the stomach, throwing him back against the wall, where he slammed his head against the stone with a grunt of pain. While he was dazed, I followed up with a series of blows to his face until he fell unconscious, his face bloodied and bruised but hopefully not permanently damaged.

I turned to look at the other two men, who were just now realizing what had happened. With cries of outrage, they charged down the hallway at me, completely unfettered by how easily I had just dispatched their two companions. Clearly, neither of them had points in whatever constituted the intelligence attribute in this world.

One of them closed the distance quicker than his companion, shooting down the hallway with some kind of *Charge*-like ability. The second man activated a protection skill, encasing himself and his ally in ephemeral purple armor that flashed around them both and then faded after a second.

Faster than I expected, the first attacker was on me. He swung his blade overhead, the blade encasing itself in fire. I frantically slapped the flat of the blade away with my hand, scorching my palm but pushing the sword to the side thanks to my high strength. I threw a quick jab at the man with my other hand, but my fist hit a purple barrier that protected him from my attack.

The second man reached me as well, stepping up next to his ally and swinging at me. I dashed backward, turning invisible and giving myself space from their attacks.

"Some sort of invisibility skill," one of the men said to the other. They both began swinging their swords in front of them, checking if I was standing right in front of them while invisible. I reappeared twenty feet down the hallway and they stopped swinging wildly, focusing on me as soon as I became visible again.

I noticed that the first man, whose jaw I'd broken, had started to rise from the ground. He was holding his broken jaw but otherwise appeared ready to rejoin the fight. These guys were much tougher than I had anticipated. I had tried to spare them, but it was time to stop holding back. I'd deal with the consequences later.

I drew my revolver. The two men who had been behind me originally helped their companion up and collected his sword for him. Then the three of them turned and faced me again. The man whose jaw I'd broken was glaring at me, clearly enraged but unable to speak. The other two were more professional, their gazes measuring me for any weakness they could exploit. I had definitely underestimated them.

I raised my revolver and fired at the man that had buffed himself and his ally. His armor flared purple as my first shot struck him, but my second bullet broke through and ripped a hole through his chest. The other two froze, turning in shock to look at what had just happened to their companion.

I lined up my next shot, targeting the other uninjured man. When he saw me pointing my revolver at him, he didn't try to flee or beg for his life. He just gritted his teeth and began to charge me again. I admired his courage, but it didn't stop me from firing twice, killing him before he could make it more than three steps in my direction.

The guy with the broken jaw didn't seem to comprehend what had happened, staring numbly at the bodies of his two companions.

I raised an eyebrow at him as I reloaded. When I finished, I pointed the gun at him, and he hastily dropped his sword and lifted his hands to show they were empty.

"I'm sure most people would want to bargain with you to try to find out who sent you and unravel the dastardly plot that set you all in my path," I said, "but it seems you aren't able to talk with your broken jaw right now, and frankly, I don't really care."

The man started to shake his head and look around fearfully.

I shot him dead.

I reloaded again and approached the last man. He lay slumped against the wall, still unconscious. Someone had to have sent the men after me, so someone would know I was the one to kill them when the bodies were eventually found. At the same time, if there wasn't a direct witness, it would probably make it harder for someone to set me up for the murders. I debated for a moment, but ultimately I had to protect myself. I didn't like my decision, but I couldn't see a better way to handle the situation.

Decision made, I drew my knife and slit the man's throat.

Emperor's guard defeated—500 experience awarded.
Emperor's guard defeated—400 experience awarded.
Emperor's guard defeated—300 experience awarded.
Emperor's guard defeated—600 experience awarded.

Nine hundred experience went to my *Gunslinger* class and nine hundred went to *Duelist*, my *Rogue* class being maxed out. That pushed my *Gunslinger* to level 11, giving me a +1 to my endurance. My *Duelist* had leveled to level 4, giving me a +1 to coordination and +1 to strength.

I searched around and recovered my bullets to make sure nobody could examine them closely. I also searched the bodies to see if there was anything obviously magical. On the man who had originally spoken, I found a strange necklace floating above his chest. It glowed purple and I was pretty sure it hadn't been there before when I had fought him.

I grabbed the necklace and slipped it up and over the dead man's neck. The necklace looked like an award of some kind, like a medal that would be given for courageous service. As I held it, the purple glow began to fade. I considered what to do with the item, but after a moment, I slipped it over my head to see if it gave me any benefits.

As I placed the medal against my chest, it began to glow purple once again. I felt a warm sensation radiate from the item and the medal began to fade, as if turning invisible. When it disappeared completely, I tried to feel for the necklace, but it was completely gone. Puzzled, I wondered what I had just done when an announcement penetrated my mind.

For your meritorious service, the Emperor has awarded you with a Triumph. You receive the perk Emperor's Guard.

Emperor's Guard: You have been entrusted with the protection of the Emperor. You are authorized to pass the wards in the Emperor's palace. You receive a +1 to all attributes.

Well, that wasn't ideal. The perk itself was great, but the fact that I had just killed one of the Emperor's own guards was very unfortunate.

I grabbed the bodies of the men and dragged them into one of the empty rooms nearby. As I carried them, I realized that this was my first time being close enough to a human corpse to truly inspect the body. I was already in as much trouble as I could get in around here, so I figured I might as well add some blasphemy to the list of my crimes.

I released a series of diagnostic nanobots into the bodies, having them gather a complete picture of the people of this world's biology.

"Huh," I said, reviewing the data as it started to come back.

Each of the four bodies had what I could only describe as a core, basically identical to the orbs that sub-bosses and bosses had inside them. I had also noticed that the dungeons I completed called the "orbs" they rewarded "cores," implying that orbs and cores were the same thing. Each of the men's cores was a different size. Three of them were nearly identical, but the fourth was very small, about half the size of the others.

I traced the differences between the bodies and compared this information to data from my world. The core wasn't the only striking difference; these men also had secondary systems of veins that ran through their entire bodies. My nanobots traced the secondary system of veins and found that none of them connected to the heart, like veins normally did, but instead connected to the core inside each man. Their bodies had adapted to make room for these extra veins, including the thickest vein that ran from the core all the way up to each man's brain, connecting the two.

I finished hiding the bodies as best as I could and collected my diagnostic nanobots. This data confirmed that the people of this world did evolve to be able to use magic, as I had hypothesized when I first came here. I had expected that was true, but I was surprised by how thorough the adaptation was. The fact that their bodies had evolved to contain a magical core was extraordinary enough, but the fact that they also had a whole secondary system of veins that spread the magic of the core throughout their bodies was astounding.

Could I ever figure out a way to adapt my own body to use magic if it required creating some kind of core inside me and an entire system of magical veins?

I shook my head, putting the thought out of my mind for now. I didn't have the time to dwell on that. Maybe someday, when I had more time and the luxury to investigate the matter further, I could work on a solution.

I had already collected all of my bullets from the hallway and the men's bodies, so I double-checked that I hadn't left any other personal traces, then made my way back to the main floor. Once there, I went in search of another guide to bring me to the armory so I could sell my troublesome skill stone and get out of here.

It didn't take long to find a young guide running past me, his distinctive robes letting me know what he did around the palace. I grabbed him and ignored his protests as I made him take me to the armory. As we walked, I kept one eye on my guide while I pulled out my personal book to review my current attributes, skills, and perks.

The most interesting thing I noticed was that my new perk that gave +1 to all of my attributes had also given me a +1 to my luck attribute. I wasn't sure if it would have only given me a boost to my "main" attributes, but it seemed to work for any attribute I had unlocked, although it didn't appear to be retroactive or my luck would have been higher from my achievements.

The fact that all-attribute bonuses improved even my luck meant I would need to keep an eye out for those in the future. Gaining enhancements to the more esoteric attributes like luck seemed rare since my class didn't seem to be awarding them.

That also meant that my new skill *Never Bring a Mob to a Duel* was causing my luck to increase as well. Whenever I was attacked by multiple enemies, not only would my normal attributes increase, but I would also get luckier, increasing my chances of survival even more.

The guide I had grabbed finally brought me to the real armory, where a guard handed me a small chest containing ninety gold orbs after I identified myself. Once I secured the chest in my backpack, the guard led me past several checkpoints manned by other guards and then ushered me into a side room protected by a thick metal door. Once the door was opened, I saw that the room was full of wooden shelving that stretched from floor to ceiling. Piled on each shelf were skill stones, more than I had thought had existed these days.

"Take your time," the guard told me, standing at the door and watching me. I nodded and walked to the nearest shelf to examine the stones on it. There had to be at least hundreds of skill stones in this room alone. Who knew if the Emperor had other rooms equally full of stones? In any case, the ones in here were enough to help hundreds of people survive the monsters that ravaged the city. It was an absolute tragedy that they just sat here, gathering dust. I felt outrage at the pure negligence and selfishness of the Emperor and his nobles. His city died around him, and he sat on a treasure trove of skills that could turn the tide against the hordes of monsters. It was outrageous.

Letting out a sharp breath of frustration, I knew there wasn't anything I could do about it right now. Maybe someday, I told myself.

For now, I just needed to find a skill I could use and then get out of here.

Hours later, my paranoia that someone would discover the bodies I had left behind had only grown. I finally finished looking over all of the skills available. Over half were magical in nature, which made them easy to dismiss. Most of them seemed rather weak as well, mostly rudimentary spells like *Firebolt*, *Chill*, *Stone Shard*, or other spells like that.

Of the physical skills, I had narrowed them all down to a couple of possibilities. First, there was a physical skill called *Leeching Strike*, which let me steal an attribute every time I landed a blow against an opponent. The theft lasted for the rest of combat, but the attribute that was stolen was random. That meant I couldn't plan to steal the attributes I needed. Plus, half of my own attributes were useless to me, so the skill wasn't quite ideal.

The next option was a skill named *Prodigy*. It was a passive effect that helped a person master weapons faster. It wasn't a flashy skill, but it applied to any weapon and seemed beneficial overall.

The last skill I was considering was called *Blood Born*. It gave me a +1 to my physical attributes every time I was injured. It would synergize well with my *Regeneration* and high endurance attribute, since I could take countless smaller injuries and heal immediately, gaining more and more attributes if I was fighting something powerful enough to injure me. At the same time, anything that could injure me was unlikely to do a small amount of damage. If something was strong or fast enough to hit me, it would probably do a significant amount of damage that would take time for even my *Regeneration* to heal. It was probably better to just not get hit at all—especially since I had just taken *Absolute Evasion*, which had some serious anti-synergy with *Blood Born*. If I had known about this skill in advance, maybe I could have planned differently, but I hadn't been so lucky.

I decided to go with *Leeching Strike*. It gave me an option for longer fights against strong opponents. Over time, I would get the upper hand as I stole more and more attributes. It synergized with *Never Bring a Mob to a Duel*, helping me boost my attributes in a fight. Even if half the attributes were useless, if I got lucky, I could take more physical attributes, and those scaled enormously well for me.

Once I had learned the skill, the thoroughly bored guard led me out of the armory and left me to my own devices. I considered seeing what kind of mischief I could get up to with my new *Emperor's Guard* perk, but I decided it was better to get out of the palace while I still could. I traced my steps back through the hallways, easily recalling the layout of the palace. It was the middle of the night by now, and the abandoned halls were eerily silent, but thankfully nobody tried to attack.

I was out of the palace enclave, halfway down the bridge to Sycae, when I heard a rapid set of footsteps behind me and heard someone call out, "Stop right there!"

I turned and saw an older Varangian man. He looked like he was important, his armor more ornate than the other Varangians I had seen, and he had a remarkable number of trinkets braided into his beard and hair. He also wasn't alone; a dark shadow-panther, just like the one I had fought in the streets of the city so long ago, stood at his side.

353

"Me?" I asked as innocently as I could, although I was clearly the only one on the bridge at this hour. The shadow-panther was sniffing toward me, as if it was tracking me by scent or some other sense.

"Yes, you," the large Varangian said. "I have tracked you from the site of several dead guards. You are to turn yourself in to me for questioning. Surrender immediately."

"I don't know what you're talking about," I told the man. "I just concluded my business in the palace and am returning to Sycae."

"That sounds like a refusal to obey a lawful command to me," the man said, giving me a bloodthirsty smile. He began to approach, clearly looking for a fight. I looked around me and saw that the other guards back near the palace hadn't approached, clearly confused about what was happening. For a moment, I debated whether I should flee or fight the man. I hadn't used my *Duel Me* skill for the day, and the fact that the man had an animal companion seriously tempted me to try my luck. Maybe I would get lucky and steal whatever skill he had that let him bond with a monster like the panther.

I reached for my revolver and whispered, *"Duel Me,"* activating the skill.

Duel activated. You and your opponent have both wagered a skill. Good luck.

I smiled as I saw the stakes of the duel.

I drew my revolver, not wanting to take any chances against the man. I aimed and fired at him, but when my bullet got close to his chest, it curved outward, missing him entirely. I swore, getting ready to fire again, when the man blinked forward, covering the remaining twenty feet of distance between us in a split second. He grabbed my arm, jerking my revolver sideways and causing my second shot to miss as well.

I immediately tried to break his grip on my arm, using my left hand to pull his hand from my gun hand, but unbelievably, his strength was greater than mine. He easily kept his hold on my hand and began squeezing. The pain radiated down my arm, making me unable to squeeze the trigger of my gun again.

I was . . . surprised by how much stronger he was than me. I knew it was possible, even probable, that people had leveled

354

classes high enough to have significantly better attributes than me. I just thought it was unlikely to find them here.

"What skill did you just use on me? Tell me and I may not kill you for your arrogance."

I seriously doubted he would stop if he learned I had just used a skill that would steal one of his skills from him if he lost his fight with me. Unfortunately, I had a sick feeling that I might have bitten off more than I could chew by dueling the man.

Seeing the two of us fighting, the guards at the end of the bridge began to run over. Several more spilled from the towers that protected the gate at the end of the bridge. My luck had definitely run out this time.

I activated *Trickster's Dash*, pushing myself backward despite the man's grip on my arm. The power of my dash was enough to pull the man off balance, but he didn't release my arm. A moment later, I reappeared, standing in the same place; my dash had failed.

The man frowned and flexed his hand, crushing the bones in my forearm with a casual strength that terrified me. I screamed, losing my grip on my revolver. It fell to the ground as the man released my broken arm.

"You have no chance against me," he said. "Tell me what you did and come with me. This is your last warning."

"I didn't do anything wrong," I told the man, "but I will not stay to be questioned."

I reached for my bandolier, grabbing a *Confusion Grenade* and throwing it forward before the man could grab my other hand and stop me. The grenade exploded into ten more copies of itself, several of them striking the man and his panther. The man seemed unaffected, but the panther looked confused for a moment and then began to growl menacingly. The man turned, surprised, and his own pet leapt forward, tackling him to the ground.

I didn't stick around to watch, knowing when I was thoroughly outclassed. I grabbed my revolver with my left hand and dashed backward as far as I could, throwing myself down the bridge until I landed on the far side. I turned and began to run, using my *Dash* at every intersection to turn invisible and hopefully lose anyone that might be trying to follow me.

When I was several streets away from the bridge, an announcement entered my mind.

355

*Winner: Akolythos! You have permanently lost your skill
Shatter Armor.*

"Damn," I muttered, cursing myself for taking the risk of dueling the Varangian. One of the downsides to my *Duel Me* skill was that I had to use it at the start of a fight, so I never really knew if the person or creature I was challenging was more powerful than me. By nature, the skill was a gamble, and this time, I hadn't felt that sense of luck I had felt in the past, so I probably shouldn't have taken the risk. The skill was just so tempting to use against interesting people because they would have the best things to steal . . . but obviously, that backfired this time and cost me one of my very few skills. I was lucky it hadn't been an even worse loss, like my *Regeneration.*

And now I might have not just the priest coming after me but some of the Emperor's guards as well. It was time to get out of the city for a bit to let things cool down. I wandered the streets of Sycae until morning came and then spent a few days across the water, not wanting the panther to track me back to Constans or the inn we stayed in. When I returned, I would plan my expedition to the north to see what I could find out about those monks who had a class that might help me deal with magic better.

Chapter 26

"So here is a list of what I want you to work on while I'm gone," I said, sliding a paper across the table to Constans. She took the paper absently as she stuffed her face with whatever food the inn was serving for dinner tonight.

"First," I said, repeating what was on the list just to make sure she understood everything, "charter a boat between here and the main part of the city so you and others you may hire can get across easier. I'm going to craft you a revolver like I use, and I want you to start getting used to hunting during the day to get yourself experience."

"Yes!" she yelled, spitting some of her food on the table in front of her. Several patrons looked over in disgust, and I despaired that the tutor was never going to be able to teach her proper table manners.

"I know you're excited," I said, leaning back in my chair as far as I could go. "You just have to promise to be extremely safe, to never get captured or reveal the revolver, and to always head back to Sycae hours before it's even close to getting dark. Can you do that?"

"Yesh," she said, biting into her food once again. "I promish."

"If you follow those directions," I told her, "when I get back, I have a very powerful class that utilizes the revolver in unique ways."

Her eyes gleamed as she stared at me in excitement, but she managed to restrain herself from yelling or spitting this time. Maybe the very obvious way I was leaning backward had reminded her to not yell when she was eating.

"Next," I said, "you're going to start putting to use what you have learned about this area and what you know about Perama."

I flipped the paper around so she could read it and drew attention to the next area I had written. She had been learning to read from the tutor and had made decent progress, considering she had been completely illiterate before.

"First, we need to do some recruiting now that we have the money and resources to pay people. Our top priority is finding a team of people who can fight for us, about four or five of them. They don't have to have any classes or experience, but I want loyal people. If we give them classes and help them level, I want to know they will stick with us."

I actually preferred people with no classes, since they would appreciate what we gave them more than those who had already earned themselves a class or two.

"Can you find us some people like that? I'm thinking more people from Perama that you might know and were in similar situations to yours."

"Hmm," Constans said, her face scrunching up in thought. "I think I can do that. I have some ideas."

"They need to be trustworthy. I don't want any criminals or people who will take what we give them and disappear."

"I have an idea of who to approach. They are trustworthy people."

"Good," I responded, "once you have them, we'll bring them over here and set them up in the inn. I want you to start working them into your training. Pay your weapons trainer to work with them. See if the tutor will take them on as well. If not, find a tutor for them. Offer to pay each person you recruit a salary on a trial basis, and if they work out, we will offer them classes and experience. You should be able to afford all this, and if you need more while I'm gone, you can always go scavenging yourself once you have your revolver.

"After that, we need two established groups that are willing to work for us, but they don't need to be as loyal. They just need to be willing to work for us and be willing to take risks. We need a group of miners and a group of sailors. I figure Sycae might have people who still know how to do that kind of work around here somewhere, hopefully. Use what you have learned of the city to find some people that will work."

"Are you going to tell me what you need them for? Am I going to tell them? They'll be more likely to join if they know what we want to hire them for."

"We are going to go on a little expedition," I replied, "once I get back. I will tell them the details myself. Just identify the miners and sailors who might be willing to work for us for now and we'll approach them together when I return. We don't need to hire them just yet. We'll start with the loyal group and get them working together with you while I'm gone."

"Wow, okay," she said, finishing her meal. "That is a lot."

"Yeah," I said, "I know it is, but we are facing some pressure from the priests and the Emperor's people, so we need to move up our timeline a bit. I will be gone a few months, I think, to give things a chance to settle down around here. Otherwise, I might get tracked back to you and you could get caught up in my problems before you're ready."

"A few months?" she said, surprised. "Where are you going for that long? I didn't think there was anywhere to go anymore!"

"I got a lead on something that might help me," I told her, leaving it vague. "I'll be fine. I just want you to focus on building a team of people we can trust. Continue with your training and work to gain experience safely across the water while you build our team."

"Will you train me in your super-secret class before you go?" she asked, a look of eager anticipation on her face.

"Yes," I said, "after you hire a boat and go hunting on your own first. Once I know you can be responsible and not get killed or caught by our enemies, I'll teach you."

"Yes!" she said, grinning. This time, thankfully, she didn't have food in her mouth.

We talked a bit more about how her training had been going and then she turned in for the night. I retired to my room but didn't fall asleep. Instead, I began crafting a revolver and ammunition for Constans and reviewing my plans for the future.

The next day, Constans went to find a boat to hire and then do her training and schooling while I relaxed at the inn and let my nanobots work on finalizing the items for her. Romanus and Valens weren't around, but I hoped they would return soon because I had an offer for them as well.

Once Constans returned in the afternoon, her revolver was ready. I showed her the different types of ammunition and presented her with a holster and ammunition satchels on a belt that was fitted for her size. They would be a bit heavy, but she would grow into them. After that, I told her to practice drawing and loading over and over as I watched and made sure she was doing it correctly.

I only gave her *Penetration Bullets* and *Explosive Bullets* to start. I figured those were already dangerous enough for a teenager to be using; there was no reason to give her more bullets to worry about right now. I just had to hope the maturity and dedication I had seen from her so far would keep her safe.

I made her practice for the next two days, which made her stir-crazy, but I had to be sure she could use everything safely. Once I was confident she knew the basics, we left for the docks. Once we got there, I saw that Constans had not just hired a boat but someone to row us across the water as well.

"How did you work out this deal?" I asked her as we watched the man she had hired get his boat ready for us.

"It was basically the same price to just keep him on retainer," she said, "and easier since we don't have to worry about storage or if someone was using the boat when we wanted to rent it."

"Good idea," I said, impressed by her planning.

We rode over together and then spent the day using our *Stealth* skill to hunt monsters. We didn't encounter any other people, thankfully, and no real surprises either. Constans was a good hunter, using her *Stealth* to get a first shot at whatever we found, often killing it immediately. Packs of creatures made her nervous, but she was able to keep her nerves about her and reload when needed. There were a few times that if she had fumbled her reload, she might have been seriously injured, but she kept her cool and handled the situation perfectly.

"This thing is powerful," she said, eyeing the gun in her hand after she had just finished killing a small pack of feral bees the size of her own head. She had rapidly dumped her *Penetration Bullets* and reloaded with *Explosive Bullets* to kill them all before they could get close to her.

"It is," I replied, "which is why we need to keep it secret and make sure that nobody gets ahold of it. It would be easy for them to figure out how to make more once they had the concept in mind. I'm sharing it with you because I trust you, so be very careful."

She smiled as she picked up the bullets she had dropped earlier. It was a bit of a bloodthirsty smile. She was happy at being trusted with such a secret and clearly enjoying her newfound deadliness. I smiled back.

"Now," I told her, "I'm not sure how this works, but I want to share my class with you. It's called *Gunslinger*. It uses the gun as its primary weapon but also focuses on tricks and luck to survive. I believe the class is based on a time I come from, when people used these weapons to fight, duel each other, and survive in a dangerous environment. That is the mythology of it, at least. The reality was a lot more complicated, but you don't need to know all that."

We found a safe building to sit in and I continued to tell her about the class. After explaining the concept, the mythology behind the class, and the style of combat, I felt an announcement overtake me.

You have initiated a class transfer. Do you wish to share the Gunslinger class with this person? I thought yes and felt something pass between Constans and me. She sat in front of me, staring into space for a minute, and then gave me a big smile.

"Wow," she said, a bit breathless in excitement, "this is the coolest thing *ever*!"

I laughed at her unbridled joy. It was undiminished by what she had gone through to survive in this dying city. It was great to see her so happy.

"Now you have a real reason to gather experience," I told her.

We finished up for the day and I took care of some chores to prepare for my trip. I bought a bigger backpack and stocked it with a sleeping roll, an oiled blanket I could string up to protect myself from rain, rope and string, an extra canteen, and plenty of nonperishable food that should last a normal person several weeks.

I also collected several large stones for a new project of mine. I carved and imbued them each with the *Concealment* rune that was on my cloak, and I tried to find a way to link them together to create a field that could hide me when I camped. Unfortunately, I was missing something; I could only make the rune cover the rock itself. It wouldn't stretch beyond to connect with another rock to form a field, as I had hoped. I had thought the shield that protected the priests' enclave might use enchantments in this way, but it was

361

clear I would need to spend more time experimenting before I could figure it out.

From crafting a new revolver and the ammunition for Constans, my *Enchanter* class leveled again, granting me another point of memory and bringing the class up to level 5. Romanus and Valens didn't return to the city in time for me to let them know I was leaving, but I had no reason to delay any longer, so I set out the next morning.

Constans and I said our goodbyes as she left to do her daily routine. I packed my backpack and double-checked my revolver, sword, armor, and cloak to make sure everything was in perfect shape.

After that, I left Sycae and hiked north for about an hour before activating my *Trickster's Dash* to throw myself upward into the air. I activated it again at the peak of my dash, launching myself forward several hundred feet in a matter of seconds. I activated it again and again, flying forward, covering miles in just a few minutes.

I became physically exhausted after just ten continuous uses of the skill and had to land to catch my breath and recover. Even with my attributes and my *Steadfast Endurance*, which reduced the fatigue from activating a skill multiple times in a row, the drain was still significant. I fell into a routine of using the skill to travel as far as I could, and then I walked briskly on the ground for an hour to recover before dashing into the air and using the skill again.

Flying through the air helped me scout the land in front of me and avoid as many monsters as possible. I could see large creatures below me as I flew. Instead of swarms of smaller creatures, the land outside of the city seemed to be dominated by gargantuan monsters that jealously guarded their territory. I saw slugs the size of buses, insect-like creatures as tall as trees, even a giant that stood twenty or twenty-five feet tall and carried a massive tree as a weapon.

When I walked, I huddled in my cloak and avoided drawing any attention to myself. I had a rough idea of where I was going, but even with the help of my *Trickster's Dash*, it would take me weeks to get there. I needed to be careful and learn how to move safely in the world outside of the city.

I rarely camped since I didn't need much sleep. If I got tired, I scouted out a safe area and curled up in my cloak during the day for an hour of rest. The monsters outside the city were active during both the day and night cycles and seemed to spend most of their time hunting or guarding their territory, but if I managed to find an out-of-the-way place to sleep, I was rarely disturbed.

I learned that smaller monsters did exist outside the city, but most of them were so busy hiding from the behemoths that they weren't easy to spot from the air. A rough ecosystem seemed to have developed in this monster-infested world, the smaller monsters surviving on whatever scraps they could scavenge, the larger monsters eating the smaller monsters and each other, and the largest monsters eating anything and everything that dared to enter their territory. It was a harsh reality, but in many ways, it was reminiscent of my world. The only difference was that instead of the predators being a pack of wolves or a coyote, it was a colossal centipede that was big enough to knock over a building.

Winter was in full swing as I traveled. When I was dashing through the air, it wasn't much of a problem since my skill let me ignore the wind that blew around me, but when I landed, I often had to trek through snow, which slowed me down significantly. The land around me had once been fairly settled; the remnants of farms and small towns dotted the countryside. I also encountered a few medium-sized cities with thick walls, but they were also empty and abandoned when I stopped to explore them.

It was the fourth day of traveling like this when I came across another regional quest.

Regional Quest Discovered: Down with the Queen.

You have discovered a regional quest. Complete this quest to receive additional rewards. Quest requirements: You must kill the queen of the ant hive to stop them from ravaging this part of the world. Reward: +2 to an attribute of your choice, 2500 experience, the skill Ant's Strength.

I was soaring through the air when the quest alert entered my mind, so I looked around and saw a large mound of earth to my left. From here, I could see a number of ants climbing up and down the mound of dirt, many of them shoveling snow off the mound to keep it clean. I dashed to the ground, alighting gently back onto the earth some distance from the hive. I took a few moments to catch my breath, eat a snack, and drink some water.

Once I was feeling rested, I crept through the lightly wooded area toward the ant mound. Snow covered the ground in places, but I stepped carefully to avoid making too much noise. I saw several ants between the trees around me. Most of them ignored me, but when I got too close to one, I saw its antennae begin to twitch, and it turned to observe me as I passed. I had been moving quietly and using my *Stealth* skill, but the ant seemed to have no problem detecting me.

I quickly walked past the ant that had detected me, but it somehow managed to silently alert the other ants to my presence. All of the nearby ants began to turn toward me, their antennae twitching frantically in my direction and their large mandibles clacking threateningly.

The ants came up to about mid-chest on me, making them the size of small ponies from my world. Their mandibles were longer than my arms and looked capable of applying significant crushing strength to anything they caught. I dashed past the closest ants, not wanting to get bogged down in a fight this far away from the nest if I could help it.

Unfortunately, when I cleared the forest and saw the nest itself, I realized it was too late for me to do this quest through stealth. The ant hive was boiling with ants, all of them alerted to the presence of an intruder. Larger and more powerful ants were coming out of the mound, presumably warrior ants here to protect the nest. The worker ants weren't shy about trying to attack me either, swarming forward with the warrior ants and trying to overwhelm me with pure numbers. A quick count showed me at least a hundred or more ants. Possibly as many as two hundred swarmed toward me.

I activated *Never Bring a Mob to a Duel*.

I felt my attributes skyrocket. My luck, my memory, and my physical abilities became so powerful I instantly knew I could kill every single one of the ants with a mere flick of my pinky. I felt flush with power, my attributes soaring so high my mind raced to try to understand what was happening.

As I continued to grow stronger and stronger, well beyond the strength of the two hundred ants that were approaching me, I realized that something was wrong. I struggled for a moment but managed to pull out my book to see how high my attributes had risen. My numbers scrolled upward and upward, well over a thousand already. I panicked, realizing my skill must have included all of the ants in the hive below me that were gathering to defend their queen. That could be thousands—potentially millions!

My body and mind froze as I stopped being able to control myself. My mind was in full overload, unable to form enough synapses to comprehend what was happening to me. I felt like I was going to explode when darkness began to creep over my vision. I welcomed the darkness, my mind retreating gratefully into unconsciousness.

When I woke up, the first thing I noticed was that I was starving. My stomach felt like it was eating itself from the inside out. It wasn't just mere hunger but a rapid pain deep inside of me. It demanded I eat anything that would give me even a moment of relief from the starving void inside of my stomach. I was only distracted from the gnawing pain of my hunger by the feeling of pressure on all of my limbs, as if something was trying to crush me and tear me apart at the same time.

My eyes shot open as my memories returned, but I saw nothing but total darkness around me. My necklace must have fallen off or been destroyed. Even with my genetically modified eyes, I couldn't see a thing.

But I could feel what was happening to me more than enough to realize that I was still surrounded by ants that were actively trying to kill me even now. The ants were crushing my body and limbs, but somehow my body was regenerating the damage they were doing so fast they hadn't managed to kill me yet.

I sat up, throwing the ants off of me. I heard the crunch of the ants' exoskeletons being crushed as I moved, and a second later, I heard the ants' bodies as they were thrown backward into walls all around me. The bodies splattered against the walls, making a loud sound in the darkened room.

I frantically felt around me, trying to find my necklace. I felt pieces of my clothing and armor; what little was left near me was shredded and destroyed completely. I dug through my clothing until I found the necklace. The string that held it around my neck had been severed, but the necklace itself was still intact. As soon as I grasped it in my hand, I felt it activate.

I looked around the darkened room, finally able to see where exactly I was. A number of ants were embedded in the nearby walls, their bodies and exoskeletons plastered to the compacted dirt like they were abstract paintings. I stood, flying upward from a mere flex of my legs, and painfully slammed against the roof above me. I realized as I fell back to the ground that I was still enhanced by my *Never Bring a Mob to a Duel* skill. The ants had never stopped trying to eat me, so I had never actually exited combat. The thousands of attributes I had gained were still in effect.

I scrambled carefully around the floor until I found what was left of my backpack. Inside, I found that my food and water had been left undisturbed by the ants. I ate everything I had brought with me, weeks' worth of food and days' worth of water gone in minutes. Even after eating so much, I had barely managed to take the edge off my hunger. I would need more food soon, or I was going to starve to death.

I was mostly naked, the scraps of my armor and clothing barely covering my body. I found my sword and revolver tossed around the room. My sword was undamaged but my revolver had been bent and crushed. I gathered my backpack and stuffed everything useful I could find inside of it. I fixed the string attached to my necklace and slipped it back over my neck, carried my backpack in one hand since several of the straps had been broken, and then gripped my sword in the other.

Once I realized I was still under the effect of so many attributes, it became much easier to control my movements. As I gathered my things and ate my food, I moved slowly and carefully, able to perform small movements much easier than I had the last time I gained a lot of attributes at once. Above ground, my mind hadn't been able to handle what was happening to me, but some part of my mind must have been overwhelmed and then adapted while I was passed out, because I felt better able to control myself now. I just hoped I hadn't broken something permanently in my brain by doing this.

I knew I was somewhere inside the ant hive, because I could sense thousands of monsters all around me. My attributes were so high that when I stepped into the larger tunnel outside the nook I had been in, the ants seemed frozen in place, their movements so slow they didn't appear to be moving at all. I walked closer to one of them and watched as it was very slowly stepping downward, its foot barely moving a centimeter every couple of seconds.

I swiped my sword through the ant's neck, decapitating the creature with ease. Its head had only just begun to separate from its body by the time I moved to the next ant in the tunnel and killed it as well. I killed every ant in sight, and none of their heads had even reached the ground by the time I turned the next corner in search of more ants to kill.

I made my way through the ant colony, slaughtering the monsters without remorse. If I hadn't had such insane attributes and my *Regeneration* perk, the monsters would have easily killed me. Each monster I killed reduced my attributes by one, but I barely felt the difference as I continued forward, killing as I went.

After killing hundreds of ants, I finally found the queen's chamber. Her chamber was a large bowl set deep in the earth, and the queen was ten times larger than the ants that stood around her. Soldier ants and worker ants filled the chamber, but none of them were moving fast enough to react to my presence.

I began killing the smaller ants first. The queen moved much quicker than the other ants, reacting to what I was doing by rearing up on her large back legs and waving her mandibles in my direction. I was surprised that she could move so quickly, but the more powerful a monster was, the higher its attributes would naturally be. She must be pretty powerful to move fast enough to even see me when I had this many attributes. If I had tried to fight her normally, I wasn't sure what would have happened. But I figured I might as well take advantage of the attributes while I had them, so I faced the queen and yelled, *"Duel Me!"*

Duel activated. You and your opponent have both wagered your experience. Good luck.

Unfortunately for her, even with a faster reaction time compared to the other ants, it wasn't fast enough. I leapt forward, slamming my shoulder into her body. My strength and speed were so powerful that I felt the queen's exoskeleton crunch as I slammed into her. I landed at her feet, but the queen's body was thrown against the wall behind her, killing her instantly.

Congratulations, you have completed Down with the Queen. You have been awarded +2 to an attribute of your choice, 2500 experience, and the skill Ant's Strength.
Ant's Strength: When you lift or carry objects, your strength attribute is magnified three times.
Winner: Alexander! You are awarded 1700 additional experience.

I killed the rest of the ants in the room in a matter of seconds. I continued through the colony, hunting as much experience as I could get while I had the chance. My enhanced memory allowed me to memorize the layout of the colony, so I only got lost a few times.

I saved the ants on the surface for last. My attributes were significantly reduced by now but still high enough for me to almost instantly kill any ant nearby. As the last of them lay dying, I turned and walked to part of the forest that wasn't covered in snow, exhaustion overtaking me. I lay down under a large tree, feeling dizzy and weak as the adrenaline of combat faded from my body, leaving me sick to my stomach. I closed my eyes as the notifications began to roll through my mind.

Congratulations, you have earned the achievement Mass Slaughterer. For killing over 1000 monsters in under an hour, you have been rewarded. You receive +3 to all attributes, and when you are outnumbered, those who dare to attack you will be overcome with dread, weakening their strikes and reducing their accuracy.

Congratulations, you have earned the achievement Attributes of a God. For having all of your attributes over 1000, you have been rewarded. You receive one divine racial evolution. Please choose from your currently unlocked choices:

Evolution of Slaughter: You do significantly greater damage to your foes. Your strikes are more deadly and your foes tremble before you. Your body size is increased and your appearance is altered to reflect your brutal nature.

Evolution of the Tinkerers: Your mind is able to process information extremely fast. Your devices are more effective and your creations are quicker, more intelligent, and require fewer resources. No physical changes.

Evolution of Leadership: Your patronage allows for those who serve you to benefit twice as fast when training or earning rewards. Loyalty from others is increased. You may form magically binding contracts. Your physical appearance is more magnetic and beautiful.

Evolution of Exploration: All of your senses are enhanced, and you gain a new sense for adventure and treasure, able to sense where to go at any time to find something interesting or rewarding for you personally. No physical changes.

Evolution of the Dungeon-Delver: You gain the power to modify existing dungeons, which includes allowing others to leave or enter the dungeon at will, keeping the dungeon from closing when cleared, and stopping monsters from leaving a dungeon once you have completed it.

That was . . . a lot to take in. I had never even heard of a biological evolution, but then again, I had never expected to get all of my attributes over one thousand either. It must be extremely rare, if not impossible, to survive such a surge of power. Other duelists had to have taken the same skill as me, although I didn't know how many duelists had actually ever existed, only that at least one person had discovered the class before me. And however many had selected the class, wouldn't most of them have focused on single-target skills since that was why they would naturally choose the class?

Of those that did take *Never Bring a Mob to a Duel*, would any of them ever dare use it on thousands of monsters at once? I had the feeling that I had only survived because of my unique mental framework and my *Regeneration* perk. I had spent the majority of my life regularly integrating and analyzing hundreds of thousands of independent pieces of data, something that seemed similar to what had just happened to me. My *Regeneration* not only kept me alive as the ants tried to tear me apart, but it likely repaired any brain aneurysms, strokes, or other critical injuries that occurred as my brain struggled to adapt to the surge of attributes. If I had been a normal person, I was sure I would be dead ten times over.

I also couldn't help but notice the achievement hadn't been for being the *first* to achieve over one thousand in each attribute, which implied other people must have done it before. Some might have even done so by leveling normally, which was a scary thought. I had only done it through abusing a skill and survived only by luck, a powerful perk, and my unique mind. It was a good thing using *Never Bring a Mob to a Duel* boosted my luck attribute at the same time as all the others.

I considered all of the possible evolutions I could pick from. I ran through my short- and long-term goals, trying to decide what was best for me and my future. I had put into motion a plan to start building a group of loyal people I could trust, so the *Evolution of Leadership* was very interesting. The ability to form magical contracts could help me find people I could rely upon, and they would grow in power significantly quicker if they benefited from the evolution that improved their training and rewards. Some of the vague, as yet undefined long-term goals I had in the back of my head could benefit greatly from such an evolution.

The *Evolution of the Tinkerers* was decent, but my brain was already able to process information incredibly fast and I didn't plan to build many creatures that could gain intelligence, although it would be interesting if it applied to my nanobots, since they had rudimentary intelligence. The *Evolution of Slaughter* was not a good choice for me, since I did not want to look like a murdering madman, as the evolution implied would happen.

The *Dungeon-Delver* and *Exploration* evolutions were very interesting as well. I could set up permanent dungeons with the *Dungeon-Delver* evolution or I could find rare treasures with *Exploration*, but ultimately those were evolutions that relied upon the random chance of finding interesting dungeons or treasures. With the *Leadership* evolution, I would be able to build a base of people that I trusted and grow my power by my own deliberate choices rather than chance or a lucky find.

I made my choice and selected *Evolution of Leadership.*

I felt the evolution envelop me. A warmth spread through me as my body began to shift and change in subtle ways. I had no mirror to check on what exactly was happening to me, but it felt odd to sense my skin and body moving without me controlling it.

The sensation passed after a moment, thankfully.

As I considered what to do next, the experience from killing all of the ants began to roll through my mind. The lesser ants only gave five experience each, but I had killed over nine hundred of them, so the announcements went on forever. The soldier ants gave ten experience apiece, and I had killed around two hundred of them. Plus, the queen awarded me five hundred experience on her own.

With the reward from the quest and the duel I had won with the queen, plus all the ants I had killed, I had earned a whopping 11,375 experience, which was split evenly between my *Gunslinger* class and my *Duelist* class. My *Gunslinger* class only increased to level 15, but my *Duelist* class shot up from level 4 to level 11. It seemed like I should have gained more levels, but I could see what people meant when they said it could sometimes be better to specialize in a single class, because dividing the experience two ways really slowed my growth.

Still, those levels gained me +2 to endurance, +5 to coordination, and +3 to strength, plus the +3 to all of my attributes from the *Mass Slaughterer* achievement, and I put the +2 for completing the quest into my luck attribute. And I earned a new *Duelist* skill at level 10 as well.

Please choose a level 10 class skill:

You Dare Challenge Me: Pick a target. You gain +3 to all attributes until you or your opponent are defeated.

Look Over There: Distract your opponent, guaranteeing one attack hits a vulnerable area.

You Fight Worse Than Your Mother: Insult your opponent, reducing all of their attributes by three and reducing their coordination by 10%. Your attributes are increased by +1 for the duration of the fight and your coordination is increased by 10%.

If It's a Fight You Want, It's a Fight You'll Get: Pick a target. The longer you fight your opponent, the higher your attributes soar. Gain +1 to all attributes once every minute you are in combat until you or your opponent are defeated.

No Retreat, No Surrender: Pick a target. Neither you nor your opponent may retreat or surrender, and nobody else can interfere with your duel until one of you is dead.

The Slow Deserve to Die: The duelist gains increased movement speed from their coordination and is able to move rapidly around any battlefield or arena. Movement speed is twice the speed of your coordination.

Weapon Master: Pick a weapon. You gain an increase to the speed with which you learn to master the weapon.

Get These Gnats Out of My Face: The duelist gains the ability to deflect projectiles with their weapon, striking projectiles from the air with a flourish.

Cripple the Fool Who Dares Challenge You: You gain a sense of where to strike to inflict crippling pain and injury on your foe.

The new skills were interesting, and I continued to appreciate the humor of the class and its skills, but *If It's a Fight You Want, It's a Fight You'll Get* was the superior choice. It was the counterpart to *Never Bring a Mob to a Duel*, helping me fight a single enemy that was too strong to take down easily, granting me a +1 to all attributes for every minute the fight dragged on. The infinitely scaling attributes of the *Duelist* class were extremely powerful, if I could manage to survive them. I selected *If It's a Fight You Want, It's a Fight You'll Get.*

Once that was done, I moved away from the ant colony. The smell of the dead ants was sure to attract something dangerous soon, and I didn't feel up for fighting, my body exhausted and my mind strained. I was also still starving; my stomach made sure to remind me that it had exhausted itself by keeping me alive while ants tried to dismember me for who knew how long.

Once I put enough distance between myself and the ant colony, I found a secure place to settle down and dumped out my backpack to see what had become of my gear. My armor, clothing, and cloak were in tatters and my gun was nonfunctional. My bullets and grenades were fine, but my food was gone and one of my canteens had been damaged and wouldn't hold water. My backpack had large rips in it, and the straps were broken when it was torn off of me by the ants. I would need to acquire some food immediately and give my nanobots time to repair my gear. It was still winter as well, and now I didn't have my clothing, armor, or cloak to protect me. My body was pretty resistant to the weather, but I couldn't continue on without some protection at least.

Chapter 27

I spent a week recovering from yet another misuse of a skill. It was so hard to know how these skills actually worked without a more thorough guide than just the vague feelings I received from whatever was communicating with my mind. How was I supposed to know my skill would target every ant nearby and give me so many attributes at once? The skill suggested that only enemies that were actively attacking me counted, although the nest must have been alerted to my presence and every single ant could have been coming to attack, so that was why they all counted . . .

I kept telling myself to stop being so reckless, but I swore my young body pumped me so full of adrenaline and hormones it made it hard to think clearly sometimes. And something about this world made it very hard to resist using skills, jumping into dangerous dungeons, or racing over at the first sign of a quest in hopes of completing it. I already knew that certain things could mess with a person's mind, such as the *Merchant* skill Constans had received. Could the world also be messing with people's minds, influencing us to complete quests, run dungeons, and use our abilities? It was clear the world tried to encourage people by enticing them with rewards and power-ups like some kind of Skinner Box dopamine reward system. Would the system also mess with our minds to make us want to play along even more?

Or maybe blaming my body and some mysterious "system" wasn't fair. Maybe I was just a bit too reckless for my own good. I *had* come to this world barely prepared and with no knowledge of what I was really getting into. That wasn't exactly the act of a responsible person.

I sighed. Admitting I had personal flaws wasn't easy, but the permanent loss of a skill, followed by almost dying from the use of another, was a hard lesson to ignore. It was frustrating not knowing all the rules that my survival depended on and trying to muddle through, but I also needed to take personal responsibility for where I was making mistakes.

I would just have to keep trying to make better decisions and just had to hope I could keep muddling through until I learned everything I could. If you counted my existence in human years, I was actually barely a few years old. Subjectively, I had lived much longer because of how much faster I processed reality in my old life, but maybe I needed to recognize that I was, in many ways, still young and could be too reckless for my own good. I had always pictured myself as firmly in control of myself and my destiny, but this world was showing me I didn't always think as clearly as I could.

I moved north and west as I recovered, but I didn't push myself this time. I took the time to hunt and gather materials for my nanobots to repair my clothing and gear. The nanobots could process the energy they needed from external sources; it was just easier and a bit quicker to use my own energy to fuel them. But since I was so drained, I decided to give them the corpses of the monsters I hunted and ate, allowing them to cannibalize what was left to fuel the regrowth of my equipment.

I wiped my sword off on a patch of grass that lay uncovered by snow under a nearby tree. I had found a sloth-like monster in the nearby trees, which made for easy hunting, although its hide was stronger than I had initially thought and the monster could move surprisingly fast when it got angry. Thankfully, my sword, my speed, and a few lucky saves from my *Absolute Evasion* kept me unharmed in the fight.

I took the time to butcher the beast for dinner later and then allowed my nanobots to use the rest of the organic matter to gather energy for themselves. I had repaired most of my gear by now, my revolver resting comfortably in my holster under my arm. The only thing I hadn't been able to repair was my armor, sadly. The drake's scales were made of something that my nanobots couldn't reproduce, no matter how much energy I fed them. After realizing nothing I did was going to work, I salvaged what I could of the armor, having my nanobots make a crude, patchwork chest piece that at least offered me some protection.

I had done decently well at hunting and cooking, although I hadn't thought to bring salt or other spices to make the meat more enjoyable. Many of the abandoned homes and farms I passed still had the wild remains of their gardens or fields, which let me scavenge for wild fruits and vegetables. They were still mostly edible, even this late in the season. My body had consumed all of my fat reserves when I was trapped by the ants, so I was eating as many calories as I could each day to rebuild my body. My *Monster Hunter* perk made hunting easy and helped me avoid the bigger monsters that could pose a danger to me.

I was searching the garden of an old manor house I had seen from the air when I caught sight of myself in the shattered remains of a window. I was shocked by how unhealthy I looked. My *Regeneration* had essentially eaten me alive, leaving behind nothing but skin on muscle and bone. My eyes were sunken and my skin looked pale and unhealthy. As I stared at myself in the window, I looked for any changes from my *Evolution of Leadership*, which would make me look more magnetic, but I couldn't notice a difference. Maybe it would be more obvious when I stopped looking like a corpse.

Now that most of my gear was back to normal and I had a good stockpile of food, I was moving quicker and hunting less. I kept heading generally northwest, keeping an eye out for landmarks that would lead me to the monastery. I estimated that I was now around what would be modern Bulgaria back home. This far from the sea, winter was in full effect, and my time on the ground was an unpleasant slog through feet of snow every time I had to land.

The monastery was located in the far west of what would be modern Bulgaria in my world. The area was a mountainous region that had to be completely snowed in at this time of year. I didn't stop or turn around, though, refusing to give up and waste more time on this excursion than absolutely necessary.

Two weeks passed without anything significant happening, other than the occasional battle with a monster I either couldn't avoid or wanted to hunt for food. I avoided the biggest of the monsters, spying them from above far enough in advance to avoid going anywhere near their territory. The few flying monsters never saw me, thanks to the invisibility granted to me by my *Dash* as I flew. I was deep into the snow-covered mountainous region when my mind flashed with another regional quest notification.

Regional Quest Discovered: Meet the Dark Elf Neighbors.

You have discovered a regional quest. Complete this quest to receive additional rewards. Quest requirements: You must become friendly with the dark elf city and solve their spider problem before they are wiped out. Reward: 1000 experience. Further rewards are determined by the dark elf house that you align with.

I stopped in midair, dashing back to the ground as I took in what the quest was saying. First, the fact that there were other races inhabiting this Earth was news to me. Had other, more fantastical races always existed? I was sure someone would have mentioned that to me at some point, or I would have found some reference to them in the books I read at the library.

Second, that I could ally myself with the dark elves or possibly gain rewards from helping them was very interesting. I ran through the mythology of dark elves from my Earth, and it wasn't good.

Most of the mythology about them was that they were evil, untrustworthy, worshiped evil gods, and were generally pests to have around. If the dark elves in this world were similar, that wasn't ideal.

At the same time, if I helped them, maybe I could get some powerful rewards . . .

I stopped myself, recognizing the urge to drop everything and go complete the quest immediately. It felt almost unnatural, the way my mind had so quickly shifted away from my own plans. Maybe there really was something messing with my mind to get me to complete quests and run dungeons.

I shook my head, pushing the urge to race off to the dark elf city out of my mind. I had a goal. If I achieved my goal or didn't find anything of interest at the monastery, maybe I would come back to see about the quest. I *was* genuinely interested in what the existence of a city of dark elves could teach me about the larger world, but if I followed up on the quest, I would do so safely and intelligently, on my own terms.

I looked around, making a mental note of where I was so I could come back to the area if I wanted to, then dashed back up in the air, ignoring the part of me that wanted nothing more than to find the dark elf city immediately and get those sweet quest rewards as soon as possible.

Another few days of travel brought me to the area where the monastery should be, and after scouting around through the air for a few hours, I was able to find it relatively easily.

The reason it was so easy to find was that after cresting a large hill, I spotted several thin trails of smoke rising into the air in the distance. I dashed toward where the smoke was coming from and found myself looking down at the monastery. And the monks that still inhabited it.

The monastery was a large compound, at least four stories tall, set on a hill above a powerful river. It was nestled in the river valley, and the river itself was fed by a wonderful waterfall further up the valley. The top of the waterfall was covered in cascading ice, like something from a winter fairy tale.

The monastery was one large building, with arches leading to a central courtyard where several monks were busy meditating around a beautiful silver tree. Surrounding the single building were large gardens, trees, and bushes, all of it covered in snow. Paths were dug around the compound, and more led to the river from the monastery. I could see several monks swaddled in heavy robes. They moved between the monastery and the river, carrying water in buckets propped over their shoulders.

I landed nearby and made my way on foot to one of the monks who was standing outside of the compound, silently staring off in the distance as if deep in thought.

"Hello," I called to the monk as I approached.

The monk was a young man, somewhere in his early twenties, if I had to guess. He had a kind-looking face, with a beard and long hair tied back in a ponytail. The young man nodded at me and bowed slightly, seemingly unsurprised by my approach, despite the fact that he hadn't looked at me once as I walked toward him. He gestured toward the monastery invitingly and then turned and led the way without saying a word.

I followed him, equally silent. I hadn't thought the monks of this era took vows of silence, but maybe I was wrong. Either way, the monk remained completely silent so I didn't pester him with questions, although I was dying to know how he and his people had survived out here for so long.

As we approached the monastery, the other monks noticed us and began to gather around. None of them spoke, but they began to walk with us in a silent group. I had a moment of paranoia, worried the monks might attack me or sacrifice me in some devilish ritual, but I had to trust I could escape with my skills if needed. And none of the monks seemed unfriendly; their faces were generally kind-looking, and many smiled at me as I looked their way. Still, I was a bit on edge after being in the wilderness for so long, so I felt tense as the group of us walked together,

Inside, an older man was waiting in the center of the courtyard. The tree that I had seen from above was even more beautiful up close. It had silver-white leaves and was in full bloom, even during the height of winter. Slow, lazy snowflakes fell around us, making the courtyard and the tree look almost surreal, like a painting brought to life.

The older monk bowed to me, and I returned the bow.

"Welcome, traveler," the older man said. I blinked, a bit surprised that the monk had spoken after the rest had been so silent.

"Hello," I replied neutrally. "Thank you for welcoming me."

"What brings a stranger such as yourself to travel during the winter seasons?" the monk asked. The other monks watched us, but none of them seemed to be intent on violence. They were just curious about a visitor—I hoped.

"I had read about your monastery," I told him, deciding to just be honest from the start, "and I came to see if anything of it remained. I'm looking for a class, and yours was one that fit what I needed. I read about it in a book in the Emperor's Library in the city that used to be called Nova Roma, or Constantinople."

"Ah," the older monk said, a sad look overcoming his face. "Yes, a great shame about the fall of that city. We are happy to welcome you and share our winter repast with you as you stay. We can discuss our class over dinner tonight. Will you join us?"

"Thank you, that would be wonderful," I said, "and I can contribute some food if you would welcome it. I have had some success hunting recently."

"Oh?" the monk said, seemingly surprised. "We wouldn't say no to sharing during the lean winter months, though normally we would decline since you are our guest. But during winter, any food would be greatly appreciated."

At my willingness to share food, some of the other monks broke their silence and talked quietly among themselves. Food must be very scarce during the winter here, and having a stranger suddenly come to stay might have worried some of them.

"Julius," the older monk said, gesturing to the young man that had first escorted me inside, "show him to a place to sleep and help him get settled. We will all talk more over dinner."

The older monk bowed to me again, and I returned the bow before following Julius. The young man led me through a wooden door and then through a small hallway to a dormitory on the bottom floor of the monastery. The windows were all sealed tightly with cloth pinned around the windowsills, and a large fireplace on the far side of the room kept the space warm. The rest of the space was filled with cots, and various pieces of clothing, blankets, and books were strewn around the room.

Julius led me toward an unused cot near the center of the room.

"You can stay here," he said to me, "and I will bring you a blanket and a small pillow. We apologize. We don't sleep in individual rooms during the winter. It's too hard to heat the whole monastery, so we all sleep in here at night."

"That's no problem," I told him. I sat down on the cot and opened my backpack, pulling out the meat and other food I had scavenged while traveling. I still had a good pound or more of monster meat and a fair amount of vegetables I had found in snow-covered gardens and fallow fields. I gave everything I had to the monks as a show of goodwill.

Julius seemed surprised by the amount of food I handed him, but he took it gratefully and bowed before leaving me. I tucked my backpack under the cot but kept my sword and revolver on me. The monks seemed nice enough, but I could never truly be sure in this world. I was surprised to find them still here and alive, so they must have some pretty powerful skills to keep themselves safe.

Better to be safe and keep my weapons on me, just in case.

Once I had dropped off my backpack, I left the dormitory and went back to the central courtyard. There, the monks ignored me or smiled politely as they passed. Hearing no objections, I explored the courtyard. I admired the silver tree for several minutes, marveling at its beauty. I was sure that if I had any magical ability at all, I would have sensed something from the tree; it was clearly magical and seemed to radiate peace to even my non-magical senses.

As the winter sun began to set early, Julius found me looking out over the river valley.

"Food is ready," Julius said. I nodded and followed him to an open room filled with wooden benches and another fireplace that only managed to keep the spacious room marginally warm. The monks wore their heavy robes the entire time, even inside, to keep themselves warm. I had noticed several glances at my cloak and the lighter clothing I wore underneath; some of the monks were clearly curious how I had survived the cold winter with so little protection.

Julius led me to a seat next to the older monk that had met me in the courtyard. Several monks served us as we sat down, placing a large pitcher of clear water on the table and a wooden bowl full of a hearty-looking stew in front of each of us. The older monk began to eat immediately, so I joined him, enjoying the flavors of the stew after weeks of eating bland, self-cooked meat.

After eating in silence for several minutes, the older monk wiped his mouth and turned to me. "Thank you for your generous gift of food. We have hunters, but most monsters leave our valley alone, so meat is getting rarer and rarer. It is a pleasant surprise for my brothers to have meat again in the middle of winter."

"I'm glad I could contribute," I said, pouring myself a cup of water.

"My name is Brother Mikael," the monk said, "and I run the monastery these days, although that is a loose term. Can you tell me more about your journey here? We are very curious about the outside world. We haven't had a visitor from so far away in a long time."

I told him about the state of Nova Roma and what I had observed in my travels. I told him how surprised I was to find them still here, since most people in the city believed the rest of the world had succumbed to the monsters many years ago.

"Ah," Mikael said, "I am not sure why your city might think that. While it is true that the world is much reduced, pockets of civilization do still exist. We trade with many small cities and one larger city just in this area alone. And through them we hear of thriving cities to the west as well."

"Oh really?" I said, genuinely surprised. "I really didn't think there would be that many people still living safely out here. Where do you trade with, if I may ask? I may want to stop there on my way back."

"We mostly trade beer and honey to Sredets, in the central part of this land," he replied. "It is a large city that has managed to do well against the monsters." He told me more about the city as I reviewed what I knew of the name Sredets from my Earth. I recognized the name as one of the older terms for what would be the modern-day city of Sofia in Bulgaria. It had been a heavily fortified city that was the capital of the First Bulgarian Empire before being conquered by the Byzantine Empire in 1018 AD. Either this region was never conquered in this world or something else had occurred so the city had kept its original Bulgarian name.

"That's very interesting," I told the monk. "I will have to visit there at some point."

"They may know more about why nobody has any contact with your city any longer," Mikael said. "I will write you a letter of introduction to a brother of ours that runs a small library in the city and he may be able to answer your questions."

"Thank you," I replied. "That is very generous of you."

"So now," Mikael said, "you came here in search of our class, you said. You know a bit about the *Monk of the Pristine Mind* class, then, I take it?"

"Just a bit," I said. "I know it's both a combat and non-combat class and that it can help me learn ways to resist spells and mental intrusions, I was told."

"Hmm," Mikael replied, "that is true. It does offer mental strength capable of resisting such things. And yes, it is both a combat and non-combat class. We prefer to think of it as a way of life, though, rather than just a class to be learned. The class encompasses both combat and non-combat because it encompasses everything in life. To properly learn the class, you must be dedicated to learning our way of life. The class cannot level without the discipline required from meditation and isolation, which takes true dedication to master."

I wasn't sure if I had the time to truly dedicate myself to mastering a class that sounded so complicated, although I had time at night to dedicate to meditating, if that was what was required to level the class. I could try to take care of my business during the day and then meditate all night to level the class.

"I see that you are considering ways to fit the class into your busy life," the monk said, smiling at me kindly, "and that is the first roadblock if you truly wish to learn the class. I am sorry to say that for us to teach you our class, you would need to commit to learning our way of life. That would require you to devote yourself to a life of meditation here at the monastery for at least a year or longer before we could teach you the class, to show that you are prepared properly."

"A year?" I said, dismayed. I had hoped to find an easy class book or something in the ruins of a destroyed monastery, not spend a year here meditating. I probably could pass their tests if I was willing to spend the time here, but I also had goals and plans that couldn't be put on hold for a year. Life was too busy right now, and I still had too many things to accomplish back in the city.

I was about to ask if there was anything else I could do to unlock the class, but before I could, Mikael raised his hand and stopped me.

"It's okay," he said. "Not many are willing to make the commitment we ask. There is no way around it, I must say. The class itself requires such dedication or you would just end up with a useless class that you couldn't even get to level 1. Trust me, this is the only way."

"Ah," I said, disappointed. "Well, that's bad news, then."

"I am sorry you came so far to be disappointed," he replied. "Stay with us for a while longer and enjoy the peace of our monastery. We can talk more when time allows."

We spent the rest of dinner discussing smaller topics such as their beer and other goods they produced at the monastery. At one point, a monk brought us both some of their famous beer. It was enjoyable, better than what I had tried back in the city, for sure.

I spent the night in the dormitory, enjoying the luxury of a bed, a blanket, and a warm room for the first time in weeks. The next morning, the monks and I ate a thin breakfast of oatmeal, and then I spent the day with Julian, seeing how the monks lived during the winter months. Their life mostly consisted of meditation, tending to a few livestock they kept in barns—which I hadn't noticed before because they were almost entirely built into the nearby hillside—clearing paths and hauling water, and more meditation. I didn't see any signs of their class skills. All of the monks instead took their time and worked with a sense of dedication and deliberateness, never once taking a shortcut or rushing through what they were doing.

I stayed another night but left early the next morning, figuring since I couldn't unlock the class here at this point, I'd better move on. I was drawn to the monastery since it gave me a sense of peace I hadn't felt since coming to this world. Maybe someday I would have the luxury to stay here and spend some time living a simpler life, but for now, I had too much to do.

As I left the monastery, I tried to decide where I should go next. I was curious about Sredets, but I also felt like the quest for the dark elves was time-sensitive. Now that the monastery couldn't give me a class that could help me deal with spellcasters better, the dark elves' rewards might. The quest had said there could be further rewards depending on what "house" I aligned myself with. Maybe I could talk them into providing me with a powerful dark elf class that could help me shore up some of my weaknesses against magic.

I dashed through the day and night, pushing myself to go as fast as I could. I quickly reached the area where I had received the quest. The quest hadn't given me exact instructions on how to find the dark elves, so I began to search the area as best as I could. Night had begun to set when I first arrived, but I didn't sense any monsters nearby, so I searched even during the night. After fruitless hours of flying over the area, I found no sign on the surface of a dark elf city, but eventually I discovered a fissure in the ground. I landed and inspected the fissure, finding that it continued downward for longer than my sight could penetrate. I climbed down carefully, spotting an unnaturally dark corner where a dungeon had formed inside the fissure, but I shook my head and moved past it, determined not to get distracted by every little thing I encountered.

I checked ahead but didn't sense anything nearby. I entered *Stealth* and began to head deeper underground, hoping this path would lead to the dark elf city. The mythology from my world said most dark elves lived underground, so I was hopeful this was the right direction.

Hours passed as the single tunnel I had originally followed branched into ten, twenty, and then hundreds of tunnels. The tunnel I followed was the largest one, so I continued to follow it downward, but I marveled at the fact that there was an entire world down here. With my *Monster Hunter* sense, I could feel monsters passing near me several times, but I managed to avoid most of them. The few I couldn't avoid were stronger than the monsters on the surface, but they were nothing my revolver couldn't handle now that it was fully repaired once again. I sensed the monsters before I got too close to them, and the ones I fought all seemed to rely on ambushing prey, so when I was the one doing the ambushing, they weren't too dangerous.

Eventually, I sensed a large concentration of thousands of monsters in the distance. At first, I panicked that I was walking into some nest of powerful monsters that dominated this part of the underground, but after a moment, I realized I might be sensing the dark elves themselves. If the dark elves technically counted as monsters, it would make sense that my perk could detect them.

Unfortunately, the tunnel that led toward the concentration of monsters was completely blocked off by thick spiderwebs. The webs were unnatural, each string as thick as a finger or wrist. They crisscrossed the tunnel, completely blocking the path forward. I could sense several monsters hiding in the webs directly in front of me, presumably guarding the tunnel. I considered what to do, but if the monsters I was sensing were the dark elves, I didn't have much of a choice but to proceed. I just had to hope I wasn't walking into a nest of thousands of spiders. If the webs didn't end in front of me, I could turn back before I got too close to the thousands of monsters I sensed in the distance, hopefully.

I drew my sword and revolver and then began hacking through the webs with my sword. The sword was magically sharp, so it cut through the thick webs without a problem. When the strands fell to the ground, I brushed them to the side with my sword, which seemed immune to the stickiness of the webs.

After the first few cuts, a loud hiss erupted from the tunnel in front of me. I sensed one of the monsters that had been hiding in the webs surge toward me. I stepped away from the webs, waiting.

After a moment, a large spider parted the webs with ease and looked out at me, its multifaceted eyes glimmering in the dark of the tunnel. It had parted the webs carefully and seemed to stare at me with disturbing intelligence, like a human holding open curtains to see who had knocked on their door.

Not waiting for the spider to attack first, I shot it. My bullet pierced through its head. The spider screeched in fury as the bullet penetrated deep into its cranium, carving a hole the size of my fist through its eyes.

Instead of charging me, as I had expected, it retreated behind its webs. I frowned, surprised it hadn't attacked and doubly surprised I hadn't killed it with a shot like that. These things were going to be a problem. Sensing the spider retreating down the webbed tunnel, I stepped forward and began to clear the webs again.

I took my time, making absolutely sure the path forward was safe before moving any deeper into the spiders' territory. I had the patience to do this right and I wasn't going to run in halfcocked this time. I kept my senses on the spider that had approached me earlier with my *Monster Hunter* perk. After its initial retreat, it had stopped about thirty feet down the tunnel and hadn't moved since.

Either it was waiting to ambush me once I got that far into the tunnel or it had eventually succumbed to its wounds. I hadn't received a notice of experience gain yet, but that could be because entering the spiders' tunnels could still be considered combat and the announcements didn't usually appear until I had settled down after a fight ended.

I cleared the spiderwebs until I reached the spider. I cut down a large portion of the webs and saw the spider slumped in its webs, dead. The wound in its head leaked viscous ichor down the webs, showing it had eventually died from my bullet; it had just taken some time for the creature to succumb to the injury.

I cut the spider down from the webs and continued forward, carefully stepping around the body to avoid touching it. I encountered several more spiders, each trying to ambush me from the cover of their webs, but my sense always revealed them to me and their ambushes failed. I continued forward until I reached an intersection in the tunnels. Forward led to where the concentration of monsters was, but if I pushed in that direction, I would be leaving several web-filled tunnels at my back.

It couldn't be helped, though; I didn't have the time to clear every tunnel I came to. I would just have to risk advancing with the web-filled passageways behind me. At first, there was no issue as I continued forward, carefully cutting through the thick spiderwebs and brushing them to the side so I could walk forward without being entangled. A moment later, though, I felt several monsters rapidly approaching, both from behind me, where the side tunnels were, and in front of me. It seemed the spiders had seen their opportunity and were trying to swarm me from multiple directions.

I took out an *Explosive Grenade* and waited, crouching down in *Stealth* several feet back from the uncleared webs in front of me.

When I sensed two monsters reaching the intersection behind me, I turned and tossed the grenade at them. The two spiders were creeping silently along the tunnel, one perched on the side of the tunnel and the other crawling along the ceiling. The explosion rocked me forward; the concentrated blast in the narrow tunnel was enough to send me stumbling forward. As I tried to recover, I felt the spiders in front of me surge forward, somehow sensing my distraction.

I wasn't as surprised as the spiders had hoped, though, having anticipated how dangerous the explosion would be in such a confined space. Unfortunately for the spiders, I had learned that lesson already from fighting in so many close-packed dungeons that punished me for using explosives several times over. I recovered from my stumble and unloaded all six shots into the narrow tunnel in front of me, not waiting for the spiders to get close enough to be seen through their webs. Even though I couldn't see the spiders, I felt them stumble and slow as my bullets ripped through the tunnel. I waited to see if they continued forward, reloading, but they stopped moving soon after they finished stumbling away.

The two spiders behind me were very dead, having been splattered and burned across the ceiling and floor of the tunnel by the grenade. The webs that had been carefully placed on the sides of the tunnel were burning, filling the tunnel with an acrid smoke that stung my lungs when I breathed in. I ducked, took several deep breaths, and then stood up and began to clear the tunnel once again.

I cleared webs for almost twenty more minutes before I finally broke through to a clear part of the tunnel. The webs continued up until I reached a ledge of stone that overlooked a massive cavern that stretched for miles in front of me. In the middle of the cavern was a city carved of stone, lit very faintly by glowing purple lights.

The city was surrounded by high stone walls, and from this high up, I could see the makeup of the city inside. There was a mix of large walled villas, massive temples that stretched higher than the walls by several stories, and then what looked like slums full of ramshackle homes of loose stone or mere clothing that provided nothing but a roof for people to sleep under. I could see thousands of dark elves in the city, the streets and buildings illuminated by faint purple lights that adorned the buildings and walls of the city.

The dark elves looked graceful and dangerous. They were taller than the mythology from my world had led me to believe they would be, some appearing to be nearly as tall as me. Some of them had pure white hair, but many others had black, brown, and even purple hair. I could also see a number of smaller beings in the city, many of which were hard to identify from a distance but appeared to be intelligent monsters of some kind. They were just as busy, or busier, than the dark elves I could see, and most of them came up to waist height on the dark elves.

I checked around me but couldn't sense any monsters nearby. I was a bit puzzled that nobody was guarding this entrance to their cavern, but maybe the spiders were their guards. The quest had mentioned needing to save the dark elves from the spiders, though, so that seemed unlikely. Maybe it was too dangerous to guard the outskirts of the city with so many spiders nearby.

I found a narrow path to my right that led down from the ledge. I followed it down to the floor of the cavern and carefully approached the city. I kept my *Stealth* active and paid very careful attention to my *Monster Hunter* sense to make sure I didn't run into any of the dark elves or other monsters. The floor of the cavern was covered in boulders and jagged stalagmites, making the area treacherous to walk through.

As I got closer to the walls, I saw there were pens carved into the stone of the floor. They looked like they had once housed livestock of some kind but were now abandoned. I also saw giant mushrooms behind stone fences. They grew like orchards would on the surface. For some reason, though, there were no dark elves tending to the mushrooms or harvesting them now; the area was completely empty and the mushrooms had been left to grow by themselves. The more I saw, the more it seemed like everything outside of the walls had been abandoned, possibly because of the spiders.

Faint spiderwebs, no more than a single strand at a time, were strung here and there across the cavern. They were hard to detect at first, but after I walked through a few, I realized they covered a large portion of the cavern. I tried to trace one briefly, and it led upward to the ceiling and then back toward one of the other tunnels in and out of the area. That tunnel was webbed closed, as were all the rest of the tunnels I could see, I realized, just like the one I had come from.

I knew spiders could detect when something touched their webs. Were these faint threads some kind of detection system used by the spiders to catch anyone who left the city? If so, it was deviously intelligent. Despite my contact with several of the threads, nothing came out of the many webbed-over tunnel entrances along the outside of the cavern to attack me, but I couldn't tell if something was watching me from the tunnels or not.

I shuddered slightly at the thought as I continued forward.

I circled the city, not wanting to get too close just yet. A number of guards patrolled the walls, diligently watching the cavern around the city. The guards all wore matching armor and carried crossbows, magical staves, and other ranged weapons. They looked professional and competent. I didn't see any of them slacking off or joking around as they patrolled the walls.

As I circled the city, I was surprised to sense a collection of monsters outside of the walls in front of me. I picked up speed and approached carefully. When I got closer, I ducked behind a boulder and watched from a distance as a number of dark elves and the smaller monsters frantically harvested the large mushrooms. The dark elves and other creatures chopped into the mushrooms with axes, as if the towering mushrooms were trees in a forest.

Whenever a mushroom fell, other workers ran forward and hurriedly piled the mushroom onto one of several waiting wagons that were hitched to monstrous beetles the size of oxen. The dark elves wore no armor or weapons and appeared poor, their clothing in tatters or barely mended. The smaller creatures were a mix of monsters I had come to recognize as brownies, goblins, and kobolds. There were also other monsters I didn't recognize, but they all appeared to be intelligent beings able to work together. The dark elves and the smaller monsters all seemed to be on the verge of panic, staring at the surrounding walls of the cavern as if expecting an attack at any moment.

I snuck close enough to overhear the workers as they spoke. The language the dark elves used was one I was unfamiliar with. I listened closely to the words, trying to get a feel for what they were saying, but before I could, I sensed several monsters approaching. I glanced in the direction of the monsters and saw several spiders scuttling through the rocky terrain, rapidly approaching the workers. The spiders were even more hideous in the open than they had been in their webs. Their legs were twice as big as their bodies, arching upward above them as they ran. They nimbly climbed and jumped over the many boulders and stalagmites, their many legs propelling them forward surprisingly fast.

A cry rang out as the workers spotted the spiders, and everyone dropped what they were doing and began to run toward the city, the beetles and the mushrooms quickly forgotten. I paralleled the workers as they raced to the walls, staying nearby in case I could help them somehow.

The retreating dark elves rapidly outpaced the smaller monsters that worked alongside them, not bothering to try helping their smaller brethren in the slightest. The dark elves were the first to reach the walls, but it did them no good, as no door was opened for them to retreat into the city. They piled up against the wooden gate, screaming and pounding on it, begging to be let back into the safety of the city. The guards above them watched dispassionately, refusing to move to open the gate. The smaller monsters finally arrived and began to add their cries to those of the dark elf workers, but they were also summarily ignored by the guards on the wall.

It was clear these dark elves were *not* good people. I almost considered leaving them to their fate, but the draw of the rewards for completing the quest kept me from leaving. And I was still curious what it meant that there were intelligent monsters in the world. If I just turned around and left, I might never get answers to my many questions about the dark elves and how they came to be here.

As the spiders approached some of the smaller workers that had lagged behind the others, I took aim and shot the two lead spiders. My bullets cut through the thorax of both spiders, causing them to stumble and slow. There were three other spiders behind those, and they immediately slowed and took cover, their legs turning their bodies back and forth so they could see what had attacked them. The two I had shot tried to turn and find a place to hide as well, but they stumbled more and eventually stopped, slumping to the ground, limbs twitching as they leaked ichor from their wounds.

The other three spiders didn't seem able to find me, frantically turning to look all around themselves. One of them had chosen to hide behind a nearby boulder, putting the boulder between itself and the wall, thinking the attack had come from the dark elves above. I snuck forward until I had a good angle and killed it with two shots to its torso.

The other two spiders gave up trying to find what was attacking them and began to retreat. I activated my *Trickster's Dash*, launching myself at an angle above the two spiders, and fired down into the back of each spider. My bullets tore through them, throwing them forward to the rocky ground. They tried to stand but eventually gave up as their strength left them.

I landed on a boulder, balancing easily on the unsteady surface, and reloaded quickly. The rest of the workers had paid no attention to what had happened, and the stragglers still running through the cavern floor arrived safely at the wall, unaware the spiders that were chasing them were dead.

I activated my *Stealth* again. Several minutes passed before the gate was slowly lifted and the frantic workers shoved each other to get inside. I waited, but no guards came to investigate what had happened and nobody came to retrieve the beetles or the harvested mushrooms.

I retreated from the area, moving further away from the city and finding a ledge on the outer wall that had a view of the mushrooms but wasn't too close to any of the webbed tunnels. An hour or more passed before the gate opened again. I watched as more dark elf workers and smaller monsters were forcibly pushed out of the city by a group of guards. Once the workers were outside, the gate was slammed closed, and one of the guards on top of the wall yelled something down at the workers. The workers, after a frozen moment, ran to where the beetles waited, still hitched to the wagons, and began to finish the work of the earlier workers.

I watched as terrified workers finished loading the wagons with mushrooms and then led the beetles back to the city. Only when the workers arrived with the mushrooms did the guards open the gate, allowing them back inside the city.

Shaking my head in disgust, I jumped down from my ledge and set off to explore the rest of the cavern. Every tunnel I found was webbed over, with no visible way for the inhabitants of the city to leave the cavern without having to cut their way through.

Chapter 28

After an hour of exploring the cavern carefully, I found a medium-sized lake on the other side of the city. It was full of pale, blind fish and had a few docks along its shore. Boats were tied up to the docks, but it didn't appear anyone had been fishing on the lake for some time.

I ignored the lake for now, continuing to circle the city to get a better sense of the entire cavern. When I finally found myself near where I had originally entered the cavern, I settled down on another ledge overlooking the dark elf city. I stared at the walls and buildings with mixed feelings. It might be for the best if the spiders killed the dark elves, even if it meant I didn't complete my quest. I wasn't sure the world would be better off having more of the cruel dark elves in it.

As I considered what to do, I felt a single monster approaching my location. I glanced toward the monster but couldn't actually see anything approaching. My sense told me exactly where the monster was, but my eyes couldn't see anything moving in front of me. I frowned, standing and drawing my sword and revolver. The monster froze when I moved, until finally it appeared in front of me, becoming visible as if by magic. Standing about thirty feet in front of me was a female dark elf in dark leather armor, a crossbow over one shoulder and a pair of large daggers at her waist.

"I don't normally get spotted like that," the woman said in formal Latin. Her hair was dark purple and hung past her shoulders, and her eyes matched her hair, glowing purple in the dim light of the cavern.

"Come on forward," I told her, lifting my weapons to make clear I was armed and prepared to defend myself if needed, "as long as you are just here to talk."

She walked forward, an arrogant tilt to her posture as if she doubted I could actually harm her even if I tried.

"I'm here to talk," she said, eyeing me up and down when she got close. "I have been sent by my matron to find out who saved our workers earlier. She wanted me to thank you."

I seriously doubted she was here with good intentions. Otherwise, she would have approached me openly.

"Not a problem," I told her. "I came across your city and I can see the predicament you are in. I'm open to helping you all, for a price."

She gave me an arrogant smirk. "I'm sure you would be very useful," she said mockingly, "a man from the surface like you. Are you here to save all us poor dark elves when an entire city of us can't save ourselves?"

"So you aren't in trouble, then? Guess I can just head to one of the nearby tunnels and be on my way. My mistake."

"Bah," she said, clearly annoyed by my reply. "My matron bids you welcome. Come with me to the city and she will speak with you."

"I'll want a guarantee of my safety from your matron," I told the dark elf woman.

She glared at me, as if insulted by my request, but eventually sighed and softened her glare slightly. "Yes, yes, you have our guarantee. You are welcomed as a guest into our city."

I didn't know if that really meant anything, but some of the mythology from my world spoke about the importance of being formally treated as a guest when dealing with creatures such as elves and other fae.

"Then lead the way," I said, gesturing for her to walk in front of me. She didn't move immediately, tilting her head to inspect me like I was a bug she was interested in studying and then squishing under her boot, but eventually she turned and walked toward the city. I followed her a few feet back with my weapons still drawn. When we approached the gate on this side of the city, the guards immediately let us inside.

The city itself was as crowded and dirty as it had looked from a distance. Poverty was rampant, mostly in the form of skinny male dark elves and the smaller monsters wearing little but rags. Up close, I also noticed that the smaller monsters were collared as if they were slaves of the dark elves. The woman I followed ignored them all, not deigning to even look at the many starving people that lined the streets or huddled in the slums that filled the city.

Next to such stark poverty, the massive villas looked even more ostentatious. Each villa was its own little walled city, the walls guarded as thoroughly as the outer wall had been. I suspected each villa represented one of the "houses" that my quest had mentioned I could align myself with. The only other well-maintained buildings were the temples, which also soared imperiously above the poverty of the city around them.

"Follow me and don't let anyone touch you out here," my escort said. "They will try to rob you or kill you if they get the chance."

Everyone turned to watch us as we passed, either with greed in their eyes or dull curiosity. I sheathed my weapons, not wanting to reveal too much to the watching crowds. I heard conversations in what must be the dark elf language. I made careful note of the words I heard, putting part of my mind to the job of deciphering the language while I focused on more immediate concerns.

We eventually arrived at one of the bigger villa compounds, its walls enclosing enough space to fill a city block. The female dark elf led me to the gate and we were admitted inside without fanfare. Male guards stood watch on the walls and the gate, eyeing me warily as I entered. These dark elves were all tall, skinny, and looked healthy and well-fed. They wore chain armor that glistened in the purple light, and each carried a crossbow and a sword.

Inside the walls of the villa was indeed like a small city. A central keep dominated the middle of the villa, but around it were shops, buildings, and workshops. I heard the ring of a smith working nearby and saw small gardens here and there being tended by enslaved goblins. A stable full of beetles took up one corner, and I saw several unarmored dark elf men tending the recently returned beetles that had helped carry the mushrooms into the city.

My escort led me around to the back of the compound, where a training yard had been set up. There, I saw a contingent of male guards standing at attention behind a tall, older dark elf woman dressed in immaculately designed clothing. She oozed power, so much so that I could feel it even from across the courtyard. She glowed a subtle purple, distinctly different from the actual purple light of the city. If her glow was like the other sub-bosses and bosses I had encountered, she was more powerful than a gold boss. I felt a prickling of danger when I looked at her and the courtyard full of her soldiers, and I realized I might have made a serious mistake in coming here.

I suspected many of these dark elves could use powerful and deadly spells, something I had very little defense against. I tensed, prepared to use my *Trickster's Dash* if there was even the slightest hint of an attack or spell cast in my direction.

The dark elf woman who had led me here stopped and bowed deeply in front of the older woman. I stopped as well and bowed deeply, trying not to reveal my growing nervousness. The older woman stared at me, not acknowledging me immediately, just inspecting me with her harsh purple eyes.

A moment of silence passed and I stared back at the woman awkwardly, unsure if I should speak first. Nobody had briefed me on the protocols for meeting intelligent monsters in this world.

Eventually, one of the men in line behind the matron stepped forward and spoke in Latin.

"I, Vornhriir Baeniryn, do challenge you, stranger. You are not welcome here. Your presence here poisons our air and brings shame to our house. You have insulted me by existing."

I blinked in surprise, looking over at my escort, who ignored me. I wanted to protest about the guarantee of safety but knew it would make me look weak. Maybe a formal challenge fell outside of such protections or maybe they really didn't care about their promise of protection at all.

I looked back at the man who had challenged me. He wore chainmail like the other male guards I had seen, but the crest of his helmet was different, as if he was a leader of some kind. He had a large sword over one shoulder and a small crossbow strapped to his left forearm. And he glowed blue, indicating he was ranked as a sub-boss. I had to wonder what it was like to have such a visible indication of one's own power. Was it helpful in establishing the pecking order in dark elf society? Or did it make one a target and reveal a person's personal power in a way that made the weaker dark elves vulnerable to the more powerful?

I cursed my mind for so often getting sidetracked by questions about the world around me, refocusing on the situation in front of me.

"I accept," I said after a moment, deciding I had little choice. If I didn't accept, I didn't know what the matron would do, but I was sure I wouldn't be able to defend myself against her if she tried to attack me or imprison me.

The older woman stepped back, clearly prepared for the challenge, and the other guards formed a square around us. The dark elf who had challenged me drew his sword, and I took several steps backward, drawing my own weapons. I debated whether to challenge the man to a duel, but the look in his eye told me that he was planning to finish this duel to the death, so I didn't have much to lose in using my skill. If I lost, I was dead. If I won, I might be able to steal something useful that could help me get out of this situation.

I felt my luck begin to tumble in my mind, telling me I had made the right choice.

"*Duel Me,*" I told the dark elf, activating my skill.

Duel activated. You and your opponent have both wagered a skill. Good luck.

The look on the dark elf's face told me he knew I had done something to him, and he raised his left arm and shot a small bolt at me before charging me. I activated my newest skill, *If It's a Fight You Want, It's a Fight You'll Get,* to give myself +1 to all attributes for every minute the fight continued. I also tried to activate *Never Bring a Mob to a Duel,* but I didn't feel any attributes empower me other than my opponent's, which confirmed the skill only worked when I was being actively targeted by multiple enemies.

I dodged to the side, narrowly avoiding the bolt the dark elf had shot at me, and then raised my sword and parried the follow-up strike the dark elf warrior had made with his sword. We exchanged several rapid blows, and I realized I was once again outclassed when it came to sword fighting. I tried using my *Leeching Strike* to steal the dark elf's attributes as we fought, but I couldn't land a single blow on the skilled warrior. He parried or dodged all of my strikes, and it was all I could do to avoid most of his attacks thanks to my high attributes and my *Absolute Evasion* skill. He began to move faster, and more and more of his attacks began to cut into me. My enhanced clothing and chest armor kept the worst of the wounds from crippling me, but I already felt the drain from my *Regeneration* as the numerous small wounds began to accumulate.

I activated *Trickster's Dash*, throwing myself backward and firing several shots from my revolver at the warrior, but at the sound of the revolver firing, he activated some kind of skill that surrounded him in a shell of blue light. The bullets pinged harmlessly off the shell, and the warrior activated another skill in quick succession. He raced toward me, leaving illusory echoes of himself behind him. I parried a powerful blow of his sword as his charge slammed into me. He quickly struck again, but as I parried the blow, he twisted his sword and somehow disarmed me, sending my sword flying several feet away from me.

Before I could react, he lunged forward to take advantage of my momentary shock at losing my weapon. I frantically dodged to the side, but the dark elf still managed to drive his sword deep into my shoulder. I reached forward with one hand and grasped the warrior's forearm in an attempt to stop him from withdrawing the sword, holding him in place momentarily. With my other hand, I threw a punch at the dark elf's head and activated my gloves. The golem's fist appeared over my own as I swung at the dark elf's head, but he turned his head to the side so fast that my fist sailed past him, missing completely.

I growled in frustration and tried to punch the dark elf again, but he drew a dagger from his waistband and stabbed me in the stomach before I threw a second punch. Panicking, I activated *Trickster's Dash* again, launching myself away from the warrior and forcing the sword and dagger to slide out of my body as I flew backward.

I couldn't stop myself from screaming in pain as the sword and dagger were violently ripped out of me by my *Dash*. My *Regeneration* kicked in immediately, healing my wounds, but it drew deeply from my energy reserves to do so.

I began to feel panic bubble up in my mind. I was clearly outclassed by the dark elf warrior. I dashed a second time to where my sword lay on the ground, then quickly grabbed it and turned to face the warrior before he could track my invisible movements. He hadn't stood idle, though, having reloaded his mini crossbow. When I reappeared, sword in hand, he fired another bolt at me. I was caught flat-footed as my *Dash* froze all of my momentum, but my *Absolute Evasion* kicked in, somehow twisting my body to the side and letting me dodge the crossbow bolt.

I tried to think of a way to defeat the dark elf, but he ran forward and continued attacking me, giving me no room to concentrate. He pressed me hard, forcing me to parry, dodge, and evade multiple attacks every second. I tried to retaliate with my *Leeching Strike*, but I still couldn't land a single blow.

Minutes passed as I frantically tried to keep the dark elf from injuring me too severely. The only good thing was that my *If It's a Fight You Want, It's a Fight You'll Get* was starting to kick in, my attributes climbing slowly but steadily. I felt myself growing slightly faster and stronger, and my *Regeneration* was draining me slightly slower as my endurance increased every minute. I was sweating and my breath was beginning to become strained, but I refused to give up.

My *Absolute Evasion* was helping me drag out the fight, as the majority of attacks that would have hit me were miraculously avoided. Without it, I was sure my *Regeneration* would have already drained me, or the dark elf would have been able to get a finishing blow on me. I continued fighting, letting time work to my favor, trusting my *Absolute Evasion* and *Regeneration* to keep me alive until my attributes rose high enough that I could hit the dark elf back.

Finally, after over ten minutes of fighting, one of my attacks was fast enough to cut the dark elf slightly on the arm. I felt my luck begin to tumble through my head again as I activated *Leeching Strike* to steal one of the dark elf's attributes. Realizing the tide was turning in my favor, I felt a surge of adrenaline and began to attack even faster, allowing him to get more hits against me in return, but I leeched an attribute from him every time I got a hit back on him in return.

It took the dark elf several minutes to realize what was happening. He stepped back and shook out his arms, as if he didn't understand why he was moving slower and his attacks were weaker than they had been before. He glared at me, suspecting I was doing something to him but not understanding what exactly was happening.

I didn't attack right away, taking several deep breaths. He shook his head and then attacked again, grimly silent even in the face of his slowing and weakening body. I took advantage of the space between us to fire another bullet at him, but it bounced harmlessly off his shield once again. Lowering my revolver, I met the dark elf sword to sword as the man renewed his attacks.

As my *Leeching Strike* stole more and more of his attributes, he finally broke a sweat, his endurance no longer allowing him to fight so effortlessly. The stolen attributes were supposed to be random, but my luck was tumbling now, suggesting that the attributes I stole might not be so random after all. I felt myself rapidly growing faster and stronger, as if my luck was allowing me to steal more of the attributes I needed, my luck influencing the random nature of *Leeching Strike* in my favor.

The warrior showed no fear or frustration as he became slower and weaker. My *If It's a Fight You Want, It's a Fight You'll Get* skill and my *Leeching Strike* had boosted my attributes high enough that I could finally outmaneuver the warrior with ease. He now appeared like a novice fighter trying to strike a master swordsman. Despite the obvious shift in power, nobody in the courtyard called for an end to the duel and the dark elf never gave up, grimly attacking even as he could barely lift his sword and he was panting like he had just finished running a marathon.

I didn't take any chances and refused to offer mercy after the man had so clearly been trying to kill me. Once I had a clear shot, I stepped forward and sliced through the man's neck. My sword cut deep and he froze, feeling at his neck where his lifeblood began to drain from his body. With a resigned look on his face, he accepted his fate, dropping his sword and standing still until his body collapsed to the courtyard.

I stared at the warrior as his blood pooled around his body. The silence of the training grounds told me everyone else was staring at the fallen warrior as well. Finally, after a minute of complete silence, I received a notification that the dark elf was dead.

Dark elf warrior defeated—200 experience awarded.
Winner: Alexander! You are awarded the skill Swordmaster.
Swordmaster: All training with a sword is doubly effective, your skill with the sword increases, and you gain an instinctive understanding of opponents when wielding a sword.

It wasn't the most powerful of skills, but it would be helpful. I felt the bonus attributes I had built up and stolen fade, and I turned to look at the matron and the other warriors surrounding me.

I could tell the fight hadn't been particularly impressive from my side. I was clearly outclassed when it came to the sword, but I had still won in the end. Not that I cared what the dark elves around me thought. After they had promised me safety, I took the duel as a violation of that promise, and my anger grew as I stared at the silent dark elves who just stood by and watched me fight for my life.

The matron finally stepped forward, deigning to address me now that I had won her staged contest. As she opened her mouth to speak, I held up my hand rudely and stopped her.

"I don't care," I told her bluntly. I heard gasps from some of the watching dark elves. "This stunt has cost you my goodwill. I believe I can help your people survive your current situation, but I will not be working with your house to do it. You have lost yourself the opportunity to be the savior of your people."

The matron's face became more and more outraged as I spoke, but I activated my *Trickster's Dash* to launch myself upward before she could retaliate. I heard her yell something in their language to the soldiers around her and they scrambled to draw their crossbows and fire bolts in my direction, but they were firing blindly and missed me completely.

I dashed again as I reached the apex of my flight, shooting forward across the city and out beyond the walls of the villa of the treacherous dark elves. I eventually flew over an alley that looked secluded and dashed downward, landing softly in the darkened alley. I lifted the hood of my repaired cloak with its *Concealment* enchantment, which I had managed to restore to working condition. I was significantly taller than the dark elves I had seen so far, but I hunched down, trying to hide my size as much as possible. I also activated my *Stealth* to try and prevent anyone from noticing me. Hopefully, my cloak and my *Stealth* would be enough to let me blend into the city around me.

Chapter 29

I was pretty hungry after the duel. My body didn't have the reserves it should have had, since I'd barely had a chance to recover from my ordeal with the ants.

I wanted to buy some food, but I didn't know the language or the currency of the dark elf city. I didn't have any food in my bag, having given all of it to the monks and not bothering to stop and hunt before coming here. Another oversight on my part.

I made my way out into the streets of the city, navigating around the busy dark elves and various smaller monsters that crowded the streets. I didn't see any restaurants or stalls selling food, so even if I had currency, I wasn't sure if there was a place to even buy it. Nobody around me looked like they had had a good meal in a long time.

I pushed down my ravenous hunger and focused on learning the dark elf language as fast as I could. That should, hopefully, help me understand more of what was going on around me and might help me find a way to get some food.

I walked through the city covered in my cloak, listening and noting every word I heard. My enhanced memory and the numerous languages I knew from my Earth helped me analyze the basic syntax and structure of the language. Each word I heard added to my understanding. After several hours, I was confident I could speak some basic form of the dark elf language, although not enough to carry on an extended conversation.

Night never fell, since we were underground, but the workers of the city seemed to congregate together and head toward the temples at some agreed-upon time. I followed the crowd and soon found myself waiting in a long line outside one of the temples, the smell of food coming from the front of the line. My stomach protested, urging me to cut the line and steal as much food as I could carry, but I ignored it.

Around a half hour later, several dark elves in voluminous purple robes gestured me forward and handed me a spongy block of food the size of my forearm. I kept my head down and my body hunched as I accepted the food, but nobody seemed to be paying attention to me. I followed the goblin that had been in front of me out of the temple courtyard, puzzling over what I had been given. It was spongy and light to the touch, almost like a bread of some kind. When I was clear of the crowd, I entered stealth again and ducked into a nearby alley. I took a big sniff of the food and sent my nanobots to inspect it, and they reported it was a variety of mushroom, likely the type I had seen being cultivated outside of the city. Apparently the mushrooms could be sliced up and served like bread and provided at least some sustenance to the majority of the city.

I took a greedy bite of the mushroom, my hunger getting the best of me. It was earthy but not unpleasant. It had no seasoning and was room temperature, but my empty stomach demanded more, so I frantically ate the mushroom while drinking the water that was left in one of my canteens. A brownie and three kobolds crouched in the alley with me while I ate, hastily eating their own food as if afraid someone might steal it. They were so busy eating they didn't even look in my direction.

After I finished eating, I waited to see what some of the creatures in the alley would do. The kobolds left together and seemed to have a destination in mind, so I followed them quietly. They led me to a plaza, where I saw more dark elves and other monsters waiting in line again, this time to drink from a central fountain. I waited patiently in line, and when it was my turn, I drank as much water as I could and then swiftly filled my canteen.

I retreated from the fountain as soon as my canteen was full, then watched the rest of the monsters as they drank their fill and then wandered away from the plaza in a number of different directions. The city around me slowly stilled, growing quiet as people began to return to their homes, or at least the place they slept if they didn't have a home over their head. I wandered the city as it slept, watching the protected villas and temples as they settled in for the night.

I quickly learned that while the rest of the dark elves and other monsters slept, the more privileged and powerful dark elves were very active. The first stirring in the night was from the walls of the city itself. I heard a desperate fight in the distance and ran toward the noise, finding the wall under attack from the giant spiders.

I sensed the spiders as I approached the wall. From below, I could see guards on the walls. They were dodging nets made of webs that flew upward and coated the top of the wall in bundles. The guards ran sideways to avoid the nets, firing bows and spells down at the spiders that were attacking them. Several female dark elves dotted the walls, casting significantly more powerful spells on the spiders below. All of the dark elf spells seemed lined with purple fire. The female dark elves summoned meteors of purple flame to crash down in front of the city walls, eradicating spiders by the handful.

I watched the fight at the walls with interest, but I was distracted by the sound of more fighting inside the city behind me. I left the walls and followed the new sounds, only to find a large number of dark elves battling each other across the rooftops of the city. They faded in and out of invisibility as they fought each other, ambushing and counter-ambushing each other all across the city. Several of the villas were under attack as well, dark elves scaling the walls and attacking the guards to force entry into the villas under attack.

Even while the walls were under attack, the dark elves spent their time and energy fighting each other instead of killing the spiders that besieged them. It was by far one of the stupidest things I had ever seen in my life. The dark elves were a people so violent, so treacherous, so self-centered that they couldn't even bring themselves to stop killing each other long enough to protect their city from certain doom. If I hadn't seen it for myself, I wouldn't have believed it.

I turned away from the sight and found a secure alley to crouch in, waiting for the "night" to pass. The next couple of days passed quickly. I spent my time learning more of the dark elf language and scouting out the different houses. As I began to understand what was said around me more, the dark elf workers became a great source of knowledge about the city. There was, indeed, a house war going on while the city was under siege. The workers were angry about the situation but had no power to do anything to change things. The workers had nothing but non-combat classes

403

and were kept weak and starved, unable to do anything but accept what the houses were doing to them. The rulers of the city controlled it with brutal violence. Any questioning by the workers or enslaved was met with torture for the offender and anyone they knew or were related to. The houses controlled all of the warriors, mages, and priests, other esoteric classes that could easily kill the classless workers.

As I listened to some of the workers complaining about their lot in life, I heard them discuss a temple they claimed was actually trying to unite the dark elves and do something about the spiders. The temple was considered heretical by many, but the hope that it might actually unite some of the more powerful dark elves against the spiders gave hope to the workers.

The majority of the dark elves worshiped a spider-goddess, which was remarkably similar to the mythology from my world. I initially thought it was strange that the dark elves would worship spiders, considering the current spider infestation threatening to kill them all, but it turned out the spiders weren't killing the dark elves for no reason. According to the gossip around the city, the intelligent spiders that besieged the cavern were escaped slaves that the priestesses had once used in barbaric sacrifices to their goddess. The spiders had escaped into the tunnels around the city and bred rapidly, cutting the city off and killing anyone that tried to leave. Despite being responsible for the current situation, the temple that had been sacrificing the spiders denied it was ever involved and refused to do anything about the spiders, claiming that killing them was sacrilegious.

The temple that was trying to unite the dark elves and stop the spiders worshiped a different goddess, Lamashtu, the goddess of the undead and vengeance. Normally, I wouldn't think a goddess of the undead would be looking out for the best interests of the city, but according to rumors, this temple was a bit revolutionary when it came to the politics of the city, and it declared the spiders an anathema, vowing revenge for what they had done to the city.

When I first heard a worker mutter the name of the goddess, I felt my luck begin to spin, telling me the temple was the lucky break I had been waiting for.

I scouted the city until I found the cathedral of Lamashtu and approached it during the busy "day" of the dark elf city. The temple was smaller than all of the other temples but beautiful all the same. It rose five or six stories and was adorned with fine stonework. Spaced around the sides of the temple were large open windows and soaring archways that led inside. The grounds were guarded by several dark elves who stood at the door of the temple, armed and alert.

The dark elves weren't the only protection around the temple. Strange ghostly monsters patrolled the area. As the spirits walked, their steps kicked up small plumes of dust as if they existed in this reality or could interact with it somehow, yet they were ephemeral and wispy, clearly ghosts of some kind. They were very dedicated to their task, endlessly pacing back and forth over their assigned ground, watching the streets near the temple grounds for intruders. The monsters were an eclectic mix, many of which I had never seen before, such as a winged gargoyle, a stone worm, a small dark dragon of some kind, and several other, harder-to-describe monsters.

Nobody was approaching the temple, so I couldn't blend in with a crowd, but I decided to take a risk and introduce myself openly. I stepped out from where I was hiding and approached the dark elf guards stationed at the door to the temple. As I stepped out to approach, I felt the spinning of a coin in my head, reassuring me that this was the place to find what I needed to solve this quest.

"Halt and state your business," one of the guards said to me in their language.

I replied in the same language. "I am here to speak to a priestess about the assistance I may offer against the spiders," I said, lowering my hood so the guards could see I was a human.

Well, a human-shaped person, at least.

The two guards exchanged a look and turned and hurried inside. The other gestured for me to wait, so I did.

A few moments later, the second guard returned and held the door open for me. I noticed that these dark elves were paler than the other dark elves I had seen. Their skin was slightly translucent and their eyes were clear white, a stark difference from the eyes of every other dark elf I had seen so far. They didn't look quite like ghosts, but considering their goddess's domain was the undead, I suspected they weren't quite alive either.

The second guard led me into the temple and down several flights of stairs underground. I saw several winding tunnels and large open areas under the temple, revealing that the worshipers here controlled significantly more space than just the temple above. A number of guards and priestesses watched me as I passed, all of them paler than the other dark elves I had seen. Their white eyes followed me as I walked past them. None of them seemed hostile, but they were all clearly curious about who I was and how I got into their city.

Eventually, the guard led me to a small office where a priestess sat reading over several scrolls she had spread out on the stone desk in front of her.

"Sit, sit," the woman said as I entered the room. A small stone bench sat before her desk, so I carefully took a seat on it. The woman in front of me was pale like the other dark elves I had seen in the temple, but she also had a faint glow of gold around her, signifying her power level. "We had heard rumors that house Baeniryn had lost track of an interesting guest that had come to visit." She looked up from her scrolls and stared intently at me. The white pupils of her eyes seemed to glow silver in the dim light of the office. "May I ask what brought you to our city and why you have now approached our temple?"

"To be honest," I told her, "I'm here because of a regional quest to try and save your city. The quest said you were dealing with a spider problem and offered a reward for assisting you. I am also hoping to get a class or find a way to assist me with a personal issue of mine while I am here."

The woman let out a small laugh when she heard about the quest. "A quest to save monsters like us? This world is truly strange. I thought the system would only ever see us as fodder here on your world, to be killed for your people for sport and experience. How charming that we have been incorporated into your quest."

"I don't know anything about that," I told her. "But I'm willing to help if I can. I'm just looking for people trustworthy enough to assist, and the information I learned in the city told me your temple might be the only one actually focused on the spider problem."

"Yes," the woman said, leaning back with a look of annoyance on her face. "That is quite true. My brethren are . . . *imbeciles*, to say the least. We are so consumed with our intrigues that we cannot unite long enough to stop our city from being destroyed. It is quite pitiful, really."

I didn't respond, not wanting to offend her by agreeing even though I did.

"Regardless, what can one person like you do to help us that we can't already do for ourselves?"

"I've thought about that," I said, recognizing the truth in her question. The dark elves I had seen were very deadly and should have been able to handle the spider problem relatively easily, except for their lack of unity and one other problem. "I think the biggest issue you have is that your people seem to rely on stealth and speed more than brute strength, and when you try to fight the spiders in their tunnels, you cannot bring any of your strengths to bear. The spiders can detect you with their webs, avoid you when you come in strength, and ambush you when you are vulnerable. You have no way to pin them down and eradicate them, from what I can guess. I could solve that problem."

"Hmmm," the priestess replied, "that is very accurate. You have been watching our people and learned so much about us already?"

"Just a few days of observing your people on the wall and your assassins fighting each other through the city tells me a lot about your people," I said, "and I cleared through one of the spiders' tunnels to get here, so I know firsthand how disadvantageous fighting there can be."

"So you have a solution for us?" she asked, clearly intrigued by what I was saying.

"Yes," I replied, "I think so. You see, I have a perk that lets me sense monsters anywhere nearby. It let me sense the spiders before they could ambush me in their tunnels. I think that my perk, combined with teams of dark elf *Warriors* and *Mages*, could be enough to push the spiders back."

I could tell the priestess was skeptical at how my perk would make a difference—and the truth was, I wasn't sure if it would be enough either—but I felt like my perk would remove one of the main advantages the spiders had. The powerful dark elves could do the rest if they united long enough to take advantage of the opportunity.

"It would be slow," I said, "but we would never be surprised by the spiders. We could clear tunnels one at a time and not have to worry about cross tunnels or ambushes from the webs we were clearing because I would know if the spiders were gathering or lying in wait."

The priestess idly scratched the side of her face as she considered what I was saying. "And what would you ask for in return?"

This was the tricky part, because I didn't want to reveal my vulnerability to magic around a dark elf that clearly had a number of magical classes. At the same time, I didn't really want any other rewards from the dark elves unless they absolutely had no class they could teach me that would fit with what I needed.

"I'm interested in your classes," I finally told her. "I like to collect rare or powerful classes, and I think that your people may have some that the surface has never seen. I would assist your people in killing the spiders. In return, I would ask for the pick of one of your non-combat classes and one combat class of my choice, from all of the classes that you have in your city."

"That is quite a demand, you know," the woman said. "We very rarely share our classes. And never with a human before. And if we are seen to be succeeding where the other houses are failing, they may unite to attack us simply to stop us from gathering the glory of saving the city. We could be killed by our own people before we stopped the spiders."

"If you don't do anything," I countered, "you will all starve to death soon enough. I have seen the exits of this cavern and they are all sealed, with no way out. If you don't do something soon, none of you will survive."

The priestess thought for a moment, rolling up the scrolls she had been reading before. "Tell me, human, where do you come from? We've hunted your kind before, but not for many years have we seen anyone come to the underdark. We suspected your kind may have expired on the surface, fallen to lesser monsters."

I considered how much to tell her, not wanting to appear like I was completely without allies. "It's true. Humans have weakened on the surface, but there are a few holdouts still left. My city has a few pockets of humanity left, fighting to survive."

"Are people from your city like you? Are they willing to work with monsters like us?"

"I doubt it," I said honestly. "They are just as scared of monsters as anyone else."

"Do you have power in your city that you could compel them to work with us? Or at least leave us in peace?"

I wasn't sure where this was going, but I was curious why she was asking about my city so much and if the inhabitants would work with her people. I decided to reveal a bit more about the reality of Nova Roma to her, interested in where she was going with her questions.

"I don't have power currently," I told her, "but I have some things in the works that might be changing that soon. I think you would be left alone in my city for a different reason, though. Most of the people left alive are huddled behind walls and rarely venture out. The vast majority of the city is overrun by monsters. I'm one of the few that has the power to deal with the situation right now, although I hope to find more people able to help reclaim the city from the monsters that roam its streets."

"Hmmm," the priestess replied, looking at me thoughtfully. "Then here is my offer: you help my people with the spiders, but not in the way you have proposed. I hold no faith in my brethren. Their shortsightedness has proven to me that my people deserve their fate. Even if we made progress in destroying the spiders that besiege us, my people would stab us in the back at the first opportunity, even if it doomed us all. They would rather starve to death than lose face, and the houses are run by arrogant matrons that believe their own power could clear the spiders at any time. They are wrong. The spiders are just as powerful as many of our matrons are now, but they are too blind to see it.

"Instead, I propose a truce between you and my people. Help us escape the city and we will resettle in your city, far away from these spiders and my people. We will coexist peacefully with your people and will assist you with reclaiming your city from the horde of lesser monsters, in return for your assistance here."

I was very interested in such a proposal, but I needed more than just assistance back home. And it would mean failing the quest here, I suspected, if I abandoned the city with just a few refugees.

"I will still need my choice of a class," I told her. "That is the main reason I'm doing this, although I'm also interested in your proposal, but without my choice of a class, I can't agree. Your proposal would mean I failed my quest, so I wouldn't receive all the rewards the quest had promised."

"Well," she replied, "I cannot promise you a pick of all the classes the dark elves have unlocked, but I can promise you a choice of one of our classes. They aren't as powerful as some of the other dark elf classes, but they have very unique skills that may serve you well. If you assist us, I promise an alliance between our people and yours and your choice of one of the classes that our temple has unlocked. If failing your quest is more important than saving some of the only decent dark elves still living in this city, then I may have misjudged you, human. That is a decision for you to make."

"Okay," I said, recognizing that what she said was true: saving some of the dark elves was more important than a mere quest reward, and so far, I had a good feeling about her and her people. They did seem more straightforward and less arrogant than the other dark elves I had met. And I had to admit, my doubts about saving the dark elf matrons and their people had only grown as I learned about them. "If we did this, where would you all settle in the city? There isn't an underground like there is here. Most of the city is destroyed these days, except for a few enclaves of humans. You would be discovered if you just moved into the city, and it isn't exactly safe."

The priestess laughed lightly. "Oh," she said, "you humans. There is always an underdark, even under your city. Trust me, the ways to our world are there. You just haven't found them yet. We will find a place. It may be occupied when we get there, but we should be able to find a solution."

She flashed me a smile, and I noticed her incisors were unusually long and sharp.

"Huh," I said, "well then."

I thought over the proposal a bit more. I really didn't have any fondness for the majority of the dark elves I had seen. They were vicious, mean, uncaring, and conniving. If the spiders wiped them out, I wouldn't lose any sleep over it. I was only here for the quest and for a chance to find a powerful class. If I could save some of the more reasonable dark elves and earn a class and some allies in Nova Roma, then it was a good bargain in my book.

"Okay," I said, "I agree to your plan. I think we can make it work."

"Great," the priestess said, giving me a broad smile. "You will not regret your decision."

"I have an ability that can immortalize our agreement," I told her, "if you would be so kind as to let me try it with you."

"Oh?" the priestess said, surprised.

I activated my ability to form a magical contract that I had recently gained from my *Evolution of Leadership*. I hadn't had a chance to try it out before, but now seemed like the perfect time. That way, there would be no confusion or betrayal between me and the dark elves I was agreeing to work with.

When I thought about activating my ability, I saw a golden scroll appear in front of me and in front of the priestess. On it was written our agreement, already laid out for us both to see. The priestess reviewed the agreement and added a few more provisions, specifically about what would happen if the dark elves that resettled in our city were attacked, making clear that the dark elves had the ability to defend themselves. I agreed with the changes and worked in a few other conditions as well. My experience negotiating contracts for my megacorp was coming in handy.

After some time, we had an agreement both of us were happy with and we both "signed" the contract. I felt it take hold, a bridge of energy forming between me and the priestess. I felt the bridge of energy, marveling at the strange sensation. As I examined it, I somehow knew that I could call up the contract we had formed anytime to review the terms of our agreement, and I could even break the agreement at will if I so desired, something other people could only do if I had included that as a term in the agreement. I had the sense that if the priestess broke the agreement without such a provision through some more powerful magical means, it would cause a significant backlash, possibly even killing her.

"I'm pleased you came to us today," the priestess said. "It was truly a blessing from Lamashtu. My name is Alaunvayas. I am the high priestess of this temple and my people will obey my will in our agreement. I will go prepare for our departure. Come with me and I will see you settled until we are ready."

Chapter 30

Things moved rapidly after Alaunvayas and I formalized our agreement. I was shown to a comfortable room in the temple, while everyone else around me erupted into action. I took the opportunity to lie down for a bit, not having slept for several days as I hid out in the city. I was invited to eat with the priestess and other members of the temple. The food was interesting and filling, mostly various forms of prepared mushrooms, but there were also a few types of meat prepared in sauces. I didn't ask too much about the meat. I speculated throughout the meal how a temple full of the seemingly undead ate regular food, but I was too sheepish to ask.

After two days, Alaunvayas found me in my room and let me know they were ready. The temple hid its preparations as best as it could, but when I left, it was "night" and a hundred or more wagons were being prepared in front of the temple. Each wagon was packed with supplies and was being swarmed over by workers, both dark elves and the other, smaller races. Pale guards stood watch, scanning the nearby rooftops for signs of any enemy dark elves that might attack them. Given the number of people and wagons in front of the temple, it was hard to hide the commotion from the ever-observant dark elves that scoured the city every night. I could sense several watching us from nearby rooftops even now.

Alaunvayas led me to the front of the wagons, where a team of soldiers and priestesses were ready. Alaunvayas herself led the way, and the wagons began to creak and groan as they were pulled forward behind us. The large beetles hitched to each wagon moved without complaint.

"This is our first squad," Alaunvayas told me as we walked, gesturing to the people around us. "They will clear the tunnels in front of us as we move. We will have several more squads ready to clear side tunnels and protect our rear and sides as we move. I can communicate telepathically with each of my squad leaders, so you and I will be in the center of the wagons. That way, you can alert me to ambushes as we move. Does that work for you?"

"This is a lot more people than I had expected," I told her, looking over the wagons. Each wagon held numerous dark elf men, women, and children and an uncountable number of smaller monsters that eagerly followed the dark elves on foot. The total number of dark elves alone escaping with us had to be several hundred.

"These are our loyal workers and their families," she told me. "We couldn't leave them behind. It had to be this way. These are all good people. They are trustworthy."

"I understand," I said quickly, not wanting to give her the idea I didn't support her saving their lives. "I'm just concerned my perk may not reach far enough to protect the front and back at the same time. With so many wagons, we will be stretched out a long distance."

"Do you have a better idea?" she asked me. "I'm open to hearing anything you suggest."

"Well," I said, "this was one of the reasons I asked for a non-combat and combat class. And I promise, I'm not just raising this now to try to take advantage of you. I did not believe we would have so many people, but if you had a non-combat class that would unlock the perception attribute, it would magnify the range and power of my perk considerably. It scales based on my perception, which I don't currently have, so it's more limited."

"I believe you," Alaunvayas said with a small laugh. "If I had known such a thing would assist you in detecting the spiders, I would have arranged for you to receive such a class right away. One second."

From the paranoid dark elves I had seen in most of the city, I assumed my request for a class right as her people were dependent on me for survival would be seen as a clear power grab. They were at their most vulnerable, so of course now was the time to take advantage, I imagined most of the dark elves would think. I actually felt bad even asking for the class, but I honestly had expected twenty or thirty dark elves at most, not this long train full of wagons and families. The fact that the priestess didn't doubt my

413

word when I said I wasn't trying to take advantage spoke well to her own trustworthiness, I felt.

"Alexander," the priestess said, waving over a male dark elf dressed in leather armor. "Follow Ryld here. He will unlock a class for you."

The man stepped forward and led me toward a nearby wagon. We jumped on the back together and he sat me down next to him.

"I'm going to unlock the non-combat class *Dark Elf Stalker* for you. It is our version of a hunter."

He explained the nature of the class, which did not sound much like a non-combat class to me. I mentioned that to him and he nodded gravely.

"Not many of our non-combat classes are really non-combat," the dark elf said. "We don't exactly live in the safest place down here. And we don't hunt deer, if you know what I mean."

I didn't know exactly, but I had an idea of what the dark elves hunted down here. Eventually, he explained enough about the class for it to unlock for me.

Ryld the Dark Elf Stalker wishes to share the non-combat class Dark Elf Stalker with you. Do you accept the class?

I accepted immediately and felt the class unlock inside of me.

Class unlocked: Dark Elf Stalker.

New attribute unlocked: Perception.

Pooled experience detected. Experience applied to your Dark Elf Stalker class.

I felt a flood of information rush into my mind from the new perception attribute. In designing my body, I had spliced in several different genes of animals in order to increase my senses, but with my new perception attribute, I realized I had been practically locked in a dark, silent room up until now. The world rushed to me, my senses perceiving everything a hundred times more finely. I heard every conversation through the entire length of the wagon train. I smelled each dark elf nearby, able to distinguish them by their individual smell somehow, and I knew I could track them like a bloodhound if I wanted. My eyes, already able to see in the dark, suddenly felt like a shader had been removed from them. Colors had been distinguishable but muted in the dark, but now I perceived a thousand new things I had never noticed before. I could even hear my own slow, steady heartbeat, a calming sound that resonated through my body.

Congratulations, you have received enough experience to level your Dark Elf Stalker class. You are now level 1.

Please choose a level 1 class skill:

Mark Your Prey: You may select one target. You will know its location at all times, and you slow your enemy slightly while gaining the speed stolen from your target, increasing your coordination once a day until you catch your prey.

Harvest Your Prey: Anything that you kill will have its most valuable or useful parts highlighted, and your intuition will show you how to properly harvest and utilize anything you kill.

Stalk Your Prey: You move silently and are nearly invisible to the naked eye. If you strike while undetected, your wounds cause bleeding that cannot be healed by non-magical means.

Sense Your Prey: Your perception is increased by 25% and you are better at spotting stealthed or hidden things.

Kill Your Prey: Mark a target for death. Any wound you inflict will cause a slow, debilitating poison to infect your prey, causing weakness, paralysis, and eventually death if your target is inflicted with enough of your poison.

These were the "hunting" skills of the dark elf class? This was basically a combat class, except you only gained experience from actually hunting things instead of just killing monsters. But how different was "hunting" monsters from just killing them normally? This was basically a combat class. Ryld wasn't kidding; they must hunt more than just deer down here. This class was designed for killers.

I could tell that *Kill Your Prey* was magical in nature, so I couldn't select that skill, but the rest were all physical skills. The clear choice for right now was *Sense Your Prey* to help the dark elves escape, but I also had to think about what was good for me in the long run, since there was no way to take back a skill once it was selected. I was very tempted to take *Harvest Your Prey* since I would gain a lot of currency from learning how to properly harvest the monsters I killed. *Mark Your Prey* and *Stalk Your Prey* were interesting, but I already had a stealth skill, and *Mark Your Prey* wasn't immediately useful to me since I didn't regularly hunt things over long distances.

That left *Harvest Your Prey* or *Sense Your Prey*. Following my plan of enhancing my attributes when possible, I decided to go with *Sense Your Prey*. It would help in this situation and it scaled with perception as it grew, and I could learn *Harvest Your Prey* through actual mentorship by someone that knew what they were doing, either from a dark elf like Ryld or from someone back in the city.

I closed my eyes and took several deep breaths, trying to regain my equilibrium now that my senses were so powerful. I slowly filtered out sounds, smells, the sensations of my body, and then all the other new data my body was sensing. Then I slowly focused on each one, imagining I was an audio engineer dialing the sensation back and able to adjust the volume at will.

It didn't quite work, but the overload of information was bearable for now. The most important thing was that my *Monster Hunter* perk was working great. I could easily sense all of the dark elves around me, both in the wagon and in the city. I could even sense the spiders that were currently attacking the far side of the city, as well as several more ahead of us in the tunnel that surrounded the city.

"I'm ready to go," I told Ryld. He nodded without a word and left the wagon. I returned to Alaunvayas and let her know I should be better able to help now. She smiled at me gratefully.

"C'mon," she told me, leading me back to the center of the wagons. "We have bribed the guards on the gate to allow us to leave tonight. We will practice our plan as we move."

I followed her and we set up in a central wagon protected by high wooden walls. I looked closely at the wood of the wagon, surprised to see such an abundance of lumber underground.

Alaunvayas must have noticed me looking at the wood.

"There are vast underground forests down here," she told me, brushing her fingers against the wood of the wagon as we settled down inside. "Our people traded with the deep dwarves for wood when things were better."

"What exactly happened that led to the spider problem? I heard rumors in the city but nothing for certain."

"The rumors are mostly true," Alaunvayas said. "Aranea, the goddess most of our people worship, is the goddess of spiders. Some of our houses raised the large spiders and began

416

experimenting, trying to find a way to fuse their own forms with the spiders, thinking they would become avatars of Aranea. The experiments angered Aranea, who is a jealous goddess. She freed the spiders, and once free, they bred in the tunnels and began to attack our hunters and traders. Years passed and nobody did anything to stop the spiders until they began to block off our tunnels. When we realized the problem, several groups tried to fight back, but the spiders were too numerous and too canny by then. Our hunters were ambushed and killed, our soldiers overwhelmed. Without the backing of the houses, we never organized enough to win."

She shook her head sadly. "That is why, even with your ability, we never really stood a chance. It is too late for the rest of my people. We can just hope to save a few of the less foolish amongst us."

We spoke more as the wagons approached and began to exit the city, the guards on the gate turning a blind eye to us as we left. I was curious what it was like being a monster, and Alaunvayas told me about her people and how they survived for this long.

I learned that when the dark elves first appeared on Earth, they came through a portal to establish a new colony. Her people came from another world, one dominated by the dark elves. She didn't consider herself a monster, of course, just another person, much like a human. But the system here classified them as monsters, and they had no way to alter that. It was strange, because according to her, the dark elves had classes, monsters, and experience on her world as well, which suggested that the gods of this world hadn't been the ones to create the system that existed here.

It was a fascinating conversation, and I learned a lot about how this world worked. The dark elves were likely one of the least friendly of the races that had come here. I wondered if there might be some that were genuinely friendly toward humans out there, just waiting to be contacted.

We practiced alerting her squad leaders through her mental connection with them. I would act like I had detected an attack from a certain location and her squad would react, grouping together and defending the wagons within seconds. She had worked out a smart way to utilize my perk, and I was thankful to have such a competent ally. I shuddered to think what would have

417

happened if I had stayed with the Baeniryn house and tried to solve this quest with them. They would have likely poisoned me or mind-controlled me, trapping me here forever and only using me for their house wars until the city was overrun with spiders.

Once we approached the tunnel that the Lamashtu followers planned to use to escape, the squad in front of the wagon ran forward and began to cast a spell that shot purple flames into the tunnel, burning the webs that blocked the way. I could sense several spiders congregating in reaction to the burning, and I alerted Alaunvayas to an incoming attack.

The squad in front stopped clearing the webs immediately and stepped back, readying themselves for an attack. The spiders stopped as well, not expecting the dark elves to be prepared for their attack. I alerted Alaunvayas to what was happening, and the mages stepped forward and began to clear the webs again.

The spiders attempted to trap several of the mages with their webs, but the other squad members were waiting and stepped forward, activating a shield that stopped the sticky nets the spiders propelled out of their tunnel. I sensed the spiders retreating when they realized they couldn't stop the mages. They scuttled upward and sideways around the tunnel entrance, preparing an ambush for when we pushed inside. Several more spiders began to arrive as well, joining the ambush and waiting perfectly still in the tunnels in front of us. I alerted Alaunvayas and she notified the soldiers.

I continued to give Alaunvayas real-time updates, which allowed the first squad to anticipate the ambush, turning it on the spiders and killing them easily. The mages immediately went back to clearing the webs, and the squad pushed deeper into the tunnel in front of us.

The train of wagons slowly entered the tunnel behind the lead squad. I turned when it was our turn to enter, watching as the dark elf city faded behind us. I wasn't sad to see it go. It had been a disturbing place, and it deserved the fate it had brought down on itself.

We made slow but steady progress. Thanks to the system Alaunvayas had set up and my perk, we were able to turn every one of the spiders' ambushes and made it out of the spiders' territory without significant harm after several hours of travel. Many of the members of the squads were hurt defending us, even with my advanced warning, but nobody died or was taken by the spiders, which Alaunvayas said was a remarkable victory. The spider attacks had become especially desperate as we approached the end of their territory. Waves of spiders tried to overwhelm the squads with pure numbers, but the dark elf priestesses kept everyone alive and got them back into the fight very quickly.

Once the way was clear, Alaunvayas slumped down in the wagon, clearly exhausted from the mental communication she had been carrying out. I handed her my canteen, offering her a drink of water, which she accepted gratefully.

"Now," she said, "we follow the underdark toward where you showed me your city is. It will be just as dangerous, if not more so, but thankfully we won't have to worry about the spiders or the remaining dark elves. Thank you for your help. I know it may not seem like much, but we would not have been able to do that without you."

At first, I wasn't sure how useful my skill really was, but as we had continued on, I realized it really was essential. The spiders had webbed over the tunnels so effectively that they could ambush the dark elves from any direction, including above. They even built false walls, hiding behind stone that they had cleverly used to disguise hidden passageways. My perk allowed me to easily sense them behind the walls and alert the squads, the same way I could sense when a group of spiders was above a squad preparing to drop down on top of them. The spiders were ingenious when it came to devising ambushes, and I could see why a fractured population such as the dark elves couldn't fight back enough to stop them.

The wagons continued to roll nonstop, the beetles seemingly tireless. People slept on the wagons in shifts, and the guards seemed to never need to sleep as they kept watch the entire time. Alaunvayas and I stayed mostly in the center of the caravan, my perk still allowing me to sense monsters and alert her squads in case of an attack from any non-spider monsters. She considered the largest part of our bargain fulfilled and began to tell me about the classes that her people had unlocked as we traveled.

"We have seven classes at this time," she told me. "Some would require you to become a devotee of Lamashtu, which I think is unlikely on your part, but the offer is there. The others may be suitable for you. The ones that require devotion to my goddess are the *Priestess of Lamashtu* class and the *Devotee of Lamashtu*. The former is what I am and gains magical power through prayer and communion with our goddess. The *Devotee* is a warrior version, similar to your *Paladin*, except ours is a darker warrior that utilizes the power of our goddess in . . . unique ways.

"The other classes are, of course, the basic *Dark Elf Warrior*, *Dark Elf Archer*, and *Dark Elf Mage*, all very unimaginative but effective nonetheless. Then we have two more classes, a rare and a legendary class. Our rare class is called *Dark Elf Necromancer* and focuses on raising the dead, death magic, and controlling the undead. And our legendary class is called *Spirit Breaker*, which unlocks spirit magic and allows you to dominate and control the spirits of foes that you have defeated."

I thought over the different classes, ruling out the two that required me to worship her goddess, as she had suspected I would. The three basic classes held no interest for me, leaving the *Dark Elf Necromancer* class and the *Spirit Breaker* class. I asked her to tell me more about the two.

"The *Dark Elf Necromancer* is an evolved form of mage," she said, "that focuses on death magic. You can raise skeletons of recently deceased people or monsters and control them for a short time. You can also take part in rituals to make more powerful and longer-lasting undead, although those can be expensive. Death magic is extremely powerful, crippling and weakening foes and strengthening yourself with the stolen energy. Some necromancers focus on combat, choosing skills that emphasize draining and empowering themselves. One of our most powerful soldiers has combined both the *Dark Elf Warrior* class and the *Dark Elf Necromancer* class, allowing her to steal the life from those she kills and healing herself so she can continue to fight near endlessly."

"And the *Spirit Breaker* class?"

"That is our legendary class," she said, "and not many people know we even have it or understand what it does. I share it with you because of your greatest assistance to my people. Only two people have the class currently: myself and the woman that discovered it. She is elderly now and does not like to be disturbed, although she is around here somewhere.

"The class isn't based on your magical or physical attributes but unlocks a new attribute called willpower and gives you access to spirit magic. You will be able to perceive the spirits of the deceased and commune with them. Your willpower determines everything about your class. The class doesn't have traditional skills, instead allowing you to dominate and control the spirit of one monster or person at level 1 and then another creature at every level that you would normally earn a skill."

"So no skills at all?"

"None," she said, "but the spirits you retain control all of their skills and knowledge from their past life and are compelled to serve you, so in some ways, you can gain many different types of skills depending on what spirit you break. But the more stubborn, intelligent, or powerful the spirit you try to break, the harder it will be. Your willpower will determine if you are capable of breaking the spirit's will and compelling them to serve you. If you fail, you could become controlled by the spirit instead. Some spirits you can keep active at all times. But if you do ever capture truly powerful spirits, they will be a drain on your willpower, exhausting you quickly. Some of the most powerful you may only be able to summon for a few minutes at a time, although that will increase as your willpower and level increases."

"Interesting," I said, thinking it over. "Anything else about the class?"

"Well," she replied, giving me a look that was hard to interpret, "I would say two things to you. First, you seem to have almost no magical power inside of you. Or you hide it remarkably well, which I find unlikely. Are you aware of this?"

"Yeah," I said, surprised she had noticed. "I'm in search of a class that might help me deal with mages for that exact reason. I find that I am particularly weak to them and need to find a way to mitigate that danger."

"I figured," she said, smiling, "and willpower will be very helpful for you there. It will not help you with spells that physically restrict your body, but your physical attributes will eventually become powerful enough that you should be able to break those yourself. What willpower can do is help you against mental intrusions and spells that affect your mind. Your willpower will resist anything that interferes with your mental clarity and self-control. Willpower is the combined power of your inner self, and you naturally do not want to be interfered with. The higher your willpower is raised, the more you will be able to break not just spirits but spells that try to influence your mind."

She reached over and patted me companionably on the arm. "That is why I suggest you take the *Spirit Breaker* class, because right now, your mind is an open book, and while it is very sweet to see such innocence in a human, you would do well to protect yourself."

I flushed, realizing she had been reading my mind the entire time we had been speaking, even from the first moment we met. I felt a bit like I was caught naked on the toilet, but I was also grateful for her suggestion. The *Dark Elf Necromancer* class would synergize well with my current skills that allowed me to gain power when fighting many foes or for long periods of time, allowing me to heal myself or leech even more power from those I fought. But at the same time, it did nothing to shore up my weaknesses, and it sounded like most of the class was magic-based anyway, which would be useless for me. Plus, *Spirit Breaker* was a legendary class, meaning I could level it to level 80, which would give me more attributes over time.

"Thank you for the advice," I told her. "I'll follow it. I'll learn the *Spirit Breaker* class."

"A good choice," she said. "Now let me teach you about spirits and spirit magic."

Class unlocked: Spirit Breaker.
Attribute unlocked: Willpower.

Chapter 31

I deactivated my *Gunslinger* and *Duelist* classes, wanting to make sure I leveled my new *Spirit Breaker* class as rapidly as possible. I was curious what my base willpower was and if I would gain an increased benefit from the attribute like I had with my other classes. I had to think it was fairly high, given that I had been nothing but a mind in a machine for much of my existence.

As we traveled slowly through the underdark, I began to join the squads in defending the wagons in order to gain experience for my new class. Eventually, Alaunvayas assigned me to my own squad and sent me out to hunt in the greater underdark. With my perk, we were easily able to find prey to hunt and monsters to kill.

The caravan had little food to begin with since so many had been starving back in the city, so hunting monsters was essential for keeping everyone fed. Ryld was assigned to my squad and helped me learn how to properly harvest the monsters we killed, as I had hoped would happen. It was slow and messy work, but I was a fast learner.

The underdark was a truly unique world and beautiful in many ways. I had originally thought it would be nothing but a series of tunnels running under the earth, but I soon saw for myself how special the world underground really was. Our wagons passed vast lakes, raging rivers, forests of mushrooms and trees, and even an ancient city Alaunvayas believed had had the misfortune of their portal opening underground, dooming a race of surface dwellers that couldn't see in the dark. I learned to navigate through the tunnels and to hunt the various creatures of the underdark. I learned which monsters to avoid as well. There were plenty of those, monsters so dangerous even the dark elves didn't want to mess with them. On a number of occasions, we had to stop and spend several days holed up in a safe cavern, waiting for some of the more dangerous monsters to pass.

I spent all of my free time training with the dark elf soldiers. Alaunvayas gladly made them available to me as tutors when I asked. My new *Swordmaster* skill made training extremely rewarding, as well as the fact that my trainers were even more tireless than me. I could push myself, training for hours, until even my body needed a rest, and the dark elf soldiers were as fresh as if they hadn't been fighting at all. The Lamashtu sect didn't have as many soldiers as some of the other houses, but I wouldn't have wanted to mess with undead soldiers that never needed rest, especially ones as skilled as these ones.

My *Dark Elf Stalker* non-combat class and my *Spirit Breaker* class leveled around the same time, gaining me a +1 to perception from *Dark Elf Stalker* and unlocking my first spirit from *Spirit Breaker*.

We were resting for several days in a safe cavern we had found when Ryld came and found me under the branches of one of the many strange, dark trees in this part of the underdark. The trees had leaves so black that they seemed to absorb darkness itself to power their photosynthesis.

"We have found a monster that Alaunvayas says would be good for you to try to capture," he told me. At his words, I stood quickly and followed him through the forest, excitement filling me. We had been on the lookout for a good monster for me to capture since I had gotten my first level, but we hadn't found anything that the dark elves felt was right for me yet. Ryld led me swiftly through a winding tunnel that led downward and away from our cavern. We traveled for several minutes until we entered a tunnel that led to a small den.

From where we stopped, I could see bones of various monsters sticking oddly out of the walls and ceiling of the cave, melded halfway into the stone as if put there by some mad artist. The room smelled deeply of musk, and I could sense a monster in the ceiling of the cave, although I could see no passageway that it could be hiding in.

"This is the den of a phase beast," Ryld told me. "It can phase in and out of any material and attack its prey. It's a good spirit beast to claim because it's not so powerful that you couldn't keep it out at all times, and it can hide under and around you, completely undetected. It also has powerful physical skills and some base magic that lets it evade attacks and turn invisible for short periods of time. It hunts primarily through ambush, and Alaunvayas thinks it would make a perfect bodyguard for you to have as your first spirit."

I couldn't disagree with Alaunvayas's idea; it sounded like a great first spirit to control. I nodded in agreement toward Ryld.

"How do we capture it?" I asked, eyeing the ceiling where it was hiding.

"That is the hard part," Ryld said. The first smile I had seen on the taciturn hunter appeared on his face. "You must enter the monster's den and wait for it to attack you. It will be angered to see you in its den, so it shouldn't be long for it to phase out of the stone and attack."

"Ah," I said, "a very straightforward and thorough plan, then." Ryld smiled more broadly at my reply. I smiled back, drew my sword and revolver, and then walked forward into the den.

As I walked in, I pretended I didn't know that the monster was above me and walked directly underneath it. Ryld had backed away, not wanting to spook the creature and unable to help since I needed to kill the monster myself if I wished to capture its spirit.

I stood for a moment under the creature before I felt it move. I could feel it when it began to move, approaching rapidly and getting ready to drop right on top of me, but I activated my *Trickster's Dash* to move just a few feet backward. The beast instead dropped right in front of me.

I got my first look at the beast, and it looked dangerous. It was all black and smooth, almost like an insect, except it was shaped like a large panther. It was longer than I was tall and stood at least to my mid-chest. Its limbs were thick and dangerous-looking. It had large teeth and claws on each of its four feet, and it looked capable of tearing me apart in seconds if I let it catch me.

"*Duel Me*," I told the beast while also activating my *If It's a Fight You Want, It's a Fight You'll Get* skill.

Duel activated. You and your opponent have both wagered your experience. Good luck.

I swiftly aimed and fired my revolver at the beast, unleashing three shots in quick succession. The monster, sensing the danger, turned invisible and dodged all three bullets. Thankfully, I could sense exactly where the beast was, even when it was invisible, so I used my *Dash* to escape its attempt to pounce on me. I shot my remaining three bullets, managing to clip the beast's rear thigh with the first shot, wounding it slightly.

The phase beast's invisibility faded and it charged me again. I evaded its attack, slicing my sword down its side and activating a *Leeching Strike* as its momentum sent it shooting past me. The beast whipped around quicker than I expected, its claw latching onto my leg, pulling me off balance and toward its jaws. Before I could free myself, it sank its massive, sharp teeth into my leg.

Trusting my *Regeneration* to keep me alive, I thrust my sword down into the back of the beast's neck as it continued to ravage my thigh. My sword struck true, sliding deep into the creature's neck. With a wrench, I pulled the sword out one side of its neck, spilling its lifeblood onto the ground.

The beast released my leg and tried to retreat toward the nearest wall, but I stabbed it several more times, holding it in place until it died.

Winner: Alexander! You are awarded 170 additional experience.

Phase beast defeated—100 experience awarded.

As the notifications came through, I sensed and saw a glow emanating from the beast's body. Since getting my new class, I had seen this in the other monsters I had slain, but this was the first time I was going to try interacting with the spirit. I reached out to it, touching the glowing energy with my hand.

As my hand made contact with the spirit, I felt the mind of the beast. I sensed the life it had led. Solitary, but satisfied to be alone. A hunter, a killer, a predator. Nothing could stop it; nothing was safe from it. I felt its fierce pride in its territory and its confidence that it could kill anything that dared to cross its path. The beast was smart, but more on an instinctive level than truly intelligent. It had no real sense of self, no personality, just a rough concept of who it was and why it did what it did.

I pushed my own willpower forward, using it to subsume the will of the phase beast. I felt it resist, but it didn't understand enough of what was happening to fight back very well. Its instincts, when it was faced with unknown danger, were to retreat into the stone that made up its hunting grounds, but it couldn't go anywhere now. I continued to push forward, forcing my will over the spirit. With a surge, my will overpowered the monster, and I felt its own will break from the pressure of my own.

I opened my eyes and saw a spirit version of the monster rise up from its dead body. It was still sleek, black, and smooth-skinned, just like it had been in life. It was only slightly ephemeral and no less deadly-looking than before. If anything, it looked even scarier now that it seemed to only partially exist in this reality. I would not want this thing finding me in a dark alley.

I mentally commanded it to phase into the ground beneath me and to protect me from any unexpected attack that might target me. The beast turned to me as it sensed me projecting my orders, and it obeyed, phasing into the ground under my feet and leaving no trace of its existence. I felt no resistance or unhappiness as it carried out the task I had given it, and I could sense it underneath me even now, watching what was happening around me.

I inspected my leg and thigh where the beast had caught me, seeing that its claws and teeth had been sharp enough to puncture my clothing. Blood was leaking down my leg, but it had slowed dramatically as my healing sealed the wounds. My thigh wasn't fully healed, but it would be soon. I felt my hunger stir as my *Regeneration* and my nanobots drew upon my body to do their work. I would need to eat something soon, but overall, I was in decent shape.

Ryld returned, glancing at the body of the monster before nodding at me as if he had expected no less. I smiled at him and then we turned and made our way back to the wagons. I sensed the phase beast following beneath me, easily able to keep pace with us. I wondered what life must look like to a creature that could exist inside solid material; it clearly didn't see with its eyes—I wasn't sure it even had eyes, now that I thought about it. It had to have a very interesting perspective on the world.

Back at the slow-moving wagons, I cleaned up my blood as best as I could and grabbed a bite to eat. Ryld had sent some hunters back to butcher the phase beast's body for us, but I decided to go with them to learn more about my new spiritual companion. The hunters showed me what they were butchering from the corpse as they worked, focusing mostly on the claws, teeth, and hide rather than the meat of the beast.

I asked them if the hide was good for anything and they said it was primarily used for armor or clothing due to its incredible stealth capabilities. Interested, I asked Ryld when we returned if I could keep the hide and if he would help me turn it into a cloak. He agreed.

With Alaunvayas's permission, we tracked down a crafter who had come with the refugees and could work with the skin of the phase beast. Ryld helped me convince her to craft a cloak in the same design as my current cloak, which draped over my shoulders and angled downward over my left arm to conceal my revolver. It looked more like a poncho than a cloak in the front, but the back hung down from my shoulders, keeping me protected and warm.

A week passed before the woman was done crafting the cloak, but when she was finished, it was a beautiful piece of work. The cloak was as black as the night and seemed to absorb any light that shone upon it. To the touch, it seemed as hard as an armored insect's carapace, yet it was so flexible that when I ran it through my hands, it felt almost like silk. The craftswoman had outdone herself.

I took off my old cloak and put on the new one. As I did, I felt a surge of approval from my spirit companion, as if I was now a recognized part of its pack, even though it had been a solitary creature before. I felt dangerous in the cloak, and it made me want to disappear into the underdark on my own, just me and my new companion, the pair of us silently stalking and killing any prey that dared to cross our paths.

I didn't get rid of my old cloak, instead sending my nanobots to extract the orichalcum thread that had been used to enchant it. Once it was extracted, I had my nanobots begin working to re-create the exact rune of *Concealment* on my new cloak, amplifying its already significant concealment properties. It was slow-going, the phase beast cloak resistant to any tampering, but I had my nanobots working on it day and night until it was completed.

I continued to level my *Spirit Breaker* class as we traveled. I began using my *Duel Me* skill every day, even on a smaller monster if it seemed like the best one I was going to encounter that day, instead of saving it for the chance to fight something powerful. The lesser monsters didn't award me much, but I got a couple of attribute points and some bonus experience that helped me level. The attributes I stole increased my magic capacity, memory, and endurance by one each.

My *Spirit Breaker* class had leveled to seven by the time we got close to Nova Roma, primarily from the hunting expeditions I led and the use of my skill to steal experience. The class gave me attribute bonuses in willpower and endurance, with a few in memory here and there. In total, I received + 3 to willpower, +2 to endurance, and +1 to memory. My *Dark Elf Stalker* non-combat class also leveled from my constant hunting, although a bit more slowly than *Spirit Breaker*. It only reached level 4, but that netted me +1 to my perception and +1 to my coordination.

Name: Alexander
Basic Class: Archer 20 / Warrior 20 / Rogue 20
Evolved Class: Gunslinger 15 / Duelist 11 / Spirit Breaker 7
Non-combat Class: Enchanter 5 / Dark Elf Stalker 4

Base Attributes:

Coordination = 41
Strength = 35
Endurance = 27
Memory = 13
Magic Power = 10
Magic Capacity = 10
Luck = 8
Perception: 3
Willpower: 4

Skills:

Stealth:
Hide in the shadows and move silently, blending into the background and attracting less attention.

Trickster's Dash:

Dash through the air, ignoring wind resistance until you land. When you dash, you are briefly invisible until your dash ends.

Gambler's Eye:
You receive a passive boost of 20% to your coordination, your vision is improved, and you gain a sixth sense that reveals when luck may be favoring you.

Swagger:
Your movement speed increases, obstacles bend from your path, and your step is sure and steady. Your movements subtly intimidate others.

Duel Me:
At the start of combat, challenge a foe to a duel. The stakes of the duel are randomly selected and may include an attribute point, a percentage of all experience gained, a perk, a mutation, a skill, or an achievement. The first to surrender, retreat, or die loses. The winner of the duel permanently steals the stakes of the duel, and the loser permanently loses the stakes of the duel. This skill may only be used once a day.

Gambler's Luck:
You push luck to the limit, changing the odds around you to guarantee a more favorable outcome. Unlocks a new attribute: Luck.

Empowered Strikes:
You magnify the power of all of your strikes. Your strength when attacking is magnified by an additional 25%.

Empowered Enchantments:
Your enchantment effects are more powerful.

Absolute Evasion:
Grants an increased chance of evading any attack or spell, even ones you may not see coming.

Steadfast Endurance:

Increases your endurance by 25%, and repeated use of your skills is less exhausting.

Never Bring a Mob to a Duel:
Gain +1 to all attributes for each nearby enemy that is actively attacking you or planning to attack you. Whenever an enemy is defeated or surrenders, you lose their bonus attribute. This skill may only be used once per week.

Leeching Strike:
Strike an enemy, randomly stealing one of their attributes and adding it to your own until the end of combat.

If It's a Fight You Want, It's a Fight You'll Get:
Pick a target. The longer you fight your opponent, the higher your attributes soar. Gain +1 to all attributes once every minute you are in combat until you or your opponent are defeated or surrender.

Swordmaster:
All training with a sword is doubly effective, your skill with the sword increases, and you gain an instinctive understanding of opponents when wielding a sword.

Sense Your Prey:
Your perception is increased by 25% and you are better at spotting stealthed or hidden things.

Perks:

Captain's Command:
Anyone obeying an order that you give will receive a morale bonus of +1 to all attributes while carrying out your command.

Swimmer's Body:
The length of time that you can hold your breath is doubled, you have improved eyesight underwater, and water restricts you less when you are moving through it.

Monster Hunter:
You can sense the presence of monsters nearby. This perk scales with your level and perception attribute.

Natural Weapons:
When using your hands, feet, claws, teeth, or any natural part of your body to strike a foe, you strike as if your strength was increased by +2.

Regeneration:
You gain the regeneration of Gromger the Mighty Troll King. Your body can regenerate from almost any wound. Injuries regenerate based on your endurance attribute and the amount of energy available to your body.

Emperor's Guard:
You have been entrusted with the protection of the Emperor. You are authorized to pass the wards in the Emperor's palace. You receive a +1 to all attributes.

Ant's Strength:
When you lift or carry objects, your strength attribute is magnified three times.

Achievements:

Dangerous Dungeoneering:
For completing ten dungeons by yourself and without a class, you have been rewarded. You receive +2 to all attributes, and rewards from all future dungeons are increased slightly.

Survive a Safe Zone:
For reaching level 10 in a class, completing a dungeon, killing at least 20 monsters, and leaving a safe zone, you have been rewarded. You receive +1 to all attributes.

Mass Slaughterer:
For killing over 1000 monsters in under an hour, you have been rewarded. You receive +3 to all attributes, and when you are

outnumbered, those who dare to attack you will be overcome with dread, weakening their strikes and reducing their accuracy.

Quests:

Make a Home:
You must establish a home and secure it from your enemies. Reward: +1 to an attribute of your choice, 500 experience.

Contribute to the Economy II:
You must sell goods or provide services worth a significant amount of money, depending on your region. Reward: Three gold cores, 600 experience.

Cull the Drakes: completed
Contribute to the Economy: completed
Clear the City: completed
Down with the Queen: completed

Evolutions:

Evolution of Leadership:
Your patronage allows for those who serve you to benefit twice as fast when training or earning rewards. Loyalty from others is increased. You may form magically binding contracts. Your physical appearance is more magnetic and beautiful.

Spirits:

Phase Beast:
A dangerous hunter of the underdark, capable of phasing through any material to ambush its prey.

Our journey to Nova Roma took several months. It was dangerous, but nobody in the wagons was ever hurt. The dark elves were very proficient hunters, and thanks to their scouting and my perk, we always managed to kill the monsters before they could get near the wagons. My skill with the sword, boosted by my new skill *Swordmaster* and countless hours of training with the dark elf soldiers, had improved dramatically. I took every opportunity to train with them, pushing my body to the brink of exhaustion, only sleeping when I absolutely had to.

As we approached the city, I could hold my own against the dark elf soldiers, all of whom had easily outclassed me when we began our journey. We didn't use any active skills when we fought, focusing more on the pure art of the sword. I was able to win a bit more often than not when we sparred, and I never embarrassed myself anymore in our fights.

On hunts, I used the full range of my skills. Using *Never Bring a Mob to a Duel*, *Leeching Strike*, and *If It's a Fight You Want, It's a Fight You'll Get* after unlocking my perception attribute took some adjustment, since those skills caused my perception to skyrocket whenever my attributes climbed too high. Whenever we fought a large number of monsters at once, my perception increased and I found it harder to concentrate. Interestingly, with my willpower also increasing, the two counterbalanced each other in many ways. As my willpower increased, my mind became more centered and better able to process the sensory overload from my high perception. It felt as if the overloading of my senses was some form of mental attack and my willpower was countering it, processing the information and protecting my mind from being overwhelmed.

Ryld also helped. Many of the dark elves had experience with adjusting to a high perception. Ryld taught me several techniques the dark elves used to manage sensory overload. The techniques mainly involved meditation and blocking out senses before slowly allowing them back in, as I had tried to do when I first got the attribute. For him, he didn't use the mental imagery of a dial but instead imagined that he was in a dark cave with no sound, light, or sensation and then slowly introduced one sense after another.

I had turned down the offer from the monks to spend a year meditating with them, but ironically, I spent months meditating with Ryld instead. He would allow me to use my *If It's a Fight You Want, It's a Fight You'll Get* in a duel with him, and then once my attributes had scaled too high for me to process the information from my perception attribute, we would sit and meditate together.

As we traveled, we also found a number of dungeons in the underdark. We avoided clearing them. The dark elves informed me that they were significantly more powerful in the underdark, and even powerful dark elf teams that attempted them often lost one or two members.

I had come to miss the sun and fresh air as weeks turned into months in the underdark. I had learned that the dark elves could technically go on the surface, even during the daytime, but that direct sunlight blinded them and weakened them, so they tended to avoid the surface as much as possible. I had lost all track of where we were as we traveled, but Alaunvayas seemed confident in where we were going.

At some point in our travels, I received a notification that I had failed the quest to save the dark elf city. I told Alaunvayas and she told me that probably meant that the spiders had completed their destruction of the dark elf city. She seemed slightly sad at the news but didn't let that stop her from leading her people forward.

Several days later, word was passed down the caravan that we were under the city. I was surprised, not seeing anything distinctive about this particular stretch of tunnels, but I trusted the dark elves to know where they were at. We stopped the caravan so the dark elf scouts could search the area for a place to settle. I joined Ryld in searching the nearby tunnels, but we didn't find anything of note in the direction that we searched.

When we returned to the wagons, another group had found a cavern they believed would be perfect for the group to settle in. The only problem was, as Alaunvayas had suspected, the cavern was occupied.

I joined Alaunvayas and Ryld and some of the other squads at the front of the caravan. Alaunvayas was preparing them to attack the cavern as I approached.

"Scouts report it's occupied by blightrats," Alaunvayas told us all. "They are deadly in numbers and can infect with every wound they inflict. They stand four to five feet tall and use their claws and teeth to bite and infect their prey. They use no armor or weapons but have a base intelligence and herd mentality that can be dangerous.

435

"The cavern is full of them. Alexander here is lucky they haven't found a way to the surface yet, because they could overrun his city if his people weren't properly prepared. We will kill them all to ensure they cannot breed somewhere else and endanger our people in our new home. Any questions?"

Nobody had any, so Alaunvayas explained the battle plan. There were several entrances to the cavern and squads would move around the area until they could all approach at the same time, coordinated by Alaunvayas's mental abilities. Once everyone knew the plan, she cast several powerful buffs on all of us, increasing our attributes and providing us some protection from disease.

Once that was done, I joined Ryld and the group of hunters I had been working with for the last few months. Our squad consisted of me and ten dark elves. Ryld was in charge, although I often took the lead since I could detect the monsters we hunted. With him were a number of hunters who were equally deadly with both the sword and the small crossbows that they used. We had two mages that used powerful shadow spells and were just as quick and stealthy as the hunters. Finally, we had a powerful dark elf necromancer named Maya who specialized in the more physical aspects of the class. She was a powerhouse in combat, although not as stealthy as the rest of the group. She had saved us from several nasty circumstances with her ability to leech the strength of our foes and heal wounds on herself and her companions, although she somehow tailored her healing for her undead allies, so I didn't benefit from the healing myself.

Together, we made a formidable team. I was able to find us targets, the hunters could prepare traps or ambush prey, and if we encountered anything that required a magical touch, our mages could likely kill it. And Maya was our ace in the hole. She did her own thing more often than not, either attacking directly or hanging back, weakening our enemies with her spells, and healing the undead members of the squad.

Since getting my phase beast companion and my cloak, I had become even deadlier at hunting and ambushing prey. I had managed to transfer the *Concealment* enchantment to my new cloak, making me almost undetectable as I hunted. Together, my new companion and I were like a wraith stalking the underdark, able to find any monster and ambush it completely unseen.

In the assault on the blightrat cavern, we were assigned one of the smaller tunnels, and Ryld led us through winding tunnels that rose steadily upward for several minutes until we reached a smaller tunnel that angled back downward sharply. The tunnel was so small that I would struggle to fit through it easily. The tunnel showed signs of being roughly carved out of the stone by blightrat claws rather than being naturally formed, as most of the underdark tunnels seemed to be, so Alaunvayas had speculated it was probably a bolt hole for the rats to escape from any predators that attacked their home.

We waited at the mouth of the tunnel until the attack began. Our job was to hold the tunnel and keep any of the rats from escaping. The narrow tunnel made it hard to utilize all of our hunters, so Ryld and I decided that once the attack began, we would move out into the cavern itself with me, Maya, and several of the hunters holding a front line while the best ranged hunters and our two mages attacked from behind us.

We waited patiently, the entire group silent and stealthed in the tunnel. When Ryld signaled us to move forward, we ran to our positions and prepared ourselves. I could see large purple explosions raining into the cavern, impacting masses of rat creatures and the crude structures they lived in. The screams of the blightrats filled the cavern and the heat from the explosions washed over us, even this far away.

The cavern itself was a third the size of the one the dark elves had come from, with a small lake in one corner. Scouts reported it was polluted now but could be cleansed easily once the rats were taken care of. With a source of freshwater and a place to build, the dark elves could settle here and rebuild their city, hopefully with less infighting and deceit this time.

We waited as the attack continued, squads of dark elf soldiers rushing forward and attacking the rats while they were stunned and confused by the magical assault. The rats began to panic and a large group of them began to flee in our direction. The mages and hunters of our squad began to pick them off as they approached, and I sent my phase beast forward to harass and kill as many as it could before they got to us.

I sensed my phase beast shooting forward, moving underground faster than most people could sprint. It materialized behind one of the blightrats that was falling behind the others, leaping out of the ground as if the hard stone was water. It pounced on the rat, killing it instantly. It shook the rat's corpse back and forth, then dove back into the stone, looking for more rats to kill. I had become very attached to the murderous monster as we hunted together over the last few months, and I never got tired of seeing its sleek, deadly grace in action.

The first group of rats running toward us never made it close; the dark elf spells and bolts, as well as my phase beast, finished them off before they could arrive. Several more groups of rats from elsewhere in the cavern also began to flee in our direction, but they posed little danger, even in greater numbers. I only used my revolver once, on a mob of over a hundred rats that rushed us from around the left side of the cavern. I had my *Explosive Bullets* ready for the blightrats and fired all six shots into the mob, stopping the charge cold and killing the majority of them.

As I reloaded, I saw Ryld give me a surprised look. He had seen me use my revolver before, but only the basic *Penetration Bullets* since we were often hunting in tight tunnels where my *Explosive Bullets* would do as much harm to us as to whatever I shot at. He was clearly surprised to see how easily I was able to kill the rats from a distance. I was happy to surprise the reserved hunter and gave him a quick smile as I finished reloading.

After that large wave, only the occasional straggler or small group tried to escape in our direction. In short order, Ryld signaled that the cavern was clear and we could move forward. As we moved inward, we hunted down several more rats that were trying to hide throughout the cavern, my sense able to detect them easily.

Realizing so many were hiding around the area, Ryld had us do a circuit of the cavern, and we found and killed all of the rats that had gone to ground. When we were done, I couldn't detect any other monsters except the dark elves. When I told Alaunvayas, she pronounced the cavern clear to the silent satisfaction of the dark elf soldiers that surrounded her.

She and her priestesses moved to the center of the cavern, the rest of us trailing after them, where they performed a ritual cleansing and dedicated the cavern to their goddess. When she finished, I noticed many of the dark elves relaxing and smiling at each other with a palpable sense of relief on their faces. For the dark elves, that kind of reaction was akin to practically jumping up and down and cheering.

I had known, of course, that this journey was risky for the dark elves, but they had all seemed so stoic that I had underestimated how relieved they all were to be somewhere safe once again.

Alaunvayas called me forward in front of the gathered dark elves and reminded them about the city above, the agreement we had reached, and several other things regarding how they would be living now that they were away from their old city.

It was hard to tell what exactly the dark elves thought of me, but I knew I had slowly won many of them over during our travels. My warnings had saved many of the hunters' lives and my squad's hunting brought in the most amount of food, helping to keep everyone well fed. Many of the dark elves watched me as Alaunvayas spoke about our agreement, and many of them nodded at me when I met their eyes, honoring me for helping them reach their new home.

Things progressed quickly from there. The wagons were brought into the cavern and the many families on them began to unpack all of the supplies they had carried for these many months. Nobody played music, and nobody served any alcohol or a special meal, but there was still an air of celebration in the cavern.

I found myself sitting alone as I watched the dark elves and their followers begin to settle into their new home. I was happy for them and glad to have such allies now. I had gained nothing but respect for the power of the dark elves while we traveled together. When they were united and working together, they were a force to be reckoned with.

At one point, Alaunvayas joined me as I watched everyone work. She handed me a bowl of traveler's stew, which was always made from whatever monster we had managed to catch that day. I ate gratefully as she sat down next to me.

"Thank you again for saving us," she told me. "I know my people do not show it easily, but we are all grateful for this chance to restart our lives. We hope to forge a new path forward, and you have helped us take the first steps on that path."

I nodded as I ate a bite of stew.

"Ryld will show you to the surface where your city lies," she told me. "And we will scout the underdark more to find resources and begin to rebuild down here. We will uphold our end of our agreement. Do not worry that we will betray you. If you need us, call on us. And until then, we will keep the pests down here from bothering you up above."

"Thank you," I told her, touched by her words. "It will be good to return to the city. I have enjoyed my time down here, but I do miss the sun."

"You will be more prepared to handle your difficulties above," she told me. "Your mind has become harder and harder to read, even for me. The foes you face above should struggle to influence you when they once may have done so with ease."

"That is what I had hoped," I told her.

"I have a boon I wish to grant you," she said. "It is from my goddess directly. We rarely grant such gifts, but my goddess feels you deserve it. Will you accept?"

I looked over at the priestess whom I had come to trust in our time together in the underdark. "Yes. And thank you to you and your goddess."

She nodded in reply. I was a bit skeptical that her goddess was real, truth be told, but apparently she could speak to the goddess, so who knew? I knew the gods of this world were real, but did the monsters that had come to this world bring their gods and goddesses with them? Or were they all a part of the same cosmos? It was a strange thing to consider, since most people on my Earth had long ago given up on the concept of real, literal gods.

Alaunvayas reached over and placed her palm on my hand. I felt an energy building against my skin, a warmth spreading from her to me.

You have received the Blessing of Lamashtu, the Dark Elf Goddess of Undeath. Lamashtu has bestowed upon you the perk Divine Sight. Your vision penetrates even the darkest of environments, and you can now see the souls of everything around you. Learn to see what a soul tells you, and you will never be deceived again.

Alaunvayas suddenly flared with color, her normally pale skin and white hair surrounded by a halo of colors so bright I had to close my eyes. When I reopened them, the halo had dimmed slightly but was still present around her.

"A great gift," Alaunvayas said, as if she wasn't sure what boon I would have received. "*Divine Sight* will serve you well. In time, you will be able to see whom you can trust, whom to be wary of, who plans to betray you, and even whether a person is telling you the truth or a lie."

As she spoke, her soul pulsed with a white light. I stared, trying to decipher what the colors around her meant. Did white mean she was telling the truth? Did it mean anything at all or did she just have a white soul? Was white good or bad or neither? I didn't think many people would consider a dark elf priestess to be "good," so it seemed unlikely the color had such subjective meaning to it.

My new sight, like much of what I had learned below ground, would take some getting used to.

Chapter 32

My return to the surface was a bit anticlimactic. I was looking forward to seeing the sun again, maybe a blue sky, maybe the smell of a fresh breeze untainted by the unending tunnels of the underdark. Instead, it was nighttime when Ryld and I left the underdark. The sky was dark and overcast, the temperature of the city cold and muggy. Snow still lingered in parts of the city and I could sense monsters nearby, the thousands of monsters that appeared at night seemingly undiminished. The city smelled of rot and buildings left abandoned for too long, like it always did.

"Thank you for everything, Ryld," I told him. "I enjoyed hunting with you."

"I did not think I would enjoy our hunts," he replied. "I thought I was stuck babysitting you for months, but you are a true hunter. It was good to hunt with you as well, Alexander. If you need our squad again, we would be glad to accompany you for more hunts. We have all agreed. When we find the rest of the paths to the underdark in your city, we will find you again and share the information with you and then we can discuss the future together."

I was deeply touched by his words. I wanted to hug the man or pat him on his shoulder, but I knew that such physical affection was uncomfortable for the dark elves. Instead, I bowed my head, and he bowed in reply before turning and heading back down the stairs into a basement that led into the underdark.

I looked around to figure out where I was in the city. The basement we had climbed out of was, thankfully, one of the few that hadn't grown into a dungeon. The building around me had fallen into ruin; nothing but loose stone walls remained. I saw a nearby building that stretched up several stories and dashed up to the rooftop to see the city better.

Once there, I found myself almost dead center in the city: the Emperor's palace lay to the north of me, and the army's walls and the priests' enclave were about equal distance to the west and east, respectively. I made a careful note of the location into the underdark in case I needed to visit the dark elves again. I had also made sure to pay attention to the twisting tunnels that led up here so I would not get lost when I returned to the underdark. I crouched on top of the building and watched the city at night, enjoying the fresh breeze that brushed my face. My phase beast followed me, flowing through the city streets and up the side of the building unseen.

I no longer needed the amulet that let me see in the dark thanks to the blessing I had received, but it had served me well in the underdark. I wasn't sure if it was some of my luck that I had received such an item, but without it, I would have surely died in the underdark many times over. Of course, I probably wouldn't have tried to approach the dark elf city if I couldn't see in the dark, so who knew? But thanks to my new divine boon, I could now see perfectly at night, just like the dark elves could. And with my enhanced vision from my body, my *Divine Sight*, my new perception attribute, and *Gambler's Eye*, which enhanced my vision even further, I could see the entire city from here with almost perfect clarity.

The biggest difference I noticed when looking at the city was that I now saw spirits . . . everywhere. Hundreds of thousands of people had died here. Many of their spirits still lingered. I saw them roaming the city, floating through the sky, and walking the streets. They were even in the buildings around me, carrying on their routines as if they hadn't died. It was eerie and sad to see how many there were. With a mental push, I turned down my *Divine Sight* with a push of willpower so I could see the city itself without being distracted by so many lost souls.

I waited on the roof until the sun began to rise, watching the monsters as they fought like the savage beasts they were. The gods, if they had actually created this system at all, had done humans a bit of a disservice by making the "safe zones" full of nothing but mindless beasts. It had made everyone think that such beasts were all that existed when, in fact, there were all kinds of "monsters" that inhabited the Earth now, many of which were intelligent and potential allies.

Once the sun had fully risen, I dashed my way across to Sycae and took to the streets as people began to wake up. The sky was still overcast and cold, but even through the cloud cover, I could feel the rays of the sun warming my body. I hadn't appreciated how nice the sensation was before. Plenty of human literature had focused on the emotional well-being that came from the sun, but for the first time since coming here, I truly understood it. As Sycae came to life around me, I took some time to just relish the fresh, crisp winter day above ground and the sights and sounds of the many different people that inhabited this part of the city.

I slowly made my way through the enclave. I stopped to buy myself some food from a street vendor that had just opened up and was surprised to have a customer so soon. I found the inn that Constans and I stayed at and ordered a warm bath from the innkeeper. Once I was clean for the first time since leaving the city, I took a bit of a nap in the comfortable bed inside the suite I had rented with Constans.

Later in the afternoon, I nursed a beer in the main room of the inn until Constans finally returned to the inn and saw me. She screamed at the sight of me—thoroughly scaring the poor innkeeper—and ran over to give me a big hug. I returned the hug, suddenly feeling a bit like a dark elf thanks to my awkwardness, and then she started punching me in the side until I had to push her away, restoring the proper order of things between us.

"You've been gone forever!" she told me.

"I know. I'm sorry about that," I said. "Things went a bit sideways where I was and it took a lot longer to return than I had planned."

"Spill it! Tell me what happened!" she said, bouncing up and down in the chair she had pulled up next to me.

I took a sip of my beer and then told her where I had been and about the journey to bring the dark elves here, making sure nobody else was nearby to listen in.

"Here? Like in the city? Real elves with magic and stuff? That is so cool!"

"Yeah," I told her, "but make sure to keep it secret for now. We don't need any overzealous people trying to hunt them."

"Of course!"

"So catch me up on what's been going on here," I said.

444

"Ugh," she said, "I can't believe you were gone for so long. I recruited a team of people for you ages ago. They've been training with me, and our tutor brought in several more people to help teach us all. We've been scavenging together, too, to get experience and because they were getting bored."

"Slow down," I said. "Who exactly did you recruit? Start from the beginning."

"Oh," she said, "right. Well, you said you wanted trustworthy people. There was this old gang in Perama that was a decent sort. They always treated me well and weren't too bad compared to some of the other gangs. I approached them and they all wanted a chance to prove themselves to you. Their leader is a good guy. Goes by the name of Basil. They are all teenagers like me, though a bit older. They have been working hard since I brought them over here."

"They sound like a good pick," I said. I could tell she was a little nervous that I wouldn't approve, but they sounded like the exact kind of people I had hoped she would find. "What about the other projects?"

"I found what you wanted," she said, "although most of the people are older and out of practice. The miners live out of an old warehouse by the docks here in Sycae. They mostly do odd jobs now since there is no more demand for their work. Sailors were much harder to find. The best I could do was talk to some of the fishermen out of Perama. A good number of them used to sail on the larger boats and are open to it again, if someone had one for them to work on. And if the pay was right and we could guarantee their safety on the open sea."

"That sounds pretty good," I replied. We spoke more and she was proud to tell me about how she was leveling her classes and had made good money scavenging and selling what she and the others found with her *Merchant* class. After we were done talking, I asked her to show me where the gang she had recruited was staying.

She led me to one of the warehouses by the docks and explained how she bought it for cheap because nobody was using it any longer. The gang helped her loot a number of cots from an old military bunker, and they had cleaned the place up and turned it

445

into a bit of a home for everyone. For most of the gang, it was the first time they had a real roof over their heads in their entire lives.

We entered the warehouse together. Inside, I saw a number of young men and women relaxing, sleeping, or playing games together. I quickly counted them, a bit surprised by how many she had recruited, and found there were twenty of them, five of them girls and the rest boys.

"Basil!" Constans yelled into the room when we entered. "Alexander is back! Come meet him!"

A tall, lanky boy with a mop of curly hair jumped up from a cot he had been sleeping on and rushed over. The rest of the crew gathered around as well, jostling each other and talking among themselves.

"He sure is a big one," I heard one of them say. "How could he be so tall?"

"And so handsome," I heard one of the young women say. "Are all the Varangians like that?"

I had forgotten that my *Evolution of Leadership* had changed me. The dark elves had seemed more or less unaffected by it, but maybe now that I was back in front of humans, it would help me charm people easier; the heavens knew I needed the help. Basil stopped in front of us and stood awkwardly, clearly unsure of how he should greet me.

"Hey," I said, reaching out to shake his hand. "I'm Alexander. I've heard good things about you and your people."

"Ah," he replied, shaking my hand. "Thank you, sir. We . . . uh . . . we are really happy for the opportunity."

"Let's sit and get comfortable," I told him and his people. "We have some stuff to discuss."

I immediately had a good impression of Basil, since he didn't try to posture or intimidate me and seemed humble even in front of his people. I wasn't sure how he had survived running a gang with his demeanor, but I was glad that Constans had found him. I also realized that part of that was coming from my *Divine Sight* perk. I could literally see his soul and it was giving me a positive feeling, one of trustworthiness. I scanned the other members and saw a mix of colors and impressions, too many to sort through right now.

I gestured for everyone to sit down around me. They weren't sure what I meant at first, but they got the idea when I settled onto the floor. Everyone eventually settled down into a semicircle with me, Basil, and Constans in front of them.

"So," I started, "Constans has probably told you some of what I have in mind, but I wanted to lay it all out for you and let you all decide if you want to work for me or not. If you have any questions, feel free to ask. I'm not a lord or some noble, so I will not be offended if you speak to me, got it?"

Basil nodded. Everyone else just watched me, clearly unsure of who I was and if what I had said was true.

"Great," I said. "So to start: why would I be hiring you? What is our goal? Well, I will be honest with you. My goal is to save this city."

The group exchanged a few looks, puzzled by what I said.

"Yes," I said, "I know that seems like a lot. But I believe that I can do it, with help from motivated and dedicated people like Constans and possibly all of you. The city is dying. It is practically already dead. You all have experienced that firsthand. You know what I'm talking about, don't you?"

"Yeah," I heard some people say quietly. More nodded.

"Well," I continued, "I can change that. I believe that we can save the city."

"How?"

"How is that possible?"

"Is he serious?"

"Yes, I'm totally serious," I said, turning and looking over the crowd of teenagers. "I have resources and some unique things that I could tell you more about if you join me and should make it possible. Now, that doesn't mean it would be easy or that we may not have to do some bloody things to make it happen, but I wanted you all to know that the end goal is something good, something noble.

"Now, to the specifics. Well, first I need a troop of loyal people to work for me. I would train you, give you classes and equipment, and help you level. In return, you would be soldiers for me. Ones that I could rely on and trust. You would be my personal guard and help me with my goals, no matter what they were."

"Can't you just hire a bunch of experienced soldiers? Why go through so many hoops to bring us on board?" Basil asked.

447

"Hey, don't discourage him if he wants to give us classes, Basil!" I heard one of his crew say, and everyone else broke into laughter.

"The issue is trust. If we want to save this city, we may end up tangling with some powerful people. The priests, for one. Possibly even the Emperor, who seems to do nothing but drink himself into a stupor each day rather than try to save the city. I need people I know will stick with me through it all. Constans vouches for you all. She says you are good people and eager for a chance to escape your current lives. I can give you all that."

"I can speak for all of us," Basil said, then paused for a moment to collect his thoughts, "and say that we are interested. We were facing another winter of starvation back in Perama. We always lose a few to the cold and hunger every year. By bringing us here and feeding us, giving us education and training and this place to live, you have already saved some of our lives. We appreciate that."

"Yeah!"

"True!"

"Agreed!" I heard some of his people say.

"Well," I said, "I'm glad to hear that. Let me give you some of the details of what I would expect from you all. Have you all heard about the legionnaires? The famous Roman army that could defeat anyone that dared come against them?"

"Of course!"

"Yeah!"

"My ma said my dad was one of them," I heard the others say.

"I know some form of the legion still survives in the army's enclave, but I plan to form my own. I would like you all to become the first of my legionnaires. Trained soldiers who could work together to defeat anyone.

"What that means, though, is that you would be signing up for a life of service. The legion before had a twenty-year term. You would be paid a fair salary, given classes, training, and equipment, and at the end of your twenty-year term, you could choose to sign up for more or you could retire. If you retired, assuming we succeeded in saving the city, I would give you a parcel of land for you to own or a part of the city, some place of your choice to call home permanently. You would be free to sell it or develop the land

and you would be responsible for protecting it. You would receive a small pension, but even after your term of service, you could be called up as auxiliaries if needed. You would be responsible for training your children or servants and sharing or acquiring classes for them, and they too would be expected to serve in the legion, if needed."

I could tell such long-term planning didn't really concern anyone in front of me, but I wanted to lay it all out so they would enter the agreement with all of the information I had to give them.

"Is he planning to run the city, not just save it?" I heard someone ask quietly, but I didn't answer them.

"Once you sign up, there would be no quitting. You would be expected to serve out your term. If you elected to stay longer than twenty years, the land you earn would grow in size for every five years after that. Your salary would go up if you were promoted as well, but for now, given how small we are, everyone will be paid the same except for Basil, who I would make your commander.

"Basil, you would be expected to maintain discipline and make sure that everyone carried out my orders. Any failures of discipline would need to be punished. Any betrayal of our secrets or desertion . . . Well, if someone betrays us, the penalty will be death.

"I know that is a lot to take in, so please talk amongst yourselves or ask me questions and I will answer. Keep in mind that during your twenty years, you will have a comfortable income, and while I can't guarantee your safety or comfort at all times, given what we need to do, I will always do my best to help you grow in power."

Silence lingered for a moment before people began to ask me questions. I answered them as they came, often just repeating what I had already said. Basil asked what sort of classes they could expect to get and if they would all get the same class or different ones.

"I have a legendary class that I will teach to each of you," I told them, "and I have some plans for some other classes. I will provide these classes for free. If you want to learn your own class, I encourage you to do so and we can learn to work your skills into the group, but you would need to save up and buy those classes on your own. I can't give you more details of the class I will give you at this time."

I saw several people eyeing the gun under Constans's arm, which she didn't conceal like I did. They had been scavenging with her for a while now, so they all probably had an idea of what kind of class I could offer. I could see that many were intensely interested in how the revolver worked.

"Can women join, too?" one of the young girls asked.

"Yes," I told her, "anyone is welcome. You will receive the same training, classes, and chance for promotion as anyone else. If anyone treats you differently, you come and tell me and I will handle it."

I knew that traditional Byzantine society had gender roles that seemed antiquated by modern standards, but most of that had apparently broken down in response to the death of most of the city's populace. I wanted to make sure that it never came back, since the class system made such ideas ridiculous anyway. Anyone could become physically powerful enough to do things that humans on my Earth would have found unbelievable. There was no reason to discriminate anymore on this Earth, as far as I was concerned.

After a few more questions, I ducked out of the warehouse and let them all talk together. Constans came to get me roughly a half hour later, letting me know that everyone had made up their minds.

"We agree to your offer," Basil told me when I settled back down on the floor in front of them.

"Yeah!" I heard people in the group say. Several even cheered.

"Wonderful," I said, smiling at the group around me. "I have a unique skill that will encapsulate everything that we have discussed and formalize our agreement. I would like to sit with each of you and go over it to make sure that you all agree and understand what you are signing."

I started with Basil, bringing up my *Evolution of Leadership* ability to form a contract. I knew this was a bit like cheating since it would enforce our agreement no matter what, but trust could only go so far. I also wanted a guarantee of loyalty.

We went over the contract, and then Basil and I signed it together. I stood and shook his hand, welcoming him as my first legionnaire. He beamed pridefully up at me, and I knew Constans had found the right man for the job when I could see his soul soaring with excitement at the opportunities in front of him.

"Welcome to the legion, Basil."

The group cheered and I smiled at the boy in front of me, my first legionnaire. He grinned sheepishly and then moved aside to let another take his place. One after another stepped forward, and I made sure they understood what they were agreeing to. I looked over their souls as they signed to try to make sure they were honest and trustworthy. I didn't know exactly what I was looking at with each individual soul, but I was generally able to get a sense of the person in front of me.

The only one out of the group that had a sour, untrustworthy soul was an older boy, possibly the oldest of all the teenagers in the room. His soul was a sickly green color and gave off the impression of cruelty and deceit. He agreed to the terms of the contract, but I could sense that he was already thinking of ways to take advantage of the knowledge I would give him.

I excused myself for a moment and explained the situation to Basil and Constans.

"Ah," Basil said after I finished explaining. "Yeah, that is Decimus. He joined us just a few months before we came here. He has been quiet so not many of us know him, but he hasn't done anything to make me worry before this."

"We can't take him," I told the two of them. "I can sense he will betray us as soon as he gets the chance. I'm concerned that he already knows too much as is."

Basil shrugged, looking uncomfortable. I could tell he wanted to defend one of his people, but he also didn't really know the kid and didn't want to disagree with me so soon after joining my legion.

"I will take him back to Perama tonight," I told the two of them. "Will everyone else understand?"

Basil thought about it and then replied, "Yeah, they should be fine. Like I said, he just joined us and not many really know him at all."

"Okay, great. I know this is hard for you, but we have to be careful."

I finished with the rest of the group, telling Decimus that we would need to talk privately after I was done with the others. The kid looked nervous and I could see him eyeing the door as he waited, but I kept my eye on him until we were done and he never bolted for it.

I left my newly formed legion to rest, the excitement of the room palpable as I escorted Constans and Decimus outside. I told Constans to head back to the inn and I led Decimus toward the water.

"Listen," I told him. "I don't fault you for who you are, but you are not right for what I am forming here."

"What?" Decimus said, immediately getting angry. "I'm just as good as everyone else in that room. Better than them! Why are you rejecting me? I don't want to go back to that shithole of a bridge!"

I could tell the kid was genuinely hurt, but not in a self-reflective way. He was blaming me and getting angry at me, not trying to understand why he might not have been selected on his own.

"You have a choice," I told him, cutting him off. "You can sign a new contract with me and you go back to Perama or I can leave you here in Sycae if you want, but you must sign the contract. Or if you don't, I will kill you."

My statement hung in the air before us, his anger evaporating in sudden fear. I felt bad for bullying what was basically a child, but I couldn't afford for him to betray us. I was either going to wrap him up in a contract he could never break or I was going to have to kill him, as distasteful as that was for me to do.

"How dare—" he started to say, but I grabbed his arm and yanked it above his head, lifting him off the ground. He dangled, trying to break free of my grasp, but he was like a small puppy compared to me and my strength.

I formed the contract and put it in front of him. "This contract states that you will never be able to communicate what you learned about me or my operations. Till your death and beyond. You will not be able to conspire against us. You will not be able to even contemplate ways to seek revenge against us. You will, in fact, forget everything you know about me and the group of kids that just joined my legion, Constans, and anything else you learned since you were recruited to come here. Do you understand?"

The boy had tired himself out trying to break free of my grasp and stared sullenly at me as I held him above the ground.

"I don't enjoy doing this," I told him, "but I can tell you were planning to betray us, even as you swore loyalty to me. You are lucky I don't just kill you immediately and be done with you. This contract will give you a chance to live, at least."

The boy tried to squirm free one more time but then slumped in defeat. "I want to live here at least," he muttered, looking away from me. "Don't make me go back to the bridge."

I put him down. "Listen, I understand some of what you have probably been through. I know it's hard to trust and that sometimes your mind thinks about betrayal because that is what you are used to, right?"

He stared sullenly at me, refusing to answer.

"I'll tell you what," I said. "I will add a provision to the contract that if you ever learn to trust and will truly never betray us, your memory will be restored and you can come find me and I will give you another shot at joining us, okay?"

"So, what? If I just become a little lickspittle like the others I can be a part of your merry little band?"

I laughed softly at his descriptions of the group. "Yes, that is it exactly. I'm pretty sure these contracts are very flexible and powerful. So I will add a provision that if you truly change, you will remember us and can find me. Maybe you won't join the legion, but I'm sure I could find a use for you. But if that never happens, you will never be able to betray us or remember anything of this time. Understand?"

"Yeah, I get it," the boy said, not meeting my eyes.

"To show you I truly don't mean you any harm . . ." I took out some currency and gave him enough to survive here in Sycae for several weeks. "This is for you. You won't remember where you got it, but if you are careful, it should help you find a way to survive over here."

He hastily grabbed the orbs and coins, eyeing me skeptically, but he was a little less sullen after he had the currency in his hands.

"Now, sign the contract. I don't want things to get messy."

He nodded and I watched as he signed the magical document in front of him. Once he did, his eyes grew dull. I could practically see the memories being locked away in his mind. I knew my evolution was powerful, but this was something else. It was borderline scary what the contract could do to a person.

I backed away so he wouldn't grow confused at seeing me and left him there on the docks, hoping someday he would find his way.

Chapter 33

The next morning, I kept Constans back from her schooling since I would need her help for the day. I gave her my amulet that let her see in the dark and a bunch of ammunition I had been crafting for her. She squealed in excitement at receiving her first magical item and more bullets, something she had been forced to carefully recover after every fight while I was gone.

"I need to start several projects today. I'm going to send you to take care of a few of them," I told her. "For this morning, find me another warehouse near where our legion is staying. Find the most secure one you can get. Location and security are more important than price. After that, come back here and we will meet up and head over to Perama for a bit. Sound good?"

She nodded with a serious look on her face.

"Great," I said, smiling at her. "Let's get to it!"

She ran off and I followed in the same direction at a slower pace. Once I was near the water, I dashed upward and shot over the channel to the other side of the city with ease. Once there, I found my way back to the passageway to the underdark, just to make sure I could find it again, and then I began scouting the abandoned warehouses all along the docks for materials that I would need. As I worked, I marked everything of interest in my mental map of the city. I also looted some more iron and some fine wood and then put my nanobots to work crafting more bullets and more revolvers in my backpack.

As the noon hour approached, I made my way back to Sycae and waited for Constans in the inn. She returned a couple of hours later. She ordered lunch, and once it was delivered, she began eating like she was seconds away from starving to death. It was almost comforting to see how little she had changed while I was gone. Once she was finished, she updated me on her day's progress.

"Got us the warehouse," she said, "but it cost a fair amount of orbs. Ownership is signed in our names and registered. Do you want to check over everything?"

"No," I said, not wanting to get into the nitty-gritty of how people bought property in a city that was dying. "I trust you. Let's go see the warehouse."

She quickly ate the last few crumbs from her plate before jumping up and leading me back to the waterfront. There, she took us to another warehouse that was kitty-corner to the one our legion was staying in. It had one entrance made of two doors wide enough for a large wagon to pass through. There were no windows or other entrances.

Inside, there were shelves everywhere and the blue glow of magical lighting. A basement held more room below, and thankfully no dungeon had formed in it. The warehouse must have once been used to store valuable goods, because it was very secure.

"Perfect," I told Constans after our tour. "Great job as usual."

There was a large wooden bar that could be lowered behind the two doors to stop them from being opened. I asked Constans to organize a guard of the warehouse with Basil to make sure two of our legionnaires slept inside and kept the door locked unless one of us was entering.

After that, we made our way over to Perama. Our first stop was the bar where I had met Nikephoros, the veteran adventurer and former legionnaire. He wasn't there, but the bartender Mehmet said he would let him know I was looking for him when he showed up that evening. After that, we visited Momma Lena, who was yet again surprised to find I was still alive and kicking.

"And you have little Constans all cleaned up, I see," she told me, giving Constans a hug. I saw Constans blush as she returned the hug.

"She's been a great help to me," I told Momma Lena.

"Yeah!" Constans said. "I am a merchant now and I'm making all kinds of money over in Sycae and organizing—"

"Okay, okay," I said, cutting her off. "No need to go into the details, right?"

"Oh, right," she said, reining herself in a bit. "Sorry, got excited!"

I laughed. "Sorry," I told Momma Lena, "just a lot of stuff we are working on."

"Are you keeping her safe and treating her okay? 'Cause if not, I will hear about it, you know."

I put my hand on my heart. "She is becoming something like a little sister to me," I said, surprised by how true it was. "I'm trying my best to help her grow into the dangerous and powerful adult I think she will be."

Constans definitely blushed at that and swatted at me, hitting me lightly on the arm.

"Good," Momma Lena said, smiling at Constans in a motherly way. "So what can I do for you, then?"

"Can someone get a second basic class and level it to try to evolve it? For instance, I leveled and evolved my *Warrior* class already, but I have an idea for another *Warrior* class I want to evolve. Is that possible?"

"You've already leveled and evolved your *Warrior* class?" Momma Lena said, shocked. "I thought you were focusing on your *Archer* class!" She looked between me and Constans, seemingly concerned about what we were really getting up to. After a moment of staring at us, she finally responded. "But yes, if someone is crazy enough to waste the experience and money to buy a class again, you can level it all over again and potentially evolve it. But you know how rare it is that anyone can level a class that high, let alone get an evolution, right?"

"Oh, I know," I said. "It's rare for most people these days. So if I buy a *Warrior* class from you, I can level it again and potentially evolve it?"

"Yes," she said, "but you don't get the attributes a second time or the skills from the base class. You can only get those once. So you would be leveling it all the way to twenty and gain nothing from it."

"Understood. Thank you, Momma Lena," I told her. "Constans, can you buy us a *Warrior* class? Bargain for the best deal you can get."

I smiled over at Momma Lena and she looked at Constans with a slight grimace.

"You're a monster," Momma Lena told me, realizing I was using Constans's *Merchant* class against her.

"Just helping her get experience," I replied with a cheeky grin.

The two of them bargained and we left the shop with a *Warrior* class book for me and some experience for Constans. I also gave her the majority of my coin and orbs, saving just a bit for personal spending money. I told her she was in charge of the legion's finances now. It would help her get experience, and she was proving to be deft at it.

Next, we made our way to the docks, where she introduced me to a few of the fishermen that weren't working out on the boats. I asked around about larger sailing ships and got some useful information. One of the oldest men that we talked to had been the second mate on a merchant ship and he gave us plenty of practical advice. He was wrinkled and deeply tanned, as if he had spent his life on the open sea under the Mediterranean sun. He was well into his later years but still spry and sharp-witted. He went by the name Theo, short for Theodosius.

"The biggest problem you'd have finding a workable ship these days is rot," he told us. "These old boats needed work every few years because the bottoms would rot away. Anything you found sitting in the water would be useless now, barely able to leave dock, if you ask me. You'd need to find something in dry dock if you wanted a real ship worth sailing anymore, and the chances of that are slim to none."

I was aware, intellectually, of the various writings and information from my Earth about ships of this era, but I hadn't connected it to how problems like rot and years of sitting idle in dock would impact my plans.

"If you wanted to try to find a ship in dry dock, where would you go? Did the empire have a place that they made their ships, back before everything fell apart?"

"Welllllll," he said, drawing out the word and looking out to the water nearby. "Your best bet would be Thessaloniki, if you could get that far. It was where many of our best ships were coming from, there at the end. Or if you could go further, some of the city-states like Venice or Genoa, which were famous for their ships. You might get lucky and find something there, but I hear it's all lost to the wild these days."

I knew where those cities were since they had been major cities in my world as well. The only issue was that they were a fair distance away, but I could reach them now that I had learned how to safely travel outside of Nova Roma. I wasn't sure about bringing a crew through the wilds, though, and then trusting them to man a ship and bring it back here.

"What about building a ship?" I asked. "Is that even possible anymore?"

"Not around these parts," Theo replied definitively. "Unless you got fine, aged lumber hidden around here I ain't seen. And the skills are long gone. Nobody with a ship-building class been seen in the city for a generation, I'd say."

"Hmm," I replied, thinking. "What about repairing a ship that has rot? If I found one of those, do you know anyone that could fix it?"

He sucked his teeth, considering what I was asking. "I don't know about that. I guess it would depend on the damage and if you had the proper lumber. It might be possible for some carpenters to make it work. I don't know. Would cost you a pretty penny, and I'd wager high that the Emperor would have something to say about seeing you repairing a ship here in Sycae. You gotta watch out for him and his cronies."

We talked a bit more and I thanked him for his information. He was happy to talk and I enjoyed picking his brain about some of my ideas. He didn't seem surprised or doubtful about what I was asking, seemingly content to just chat with us and consider the questions I asked him.

After that was over, Constans and I retired to the bar, where we found Nikephoros sipping a drink at one of the tables. I ordered another round and we joined him.

"We spoke before, yeah?" he said as I sat down with Constans and slid another mug in front of him.

"Yeah," I replied. "You helped me learn a bit about dungeons and hunting in the city. I appreciate the information you shared. It helped me survive out there."

"Mmm," he replied, unmoved by my thanks.

"I have a proposal for you," I told him after an awkward moment passed, "if you are interested in some work."

"What kinda work? I'm not going back to the adventuring life, if that's what you're after. That's a young man's game."

"No," I said, "nothing like that. But I have a group of young men and women that need training. I heard you used to be in the legion, and I wanted to see if you were interested in training up a group of people for me. I'd pay well."

He eyed me skeptically, clearly thinking I was disturbed in some way, but after a moment of consideration, he replied, "What's the pay?"

"Constans here will work out a salary for you," I told him, "but it will be fair and include room and board over in Sycae. We would need you to travel a bit, so we could train in private, but you would not need to fight if we encountered any problems. We would protect you. You would also be expected to remain silent about what you learn about us, even if you leave our employment."

"I'm not worried about needing protection," he said, "but I want to know my pay and how long you'd be hiring me for."

"We'll start with six months," I told him, "and if I like your work and you want to continue with us, we can renew for longer the next time. Constans and you can discuss the salary."

I let her talk to him about the details, surprised by how capable she was even when dealing with an old veteran like Nikephoros. She also knew him, which might have intimidated her, but instead, it just gave her ammunition; she pointed out what a layabout he had become and how he was always grumbling about how soft the youngsters were these days. I had to look away to hide my smile as she laid into him.

Afterward, he shook her hand, looking almost embarrassed by how she had called him out, and she turned to me with a serious look on her face.

"He agrees," she said, a mischievous smile peeking through her serious expression when she caught my eye.

"That is wonderful," I told him. "I have a skill that will capture our agreement. Please review what you see and let me know if you have any questions."

I summoned the contract between us, making sure to include the portion about him remaining silent even if he left our employment.

Nikephoros reviewed the contract and signed with a grunt. "Now what?" he said, finishing off the drink I had bought for him.

"You need to gather anything before we go to Sycae? We can come back for you tomorrow if you need some time."

"Achh, no," he said. "Sold everything I own a long time ago. What you see is what you get."

He looked at me as if daring me to take back our deal, but I just nodded politely.

"Perfect, then," I said. "Let's get going."

I let Constans guide us through Perama, Nikephoros following steadily despite having a few drinks in him already. I dashed us across the water—Nikephoros did not enjoy the experience in the slightest—and then put him up in the same inn as us and let the innkeeper know food and two drinks a night were on me.

I gave Constans some orders for the next day, primarily to get Nikephoros cleaned up and get him some new clothes. She had already purchased new clothes for the others when she recruited them, so I told her to just get some more of those so everyone looked similar for now. We didn't quite have a uniform yet, although I hoped to change that at some point. After that, I left Constans at the inn and went out just as the sun was setting.

I had a few more things to do and wasn't feeling tired, so I went north and convinced the guards to let me out of the city before night fell completely. I could tell they thought I was going to get myself killed, but they didn't protest too much when I insisted.

Once clear of the city, I pulled the *Warrior* book from my backpack and learned the class for the second time.

Class reset: Warrior. Your Warrior class is now at level 0.

I kept my *Spirit Breaker* class active, wanting to get it to level 10, but left my *Gunslinger* and *Duelist* classes inactive. Once I learned the class, I sensed around me for the nearest monsters and began to hunt.

The night was cold but clear, the moon above giving plenty of light. My enhanced vision made it seem like the middle of a sunny day to my eyes, especially after months of hunting in absolute darkness underground. My ability to detect monsters made it easy to hunt, and unlike in the city, there weren't so many monsters out here that I could get swarmed and overwhelmed. It was actually easier to kill monsters outside of the city, even if they were stronger, because they mostly kept to themselves. I was able to pick my prey and track it down easily, ambushing it and killing it with either my revolver or my sword with relative ease.

I spent the night hunting and harvesting all of the monsters near the city. I didn't try to be fancy with my hunting or push myself or test my skill. I went on a purely utilitarian hunting spree, killing anything and everything I could find in the most efficient way possible. Using my revolver while stealthed, I managed to kill most of the lesser monsters I encountered. If anything could survive my opening salvo, I followed up with my sword and fought the monster long enough for my attributes to soar with *If It's a Fight You Want, It's a Fight You'll Get* and *Leeching Strike*, with a few grenades or shots from my reloaded revolver as needed.

By the end of the night, I had a pile of monster corpses stashed in a building near the city gate and had leveled my *Warrior* class back up to level 1. It still struck me as notable how little experience the general monsters gave, even the larger ones outside the city. The system pretty heavily favored clearing dungeons and completing quests, it seemed to me. And most people didn't even know how to do that anymore, leaving the slow grind of killing monsters as their only way to level.

As the sun rose, I returned to the city. I found Constans before she could start on getting Nikephoros all cleaned up.

"Can you hire me a wagon for the day? And run and tell Basil to bring everyone to meet me here?"

"Sure!" she said, grabbing the breakfast pastry she had been eating off her plate and running off to do what I asked. I shook my head, as disgusted as I was amused by her obsession with food.

"Oh, and buy several large tarps or blankets for me!" I yelled after her. She threw her hand in the air in acknowledgment as she raced down the street.

I waited at the inn until Basil showed up with the other legionnaires. Constans returned with them to let me know she just ended up buying the biggest wagon outright, not seeing the point of renting anything when we might use it again. The only issue was that nobody in Sycae had livestock or draft animals for pulling wagons; most of the work was done by laborers around the city. Only the richest merchants had horses to pull their wagons, and those were all loaned to them by the army and could only be used for trading with the other enclaves.

I led Basil and the legion to collect the wagon. It was a monster of a wagon, bigger than the ones used by the dark elves, as if it had once been used to haul lumber to the city. It would work perfectly. I got in front of the wagon and placed the harness around my neck. With a surge of strength, I easily got the wagon moving. Basil and several of the others jumped in to help me by pushing the wagon, but I felt little actual strain from the work; my attributes and my *Ant's Strength* perk made it more than easy.

We drew quite a lot of eyes as we made our way through the city. The sight of me pulling the wagon was only part of it. The other part, I noticed, was the number of people with me. Not many people traveled in groups as large as ours, unless they were up to no good or protecting a rich merchant. I heard a number of people speculating on who we were and what we were up to. I should have considered the attention we would draw by traveling in such a large group and had some of the legionnaires stay at the inn and travel separately. It was too late now, but hopefully nobody in power would bother to investigate what we were up to.

After a tense exchange with the gate guards, we were allowed outside the city. The young men and women around me whispered excitedly among themselves, staring at the ruined buildings and streets that filled the area. The guards watched us as we pulled away from the gate, clearly convinced we were all insane but not concerned enough to try to stop us.

Outside the city, I pulled the wagon over to the remnants of a house I had stashed the monsters' corpses in the night before. I gestured for Basil to come over.

"Inside here are a number of corpses we need to bring back to the city. Can you get your people to load everything up and then cover it with the blankets Constans bought for us?"

"Yes, sir!"

I let him give the orders, wanting everyone to get used to seeing him in charge. The men and women worked quickly, only complaining slightly about the blood and smell coming from the bodies of the monsters. Once everything was loaded up, we pulled the covered wagon back into the city, the guards now staring at us in shock. My legionnaires smirked back proudly, holding their heads high. We took a few of the less popular roads down to the docks and then pulled the wagon into the new, secure warehouse Constans had bought for us.

I had Basil get everyone to carry the corpses down into the basement and pile them on the floor. There was plenty of room, although little fresh air, but it would serve the purpose for what I had in mind.

"What do you need all this for?" Basil asked me after we finished.

"I need the raw materials to start working on some projects for us," I told him, not willing to go into details. He just stared at the pile of monsters and shook his head, already resigned to putting up with my strangeness, which I thought was a good sign for our future together.

I instructed Basil to have the others clean up the blood while I sent Constans off to get Nikephoros squared away.

I separated the monsters into three piles spaced around the basement. Once I had three equal-sized piles, I injected some custom nanobots into each one, something I had been designing as I traveled back from the dark elf city. Each nanobot sacrificed diversity for production speed, something I couldn't do with my other nanobots without sacrificing too much utility. These nanobots only had two functions: reproduce and craft the very specific blueprints I had programmed into them. I left them in each pile to begin consuming the resources so they could mass-produce themselves.

I could have used any material for them to consume, but monsters were actually the only truly abundant resource in the city these days. If I were to buy enough metal or wood for my nanobots to consume, I would quickly bankrupt myself and deny the city a much-needed resource for people's survival. Monsters, while inconvenient to kill, both fueled my nanobots and gave me experience, so they were the ideal resource for now. Of course, my nanobots would rapidly burn through the piles of corpses, so I would have to spend a significant amount of my time hunting for more, which would be quite time-consuming. Hopefully I could get Basil and the others to do some of it once I was confident they wouldn't get themselves killed.

Back upstairs, I told everyone to stay out of the basement for now and to finish cleaning up here and then wait for me to return. I left them to it while I went and found Constans and a cleaned-up Nikephoros and led them back to the warehouse. Nikephoros grumbled as we walked, complaining under his breath about the mandatory bath and clean clothes. I politely ignored him, while Constans poked him every time his complaints got a bit too loud.

"Everyone," I said, getting the young men and women's attention as we closed the warehouse doors behind us. "This is Nikephoros. He used to be a legionnaire. I've hired him to start training you. He is only with us for a short time, but as he trains you, I expect you all to respect his authority. He knows the methods used to train legionnaires in the army, and you all will benefit from his training."

Everyone perked up, looking at Nikephoros with interest.

"Nikephoros," I said, turning to him. "Basil here is the centurion for what will become our legion. You will act as prefect. Train them however you see fit, and Constans will get anything you need. Don't worry about weapons for now. I'm working on those. The main thing I want you to focus on is training them to work as a unit and learn the discipline that distinguished the legion from the rest of the world."

I could tell he thought I was crazy, a recurring theme for the day, apparently, but he didn't say anything. I left him standing awkwardly in front of the eager young legionnaires, looking a bit lost on what to do first, but I took Constans and left, closing the doors behind us. Before we got more than a couple of steps, I heard him start yelling orders.

"Sounds like he remembers what to do just fine," I told Constans as she looked behind us in concern. "Constans, find me some work benches, stools, a few desks, and anything you can think would be needed in a workshop. Paper, blank books, things to write with, stuff like that. The only thing I won't need is tools. Don't worry about those. I'm going to turn this warehouse into my work area. Have them delivered here, if possible, but don't let anyone inside that isn't a part of our organization."

"Got it!"

Once she took off, I dashed back over the water and began collecting all of the resources I had marked the other day and what I had found so long ago in some of the warehouses near the ancient harbors. I made trip after trip, ushering it all back over to the new warehouse. I considered having Basil and his team help, but trying to get everything back over to Sycae by boat would be more trouble than it was worth. With my *Ant's Strength* perk, I could carry a significant amount of weight and still use *Trickster's Dash* to get me across the water, so it was faster for me to do it by myself.

Even with my speed and the amount I could carry, it took me several days to transfer everything to the warehouse. During that time, I sent Constans back to her tutoring and training and ignored Nikephoros, who clearly felt none of the teenagers were in good enough shape to serve as proper legionnaires. I did not envy them, considering the workout he was giving them. Their once-eager smiles had significantly dimmed, but none of them slacked off or dragged their feet. Every time I stopped in with another load of goods, they were doing some exercise or another while he yelled at them to push themselves harder. The yelling was interspersed with lectures about how important your body was for magnifying the attributes you received from your classes.

I filled my workshop with the goods I had salvaged, organizing everything onto shelves I had dragged down into the basement. My three piles of nanobots were progressing well, slowly consuming the raw materials they would use to reproduce themselves. The smell was revolting, but there wasn't much I could do about it, so I tried my best to ignore it.

Once Constans had all my furniture and supplies delivered, I organized the basement into three separate workstations. Each group of nanobots had a workbench next to it, and I placed the iron that I had salvaged around each station to make it easier for the nanobots to work the iron.

By the time I finished setting up the workstations and brought over the last of the goods I had found, my nanobots had finished consuming all of the monsters' bodies. I gathered the specialized nanobots together and placed each of them on its respective workstation. They would need a ton of resources for what I had planned, but I was excited about the potential of my little specialized machines.

The first group of nanobots was programmed to make *Penetration Bullets*. They would take the iron and scrap steel I had provided them, turn it into fine steel, form it into the shape of a standardized bullet, and then carve out the three runes required to make the bullet fly. It was still going to be a slow process, even with the specialized nanobots, and would take a lot of resources, but making the bullets wouldn't require my constant attention once I provided the necessary resources.

The second group of nanobots was programmed to make my revolvers, each one with a *Durability* rune on the handle to match the revolver I carried. The third group of nanobots was programmed to make nothing but *Explosive Grenades*. I would eventually have to salvage more pottery to make the grenades and more iron to form the revolvers and bullets, but for now, I should hopefully have enough to outfit my legionnaires before I ran out.

I watched as the specialized nanobots began to work, but they quickly ran out of material to consume and could no longer power themselves. I sighed and left the workshop, making my way north to the enclave's wall. It was time to hunt once again.

Several days later, I settled back into my workshop. The specialized nanobots greedily consumed the many monsters I fed them, so I began work on a separate project of my own. I gathered some of the iron and wood and settled down in a nearby chair, humming a bit as I watched my nanobots working nearby. During my time with the dark elves, I had been thinking a lot about what I wanted to do once I got back to the city. One of the projects was to design something that had more range and power than my revolver. I carefully reviewed the blueprints I had designed as I traveled through the underdark until I was sure of exactly how I wanted the design to work.

Even with months of theory-crafting, I ended up working through the night and the next day, making prototypes and reworking them over and over whenever I found an inefficiency or flaw in the design.

When I was finally done, I was exhausted but pleased with my creation. On my Earth, it would have been called a carbine. It had a pump-action lever under the barrel, which would draw from a small magazine that held the same ammunition as my revolver to avoid having to produce two different kinds of bullets. The magazine could hold twenty bullets before it had to be replaced.

The rate of fire was slower than that of the revolver, but it could still be fired just as fast or faster than a bow and significantly faster than a crossbow. A person could aim and fire, pump the lever on the bottom of the rifle to reload, and fire again within a second. With twenty deadly *Penetration Bullets* being fired every twenty to thirty seconds, each one accurate up to a thousand feet or more, my legionnaires should be able to devastate most things in this world. It was hard to imagine what could stand up to a line of properly trained legionnaires armed with such weapons. And when the first magazine ran out of bullets, it only took a matter of seconds to reload the rifle.

It was, in many ways, a savage weapon. The people of this world were used to honorable warfare, but the rifle refused to play their games. There would no longer be honorable duels or carefully orchestrated battles where the skills of the soldiers or an individual fighter won the day. I knew I was ushering in a new era, one that could be even more brutal and oppressive than the one that existed now, but I couldn't see another way that gave humanity a chance to survive. The class system favored individual strength and courage, but if people didn't step forward to do their part, the whole system fell apart. When people selfishly hoarded their classes, their skill stones, and their knowledge, the common people paid the price. Guns were the great equalizer, even though they came with their own dangers. I just had to hope the good would outweigh the bad in the long run. Maybe someday I would be cursed for introducing such weapons to the world, but as it was right now, I wasn't sure humanity was going to survive much longer. If people were still around in the future to curse me, I would take that as a success.

I grabbed twenty of my own *Penetration Bullets* and loaded a magazine, slotting it into the rifle with ease. I had used some of the cloth I had looted to make a strap from the bottom of the barrel to the stock so it could be thrown over a shoulder or across a person's chest. I also made a larger satchel that would hold several magazines on a person's belt. I primed the rifle, loading the first bullet into the chamber with a single pump of the lever, and then tossed the rifle over one shoulder. I strapped the satchel full of magazines to my belt and then looked around my workshop.

I was tired, but excitement burned in me; I was looking forward to testing out my newest creation. My nanobots had already burned through the corpses I had given them, days' worth of hunting gone overnight, but there wasn't much I could do about the enormous resource drain right now, other than go hunting once again. With my rifle over one shoulder, my revolver under my arm, and my sword on my hip, I left the warehouse to go kill some more monsters.

Chapter 34

The first monster I found was a mammoth covered in thick and deadly-looking spikes, much like a porcupine but with the tusks of an elephant. It stood half as tall as the nearby trees.

I hid in *Stealth* as far away from the creature as I could get while keeping it in sight, my rifle in my hands. I aimed and began to fire at the beast. Each bullet was followed by the satisfying sound of the pump-action lever loading another bullet. The monster spun in confusion as the first bullet struck and penetrated deep into its thick hide. Before it could find me, more bullets struck it, each one driving deep into its body, causing horrendous wounds that sprayed blood each time a bullet impacted its hide. It finally determined the direction the attacks were coming from and turned toward me, but that let me focus on its head as it tried to charge me. Soon, it was blind and stumbling, too injured to take more than a few steps in my direction. I unclipped the magazine I had been using, slapped another into the rifle, and finished the beast off as it charged forward and crashed into trees in its blind rage. With just a few more bullets, it slumped to the ground, too wounded to continue its rampage.

I tossed the rifle over my shoulder and jogged over to the monster. The *Penetration Bullets*, fired from the extended barrel of the rifle, traveled faster than those fired from my revolver because of the way the rune magnified the underlying speed of the bullet when it was fired. That meant when the bullets hit, they penetrated even deeper, all while being fired from significantly further away. Aiming was easy as well; the bullets moved so fast that I barely had to account for wind or gravity when I fired.

As I watched the mammoth slowly dying in front of me, I felt a grim satisfaction with my design. The poor mammoth hadn't stood a chance. I was confident the rifle, used for long distances, and the

470

revolver, used for anything that got too close, would be an unstoppable combination.

I dragged the mammoth's corpse behind me once I was sure it was dead, able to drag it with ease thanks to my attributes and *Ant's Strength*. I knew I made a bit of a ridiculous sight, if anyone had been there to see me. I thought I looked a bit like a toddler dragging their favorite teddy bear, except mine was a gargantuan mammoth that left behind a trail of congealing blood as I walked. I dragged it back toward the city gate, then went back to the hunt.

Days of exhausting work later, I had replenished the corpses in my basement and the nanobots went back to work. I added a fourth pile and programmed a fourth set of customized nanobots, these ones designed to produce the new rifle design.

I found Nikephoros and the legionnaires busy doing push-ups in the other warehouse, where the beds had been pushed to the side to make room for their workouts.

"I should have a new type of weapon for them in a month or two," I told him. "I'm going to be gone most of that time, stopping in to drop things off every so often, but not staying long. Keep training them until the weapons are ready."

"We're gonna need more space," he told me. "We can't properly train in formation, and their stamina is weak. We need space to stretch ourselves."

I thought for a moment. "I think there are two options. You can get Constans to buy more boats and you all can go over to the city every day to train. That would let you practice formations in an empty part of the city and they could learn to fight the monsters there as a group. That could be helpful.

"You could also go north of the city. I have killed most of the nearby monsters, so it should be safe to be out there if you stick close to the walls. The guards might wonder what you are doing, but hopefully nobody will object too much. That should give you room to practice."

Nikephoros grunted at me and looked thoughtful. "We need weapons. I know you said you can supply them in a month or two, but to train as a group, they need to fight together."

"Sure," I said. "Talk to Constans. She can get them some better weapons."

471

They had a hodgepodge of weapons from their time as a gang and what Constans had bought them when they went scavenging with her while I was gone, but they could use more professional weapons if they were going to be picking fights more regularly across the water.

Satisfied with what I'd told him, Nikephoros grunted again and turned back to the legionnaires. I gave the exhausted-looking men and women a hearty wave and then left them to their workouts.

When I found Constans later that night, I told her to join the legionnaires while I was gone. She could use the training and it would help her form a stronger bond with everyone. She groaned theatrically at the order but agreed.

The next day, I packed up my gear and bought some supplies to supplement any hunting I might need to do, replacing one of my lost canteens and stocking up on nonperishable goods. Then I set out for the north of the city once again.

Before I could reach the gate, a person covered head to toe in a large robe flagged me down. The person had a thick hood over their head and I immediately tensed, worried it was a priest here to attack me. I paused, reaching for my revolver, but when the person didn't act aggressively, I walked closer, curious what was going on.

When I got close, the person looked up at me from within their hood, and I saw it was Ryld, out during the daytime.

"Alexander," he said, deadpan, by way of greeting.

"Ryld, it's great to see you," I replied, surprised to see him. "How is resettling going?"

"It's going well," he said. "We have not encountered any monsters that we couldn't handle, and work on dwellings for us all is progressing rapidly."

"I'm glad to hear that. What brings you up here?"

The sun was clearly making him uncomfortable, his pale eyes narrowing in pain even under the heavy hood that covered his head.

"We have found all the entrances to the underdark around your city and wanted to give you this so you can find your way," he said, handing me a rolled-up scroll.

I took the scroll and unrolled it, seeing a simple map of the city with markings denoting the location of all the underdark passages.

472

I saw several in the main part of the city, one in Sycae, one in the palace, and several outside of the city proper, but they were near enough they could be used in an emergency. Next to each entrance was a brief description in Latin on how to find the dark elf city from that particular entrance.

"This is very helpful, thank you," I told him, rolling up the scroll.

He nodded in reply. "Find us if you need us," he said before turning and walking away.

I watched him leave, bemused by his stoic hello and goodbye.

After he was gone, I memorized the map and then sent my nanobots to destroy it to prevent anyone from ever finding the passageways. As my nanobots began to break down the map, I continued on my way out of the city. I had already killed most of the nearby monsters, and unlike in the city, once a monster's territory was cleared out here, it took some time for new monsters to venture into the region. That meant I had to travel further and further to find things to hunt, and it took even longer to drag the bodies back to the city. It was an annoying chore, but it was necessary for producing the rifles and other weapons my legionnaires would need. As I trekked north, though, I vowed to figure out a better setup someday.

A dirty month and a half followed, until I had built up such a glut of monsters' bodies in the basement of my warehouse that I could finally spare some time to go handle another project of mine. The legionnaires had also started collecting the bodies of the lesser monsters they killed in the city, dragging them back to Sycae by boat, which helped supplement the demands of my nanobots somewhat. Nobody knew why I was still piling up so many corpses in the basement or where they all kept disappearing to, but none of them objected to the chore of gathering them for me. I left Constans in charge of the basement, making clear that she was to keep everyone away from the workstations at all costs.

Finally free to pursue my next goal, I left the city once more, eagerly dashing west, away from the city. I traveled quickly, following the coast toward where Greece would be on my world. I hugged the coast, stopping in every harbor to look for a ship of some kind that wasn't completely ruined. The coast was full of beautiful natural harbors and picturesque cities and towns ruined by the infestation of monsters that had moved into each of them.

It wasn't until over a week later that I reached a city named Heraclea, where I found a harbor that had ships floating in it. I had found an old Roman road that ran along the coast and followed it to the city. Spotting the harbor from a nearby hill, I was excited to see several ships still bobbing in the waves that lapped against the stone docks. The ships floated low in the water and seemed to be in poor repair, but after a week of empty harbor after empty harbor, I felt a surge of hope that one of these would work for what I had in mind.

When I got closer to the city itself, I was shocked to see that the entire city had been destroyed. It looked like some natural disaster had struck the city, destroying every structure in sight, scattering the stone and wood around the area haphazardly, and leaving almost nothing standing. Extensive stone docks lined the waterfront, one of the only things still in one piece for as far as I could see.

As I stopped to take in the scope of the damage to the city, I realized the city hadn't been struck by a natural disaster. What I had originally taken to be a small hill in the middle of the city was, in fact, the monster that had caused so much destruction.

Regional quest discovered: Giant Problems Require Giant Solutions.

You have discovered a regional quest. Complete this quest to receive additional rewards. Quest requirements: You must kill Mitkos the Giant King to save the city from his wrath. Reward: +3 to an attribute of your choice, 2500 experience, the achievement Giant Killer, King Killer.

Mitkos the Giant King? That seemed . . . dangerous.

The giant slept in the middle of the ruined city. He slept like a toddler, splayed out on his back with his arms stretched wide, as if he didn't have a care in the world. He was significantly larger than other giants I had seen, at least thirty feet high and as wide as a school bus from shoulder to shoulder. He also glowed with a faint purple light.

I sighed in frustration. Could I risk fighting a purple monster? A purple monster with a name like Mitkos the Giant King? But if I didn't, I might not find another usable ship for weeks—possibly months—and I had already wasted too much time hunting just to keep my nanobots fed. I couldn't afford to waste months searching for a ship in a safer area.

I planned to have my nanobots work to repair one of the ships, if they weren't too badly damaged. I couldn't risk sneaking aboard one of them and hoping to avoid the monster's attention, though, because the nanobots would require time to work. I would have to kill him if I wanted to use one of the ships here.

And once again, I felt the draw of rewards urging me to complete the quest. If I did want to kill the monster, now while it slept would be the ideal time to try. And chances were, if things went sour, I could escape with my *Dash* . . .

I knew I was finding reasons to justify a risky decision, but at the end of the day, I couldn't afford to pass up the ships here. I would need to kill Mitkos the Giant King.

I scouted around the ruined city to get the lay of the land. The city had originally been built on a stretch of flat land between the coast and the rolling hills further inland. It was once a large, sprawling city, but now it was nothing but a sprawling mess of loose wood and stone scattered everywhere.

When I felt as prepared as I was going to get, I approached the sleeping giant under the cover of *Stealth.* When I got close enough to really look at the giant, I realized I might have underestimated the size of the monster. He was definitely over thirty feet tall, but that didn't properly capture how substantial the creature was. He was thick . . . everywhere. His arms were long, stretching nearly to his knees and bulging with so much muscle it looked like the arms of a gorilla had been attached to a man. His chest was thicker than I was tall, and his legs were as thick as a house. Thankfully, he wore a crude loincloth, because I did not want to know the size of what was underneath it.

Whereas the other giants I had seen often carried an uprooted tree to use as a weapon, resting next to Mitkos was a dull gray pillar of pure metal, twenty feet tall and as thick as the giant's arm. It was carved with numerous runes I couldn't decipher. None looked to be human, but all of them glowed with power. I had no doubt that after a single hit from his weapon, my *Regeneration* would have nothing but paste to work with.

At the sight of his weapon, I really considered just leaving, but I shook my head and stepped closer to the sleeping giant instead. When I got close enough that I could spit on the giant, I reached into my grenade pouch and withdrew all of my *Explosive Grenades*. I had over thirty, each one capable of killing most normal monsters on their own and doing significant damage to even the most powerful ones. With both hands full of grenades, I aimed carefully and tossed the entire bunch into the open mouth of the giant. I paused for only a second, making sure every single one of them landed inside his mouth before dashing backward and putting as much distance between me and the giant as I could. I couldn't use my *Duel Me* skill this way, which I regretted, but it was more important to kill the giant and complete the quest rather than alert him to my presence by using the skill. Too many monsters seemed to be able to detect when I used *Duel Me* on them, so I shouldn't risk it on such a dangerous fight.

A moment later, a muffled explosion rang out behind me. I turned to see if my grenades had managed to kill the giant, but sadly, he was lurching to his feet, still very much alive. My grenades had managed to do some damage to the monster; his lower jaw and part of his throat were torn out, blood and gore dripping down his chest as he rose from the ground. The grisly remains of a massive tongue lolled down from his mostly jawless face as he turned and spotted me instantly. He roared. The sound was muted from his injuries but still powerful enough to spray spittle and blood twenty feet or more into the air in front of him.

As the giant pushed himself upward with one of his arms, he reached back and grasped his weapon, using it to help him stand. I dashed backward again, putting hundreds of feet between the two of us, then swung my rifle off my shoulder and began to fire at his eyes and face. My aim was perfect, my bullets punching large holes in his eyes. Clear liquid spilled from them, joining the rest of the mess that was his face. He finished standing and began to run toward me, his lumbering steps shaking the ground I was standing on even from hundreds of feet away.

I continued to fire bullet after bullet into his eyes until there was no way the giant should have been able to see any longer. I dashed out of the line of the monster's charge and waited, seeing if he would change course and pursue me, but he continued forward, unable to tell that I had moved.

Sighing in relief, I began to pepper the giant with bullets, dashing to a new location when he finally realized I wasn't in front of him any longer. He eventually slowed and turned himself around to charge toward my new location. The giant was a powerhouse—there was no doubt about that—but his greatest weakness was his vulnerability to ranged attacks and just how massive he was. He couldn't change directions easily and he had no way to close with me. This allowed me to continually dash around and fire bullet after bullet into him.

I burned through almost every single bullet I had on me, including my more esoteric bullets like my *Light Bullets* and *Darkness Bullets*, using them just for their penetrating power rather than their light or dark effects. Finally, over an hour of steady firing later, the monster succumbed to his injuries, toppling forward and landing on the ground with a resounding crash.

Congratulations, you have completed Giant Problems Require Giant Solutions. You have been rewarded with +3 to an attribute of your choice, 2500 experience, and the achievement Giant Killer, King Killer.

Giant Killer, King Killer: For killing Mitkos the Giant King, you have been rewarded. You receive +5 to strength and +5 to endurance.

The experience was enough to level my *Spirit Breaker* class to level 10. As soon as I got the notification of it reaching that level, I deactivated the class, funneling the rest of the experience into my *Warrior* class, which had reached level 8. My *Dark Elf Stalker* class had also leveled, reaching level 9 from the experience I received for "hunting" Mitkos and all the hunting I had been doing back in Nova Roma.

Congratulations, you have received enough experience to level your Spirit Breaker class. You are now level 10. You may now bind a second spirit to your service.

I immediately put my +3 attributes from completing the quest into willpower, bringing it up to nine after I received +2 to willpower and +1 to endurance for the *Spirit Breaker* levels. Then I focused on the spirit rising from the corpse of Mitkos the Giant

King. With my willpower now at nine, I reached out to the spirit of Mitkos and formed a connection with the king.

I could immediately sense what a stubborn will the king had. His mind wasn't the quickest, but what he lacked in intelligence he made up for with pure bullheadedness. I set my will against the spirit, forcing it to concede to me. It was like trying to break down a wall with a plastic straw, yet the king's will couldn't do anything more than stubbornly resist me. It never pushed back, affording me the time to slowly wear it down bit by bit. Time had no meaning there, but my will was implacable. I refused to give up. Slowly, centimeter by centimeter, I wore down his will with my own. Gradually, painfully, slowly, the king's will began to give in. I didn't rush. I didn't let up. I just kept slowly wearing him down until I, finally, found myself in control of Mitkos the Giant King's spirit.

I came back to myself slowly. In front of me towered the king of the giants in all his glory, restored to his original form. It was dark out by the time I finished subduing his spirit, but his presence above me blocked the night sky completely. I instinctively stepped back at the sight of the gargantuan giant staring down at me, but I sensed no malice or danger from him. He was simply staring down at me, not even mild curiosity filling his mind.

I took several large steps back to get a better perspective on the king. He held his weapon in one hand, its runes glowing a vibrant blue and orange in the dark night. I could already feel the drain of such a powerful monster on my willpower. After having him summoned for less than a minute, I already felt more tired than I had from the entire fight to kill him. With a thought, I pulled at his spirit, willing it back inside me. The king slowly turned into an ephemeral golden energy and then spiraled down into my chest.

The sensation of having the spirit inside me was strange, but not unpleasant, almost like I had consumed a very filling meal just moments before. I felt slightly stretched thin, as if his spirit couldn't quite comfortably fit inside of my own, but having Mitkos on my side was worth any amount of mild discomfort.

I looked over at the corpse of the monster and saw that it no longer glowed purple, yet I hadn't been able to collect a purple core from the body. Maybe the act of taking its spirit made it impossible to collect its core as well. My phase beast hadn't glowed, so I hadn't had a chance to see if its corpse still produced an orb upon its death. I was a bit disappointed that I hadn't received a purple orb, which would have made me extremely wealthy, but like the slight discomfort I felt, losing the orb was a small price to pay for Mitkos.

Chapter 35

After unsummoning Mitkos, I made my way through the devastation of the city to the docks where the ships were moored. I inspected each one, finding them covered in rot, as Theo had predicted. One ship was empty of cargo, but I was surprised to find the other two had holds full of trade goods. One had rotted foodstuffs that were long past their expiration date, but the other had a variety of goods, including some metals, clothing, rugs, and other fairly useful things that had managed to hold up fairly well over the years.

I stripped down, setting my phase beast to protect me in case something tried to ambush me while I was vulnerable, and then swam under the ship with the more useful cargo in its hold. I took a close look at the rotting wood that covered the bottom of the ship, carefully inspecting the hull to determine if it was salvageable.

When I surfaced, I did some quick calculations to see how long it would take to fix the amount of rot I had seen. The wood itself was fairly easy to fix since I could cannibalize the good wood in the other two ships. My nanobots would help me strip out the rotted wood without sinking the ship and help me replace it with wood that was in better condition.

The first thing I did was create another specialized nanobot and let it feed off Mitkos's body so it could reproduce itself as rapidly as possible. Then I combed through the wreckage of the city, finding iron and even a few pieces of crude steel, which I used to craft a set of tools that would assist me with the work.

Once the tools were done, the sun had risen on a new day and I was eager for my nanobots to consume Mitkos's body. The stench wafted down to the docks every time a breeze blew through the city, threatening to make me gag. Trying to ignore it, I got to work on the two ships I wanted to cannibalize, cutting and prying apart the healthiest wood I could find. It wasn't easy work; the wood was seasoned and fit closely together, a testament to the original shipbuilders who had made the two craft. But with my strength, I was able to make quick work of it once I figured out the best process for taking apart the other ships. As I worked, I piled the good lumber on the dock in front of the ship I planned to fix, quickly accruing a large pile of good wood.

I salvaged all the usable wood I could from the two ships for the rest of the day and then ate a quick meal. Once I was finished eating, I stripped down and dove back into the water of the harbor. The process of replacing the beams of the ship while underwater was tricky, but the first thing I did was spread my nanobots along the beam I was planning to remove, having them form a net to stop water from rushing into the ship when I pulled the beam free. Covering the large beams drained me of almost all of my nanobots, but I had my phase beast scouting the waters around me constantly, protecting me from any attackers, so I felt safe enough.

Once I was confident I wouldn't sink the ship, I started slowly replacing the beams. I ripped the rotted wood out in bits and pieces with either my hands or my tools, letting it sink to the bottom of the harbor below me. Once that was done, I grabbed some of the good wood and placed it in the hole I had made, ordering my nanobots to secure it for me and making sure it fit perfectly. I had no caulk or other substance to seal the gaps between the beams, so I had my nanobots produce a similar substance. They consumed the minuscule lifeforms in the water around us to power the conversion of matter.

It was a slow process, but as the days passed, I found it to be rather enjoyable. I could hold my breath underwater without issue, so I was able to take as long as I needed to strip the old wood and replace it with new wood. As I worked, I basked in the warm summer sun, finding pleasure in the feeling of it beating down on my mostly naked body. Working on the ship almost felt like a bit of a vacation, something I had never experienced before. The area was peaceful—the other monsters had likely been scared away by Mitkos—so I was able to truly enjoy the beautiful Mediterranean weather. With my phase beast to keep watch, I found myself taking the occasional break from work, simply floating in the water near the docks or even napping on the shore, my sleep untroubled by the nightmares that often plagued me.

Finally, though, I finished with my task, having replaced much of the ship's rotten wood with clean, serviceable wood that would at least hold water for now. I wasn't done yet, though. My nanobots had finished consuming Mitkos and were ready to start their work. I gathered them up and released them into the ship, their single-minded programming going to work immediately. I had tasked them with finishing what I started: rooting out all traces of rot from the ship, generally reinforcing the beams, and patching the many areas where I hadn't done a perfect job of replacing the wood. I was proud of the work I had done, but I wasn't kidding myself. I was no shipwright and could not repair a ship so easily. But I had done enough to let my nanobots take over where I left off, and they would finish the job, hopefully making me a ship capable of sailing the sea once again.

It would take some time for the nanobots to finish, and I didn't want to just sit around and wait even though I had enjoyed my time in the harbor. I gathered all of the bullets that lay exposed on the ground where my nanobots had consumed Mitkos's body and then took to the air, flying back to the city as fast as I could.

I checked in with Constans, Basil, and Nikephoros when I returned to the city and made sure they were doing well. I also ran into Romanus and Valens, finally, as I returned to the inn that evening. I found the two of them drinking in their usual spot in the common room and happily joined them for a few drinks. We caught up and they told me about some of their adventures, which included clearing several more dungeons, apparently.

We spoke late into the night, and at one point, I told them about my plan to level *Warrior* to level 20 for the second time. They both thought I was crazy but offered to complete dungeons with me to help me get experience if I wanted. I would have refused their offer in the past, but I was starting to recognize the importance of friends and building connections with other people, so with a grateful smile, I took them up on the offer.

It felt good to be so . . . normal, if that was the right word. To be so human, if I was being honest with myself. My time hunting north of the city had reminded me of how lonely my existence had been before, and I didn't want to go back to that life.

The next day, I found Constans and invited her to go with us to complete the dungeons. After she stopped screaming at me in excitement, I gave her a list of things to buy and she ran off to buy everything as fast as she could. I shook my head, constantly surprised by her endless energy and enthusiasm, even after everything she had lived through.

The next morning, the four of us met up and took one of our boats across the water. Constans had a backpack stuffed so full she could barely carry it, but she refused to let me help by carrying some of her supplies. Romanus, Valens, and I shared a smile when she looked away. Once on the other side of the channel, we scouted out a safe place to make our home base in and then began to search for dungeons nearby.

Surprisingly, the first dungeon we found was in a closet in the very home we had chosen for our safehouse. Constans was poking around the house, digging into the nooks and crannies, when her voice suddenly cut off. I froze, recognizing something was wrong, and ran over to where I had last heard her making noise. To my shock, I found an open closet door with a pit of pure blackness indicating a dungeon.

"Romanus! Valens! We got a dungeon here and Constans fell in! Can you grab her gear for me?"

Once I made sure they were moving, I dove into the dungeon after Constans.

Inside, Constans was backed up against a wall to my left with her revolver in hand, eyeing everything around her nervously. She jerked the gun toward me as I appeared but hastily lowered it when she saw it was me.

"Finally!" she yelled. "I've been here forever!"

"No, you have not," I said, smiling at her. I checked around us and saw nothing immediately threatening. Romanus and Valens appeared next to us, popping into existence out of thin air, something my rational mind immediately struggled to accept, but I pushed past it.

"Well, it felt like forever!"

I grabbed her backpack from Romanus, emptied out all the extra weight she didn't need to be carrying, and put it in my own pack. Once that was done, I handed it to her. She eyed me suspiciously, like I had just stolen some sacred treasures from her, but she holstered her revolver and put the backpack on anyway.

I looked around and saw we were in a swamp. Stagnant and murky water surrounded us in all directions. Here and there, the occasional mound of solid ground rose out of the water. The ruins of old buildings remained on many of them. Valens had drawn his sword and was checking around the mound of earth we had appeared on, looking down into the murky water in case of a surprise attack. He had already taken watch and was checking out the surroundings. I could sense my phase beast had transitioned with me and was keeping a vigilant watch in the ground underneath me for any attackers as well.

I could also sense a number of monsters in the distance, but none were in our immediate area, which apparently didn't reassure Valens, who still thoroughly searched around us for any hidden dangers.

"We got stuck in a dungeon with a lot of traps," Romanus told me, seeing me watch Valens. "Can't sense those with our *Monster Hunter* perk. Almost cost me my life, so Valens has been relying on his *Danger Sense* as well and scouting very . . . thoroughly since then."

I shrugged, trusting Valens to do what he thought was appropriate.

"Constans, you stick in the middle of our formation and keep your revolver holstered unless you are really in danger, okay?" I said, turning to her. I expected her to complain about being told to restrain herself, but she showed her maturity once again by simply nodding and stepping forward to stand beside me and Romanus. I led the way forward, with Valens ranging forward and around us to scout with his *Danger Sense*. Romanus took up the rear, watching behind us and above in case of a surprise attack that we somehow couldn't sense. It was nice having such dedicated companions with me, even if it slowed me down.

We moved toward one of the nearest monsters, stepping carefully down from the mound of earth and into the tepid water. We moved slowly, the mud grasping at our feet every time we took a step, wary of traps or other dangers. Each time we reached a mound of earth, we stopped and rested. Constans was still young and had significantly fewer attributes than the rest of us, so we tried to be mindful of her as we traveled. She never complained and never slowed, keeping up with us with steadfast doggedness.

When we spotted the first monster, Valens and Romanus both let out a groan of distaste. In the distance was a large green slime, slowly slinking forward through the muddy water of the swamp. It was taller than us and as wide as a house, but it seemed slow and docile, at least from here.

"It will be resistant to our weapons," Valens said, eyeing the slime. "And none of us are magic users. This dungeon is going to be a pain."

Romanus agreed.

I drew my revolver and switched ammunition to my *Explosive Bullets.* I fired a single shot at the slime, the bullet piercing into the slime's body before exploding out of it, spraying scorched goo everywhere. The slime didn't make a sound but began to turn in our direction. I fired two more shots, the second one finally causing the slime to shake and then disintegrate into the swamp water beneath it.

"Not ideal," I said, "but we can make it work."

It turned out my rifle worked decently at killing the slimes, although it took five or six *Penetration Bullets* to put one down. They moved so slowly it wasn't an issue, thankfully, and I had a lot more *Penetration Bullets* than I did *Explosive Bullets.* We gave Constans a chance to hunt and kill them with me, but Romanus and Valens stayed mostly in the back since their melee weapons would only get damaged when they tried to kill the slimes.

We rested in one of the less-destroyed stone buildings we found and I kept watch while the others slept. The next morning, we shared a breakfast in companionable silence and then continued forward, killing slimes until we found the final boss of the dungeon.

It was, of course, a giant green slime. It was twice the size of the other slimes, towering over us like an apartment building made of green goo. I challenged it to a duel, in case it might give me something interesting, but the stakes were only experience. At my challenge, it began to slowly crawl toward us, so Constans and I began to shoot it in unison. The gigantic slime had some kind of regeneration ability, because our shots were doing visible damage, but it rapidly healed the wounds, seemingly unconcerned by them.

I dug out my *Explosive Bullets* again and gave some to Constans. Then I holstered my rifle, grabbed my revolver, and fired six *Explosive Bullets* into the boss, one after another. The bullets penetrated several feet before exploding, throwing chunks of slime everywhere as the fire expanded inside the boss's body. Even with me and Constans both firing *Explosive Bullets* into it, though, it seemed to be regenerating faster than we could damage it.

"Everyone step back a bit," I said. "I'm going to use something new."

They all followed my directions and I concentrated, summoning Mitkos. It took several seconds for him to appear, and I felt the drain on my mind and body immediately as he coalesced behind the slime. I heard my companions gasp at the sight of the giant king.

"What in the world?" Constans said.

Mitkos, meanwhile, had no patience for the slow-moving slime and immediately slammed his metal club down on the boss, splattering it into the ground. Surprisingly, that still didn't seem to kill the boss. It reformed around the club and began to slowly crawl up it toward Mitkos's arm. Enraged that something dared to survive his strike, Mitkos began slamming his club into the ground over and over, the slime boss getting the worst of the impact every time.

The four of us had to brace ourselves as Mitkos's attacks threatened to throw us to the ground. We hurriedly backed up even further. Mitkos gave up on slamming the slime into the ground and instead began rending and tearing the boss with his own hands, pulling it apart like putty. I started to feel the strain of keeping Mitkos summoned, my vision beginning to dim and my breath coming faster, as if I had just run for miles. I dismissed my phase beast to help me keep Mitkos active, closing my eyes to focus on maintaining the spiritual connection that allowed Mitkos to appear in the world and do my bidding.

Even the slime's regeneration couldn't keep it alive in the face of Mitkos's brutal strength. After a minute of him tearing and rending the slime into tinier and tinier pieces, it finally stopped reforming, becoming nothing but a mess of green ooze covering Mitkos's hands and body. He roared to the sky in triumph. I immediately dismissed him, feeling sick to my stomach from the drain of maintaining him for even a couple of minutes.

"That was . . . something right there," Romanus said.

"Yeah," Valens said, turning to me, "how did you manage that?"

"Got a new class," I said, trying to control my heavy breathing. "Seems pretty powerful. First time I've used that guy."

Romanus keeled over in laughter while Valens just raised an eyebrow at me. Constans was still eyeing where the giant had destroyed the slime, a look of pure awe on her face.

Congratulations, you have completed this dungeon. You have earned the following rewards: 1 gold core, 11 blue cores, 1000 experience.

Chapter 36

Once we were back in the city, we cleaned the muck of the swamp off ourselves as best as we could, and the others went to rest while I scouted for more dungeons. While the others were resting, I also took some time to dash away and scout the entrances to the underdark that Ryld had given me. I wanted to see if I could find one near a mostly intact home or a location safe enough for us to set up a more permanent base.

Luck must have been on my side, because one of the entrances to the underdark was inside an old temple that sat in a secluded part of the city. It was some distance from Perama and Sycae, and a little close to the army's enclave, but the temple was large enough to house me and my legion with ease. A thick stone wall protected the temple and the grounds around it.

Inside the temple were plenty of rooms and even a full kitchen and bath, all hidden underground in rooms carved beneath the temple. The rooms were dirty and long since unused, but they seemed serviceable enough after some spit and polish. The path leading down to the underdark was behind a stone doorway with beautiful engravings of a goddess of some kind. Whoever had worshiped at the temple must have known about the underdark, because the door seemed to be a special part of their worship. Not much else remained of the goddess, but from what little I found, I suspected she had been a dark-affiliated god that was associated with the underdark in some way.

I went back to find the others and told them about the temple. They were more than fine to move locations, so we moved our safehouse to the temple. I kept the door to the underdark closed for now, not wanting to explain the situation with the dark elves to Romanus and Valens. Since we were going to be completing dungeons anyway, it made sense to do so around the temple since it would help make the temple safer if I decided to make this a more permanent base of ours.

After we moved to the temple, we found a number of nearby dungeons and completed them without issue. We spent the nights in the temple and I kept watch, only taking a small nap every so often in the afternoon when the others were awake. After several days of completing dungeons and resting, the others were burning out and needed a break so we traveled back to Sycae. Thanks to my *Duel Me* perk, I got more out of the dungeons than the others and managed to level my *Warrior* class to level 12. I also stole some random attributes in magic power and memory and one in willpower from an especially obstinate goat-like boss that refused to stop fighting well after he should have died.

Constans reported she had reached level 8 in her *Rogue* class, which was impressive for her age. Back in Sycae, I checked in with my crafting in my workshop and saw that I had thousands of bullets, hundreds of *Explosive Grenades*, and enough revolvers to arm the legionnaires, although the rifles weren't done yet. It had taken two months of intense hunting, but I had finally made enough to equip everyone with at least a revolver.

I charged as many runes as I could with the currency I had collected from the dungeons, but I had to borrow some from Constans to finish charging everything. It cost us a fair amount, another downside to making more of the weapons for the others. It also took a painful amount of time to charge them, Constans and I working in shifts to drain our money into the ammunition until our eyes crossed.

Once everything was finished and ready for us, I told Nikephoros and Basil to organize an overnight trip north and to let everyone know we were going outside the city for something special. It took a few days to get everyone properly equipped with backpacks, canteens, blankets, food, and the other necessities for a trip out of the city. I hunted monsters to keep my nanobots working and completed a few dungeons to gather experience and get more cores for Constans. We could also use them to charge our weapons.

Once we were ready, Basil led us out of the city. The guards on the gate let us pass without a word. They had finally gotten used to us coming and going and trusted that we knew what we were doing. I dragged the wagon with us, although this time it was loaded with extra supplies and the weapons I had crafted for everyone; they were hidden under blankets so the surprise wouldn't be spoiled. Given the number of bullets and grenades in the wagon, there was probably enough explosive power that if something set it all off, people would find parts of our bodies back in Sycae.

The legionnaires fell into a marching line around the wagon once we were clear of the wall. They marched in unison, looking like professional soldiers, except for the eager gleam of their eyes when they snuck glances at the countryside as they marched past it. I told Basil to keep us going for most of the day, until we found a small hill with an old manor on top, surrounded by extensive farmland gone fallow. The manor was almost entirely intact and had a commanding view of the surrounding area.

When we arrived, Basil barked orders and had everyone scrambling to clear the manor and make sure it was safe. Once we were sure the place was safe, the legionnaires began to fortify the manor under the direction of Nikephoros, who ordered them to get to work barricading doors and windows so only the front entrance and one side door were usable.

I waited patiently near the wagon, sensing no monsters nearby, while everyone worked. Constans stood with me, happily watching the others work while she got to stand around. I let her enjoy the moment since she would be working hard soon enough.

Once everyone was done, they gathered around me and Constans.

"Great job, everyone," I said. "I'm very impressed. Thank you, Nikephoros, for your work so far. Basil, your people are living up to all of my expectations. Thank you."

They all saluted as one, slamming their fists into their chests, something Nikephoros must have taught them recently. The gesture took me by surprise, and I looked over at Nikephoros, who stared at me as if I shouldn't be surprised that he was teaching them to salute like real legionnaires.

"If we are going to do this," he told me, "we are going to do it right."

I bowed my head to him, acknowledging his good point.

"As a reward," I continued, "for all your hard work and your loyalty, you are going to be getting your first class today. All of you."

Cheers broke out around me. Nikephoros growled, clearly embarrassed by the display, but I let them celebrate. I knew it was a big moment for them all.

They eventually settled down and I ripped the blanket off the top of the wagon, exposing the revolvers and several crates full of bullets and grenades. Everyone gathered around excitedly, talking about the weapons and crates and speculating about what class they were going to get.

"I unlocked a unique class," I told them, "thanks to some technology that I invented. It's called the *Gunslinger* class."

"A unique class? No way!"

"Is that what we're gonna learn?"

"That is so cool! But what's a *Gunslinger*?"

I drew my revolver, pulled one of my bullets from my belt, and held them both up for everyone to see.

"This is a gun," I said, showing them the revolver. I held up the bullet next. "It fires these. These are called bullets. They can go faster and further than most ranged weapons, and you can fire them quicker than any bow or crossbow."

I holstered my revolver and put the bullet away, then pulled out a grenade.

"These are grenades," I said, showing everyone the round ball I held. "They explode on impact, much like a fireball or other spell."

I tossed the grenade down the hill, away from everyone, and they all turned to watch it fly through the air. It landed, sending an explosion of flame skyward. The legionnaires all ducked, staring at the flame with awe on their faces. Even Nikephoros looked impressed.

"These will be the first part of what makes you soldiers," I continued. "The second part will be this rifle I have here, although that isn't ready for you yet."

I showed them the rifle.

"The rifle will be the main weapon you use," I said. "It has great range and significant stopping power. Think of it like the old ballista of the legion, but much lighter, and you can fire twenty bolts before you have to reload."

More excited muttering broke out at my words.

"Now," I said, "the thing about these weapons is that they are dangerous to not just others but to yourselves. If you point it in the wrong direction, you can easily kill one of your friends. Your training will be focused on two things. First, safety. How to carry the weapons safely, how to use them safely, how to reload them safely. Second, accuracy. These guns do you no good if you can't hit what you aim at. You will learn to fire quickly and accurately. It will be essential to your survival.

"Your rifle will be for long distances, your revolver for if things get close to you, and your grenades for swarms of enemies that you can't kill fast enough to stop. Combined, you will form the deadliest concentration of power that this world has ever seen. And with that power, we will take back this city and secure it once again."

They roared in approval at my words, saluting me as one, their fists slamming against their chest with a thump. All of them beamed with pride at their new purpose in life.

"Constans, start handing out the revolvers. Wait on the bullets and grenades for now."

As she jumped into the wagon and began grabbing revolvers to distribute, I pulled Nikephoros aside to have a private conversation.

"Are you interested in learning this class as well?"

He hemmed and hawed a bit, but I could tell he was interested.

"I'm willing to teach it to you as well," I said. "In fact, it's in my best interest for you to learn it because it will make it easier for you to understand how to train everyone. But if I'm going to give you such powerful secrets, I would need to modify our contract and have you formally become a part of our legion. It would be a ten-year term for you, with the option to renew or retire after that. Same deal as the others got, with salary while you serve and land once you retire."

We discussed the details a bit more, but I could tell I had him hooked. He was bored with his old life and he had come to like these young kids—it was hard not to. They had come from a rough place but hadn't lost their excitement and enthusiasm, much like Constans. The people of this city were hearty folk, able to overcome adversity and persevere in the face of almost total extinction. It was hard not to admire them.

By the time we were done discussing the contract, and with help from a shout from Constans telling him to stop being such an idiot, he agreed to a ten-year term. We signed the contract together and I clapped him on the arm.

"Welcome to the legion," I told him with a smile.

He grunted, trying to look unimpressed, but his eyes kept being drawn to the young men and women excitedly fondling their new weapons nearby.

"Now," I said, turning back to the group, "I'll meet you one at a time and share my class with you. While I do that, Constans here will start training you all to use your new revolver. Get used to drawing and holstering the revolver first, and then she'll explain how reloading works. Practice that until everyone has unlocked their new class and then we'll move on to a new subject."

I signaled for Basil to come first, and the two of us entered the manor together. I found a comfortable place to sit down in the foyer and I began to explain about the class, willing him to receive the class from me. After he managed to get it, I called in Nikephoros and then, one by one, the rest of the legion. They all managed to learn the class surprisingly fast, and when we finished, I stepped outside and watched Constans showing them all how the revolver worked.

I pulled Basil and Nikephoros to the side and explained that Nikephoros was joining us more permanently and would be second to Basil in command. Since he had considerably more experience, though, I made clear that I expected Basil to listen to his suggestions.

After that, Constans and I began to drill them all on firearms safety. We taught them all to never point the gun at something you didn't want to kill, about not resting your finger on the trigger, and about cleaning and caring for the revolver. We ran everyone through drills. They drew, mock-fired, and re-holstered their revolvers over and over until the sun started to set and we broke for dinner.

I left them to cook while Basil and Nikephoros set up a watch schedule to patrol around the manor in case any monsters strayed too close. I stayed out all night to make sure that didn't happen, but

I didn't tell the others, wanting them to get used to the seriousness of standing guard.

Over the next few days, we slowly introduced everyone to loading and unloading the revolver, and I had everyone collect rocks and practice throwing them as if they were live grenades. I set up targets using the old furniture in the mansion, and we kept track of who could hit the targets with their rocks the best. The young men and women had a blast seeing who could throw their stones the furthest and the most accurately, while I watched and judged the winners of their competitions.

Once I was sure they had a good sense of safety, I finally let them practice firing their revolvers with live ammunition. I placed more furniture on the backside of the hill the manor rested on so we could try to recover as many bullets as possible. I lined everyone up, including Constans, who I hadn't had a chance to train as much as I wanted, and I showed them the proper form for firing the revolver and how to aim down the sights. I signaled to Basil, who I had coached on what to say.

"Draw your weapon!" he yelled. "Aim! Fire!"

Even without gunpowder, the sound of twenty-two revolvers firing at once was loud. I watched as a wave of bullets impacted the hillside, but only a few bullets actually hit the furniture I had set up.

"Fire!" Basil yelled again.

"Fire!" he continued until everyone was out of bullets.

"Reload!" he yelled and everyone scrambled to reload, some managing to finish the task faster than others. I stood behind the line of fire and kept track of who needed help with their stance, with their aim, or with their reloading. Once they had all reloaded, I moved down the line and began to coach each person individually.

"Now," I said, "in the heat of combat, your revolver is going to be more about drawing and firing as many shots as you can, as fast as you can. But we want to learn volley fire for when you have your rifles, so we are practicing it now. You can see that when you all fire at once, the effect on your enemies will be devastating. Imagine a swarm of monsters trying to charge into the wave of bullets that you all are firing at once. Very little would survive such concentrated firepower. Keep practicing for now."

Basil and then Nikephoros led them through more rounds of volley fire and then I signaled to Basil, who quickly called for grenades. The legionnaires grabbed the stones they had placed in their bandoliers and tossed them at the distant furniture before returning to the ready position to fire their revolvers once again. Their accuracy slowly improved, as did their reload time, but they were painfully slow compared to me. Once we got their coordination attribute higher, though, they would do better.

I let Nikephoros take over their daily training after we had exhausted all of the bullets I had brought with us. He ordered everyone to go collect the bullets first, then began to drill them through the volley fire and grenades exercises over and over until they responded to his or Basil's orders instantly.

He woke them early each morning and ran them around the manor, followed by an hour of strengthening exercises, and then marched them around the area. That took up the morning. In the afternoon, he drilled them in volley fire for hours and then broke them into two groups, having them engage in mock battles around the manor. He often incorporated the manor itself into the battles, ordering one team to take it from the other. He didn't give them live ammunition but had them use their stones to mimic grenades, and anyone that had a gun pointed at them was considered "dead" and had to lie down and play dead. It was fun to watch the mock battles, and it was clear the young legionnaires loved that part of their day the most.

I made Constans join them for the exercises and she took to it with a passion as well. The entire cohort was brimming with energy. The legionnaires were excited to be getting such thorough training and to have been given a class of their own, especially such a powerful and rare one. To them, this was something that happened to people in the stories, not regular orphans like them.

After two weeks of drills and practice, I took the legionnaires out for their first real hunt. They exchanged nervous looks when I announced the hunt, but Basil ordered them into formation and they jumped to obey without question. Basil led the group and Nikephoros took up the rear, while I walked beside them. While they drilled, I scouted around in search of something that would be a good test run for them, and I found a nest of monsters that I felt would be perfect. They were some kind of monstrous jackals with a den nearby and numbers to give the legion a challenge that shouldn't overwhelm them.

I gave my summoned phase beast orders to guard the legion just in case something went wrong and I couldn't protect them in time to stop it.

I gave everyone live ammunition and grenades and then gave Basil and Nikephoros free rein to plan the attack on the jackal den. I moved ahead and hid between the two forces to observe how they did.

I watched Basil, Nikephoros, and Constans huddle together briefly before Constans ran ahead in *Stealth* to scout the den.

When she returned, she met with Nikephoros and Basil again before they led everyone toward a small hill that overlooked the den. Everyone quickly and quietly got into position, but before they could finish, loud barking came from the den. The jackals had smelled the gathering legionnaires. Basil ordered everyone to draw their revolvers. A snarling group of the beasts came charging across the open ground toward the legionnaires, but thanks to some loud yelling from Nikephoros, everyone managed to get themselves squared away before the jackals arrived.

"Fire!" Basil yelled. The first group of jackals was cut down easily, even though many of the shots missed. There were only five of the beasts in the first group, and all twenty-two revolvers being fired at once was enough to cause each jackal to be hit multiple times.

More jackals followed and Basil gave the order to fire again. This time, a number of jackals survived the volley. I saw several of the beasts hit by four or five bullets, while others had gone completely unharmed. The legionnaires had concentrated their fire too much. The unharmed jackals raced forward, closing the distance at full tilt.

"Fire at will!" Basil yelled, a slight edge of panic in his voice. The legionnaires cut loose at his order, firing all of their remaining bullets into the handful of jackals that were closing in on them.

I rubbed my forehead in frustration at the sight. They were just a little scared, a little eager, and wanted to make sure they killed all the monsters before they could reach them. Which was, generally, a good philosophy to follow. It would take time for them to learn how deadly their weapons truly were so that they stopped wasting so many bullets when just a handful of their best shooters could have picked off the jackals with ease.

After the cohort finished reloading, they all stood frozen for a moment, until Nikephoros nudged Basil, who seemed to gather his wits about him and ordered Constans forward to scout the den once again. When she returned, reporting no more jackals in sight, the legionnaires relaxed.

I left *Stealth* and approached the legionnaires on the hill.

"Nicely done!" I said. "A bit overkill for the poor beasts, I'd say, but a true show of how deadly you all can be now. Great job."

They all holstered their revolvers and then gave me a salute, smiling in relief at having killed the jackals so easily.

Basil ordered half the legionnaires forward to collect our spent bullets, while he had the other half keep watch for any other monsters. They managed to find most of our bullets and a blue core from one of the jackals. I gave it to Constans, who was essentially acting as the legion's quartermaster. I showed a few of the legionnaires how to harvest the beasts and we gathered enough meat to last us several days.

Chapter 37

Back at the manor, I sat everyone down to discuss ways we could improve the performance of the legion. I didn't just lay into them with everything they did wrong. Instead, I encouraged them all to talk openly about their own ideas and ways they could improve. I made it clear that Basil should hold such a meeting after every engagement and treat each person's ideas with respect. I guided us around to the issues I had seen and had them speak about ways to use less ammunition and how to pick targets better. Basil came up with several good ideas on his own for how to handle fighting a small number of enemies that didn't require the entire cohort to fire.

After I got the conversation going in the direction I wanted, I left it to them to hash out plans for improvement. There was nothing like teenagers full of energy and the excitement of their first successful hunt to spur creative conversation. They spent half the night celebrating and discussing tactics and strategy together.

Even Nikephoros joined them after a while, drawn to the companionship despite his best attempts to act like a lone wolf. As the night progressed, he even shared some of his stories from his time in the legion, before the city had been completely lost to the overwhelming number of monsters that attacked every night. Even I listened raptly to his stories, fascinated by what he had lived through.

I stood outside the front door of the manor, keeping watch so all the legionnaires could be inside together. Constans came out to check on me a couple of times, but I shooed her back inside each time, wanting her to enjoy the night. She deserved to share in the camaraderie, just like Nikephoros did. I was hoping to build more than just a legion here; I was trying to build a family for everyone. It would help them stay strong and make them more motivated to fight for each other, but these reasons aside, they all deserved to feel a part of something bigger than themselves.

We spent one more week at the manor, hunting monsters and discussing ways to improve the legion after each battle. By the end of the week, everyone had received enough experience to unlock level 1 in *Gunslinger*. The legionnaires showed remarkable growth, earning experience and learning from their training at a record-setting pace. My *Evolution of Leadership* doubled the experience and rewards for anyone that followed me, which made a noticeable difference. They were all also benefiting from my very first perk, *Captain's Command*, which gave everyone +1 to all of their attributes when they were following my orders.

Once everyone was level 1, we sat down as a group and discussed what skill each of them should pick. I let them know that I reserved the right to pick skills for them when it came to the core classes I had provided, but I would take their input into account, and if they ever bought themselves their own classes, they could do whatever they wanted with them.

As we began to discuss what skill to pick, I realized they had been given the choice of some different skills from the ones I had been able to choose from when I leveled the class. That didn't happen with the basic classes, at least from what little I had seen. Maybe it was the nature of a legendary class at work or had something to do with the unique way they learned the class. I didn't know.

They had the same choice of *Elemental Adaptation* and *Rapid Reload* that I had, but their other three skills were called *Fire at Will*, which increased their accuracy, *Bringer of Justice*, which gave them passive attribute bonuses when they were pursuing what they believed was a just cause, and a movement skill called *Gather Your Posse*, which let them move quicker when they were surrounded by other people with the same skill.

They debated the merits of the various skills while I just listened in. I ruled out *Bringer of Justice* immediately because it was too vague and each person would have their own idea of what justice was. And the truth was, there would be times that what we did wasn't necessarily going to be just, which I told them honestly could be the case more than any of us might want in this world. They agreed with me and decided that skill wasn't for them. They only had the four basic elements for *Elemental Adaptation*, unlike my skill, which had given me the choice of a few more esoteric elements such as demonic, space, and dimensional magic. Still, having an entire legion being able to fire bullets infused with fire or ice could be very powerful. I didn't think it would be that helpful, ultimately, because the bullets already did so much damage to whoever was shot—any more was just overkill—but I let them discuss it in case any of them could change my mind.

Rapid Reload, they all agreed, wasn't needed because they would practice until they got fast enough to reload without needing the skill. I agreed wholeheartedly that the skill was a waste and encouraged their positive attitude toward training rather than taking a shortcut. They ruled out *Fire at Will* for the same reason, reasoning that they would learn to be more accurate and thus didn't need to waste a skill.

That left *Gather Your Posse*. It wasn't the flashiest skill in existence, but it scaled when more people nearby had the same skill, which was perfect for the legion. Nikephoros was a big believer in the skill because, according to him, the legion won wars mostly because of how fast it could march. According to Nikephoros, the official legion had a powerful marching skill that scaled based on how many other legionnaires were also using the skill, which let the legion cover vast distances extremely rapidly. After he finished explaining how powerful a marching skill truly was, everyone was convinced and chose *Gather Your Posse* as the skill they thought was best. I agreed and ordered them to take it.

Of course, once they chose their very first skill, they all had to go practicing it together. They formed up and began to march away together, Nikephoros staring at them in fond amusement. Constans stayed near me as they left as well.

"Nothing works better to get the recruits voluntarily marching all over the place than giving them their first marching skill," Nikephoros said. I laughed, enjoying the slightly less grumpy Nikephoros that had been slowly showing his face since he had been with us.

"You don't want to go march with them?" I asked Constans, turning to her.

"Nah," she said, "I didn't get the same skills as the others so I haven't picked one yet."

She seemed upset until I had her tell me what skills she was offered. I told her that she had received the same skills that I had received when I first leveled my class. After that, she changed from morose to excited in a second and we discussed which skill would be best for her. I told her I wouldn't pick the skills for her, but I thought *Duel Me* was the best skill available at level 1. It would significantly speed up her rate of experience gain and give her the chance to steal more power bonuses.

She agreed after she realized how the skill could be used. She immediately wanted to go out and start dueling monsters, but I cautioned her about the skill and warned her to never duel something she wasn't sure she could defeat. I told her about how I lost one of my skills and that sobered her up a bit.

Still, I wasn't one to discourage her, so we went on a little hunt while the others marched around the manor, playing with their new skill. I scouted through the air until I could sense a nearby monster and then led her toward it. As I watched, she dueled it and killed it with three shots of her revolver.

"I got an attribute!" she said, jumping up and down.

"Well done!" I called to her. "Maybe don't celebrate with a gun in your hand and potential monsters still around next time, though!"

I looked at the human-sized bullfrog she had killed, deciding not to harvest its slimy corpse. She glanced down at it and then around us, holstering her revolver. When we returned to the manor, the rest of the legionnaires were done trying out their new skill and were relaxing and celebrating around an open fire. Constans went and joined them while I scouted around the manor to make sure everything was still safe.

The next morning, we traveled back to the city and I had everyone hide the revolvers in the wagon to avoid any suspicion from the guards. I told the disappointed teenagers, who were sad about having to give back their new favorite toy so soon, that I would design something that would conceal the revolver, but until then, we needed to avoid too much attention. They understood, of course, but many of them stared lovingly at their revolvers as they handed them to me, sad to be giving them up already.

I gave the order for everyone to take a day off in celebration of our foray outside the city. They saluted with grins on their faces and then broke into more cheers, patting each other on the back and excitedly discussing what they should do for the day. I had Constans give them their pay and then went and checked on my workshop. We had made sure to collect the corpses of the monsters that the legion had been hunting for the last week, so I dragged them down into the basement myself and dumped them near the nanobot worktables. Most of them had stalled out, starved for resources and unable to continue manufacturing the items I had ordered them to make. The rifles were nearly done, and the nanobots had made a decent number of bullets and grenades before going dormant.

I dragged some of the raw cloth I had salvaged down to the basement and began designing some cloth armor, but after a few hours, I wasn't happy with any of the designs I was coming up with. It was much easier to design a firearm, I discovered, than something as subjective as stylish clothing.

Giving up, I went and met with a few different crafters in Sycae until I found a leatherworker who was willing to work with me to design what I wanted. We bounced ideas around until we had a working design I was happy with.

The armor would be part cloth armor and part leather armor. The outer layer was leather, with an inner layer made of thick cloth for comfort and added protection. The upper body armor covered the torso completely, down to the wrists, and had two overlapping folds from each side that gave two layers of protection. It was secured by first folding the left side of the jacket across the chest and then folding the right side over the left. It could be secured tightly along the ribcage with leather ties or tied loosely and left partially open for more breathability. It had a high, stiff collar around the neck and made for a sleek and form-fitting bit of armor that looked a bit like a formal jacket mixed with an eastern robe.

Along with the chest armor, I commissioned leather pants and boots and a cloak identical to the one I had made for myself when I first came to this world. It would allow each legionnaire to conceal their revolver on one side of their body while keeping their other arm free.

After placing an order for thirty sets of the new armor, I left Sycae and returned to the temple with the passage that led to the underdark. I moved rapidly through the underdark, sensing my phase beast getting excited that we might be hunting together like we used to. I promised it we could do some hunting on the way back, after I found the dark elf city and took care of my business. The underdark would be a good source of monsters' bodies for my nanobots back in my workshop, and it would make my companion happy at the same time, so I vowed to spend more time hunting down here in the future.

When I entered the dark elves' cavern, I barely recognized the place. In the center of the open area was a growing city, stone houses sprouting from the ground everywhere. Baby mushrooms were growing over the back half of the cavern, and all of the beetles the dark elves used to pull their wagons were in pens near the mushroom farms or wandered freely nearby.

An earth mage of some kind was building a house as I approached the city, manipulating stone like she was playing with wet clay, raising walls with nothing but a gesture of her hand. The dark elves and the smaller monsters that had come with them were everywhere, building, farming, trading, socializing, or just relaxing and enjoying themselves. The city had an air of happiness and relaxation to it, something that had been severely missing from the old dark elf city.

I felt a monster approaching and saw one of the dark elf scouts walking toward me. I waved and the dark elf bowed in greeting. I didn't recognize her, but she seemed to know me and led me toward the growing city.

The scout and I made our way through the chaos of the dark elf city until we found Alaunvayas and Ryld, who were waiting for me. We bowed in greeting to each other. Alaunvayas invited me to relax with a meal and the three of us caught up over some mushroom and traveler's stew. I enjoyed the meal and hearing about the growing city, impressed even more by the dark elves as I saw how different this city was from the old one. Part of me had worried they might resort to old ways once they settled down, or factions would develop that would ruin the peace of the city, but it seemed like things weren't heading in that direction.

I told Alaunvayas about Mitkos, the spirit I had captured, and she was very impressed. She warned me about the drain of summoning such a powerful spirit, which I had already experienced firsthand. We talked more about our mutual class and my adventures on the surface until I got around to bringing up why I was there.

"I'm planning an expedition," I told them. "I'm hoping to borrow the squad I had hunted with to travel with a group I have formed above ground. It may be dangerous, but their skills could help a lot."

Ryld and Alaunvayas exchanged a look, and then Ryld nodded.

"We will be glad to accompany you," he said. Alaunvayas smiled at the two of us.

"That's it? No questions about what the mission is or anything like that?"

"No," Ryld replied, deadpan. Alaunvayas laughed.

"Alright," I said, holding back my own laughter. "Glad you're all on board."

"You end up in interesting places," Ryld explained. "We all volunteered to be in a squad with you because we enjoy adventure and are looking for challenges. We have been waiting for you to need us so we could go explore above ground in this new area. We are looking forward to it."

"Wonderful," I said, surprised he had explained so much. "I will try not to drag you all to anything too dangerous, but you are right. I plan to go to some interesting places, that's for sure."

I asked about whether dark elves used enchantments in the same way that humans did, but Alaunvayas told me that they didn't have the knowledge; they only crafted with the parts of lesser monsters. I had figured that was the case, judging by how none of the dark elves had enchanted goods, but I wanted to check. I asked Ryld to have the squad move into the temple above us and to plan for a couple months on the road when they selected their equipment.

I traveled back to Sycae and retreated into my workshop to check on the progress of my rifles and to work on another new project: making goggles that would protect the dark elves on the surface.

I used leather to form a head wrap and then reformed some glass I had salvaged earlier, adding a mixture of iron filings to stain them dark gray. The first few attempts were too dark or too light, but eventually I got the formula right and made a rudimentary pair of protective goggles. I grabbed the necessary ingredients and tossed them in my backpack, ordering my nanobots to craft nine more pairs for me.

Finally, out of immediate projects, I went back to the inn and got some food and rest.

Chapter 38

The next day, while the cohort was nursing hangovers, I had them pack up as many supplies as they could and I had us move to the temple as well. The walls were high enough that hopefully, if we cleared the nearby dungeons, we wouldn't get swarmed by monsters during the night. And it would give us more privacy for practicing and allow everyone to carry their revolvers openly.

When we arrived, the dark elves were already inside the temple. Several of the legionnaires noticed a robed dark elf watching as we approached and became nervous. I gestured for them to relax, not bothering to tell them that if the dark elves let themselves be seen, it was because they were being peaceful. It was the dark elves you didn't see that you had to worry about. After a tense moment as everyone stared at the dark elves, we were welcomed inside the temple and I made introductions.

Questions immediately broke out, mostly about the existence of intelligent monsters. I watched as most of the legionnaires went through the same process of surprise, questioning, and then acceptance. I told them about my journeys with the dark elves and everyone accepted the dark elves as allies soon after, taking my word that they were trustworthy.

I left the two groups to talk in the temple while I did a quick scout around to make sure things were safe. When I returned, the taciturn dark elves were sitting with the young men and women of my legion, answering numerous questions from the humans with great patience.

"Listen up," I said after the conversation started to lull a bit. "We are here for a reason. We are going to train together before we leave for an extended trip outside the city. We need to get everyone to level 10, and we will need to complete a dungeon for each of you, for reasons you will understand later."

There were more questions but also excitement at the prospect of completing dungeons. After answering a few of the questions, I explained how we would clear the dungeons together.

"First, we'll try to go as one big group. It should be possible to go with a group our size, but the dungeon will react by sending more monsters after us. It will be significantly more dangerous than if we went in smaller groups, but it will also be a great training ground for all of us to learn to work together.

"The other aspect of dungeons are rewards, as many of you may know. Everyone will earn a share of rewards we all receive and you can keep any equipment that drops for you. The share of the currency you get personally will depend on your rank, but the majority will go to the legion itself to pay for our expenses, such as charging your bullets and grenades and other operational costs. Believe me, making and charging those weapons of yours is *not* cheap. I believe in transparency, though, so Constans will be tracking everything, and at any time, any person may ask for details on their share and where our money is being spent so you know we aren't taking advantage of you."

"I will be?" Constans asked, surprised.

"Yep," I said, "that's why you're the quartermaster. It isn't all fun and games, Ms. Merchant."

She gave a mock-groan and the legionnaires all laughed good-naturedly at her.

"For the dark elves," I said, "since we don't provide your equipment, you all are considered irregulars. We don't support you in the same way, so what you get in dungeons is yours to keep, but at the same time, your weapons and supplies come out of your own pockets. The currency you earn should help reward you for coming with us. Let me know if that isn't satisfactory to any of you.

"Ryld, I should have thought of this sooner, but I have a skill that will benefit all of you greatly if you pledge yourselves to my service. Those of you in the legion may have noticed the changes already, but if you are in my service, you will train twice as fast, receive additional rewards like experience or loot, and receive a +1 to all your attributes when you are following my orders."

"Really? Wow!" I heard several people exclaim. Nikephoros nodded at the back of the room, as if my words had confirmed something he had been suspecting for some time.

"So normally I wouldn't ask it of you, but I think it will benefit you all greatly," I said, turning to Ryld and the other dark elves who had agreed to join me.

Constans also hadn't technically pledged herself to my service, so she signed up immediately. Instead of making her a member of the legion, I simply named her my apprentice and the contract consisted of loose conditions of not betraying me in return for my pledge to train her and assist her until either one of us decided to end the apprenticeship.

She signed quickly and I might have missed it without my enhanced vision, but she had a little bit of water in her eyes when she got to the part where I considered her my apprentice. Neither of us said anything, and she hastily turned away after signing so I couldn't see her reaction any further. I didn't want to embarrass her, so I pretended to have not seen anything, but I felt a surge of affection for her. She had been through a lot and had come out a strong, motivated young woman. She deserved far better than what life had dealt her so far, and I planned to make sure she got to pursue whatever goals she had for herself in this life.

The dark elves were more than happy to sign a contract as well. It designated them auxiliaries to our legion for a period of six months and could be renewed or terminated at the end of the six months by either party. I included provisions of not betraying us or the secrets they learned in my service. In return, they would not receive a salary or equipment but would keep any loot or goods they received.

Everyone signed and I looked over my newest followers as we sat comfortably around the spacious temple. It was a good sight. I had found loyal and skilled people that I could trust. I felt like there wasn't much that could stop us when we worked together, and I was not only impressed by the people I had gathered, but I liked them, too. I was on the way to building something that felt a bit like a family for us all.

We learned quickly that bringing over thirty people into a dungeon was possible, but I was correct that the dungeon would be full of significantly more monsters as a result.

The enemies scaled in number, size, and difficulty. When we all stepped into the first dungeon, we found ourselves standing on a steep hill, staring upward at a mountain in front of us. The hill was covered in loose rock. Several of the legionnaires had to catch themselves as they started to slide backward. Before the others had time to adjust to their new surroundings, a swarm of very angry-looking monsters charged down the hill toward us, screaming bloody murder at the sight of so many intruders. The monsters were large and covered in white fur like the mythological yeti from my world, and they carried crude axes and spears, the weapons made from sticks and sharp stones.

Basil hastily ordered the legion into a line and gave the order to fire. The legionnaires responded admirably, forming up and firing into the charging yeti within just a few seconds. The dark elves moved behind the legion's firing line, aiming crossbow bolts and spells over the legionnaires' heads. The legion's bullets were deadly, killing many of the yeti immediately, but there were over forty of the monsters charging at us and many of them took two or more bullets to put down. The bolts and spells of the dark elves helped, but over half of the monsters were still standing as Basil ordered the legionnaires to reload. They began to frantically dig at their satchels, grabbing for their bullets, when Nikephoros interrupted them.

"Grenades!" he yelled. The legionnaires, realizing their mistake, frantically stopped trying to reload and grabbed their grenades instead, tossing them forward at the charging yeti. Basil grimaced at his mistake but threw his own grenade with precision. The resulting explosions rippled down the line of yeti, throwing them back and off their feet, stunning the ones that weren't outright killed by the explosions.

"Now reload!" Basil yelled, and this time the legionnaires had enough space to grab their bullets and reload their revolvers. The dark elves, not needing to reload, had continued to attack, and their bolts and spells managed to kill the few yeti that remained alive after the grenades had done their work. My phase beast and I had been prepared to step in, if needed, but I was happy to see that it hadn't been necessary.

It was daytime on the mountain, so the dark elves were suffering under the direct light. I only had two goggles that were finished so far, so I gave them to Ryld and one other dark elf. The rest weren't going to be at their best under the sun without the shaded lenses to protect their eyes. Still, I was confident that Ryld would be more than enough for now. He vanished in front of the legion's eyes to go scout around us while I tracked his progress with my *Monster Hunter* perk. The legionnaires waited patiently, eyeing their surroundings and fingering their holstered guns, paranoid something might jump out at them at any moment.

If not for Nikephoros calling for the grenades, they all knew they could have been seriously hurt. I could tell Basil was being hard on himself, but that didn't stop him from walking the perimeter and making sure everyone was fully prepared for the next fight. I took that as a good sign. A leader didn't have to be perfect; they just had to learn from their mistakes and not let the mistakes stop them from doing what they needed to do.

When Ryld returned, he reported there was a rough path up the mountain ahead of us. I could sense monsters in the distance above us, so I gave Basil the order to head up the mountain. Even impaired, the other dark elves spread out around the legionnaires, blending into the rough scrub and rocky ground around us as if born of the environment. Even in direct sunlight, they were extremely hard to see. The legion formed up and marched up the path, Basil in the lead and Nikephoros taking up the rear. Constans and I followed behind them, walking together in companionable silence.

Almost an hour of steep hiking later, we reached a flat and wide shelf that curved gently around the mountain to our left. Ryld appeared next to Basil, and I heard him reporting that there was an ambush ahead, around the curve of the mountain. The yeti had constructed hidden redoubts above the trail and were waiting for us to approach. The dark elves estimated there was about the same number of enemies as in the last group we fought.

I let Basil and Nikephoros discuss tactics for dealing with the ambush, while Ryld stood by patiently. Nikephoros suggested just triggering the ambush; our grenades and bullets were more than enough to kill the yeti if used properly. Basil wanted to send scouts to attack and try to lead the yeti back to a secure position where we were now.

They spoke quietly for another moment before deciding to follow Basil's plan. They asked Ryld and the other dark elves to try springing the trap and drawing the yeti back toward the legionnaires. Ryld listened and then left with a nod.

Basil and Nikephoros spread everyone out across the length of the open shelf, ordering them to drag the nearby boulders into a rough line for them to crouch behind. Constans was acting as a member of the cohort for now, so she stepped forward and joined them in setting up the counter-ambush. I waited behind them all, sliding my rifle off my shoulder in case it was needed.

A couple of minutes after the legionnaires finished making a low wall to crouch behind, the dark elves came racing down the path, the cries of angry yeti echoing across the mountainside behind them. I took aim and began to pick off the first few; the range of my rifle was significantly better than that of the revolvers the legionnaires were using right now. I killed five of them before the dark elves reached the line of legionnaires, leaping over them and settling down behind the boulders to stand shoulder to shoulder with the men and women of my legion. A moment later, as more yeti poured down the path, Basil gave the order to fire.

A wave of bullets, spells, and bolts slammed into the mass of angry yeti, throwing them into confusion. The front yeti fell, wounded, tripping up the ones behind them. I continued to fire with my rifle, each shot killing a yeti. This time, we didn't need the grenades; the effectiveness of the volley fire was enough to disrupt the enemies' charge, allowing the legionnaires and dark elves to kill the yeti as they tried to pick themselves back up from the entangled mess their charge had become.

"Great job!" I called out, sensing no more yeti coming to attack us. Basil and Nikephoros checked over everyone and then they stood, admiring the effectiveness of revolvers when used together. I let them have a moment before signaling to Basil that we should get going.

We faced several more charges from the yeti, but thanks to the dark elf scouts and my own ability to detect the monsters, we were able to turn every ambush and fight on advantageous ground each time. As we continued up the mountain, the sun began to set around the same time we reached the snow line, the temperature dropping sharply as the sun began to disappear behind us. Ryld found a cave just a bit further up the mountain for everyone to shelter in, so Basil ordered everyone up the path at a jog. We hadn't brought any winter clothing or firewood, an oversight on my part. I was so used to being able to survive in almost any environment that I had forgotten the need to be more fully prepared when bringing regular people into the dungeons.

It was right before we reached the cave that we suffered our first injury. The legion was crunching through the light snow that covered the path in front of us when a cry rang out.

"Make room!" Nikephoros yelled, bullying through the troops to see what had happened. I pushed my way through as well and saw the snow had been covering a crevice on the side of the trail that led downward. Whoever had fallen must have just stepped slightly to the side, not realizing there was a crevice there covered by snow. I heard a scream from down below, and I hastily pushed past the last few gaping legionnaires and leapt down the crevice, unconcerned with what I might find below.

I scraped against the walls of the cavern as I fell, but I arrested my momentum with a short dash when I reached the bottom of the crevice. It was dark down below, but my vision let me see what had happened perfectly. One of the younger legionnaires, Aykan, one of the boys I suspected was of Turkish origin, given his darker skin, had fallen and broken both of his legs. His arm was also twisted under him and he was losing a significant amount of blood.

Cursing, I grabbed him and dashed upward, flying out of the crevice, where I landed softly with Aykan cradled in my arms.

"Maya!" I yelled, calling over the dark elf necromancer. She came running and took the fallen legionnaire from my arms, laying him gently in the snow. She didn't have many healing skills for non-undead, but she still had more than the rest of us. After Maya worked on his body for a moment, I saw his wounds mend slightly; whatever magic she was able to use on his human body helped stop the blood loss. As I watched her work, I realized another major oversight on my part. We had no healers in the legion. A single injury could spell doom for a legionnaire. All of my hard work building a team and training the men and women could be lost by something as small as a fall into a crevice. I was angry with myself at the oversight, and I vowed to fix my mistake as soon as we were out of the dungeon.

Nikephoros designated two people to carry Aykan with us until we could reach the cave. Inside, the legionnaires cleared a space for Aykan, many of them giving him concerned looks as they worked, and then began to make camp for themselves.

512

The cave was made of ice and led gently upward, continuing through the mountain in front of us. The dark elves kept watch, their tireless undead bodies not needing to rest, while the legionnaires rested and recovered. Maya kept an eye on Aykan throughout the night, making sure he didn't get any worse.

A day of strenuous hiking and multiple tense engagements had exhausted the others, who quickly fell into a light sleep after a cold meal. They all huddled together, sharing body warmth and blankets freely among themselves. I found it a bit odd to see them sleep so close together until I realized they must have done it many times in the past when they were surviving in Perama. I felt sad for what they had been through, watching them sleep like that, but also proud of how far they had come already.

Ryld and I stood watch together nearby. The other dark elves were out in the night, scouting the mountainside to get us more information on what we faced ahead. Now that it was nighttime, the dark elves were impossible to detect as they explored the dungeon, and reports began to trickle in through the night on what they had found. The ice cave we were in continued forward for almost a mile until it opened into a large room where a sub-boss waited. He was another yeti, larger than the others, and wielded a large, crude-looking axe in each hand. Large icicles with sharp points hung from the ceiling, and the floor was covered in slick ice.

I let the cohort rest for most of the night but woke up Basil and Nikephoros when there were still a few hours of darkness left. Groans rang out as the two of them went around and woke the others, but eventually everyone was awake. Nikephoros made them eat another quick meal and then had them do some light exercises to limber up.

Once everyone was more awake and fed, Ryld led us forward through the darkened cave. I took out one of my first inventions, the *Light* stone I had made so long ago, and gave that to Basil to help light the path forward for the legionnaires. I told him to keep it, since it would do more good with the legion these days than in my belt pouch.

The sub-boss was staring at us as we approached, the *Light* stone easily giving us away, so Basil ordered everyone to spread out around the entrance of the room. He left Aykan, who had recovered somewhat, in the cave behind us, where he held the

Light stone to provide light for everyone else. The sub-boss roared, slamming his axes against his chest, and as his roar echoed around the cavern, the large icicles on the roof began to shake and loosen.

"Watch out! The ice is falling!" someone yelled. Everyone looked up, and several of the icicles hanging from the ceiling fell free, plunging downward toward the legionnaires. People scrambled out of the way but slipped on the floor as they hurried to escape the falling icicles.

The yeti used the distraction to toss both of his axes at the group. The axes flew toward two separate groups of legionnaires who were still trying to recover from the icicles. I dashed forward and put myself between them and one of the axes. I slammed it to the side with both of my hands, stopping its momentum cold. The other axe spun through the air, threatening to cut through four or five of my legionnaires, when Maya dove in front of it. The axe struck her, cleaving deeply into her shoulder and throwing her into the legionnaires she had just saved. They were scattered across the ice but had been saved from being cut to pieces.

I didn't see much blood, thanks to her undead body, and Maya immediately sat up and began casting a spell on herself to heal her wound. I reached down to grab the axe that I had blocked, but before I could, it disappeared. I turned to the boss and saw he had recalled both of his axes to his hands with some kind of magical skill.

"Shoot him!" I heard Basil yell. The recovering legionnaires drew and fired swiftly, peppering the yeti with *Penetration Bullets*. The remaining dark elves hadn't been idle either; shadow bolts had been launched by the two dark elf mages, and bolts empowered with skills of their own, fired from our hunters, were sticking deeply into the yeti's body.

The yeti roared again, seemingly uninjured, and everyone was forced to scramble as more ice began to fall from the ceiling. Not wanting to risk any more injuries, I drew my sword and used *Trickster's Dash* to appear at the side of the yeti. I plunged my sword deep into his thigh and ripped it out one side. Gushing blood followed my sword as I tore it free.

The yeti staggered from the wound, turning to stare downward toward me in shock. He tried to bring an axe down on my head, but I dashed backward. Seeing me clear, the legion unloaded all of their remaining bullets into the yeti. Overpowered by his weakened leg and the momentum of so many bullets hitting him, he slowly tipped over backward, slamming into the icy ground behind him. As the legionnaires reloaded, I dashed forward again and slid my sword deep into the yeti's throat, where he rapidly began to choke on his own blood. With a twist of my wrist, I tore out his throat and stepped back until he bled to death on the ground in front of me.

Ryld went to check on Maya, who was recovering fine from her injuries; the gaping wound in her shoulder was slowly stitching itself back together. We took a moment for everyone to recover from the sudden violence before one of the dark elf hunters showed us the stairs leading upward, out of the sub-boss's cavern.

At the top of the stairs, we exited onto a flat expanse of ice and snow that stretched a mile or more in front of us. In the distance, the mountain continued but was partially blocked by large ice walls. The dark elves had scouted the walls as best as they could and reported yeti in great numbers patrolling the top of the wall, waiting for us. One of the dark elves had scaled the walls and found a castle made entirely of ice, and it was full of more yeti. The walls stretched fifty feet or higher into the sky and there was no visible gate. I heard several people wondering how we were supposed to get through, but Basil quickly quieted the speculation.

I wondered what I would have encountered if I had come here by myself. Were the walls and castle a manifestation of the increased difficulty of the dungeon due to the number of people we had brought inside? If I was by myself, would it have been a small tower or some other easier challenge?

A clear night sky gave us enough light to see by for now. I told Basil to lead us forward as fast as he could so it was dark enough for the dark elves to fight comfortably but light enough for everyone else to see. The dark elves were our most experienced fighters, so I wanted them to be at the top of their game for tackling the ice walls.

We marched across the snowy plains toward the castle. There was no reaction from the wall, so we kept going until we were less than a hundred feet from it. The legionnaires were a bit winded from the rapid hike and the use of their skill to speed them along, so I gave them just a few minutes to recover as best as they could and then started the assault.

"Get ready," I said to Basil, who stood next to me. He passed the word quietly through the troops, and everyone drew their revolvers and crouched, staring at the wall in front of us.

"How are we going to get over the wall?" Basil asked me. This was what many others had been wondering as we got closer and closer to the enormous walls. The walls were made of pure, slick ice, and even the dark elf hunter that managed to climb them had struggled to do so. Normally, it would be impossible for our legion to scale the wall, especially if the yeti saw us and began to attack us as we tried.

Thankfully, I had an ace in the hole. Well, not so much an ace as a king. I concentrated for a moment and summoned Mitkos the Giant King.

His golden spirit spiraled out of me and spread out in front of everyone, his gargantuan body slowly forming. The legionnaires and the dark elves both stared, entranced by the sight of the giant forming in front of us. When Mitkos was fully formed, several people gasped, while others stared in awe at the king.

Mitkos, never one for stealth, took the wall in front of him as a personal insult and roared a mighty challenge. Everyone covered their ears, the roar shockingly loud in the still night air. When his roar died down, the many yeti on the wall tried to respond with their own yells, but they sounded weak compared to Mitkos's roar of pure fury.

Mitkos raised his metal pillar and charged the wall, building momentum rapidly. He covered the distance in seconds and slammed into the wall. The yeti along the stretch Mitkos had collided with were thrown backward, sailing off the wall. The wall buckled but held.

Even more offended by that, Mitkos stepped back and began to slam his rune-carved pillar into the wall, breaking off chunks with every strike. Blocks of ice and sprays of ice shards began to fly into the air. Without needing any orders, we all ran backward as the ice began to fall all around Mitkos, some of the blocks of ice as large as a house.

By the time we had run far enough away to feel safe, Mitkos had bludgeoned his way through the wall. The strain of keeping him summoned was beginning to make me light-headed, but I ordered him to kick a clear path through the wall so we didn't have to climb over anything when we attacked. He roared again, kicking the base of the wall with his mighty feet, sending chunks of ice rolling forward into the space behind the wall. Before I collapsed from the strain of keeping Mitkos summoned, I ordered him into the city to kill as many yeti as he could.

I signaled Basil to move forward, unable to speak from the strain on my willpower. Basil understood my gesture and yelled for everyone to run for the wall. Impressed by the might of the giant, the legionnaires let off a yell and charged forward, their revolvers in hand and eager smiles on their faces. The dark elves raced ahead of the slower-moving humans, turning invisible when they reached the wall. I followed behind slowly, barely able to think clearly as Mitkos continued to rampage behind the wall.

I kept him summoned until I sensed he was out of immediate enemies to kill. I gratefully released him, feeling as if I had just run for a week straight while trying to understand seven new languages at the same time. It was a complete physical and mental exhaustion, unlike anything I had experienced before.

Maya stayed behind, still not fully recovered from the axe she had taken to the shoulder, and helped Aykan limp toward the wall. I forced myself forward, sliding my rifle off my shoulder and carefully picking my way over the icy ground.

I didn't try to get involved in the fight this time, just tried to stay awake long enough to make sure nothing attacked me, Maya, and Aykan. I wasn't sure how much time passed, but I eventually heard Nikephoros start bellowing orders at the legionnaires. The legionnaires slowly began to trickle back toward where I stood, while the dark elves unstealthed when they arrived. I had only caught glimpses of the dark elves here and there as they appeared from stealth, killing yeti from ambush all around the courtyard and keep in front of us.

Mitkos had only partially damaged the keep. Some of the chunks of ice he had kicked clear of the wall had struck the front, but otherwise, it was mostly intact. The courtyard in front of the keep was another matter; the ground was torn up and covered with blood and so many different yeti it was hard to tell where one ended and another began.

I ignored the devastation around us and pointed at the doors to the keep. Basil gave the order, sending everyone forward to assault the keep.

I followed them, shaking my head to stay awake. Keeping Mitkos out for that long was dangerous. If I had been alone, I would be extremely vulnerable right now. I heard gunshots ring out inside the keep but had to trust that my people could handle themselves without me for now. When I finally made it inside, the sound of fighting had died down.

Inside, a pair of white wolves were lying dead in the center of a banquet hall. Tables were spilled over, and food and drinks were thrown everywhere. It looked like over a hundred yeti had been in here but had made a hasty exit when they heard Mitkos begin his attack. A wooden throne dominated the far side of the hall. A large table had been tipped over in front of it and now lay on its side.

The two wolves had been chained up to the wall behind the throne. The chains had allowed the wolves to reach almost halfway across the hall, but someone hadn't had the time or foresight to free them for the battle outside. The dark elves and legionnaires had killed them while they strained at their chains, trying to attack.

Behind the throne, resting on a pedestal, was the white dungeon core. I looked around, surprised. Had we already killed the final boss? Surely the two wolves weren't the boss.

I hobbled back outside and tried to find a body that stood out from the other dead yeti, but Mitkos had done such a thorough job it was hard to tell one from another.

Shrugging, I went back inside.

"I guess we killed the boss already," I said to the waiting legionnaires. They exchanged glances, surprised that we had already beaten the dungeon, before clapping each other on the backs and hugging, smiles of relief breaking out on their faces.

The celebrating legionnaires grabbed Basil and Nikephoros as well, forcing them to join in their celebration. Basil looked relieved that nobody had any hard feelings for his mistake earlier in the dungeon. Nikephoros tried to act gruff, but I could tell he was warmed by the gesture. Constans walked over to me and grabbed me by the arm, dragging me over to the celebrating legionnaires as well. I tried to glare at her, but she didn't stop, so I reluctantly let her pull me over to them.

"To Alexander!" she yelled, pushing me into the middle of the pack of legionnaires.

"To Alexander!" they all yelled, crowding around me, jumping up and down, and slapping me on the back in celebration. I couldn't help but smile at the legionnaires, warmed by their camaraderie.

Congratulations, you have completed this dungeon. You have earned the following rewards: 1 gold core, 2 blue cores, 1 perk, 1000 experience.

Perk obtained: Natural Born Leader. You command the battlefield with grace and poise, lending confidence to your troops. Any troops or followers under your command receive +1 to all attributes, are immune to fear-based attacks, and are less likely to break or retreat unless ordered to do so.

When everyone materialized outside the dungeon, people immediately began to share what lessons they had learned. I sent Constans around to collect the cores while Basil and Nikephoros ushered everyone into some semblance of order and got us back to the temple we were using as a base.

Chapter 39

Back at the temple, Nikephoros had some people preparing food while everyone else gradually began to relax. I took a tally of who had received what from the dungeon. Most everyone had just received experience, but Basil, Ryld, and Nikephoros had also received a perk that gave them bonuses to the troops they commanded. Basil's and Nikephoros's made them more likely to be obeyed by their troops and gave everyone a +1 to all attributes. Ryld's gave his troops a bonus to stealth and perception. It was good news to me, since stacking such bonuses in the leadership of an army would be a great benefit for everyone.

Once the food was ready, I pulled Constans, Ryld, Basil, and Nikephoros aside for a conference.

"We need to get secondary roles for everyone," I told them, "not just their primary classes. It was a mistake on my part that we didn't have healers with us. Let's figure out what secondary classes or non-combat classes we need to make sure something like that doesn't happen again."

We talked as we ate and came up with a list of support classes that we should get for the legion. We came up with five roles we needed. First, a healer who could heal any injured legionnaire but would also have access to group enhancements and other magic. Second, a cook. We couldn't survive forever on nonperishable foods. Third, a hunter and butcher. We couldn't always count on the dark elves to hunt for us and needed to be self-sufficient. Fourth, a scout with enhanced vision and senses for detecting traps or spotting enemies. And fifth, unit leaders that would hopefully unlock their own bonuses for commanding their smaller units, much like we were getting for ourselves already.

I decided we would organize our cohort a bit differently to take advantage of these roles. We would form squads of five people, and each one would be assigned one of the roles we designated.

Nikephoros and Basil would pick who they thought should be small-unit leaders. After that, we would ask what people preferred and try to match them to a role we needed to fill. Having a healer in each unit of five would mean quick and easy healing for everyone, which should help keep people alive, get them back into the fight in seconds, and prevent injured legionnaires from being out of commission for the entire mission, like what had just happened to Aykan.

We had made a good amount of currency from the dungeon run, each person having received at least one gold core and several blue cores, which Constans collected and kept track of as our quartermaster.

Once everyone was recovered, I decided we weren't going to try staying in the temple overnight, as I had initially planned, since we needed to get some more classes for everyone. I sent the dark elves back to their city and led the cohort back to Sycae, letting everyone have a good night's sleep back in the warehouse, where it was safe.

The next morning, I sent Constans to begin working on getting the classes we needed. The dark elves were willing to train our hunters for free, so we just needed to get the non-combat class *Cook* and the *Scholar* class, which was a healer and enhancement class. For those in a scout role, I decided we would buy them the *Rogue* class, and for leaders, we would get them the *Warrior* class, with the hopes that they would evolve it into something more specific once they hit level 20. That left the cooks and the hunters without a combat class that could evolve, which I felt was unfair, so I added to our list to get the hunters *Archer* and the cooks *Scholar* as well, wondering if cooks could learn some interesting ways to enhance troops through food.

And that led to us deciding that it was unfair if people only had a combat class as well, so we found a non-combat class called *Medic* for the healers, which used non-magical means for healing people, like doctors or nurses did in my world. And Constans found an old man willing to teach a class called *Principales* from his time in the legion. A *Principales* was a rare non-combat class that gave bonuses for organizing people, supplies, and other things like that. Nikephoros was familiar with the class but had never unlocked it because it was held back as a reward for a select few in the legion and never widely distributed. It should help run the squads more efficiently, so we paid the veteran to teach it to each of our unit leaders and to Basil, Nikephoros, and Constans as well. He was happy to take our money.

Finally, Constans told us that the guards who protected Sycae actually had a non-combat class called *Guard* that gave bonuses to spotting suspicious activity and detecting thieves or traps. It even gave some truth-sensing abilities at higher levels. They could act as both military police and watch out for external threats. Constans found a down-on-his-luck guard who was willing to train our people in the *Guard* class in exchange for just a few orbs.

In the end, each squad would have one legionnaire with each *Scholar/Medic, Warrior/Principales, Archer/ Dark Elf Stalker, Cook/Scholar,* and *Rogue/Guard.* And everyone would, of course, have the *Gunslinger* class for their revolver and hopefully something else for their rifle, if my plan worked out.

Of course, we couldn't afford all of that right now, so I told Constans to focus on the healers first, and then we paid for the *Guard* class and the *Principales* class since those were limited opportunities I didn't want to pass up.

Once that was done, I checked in on my workshop and gathered the newest crop of bullets and grenades for the legion. The rifles were actually almost done, but I didn't want to introduce those to the troops until I had, hopefully, unlocked a new class I could teach them for free. My greedy nanobots were out of resources once again, and I didn't have time to go hunting right now, so I ended up having to feed them a portion of the trade goods I had been holding on to just because I really needed the rifles to get finished sooner rather than later. It cost me the majority of the cloth, wood, glass, and other resources I had been stockpiling. I left only the iron I had salvaged, the pottery and clay to form the grenades, and enough wood and cloth to put the finishing touches on the rifles.

Once Constans was back, having drained our reserves to buy four *Scholar* classes and the *Guard* and *Principales* classes, Basil and Nikephoros had worked out who would take what role in the groups of five, so I gave the classes to the four newest healers of our legion. Three of them were young men and only one of them was a woman. Our *Guards* and *Principales* had been taken to learn their new classes early that morning and were eager to level them by, presumably, guarding things and organizing things, respectively.

Once everyone that could get a class right now had theirs, Basil rallied the troops and we set out for our temple once again. The healers would be level 0 for one more dungeon, but that couldn't be helped unless we went hunting outside of the city for days to level the *Scholar* class to level 1. We would just have to be extra careful and make sure nobody got hurt.

When I expressed my worry about not having the healers at level 1, Constans surprised me by handing me a satchel full of healing potions. I knew that alchemists existed in this world but hadn't really investigated the class much. Apparently Constans knew that alchemists sold healing potions and had stocked up since our last dungeon, just to be extra prepared.

"I'd give you a promotion," I told her as I gave her back the potions and told her to distribute them to the new healers for emergencies, "if you weren't already basically in charge of everything."

Constans ran off, pleased, and handed them out to the healers. Once we arrived at the temple, the dark elves were waiting. I had managed to craft several more of the new shaded goggles and gave them to Ryld to hand out for me. I promised to give them the rest once they were finished being made.

The next dungeon we found was a mystical forest, filled with will-o'-the-wisps that tried to confuse us and beastkin that tried to ambush us. The beastkin were humanoid versions of forest animals without tools or weapons, but they were still cunning and dangerous. The dark elves weren't tricked by the will-o'-the-wisps and were able to keep us all on track, and the ambushes were easily turned as usual. The forest was beautiful but sinister, full of glowing bugs and plant life that was in a constant state of flowering. The smells were heavenly and I worried for a second about a biological attack from the flowers, but nothing bad seemed to happen so maybe it was just a nice-smelling dungeon.

We fought five different bosses, each one representing a type of beastkin that tried to ambush us in the forest. We fought deerkin, boarkin, wolfkin, and birdkin. The final boss was a monstrously large bearkin that I ended up having to summon

Mitkos to kill because our bullets and arrows just didn't penetrate its hide at all.

We practiced having the individual squad leaders relay orders from Basil and Nikephoros, but none of them reported gaining a perk yet at the end of the dungeon. Constans and I both tried to duel the final boss, but only one of us was allowed to use the perk. I had let Constans go first so she ended up with the duel bonus. She excitedly told me, after the boss was dead, that she had won a perk called *Bear's Hide*, which increased her skin's ability to resist attacks for five minutes on a cooldown of a half hour. I half expected her to sprout fur all over her body. When I warned her about the possibility, she was even more excited to try the skill, but sadly, no fur appeared when she activated it. She pouted for a moment, but then she tried to cut herself with my knife and it didn't scratch her, and she got excited once again.

Constans collected the orbs from everyone and documented everything in the company logs I had made her buy once we exited the dungeon. We hadn't ended up needing the healing potions, thankfully, and now everyone had earned enough experience to skyrocket their main class and level their secondary class as well.

I asked Basil to check in with the legionnaires and ask if they were up for another dungeon. He reported back that they were all in good spirits, so we found another dungeon nearby and completed that one as well. I used my rifle exclusively throughout the dungeon and began joining the firing line with the other legionnaires, mentally imagining what I wanted my *Warrior* class to evolve into. I had chosen *Warrior* for a specific reason, and I had hoped that my use of the class and my unique weapon would give me an evolution similar to what I had in mind. It had worked with my *Gunslinger* class, pulling from how I used the class and my own recollections of how a six-shooter revolver was used on my world. I hoped whatever determined the evolution of classes would do the same with my rifle.

Since *Warrior* was my only currently active class, it was rapidly gaining experience from the dungeon runs. I sent Constans back to Sycae to buy more classes for the legionnaires and supplies as needed, and by the end of two more weeks, everyone had reached over level 10 in their primary class. They all had their secondary classes unlocked as well, and we had replenished our dwindling finances somewhat. And finally, I reached level 20 in *Warrior.*

Congratulations, you have unlocked an evolution of your Warrior class. Based on your unique use of the class, you have unlocked Rifleman. Your class rating is Unique. Do you wish to adopt this class now?

Congratulations, you have reached level 20 in your Warrior class. Your actions have unlocked a possible evolution to your class. You have unlocked the class Sniper. Your class rating is Rare. Do you wish to adopt this class now?

That was interesting. My use of the rifle to kill from a distance must have met the criteria to unlock a class called *Sniper*, but it wasn't unique, meaning someone had already unlocked it in the past, likely an *Archer* who had been especially proficient with killing from a distance. I was intrigued, but that wasn't why I went through the trouble to re-level my *Warrior* class all over again.

You have evolved your Warrior class into the unique Rifleman class. There are no Warrior skills eligible for evolution with your evolved class.

Congratulations, you have earned the achievement Evolve a Second Unique Class. You have managed to evolve not one but two unique classes that have never been seen before. You have earned a +1 to all attributes and may pick one skill from any level of the Rifleman class.

A long list of skills suddenly filled my mind, all of the skills from level 1 all the way to level 100. As my mind processed the information, I felt a moment of vertigo and had to steady myself on a nearby wall. I told Constans I was going to be distracted and she helped me back to the temple while the rest of the legion marched nearby.

Having so many skills to process and review took hours. I started at level 100 to see the most powerful skills and then made my way down the list, not skipping a single one in case something of lower level would synergize better with my current skills.

I was tempted by all of them, but some were especially powerful. One of the level 100 skills, *Ultimate End*, could only be used once a week but charged up and fired a bullet so powerful it could level cities. Another, *Bullet Time*, stopped time whenever I aimed, allowing me to get the perfect shot every time. Of course, I didn't really have much of a problem aiming with my high attributes and enhanced body and mind, so that wasn't completely useful but still remarkably powerful. And I didn't really need a city-killer skill, now that I had Mitkos, but still, they were impressive.

Many of the *Rifleman* skills were best used in a group, gaining power when more nearby people also had the skill, but I wasn't looking for something like that right now since it would be a very long time before the others leveled high enough to get some of the more powerful skills.

Of the skills that were focused on individual power, I debated between three. The first was a skill called *Metal Mind*, which allowed me to control all forms of metal with my mind out to a distance that scaled based on my memory and willpower. It would allow me to bend or stop my bullets or to protect myself from metal weapons, and I could use it for crafting, which could let me do some pretty interesting things. The second skill was the *Ultimate End* skill, even though I had Mitkos. Sometimes, overwhelming force was just something that came in handy. Third was a skill called *Absolute Inspiration*, which increased the attributes of me and all of my allies nearby by +50 for an hour, although it could only be used once a week like the *Ultimate End* skill.

After reviewing every skill several times, not wanting to get such an important choice wrong, I chose *Metal Mind*. It synergized with all of my current weapons, it offered offensive and defensive capabilities, and it could be used to help me do some unique things with metal and my crafting. It was a hard choice, because *Absolute Inspiration* could have made any army I someday fielded extremely powerful, while *Ultimate End* could end a war for me in a single shot, but ultimately *Metal Mind* gave me the most personal power and diversity while synergizing with my current skill set the most.

As the skill blossomed in my mind, I felt my perception of the world around me expanding. I could feel every bit of metal around me for hundreds of feet. I knew exactly where each piece of metal was, including all the impurities inside the metal. I could also feel how, with just a slight tug of my mind, I could pluck the metal to a tune of my own making, making it do whatever I wanted.

Congratulations, you have received enough experience to level your Rifleman class. You are now level 1.

I had just enough experience to hit level 1 in the *Rifleman* class after hitting level 20 in *Warrior* since no other combat class of mine was currently active. I reviewed the level 1 skills again, which seemed fairly lackluster compared to so many that I had just seen from my achievement.

Please choose a level 1 class skill:

Hold the Line: You and any nearby allies receive a bonus to your strength and coordination, cannot be moved by physical force, and are immune to fear or magic-based fear effects.

Aim True: Your aim is improved and you may fire further with your guns. Your bullets are not slowed by air resistance or the pull of gravity.

Shield Wall: Project a barrier that blocks incoming magical or physical attacks but allows you to fire through it. This barrier is strengthened if others nearby also have a Shield Wall active.

Volley Fire: The power of your bullets is magnified by the number of other people nearby who fire at the same time as you. Each bullet fired at the same time as yours increases the velocity and penetrating power of your bullet by a small amount.

Tactical Withdrawal: Leap backward, landing smoothly behind you. If you are in formation with others with Tactical Withdrawal, you land in the same position that you had leapt from.

The skills were exactly what I had hoped for by evolving such a class from the *Warrior* subclass instead of the *Archer* subclass, since they focused more on formation fighting and working as a cohesive whole rather than on individual skill or one-on-one combat. If I had taken the *Sniper* class, it probably would have been more solo-focused, but this class was what I had imagined every time I used my rifle. With this, my legion would finally reach its true potential.

I selected the *Aim True* skill, since it seemed to imply it worked for any bullets, making them no longer slowed by air resistance or the pull of gravity, which seemed like a subtle but powerful boost. I then deactivated the *Rifleman* class and reactivated my *Gunslinger*, *Spirit Breaker*, and *Duelist* classes. I didn't have much of a preference which one leveled from here, so I activated them all at once.

After everyone else had leveled up at the temple, we returned to Sycae and I gave everyone three days of leave to celebrate reaching level 10 in at least one class. This time, we discussed the skills but they were all more or less decent, so I didn't get involved with them as they chose their skills, figuring it was fine for them to pick whatever they wanted for this level. Variety of skills wasn't always a bad thing. Plus, the *Rifleman* class was going to be the real powerhouse of the legion once I shared it with everyone.

While they were on leave, I checked on our armor, which the leatherworker had finished. I had him deliver the crates of uniforms to the warehouse where the legionnaires stayed, excited to show them the new uniforms. The rifles had finally finished as well. I had also crafted an entire second set of revolvers by the time the rifles were finished.

When everyone was back from leave, I gathered us up in my workshop and presented my newest creations. First, I gave everyone the armor I had crafted. They were excited and rushed to the private areas that had been set up for them to change clothes. Once they were back, I admired how nice they all looked. The armor fit well enough on each person, and having everyone wearing matching armor and a matching cloak gave us all a more professional, polished look. It also hid their revolvers, which meant they could wear them more often in the enclave.

When everyone was dressed, I formed them up into a line. Basil, Nikephoros, and Constans stood in front of the rest of the legion. I walked up and down the line, inspecting uniforms, belt satchels full of bullets, bandoliers, and revolvers where they rested in their holsters. They all looked like real, professional soldiers. They were practically veterans at this point, having fought through a number of difficult engagements in the dungeons that we raided as a team. Their uniforms looked slick and made them look downright dangerous. I wouldn't want to tangle with a group of them in a dark alley if I saw them coming toward me.

"We look fucking amazing!" Constans said, no longer able to hold in her excitement as I inspected them all in silence. That broke the tension in the air, causing everyone to break down in laughter. I joined in, pushing her out of line, which the rest of the legionnaires took as an excuse to break formation and mob us, giving us hugs and slapping us on the back and arms affectionately.

Once order was finally restored, I unveiled my second creation. "This," I said, holding up my rifle, "is now ready for you all to use. It's called a carbine, and it's capable of firing further and with greater accuracy and stopping power than the revolver. It holds twenty bullets in what's called a magazine. I have a new class to share with you all as well. It will be the core of our legion, the primary class from this point forward. I would ask you all to put your other classes on hold and level this one exclusively until further notice."

Excited chatter broke out, and I began to hand out a rifle to each person. They weren't loaded, but I showed how there was a small magazine attached to the bottom of the gun, and I showed them how the pump-action lever under the barrel worked to prime the next bullet.

"One shot, one pump, and then shoot again. It is slower than the revolver but more consistent over long distances, and you can fire it twenty times. It will let you fire more rapidly than a bow or crossbow and has significantly more power in each bullet than your average arrow or bolt. Now line up and I will give you all the main class of our legion: the *Rifleman*."

I gave everyone the class, including Constans, Basil, and Nikephoros. Everyone agreed to make it their primary class and deactivate all of their other combat classes for now. Once that was done, I gave everyone more bullets for their pouches and showed them how to reload the magazines for the rifle.

We gathered our dark elf auxiliaries and traveled back across the water to do one more dungeon to get everyone level 1 in their new class. The dark elves quickly found another dungeon and we jumped right in. While we completed the last few dungeons, we stayed in the temple when night fell so we didn't have to keep traveling back and forth across the water every evening. It had been nerve-wracking for the first few nights, but we closed up the temple tightly at night and made as little noise as possible. With the dark elves able to keep watch all night and us remaining quiet, we were lucky and had no monsters disturb us. We had also cleared several of the closest dungeons, which helped reduce the number of monsters spilling out into the immediate area as well.

With the addition of support classes, running the dungeons had become routine. The legionnaires and the dark elves had meshed well, and the varied dungeons helped us all learn and grow as a team. The legionnaires thus gained valuable experience that most soldiers would have never received. Whereas a typical army might fight a couple of battles a year, the dungeons pitted us against monsters over and over again in wildly different environments and gave us all kinds of different objectives to conquer. By now, my people were veterans of more battles than some legionnaires might see in their entire lives—back before monsters, at least.

All of this was helped by my skills that boosted their training and rewards and perks that enhanced everyone's roles in the legion as a whole. As I had hoped, our leaders had started to receive a few perks that benefited their squads. The other legionnaires were also receiving perks that enhanced their support roles. Our healers, for instance, now had access to a healing spell that also granted bonus attributes to whoever they healed.

Our coordination and growing skill showed in the newest dungeon, the rifles making the dungeon even easier. The legionnaires formed a line and the dark elves scouted, flushing out any enemies and leading them back to the waiting line of riflemen. Monsters were shot down well before they could get close enough to hurt anyone, the volley fire of the rifle too powerful even in the hands of just twenty men and women. The very few groups of monsters that survived the first twenty volleys from the riflemen, either through numbers or pure strength and endurance, were met with grenades and revolver fire. With their charge disrupted, the dark elves and legionnaires finish them off with ease.

It had taken a lot of planning to come up with the various tools of the legion, but as I watched them fight, I felt extremely proud of what we had accomplished together. They were a smooth, organized, and deadly group, and the tools I had provided them synergized extremely well, making them nearly unstoppable. At least here in the dungeons we were unstoppable, since the dungeons always scaled the enemies to be a challenge but to not be too powerful.

When we finished the dungeon, everyone got enough experience to level *Rifleman* several times. This time they all got the same skill options I had received, and I told them all to take

Shield Wall to give us some necessary defensive options, something we were currently lacking. Everyone agreed, and when we practiced it outside the dungeon, the shield wall sprang up in front of the line of riflemen immediately. It formed a thick blue barrier that shielded the entire group from the ground to above their heads, curving overhead to offer protection above them as well. I could see through the blue shield easily from behind, but when I moved in front, everything was obscured, making it harder for attackers to target the legionnaires individually. I tried pushing through the barrier and found it resistant to my entry, meaning it would help resist enemies that tried to attack in melee as well as from range.

Chapter 40

Now that we had the core of our classes and plenty of practice working as a team, it was time to move to our next phase of operations: recovering the ship I had repaired weeks ago. I sent everyone back to Sycae while Constans and I went and tracked down Theo, the former sailor, and some of the other fishermen Constans had spoken to so long ago. When I finally explained that we wanted to hire them to leave the city with us, nobody was interested except Theo. Even after we offered very good compensation, nobody was willing to trust that we could protect them outside the city. Everyone seemed to have a bit of a fatalistic attitude that there was nothing worth looking for anymore and that it was just a matter of time before even these last few enclaves were overrun. Why rush their death by leaving the city? They were happy to just stay here, even though they knew full well they were all slowly being choked to death by the monsters that surrounded them.

Theo, on the other hand, was more than willing to go with us. When I told him the plan, he thought I was completely crazy, but that only interested him more.

I had been hoping to get a crew of experienced people who could man the ship for us, but since none of the other fishermen were willing to go, I asked if Theo thought he could get a ship back to the city with a crew of untrained men and women.

"If they're willing to listen," he replied, "they'd already be a step above these sorry sacks of flesh. If you really found a ship out there that's seaworthy, I can guide a novice crew back here."

"Then consider yourself hired," I told him, shaking his hand.

With Theo on board, Constans and I took him over to Sycae and got him settled at the inn. I told Basil to have everyone ready to go the next morning.

I decided to let the legionnaires walk openly through the city as we left. Their pride in their new uniforms and the new, hard-won skills they had earned made them hold their heads high as they marched through the city. I could tell it meant a lot to them as they saw so many people stop and stare in admiration and surprise. They tried not to show it, but they all beamed with pride in themselves and their companions.

And truth be told, we made a damn impressive sight as we left the city. With rifles slung over their shoulders and matching uniforms and cloaks, the legionnaires marched in perfect unison. The men and women of the legion looked like truly professional soldiers. The dark elves surrounded the legionnaires, heavily cloaked and wearing the goggles I had made for them, adding even more mystery to the sight of us.

We marched west, away from the city, tracing the route I had taken previously when I found Mitkos and the ship I had worked on. It was much slower-going than when I had been on my own, but I couldn't bring the ship back by myself.

Once we were about a mile outside of the city, I heard a number of cries of surprise from the legion. I signaled for Basil to stop everyone, since they would need a moment to understand that they had just earned an achievement for completing the "safe zone" they had spent their whole life in. Everyone huddled up. I explained what I had learned about the achievement system, the "safe zone," and regional quests, and I answered a number of questions from everyone. There were some I couldn't answer, but I let everyone talk it out while the dark elves kept watch. I had expected this reaction once we left the city, so I made sure we had the time to stop and discuss it while there was plenty of daylight left for us to travel by.

Once everyone had come to terms with so much new information, we set out once again. Ryld joined me as we traveled and seemed to have something on his mind, but it took a while for him to speak up. I was used to his silence, so I didn't push him, waiting patiently until he felt ready to talk. Finally, Ryld turned to me with a serious expression on his face—more serious than even his normally stoic expression.

"Alexander," he started, "the other dark elves and I have been talking. It has been a rude awakening to see how powerful your

533

devices can be. We knew your revolver was deadly in the underdark, but you have shown us something we have never seen before with your legion." He paused, considering his words. "Your rifle is better than our crossbows, your revolver is better than our swords, and your grenades are almost as good as our spells. It's a very humbling thing to witness."

I wasn't sure if I should apologize or be proud of his compliments, but he continued before I had to come up with something to say.

"For that reason," he said, "we have all decided that we want to formally join your legion. We understand that means we would pledge ourselves to your service for twenty years and we are willing to do that. In return, we want to learn your new classes and be equipped with your new weapons."

I was surprised by his words but also happy that they were all willing to join my legion. I hadn't wanted to pressure them, but they were a powerful group that I trusted, and they had become a vital part of our tactical approach to battle. Arming them with my classes and modern weapons would make them even deadlier.

"When we stop for a rest, gather the dark elves together and we'll sign the contract. I don't have enough weapons immediately, but I will work on getting enough so everyone has a rifle and revolver as soon as possible."

"Thank you, Alexander," he said. "We live a long time, by human standards, but twenty years is no small amount of time. We pledge to do our best to work toward your goals and protect you. Your new ideas will bring dangerous enemies as knowledge of what you have made spreads, but we will be there by your side to see you through the danger."

I was touched by his pledge and bowed respectfully to him. When we broke for lunch, I swore in the dark elves and taught each of them the *Gunslinger* and *Rifleman* classes. The legionnaires clapped as I swore in each dark elf, welcoming them to the legion. The taciturn and reserved dark elves simply bowed back but seemed happy with the welcome.

I gave Ryld my own rifle and had Basil, Nikephoros, and a couple of the humans loan their rifles to the other dark elves so they could begin practicing. Then I assigned Nikephoros to work with them to train them in gun safety and the use of their new weapons.

The dark elves were already naturally quick learners and disciplined fighters, so with the help of my bonuses, they mastered their weapons in record time. When we got back on the road, Basil sent the human scouts out to practice while the dark elves drilled with their firearms on the march.

We were attacked numerous times as we traveled, but our experiences in the dungeons had made everyone into professional soldiers. Even when we were swarmed by a flock of griffons from the air, upset because we accidentally traveled too close to their nests, everyone calmly formed a line as the angry birds took to the sky. Before they could get anywhere near us, the legionnaires shot them down.

Theo watched in awe as we slaughtered the monsters that attacked us. The first few nights, he drank himself into a stupor from nerves, but after he saw us fight a few times, he started to become almost too comfortable with the trip. He often wandered off to enjoy the seashore or other sights, relishing his time out of the city. I eventually had to ask him to at least take me or Constans with him just to make sure he stayed safe, which he was more than happy to do.

The trip to recover the ship took over three weeks on foot, even with the movement speed skill that most of the legionnaires had. We still had to sleep and rest since the legionnaires' attributes were still not particularly high yet. And after every fight, Nikephoros sent the legionnaires to go recover their bullets which slowed us down considerably. We just didn't have enough bullets to spare, so we had to take the time to get as many of the bullets back as we could. Theo and Constans also didn't have the same movement skill as the legionnaires, so once they got too tired, we had to slow down. Constans hated every time it happened, but I didn't mind the more leisurely pace.

The biggest surprise of the trip took place about two weeks into our journey. I had sensed a large monster in front of us for a while now, and when we got close, a dark elf scout came running to report that I needed to follow her. I ordered Basil to form up in case of attack and ran forward with the scout.

I could sense the monster ahead and I could hear a battle taking place, but there was no sign of another monster nearby. What was the monster fighting if there wasn't another monster nearby?

When I followed the scout over the nearest hill, I got a look at what was happening and almost gasped in surprise at what I was seeing. The monster I had sensed was a large drake, brown in color and standing almost a story and a half tall. It was battling a person wearing heavy plate armor and riding a horse equally covered in heavy armor. The light reflected off the armor, making the horse and man shine like something from a storybook. The knight— because what other class could I be looking at?—wheeled around, twirling a large halberd in his hand, and raced toward the drake as it reared up to strike him with one of its claws. The drake was slowed, though, from a lance that had been driven completely through the beast from its breast to its back.

As the scout and I watched, the knight and his steed moved too fast for the drake, easily racing past its attack and under its arm, stabbing his halberd deep into the side of the beast. The knight urged his horse forward even faster, dragging the tip of the halberd through the side of the drake from its chest to its tail in a split second.

The drake let out a great howl of pain as its entire side folded open like a slice of cheese, exposing its guts and soft tissue. The knight turned and activated a skill of some kind. He and his mount became cloaked in a shining radiance, and then they shot forward, slamming into the drake like a wrecking ball, knocking the wounded monster onto its side. When the light faded, I saw the halberd buried deep in the drake's skull.

I was impressed, not only by the power and speed of the knight but by the bravery it took to fight a drake that size in single combat. I could have managed it myself, but I would have had to kill the drake from a distance, using cheap tactics to wear it down and kill it before it could get close enough to touch me.

The knight dug his halberd out of the drake's skull and then climbed down to grab the end of his lance and slide it out of the monster's body. He turned and looked in our direction, giving a wave, and then mounted his horse and rode over, seemingly unconcerned about us watching him.

"Hello!" I called out in Latin as the knight approached.

The knight secured his lance in a large holster on the side of his horse and strapped his halberd onto his back in some fashion. Once his weapons were put away, the knight removed his helm to reveal a sweaty man with a wide grin on his face.

"Well met!" he said to me. "I am sorry I couldn't greet you a moment sooner. I had a pest to vanquish first!"

He approached and stepped down from his horse in front of me and the dark elves. Once he was down, he bowed deeply with an elegant flourish that hinted he might come from some noble's or king's court. I bowed in return, impressed that he could bow so elegantly while wearing heavy plate armor.

"Where are you from?" I asked him. "We didn't expect to find anyone alive out here."

"To say I feel the same would be a great understatement," he said. "I come from the Kingdom of Champenois. I am on a holy quest to find if any civilization remains in the east, but I have traveled for many months and found nothing but devastation. But now, right before I feared I may have to give up and turn around, I find people! It is a miracle!"

I didn't think that finding us was a miracle, although stranger things did happen in this world, but the fact that he came from something he deemed worthy of calling a kingdom sounded promising to me. I invited him to camp with us and he happily agreed. I sent the scout back to warn everyone. Then the knight, who was named Oudinet Toussaint and who, indeed, had the *Knight* class, joined me as we walked back.

When he saw my troops, he became even more excited.

"A fine company! It is good to see there is real civilization out here after all!"

"There are a few people holding on," I told him, not wanting to get his hopes up too much, "but it is a far cry from civilization at this point."

We stopped early for the day and set up camp, our cooks preparing some freshly killed monsters from earlier in the day to welcome our guest. Oudinet had saddlebags full of supplies and shared some wine with me and my other leaders as we ate. He expressed no surprise over learning about the dark elves' presence, which hinted to me that wherever he was from, the people there knew about intelligent monsters. Or perhaps he simply accepted them since he was a guest and didn't want to offend us.

He was an amicable and boisterous man. It was charming, although I wouldn't want to spend every night around a fire with him. He was loud and told outrageous stories, but he was clearly good-natured and seemed to have no hidden motives that I could sense. His soul was pure, full of the thrill for adventure.

We spoke late into the night about where he was from and our part of the world. His enthusiasm wasn't dimmed when he learned that our city had truly barely survived. After I told him about our region, he relayed stories of his homeland. Apparently medieval France was in full swing, full of small warring city-states and kingdoms, each claiming the right to ascend to the French throne. I learned a lot from him. A lot of what he shared he seemed to assume was common knowledge, although it wasn't to me.

His area of the world was more tamed and full of real, actual kingdoms. Large cities, towns, and villages had all survived the monsters and changes to the world. Life still wasn't as easy as it had been before, but it was very obvious that his area of the world had adapted significantly better than ours. Some of the Italian city-states had also survived, I learned, Venice and Genoa being the two biggest on the international stage. Rome had fallen and never recovered. Expeditions to explore it never returned to speak about what had taken the city. The far north, where Scandinavia was, and all of Britain were apparently considered the frontier. The French people were actively trying to settle the region to claim their resources and battle the more powerful monsters that populated the area. Monster hordes attacked from the frontier regularly, and only the hardiest and strongest of settlers tried to claim land, backed by various French kingdoms.

"The larger the population when the monsters appeared," Oudinet said, "the more dungeons spawned and the more monsters attacked, as I'm sure your people must have found out. The biggest cities were destroyed and we don't have the armies to take them back anymore. It's impressive that such a mighty city as Nova Roma survived at all, truly."

That bit of information helped explain more of what had happened and why so many dungeons existed in the city. Apparently his people survived primarily because they were so spread out. These days, they were very careful to keep their populations dispersed and had unlocked classes that could tame dungeons and make them permanent so they wouldn't spawn wildly and could be used by people to train and gain power in a more controlled environment. It truly did sound like actual civilization compared to where I had been living.

"Our biggest city is Paris," he said, "which was originally lost but has been reclaimed and is now the center of our region. Almost all trade passes through it, although no king will grant supreme authority to Paris. Everyone respects the power of the king that rules the city, though."

"I should visit someday," I said, imagining what the city must be like.

"You should visit my kingdom first," Oudinet said. "I will put in a good word with my king and you will be treated like a foreign prince. I give you my word!"

"We are continuing on along the coast for now and have a lot to do around here, but maybe someday I can visit," I told him, touched by his invitation. "If you want to join us, you would be welcome company."

"I will travel with you for a few days," he replied, "but then I must head back home. I was already planning to return soon, but now I have good information to share so I must make haste. My king will be ecstatic to learn of the success of my mission. He may send a delegation to visit your city and reestablish trade! It could be a great boon for my people. I am truly blessed to have run into you!"

After a few more drinks and some more conversation, we turned in for the night, the dark elves keeping watch as most of the humans slept. For the next couple of days, we traveled with Oudinet. We encountered a number of monsters, but I didn't want to reveal how our weapons worked, so I invited the knight to go hunting with me whenever a monster was spotted by our scouts or I sensed one nearby. He took it as a deep compliment that I wanted to go hunting with him so often. Apparently hunting was a sign of deep friendship between people and he was touched that I extended him so many invitations. I didn't have the heart to tell him I was just doing it to hide our weapons from him, so I kept up the charade multiple times a day as monsters came close to us, feeling bad about the deception.

I only used my sword on the hunts, but I was barely needed. Oudinet was a powerful knight. Significantly more powerful than me, even, if you didn't count the way I used my inventions and tricks to kill monsters. He clearly had more attributes than me. Although he was about as fast as me, he was significantly stronger, able to lift entire monsters easily whenever the need arose. He did this more frequently than I thought a sane man should, joyously charging in headfirst and relying on his strength and power to get him out of tough situations.

One time, I saw him lift a boulder as large as a small house and toss it effortlessly at a charging snake, crushing its head completely. I could have maybe lifted the boulder if I really tried, especially with my *Ant's Strength* perk, but there was no way I could do it so easily or throw the boulder so accurately.

Oudinet laughed uproariously after squashing the snake with the boulder, finding it the height of hilarity. I couldn't help but laugh at the absurdity of a human man throwing such a large rock so effortlessly. It looked unreal, like watching a bad movie back on Earth.

I enjoyed fighting with the knight. He taught me a valuable lesson in how different this world truly was. Most people were fairly reserved with their power in this world, but Oudinet wore his power on his sleeve and loved every moment of it. It was refreshing to see. Seeing the superhuman feats he was capable of helped me come to terms with how different a person with high attributes truly was in this world. And despite my best efforts, I couldn't resist Oudinet's infectious laughter and congenial attitude. The pure, unadulterated pleasure he took from fighting monsters had me laughing more than I had ever laughed before in my life. Watching him fight was like watching a toddler given permission to destroy a room full of toys, with the exact amount of smashing, laughing, screaming, and destruction you would imagine.

After several days of hunting together, we parted with a hug. He promised to look me up if his king sent him with a future delegation and I promised to do the same if I ever found myself in Toussaint. I was surprised by how easily I had come to like the man. Despite how tiring his boisterousness could sometimes be at the end of a long day, I found myself missing him after he was gone. It had been a nice diversion to meet someone new, and his good-hearted enthusiasm for life was a pleasure to be around. I hoped I would be able to see him again someday.

When we finally arrived at the ruined city where the boat was docked, we found the area still empty of any other monsters. The memory of Mitkos was apparently enough to keep the local monsters far away, even after he had been dead for so long. I had Basil secure the city anyway, and he posted sentries and fortified the area at the end of the docks in case of attack. The legionnaires jumped to it, dragging stones from around the ruined city to form a small wall at the end of the dock that held our ship.

As they worked, I inspected the ship from the inside and from underwater. It looked fully repaired; even the wear and tear of the deck had been cleaned and repaired. The ship practically sparkled.

Theo was dumbstruck upon seeing the condition of the ship, thinking it must have just been built since it was in such fine condition.

I gave Theo free rein of the ship and watched the legionnaires as they prepared our defenses. The dark elves were hidden around the city, keeping watch for anything that might approach while the others worked. The legionnaires worked swiftly, building the short wall with enthusiasm and good-natured competition to see who could build their section the fastest. Basil and Nikephoros directed everyone on where to place their stones, and Constans worked beside the others, not sparing herself the physical labor.

When they finished, a short wall about five feet tall stretched in a semicircle around the dock. The dark elves stayed in the city as night fell while some legionnaires kept watch at the wall. The rest of us entered the ship and everyone was shocked to find hammocks in the hold, perfectly repaired and ready to be used. I hadn't exactly ordered the nanobots to repair even the hammocks, but I had been gone longer than I had planned, so they must have just kept going, repairing more and more of the ship as they consumed life from the water around the city.

When everyone awoke the next day, Theo began a crash course on how to run a ship. I had the dark elves keep watch in the city and had only the humans learning from Theo since I wanted the dark elves' superior marksmanship and attributes to protect the

541

ship in case we were attacked at sea. While the humans had been using the firearms for longer, the dark elves had been hunters before the humans had even been born. The dark elves were quick learners and could borrow the humans' rifles to protect the ship while we were at sea, so it made sense to have them protecting the ship while the humans ran it.

It was two weeks before Theo felt we were ready to leave the harbor, and he expressed surprise at how fast that was. He had expected it to take a month or more, but working nonstop to learn the ship and my bonuses had resulted in everyone learning remarkably fast. It was an enjoyable two weeks for me, since I mostly just watched them work, dashing back to the city only once to go hunting for a few days to fuel my nanobot workstations.

Once we were ready to go, Theo took the helm, guided us out of the harbor, and navigated us back toward the city. The dark elves kept watch in the sails and rigging for any monsters, their keen eyes able to partially see into the water, even during the day, thanks to my goggles. I also kept watch, climbing up to the crow's nest since I had the best vision of everyone.

I could see a number of monsters under the water, and at first, I raised the alarm each time, but none of them seemed to bother us as we traveled along the coastline. Most of them were further out at sea, and the few that were close were smaller than our ship and seemed more intimidated by us than we were of them.

We were attacked a couple of times, once by a flying sea monster that leapt out of the water on wings too tiny for its long, sinuous body. I called the alarm, but the dark elves had already spotted it and began peppering it with devastating shots from their rifles. By the time it got close to our ship, it had realized it was seriously out of its depths and turned around and dove back into the water, trailing a thick line of green blood in the waves behind it as it fled.

The second attack came at night, while most of the humans were sleeping, but the always-alert dark elves spotted the danger once again. I was keeping watch in the crow's nest but didn't see the danger because I had been focused out in the distance. When someone yelled the alert, I looked down to see a swarm of large crabs climbing up the side of the ship. I echoed the alarm, calling for everyone to get up to the deck right away, and then jumped down from the crow's nest and drew my sword.

For the first time in a while, I was forced to fight hand to hand. The number of crabs was too great to keep off the ship, and I had no good angle to shoot them. When I landed on the deck, I activated *Never Bring a Mob to a Duel*, gaining a surge of power, and then began to lay into the crabs closest to me. I wasn't subtle this time, diving into their midst and cracking carapaces with my hands and feet, cutting off limbs with my sword, and becoming a whirlwind of destruction among the monstrous crabs.

I took numerous wounds for my recklessness, counting on my *Regeneration* to keep me going. By the time the sleeping crew began to boil up from belowdecks, I was covered in blood and the guts of the crabs, but I had left behind me almost fifty dead or crippled crabs.

The legionnaires, seeing the situation, began to fire on the swarming crabs as they reached the deck. I did a short dash backward as more of the crabs continued to climb over the railings of the ship, grabbing as many bullets as I could from my belt satchels. With my hand full of bullets, I threw them in an arc toward the railing covered in crabs, *willing* the bullets forward with my new *Metal Mind* skill. The bullets shot forward, almost as fast as I could fire them from my revolver, slamming into the entire front line of crabs as they tried to climb onto the boat further.

The injured crabs weren't killed but were staggered enough that they fell back off the ship or blocked more of their brethren from getting on board. The staggered and injured crabs also made for easy targets. The rest of the legionnaires hurriedly followed up and killed most of them with shots from their rifles and revolvers.

I looked to the other side of the ship and saw several legionnaires trying to hold off crabs that had gotten too close. They were using their rifles to try to block the grasping claws of the crabs, but they weren't very effective. I dashed over and began to cut down the crabs from behind, giving the threatened legionnaires space to recover.

"Form a square!" Nikephoros yelled, stepping toward the center of the ship's deck. The seasoned legionnaires responded quickly, forming around him. It was clear they had practiced the formation many times, because within a matter of seconds, the legionnaires had formed into a square with Basil and Nikephoros in the center, rifles and revolvers bristling outward in all directions. I ducked inside the square next to Basil and Nikephoros, not wanting to be caught by friendly fire.

"Shield wall!" Nikephoros yelled. The newest skill of the legionnaires was activated, a blue wall springing up around the square formation. The closest crabs charged and impacted against the shield, no longer able to reach the legionnaires.

"Fire at will!"

With a blast, a volley of bullets was shot outward in every direction, mowing down the closest crabs. A second later, another volley erupted, and then another and another. By the time Basil gave the order to reload, all of the crabs on deck were dead or so injured they couldn't continue attacking.

The healers for each squad were moving around the inside of the square, healing everyone who had been injured by the crabs. Several people had wounds from the large claws, but the healers kept them alive, and once the fighting ended, they gathered around the most severely wounded and began to concentrate on healing them.

When everyone was healed and we had recovered from the sudden attack, Theo told us we should harvest the crab meat and he would show us how to make a delicious soup from his old sailing days. Apparently sea crab swarms were fairly common, although he said there were normally only thirty or so of the monsters, not the hundred or more we had fought.

The legionnaires took to harvesting the crabs with gusto, excited to eat something better than roasted monster meat and trail rations. Under the guidance of Theo and our cooks, a delicious soup was made for everyone to enjoy.

I ate quietly on the deck as I considered my newest skill, *Metal Mind*. It had been very effective, essentially firing a large number of bullets rather than one at a time like from my revolver or rifle. I had become accustomed to my new sense of metal while waiting for the legionnaires to learn to sail, but I hadn't used it actively until now. I could sense every bit of metal, no matter how small, on the ship and people around me, and even get a sense every so often from the seabed as we traveled. It also helped with gathering my used bullets back to me, allowing me to pull them from the corpses of the crabs I had killed while everyone else was busy harvesting them. A few of the bullets were wedged too deep into the wood of the ship for my skill to effectively grab, and more had missed and launched themselves so far away I couldn't sense them anymore, but the skill should still help me to recover more of my bullets than I could normally do by hand alone.

After the swarm of crabs, we were thankfully unmolested as we traveled along the coast toward Nova Roma. What had taken weeks of travel by land ended up only taking us two days of sailing. When we turned up the channel leading to Nova Roma, everyone cheered, including Theo, who was visibly thrilled to be piloting a ship home for the first time in many years. He threw his hand in the air and did a small jig, dancing in place as Nova Roma came into view.

When he calmed down, I told him to take us to the Sycae docks and to avoid getting too close to the main city. He saluted with a grin on his old, scraggly face and guided us forward.

As we coasted past the main part of the city, I could see men and women rushing to line the wall all along the Patriarch's enclave. They stared at us in silence, but thankfully, none of them tried to attack us or cast a spell in our direction.

When we reached Perama, I saw people lining the side of the bridge and climbing the ramshackle buildings all along the eastern side, many of them cheering and screaming at the sight of a ship approaching the city once again. The fishermen on their boats in the nearby water stopped their work and rowed in our direction, calling up questions about who we were and where we had come from.

By the time we reached the docks of Sycae, word had spread and the docks were packed full of people. Men and women, many with their children on their shoulders, were packed into every free inch of space all along the docks. The sounds of their cheering and cries of joy echoed across the water toward us as we approached the dock. As we got closer, I saw many openly weeping, even the men, at the sight of a ship returning to the city for the first time in so many years.

545

Even the legionnaires, who had basked in the attention they had received when they left the city, seemed shocked by the reception.

As we finished tying up to the dock, I could see a delegation of merchants pushing through the crowds, surrounded by guards that were shoving people out of the way as they came toward us. We lowered the gangplank and I walked down first. People swarmed me on the dock, asking questions about where I was from and if other parts of the world were still surviving.

I felt bad having to tell them that we weren't from another city. I explained to those nearby that we were from here, just returning with a ship we had salvaged, but not many heard or understood me in the press of the crowd.

When the merchants arrived, I finally got to see the merchant council that ran Sycae for the first time. Their guards pushed their way down the dock until the merchants could speak to me. I invited them onto the ship to give us some more privacy, figuring there was no way to avoid talking to them and I might as well get it over with as soon as possible.

On the ship, the four men and one woman that made up the council stared at everything excitedly, marveling at the crew and the fine condition of the ship. Their enthusiasm made me like them a little more, despite the poor introduction they had made by bullying through the crowds to reach us.

I started by breaking the bad news to them immediately, telling them that we weren't from another city and that we had just recovered this ship for our own purposes. They took the news well, immediately shifting to talk of whether I would be trying to find other cities and if I would be selling cargo space on my ship. I admired how quickly they could adapt and immediately try to turn a profit from us, although I didn't commit to anything and didn't tell them about what I had learned at the monastery or from Oudinet, still unsure why nobody had come to the city in so many years when it was clear other cities and regions had survived.

Instead, I told them I would contact them when we returned from our first expedition and that, if things went well, I should have something that would interest them greatly. They tried to pry for details, intrigued by what I'd said, but I refused to share more than that.

Eventually, after almost an hour of talking back and forth, they realized they had learned all they could and we said our goodbyes. I was eager to see them gone, already tired of having to make small talk and resist their prying questions.

News trickled slowly through the crowd that we were from Nova Roma and had returned with a salvaged ship. Despite some disappointment, others seemed even more excited by the idea that Nova Roma had a trade vessel once again. Eventually, the excitement of our arrival faded and people began to return to their homes and work. When the crowd finally dispersed, we all shared a sigh of relief. Our return had been more intense than any of us had expected, and it was clear we had underestimated the hunger for even a hint of prosperity and trade returning to the city.

"Constans," I told her once everything settled down a bit, "get a list of what we have on the ship and go sell it all except for the iron ore. Leave that here for now. Price doesn't matter for the rest, although do your best. Once you sell everything, buy us food and water to stock up enough for a month at least, longer if you can get a good deal."

"On it!" she yelled.

"Basil," I said to him, "we want a heavy watch at all times. Nobody on or off the ship unless they are with their entire squad. We just painted a very large target on ourselves so everyone needs to be careful. Nobody is to go back to the warehouses. Assume that we are all going to be watched at all times. We don't want anyone knowing where they could attack us when we leave, and we won't be able to protect the warehouses, so we don't want anyone to know they are ours, got it?"

He saluted and turned to pass word on to everyone else.

"Ryld, you and the other dark elves stay on watch at all times. Keep an eye out for someone trying to do something under the water as well. There is a reason other cities stopped coming here, and until I know why, I want us to be very vigilant. Someone could try to sabotage the ship or steal it from us."

"Understood," he said.

I dashed upward, my invisibility allowing me to hide from those that were still lingering nearby and watching us. I soared over Sycae until I found our warehouses and then dashed into a nearby alley where nobody would see me.

I let myself inside and gathered the weapons and ammunition that had been completed since I left. I loaded them all into crates and dashed back and forth to the ship, depositing them in the hold after giving the dark elves the newest batch of rifles. Back at the warehouse, I found the four largest clay pots I had salvaged and ordered my specialized nanobots into them. I packed up their workstations and then made several more trips, bringing all of them to our ship and setting them up in the bottom of the hold.

Once those were secured, I gathered up the rest of the raw materials I had left and brought them to the ship at a more leisurely pace.

Afterward, I returned to the warehouse and scoured the basement to make sure no trace of what I had made remained, just in case anyone found it and investigated.

It took several days for Constans to sell the goods that had come with the salvaged ship when I found it. She made a killing with her deals, though, primarily because of the novelty of buying goods from the first ship to dock in the city in almost ten years, she said. While she was busy selling everything, barrels of water and dried food began to be delivered. The legionnaires loaded the barrels themselves, not allowing the eager delivery people onto the ship.

While she was busy with all of that, I approached the miners that she had found so long ago and spoke to them about coming with us. They were extremely skeptical until they realized I was the owner of the ship that had docked in the harbor. Once they realized that, they agreed to go with us, although it still wasn't cheap to hire them and they insisted I pay their families even more if they died. I didn't take their lack of trust personally and was just glad they ended up agreeing to work for me. I had each of the miners sign a year-long contract with a provision of complete secrecy for life and guarantees of a good salary and death benefits if something happened to them while in my service.

Then I grabbed Theo and approached the fishermen again. This time, the bunch of curmudgeonly old men and women were much more open to what I had to say, but many of them were still nervous and unwilling to leave the city. They were too afraid of the open sea these days and many of them had families that relied on them and the food they brought in.

Theo wasn't surprised and suggested that we recruit some of the younger men and women and train them up rather than try to find old veterans. Not having much of a choice, I deferred to him and told him to find me some people that we could trust. I would then vet them and bring them on board. When our supplies were all delivered, he came to me with a group of fifteen young men and women. They were eager to try their hand on the ship and many of them had already been taught the *Sailor* class by one of their parents, but had never had a chance to gain much experience in the class. Theo promised to get them enough experience to finally level them up and let them gain useful skills if they joined with us. *Sailor* was a non-combat class but could come with some combat skills for defending a ship as well as skills to help run a ship faster and more efficiently.

I interviewed each one individually and found them to be earnest and generally good-hearted. I only rejected two of them, not for anything as serious as the young man I had rejected from my legion, but just because they didn't really want to go with us and were only going because they were being pressured by someone—I couldn't tell who, but I could see the pressure weighing on their souls when I observed them.

I signed on the others for a one-year contract, promising them a salary, training, a class if they didn't have *Sailor* yet, and food and board for the year. In return, they pledged loyalty for the year and secrecy for life.

Once every one of them had signed up, I officially made Theo the captain of the ship and told him he was in charge of the ship from now on.

He smiled, his wrinkled face lighting up as he looked over the ship.

"I never thought—" he started to say when a shocked look came over his face.

"What happened?" I asked him, hastily looking around, afraid we might be under attack. I reached for my sword but couldn't see anything dangerous nearby.

"My *Sailor* class just evolved," he said, closing his eyes. "I didn't know it could do that. Captains don't share how they get their class with lowly sailors, even their seconds. As soon as you

549

made me the captain of your ship, my *Sailor* class became *Captain*. Wow."

I clapped him on the shoulder and congratulated him.

He turned to look at me, a stunned look on his face.

"All of my *Sailor* skills upgraded," he said. "And it reset to level 1, so it should level again in a hurry. Thank you, sir. I never thought I would live to see such a thing."

"You earned it for being willing to take a chance with us, Theo," I told him. "You saw how few were willing to take such a risk. You put your faith in us and you were deservedly rewarded. You earned it."

He didn't respond, focusing internally, likely reading all his new skills. I left him to it.

As his first job as captain, I had him take us out of the dock with my legionnaires as crew, not wanting to wait for his sailors to get trained in the practical aspects of running a ship while the entire city seemed to watch everything we did. Thankfully, the evolved class *Captain* could still teach people the *Sailor* class, so we didn't have to worry about that with the new recruits who hadn't been a taught the class yet.

My legionnaires taught the new sailors as we left the dock, joking and teasing the new recruits who were around the same age as the young legionnaires. The sailors were good-natured and took the teasing well, jumping to learn from the legionnaires without complaint. Theo regained his composure and began yelling orders at the legionnaires and sailors as we pulled away from Sycae. As we drifted out into the channel, a small group of people gathered at the dock, waving goodbye to us, some of them clearly family of the sailors we had recruited, who waved back. I was touched by the normalcy of the sight, nervous and proud parents saying goodbye to their children as they left home for the first time. I vowed to do my best to make sure everyone returned home safely.

The people of Perama turned out as well. Only slightly less subdued than last time, everyone rushed to get a spot where they could watch us as we sailed past their bridge, cheering and waving from the bridge and the sides of the buildings. With how many were rushing to see us, I worried they would collapse the buildings or push people off the bridge entirely. Many of the sailors and even some of the legionnaires returned their waves, which only encouraged them to yell and scream more in excitement. I could even see Momma Lena up there, watching us from in front of her shop as we passed the bridge. I wasn't sure if she recognized us, but I didn't doubt she could tell exactly who we were and what we were up to.

Once we were past the city, I called up the people I considered the leaders of my little band of misfits. Theo, Basil, Ryld, Constans, and Nikephoros joined me on the top deck, and I finally revealed our destination to them all. When I told them we were going to find an old orichalcum mine that had been lost generations ago, none of them objected or called me crazy, a sign that I had either finally worn them down or they really had come to trust me by now.

Theo knew the way, having worked these waters before, so I left him to guide the ship south. The rest of us talked about our destination and what we planned to do when we arrived. I told them how I had learned the destination of one of the largest mines for orichalcum in the old empire and how I planned to reclaim the town to mine the precious metal.

"You know that to the best of our knowledge, everything east of Nova Roma has been overrun by the undead, right?" Nikephoros asked.

"I've heard that," I told him. "But I think our legion can manage it. We'll see soon how true the rumors are. Spread the word on what you know about the undead so everyone can be as prepared as possible."

He and Basil saluted and left to organize the legionnaires. I had Constans run through what she had sold and how much she had made in the city, and when she finished telling me, I received notice I had completed one of my first quests, *Contribute to the Economy II*. As the rewards materialized, I gave the cores to her and reviewed the next quest, *Contribute to the Economy III*, which came as no surprise to me.

Contribute to the Economy III: You must sell goods or provide services worth a very large amount of money, depending on your region. Reward: 10 gold cores, 200 experience.

I smiled at the quest description. That was the plan, mysterious quest-giver, whoever or whatever you were. It was time to reintroduce some orichalcum ore to the world.

Chapter 41

We made good time down the coast and managed to avoid being attacked by any sea monsters as we traveled. I stayed in the crow's nest, watching the coast of what used to be Turkey in my world. I saw numerous cities and towns dotting the coast, but none of them were occupied. I also noticed that the area didn't seem overrun with monsters like the cities and harbors had been when I traveled to the west of Nova Roma. Here, the cities and towns were completely abandoned, but I couldn't see any damage to the buildings, only empty streets and homes. It was as if a plague had swept through the region, killing everything that lived but leaving the rest of the area untouched. There was no movement, no life, no birds above, no monsters or smaller animals scurrying through the remains of the towns and cities we passed. There was no sign of movement except the soft breeze as it rustled the trees, bushes, and grass that had started to reclaim the land.

It was eerie and unnatural to see so many picturesque cities and towns so empty of life. Even the monsters would have been better, in many ways, at least giving us an explanation for why everything had been abandoned. Here, there was just . . . nothing.

Nobody else seemed to really notice, too busy with their day-to-day duties on the ship, but I caught the dark elves eyeing the shore from time to time, so I suspected they shared my disquiet.

It was just a couple of days down the coast to Miletus, the town that had been one of the major sources of orichalcum ore for the now-fallen Roman Empire. When we arrived, we approached the town cautiously, but everything looked just as dead as everything else had. A small, quaint dock only big enough for a few large ships jutted into the small harbor the town had been built around.

The town itself was full of beautiful stone buildings and surrounded by high cliffs. There was only one large warehouse next to the dock, and the rest of the town appeared almost wealthy, the houses large and multi-storied. At the very back of the town was a large, gaping hole carved into the cliffside. It seemed out of place in such a beautiful town. Mining equipment left exposed to the weather was piled up around the hole.

As we approached the dock, everyone was on deck and alert for any sign of an attack. This close to the shore, I could see bodies lying in the streets and along the docks, many of them splayed out as if they had fallen in surprise, unaware of whatever had killed them. The bodies didn't look nearly decayed enough for having lain exposed to the elements for the better part of a decade or more.

"Anyone wanna take a bet those corpses attack us as soon as we land?" I heard Constans say.

Several people laughed, but nobody took her up on the offer.

"Form a line along the starboard side and prepare to repel boarders!" Basil yelled.

Everyone got into position and we eased closer to the dock under Theo's expert direction. We docked, and several legionnaires rappelled across to the dock and tied us up before hastily climbing back aboard the ship. The rest of us waited, the silence of the town eerie and unsettling. I finally jumped down, figuring I was the best one to trigger any surprise attack if it came. I approached one of the nearby corpses on the dock. A partially broken crate lay in front of the body as if the person had been carrying it when they died.

When I stepped within a few feet of the body, it began to twitch slightly. I drew my sword and waited. The body twitched more and more rapidly before it began to pull itself upward, a groan escaping from it as it slowly rose next to me.

I sliced the zombie through the neck, aiming to decapitate it, but was surprised to find my blade only cut halfway through. With my strength and my magical sword, I had expected to cut through its neck with ease. I wrenched my sword out and swung again, putting all my strength into the blow. This time, my sword passed through its neck and the corpse collapsed back to the dock.

"Shoot for the head!" I called up to the ship.

A wave was spreading down the dock and into the city, originating from where I stood. It wasn't visible to the naked eye, but I could see it with my spirit vision. It was some kind of spiritual alarm. When it passed, the bodies of the zombies reacted, beginning to twitch rapidly. A moment later, the many bodies that littered the city began to rise.

I jumped back onto the ship. Legionnaires took potshots when they had a good angle, picking off the rising undead. Their accuracy had improved significantly since those first days I trained them to fire, and more often than not, their shots hit the zombies in their heads, instantly killing them.

Of course, in typical zombie fashion, there were more bodies pouring out of the houses of the town. A wave of zombies even came pouring out of the mine, all of them carrying mining equipment and pickaxes. The zombies began to stumble toward us, moving slightly faster than I expected.

To my shock, several of the zombies stopped when they got near our ship and began casting magic at us. Bolts of sickly-looking green magic shot toward some of the legionnaires who were positioned at the front of the ship. The legionnaires reacted calmly, raising their magical shield in front of the ship, which managed to stop the spells for now.

"Take out those mages!" I heard Nikephoros yell. The dark elves in the rigging of the ship responded immediately, shifting their aim to the zombies casting magic at us. The zombie mages seemed unable to defend themselves, purely focusing on casting their spells over and over again, so the dark elves were able to kill them quickly. Meanwhile, a large wave of zombies was approaching down the central road, including the zombies from the mine, who had swelled the ranks of the zombies spilling from the homes nearby. Basil and Nikephoros were ready, though.

"Grenades!" Basil yelled. Legionnaires all over the ship pulled out their *Explosive Grenades* and launched them into the middle of the zombie horde. The explosions rippled through the crowd, throwing them in the air, killing and injuring a hundred or more in a second.

Some of the zombies struggled back to their feet, burning as they tried to stand, but were rapidly met with rifle shots to the head. Others continued to crawl toward us as they burned but were ignored for now because they moved too slow to be a real danger.

Once the main wave of zombies was killed, it became more of a matter of cleanup than a real battle. Any group of ten or more zombies was met with a grenade, the individual zombies picked off

554

before they could get anywhere near the ship. It became a game for the legionnaires and the dark elves, the youthful men and women of the legion trying to kill more of the zombies than the dark elves, but if you didn't count the grenades, the dark elves were clearly the winners. Their position in the rigging and years of training with ranged weapons and hunting made them the superior marksmen by a long shot.

Once Basil gave the word to stand down, everyone let out a cheer. The sailors and miners who were watching from the back of the ship were the loudest of them all. They had never seen us fight before, and it was clear most of them had expected us to be overwhelmed and killed when they saw the number of zombies attacking us. When they realized we had won, they jumped for joy, calling out their thanks to the legionnaires and dark elves that had saved them. The men and women of the legion took the praise with humble smiles, while the dark elves ignored the celebrating humans to keep an eye on the city, occasionally shooting down one of the moving zombies that still appeared every now and then.

Once even the dark elves couldn't find anything to shoot anymore, Ryld sent them forward to scout the town and finish killing the injured zombies that were still trying to crawl toward us. The dark elves swung themselves out of the rigging to the dock below with superhuman agility and then turned invisible, fanning out into the city to hunt down the rest of the zombies.

Ryld went with them but returned within just a half hour to let me know the town was safe.

"Unload everyone from the ship and find us somewhere safe to stay," I told Basil. "And then have some people clean up this mess. Pile the bodies in one of the larger houses. I can use them in the future." He saluted and hurried away, not even asking why I wanted hundreds of zombie bodies. I didn't have the heart to tell him they would fuel the creation of even more bullets and grenades for his men.

I jumped down to the dock and went to scout the nearby warehouse. The doors were open, partially broken off the hinges, so I was able to enter easily. Inside, I found crates and crates of orichalcum ore, a shipment that had been ready to be picked up, but nobody had ever come for it. I had sensed the metal from the dock, shocked to find such a concentration of the rare metal just

555

sitting here unused. I had brought the miners along with the expectation that we would have to stay here for months before I could enact the next stage of my plans, but with the warehouse full of orichalcum ore, I could move up my plans significantly. I would still have the miners begin working in the mine, but I no longer had to wait around for them to start gathering the ore from the mine.

I found Theo and told him about the ore. I also told him to have the sailors load it onto the ship for us. After that, I went and explored the mine. I kept my sword drawn and my eyes open as I explored, but I found nothing but rusted tools and empty passageways spread deep into the earth, radiating outward and down from the mine's entrance. My *Metal Mind* told me that there was a massive deposit of orichalcum ore all around me as I walked, enough to feed an empire's demands for generations to come.

I hadn't noticed at first, but now that I had a moment to reflect as I explored the empty mine, I realized that none of the undead had registered as monsters to my *Monster Hunter* perk. Was it because they had once been human? Were they still classified as human, even after they had turned undead?

And what had caused such an outbreak? And how far east had it spread? Was all of Asia nothing but an undead wasteland? The population of those areas, even during this era, was fairly high. A plague like this would be very dangerous if it spread into the more populated regions of the Far East.

I put my questions aside as I finished exploring the mines and then returned to the surface. Up top, most of the zombies' remains had been piled into one of the larger houses along the cliffside and the sailors were working on loading the ship full of the ore from the warehouse. I approached Ryld, who was standing watch near the docks, still vigilant despite the all-clear he had given me earlier.

"Any passageways or paths to the cliffs above we need to guard?" I asked him.

"It looks like the town is only accessible by the sea," he replied, gesturing up at the tall cliffs that surrounded the town. "I sent a few scouts up to the top of the cliffs to keep watch, but it doesn't seem like there is anything nearby. I think this place was hidden pretty well from the locals back in the day. Probably one of the reasons the mine was dug here."

I nodded. "Good, keep the scouts on the cliffs just to be safe."

"Of course," he replied. I left him and checked in with everyone else, but they were all busy doing their assigned jobs or helping others, so I wasn't needed. The sailors were loading the ship full of ore under Theo's careful scrutiny. Constans was showing the miners to the mine and helping them find housing near the entrance. Now that the zombie bodies had been moved, Basil and Nikephoros had the men cleaning a few houses near the docks so everyone would have a place to sleep. Zombie parts and blood still littered the streets. Part of me wished we had some kind of water mage to just wash it all into the sea, but some of the less squeamish legionnaires had found a few brooms and were slowly cleaning up the streets as best as they could.

I unloaded my nanobots, their workstations, and all the resources I had brought from Nova Roma into the house full of zombie bodies, then fed the bodies to the nanobots to get our weapons production back up and running. Once that was done, I didn't have anything else pressing to do, so I returned to the ship and watched as the town bustled with new life. By the time night arrived, everyone was settled into a few select houses, the dark elves were watching over the town, the ship was fully laden with ore, and the miners had claimed their own houses near the mine.

I stayed up late, just enjoying the sight of the town and knowing that it was mine. Securing the ore and a home base that was almost impossible for anyone to get to but us was the first step in my plan for true independence from the factions of Nova Roma. It felt good to look out and see a town that was mine, full of people whom I trusted and who trusted me in return. I felt whole in a way that I hadn't for a very long time.

When the sun rose on a new day, it found me seated in the crow's nest and staring out to sea, enjoying the peace and quiet of dawn. I told my leaders that we were heading back to Nova Roma already but only taking a portion of our strength this time to make sure the town stayed secure. I left Basil in charge of Miletus, with Ryld as his second. I took Nikephoros and Constans with me and had half the dark elves and half the legionnaires come with us.

A few flying harpies tried to harass us as we passed a small jut of land in the middle of the sea, but a few volleys from our rifles killed enough of them that the rest flew away, angrily squawking at us as they retreated.

Back in the city, there was thankfully less of a crowd as we docked, although a number of people still stopped what they were doing to watch us. A representative from the merchants council approached soon after we had tied up. I let the man know I had a cargo that the merchants would want to buy but that I wanted to talk to the whole council before I chose whom to sell it to.

The representative ran off to inform the council, and within the hour, I was escorted to them by a handful of guards. I brought Constans to negotiate for me and a few legionnaires as guards to keep us safe. The guards led us to a finely adorned villa. We were ushered into a dining hall where a large table had been set up for us. The members of the merchant's council were already present, seated at the table. Their clerks stood behind them, taking notes or holding books or other instruments they might need.

After introductions and pleasantries were exchanged, I made my offer.

"I have a shipment of orichalcum ore," I told them all, "that I'm willing to sell to the highest bidder."

Loud conversation immediately broke out among the merchants, although I noticed a few didn't seem as surprised as I had thought they would be. Maybe they had been sitting on the location of Miletus or another mine and had hopes of someday securing the mines for themselves.

"I also have one condition," I said, "and that is that the highest bidder must also be able to provide me with a tome of every enchantment known in the city. There will be no negotiations on that point. If none of you can acquire such knowledge, I will begin offering contracts directly to enchanters, who I am sure will be very interested in getting to work with orichalcum once again."

That caused an even greater reaction, some of the merchants cursing me for even suggesting such a thing. I ignored them until they settled down. Then I introduced Constans. I told them that she would be taking their bids and that they should only contact her with serious offers. I left the legionnaires with her and returned to the ship.

Constans returned hours later, visibly annoyed.

"How'd it go?" I asked her.

"They spent the majority of the time trying to bully me into taking ridiculously low prices or to get me to sign a contract not requiring them to provide you with the enchantment knowledge," she said. "They were so infuriating I almost wanted to shoot them."

"Did you get through to them?"

"I told them if they didn't have realistic offers by tomorrow," she replied, "that we would stop negotiating entirely. That helped them focus better. Hopefully tomorrow will be more serious."

She went to grab some food and get some sleep belowdecks, so I continued to watch the city with the dark elves, who also kept watch. Nobody tried to attack us during the night, although I witnessed a number of people watching us from stealth as the night wore on. They all thought they were well-hidden, but my advanced perception and divine boon from Lamashtu let me see them easily.

The next morning, Constans and her guards left to continue negotiations, and I debated whether I should stick around and keep guarding the ship or go try to run a dungeon real quick for some experience. However, the decision was made for me.

Soon after Constans left, one of the dark elves silently signaled to me, indicating that someone was approaching our ship under the water. I entered stealth and ran to the side of the ship the dark elf had indicated and watched as a man swam closer. He was mostly naked and had a strange bubble of air around his head, presumably what was allowing him to breathe underwater for so long. I couldn't tell who had sent him from here, so I unstrapped my weapons and took off my cloak so I wasn't too encumbered in the water.

Once that was done, I dove over the side of the ship above where the man was swimming. I pierced the water headfirst and shot downward toward the man, my *Swimmer's Body* perk from so long ago coming in handy. I wrapped my arms around the man when I reached him, one arm around his neck and the other around his body. The man flailed, trying to break my grip, but I was significantly stronger than he was. I began to kick us both toward the surface, forcing him upward with me. I couldn't hear anything the man said, but it looked like he was yelling as he tried to fight me off. We surfaced together and I dragged him toward our ship, paddling awkwardly with one hand while I held his two arms with my other. Several legionnaires stood at the railing, their rifles pointing down at us as we approached. They lowered a rope ladder, and a few of the sailors climbed down, helping me tie up the man and then haul him up the ladder.

On the deck, I could see the man was small and thin and seemed like he would be more at home in a library than swimming underwater to attack a ship like ours. His struggles had ceased as he realized his situation and he looked terrified, staring wide-eyed at the legionnaires and dark elves that surrounded him.

"So," I said, not sure where to start exactly. "What brings you swimming up to our ship on this fine day?"

He was shaking in fear but refused to answer my question. I crouched down and took a deep look at his soul to see if I could figure out what his motivations were. I stared for a minute but couldn't really find anything useful from gazing at his soul.

"Listen," I said, "you were clearly just about to attack us or try to sabotage us in some way, so we are within our rights to kill you. If you tell me who sent you and explain what they wanted you to do, I will let you go. I have no personal animosity toward you, only the person or people that sent you to attack us."

I didn't really have any experience trying to coerce a confession out of a person, but it seemed like a reasonable offer to me.

He shook his head and muttered under his breath, "You are going to kill me anyway."

I waited for him to say more, and after a moment, he said very quietly, thinking I couldn't hear him, "I knew this was a stupid idea. I should have never agreed." He closed his eyes, tears beginning to leak down his face and fall onto the deck where his face was resting.

I pulled up a contract between me and him.

"This is a magical contract," I told him. "It is unbreakable. If you look at the terms, you can see we can reach an agreement where you get to live through this experience and you can be sure I'm telling you the truth."

I proposed terms that we would spare his life for unprovoked aggression against us. In return, he would answer all of our questions honestly and never act against me or my interests in the future.

I saw him look over the contract reluctantly. He clearly did not want to agree to the contract but was scared of what would happen if he refused. I gave him plenty of time, not pressuring him as he stared at the contract.

"Is this for real?" he finally asked, looking around at the others to see their reactions. Many of them nodded at him with sympathy on their faces, clearly also not wanting to kill the man if they didn't have to.

"I have contracts with all of my people," I told the man. "They can assure you that they are ironclad and bindable on both parties."

We talked more, but I could tell I had him. He was definitely not meant for this line of work; he had clearly been set up in some way or had been pushed into this by someone. I wasn't sure the man had ever been in a fight in his life, judging by his body and how easily he caved to our demands.

"Okay," he said, looking down in shame as he signed the contract. I saw the contract stretch between us and form a permanent bond between his soul and mine.

I interrogated him thoroughly, not leaving a single question unanswered. I was disturbed by what I learned, but I never took it out on the poor man. As I had suspected, he was nothing but an unwitting tool that had been sent here because he was easily expendable.

He told me that he was a priest from the Patriarch's enclave and had been sent here because he had water magic and could make the trip through the water. He was supposed to sneak up on the ship at night and use his magic to punch a hole through the hull, but he was a scholarly priest and it had taken him significantly longer to swim here than he had thought it would. He was exhausted, even with his water magic, and hadn't wanted to do the mission in the first place but had pushed forward because he had been ordered to do so. It hadn't occurred to him how much easier it would be to see him during the day, showing once again he had no business trying to be a saboteur.

I got a description of the priest that had put him up to it, and it matched the man I had tangled with several times now. He must have learned of my connection to the ship, which probably wasn't hard since we drew so much attention when we arrived and I stood out quite dramatically from the rest of the people of this city.

I let the priest go, as promised. I didn't even send a dark elf to assassinate him, which I had specifically left as a possibility in the contract since I would be doing it to silence the man, not as punishment for his aggression against us. He was an honest dupe, though, and didn't deserve to die. He had been used to strike a blow against us, one that the priest who sent him probably didn't think had much chance of success. The priest clearly did not care about the life of one man if it meant the chance of a successful attack against us.

I had kept telling myself I would need to deal with the annoying priest at some point, but it never seemed convenient or that important in the overall scheme of things. The Patriarch's enclave was just a big hassle to my mind, since I couldn't risk openly attacking the priests without upsetting the Emperor and the army. That left trying to infiltrate the enclave, which seemed dangerous since I didn't even know how to get inside, or spending weeks of my time waiting outside the enclave in the hope of seeing the priest again, which I just didn't have the time to do.

Sighing, I watched the priest scramble onto the dock and flee into Sycae. Once he disappeared into the city, I moved back up to the crow's nest and kept watch throughout the day until Constans returned with news of the negotiations.

"Well," she said, "we have a couple of options that are decent." I walked with her to the galley, where she grabbed some food and began to eat hurriedly.

"First," she said, only slightly spitting her food out as she spoke, "we have one guy that is offering us a high price for the ore, but he only has access to one book of enchanter's runes. He has a stake in an enchanter's shop, but the enchanter only specializes in arrows and other disposable weapons so the selection would be limited.

"The other offer worth considering is from the newest merchant on the council, a young man who showed some actual work ethic, in my opinion. He went around to all of the enchanters' shops and struck a bargain with them that he would sell each of them orichalcum ore for a reduced price for five years if they all gave him their runes. He also offered them an initial payment that was quite high, so his actual price for our ore is the lowest of them all, but he promises us the runes from every shop except the one owned by the other merchant. There is another enchanter who makes arrows so we wouldn't be losing anything—except a very large amount of silver, gold, and orbs, of course."

I didn't have to think twice, since money wasn't the main goal here.

"Take the young man's offer," I told her. "And I'll have Ryld send some dark elves to guard him until we get what we need, in case anyone tries to interfere with our agreement."

"Oh, good," Constans said. "I wanted to take his offer as well but wanted to make sure you agreed first. He's pretty smart. For a merchant from around here, I mean."

I raised an eyebrow at her and she looked away, blushing and muttering improprieties about me. I stifled a laugh and left her to her meal.

It took several more days before everything was finalized, but Constans delivered to me not just one large enchanter's tome but seven of them. They had been hastily copied by scribes at no small expense. I looked through them immediately and was impressed by how thorough each of them was. I couldn't tell if the enchanters had held things back, and chances were good that they had, but there were just so many runes here I should finally be able to figure out the underlying logic of the rune system. Runes were essentially a type of language, and now I had the dictionary.

"Perfect job," I told Constans. "I couldn't have asked for better. You outdid yourself, negotiating with some of the most powerful merchants in the city, and you got us exactly what we needed. Thank you."

A large chest was also delivered with the tomes. When I opened it, I saw hundreds of silver pieces and blue orbs filling the chest almost to the brim.

"I thought you said he wasn't paying us much?"

"Pssh," she replied, "this is nothing compared to what the others offered. That ore is worth a kingdom's ransom. The merchant will make double what he paid, if not more. And the enchanters will finally be able to craft real magical items again, which will sell for high amounts to the Emperor and the army, which will trickle its way back into the economy and stimulate all kinds of growth in Sycae. This is a very small amount compared to what some of the merchants offered us."

I was impressed yet again. She had clearly been paying attention to her tutor for her to fully understand the economic impact of the ore being sold in the city. There was enough wealth inside the chest in front of me to keep our legion armed with weapons and ammunition for a year or more, at least. And that was assuming we didn't go make our own wealth that entire time, which was fairly easy to do with how skilled we had become at completing dungeons.

"Amazing job, Constans," I said. She had grown so much since I had first met her and I was prouder of that than I was of anything else I had done in this world so far. She smiled at me and tossed me a legionnaire's salute.

"Just doing my job, sir," she said, only slightly mockingly.

"Restock some supplies and then tell Theo to take us back to the mine," I told her, returning the salute with a big smile on my face.

Once she was gone, I brought all seven of the tomes down to the hold where my nanobots and supplies had been stored. I stayed down there for our entire trip back to the mine so I could pore over the books, greedily drinking up all of the knowledge they contained. I didn't break for food or sleep, and thankfully, I wasn't interrupted by a monster attack either.

Two days later, when we reached the mine, I had memorized every rune and formed a basic understanding of the language of enchanting. It was unlike any other language I had ever encountered, but it had some similarities with ancient Egyptian or the Chinese written language adopted by much of Southeast Asia. Where this language differed, though, was that the enchanting runes had their own internal logic system, much like the programming languages of Earth, but they were based on esoteric principles of the flow of energy, energy conservation, and energy concentration. With so many examples, I finally began to understand how energy moved, was stored, and created the effects that powered the enchantments.

As I was poring over the tomes, rapidly memorizing the new runes, I realized I was having fun. I had always loved puzzles, but none of the puzzles on my old Earth had lasted more than a nanosecond once I had dedicated the full capabilities of my artificial intelligence to solving them. Here, I had been so busy surviving that I hadn't had time to dig into any real intellectual pursuits. I missed the pureness of learning knowledge for knowledge's sake.

It was . . . a hobby of mine, I decided. I hadn't had the chance to develop my own hobbies before. Even my enjoyment of playing virtual reality games came from the time I had spent with Michael and less from my own personal enjoyment of the games. It was nice to discover an aspect of my personality that I hadn't explored much before. I enjoyed puzzles. I enjoyed intellectual challenges. I enjoyed learning languages. I felt a bit like a child, having found a hobby all of a sudden, but I welcomed the information about myself with open arms.

Tired but happy, I climbed up to the deck as I felt us pulling into the harbor of the mining town.

I greeted my companions, who mocked me a bit for hiding away for so many days, but I just smiled and bantered back with them. I *had* gone a bit crazy locking myself in the hold for two days, but I almost never took time for myself so I didn't apologize for my actions. They didn't seem upset anyway, more amused than anything, so it was all good-natured teasing.

The streets of the town had finally stopped looking like a battlefield and I saw that many of the homes had been cleaned somewhat, lending the town a much warmer appearance than before.

Basil walked toward us down the dock as we finished tying off, so I jumped down and joined him.

"All clear here," he told me. "No surprises and no attacks."

"Great," I said. "How are the miners doing?"

"They started work as soon as you left," he told me. "They were able to restore enough tools to let them get to work immediately. Apparently several of them have skills that repair equipment for them. We have been collecting the ore in the warehouse."

I had Basil give me a quick tour of the town. He had selected a house for me, one of the nicer ones along the eastern side of the town. Built into the cliffside, it wasn't overly large, but it had a nice view of the water, so I accepted it. I felt like we were making a more long-term base here than we ever could in the city so it made sense for me to have a house to myself. We had access to the mine, it was secure from attack on land, and we seemed to have the only workable ship in the region, so it was a perfect place to set up something more permanent. Having a nice house with a view was the cherry on top.

Congratulations, you have completed the quest Make a Home. You have been rewarded with +1 to an attribute of your choice and 500 experience.

It wasn't much these days, but I would take the free experience and an attribute point. I put the point in willpower and then reviewed my book to see how much had changed with my attributes, skills, and perks since the last time I had looked.

Name: Alexander
Basic Class: Archer 20 / Warrior 20 / Rogue 20
Evolved Class: Gunslinger 15 / Duelist 11 / Spirit Breaker 10 / Rifleman 1
Non-combat Class: Enchanter 7 / Dark Elf Stalker 9

Base Attributes:

Coordination = 42
Strength = 40
Endurance = 34
Memory = 14
Magic Power = 11
Magic Capacity = 10
Luck = 8
Perception: 6
Willpower: 11

Skills:

Stealth:

566

Hide in the shadows and move silently, blending into the background and attracting less attention.

Trickster's Dash:
Dash through the air, ignoring wind resistance until you land. When you dash, you are briefly invisible until your dash ends.

Gambler's Eye:
You receive a passive boost of 20% to your coordination, your vision is improved, and you gain a sixth sense that reveals when luck may be favoring you.

Swagger:
Your movement speed increases, obstacles bend from your path, and your step is sure and steady. Your movements subtly intimidate others.

Duel Me:
At the start of combat, challenge a foe to a duel. The stakes of the duel are randomly selected and may include an attribute point, a percentage of all experience gained, a perk, a mutation, a skill, or an achievement. The first to surrender, retreat, or die loses. The winner of the duel permanently steals the stakes of the duel, and the loser permanently loses the stakes of the duel. This skill may only be used once a day.

Gambler's Luck:
You push luck to the limit, changing the odds around you to guarantee a more favorable outcome. Unlocks a new attribute: Luck.

Empowered Strikes:
You magnify the power of all of your strikes. Your strength when attacking is magnified by an additional 25%.

Empowered Enchantments:
Your enchantment effects are more powerful.

Absolute Evasion:

Grants an increased chance of evading any attack or spell, even ones you may not see coming.

Steadfast Endurance:
Increases your endurance by 25%, and repeated use of your skills is less exhausting.

Never Bring a Mob to a Duel:
Gain +1 to all attributes for each nearby enemy that is actively attacking you or planning to attack you. Whenever an enemy is defeated or surrenders, you lose their bonus attribute. This skill may only be used once per week.

Leeching Strike:
Strike an enemy, randomly stealing one of their attributes and adding it to your own until the end of combat.

If It's a Fight You Want, It's a Fight You'll Get:
Pick a target. The longer you fight your opponent, the higher your attributes soar. Gain +1 to all attributes once every minute you are in combat until you or your opponent are defeated or surrender.

Swordmaster:
All training with a sword is doubly effective, your skill with the sword increases, and you gain an instinctive understanding of opponents when wielding a sword.

Sense Your Prey:
Your perception is increased by 25% and you are better at spotting stealthed or hidden things.

Aim True:
Your aim is improved and you may fire further with your guns. Your bullets are not slowed by air resistance or the pull of gravity.

Metal Mind:
Your mind has evolved. You understand metal on a fundamental level and are able to manipulate all forms of metal at will. The distance from which you may manipulate metal and the power and

precision of your control scales based on your memory and willpower.

Perks:

Captain's Command:
Anyone obeying an order that you give will receive a morale bonus of +1 to all attributes while carrying out your command.

Swimmer's Body:
The length of time that you can hold your breath is doubled, you have improved eyesight underwater, and water restricts you less when you are moving through it.

Monster Hunter:
You can sense the presence of monsters nearby. This perk scales with your level and perception attribute.

Natural Weapons:
When using your hands, feet, claws, teeth, or any natural part of your body to strike a foe, you strike as if your strength was increased by +2.

Regeneration:
You gain the regeneration of Gromger the Mighty Troll King. Your body can regenerate from almost any wound. Injuries regenerate based on your endurance attribute and the amount of energy available to your body.

Emperor's Guard:
You have been entrusted with the protection of the Emperor. You are authorized to pass the wards in the Emperor's palace. You receive a +1 to all attributes.

Ant's Strength:
When you lift or carry objects, your strength attribute is magnified three times.

Natural Born Leader:
You command the battlefield with grace and poise, lending confidence to your troops. Any troops or followers under your

command receive +1 to all attributes, are immune to fear-based attacks, and are less likely to break or retreat unless ordered to do so.

Achievements:

Dangerous Dungeoneering:
For completing ten dungeons by yourself and without a class, you have been rewarded. You receive +2 to all attributes, and rewards from all future dungeons are increased slightly.

Survive a Safe Zone:
For reaching level 10 in a class, completing a dungeon, killing at least 20 monsters, and leaving a safe zone, you have been rewarded. You receive +1 to all attributes.

Mass Slaughterer:
For killing over 1000 monsters in under an hour, you have been rewarded. You receive +3 to all attributes, and when you are outnumbered, those who dare to attack you will be overcome with dread, weakening their strikes and reducing their accuracy.

Evolve a Second Unique Class:
You have managed to evolve not one but two unique classes that have never been seen before. You have earned a +1 to all attributes and may pick one skill from any level of the Rifleman class.

Quests:

Contribute to the Economy III:
You must sell goods or provide services worth a very large amount of money, depending on your region. Reward: 10 gold cores, 200 experience.

Cull the Drakes: completed
Contribute to the Economy: completed

Contribute to the Economy III: completed
Clear the City: completed
Down with the Queen: completed
Meet the Dark Elf Neighbors: failed
Make a Home: completed

Evolutions:

Evolution of Leadership:
Your patronage allows for those who serve you to benefit twice as fast when training or earning rewards. Loyalty from others is increased. You may form magically binding contracts. Your physical appearance is more magnetic and beautiful.

Spirits:

Phase Beast:
A dangerous hunter of the underdark, capable of phasing through any material to ambush its prey.

Mitkos the Giant King:
The king of the giants, this proud monster once ruled the giant race for over 1000 years before his exile.

Divine Boons:

Divine Sight:
Lamashtu, the dark elf goddess of undeath, has bestowed upon you the perk Divine Sight. Your vision penetrates even the darkest of environments, and you can now see the souls of everything around you. Learn to see what a soul tells you, and you will never be deceived again.

I still hadn't evolved my *Rogue* class. I had the class *Pirate* waiting, which might be more useful now since I could teach it to

571

our sailors and give them a combat class, but it just wasn't that exciting for me personally. I was still holding out hope for a more powerful class, although now that I knew I could get the *Rogue* class again, maybe I could evolve the class into something better the second time.

I debated what to do but ultimately decided to wait on taking the *Pirate* class. Our sailors were new and they hadn't officially joined my legion, so it wasn't worth getting a class just for them. Maybe if they decided to swear allegiance, I would consider it.

I decided to start by looking over my new home. It was larger than I would ever need, but most of the houses in the town seemed to be that way. Either the people that had once lived here were wealthy or the empire had taken great strides to make sure they were all happy, with large houses for everyone and probably other luxuries that hadn't survived. I took the master bedroom upstairs as my own and then turned another bedroom nearby into a study, where I unloaded my enchanting books and some supplies Constans had gotten for me for drafting enchantments.

The town ran itself fine without me so I took a week to myself and worked on several projects that had been kicking around in my mind for months now. Now that I had the orichalcum ore, I could finally craft truly powerful enchantments, unlike the more basic version I had been using that didn't require the ore and required orbs to charge the runes.

First, I finally worked out a way to extend the *Concealment* enchantment into a field that would protect a large area. It required several runes that worked to connect the runes and broadcast a field between them. It also required a token keyed to the field. Otherwise, it would be so powerful people would forget about what was hidden behind the enchantment even if they made it themselves. I crafted one set of stones that would be large enough to conceal the legion's entire camp and then crafted tokens that could be sewn onto each person's uniform to key them into the *Concealment* enchantment so our people wouldn't be affected by the powerful enchantment. I designed the token as a little revolver and rifle crossing over each other. The words *Domus, Virtus, Fides*, which meant family, courage, loyalty, were written underneath them. When the tokens were finished, each legionnaire got one. They all admired them and proudly pinned them to their uniforms.

Next, I designed and drew a larger version of the same enchantment but added several more runes to make it multifunctional. I didn't craft this one yet, simply drawing the runes out in my drafting book to make sure I got everything right. I combined a *Concealment* rune, a *Durability* rune, a *Water Repelling* rune, and a *Shield* rune. The *Concealment* and *Shield* runes were placed into a field design, allowing them to be spread around a designated area, and I also created a switch rune to allow either enchantment to be turned on or off.

These enchantments were large and complicated, requiring a significant amount of orichalcum, but for what I had in mind, it was a worthwhile investment. Once I was sure I had everything correct, I went down to the ship and began shifting some of the orichalcum ore over with my *Metal Mind*, using the skill to embed the ore into the sides and bottom of the ship in the exact pattern of each rune.

It took me days and almost all of the ore that had been mined so far, but when I was done, our ship was covered in large runes spaced about every ten feet along its length. I tied the *Concealment* and *Shield* activation to several tokens that I put at the helm and gave additional copies to Ryld, Basil, Theo, Constans, and Nikephoros, I kept one for myself. I also tied the legionnaires' tokens to the ship's *Concealment* and prepared a modified version that only worked with the ship's *Concealment* field for the sailors as well. Their tokens displayed a ship's sails with the crossed rifle and revolver to distinguish them from the other legionnaires. When I handed the sailors their tokens, they all looked immensely proud to be considered enough a part of the legion to get one. They eagerly pinned the tokens to their clothing.

Everyone had been watching me work as I affixed the runes to the ship, but when it was done, I gathered my leadership together and we all stared at the ship. The water seemed to flow around the hull of the ship, the *Water Repelling* rune making it so the water never actually came into contact with the wood of the ship, which should keep it from developing rot in the future and let us skim through the water faster than before. The runes all glowed with energy that pulsed blue and gold, making the ship look dangerous and exotic. It made the ship look like something from a futuristic science fiction story from my Earth, I thought.

"You know the amount of ore you used on this one ship could buy us almost all of Sycae, don't you?" Constans asked me, staring at the glowing ship with a bit of awe and a bit of disgust.

"Sure," I replied, "but I like our ship. I don't want to buy Sycae."

Theo laughed loudly at that, and Constans joined him a moment later.

"That *Concealment* rune should let us avoid monsters, shouldn't it?" Nikephoros asked, staring at the ship more seriously.

"Yeah," I said, "it should basically make us invisible and forgettable to anything we pass. It's powerful enough that I don't think anything short of a platinum boss could detect us. And the *Shield* rune can be activated to give us a strong defense that should stop almost anything that tries to sink us."

"Impressive," Ryld said, staring at the enchantments with a raised eyebrow. For the stoic dark elf, that was practically jumping up and down in excitement.

I grinned. It was impressive.

After we finished staring at the finished ship, I returned to my home and got back to work. My next project was to enchant the legionnaires' armor to help keep them safe and to deal with the slight problem of smell that had arisen as the men and women wore their uniforms for such an extended period of time. I designed enchantments that would increase everyone's coordination by ten percent, make the uniforms self-repairing and self-cleaning, and would offer greater protection from piercing attacks. I had to wait for more ore to be mined, but I took one of our spare uniforms and enchanted it to test everything out, finding that my designs worked perfectly.

I decided to change into the same uniform as my troops, except I used my own phase beast cloak instead of the half cloak I had designed for them. The newly enchanted uniform didn't offer quite the same protection as the bits of drake armor I still wore over my chest, but it was more comfortable and more flexible, and me looking like the other legionnaires would be good for morale.

I didn't end up needing the self-repairing or self-cleaning enchantments, though, since my bots did that for me, so I ended up replacing those with runes that increased my strength and endurance by ten percent to match the runes that did the same for my coordination. That was the maximum number of enchantments the uniform could hold. I hid the enchantments along the back as much as I could, but some of them ended up spiraling under the arms and onto the chest of the uniform. Hopefully the cloak would hide most of it, or people might start trying to kill my legionnaires just to get the metal in their uniforms.

The next project I turned to was creating what enchanters called a spatial bag. The runes for making one were included in only one of the tomes I had received, so either the enchanter who had shared that enchantment was a very honest sort or he had forgotten what he had sent to be copied, because I couldn't imagine anyone sharing such a series of runes without serious compensation.

It was an extremely difficult enchantment to get right. I ended up working night and day to get it right, and even then, it took me over a week and numerous failed attempts, some of which backfired dangerously.

When I was done, though, I had a small satchel that I could strap on to my belt and held 150 pounds of matter inside it without any weight at all. By merely reaching into the spatial bag, I could call to my hand anything that was inside with a mere thought. It was a marvel of the enchanting profession. The satchel was covered with runes so small most people would need to be inches from the bag to read them. It wasn't a subtle satchel—it practically glowed with a sign that read "try to steal me!"—but it was worth it.

I loaded all of my bullets and grenades into the satchel. I kept my sword and revolver on me, the sword strapped to my belt and the revolver in its holster under my left armpit, but now I could call forth grenades or any of my bullets at will rather than having to pick through my various satchels to grab what I needed.

With what I had discovered with my *Metal Mind* skill, I likely didn't even need the revolver any longer. I could pull bullets from the pouch and launch them with my mind so rapidly that the revolver actually slowed me down. The rifle was still better than what I could do with the skill, though; its accuracy and distance were still superior for shooting single targets far away.

No longer having to wear so many satchels and pounds of bullets and grenades felt good. I could move more easily and felt slightly less weighed down. Although none of the satchels had actually slowed me at all, I still had to be more careful so they wouldn't snag on things or fall open. It was mostly a psychological thing, I fully realized, yet when I was done crafting the satchel and put on my new uniform, I felt sleeker, faster, and deadlier than ever before.

My very final project used a combination of runes to do something I had been hoping I could figure out for a while now: a way to empower my nanobots that didn't require me to farm monsters for days and weeks at a time to make our weapons. A combination of the *Battery* rune and a massive amount of orichalcum ore let me produce batteries of pure energy the size of a small child. Each one drew power from the world without needing to be recharged, thanks to the large amount of orichalcum inside each one. I then converted that magical energy into something my nanobots could interact with: life itself. I found a *Growth* rune that was traditionally used to help farmers produce better yields from their crops. I took it a step further and used the idea I had when I repaired our ship, having my nanobots draw energy from the tiny picoplankton and phytoplankton that lived in the Mediterranean Sea.

I tore out the walls of the largest home next to the dock and converted the home into a series of large pools. Using my *Metal Mind*, I crafted a series of pipes that would bring in fresh sea water and then carved a *Growth* rune in the middle of the pool. As the pools filled with plankton, the *Growth* rune, connected to the superpowered battery I had made, stimulated the growth of the tiny organisms. I watched as the *Growth* rune caused an explosion of life, instantly turning the water from a light blue into a solid green mush. I sent the nanobots into the pool to begin consuming the plankton. I waited several hours until the pool finally reached an equilibrium, the nanobots able to consume the plankton fast enough to keep up with the *Growth* rune's effect.

I made four more pools and placed my specialized nanobots in each one. I redesigned the worktables to make sure the nanobots deposited their finished projects at the front of the building. I didn't want the weapons or ammunition falling into the pool where the powerful *Growth* rune might do some strange things to them.

The results were impressive. While the nanobots still weren't churning out weapons and ammunition like a modern-day factory, the fact that they could work day and night without needing to be recharged by hunting monsters any longer meant we would finally have enough ordnance to supply a real army, if I ever decided to expand my operations any further.

I carefully watched the pools for a few days to make sure there weren't any problems. When nothing arose, I told my leaders about the pools and made them promise to only come to the building to collect weapons and ammunition and to never touch the pools or the batteries. That much power channeled into a *Growth* rune was liable to give a human cancer in seconds if they ever touched a pool, so I tried to really emphasize how dangerous it was to mess with anything inside.

By the time we had enough ore for all of my projects and for me to enchant everyone's uniforms, the sailors under Theo were fully ready to take over the ship's duties. Nikephoros had resumed training the legionnaires and the miners were settling in well, even discussing bringing their families here and settling permanently if we stayed, according to Constans.

We were running low on food, so I took the ship back to the city to resupply. The trip back took around two days before, depending on the wind, but with the new enchantments on the ship, we made it back in less than a day. And nothing bothered us, our passage completely silent and unnoticed by the monsters of the sea. I was immensely proud of the work I had done on the ship and was glad to see it worked as well as I had hoped.

I had us stay under *Concealment* until we docked, appearing suddenly at the pier. The sailors then rappelled down and tied us up. Several people cried out at the sight of our ship appearing out of nowhere. The bystanders calmed down when they recognized us, until someone noticed all of the runes that now covered our ship and began to point them out to the others. That caused an explosion of even louder conversations, people coming to stare at our ship more and more as word of the enchantments spread. I had Theo raise the shield just to be safe. It partially obscured the ship and prevented anyone from trying to attack us unless they brought significant firepower with them.

Of course, the shield drew even more attention, but it couldn't be helped. I sent Constans with a full squad of legionnaires to buy food for us. I also told her to see about making us self-sufficient at the mine in case we needed to leave the city for any reason. We had plenty of drinkable water, Basil had told me, since there was a natural spring that ran down one part of the cliff and fed into a large cistern under the town. The only thing we needed was a way to grow food, but with limited space and no good soil, that seemed unlikely. Maybe some kind of domesticated animals to supplement the food we bought in Sycae?

The problem was that most of the food in Sycae came from the army through the Emperor's enclave. Sycae didn't have much of a food industry, primarily being filled with crafters and merchants. They produced the quality items needed to defend the army's walls and provide luxury goods to the Emperor. In return, they got the food they needed to survive and some currency. It wasn't a very healthy system, but the Emperor maintained a stranglehold on the only bridge between the main part of the city and Sycae, so he preserved the delicate situation to guarantee his own relevance.

I had Constans make some inquiries just in case, but she didn't have any luck. I started to think about some monsters that we might capture to eat, instead of the traditional livestock humans used. Ryld was with us this time, and when he overheard me and Constans talking about the problem, he suggested we just cultivate the mushrooms the dark elves ate, which could grow easily in the unused parts of the mine and provide enough nutrition for most people to live on.

I sent Ryld to get us the mushrooms while I considered if there were any other options that could help us. The dire rats that infested the city bred quickly and had a decent amount of meat on them, but during my time, humans had a taboo against eating rat meat. I talked it over with Constans, Basil, and Nikephoros, and I was surprised to find they had no problem with eating rat meat. Apparently the people of this era, especially those that survived in Nova Roma these days, weren't quite as picky about food as the people from my world had been.

I had Constans buy us twenty large cages, which she paid a premium for since they had to be made from scratch. We made a run to Miletus to drop off supplies, and when we returned, the cages were ready. I had Constans go see if she could find us someone that had a class that could help with breeding and harvesting livestock, while I went and caught twenty of the rats back in the city. They were an angry bunch and smelled terrible, but I dragged them one by one into the sea and cleaned them off before stuffing them in their cages and loading them onto our ship. They were sort of like large pigs, if one tried to look at them in the best light possible.

Constans wasn't able to find anyone in Sycae that had a class that let them breed animals, but she found several older workers in Perama that had the skills we needed. She hired us a butcher, breeder, and farmer. The butcher and breeder were both older women, and the farmer was a nice middle-aged man who had been raising sustenance crops on a rooftop for so long he was willing to do anything to grow something new. The farmer primarily had experience with crops, but Constans figured he could help with the mushrooms. I applauded her foresight once again and told her to hire all three immediately.

I inspected their souls and then had them sign my now-standard contract for workers. Then we whisked them and twenty cages full of monstrously large rats back to our new town. Ryld told the farmer a bit about how the mushrooms worked, and he eagerly got to work planting them everywhere he could inside the extensive mine.

Basil had his troops construct a rough pen for the rats and the breeder got to work on them. I wasn't sure that monsters bred the way normal animals did, but I hoped the breeder would figure it out. The pen for the rats was extra secure just in case, made from blocks of stone so the rats had no chance to escape. I even enchanted them with a few runes—one *Durability* rune and several *Ward* runes—to repel monsters and keep the rats from breaking out of the pen.

By the time everything was finished, weeks of hard work had passed in a blink. It was the slowest period of my own growth since I had come here. I hadn't gained much experience at all except for two levels in *Enchanter*, yet I felt a deep sense of satisfaction as I watched our town grow around me.

As we finished the last touches on the pen of rats and finished filling the ship with another load of orichalcum ore, I told everyone that we would throw a large celebration once we returned from the city. Everyone cheered at the announcement.

Chapter 42

We arrived back at the city and Constans contacted the young merchant I suspected she had a bit of a crush on, offering to sell him our next shipment of ore. As she left to go negotiate with him, I went over to Perama and contacted Mehmet at the bar Constans and I had first visited. I asked him about his work and life and he was more than happy to share, telling me he was an orphan as well—something that Perama had hundreds of, I had been learning. He had been given the chance to run the bar, but the owner barely paid him and had never even given him a class to help him run the place.

I told him about our new town and that there was an empty inn that I was thinking about filling. His eyes lit up when he figured out what I was offering and I laid out my terms, which he quickly accepted.

"Can I bring my friend that brews for us? He's in the same situation as me, although he has the *Brewer* class at least."

"Absolutely," I told him, "and anyone else you think would want to come that could help you run the inn. Just let me know."

He ended up bringing a cook's apprentice and a young woman that he said would help him clean and run the place. I suspected she was his girlfriend, but I didn't mind. I brought them all over to our ship and had Constans go buy some non-combat classes for them when she returned from selling our ore. I got Mehmet and the girl he invited an *Innkeeper* class, and the other two already had the *Brewer* and *Cook* classes, although we bought both of them their own supplies and materials to do their jobs.

I also hired several actual guards to protect the town when we left, so I wouldn't have to leave a complement of my legionnaires behind. There was an abundance of older guards who had been retired with little in the way of money or skills, other than being a guard. Constans found ten of them working odd jobs as bouncers at

581

inns or security at some businesses. They accepted our offer when they saw the salary I was willing to pay but insisted that they be able to bring their families, which I agreed to as long as all of them were willing to sign my contract ensuring secrecy for life. Every one of them agreed and signed happily.

Miletus was large enough to easily house over a hundred people, so we had plenty of space to spare. The mushrooms were already thriving in the dark of the mine, and while the livestock was still in the experimental phase, the breeder thought she might have a way to get them to procreate based on one of her skills.

Along with the guards and Mehmet and his people, I convinced a few fishermen to join us on the condition we would bring their families as well. I hired two families. Each had their own boat but hadn't had as much luck fishing around the city as of late. They were willing to try somewhere new now that they saw how well we treated the sailors.

We loaded everyone on the ship, including the two fishermen's smaller vessels, as well as more supplies and a generous amount of alcohol. And of course, another generous chest full of gold, silver, and orbs we acquired from the sale of the ore was kept secure in Theo's cabin. Once everything was on board and all the ore had been unloaded, we set sail back home.

When we arrived back at Miletus, we unloaded everything and then I introduced Mehmet and his people to the inn they would be owning. While I was doing that, Constans showed the guards and fishermen to their new homes. After setting Mehmet up in the town's inn, I let him know he only had a day to get acquainted with his new home before I planned to throw a huge party. He and his team yelled at me, but I ducked out of the inn in a hurry, promising them it would be fine. For some reason, they didn't believe me, but the threat of the party sure motivated them to start unpacking their new supplies.

I would, normally, have spent most of the party working or sitting by myself, but I knew how important it was to bond with my people, so I tried not to be so standoffish. I forced myself to have a few drinks and relax with my leaders and some of the other new townspeople. What started as a bit of an effort eventually turned into genuine enjoyment after I let myself relax a little.

By the end of the night, Mehmet's girlfriend—he confirmed their relationship—had brought out a musical instrument and was playing and singing for the rowdy crowd that filled the inn and spilled out into the surrounding streets. We all danced and sang along with her, and drinks and food were free for everyone, courtesy of Constans and me.

I had given everyone the next two days off as well, to help them recover, so the town was in a relaxed state the next morning despite everyone's hangovers. I spent the day puttering around with my enchanting tomes, thinking of some new experiments to run and planning what my next steps would be now that we had some financial security and a safe place to call home.

For the next two days, the town had an air of peace and comfort I had never felt in Nova Roma. People swam off the dock, took time to decorate their new homes, or just met their neighbors and began to get to know each other. When the two days were over, everyone was excited to get back to work. The town had turned from my town into *their* town, and they were invested in making a new start of it.

The miners eagerly got back to work, our new fishermen explored the waters near our harbor for fish, and Mehmet officially opened his inn.

I made the rounds of the town, making sure nobody needed anything from me, and then spent more time tinkering with enchantments and planning my future. I was starting to feel the itch to level and explore again despite how much I loved spending time in the town. I was still at a relatively low level compared to the rest of the world. I had some unique classes, skills, and attributes that made me more powerful than my levels would make it seem, but I still had a lot of growth to go.

We made another run to the city, this time with our full complement of legionnaires since the guards could keep the peace back in Miletus. I had also given the sailors and Theo revolvers and rifles, just to help them protect themselves and the ship in case of trouble. I had been churning out bullets and weapons, so we finally had enough to spare, although we would need to start buying iron more regularly now to keep up with the new demands of my nanobot farms.

When we coasted into the docks this time, I could immediately tell that something was wrong. The normal crowds of people on the streets were gone, and from the crow's nest, I could see faint blood stains in the streets and some broken doors on some of the buildings nearby.

"Don't deactivate the *Concealment* enchantment," I called down to Theo, who stood at the wheel. He nodded, having seen what I had seen as well. We didn't tie up to the dock, instead just bobbing next to it as we watched the city carefully. The legionnaires, sensing something wrong as well, got into position at the railings, rifles raised in case of trouble.

All of the houses and warehouses nearby seemed deserted. Had the city been attacked? Or was something waiting to attack us? The normally loud and busy Sycae was as empty as a ghost town.

"I'm going to go scout out what's going on," I told Basil. "You all stay here and be prepared in case of trouble."

Before I could carry out my plan, I heard a cry from one of the buildings ahead.

"I can sense something magical at the dock," a voice said. "I think the ship is there!"

"Order the attack!" another voice yelled.

"Drop *Concealment* and raise the shield," I yelled at Theo immediately.

Before Theo could raise the shield, a barrage of spells and arrows struck the front of the ship, hitting a number of sailors and legionnaires who had been preparing to defend us. I watched in horror as one of the sailors was struck by a pool of green liquid that began to eat away at his skin the second it landed on him. He screamed and tried to roll on the deck to get the liquid off of him, but that only spread it further. One of our healers tried to help him, but it was already too late. His screams slowly quieted until he lay, slowly dissolving, on the deck of our ship. Several more sailors and legionnaires were injured, many of them severely.

I felt rage consume me at the sight. I had allowed the priests and their insanity to stand too long, and now my people were paying the price for a conflict that was solely between me and the priest who had attacked me so long ago. How *dare* he invade Sycae and do something like this to innocent people. How *dare* he

584

attack me when I was the only one doing anything to help the people of this city.

Our healers were swiftly getting the wounded healed and back on their feet as the *Shield* rose to protect us. A second barrage of magical and mundane attacks was launched from the windows and doors nearby, but the shield managed to hold, causing many of the spells and arrows to impact with no effect. Some of the spells lingered, sizzling and boiling on the surface of the shield, however, causing constant damage to it.

"Return fire!" Basil yelled, and a volley of bullets rang out. I saw a number of people hiding in the windows fall backward, killed instantly by the powerful rifles.

"We have incoming from behind as well," Theo yelled. I turned to look and saw that a small fleet of fishing boats had appeared in the middle of the channel, as if they had been concealed by some spell powerful enough to hide them even from my sight. The boats were full of Varangian soldiers, all of them dressed for war. They looked dangerous.

"Basil, get a squad to the back of the boat. Ryld, have your people focus behind us and try to sink those boats!"

People began to run out of the buildings in front of us, charging toward the ship as the boats closed in on us from behind, the powerful Varangians propelling the boats with swift jerks of their oars. The attackers on the docks of Sycae were dressed like warrior-priests. They wore a mix of heavy armor and robes and wielded more esoteric weapons like holy symbols and ornamental staves. A few even just carried books in their hands, the tomes glowing with light as they charged. Many of the priests were tainted with dark energy. The black veins covering their bodies swelled as they gathered power to attack us.

"Grenades!" Nikephoros yelled. The squads at the front and back both drew and tossed grenades overboard immediately. The resulting explosion was devastating, shattering the boats coming up behind us. The majority of the Varangians were thrown overboard as their boats were destroyed, many visibly injured by the fiery explosions and the shrapnel from the wooden ships. Unfortunately, it looked like all of them survived, too powerful to be killed so easily. They rapidly recovered from the explosions and began to swim toward our ship, although many had lost their weapons when they were thrown overboard. I raised my rifle and began to pick off the swimming Varangians as fast as I could.

The impact of the grenades on the priests was less effective. A multicolored shield sprang up to protect the charging warrior-priests, absorbing all of the blasts from the grenades without flickering in the slightest.

"Theo, get us out of here!" I called out to him. We had barely trimmed the sail before we reached the dock, so his sailors jumped as he ordered them to turn us around. It was a painfully slow procedure and I could tell we wouldn't escape before both forces reached us.

Resigned to exposing more of my power than I wanted, I concentrated and began to summon Mitkos. As he formed above the priests who were storming down the docks toward us, I ordered Basil to concentrate our troops on the Varangians fast approaching behind us.

Mitkos smashed onto the multicolored shield the priests had summoned to protect themselves. Their shield couldn't stand up to his pure mass, buckling under the pressure before shattering a moment later. This allowed Mitkos to land in their midst and disintegrate the wooden dock under their feet, sending the warrior-priests flying into the water around the angry giant. Mitkos roared in pure rage and began smashing the flailing priests as they tried to right themselves in the water, their heavy robes and armor slowing them down. His massive weapon cleaved into the water, sending sheets of sea spray mixed with blood cascading up into the air. It splashed on our shield and all over the nearby docks and waterfront in a tsunami of blood-stained water.

Basil had followed my orders and gathered the legionnaires at the back of the ship, where they were firing shot after shot into the Varangians, who were trying to swim toward us. The dark elves in the riggings join them, firing bullets and spells down on the Varangians, showing them no mercy. Over thirty rifles firing a bullet a second was too much for even the powerful soldiers to survive.

It was the proverbial shooting fish in a barrel, except this time they were human, and if they reached us, they could kill us all in a matter of minutes. Blood began to turn the sea behind our ship red. By the time the quickest swimmer of them all had barely gotten within fifty feet of our ship, all of them were dead in the water. The very last Varangian didn't go down without a fight, taking bullet after bullet and refusing to die. I tried to get a good look at his face, but I couldn't tell if it was the man from the Emperor's palace I had fought before on the bridge. Either way, if it was him, he had tried to attack me one time too many. I had no mercy in me this day for any of my attackers. I drew my rifle and placed a perfect shot directly through his forehead, finally ending his struggles.

On the other side of the ship, Mitkos had made short work of the priests in the water and was stomping ashore, attacking anyone who was stupid enough to have lingered nearby. Before he could do too much damage to the city itself, I dismissed him. I was tired from summoning him for so long, but it hadn't been long enough to make me feel ill like the last time I had kept him out.

With the last of the Varangians dead, Basil ordered the legionnaires back to the front of the ship. I could see a number of priests still struggling in the water and hiding in the nearby buildings. I reluctantly ordered Basil to hold his fire since none of them seemed to be trying to attack us any longer. They were all too overwhelmed by what had happened to them, and the ones in the water were just trying to make it to shore in their heavy armor and robes.

"Keep us moving away from the dock!" I yelled to Theo. Then I dashed forward until I could land in front of one of the older-looking priests where he huddled in a doorway, injured with a bullet wound and unable to escape. He had no visible weapon and his robe was finely adorned with gold thread, making me think he might be one of the leaders behind the attack.

When I appeared in front of him, he flinched and tried to scramble back, but I grabbed him and slapped him several times. My blows rang against his head, stunning him and causing him to go limp instantly. Before he could recover, I lifted him up and dashed backward until I landed on my ship once again.

"I sure am getting tired of kidnapping priests," I said to the stunned man as I threw him down to the deck, uncaring if he was injured from the fall. I called over one of our healers, just to make sure he didn't die of his bullet wound, and then shooed her away to take care of our own injured again. Theo slowly got us away from the dock as I stripped the priest, slicing the richly adorned robe into strips with my sword and pulling it apart around the man. He stared in shock at what I was doing, trying to understand what was happening to him.

When I was sure he had no weapons hiding on him any longer, I knelt next to the naked priest and stared him in the eyes. He tried to stand, some of his arrogance returning as he looked me in the eye, but I held him down with one arm. He struggled in an attempt to push past me, but when he realized he couldn't move my arm an inch, he finally gave up.

"You don't deserve to stand," I said, glaring at him. I shoved him harder into the deck, deliberately pushing on his injury. He winced and cried out, but I ignored his pain.

"Tell me why you attacked us," I told him, "or I will kill you and go capture another priest and another one until I get the answers I want."

My legionnaires surrounded us, staring down at the priest with as much anger on their faces as I felt. They had all seen the young sailor die just like I had, and all of us wanted our revenge.

"You've been declared an outlaw," the priest replied, attempting to sound self-righteous but failing, as the fear was evident in his voice. "The Emperor has declared you a murderer and the Patriarch has declared you a heretic. We were sent by both to seize your ship and your goods in the Emperor's name, for the good of the city."

"And you believe that, do you?" I said, looking at the priest's soul as well as his face. His soul was tainted with dark energy, but even he knew what he said was a lie.

"Is this what happened to the other ships that used to dock here?" I asked him, reading something in his soul that told me this wasn't the first time he had participated in such an attack, justified as it was by such flimsy rationale. "Or was this more personal?"

I sensed no shift in his soul at my second question. So was it both? I had upset the Emperor and a priest, so it wasn't a surprise that they might try to attack me in some way, although I had never expected this. But from the glimpses of what I saw in the priest's soul, I got a darker picture of what was going on. I stared deeply into the man's soul, pushing my mind inside and demanding answers to my questions. After initial resistance, I felt the soul cave to my will and open itself to me. I ransacked the priest's soul, uncaring for the damage I did, as I searched for answers.

I found what I was looking for in the priest's memories from over a decade ago. A memory played in my own head, as if I was living it. I experienced the priest in front of me at a meeting with the Emperor and his advisors. The Emperor ordered the Varangians and the priests to seize the remaining ships that were docked in Nova Roma, ordering that they be confiscated for the good of the city. Some had objected, arguing that the ships were practically national treasures for beleaguered cities that had sent them. If we seized them, they claimed, these cities would never send more trade to Nova Roma.

The Emperor ignored such arguments, demanding the seizure of the ships. Otherwise, he would take to the field and do it himself. Images of the Emperor recklessly destroying much of the city with his power flashed through the priest's mind, and everyone soon agreed to the young Emperor's demands. The priest hadn't been one of the voices arguing against the seizure of the ships. His mind betrayed his eagerness to loot the ships, and he had clearly hoped he might be able to capture someone he could bring back to his temple and use to perform forbidden rituals that would grant him more power. I avoided learning more about what kind of rituals were involved, not wanting to taint my mind any further with his memories.

When the memory finally finished, I drew my sword and stepped back from the priest. He looked up at me, seeing the look on my face, and opened his mouth to beg for mercy, but I didn't give him the chance. I struck his head from his body in a single blow. It landed on the deck of the ship and rolled several times before coming to a stop. Blood began to pool on the deck nearby, but I flicked my sword, shedding the blood off my blade. I re-sheathed it, ignoring the spreading pool of red.

When I looked around me, the legionnaires and Constans were watching me carefully. For a moment, I worried she had lost her high opinion of me, but her face held only concern for my well-being. I turned to the legionnaires and ordered the body dumped in the water.

"I'm going to take care of the rest of these bastards," I said. Several legionnaires raised their rifles in a cheer, wanting to come with me, but I silenced them with a wave of my hand.

"Protect the ship," I told them before vanishing upward with a dash. I quickly dashed across the water and landed behind the buildings that lined the docks. Entering stealth, I began to stalk through the buildings, hunting down the priests too cowardly to attack us directly. My phase beast, which had waited so patiently for me for so long, finally got to come and hunt with me once again. I felt a surge of primal pleasure from the beast, his bloodlust matching my own as we stalked the streets together. We moved swiftly and silently through the city, a pair of killers ready to exact our revenge.

Many of the priests had already fled, but without the ships of the Varangians, they had no way back across the channel. I tracked them through the streets of the enclave, murdering any that refused to surrender immediately.

Many of the priests tried to fight back, but I flung bullets from my spatial satchel, willing them forward with my *Metal Mind*, and then dashed forward with my sword while my phase beast rose behind them, crippling them with devastating attacks. The brutal aggression of our attacks left the priests who tried to fight me overwhelmed before they could even think of a way to defend themselves.

I felt . . . disconnected as I hunted. It wasn't like hunting in the underdark. There was no pleasure to the hunt, only rage and hate and fury. I felt like I had lost a bit of the humanity I had worked so hard to obtain since coming here. And yet, at the same time, I felt more human than ever before. Righteous anger filled me. I reveled in the violence. I stopped holding back, using all of my strength, speed, skills, and training to massacre the priests that dared stand against me. The never-ending screams of the sailor who had died echoed in my mind as I hunted, urging me onward faster and faster.

I found the priest who had started the whole thing huddled in an alley at the edge of town. He was desperately trying to open a portal to summon another demon to protect himself, but nothing worked. It appeared even his demonic allies had given him up for dead.

I had no interest in talking to him, or gloating over his defeat, so I just stood on a rooftop above him and launched a barrage of bullets with my *Metal Mind* at him. My phase beast rose from the alley floor at the same time. It bit through his neck and shook him back and forth like a ragdoll. My first few bullets struck his shield, but the magical bubble surrounding the priest rapidly collapsed under the strain of my phase beast's deadly attack. The bullets continued coming as I willed more and more of them forward. They struck the priest's chest over and over until I was sure he was dead.

Of the priests that did surrender, I ruthlessly plunged into their souls to see if they were tainted by unholy magic or had participated in any of the events that caused the city to be so abandoned. I found a handful that were completely innocent and I let them live, but the majority were guilty. They had committed such horrendous acts in the name of gaining power that it was practically a good deed to kill them in cold blood.

Chapter 43

Once I had killed the last of the priests who deserved to die, I returned to the ship. I was glad to see it was now safely anchored in the middle of the channel between Sycae and the main part of the city. It was also back under *Concealment* and still had its shield active just in case of another attack. As I dashed across the water, I could see the legionnaires and dark elves still on deck, watching the city warily, rifles ready.

When I landed softly on the deck, several guns swung my way, but the legionnaires hurriedly lowered them when they recognized me.

Basil, Nikephoros, Ryld, and Constans ran over to check on me. I knew I was a mess, covered in blood and disheveled from my many fights.

"What happened?" Basil asked as he stopped next to me.

"Are you injured?" Constans asked, concern filling her voice.

"No," I replied, trying to shake off the sense of detachment I felt from the world. "No. I'm okay. The priests shouldn't bother us anytime soon now. I should have done what I did much earlier, but I didn't have the courage to act."

"Good!" Nikephoros, of all people, said. I was surprised and then grateful for the anger in his voice. He was a former legionnaire of the army, but even he seemed outraged by such a cowardly ambush. He must also know how close we came to being overrun. If not for the shield I had just recently added to the ship or the grenades that threw the Varangians into the water, we would have been killed.

"Bring us back to the dock," I called up to Theo, who still stood at the helm. "We should be safe for now. We have some things to do before we leave the city this time."

Theo gave the order and the sailors jumped to obey.

"I had heard rumors," Nikephoros told me, "of ships taken in the night or caravans raided as soon as they left the city, but there was never anything concrete. Over time, fewer and fewer people started to come to the city until everything just stopped and we never knew why. Was the Emperor attacking ships and caravans? You were muttering about the Emperor attacking ships while you stared at that priest."

"Yes," I said, "I was able to relive some of the priest's memories and I saw the Emperor order the seizure of the last few ships that ever visited the city. Many of the priests were eager for the spoils and joined him willingly."

"It's so stupid!" Nikephoros said, stamping a foot down on the deck of the ship. "All it did was leave us here to rot for good. All to line the pockets of the Emperor and his cronies for a month at most."

"We can't stay here long," I told them all. "The Emperor will inevitably try again and he has some very powerful magic and soldiers available to him. I don't know exactly what he can do, but even the priest I had taken was afraid of what would happen if he used his power near the city. We were lucky they tried to take our ship instead of just trying to kill us."

"Where will we go?" Basil asked, looking over at the only real city he had ever known.

"We will need somewhere to trade," I replied. "I hear there are still ports active to the west. I'm sure we can find some people to trade with there, especially with all the orichalcum we will have. That will open many doors for us."

Everyone turned to look back at the city. It wasn't a good city. It wasn't even a semi-decent city anymore. It was more ruin than anything, but it was still home to everyone on board except me.

"Give the sailors an option to leave if they want," I told them. "Anyone that wants to stay that hasn't signed up for the legion can go, with a bonus for good work. Let everyone know."

I handed Basil my weapons and dove overboard, letting the clean water of the sea wash the blood off my clothes and body faster than my nanobots could clean it up. The cold of the sea was refreshing, bringing me back to myself a little bit, helping me feel less disassociated from reality. I let myself sink downward into the cold water, my clothes pulling me toward the bottom as I let my muscles relax completely. The silence of the water was a balm on my mind, and I let it wash over me and finally calm the last of my anger.

When I was as clean as I was going to get, I swam to the surface and dashed back aboard the ship. Basil handed me my weapons and I ordered my nanobots to begin drying me off as quickly as they could.

We docked soon after. This time, sailors swiftly jumped off the ship to tie us up. We kept the shield up and remained concealed, not wanting to chance another surprise.

I walked off the ship and took an escort with me as I surveyed the docks of Sycae. Corpses were being washed against the waterfront as the waves pushed the many dead Varangians and priests against the stone sea wall that lined Sycae. I ignored the bodies, moving deeper into the enclave. I made my way toward the home of the merchant we'd been working with to sell our ore.

I found his estate heavily guarded, the walls bristling with men and women ready to repel any attackers. When I identified myself from a distance, they summoned the merchant and he hurriedly ushered me inside the front gate.

"What happened here?" I asked the merchant as he closed the gate behind us. He grimaced and led me toward a set of benches in his garden before answering.

"The Emperor and priests attacked us," he said. "We tried to resist at first, but they overpowered us easily. The members of the merchant council have been ordered to remain in our homes under threat of death. Those who resisted were killed. This has happened before, my father told me before his passing, but not for a long time. We thought we had found a way to appease the Emperor enough to stop his raids."

"He's attacked you before?" I said, a spark of outrage reigniting inside of me.

"Not for many years," the young merchant said, sensing my tone and trying to keep me calm. "Before I was even on the council. He used to raid us for our wealth and demand tribute like we were a conquered nation of his. We never had the power to stop him and the army won't help us against the Emperor."

I didn't know what to say.

594

"I see you survived, though," he said eventually. "I heard they were planning to ambush you but I had no way to warn you. I am sorry."

"It's okay," I told him. "There would have been no way for anyone to warn us. We did survive and the Emperor and the priests are going to be regretting what they did here for a long time."

I had estimated we had killed at least forty of the Emperor's Varangian guards and that an equal number or more of the priests had died as well. That had to be a significant amount of their strength in the city, although I still feared what the Emperor himself was capable of if he got involved. The fear in the priest's memory had been very real.

"What will you do now?" he asked me.

"We're going to get what we need from the city and then leave for now," I told him. "We might return someday, but not for a while. There are other cities out there to trade with and the Emperor just cost his city the chance to rebuild, at least for now. With the Emperor in power, there is no way for us to stay here. Maybe that will change, but until then, we will take our trade somewhere else."

The merchant sagged at my words, visibly sad for his city. He didn't seem concerned for himself or the trade we had brought him but for the city as a whole. My respect for him grew.

"Thank you for treating us fairly," I told him. "I hope that the Emperor won't take it out on you that we killed so many of his men."

"Me too," the young man said, sagging further into his chair. He didn't speak for several minutes, and I realized I had nothing left to say, so I left him there, the poor man seemingly weighed down by responsibility beyond his young years.

I made my way back to the docks, passing Constans. She was banging on shop doors with a squad of legionnaires behind her, demanding shops open up and sell us what we needed. I didn't want to upset the merchants who had treated us right, but we needed supplies now and then we needed to be gone before night set in the city. Constans was buying up as much food, clean water, and other supplies for the ship as she could get.

When I returned to the docks, I saw a small crowd had formed. Many of them had backpacks on or were carrying whatever they could hold in their arms. When they saw me, they rushed over to try to talk to me. I froze, unsure of what was happening. Seeing me, Nikephoros came running over, interrupting the approaching people to speak to me first.

"Sir," Nikephoros said. "Several of the sailors wanted to check on their families, and when people heard we had survived, many of them wanted to come with us. Theo says there are some good sailors amongst the bunch and many want to bring their families to our town. They don't want to stay here any longer after what the Emperor did."

I stared at the anxious and frightened faces of the people waiting to talk to me. They clutched desperately at the few items they could carry, equal parts hope and fear appearing on their faces.

"I'll meet them all and let you know who can go with us," I said. I looked over at Perama, where the Varangians had likely stolen the boats they used to attack us. I suspected they didn't take them peacefully and there would be people over there hurting in the days to come.

I quickly met with and approved of everyone on the docks, having them all sign contracts of secrecy with me and then telling Nikephoros to get them situated on the boat. Once that was done, I dashed across the water and found Perama in a similar state. Blood and wreckage lined the streets and floated in the water near the buildings below the bridge.

Had the Emperor killed even the fishermen his city relied upon? How would his people feed themselves now? Did he not care that thousands of people in Perama and the rest of the city relied on that fish to survive? The sheer stupidity and callousness of his actions angered me almost as much as the murder itself.

I climbed the ladders up to Momma Lena's place, finding her repairing some damage to a neighboring shop with several others. People lingered on the streets, seemingly in shock. When she saw me, she rushed over and gave me a hug, which surprised me greatly.

"Is Constans okay?" she asked, pulling back but continuing to hold me by the shoulders.

"Yes," I reassured her. "We survived. Are the people here okay?"

"No," she said, looking around. "We aren't sure how we will survive now. Without our boats, we can't get enough food to last the next winter. The Emperor has never attacked us before. They overran us in seconds at the wall and killed people in the streets just for slowing them down. Our guards tried to stop them, but they were too strong and many of them are dead now. We will struggle to hold the walls at night and will never be able to feed so many anymore."

She began to cry and I hugged her back, offering what comfort I could. I tried to think of what I could do. I couldn't just leave them here to starve or be overrun by monsters, but I also couldn't bring so many people with me to Miletus.

"What if . . ." I said to her, thinking out loud. "What if I could bring everyone over to Sycae? It would mean leaving your homes, but you could survive over there and they lost a number of people as well. It would be a tight fit but it might work."

She stepped back, wiping the tears from her eyes as she considered what I said. "Could you do that? Would they even take us? They've never reached out a helping hand to us before. Why would they start now?"

"I think I can make it happen," I told her. "In fact, I'm sure of it. If they won't take you willingly, I can force them to take you if need be. Once you are there, they don't have the manpower to force you out. Can you talk to people and try to get everyone organized? Time is of the essence here. If the Emperor finds out what we are doing, he might intervene to stop us."

"Yes," she said, eyeing me with a small glimmer of hope. "Yes, I can talk to people and get it started."

She began to yell for some of her neighbors and I left her to it. I dashed back across the water, thinking of how to evacuate several thousand people as rapidly as possible. It was only a short distance across, but with the Emperor breathing down our neck, it felt like miles of water.

Back in Sycae, I approached the young merchant again about what had happened in Perama. It took some convincing, but he agreed to call the council together so I could discuss the issue with them. While I waited, I told my leaders what was happening and explained my plan for ferrying the people over to Sycae. Theo immediately started to take us back to the Sycae dock to unload our current passengers. I told him to start loading as many people on the ship as he could while I went to talk to the merchant council.

A frustrating hour later, I sat around the familiar table and raised the issue of bringing the people of Perama over here.

"We can't take them!" one of the older merchants yelled. "We can barely feed ourselves. You would have us all starve!"

"It will inflame the Emperor even more," another merchant said. "He can cut off our food at any time. What will we do if he does that? We would be left with nothing."

"If I'm not seen to be involved," I replied, "the Emperor should have no reason to retaliate. It will look just like refugees seeking shelter in your enclave. He barely cares enough to know that Perama's people exist. He won't care if they come here."

"How would you get them here without him knowing?"

"We can move a number of people under *Concealment* in my ship," I replied. "Nobody should be able to break *Concealment* from so far away. I will need your assistance to unload the people as fast as possible, though, so it's not obvious what we are doing."

"But why should we take them? What can they offer other than more mouths to feed?"

Part of me was very tempted to leap across the table and make the merchant that had said that learn firsthand why he should take the refugees, but I restrained myself despite the surge of rage pushing me to do it.

We talked back and forth about the issues until finally, after some not-so-subtle threats from me, and having to part with most of the money we had made from selling the orichalcum ore, we had an agreement. I told the young merchant we had worked with before that we would have the money delivered to him and him alone. I also made him sign one of my contracts to guarantee that all of the money would be spent resettling and helping the people of Perama exclusively.

I ran back to the dock to see the first of the refugees being unloaded from our hidden ship. A group of guards helped them down the docks as fast as they could, carrying their things for them and rushing them into a nearby warehouse. Once they were unloaded, Theo turned the ship around as quick as he could and set sail back for Perama.

It was a painfully slow process, the ship only able to hold one or two hundred people at most, while there were thousands of people packing the tenements of the bridge city. I helped carry as many as I could as I dashed back and forth across the water, contributing what little I could to the resettlement. Many of the people of Perama refused to leave, despite the urging of Momma Lena and the other elders of the enclave. I ended up having to forcibly evict the most stubborn of the bunch, dashing with them across the water and leaving them on the docks of Sycae.

Night came and went, with no sign from the Emperor or the priests. I thanked my lucky stars that he either didn't care what we were doing or hadn't spotted us. It was also possible that nobody had dared to tell the Emperor what had happened to his Varangians, which helped buy us time. I could only imagine what would happen to the unlucky messenger that had to give the Emperor that bit of bad news.

As dawn rose, the Sycae enclave was swollen with refugees. The people of Sycae, despite the complaints of the merchants, welcomed their neighbors with open arms, bringing them into their homes and preparing food for them to eat as the night turned cold. I was moved by the generosity of the people of Sycae and vowed to do my best to save them from the Emperor when I someday had the power to do so.

With the last of the refugees being housed, I was finally able to review all of the experience announcements from the battle with the priests and Varangians. There were quite a lot of announcements and I got credit for every kill Mitkos made as well, some of which were very experienced priests. Since my experience was split among *Gunslinger*, *Duelist*, and *Spirit Breaker*, though, I only gained a few levels in each class. My *Gunslinger* went up to level 17, gaining me a +1 to strength and a +1 to endurance. My *Duelist* went up to level 14, gaining me a +1 to coordination, a +2 to strength, and a +1 to endurance. And my *Spirit Breaker* went up to level 14 as well, gaining me a +3 to willpower and a +1 to endurance.

The group of people that had wanted to come with us before had swollen as the night passed. Several of the refugees from Perama joined them when they learned what they were waiting for.

I was surprised to find Asylaion, the merchant who had first helped me out in the city, standing with them, surrounded by his guards.

"When I heard the rumors a rogue Varangian had bloodied the Emperor's nose," he said, grinning widely at me when I stopped in front of him, "I knew it had to be you. It is good to see you still live, Alexander. I had been worried since I hadn't seen you in so long."

I embraced the merchant, happy he had survived. He returned my hug warmly.

"Are you doing okay? What will you do now?" I asked him after the hug.

"Ah," he said, "it will be hard for me here. Too much competition for my old bones. Many of us feel the same."

He gestured to the slowly growing group of people from Perama who stood next to the men and women from Sycae who were going to come with us.

"We hear you have a place," he said, "safe from the Emperor. We are wondering if you would take more people. Some even want to join your soldiers. They have heard how powerful you are and that you treat your people well and help them get classes. Many want to sign up for that reason alone."

I looked over the crowd again, eyeing them with interest. We had room to expand, it was true, although I would need to be careful to make sure I got the right kind of people.

"I would also like to join," he told me. "I can work as a merchant for you or in some other capacity. My men are trained warriors and archers and would join you as well."

"I would be happy to have you join us," I told him genuinely. "We can discuss the details later. Can you go find a man named Basil on the ship and tell him that you and your men are joining us? He will find you space on the ship."

"Thank you, lad," he said, embracing me again. "We will serve you well."

I approached the people in the crowd and called over Constans. I had her start on one side and told her to catalog who everyone was and what they hoped to get from joining us. When we met in the middle, I found we had a mix of young orphans who wanted to join our legion, like I had recruited before, and older crafters who wanted a safe place to work, fearing they wouldn't be able to compete in Sycae.

I spoke to each person and weighed their soul and found them all to be trustworthy and genuine in their desire to join us. I could use the crafters, for sure, and I was open to expanding our legion more, so I told them they could all come with us.

By midmorning, I had accepted another one hundred legionnaires into my service, Asylaion and his guards, and a leatherworker, a blacksmith who could produce both weapons and armor, an enchanter, several more fishermen, and Momma Lena as well. The families of Asylaion's guards, the crafters, and the fishermen also joined us, straining the number of people we could fit on our ship, but I didn't have the heart to turn any of them away.

I had Constans buy even more food. It put a strain on Sycae's markets, but we needed to stock up with as much as we could carry now that so many people would be moving to our town. I sold the remaining orichalcum ore to the young merchant to pay for everything as well, leaving us with a much smaller treasury but enough to survive for a bit. Food was more important right now, so none of my people would go hungry.

Once everyone was situated on the ship and all our supplies were loaded, we bid farewell to the city for now. Many people were openly weeping on the ship, sad to be leaving the only home they had ever known. Others were smiling and joking with friends or family, excited to finally escape a place they assumed would kill them someday.

I found my leaders and had everyone meet at the helm next to Theo. I invited Asylaion to come with us as well as we planned our next steps.

"Theo," I said when everyone had gathered, "how many sailors do you have now?"

"We are up to twenty-five men and women now," he replied. "It's a bit heavy for a ship this size, but it will give us better protection if we're attacked when you aren't around. I'm training up the new people you signed up earlier."

"Great," I replied. "Basil and Nikephoros, start working with the new legion recruits immediately so they know what to expect. Divide up our veterans and make them the leaders of new, larger squads. Each one of our old squads will get twenty new recruits, making twenty-five-person squads with our leaders in charge of each."

"Yes, sir," Basil said, saluting.

"Asylaion," I said, turning to him. "How do you feel about running our small town? We need a mayor and you would be a perfect fit. You can merge your guards with the ones we have back home to protect the town in case of danger and I trust you to run the place fairly."

"If that's what you need me for," he replied, "I can do it. I always wanted to be in charge!"

He laughed and I gave him a small smile in return, appreciating his attempt at humor.

"Constans can show you around town when we get there and introduce you to everyone," I continued. "Get the new crafters settled and let Constans know what they need to do their job. Constans will be the go-between for the town and our ship and soldiers. Any issues, bring them to her."

We discussed various problems that might arise and came up with some plans. Then I sent everyone to get some food. It had been an exhausting couple of days and everyone was running on little to no sleep and still recovering from the battle we were lucky to have survived. I climbed up to the crow's nest to have some privacy. We were so full that people crowded the deck; they were leaning against the crates of food and supplies that littered the area.

I wasn't sure how I felt about what had happened in the city. I had formed a lot of plans for the city and had high hopes I could stop the spread of the dungeons and monsters, but now life had dealt me a new hand of cards. Now I had people that looked up to me and trusted me to keep them safe, and I couldn't just abandon them. We were on our way to our new home, which I hoped to make into something special. Maybe someday we could return and set things right for the rest of the people in the city, but that just wasn't possible today. I didn't have the power yet, but someday when I did, I would return.

I looked over the clear, pure water of the sea as we sailed away from Nova Roma. It was a beautiful day and our ship, packed full of people that trusted me, cut through the waves like a predator ready to take on the world. The lightest of spray reached me in the crow's nest, and the sun warmed me from above. With a sigh, I let my sadness and regret at having to flee the city fade away, focusing my mind on the future instead.

When I had first come here, I had been lost in more ways than one. I had no real purpose. I was unable to cope with my grief and had thrown myself into danger recklessly. Only now, looking back, was I able to recognize how self-destructive my actions were. A part of me had hoped to die, or at least was more accepting of that possibility than I should have been. Instead of dying, though, I had come out of the crucible of my own making, stronger than ever before, thanks in large part to the people I had learned to rely upon.

I had survived the streets of Nova Roma and the machinations of the last Emperor of Rome. Those were no small feats. I had made some mistakes, but I had learned from them. I had found a good group of companions and a town full of people that had come to trust me. And now, with a purpose for living and a reason to grow stronger, I felt more motivated than I ever had before. I had failed to protect my only friend back on Earth, but I wouldn't make the same mistake here. I would do whatever it took to protect the people that had come to follow me.

On the deck, Constans was arguing with Basil about something inconsequential. Theo was at the wheel on the quarterdeck, occasionally shouting out orders to his sailors. Nikephoros was somewhere belowdecks, presumably harassing the legionnaires in some way to keep them on their toes. Ryld was up in the rigging near me, keeping watch for any dangers that might approach.

When I looked his way, he turned his head and nodded at me companionably. I nodded back and then turned toward the sea once again, a sense of excitement filling me as I looked out on the vast, magical world that I found myself in. I had never imagined life would take me to a place like this, or surround me with so many strange, good-hearted people, but I was happy that it had. I didn't know what the future would bring for us all, but I was looking forward to finding out.

Afterword

Thank you for reading my novel!
If you liked this book and haven't read my other series, please check out *Jake's Magical Market*. Available here: https://www.amazon.com/Jakes-Magical-Market-J-R-Mathews-ebook/dp/B09HWX11N9.
It's a very different story from Nova Roma, but if you're interested in reading about how a slacker who works at the neighborhood market under his apartment manages to survive the magical apocalypse, you may like the book! It was also the first to set a lot of the groundwork for the new "magical deckbuilding" sub-genre that has developed lately, so if you want to see the origin of some of those ideas check out the book!
Jake's Magical Market 2: A Trek Through Time is also now available and book three in the series, Jake's Magical Market: Home Sweet Home, will be out in April 2024. That will complete the series if you are like many readers in this genre and are looking for a finished series to read!
Please help support me as an independent, self-published author by leaving a review or rating on Amazon. The reality right now is that Amazon ratings can make or break an author, so please help authors whenever you can by rating their books and leaving a review!
Also, if you liked the book, please don't be shy about sharing it with friends, family, or on social media. Genuine fan recommendations carry more weight than any advertisement or Amazon algorithm ever could, and it means the world to me when I see people talking about and sharing my book. You are all wonderful people, and you really make a difference in helping authors like me keep writing for you.
I do have a Patreon if you wish to help support me more directly: patreon.com/JRMathews. I tend to release advance copies

of my books there to my patreon supporters, and you can even subscribe at the Artifact level to get beta versions of my books once they are ready - sometimes months in advance of publication! **Thank you to all of my amazing Patreon supporters.** You are all wonderful for supporting independent authors like you do.

You can also follow me on Facebook for more casual updates: https://www.facebook.com/JRMathewsAuthor.

Or join my discord here where I am fairly active and you can discuss the book with me or other fans:https://discord.com/invite/9xpddKgGBw.

I have also opened a store where fans can buy t-shirts, posters, and more. Check it out here: https://www.etsy.com/shop/JRMathewsBooks.

Thank you to the fans, authors, critics, and supporters that have messaged me or posted on Reddit or Facebook about my book. I appreciate all of you so much. The community at r/LitRPG and r/ProgressionFantasy is amazing, and I would never have had the courage to become an author without those subreddits. Thank you as well to the many wonderful Facebook LitRPG/GameLit communities, especially the LitRPG Author's Group, LitRPG Books, LitRPG Releases, LitRPG, GameLit Society, and LitRPG Forum. Thank you as well to my amazing editor Bodie Dykstra and my cover artist Sevenchi!

Finally, last but not least, a *huge* thank you to my beta readers: Zechariah, Trevor, Steve, Daniel, Frank, and Carlos. I hope that you are able to see how the feedback you gave me ended up in the final version of the book and are happy with the results. I can guarantee you all had a big impact on the story, and I truly appreciate all of you taking the time to read the early versions of *Portal to Nova Roma* and give me such amazing, detailed feedback.

Thank you all for reading my book from the bottom of my heart. I appreciate you all so damn much.

- J.R. Mathews

Made in the USA
Middletown, DE
09 March 2025